Franciscus Schottus, Edmund Warcupp, David Loggan

Italy, in its Original Glory, Ruine and Revival

being an exact survey of the whole geography, and history of that famous country :

with the adjacent islands of Sicily, Malta

Franciscus Schottus, Edmund Warcupp, David Loggan

Italy, in its Original Glory, Ruine and Revival
being an exact survey of the whole geography, and history of that famous country : with the adjacent islands of Sicily, Malta

ISBN/EAN: 9783337381417

Printed in Europe, USA, Canada, Australia, Japan

Cover: Foto ©Andreas Hilbeck / pixelio.de

More available books at **www.hansebooks.com**

ITALY,

IN ITS ORIGINAL
GLORY, RUINE and REVIVAL,

Being an Exact SURVEY

Of the Whole

GEOGRAPHY,

AND

HISTORY

Of That *FAMOUS*
COUNTRY;

With the Adjacent Iſlands of *SICILY*
MALTA, &c.

And whatever is Remarkable in

ROME

(The Miſtreſs of the WORLD) And all
thoſe Towns and Territories, mentioned in Antient
and Modern Authors.

Tranſlated out of the Originals, for General Satisfaction.
By EDMUND WARCUPP, Eſquire.

LONDON,
Printed by *S. Griffin*, for *H. Twyford*, *Tho. Dring*, and *I. Place*, and are
to be ſold in *Vine* Court middle Temple, at the *George* in *Fleetſtreet*, and at
Furnevals Inne Gate in *Holborn*, 1660.

TO THE
RIGHT HONOURABLE
WILLIAM Lord LENTHAL.

My Lord.

O repeat your Lord-ships Tytles, and the Merits by which you atchieved them, and your just Administration under them, requires a larger volume then I here present you, nor had you received any other demonstration of my duty, till I had payed it in that kind, could I believe my self fit for so great an enterprize. To contract them into the narrow compass of an Epistle, is a diminution I dare not think of, since no Reader capable of this treatise can be ignorant of more then I could here tell him, should I extend it much beyond the ordinary limits : and Posterity can turn over no leaf in the English History (during our last twenty years transactions) wherein he will not find frequent mention of your Lord-ships name so involved in the principal affaires, that no alteration the Island can suffer (whil'st inhabited by men) can extinguish your memory. A change of language in our Nation by foreign Conquest or confusion like that of Babel, would for a short time obscure it ; but retained by all other parts of the knowing world in their memorials of our stupendious changes, how soon will the next commerce bring it back again ? and consecrate your name to the utmost extent of time. Amidst these considerations I make humble tender of all I can. The Itinerary of Italy, translated long after my return thence, in those vacant hours which I allowed to diversion, without farther intention then to renew that language by a re-translation (which occasioned my so close keeping to the Italian

B 2

names

names and Idiome) and once more to travel that celebrate Countrey in this exact description, whither in my earlier years your Lord-ship addressed me. Taking wing therefore from your Lordships Hand, and persuit from your direction, the Quarry (such as it is) ought to be your Lordships at the retrive; and though perhaps you will not esteem it fit to range in the first course of Books on your Lordships well furnished Table, yet it may deserve a share in the second, affording a pleasant repast even to those, who require a more substantial meal. To advance that thought a little, and call it Manna (such in every mans mouth as he best liked) though proper enough to the Countrey where it abounds in great perfection, and agreeable to this work, where all appetites, all tasts, may be delighted, would perhaps appear arrogance in me, who deliver it not pure from the tree (on which it falls) but as from an Apothecaries shop, where it may have received some taint. Yet those imperfections your Lordship will pardon, and for your Lordships sake this Nation, (at least in some measure) because devoted to you upon the score of publique gratitude as well as the particular obligation, of

My Lord,

Your Lordships most affectionate

Nephew, and most obedient

Servant

EDMOND WARCUPP.

A
PREFACE
TO THE
READER.

OU have here the Itinerary of *Italy*, a guide to all that travel thither, a memorial after their return, a juſt entertainment to the learned, & a pleaſing diverſion to thoſe who have not given themſelves the trouble of unneceſſarie letters; whilſt with eaſie Journies they paſs through the moſt celebrate part of the habitable Earth, directed by this Treatiſe to the view or contemplation of all that is excellent in art, or nature. Such indeed is the ſcituation of the Country, ſuch the nature of the ſoile, ſuch the antient manners of the people, as gave them a juſt Prerogative to the Empire of the world: proportioned to their dominion were their actions, the great examples of enſuing ages in all that was imitable, their wonder

A

and

and amazement in what exceeds the hope of imitation. Of both you have a tranſitory account ſo interwoven with the general ſurvay, that it is ſcarce poſſible a volume of this ſize, can contain more, or more worthy remarques of perſons, places, things, from the remoteſt of times to this inſtant. For beſide the neceſſarie inſtruction in the number of miles, & conveniences of paſſage from Town to Town, through every part that can recompence the trouble of a journey, you find a breif and yet a lively deſcription of their ſeveral ſcituations, a repetition of their Hiſtorie, Government, capital Families, eminent perſons, ruined Amphitheaters, Arches, Bathes, old Temples, later Churches, Palaces of both ſorts with their various ornaments; what they have bin & what they are, when, and by whom founded, ruined, or reſtored. Not any thing antient or modern, which a man upon the place ought to underſtand, ſeems omitted, nor is there any thing inſerted to the unneceſſary burthen of his memory: no Treatiſe in the Italian tongue was ever ſo acceptable to ſtrangers, none on this ſubject deſerved ſo well from the natives. Whatever therefore the ſucceſs be in the tranſlation, you cannot but commend this Gentlemans choice, who after many years return from that pleaſing journey, intended only a recollection of the language, and review of the Countrey, without any deſigne of making his papers publique, till aſſured by his friends they would in all hands meet a fa-

voura-

vourable reception; fince the early progrefs of
our Englifh youth, and fhort abode there, feldom
gives them opportunity to arrive to any perfection in that fpeech, till they are ready for departure, nor do many of them long retain it. Of
thofe how few are there that prefer not difcourfes in their own? efpecially on a fubject wch admits no continued elegancie of ftile, or contains
any thing not eafily reducible to another Idiome Such as have traverft the Hiftory only, will
find in every leaf a new delight by the brief
recitals of the beft Authors, enlightned with
Chronologie, & many doubtful paffages reduc'd
to certainty by the fite and diftance of the moft
memorable Cities, Fields, & villages celebrate
in Latin & Italian ftories. Thofe who are hitherto
unacquainted with either, will here find enough
to inform themfelves, & fatisfie others, that they
are not ignorant of any thing worth knowledge
in that Country. Nay even to them who little
regard the Hiftory or Geography, devotion wil
render it acceptable, the moft important ceremonies of the Roman Church being briefly dif-
cours'd, and expofed to the different cenfures of
thofe that read them with fcorn or reverence.
If there are any in the number of Readers who
believe themfelves unconcerned in all that is
hitherto offred, there yet remains for them fufficient entertainment, in the magnificent buildings, elegant Gardens, Statues, Embofments,
Paintings of all forts, and in every fort more excellent then all the other parts of *Europe* pretend
unto. Hence did the barbarous *Britains*, *Gauls*,

Ger-

Germans, &c. derive their firſt civility, and hence in all ſucceeding ages received their beſt ſupply. Who in theſe nations leſs barbarous then their Anceſtors, can think of that Country without reverence? who can peeviſhly reſolve to be ignorant of their ſtory by refuſing this Treatiſe? though I confeſs the Originals whence this Gentleman derives it, are not without manifold errors by the tranſlation of Greek and Latin names into Italian, and extreme negligence in the impreſſions, ſo that the engliſh verſion wants a double Apologie, whilſt it oft-times follows thoſe miſtakes, and is in the phraſe far from the perfection it had appear'd in, had our Tranſlator intended it for publique view. Yet is there no real lapſe in the main, & every where intelligible: the faults of the preſs are as carefully corrected as the Printers importunate haſt will permit. And whatever imperfections the curious Reader ſhall after theſe reaſonable excuſes diſcover, it is to be hoped he will gently pardon, or vouchſafe to the Book-ſeller ſomthing of his own more excellent then what he now recommends to the Nobility, Gentry, and Merchants of the Nation.

Farewell.

A

TABLE

OF

THE FIRST

PART

THE
SECOND PART
contains the Description of
ROME:

THE
TABLE
OF THE
THIRD PART.

THE POSTS and STAGES TO divers Parts of ITALY.

Posts from *Rome* to *Naples*.

The City *Rome*.	Posts
To the *Tower Mezza Via*,	1
To *Marino*,	1
To the City *Velletri*,	1
To *Cisterna* where pass the River *Astura*,	1
To *Sarmonetta*,	1
To *Casa Nova*,	1
To *Badia*,	1
To *Fondi*.	1
To *Molla* behind *Marina*,	1
To *Garigliano* where you ferry over the River *Garigliano*,	1
To the *Bagni*	1
To the Castle *Castello*,	1
There pass the River *Volturnus*,	1
To *Patria*,	1
To *Pozzuolo*,	1
To *Naples* a most famous City and fair Port,	1
	Posts 16

Posts from *Naples* to *Messina*.

The City *Naples*.	
Near whereto pass a small Rivolett——	
To the *Torre del Greco*,	1
To *Barbazona*,	1
There pass the River *Sali*.	.
To the City *Salerni*	1
To *Taverna pinta*	1
To *Rivole*,	1
To the *Duchessa*,	1
To the Castle *Goletta*,	1
To *Sala*,	1
To *Casal Novo*,	1
Near whereto pass the River *Molfe*,	1
To *Rovere Negra*,	1
To *Alpicia*,	2
Pass the River *Lavo*,	.
To *Castelluccia*,	1
To *Val S. Martine*,	1
To the Town *Castro*,	1
To *Esaro*,	1
To *Regina*,	1
Pass the River *Busento*, to the City *Cosenza*,	1
To *Caprosedo*,	1
To *Martorano*,	1
Pass a small River,	
To *San Biasio*,	1
To *Aqua della Fica*,	1
To *Montelione*,	1
To *S. Pietro a Burghe*,	1
To *Rosa*,	1
To *Sant' Anna*,	1
Pass the River *Mettauro*,	1
To *Fonego*,	1
To *Fumarade Mori*,	1
Here embarque on the River *Farto*, for eight miles and four afterwards by Land,	2
To *Messina* a City and fair Port,	
	Posts 36.

Posts from *Messina* to *Palermo*.

FRom the said City *Messina* to *Palermo*, there are not fixed posts from place to place as abovenamed, but provide and hire Mules from *Messina*, there to be found for that service, accustomed to pass over those Mountains both speedily and securely; this journey is 180 Miles; wherfore (with the greatest diligence) it cannot be attained in less then two daies and a half: which voyage when any Messenger or other person is obliged to expedite, they pay for the said Mules as for twenty Posts: P. 20

This journey leads over several Mountains, particularly, *Namari*, *Atrei*, and *Mondon*. And obligeth the passing of several Rivers, the chief whereof are, *Castriregali*, *Oliveria*, *Trajano*, *Furiano*, *Salus*, and *Termini*,

P. 20.

Posts from *Naples* to *Lezze* by *Puglia*, and the Province of *Ottranto*.

The City *Naples*.	Posts
TO *Marigliano*,	2
To *Cardenale*	1
To *Avellino* a City and Principality,	1
To *Adente cante*	1
To *Poracutia*	1
To *Ascoli*, a City and Principality,	2
To *Acquaviva*	1
Traverse the *Apenine* Hills.	
To the house of the Count	1
To *Cirignola*,	2
To *Canossa*,	2
To *Udria*,	2
To *Ricco*,	1
To *Bisonto*,	2
To *Caporto*,	1
To *Conversono*,	2
To *Monopoli*, a City on the coasts of the *Adriatick Sea*,	2
To *Fagliano*	1
To *Astone*	2
To *Sant Anna*	1
To *Busveglia*	1.
To *San Pietro*,	1
To *Lezze* a City of *Puglia*: Thence to *Ottranto* are 24 miles.	

miles, reputed and payed for
poſts, 3

Poſts 33.

Poſts from *Rome* to *Na-*
ples, by the *Valmone* and the
Aglieri.

The City Rome.   Poſts

TO the *Torre Mezza Via*, 1
   To the *Cava del' Agli-*
eri, 1
To *Volmontone* 2
To *Caſtel Matteo*, 1
To *Florentino Caſtello*, 2
To *Torci*, 1
To *Crepano*, 2
To *Ponte Carvo*, where paſſe
   the River *Garigliano*, 1
To the *Frate Villa* 1
To *Carigliano*, 2
To *Bagni*, 2
To *Caſtel Caſtello*, 1
Paſs the River *Volturno*
To *Patria* and *Pozzuolo*, 3
To *Naples*, 1
         Poſts 21.

Poſts from *Rome* to the holy houſe of *Loreto*.

The City Rome.   Poſts

TO *Prima Porta*, M.7 P.1
   To the *Caſtle Nova Ca-*
ſtello,
To *Rignano*, 1
Paſſe the *Tyber*,
To the City *Cività Caſtella-*
na, 1
Paſſe the *Tyber*,
To *Ottiricoli*, 1
To *Narni*, a City, 1
Repaſſe the *Tyber*
To the City *Terni*, 1
To *Strettura*, 1
To the City *Spoleto*, 1
To *Paſſo di Spoleti*, 2
To *Varchiano*, 2
Paſs the River *Trent* in the
   plain of *Dignano*, 1
To the *Mutia Caſtello*, 1
To *Valcimara*, 1
To the City *Tolentino*, 1
To the City *Macerata*, 1
Here paſs the Riveo *Patenza*
and go to *Recanati*, whence to
Loreto is,   poſt 1
         Poſts 19.

Poſts from *Loreto* to *Ancona*.

The City *Loreto*.   poſts

To the City *Recanati* 1
paſſe the River to the City
Oſmi, 1
To *Ancona* a City & Seaport 1.

         Poſts 3

Poſts from *Rome* to *Florence*
by the way of *Valdarno*, and
Orvieto.

The City Rome,   poſts

TO the *Iſola Storta* 1
   To *Bacano*, 1
To *Monteroſa*: 1
where ends the Eccleſiatical
State
To *Ronciglione* a Caſtle, 1
return into the ſtate of the Ho-
ly Church.
To the City *Viterbo*, 1
To the City *Monte Fiaſcon* 1
To *Gapafrica*, 1
To *Nona* under *Orvieto*, 1
To *Ponte Carnaiole*, 1
To *Caſtel della Pievi*, 1
To *Caſtigliori de Laco*, 1
To *Lerſaia*, 1
To *Caſtillon Artino*, 1
To *Baſtardo*, 1
To *Ponte alle vane*, 1
To *Fighino*, 1
To *Treghi*, 1
To *Florence*, 1

         poſts 18.

Poſts from *Florence* to *Lucca*

The City *Florence*.

PAſs the River *Biſenzi*
   To *Poggio Cajano*, 1
paſs the *Ombrone* to the City
   Piſtoia,
paſs the River *Peſcia* to *Bor-*
go Begia, 1
To the City *Lucca*, 1

Poſts 4.

Poſts from *Milan* to *Ve-*
nice by the way of *Breſcia*
and *Bergamo*,

§. The City *Milan*,
paſs the River *Lambro* to the
   Caſſina di Pecchi,
paſs the *Navilio*, to the Cano-
nica where paſs the River
Adda, 1
At two miles diſtance from
whence begins the Venetians
Dominion

To the City *Bergamo*, 1
paſs the Rivers *Serio* and *O-*
glio, to *Palazznolo*, 1
To *Ospedaletto*, 1
paſs the river *Mel* to *Breſcia* 1
paſs the rivers *Naviletto* and
Chies. To *Deſenſano* 1
To *Ponte di. S. Marco*, where
   paſs the River *Menze*. To
   Caſtle Nuovo, 1
To the City *Verona*, 1
Here paſs the *Adice* to *Scalde-*
re, 1
paſs the River *Agno* to *Mon-*
tebello, 1
To the City *Vicenza* and paſs
   the River *Bacchiglione* 1
To the City *Padona*, 1
There paſs the River *Brenta*
   To *Lizaſuſina*, 2
Where imbarking after five
miles on the Sea you arrive at
Venice.   poſt 1

         Poſts 18.

Poſts from *Milan* to *Udi-*
ne in *Friuli*.

The City *Milan*.

TO *Caſſina di pecchi*, 1
   To *Canonica* where paſs
   the River *Adda*, 1
and there you leave the *Mi-*
laneſe Territory and enter
the Venetians.
To the City *Bergamo*, 1
Paſs the Rivers *Serio* and *O-*
glio to *Palazuolo* 1
To *Hoſpedaletto*, 1
Paſs the River *Mel* to the City
   Breſcia, 1
Paſs the *Naulietto* and then
   Chies, to *Deſenſano*, 1
To *Ponte S. Marco* paſs the
   Menzo. To *Caſtel Novo*, 1
To *Verona* where paſs the *A-*
dice, 1
To *Scaldere*: 1
Paſs the river *Agno* to *Mon-*
te bello: 1
To the City *Vicenza*, 1
There paſs the *Bacchiglione*
   and the rivers *Teſena* and
Brenta to *Citta Della*, 1
At *Caſtel Franco* paſs the
   Muton, 1
Paſs the rivers *Piave* and
Mondegan to *Uderzo* 4
To *Motta* where paſs the *Li-*
venza to *San Vito*, 2
         To

To Codroipo, 1

Pass the River *Torre.* To *Udine* the chief City of the *Friuli,* 1

Posts 23.

Posts from *Milan* to *Brescia.*

The City *Milan.*
To *Cassina Bianca,* 1
To the Castle *Cassano:* where pass the River *Adda,* 1
To *Martinengo,* 1
To *Coccai,* 1
To the City *Brescia:* 1

Posts 5.

Another way from *Milan* to *Brescia,* where heretofore the Posts were layed now not

The City *Milan* Posts
To *Cassina Bianca,* 1
To the Castle *Cassano* pass the River *Adda,* 1
Pass the River *Serio.* To *Martinengo,* there pass the *Oglio* 1
To *Cocci,* a 1
To the City *Brescia,* 1

Posts 5.

Posts from *Mian* to *Venice* by the way of *Cremona* and *Mantona.*

The City *Milan.*
To *Meregnano,* pass the River *Lambro,* 1
Pass also the River *Muzza* to the City *Lodi,* 1
To *Zorlesco,* 1
To *Pizighitone* there pass the River *Adda,* 1
To the City *Cremona,* 1
To *La Plebe di san Giacomo* 1
To *Voltino* the last post of the *Milanese,* 1
Enter the *Mantouan* Territory, and pass the river *Oglio*
To *Marcaria,* 1
To *Castelluccio'* 1
To the City *Mantoua,* 1
Here you pass the Lake over Bridges pass the River *Teyone*
To *Castellaro,* 1
pass the River *Tartaro* To *Langoneo* in the *Veronian* Territory, 1
pass the River *Daniella* and

at *Legnano,* the Castle ludes to *Bevilacqua:* 1
At *Montagnana,* pass the River *Lagno* to *Este,* 1
To the City *Padoua,* whether a conveyance lies also by water, 1
To *Lizasuzina,* one may go by water, 2
To the City *Venice* by water 1

posts 18.

Posts from *Milan* to *Ferrara*

KEep the foregoing posts from *Milan* to *Mantoua,* which are, 10
To *Governolo,* where the *Mens* issues out of the Lake of *Mantoua,* 1
To *Hostia,* 1
To *Massa* of the holy Church 1
To *Palantone,* there pass the *Poe,* 1
To *Ferrara* there repass the *Po,* 1

posts 15.

Posts from *Ravenna* to *Ferrara* the City *Ravenne* to *Fusignano,* 1
To the *Casa de Copri,* 1
To *Argento* pass the *Po.* 1
To *San Nicolo,* 1
To the City *Ferrara,* 1

posts 5.

Posts from *Ferrara* to *Bolognia.*

The City *Ferrara,*
To *Poggio,* 1
To *San Pietro in Casale* 1
To *Fun,* 1
Xo the City *Bologna,* 1

posts 4

Posts from *Milan* to *Ferrara* by *Parma.*

The City *Milan.*
To *Meregnano* : pass the *Lambro,* 1
To the City *Lodi,* 1
To *Zolesco,* 1
Leaving the *Milanese* territory and entring that of *Ple-*

centia. To *Fombi,* 1
To the City *Piacenza* pass the *Po,* 1
Pass the Rivers *Nuro* and *Reilo Arta,* 1
At *Fiorenzuola* pass a rivolet, 1
To the *Borgue san Dunino,* 1
Pass the *Tarro* then the *Parma* Rivers. To the City *Parma,* 1
To *Sant' Ilario,* 1
Pass the River *Lenza* where the Territory of *Parma* ends and that of *Modena* be, ins.
To the City *Reggio,* 1
Pass the Rivers *astrola* and *Secchia.* To *Marzaia,* 1
To the City *Modena,* 1
To *Bon Porto* pass the *Secchia,* 1
To *Vo,* 1
To *Bonizo,* 1
To *Finale* pass the River *Castrola,* 1
To *Bondinello,* 1
Pass the river *Reno,* then the *Po* to the City *Ferrara,* 1

posts 20.

Posts from *Milan* to *Bolonia,* by the shortest way.

posts
KEep the above written way from *Milan* to *Modena* 14
Then pass the river *Panara,* where you quit the Territory of *Modena,* and enter that of *Bolonia,* pass the *Imola.* To *Sumoggia,* 1
Pass the rivers *Canto* and *Reno* to *Bolonia* a fair City, 1

posts 16.

Posts from *Bolonia* to *Rome* by the way of *Florence.*

The City *Bologna*
PAss over the Bridge and afterwards to *Guazzo* pass the River *Savona.*
To *Pianoro,* 1
Here begin the *Apenine* Hills.
To *Loiano,* 1
Here you determine the Territory of *Bolonia,* and *Florentine* begins. To *Felagaia,* 1
To *Fiorenzuola,* 1
To *Zovo,* 1
Pass the River *Siene.* To *San Pietro a Sieno,* 1
To *Ucellatoio,* 1
To *Florence* pass the River *Arno,* 1
To *San Cassiano,* 1

To Le Tavernelle, 1
To Sugia, 1
To the City Sienna, 1
To Lucignano, 1
To Ternieri, 1
Pass the River Orcia to
Scala, 1
Pass a rivolet, and then ascend
the Mountains to Radicofani,
a Castle and good Inn, 1
At the foot of the Mountains,
pass a Rivolet. To l'ontecenti-
no, there pass a Rivolet trouble-
some: in rainy weather, 1
Thence a little pass the Paglia
by bridge. To Acqua Pendente
of the holy Church, 1
To the City Bolsena, 1
To the City Monte fiascone, 1
To the City Viterbo, 1
To Ronciglione, 1
To Montrossa, 1
To Baccana, 1
To Storta, 1
To the City Rome. 1
Posts 26.

Posts from Fossombrone to
Perugia. At Fossombrone pass
the River,

To Quaiana, 1
To Cantia pass the hills 1
To the City Giubileo. 1
To the City and university Pe-
rugia, 1
Posts 4

Posts from Rome to Venice.

The City Rome, posts
To Prima Porta, 1
To Castel, a new Castle 1
To Riguano pass the Tyber, 1
To Civita Castellana: 1
Repass the Tyber,
To Otriecli, 1
To The City Narny, 1
pass the Tyber again to the Ci-
ty Terai, then to Strettura, 2
To Prote and to Sant Horatio 2
To Pontecentemsio and the Ci-
ty Nocera, 2
To Gualdo and to Sigillo, 2
To Sheggia, 1
To Cantiana & Acqualagna 2
To the City Urbine, the state of
that Duke and a Sea Port, 1
To Foglia, & to Monte Fiore 2
§. To Coriano and to the City
Rimini, 2
To Ballaere and Cesenatico, 2
To Savio, and to the City Ra-

venna, 2
To Primaro & to Magnava-
ca, 3
To Volani, 2
To Gorro pass there the Po, 2
To Fornase repass the po, 2
pass the River Adice, 1
To the City Chioza, 2
There embarque for Venice, 3
posts 40.

posts from Rome to Bolonia
through the province Romagna
The City Rome,
§. Keep the same posts
as above till arri-
ved at this mark, that is to the
City Rimini, 21
To Savignano, 1
To the City Cesena, 1
To the City Forli: 1
To the City Faenza, pass the
river Lamone, 1
pass the river Senio to Imola, 1
pass the River Santerno, 1
pass the rivers, Salerin, and
Giana, 1
To San Nicolo, 1
pass the rivers Adice and Savona, 1
posts 29.

Posts from Rome to Perugia
The City, Rome, pass the
Tyber, to Prima Porta, 1
To Castel, novo Castello, 1
To Riguano, pass the Tyber, 1
To Civita Castellana, 1
Pass the Tyber to Ostricoli, 1
To Narni pass the Tyber, 1
to the City Terni, 1
To Strettura, and to Proti, 2
To Sant Horatio, 1
To Santa Maria de gli An-
geli, 2
To Perugia a City and Uni-
versity.
posts 12

Posts from Perugia to Flo-
rence.
The City Perugia.
To Tortè, and Orsaia, 2
To Castello Nartino, and
to Bastardo, 2
To Ponte allè Valle, 1
To Fichini, and to Treghi, 2
To Florence, passing the Arno 1
posts 8.

Posts from Milan to Pesaro.
From Milan, you must
go to Bolonia the way and posts
whereto, you have before, 16
pass the rivers Savona and

Adice 1
To San Nicola, 1
pass the river Salerno to Imo-
la, 1
pass the river Santerno, then
the Senio 1
In the City Senio pass the
Amone, 1
To Forli, 1
To Cesena and then to Sevig-
nano, 1
§. To the City Rimini, 1
To Cattolica, 1
To the City Pesaro, 1
26

posts from Milano to Ur-
bino.
From Milan keep the a-
bove written posts to the
City Rimini, 24
To Coriano, 1
To Monte Fiore, 1
To Foglia an Hostery, 1
To the City Urbine, 1
posts 28

Posts from Lucca to Genoua
At the City Lucca pass
the River Serchio A
Mazaroso in which stage, you
leave the territory of Lucca, entring the Florentine. 1
To Pietra Santa, 1
To Massa del Principe, 1
pass the River Versiglia to
§ Sarezana, a City of the state
of Genoua, 1
pass the River Marca to Lerci
whence you may pass to Genoua
by water as well as Land, 1
To San Simedio, 1
To Borghetto, and to Mante-
rana: 2
To Biacco and to Sestri, 2
At Sestri, you may imbarque
also for Genoua, being five
posts by water but in an ill season pass on by Land.
pass the River Lugna. to Chi-
avara pass the River Sturla 1
To Repalo and to Recco 2
To Bolignasco, pass the River
Besagna, 1
To Genoua a City, and Sea
Port, 1
posts 15

Posts from Venice to Genera
by the way of Parma.
At Venice imbarque for Liza-
fusina, 8
To Padoua, pass the River
Brenta, 1

A

A Este, 2
At Montegnana, pass the River Lagni, 1
To Bevilacqua, 1
Passe the River Daniello to Sangoneto Veronese, 1
Pass the River Tanaro To Castellaro, pass the Teyone, 1
To Mantoua, pass the Mantouan Lake, 1
To Borgo Forte, 1
To Mora, pass the Po, 1
To Guastallo, a Principality, 2
To Borsello, pass the River Lenza, 2
To Parma, pass the River Parma, 1
To Fornonovo, on the River Parma, 2
To Borga di val di tarro, 2
Pass the Hills, the Marca, & the River Vogliasco. To Varasi, and to Sestri, 2
Pass the River Lavagna To Chiavari, pass the Sturla, 1
To Repalo and to Rtcco, 2
To Bolignasco, pass the Besagna, 1
To Genoua City a Sea Port, 1
Posts 27

Posts from Milan to Genoua.
To Binasco, 1
To Pavia a City and Colledge pass the Tioino, 1
pass the Rivers, Gronolone, and the Po, Pancarana, and to Voghera, 2
Pass the Stafora and Curone to the City Tortona, pass the Scrivia to Bittola, 2
To Scravalle, and to Ottagio, 2
Ascend the Zovo, and go down it. To Ponte Decimo, 2
Pass the River Soferia, to Genoua, 1
posts 11

Posts from Genoua to Venetia, by Piacenza and Mantoua.
The City Genova pass the River Seria To Ponte Decimo, 1
Ascend and descend the Zovo To Ottagio, 2
Near Gavio pass a small stream To Seravalle, a Castle of the Milanese, 1
To Betola, 1
To the City Tortona, 1
pass the Stafora to Voghera, 1
pass the River Coppa To Schiatezza, pass the River Versa 1
To Stradella, 1
Here you quit the Territory of Milan, and enter that of Piacenza to the Castle St. Gioanni: 1
pass the River Tidone, To Rottofrenoa Castle, 1
pass the River Trebia to the City Piacenza, 1
pass the Rivers Nuro Relio, Vezeno, and Chier all in one stream, and near Cremona, pass the River Po, To Cremona a City of the state of Milan, 3
§ From Cremona to Venice you will find the posts in the journy from Milan to Venice by Cremona and Mantoua marked as is here marked, 14
Posts 29

posts from Milan to Guastalla
The City Milan pass the river Lambro to Merignano, 1
To the City Lodi, and to Zorlesco, 2
To Pizighitone Castello pass the Adda, 1
To the City Cremona, 1
To plebe di San Giacomo, 1
To Volti. 1
§. To Casal Maggiore, 1
To Barsello and to Guastalla, 2
posts 10

Posts from Milan to Corezzo by the aforenamed way
The City Milan.
§ Take the foregoing posts from Milan to Casal Maggiore, marked as in this place, 8
To Bersello pass the Po, 1
From Bersella to Corezzo are thirty five miles, which according to the custome of the Modeneses are divided into 4 posts
posts 13

posts from Milano to Trento.
§ The City Milan posts
From Milan to Castelnovo the posts are set down in the posts from Milan to Venice, by Bergamo and Brescia 10
to Volgarna, 1
To Peri, 1
To Vo, 1
pass the River Adice
To Revere, 1
To Trente a City of Italy and Germany, 2
Posts 16.

FRom Brescia to Trento there is another way to wit, by the Lake Garda, but the posts are not layed that way nor is the Lake Garda, at all times passable without danger.

Errata.

Page 2. l. 13. r. the Germans. p. 10. l. 32. r. behold. p. 12. l. 35. r. Grisons p. 20. li 7. r. cartel p. 33. l. 10. 11. r. when I was in *Italy* in honour of whom p. 38. l. 41. r. malignity it, ib. l. 42. 1. in by. p. 46. l. 39. r. Vicenza, p. 48. l. 41. r. for, p. 50. l. 48. r. faith. p. 54. l. 36 r. likewise, p. 55. l. 25. r. viscounte. p. 59. l. 10. for table r. *pretend* p. 59. l. 34. r. *Pompeis* p. 64. l. 3. r. storm. 69. l. 27. r. many, p. 72. l. 2. r. me, p. 75. l. 7. r. dele re a, p. 76. l. 38 r Lake p. 81. l. 1. 1. as p. 83. l. 26. r. or, p. 84. l. 35. r. such as have, p. 87. l. 15. r. by for *be*, p. 85, l. 4. r. ruines, p. 92. l. 30. r. passing, p. 93, l. 36 r. in those, p. 98. l. 45. r. *Florence*. p. 99. l. 6. r. *Ombrosa*, p. 139. l. 16, 17. r. incomparablenesse. page 144. l. 32. r. entire. p. 150. l. 1. r and by. p. 163. l. 13. r. God p. 163. l. 35 r. Oratorians reside. p. 165. l. 22. r. Pallas. p. 167. l. 45. r. Cardinal Presideut, p. 170. l. 4. r. Martyr, ib. l. 43. r. old the Temple, p. 174. l. 18. r. *Pliny* in the, ib. l. 19. dele in, ib. l. 46. r. time, p. 178. l. 43. r. deputed to him p. 170 l 7. r. carcasses, p. 182. l 38. r. diseased. p. 182. l. 4. dele and, p. 191. l. 31. r. *Tyber*. p. p. 208. l. 39. r. ran into the, p. 210. l, 18. r. denominated, ib. l. 32. r. Palme, p. 235. L 47. r. Salutation, p. 236. l. 25. r. 1465, p. 292 l, 17. r. same, ib. l. 19. r. *Tully*, p. 245. l. 18. r. bring, p. 248. l. 10, 11. r. Artemisio.

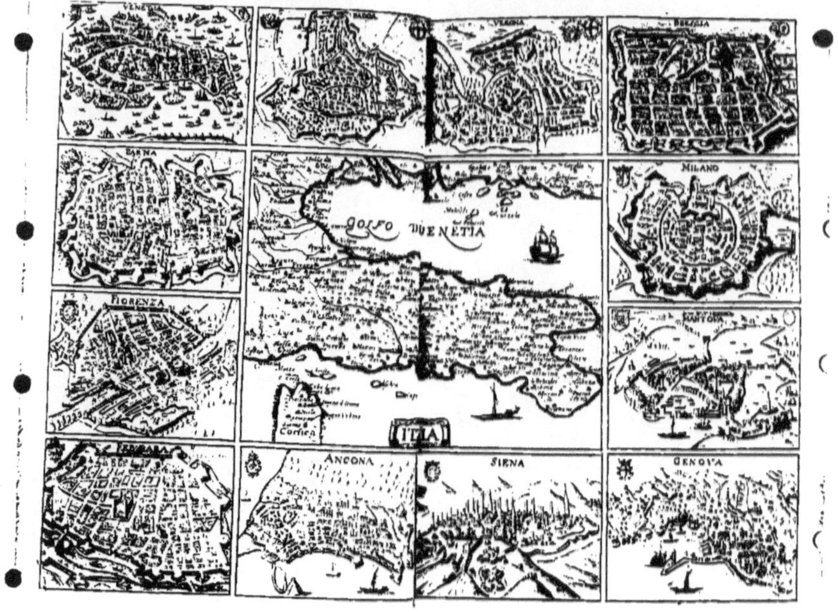

VENETIA
PADOA
VERONA
BRESSIA
PARMA
MILANO
FIORENZA
MANTOVA
GOLFO DI VENETIA
FERRARA
ANCONA
SIENA
GENOVA
ITALIA
Corfica

THE
HISTORY
OF
ITALY,

BEING

An exact Description of all the Cities, Towns, Castles, and Villages of *ITALY*, with the most remarkable particulars in each of them.

The first PART.

Wherein is conteined the Journeys, or Voyages, from *Trent* to *Venice*, from *Venice* to *Milan*, from *Milan* to *Rome*.

The way from *Trent* to *Venice*.

Rento, or *Trent*, is a City of the Province of *Marca Trivigiana*, or *Marquisate* of *Treves*, and is seated in a Valley on the confines of the said Province. It hath Walls round it, which are about the compass of a mile, and are washed by the River *Ladice* towards the North; Large and Fair Streets, paved with Flint-stones, and stately Houses: Its Churches are very beautiful, though not large. There is one most sumptuous, and Royal Palace, which was lately restored by *Bernardo Clessio*, Bishop of the said City. Towards the East part thereof enters a little River, upon which are raised many edifices, to work Silks in, as also to grind Corn; and from the said little River are brought many Rivolets, which run along the Streets, and into the Houses of the Citizens. Without the Gate called

B

Saint

Saint *Lorenzo*, upon the *Ladice*, there is a magnificent Bridge, of one hundred forty & fix paces in length (but of Wood)which conjoyns the *Ladice* with the other little River. The furrounding Mountains by, being continually covered with Snow, precipitous, and fo high that the heads thereof feem to touch the heavens, are rendred inacceffable. Between thefe Mountains, are two wayes, the one goes towards the North, the other towards *Verona*. It hath but little Champaign, or Fields, but thofe are pleafant and Rich, planted with Vines, and fruitful Trees, amidft which paffeth the *Ladice*. In this place, may be feen the Caftle, and Fort, called *Pelen*, appertaining to the moft Noble Family of the *Troppi*. The Citizens fpeak good *Dutch*, and not ill *Italian*. *Trent* is now reduced under the power of *Germans*, and is a refuge for all *Italians*, when any difgrace happens to them in their own Countrey. They gather but little Corn, but, in lieu thereof, they have good quantity of delicious Wines, both White, and Red. In the Summer, the Air is good, but the Sun beats upon it moft vehemently on thofe dayes it remaineth in the fign *Leo*; And in the Winter, 'tis fo very cold, by reafon of the Frofts and Snow, that there is no living;their Stoves are not fufficient to provide againft it, becaufe the cold is fo fierce, that it turneth the Rain into Snow, before it can fall to the Earth; and that which occafions the greateft wonder here, is, that in that time their Wells, or deepeft Pits, are void, and empty of Water. In ftead of Mules, Affes, and Horfes of Burthen, they ferve themfelves of their Oxen, and Cows, with Charrets fo eafie to carry goods, that they run up by the Mountains, as if it were in a Plain; though 'tis very true, that the wayes are fo well helped by the Cliffs, or Craggs, that the Beafts may go any where with little labour.

This City was greatly illuftrated, and enriched certain years paft, by the General Council held here: for that there met then five Prefident Cardinals; Two Legats of the Council, for his Holinefs, *Pius* the fourth, Chief Bifhop, or Pope of *Rome*, being Cardinals alfo, that is to fay, Cardinal *Loreno*, and Cardinal *Madruccio*; Three Patriarchs, Thirty two Arch-bifhops, Two hundred and thirty Bifhops, Seven Abbots, Seven Generals of *Religion*, One hundred forty and fix Doctors of Divinity, between Seculars, and Regulars; The Embaffadour of *Ferdinand* the Emperour, as well in the name of the Empire, as of the Kingdoms of *Hungary*, and *Bohemia*; as alfo the Embaffadours of the King of *France*, of the King of *Spain*, of the King of *Poland*, and of *Portugal*, of the Dukes of *Bavaria*, of *Savoy*, of *Venice*, of *Florence*, and of the other Catholique Princes.

The Council was held in the Church of Saint *Mary*, where there is a very fair Organ. In the Church of Saint *Peter* are the Afhes of the bleffed *Simeon*, Martyred by the wicked Jewes. In the Church of the Fryers *Heremitans* lies buried Cardinal *Seripando*, who was Legate of the Council, a man famous for Holinefs, and Doctrine. The Cannons are all illuftrious perfons, and have authority to choofe the Bifhop, Lord of the City, and Prince of the Empire, which dignity, three Cardinals of the moft Noble Family of the *Madrucci*, have enjoyed fucceffively, of which one named *Altiprando* lives at prefent, a religious Perfon, and a lover of Learned men.

BASSANO.

B A S S A N O.

FRom *Trento* the way lies to *Baſſano*, travelling towards the Eaſt by the Valley of *Sugana*, called by the Antients *Euganea*, becauſe a People of that name dwelt there; This Plain is eighteen miles in length, and two only in bredth, whence you may go to *Venice*, but 'tis too long a journey. Five Miles forth of *Trent*, is ſituated the rich, and populous Countrey of *Terzene*.

At the Head of the Valley, near *Primolano*, are the confines between the *Venetians*, and *Germans*. Upon the high Mountain of *Primolano* is there built a moſt ſtrong Bulwark of the *Venetians* called *Strada*, where a few Souldiers can repel the Dutch, when ever they offer by violence, or force, to advance forwards. At twelve miles diſtance from thence towards the Eaſt, among the *Alps*, is the City of *Feltre*, by the which way at the right-hand-ſhore of the River *Brent*, three miles diſtance from *Scala*, is ſeated *Cavolo*, a Fort of the *Germans*, inexpugnable, in reſpect that 'tis founded upon a great Rock directly hanging over the high-way, with a Fountain of living water in it, whereto neither Man, nor Goods can be mounted from the Earth, unleſs faſtned to a Rope, and that wound up upon a wheel, from which (becauſe 'tis a very narrow way underneath, between the Mountain and the River) with ſmall labour, may their enemies be ſlain with Stones caſt on them, as they march along. Thence five miles diſtant, is the River *Ciſimone* (wch diſembogues it ſelf into the *Brenta*) where the Dutch and *Feltrini*, daily load great qnantities of Timber and Wood, as well for the uſe of Building, as for firing, which they afterwards tranſport to *Baſſano*, to *Padoua*, and to *Venice*. Seven miles diſtant from *Baſſano*, on the Right-hand-ſhore of the *Brent*, lies the Countrey of *Valſtagna*, placed at the foot of the Mountains, and famous for the Sawes there made: thence diſtant three miles, lies the Countrey of *Campeſe*, where in the Church of the Fryers of Saint *Benedict* lies buried he that wrote *la Machaᵣonea.*

Baſſano lies at the foot of this ſtreight Valley, and is waſhed towards the Weſt by the *Brent*, called antiently *Brenta*, or *Brenteſia*, the which hath its Sourſe, or head, beyond the *Alps* of *Trent* twelve miles, near *Levego.* Over the *Brent*, a little forth of the Gate of *Baſſano*, is built a great Bridge of Wood, which conjoyns both the Rivers. Between the *Alps*, and this Caſtle, there are ſome Hills, which produce moſt abundantly all things requiſite, as well for neceſſary living, as delicacy, but moſt particularly, they abound with Olives, and precious Wines. The River *Brenta* runs thorow the Territory of *Vicenza*, paſſeth by the City of *Padoua*, and in the end diſchargeth it ſelf, by the Fenny, or Mooriſh grounds, into the Sea. In this River, they take excellent Fiſh, as *Trouts*, *Pollard*, or *Chieven*, *Eyles*, *Pyke*, *Tench*, *Lampreys*, *Barbel*, and *Crabfiſh.* In no place are the men more ingenuous in Merchandize than in this: particularly in weaving of Cloth, in turning moſt neatly in Ivory, and in Carving in Nut-Trees. There is never a year, that they dreſs leſs than fifteen thouſand pound weight of Silk, and notwithſtanding that, that which is made in *China* is eſteemed better than is made in any other part of

the world, neverthelefs 'tis known, that this of *Baſſano* is more fub-
tile or thin, and more light. Hence the Family of the *Carrareci* drew
their Original, and *Eccellino* the Tyrant, as alfo *Lazaro*, furnamed *Baſſano*, a perſon not meanly learned, nor lefs acquainted in the Greek
tongue than in the Latine: he lived a long time in *Bologna*, with great
fatisfaction to the learned, afterwards he rendred himſelf at *Padoua*,
to the end that he might illuminate thoſe who were ſtudious of good
Letters. At preſent *Giacomo dal Ponte*, an excellent Lymner,
greatly illuſtrates this Country, together with four of his Sons, called vulgarly, the *Baſſani*. *Baſſano* hath under it twelve Towns, which
with it felf contein to the number of twelve thouſand Souls.

MAROSTICA.

AT three miles diſtance from *Baſſano* towards the Weſt, is ſeated
a ſtrong place, named *Maroſtica*, a Caſtle built by the Lords of
Scala, near the Mountain, and fortified with Walls, and two Sconces.
Antiently this Caſtle ſtood in the neighbouring Mountain, which
looks towards the Eaſt, where, at this time are to be ſeen the Foundations. Here the Air is moſt perfect, and the Countrey as pleaſant,
and produceth excellent fruits, in great abundance, but it moſt excels in Cherries of all ſorts, which are ſo infinitely pleaſant, and ſo
well reliſhed, that therefore in many places they are called *Maroſti-
cane*. There are many Fountains of clear Water; and thence about
two miles, is a Lake called *Piola*, whoſe waters abate, and riſe, in the
ſame manner as they in the Golf of *Venice*, with great admiration to
the beholders. The Inhabitants of this Caſtle are extreme conten-
tious, whereupon an Elegant Poet wrote thus,

> *Reſtat & in Civibus Marii diſcordia vetus,*
> *Quæ cum Syllanis ſævit in urbe viris.*

Within this Caſtle, are many Churches, among which is that of
Saint *Baſtiano*, where the Fryers of Saint *Francis* dwell, wherein lies
the Body of the bleſſed *Lorenzuolo* the Child, Martyred by the wicked Jews, who antiently there inhabited. *Franceſco* of the Family of
the *Freſchi*, hath much illuſtrated this Caſtle, who publickly Read
the Civil Law in *Padoua*, and likewiſe *Angelo Mateaccio*, who hath
compoſed ſome Books of the Laws. At this preſent, adds no ſmall
Fame to this his Countrey, *Proſpero Alpino*, the moſt excellent Phyſician, publique Reader of the firſt matter of Simples, in the Academy
of *Padoua*, who hath written *De plantis Ægypti, De Opobalſamo*, and *De
Præſagienda vitâ, & morte Ægrotantium*, lately publiſhed, And is now
employed (beſides his publick Reading) in compoſing, and ripening
ſome other noble Work for publick view. Thorow the middle of
this Caſtle, runs the little River called *Rozza*, whence about a mile
paſſeth the *Sillano*, ſo called, becauſe in Antient Language, it ſignified
a Stream of running water. 'Tis believed, that the Antient *Romans*
much frequented this Place, for that the Inhabitants to this day retain certain Latine words, though ſomething corrupted. Before
the

the Church of Saint *Floriano*, stand two Marble Stones of great antiquity, upon the one whereof is written thus,

> *T I Claudio Cæſ.*
> *M. Salonius .·..·. es*
> *Martina Chara Conjux quæ*
> *Venit de Gallia per manſiones*
> *L. Vi commemoraret memoriam*
> *Mariti ſui*
> *Bene quieſcas dulciſſime mi Marite:*

TREVISO.

THe Antient City of *Treviſo*, is ſituated on the Eaſt of, and at the diſtance from *Baſſano* twenty five miles. This City was founded by *Oſaride*, the third King of the *Grecians*, who being adopted Son of *Dioniſius* (therefore conceded unto him *Ægypt*) and Reigned in *Italy* ten years : And becauſe after his death, there appeared to the *Ægyptians* an Ox, they ſuppoſing it to be their King *Oſiris*, worſhipped it as a God, and called it *Api*, which in their language ſignifies an Ox, for which reaſon in many places of *Treviſo*, is found an Ox painted with this Motto: *Memor:* in memorial of their firſt founders. Others ſay that *Treviſo* was built by the Companions of *Antenor*; Others by the *Trojans*, who went from *Paflagonia*; but whoſoever it was built it, imports not much, ſince 'tis moſt certain, 'tis a City of great Antiquity. They oftentimes came to Warlike diſputes with the *Padouans*, as alſo with the *Altinati* for maintenance of their confines, and although through their vigilancy, and victory over the power of their Enemies, they had much enlarged their Territories, almoſt over the whole Champain, yet to ſecure themſelves the better, they erected ſeveral Towers, whence they might diſcover their Enemies, obſtruct them from too near approaches, and as neceſſitated therein, make their own retreat ſecure: and for this reaſon, was it along time called the City of *Towers*, bearing for its Arms three Black Towers in a white Field. This City either for that it was the moſt noble of all the other, or for that it became firſt under their Dominion, the *Longobardi* made the ſeat of their *Marqueſate*, *Marca* ſignifying in their language, Confines : whence all this Province is called by the name of *Marca*; Wherein antiently were ſix principal Cities, (at preſent but four) with many other Cities, and great Caſtles. Its Territory is in length from Eaſt to Weſt forty miles, and from North to South, fifty miles. It was ſubjected to the *Hunnes*, to the *Longobards*, Then to the *Hungarians*, afterwards to the People of *Scala*, after them to the *Carrareſians*, and laſtly in the year of our Lord, One thouſand three hundred eighty eight, it was reduced under the Dominion of the *Venetians*, to whom from that time to this day, they have maintained conſtant Faith and Obedience. This City was converted to the Chriſtian Faith, by the Preaching of Saint *Proſdocimo*, Diſciple of Saint *Peter*, from whence they took, a white Crosse in a Red Field for their Arms, in liew of their Black Towers. About *Treviso* runs the River *Sile*, with many other Rivolets, which incorporate with it, and towards the East, it hath the great River of *Piave*, wherein they take the largest Crabfish. The Countrey abounds in all things, but principally it breeds the Fattest Calves. It conteins many sumptuous Pallaces, and not a few Noble Families. At eight miles distance from this City, stands *Altino*, which was founded by *Antenor*, but afterwards layed wast by *Attila*; between *Treviso*, and *Padoua* presents it self the Rich and Civil Castle of *Noale*. Upon the Mountains towards the North, stood the noble Castle of *Asolo*, heretofore a Colony of the *Romans* as report saith, where with great delight, dwelt the Queen of *Ciprus*, having four miles off *Asolo*, built a most beautiful Cittacel in as pleasant a Plain, with Gardens, Fountains, Fish-ponds, and all other recreations. Eloigned from thence ten miles stands *Castel Franco*, a famous Castle, which was built by the *Trivisani*, in the year of our Lord, One thousand one hundred ninety nine. After which towards the East, between the Rivers *Piave*, and *Livenza* shewes it self *Conegliano*, part whereof stands erected upon the Hill, and part upon the Plain, which is replenished with beautiful structures, and a numerous People; and enjoyes an Air so temperate, that it acquired the name among the *Germans* of *Cunicla*, which is as much as to say, a Residence for a King. This was the first place, that the *Venetians* possessed upon the firm Land. Adjacent hereto stand *Colalto*, *Narvisa*, and the Castle of Saint *Salvadore*, to the most Noble Family of the *Collalti* appertaining. A little further lies *Oderto*, whereto in the time of the *Romans*, the *Adriatique* Sea rise, which encouraged the *Oderzesians* to set a Fleet to Sea. Near thereunto lies, *la Motta*, the Countrey of *Girolamo Alexandro* created Cardinal, by his Holiness *Paul* the third Bishop of *Rome*, for his most excellent Doctrine; being no less learned in the Greck, and Hebrew Tongues than in the Latine. Travelling from *Treviso*, over a large and spatious High-way, at ten miles distance, is met the Castle of *Mestre*, and two miles off that *Margherd*, where taking Boat, after rowing the space of five miles, you arrive at *Venice*.

1199.

VENETIA, la *Ricca*, or *VENICE* the *Rich*.

Sholes.

HAving attained *Le Lagune*, or the (M O O R E S, or S H O L E S) now the Streets of *Venice*, you behold many proud Pallaces, built of Marble, adorned with Columbes, Statues, and Pictures of great value, erected by those Noble Senatours, with inestimable Expence, and Artifice; among which is Seated the Pallace of the *Grimani*, imbellished with Statues, Figures, Pourtraicts, high and great Colossuses, and Vaults; some of Marble, and others of Brass, very artificially Carved, and Engraven, being brought hither from *Greece*, and the Ruines of *Aquileia*. In the open Gallery, whereof are divers Marble Stones, with excellent Inscriptions, amongst the which

we

we will hereunder set down some, which are engraven upon some
Altars dedicated in honour of *Beleno*, who was held in exceeding
great veneration by the Inhabitants of *Aquileia* as the Histories of *E.*
rodian, and *Giulio Capitolino* do averr and justifie ; The Titles of
which Inscriptions, I believe will be very welcome and pretious to
the Lovers of Antiquity.

Upon one four squared Altar, is
  inscribed.
    Beleno.
    Mansuetus.
    Verus.
    Laur: Lau:
  Et Vibiana
      Jantula
      V. S.

Upon another.

Apollini
Beleno. Aug.
    In honorem.
C. Petti. C. C. F. Pal.
Fbiltati. Eq. P.
Præf. Æd. Pot.
Præf. Et. Patron.
    Collegiorum.
Fabr. Et Cent.
  Diocles Lib.
Donum. Dedit.
L. D. D. D. D.

Upon another.

  Belino. Aug.
    Sacrum.
  Voto suscepto.
  Pro. Aquillio
C. F. Pomp. Vatente
  IIII. V. I. D. Design.
  Phœbus Lib.
V. S. L. M.

Upon another.

  Beleno.
Aug. Sacr.
L. Cornelius
 L. Fil. Vell.
  Secundinus

    Aquil.
Evoc. Aug. N.
Quod. In. Urb.
Donum. Vou.
    Aquil.
Perlatum.
Libens Posuit.
  L. D. D. D.

Upon another.

Beleno. Aug.
  In. Memor.
    Julior.
Marcell. Et.
Marcellæ. Et
    In Honorem
      Juliarum.
Charites. Et
Marcellæ. Filiar.
Et. Licin. Macron.
  Iunior Nepotis.
  C. Iul. Agathopos
V I. Vir. Aquil.
  L. D. D. D.

Upon another.

  Beleno
    Sex
Græfernius
    Faustus
V I. Vir.
V. S. L. M.

Upon another

  Eonti. B.
Upon another.
V I. Divinæ
  Sacrum
C. Verius.
C. F.
Gavolus.

The next object worth a view, is the Royal and Proud Pallace of the Duke of *Venice*, which was firſt begun to be erected by *Angelo Participatio*, in the year of our Lord, Eight hundred and nine, ſince when though ſix times burnt either in part, or in all it riſe again, and recovered much more beauty and luſtre. Its Form, is not altogether ſquare, the length ſomewhat exceeding the Bredth. Towards the North of it, ſtands the Church of Saint *Marco*, towards the Eaſt, the Grand Canale, or Channell, towards the South the Sea Coaſt, and towards the Weſt, the *Piazza*, or broad Place of *Venice*. From the principal Gate of this Pallace, to that Coign which ſtands next the Bridge, called *Paglia*, or (*Straw Bridge*) towards the South: It hath an Arcade of 36. Arches, every one wherof are ten feet large, which ſpace comprehending thirty three Pillars, affords in length three hundred foot, which Collumns have no Baſes, but excellent HEADS. The two Frontiſpieces thereof, appear Pargetted with White and Red Marble, in the midſt whereof are little Aſcents or Hills, whereon are ſet thirty ſeven Collumnes, made in the Form of *Pyramids*, with ſeventy two Arches; The Facade or Frontiſpiece backwards was lately beautified with *Iſtrian Stone*, and is contignous towards the North, with the Church of Saint *Marco*. The Roofs of this Pallace were heretofore covered with Lead, but the fire that happened in the year, 1574. cauſed it to be covered inſtead of lead, with Slat of a certain Mettle. Every Front hath one Gate, The principal which is conjoyned with the Church, (of a Piramide Figure) looks towards the *Piazza*, or broad Place, juſt before which ſtands the winged Lion, and the Duke *Foſcaro*, Carved in White Marble. Next within on the right hand, is found a ſpatious Court, wherein are two Wells of ſweet Water, whoſe mouthes are made with Braſs, garniſhed with Spouts, and other Curioſities. At the end of this Court, is the Gate which anſwers to the Sea. Then having aſcended the cloſe Stairs called *Foſcara*, on the left hand, you may go round the Pallace upon the Tarrace. The two Fronts backwards, the one whereof looks towards the Sea, the other towards the *Piazza*, parallell them that are forwards, except that they have neither Arches, nor Collumnes below. The Front towards the Eaſt on the even ground, hath thirty ſix Arches, and as many Pillars of *Iſtrian Stone*, over the which, there is an open Gallery of fifty four Arches, and fifty five Collumnes. On the Top is drawn a Wall of *Iſtrian Stone*, adorned with beautiful Corniſhes. Juſt againſt the Principall Gate, ſtands the large Stayer-caſe of the Pallace towards the North, which leads directly to the Lodging of the Prince, at the foot of this Stayer-caſe ſtands two Coloſſuſes, the one of *Marſe*, the other of *Neptune*, Upon the top thereof likewiſe, juſt oppoſite to them, ſtands two moſt excellent Statues, the one of *Adam*, the other of *Eve*. The Front below towards the Canale, or Channel, hath two Stayer-caſes, by the which, they aſcend to that moſt Royal Corridor, or open Gallery, wherein ſtand many Tribunals, or Courts of Juſtice. Oppoſite to the Chief Stayer-caſe, is a Memorial of *Henry* the third King of *France*, engraven in Marble with Letters of Gold. From the South Eaſt, they aſcend that moſt ſplendid Stayer-caſe, which upon the left hand leads to the Chamber of the Prince; and on the right hand to the Colledge. Where the Eye is wholly taken up with beholding

holding

beholding the moſt ſumptuous Vaulted, or Arched Roof, or Seeling, Richly garniſhed with Gold.

This College ſtands towards the Eaſt, over the Chamber of the Prince, whoſe vaulted Roof (as at *Venice* they call it) is partly guilt, partly Carved with great Artifice, partly Painted, and wrought with Hiſtories, even to Admiration; At the upper end of this Hall, is exalted the Imperial Throne of the Duke, and the Images of *Venice*, figured by a Queen, who diſpoſeth the Crown upon his Head. Here the Duke with the Senatours tranſact the affairs of State, and give Audience to Embaſſadours, as well ſuch as have recourſe to them from their own Territories, and Cities, as of Foreign Princes. Out of which leads a door into another great Hall, wherein are figured all the Provinces, which the *Venetians* poſſeſs upon the firm Land, where alſo are erected eleven moſt excellent Statues of Emperours. Iſſuing forth of theſe Places, and walking towards the Sea, you meet the dreadful Tribunals of the Counſel of *Tenne*, where every Place gloriouſly ſhines with Gold and coſtlineſs.

A little more forwards is the ſpacious Hall, or Senate Houſe of the Great Counſel, where they diſpoſe the publique Offices, and Ballott the Magiſtrates; which Counſel orders it ſelf in this manner. Firſt the Duke royally clad, ſits on a Throne, raiſed a good higth from the Ground. On his Right Hand, he hath three Counſellors near him, accompanyed by one of the Chief of the Magiſtrates of forty, for Criminal Offences: Juſt oppoſite to the Prince at the other End of the Great Hall, ſits one of the Chief of the Illuſtrious Counſel of the *Tenne*. A little from whence ſeats himſelf one of the Advocates of Comminalty. In the Angles, or Corners of the Great Hall, ſtands the Old and New Auditors. In the middle are the Cenſors. The reſt of the Nobles of *Venice* ſit promiſcuouſly in other Seats leſs raiſed from the plain ground of the great Hall. Into which Counſel cannot be admitted any that is not Noble, and who is not above the age of twenty five years. Afterwords the Grand Chancellour (having firſt recommended to every One their duty, to elect a Perſon fit for that Magiſtracy) names the firſt Competitor. Then certain little Lads, go up and down the Hall with double Boxes, the one wherof is white, the other green; The White forwards, the Green more inward gathering the Balls, which Balls are ſmall, and made of Cloth, that by the ſound of the fall into the Box, may not be judged into which 'tis caſt, and before he caſts in, the ſuffrage giver, muſt ſhew that he hath but one Ball, and alſo tell the name of that Gentleman who ſtands for thoſe that perhaps have not well heard who 'twas, do it (many times) over again; He that would exclude the Stander caſts the Balls into the Green Box, and he that would have him choſen caſts them into the White Box, which are made in ſuch a Form that none can diſcern into which of the Boxes they put their Balls, The Procurators of Saint *Mark*, never enter into this Great Counſel, Except at the Election of the Duke) but ſtand under the Lodge with the Maſter & Officers of the Arſenal, while that great Counſel is gathered together for its Guard, dividing among themſelves thoſe dayes, whereon they ought to have this Charge. But of theſe things for further ſatisfaction we referr the Reader to ſuch, who treat of them at large, herein intending only to glance briefly at the moſt remarkable things.   D   This

This great Hall, is ſeventy three foot broad, & one hundred & fifty foot long, and was begun in the year, One thouſand three hundred & nine. On its walls were drawn by the moſt excellent Painters of that Age, the victories of this Commonwealth, Its Princes, with many other famous Men of *Jtaly*, which being ſpoyled by the ſmoak of that Fire, which happened in the year, 1577. in liew thereof, was Painted the Hiſtory of *Alexander* the third chief Biſhop of *Rome*, and *Frederick* the Emperour, with the ſubjection of *Conſtantinople*, to the *Venetian* Republique. The Floors are wonderful neat : Towards the Eaſt, is ſeated the Throne of the Prince, over which is a Paradiſe Painted by the hand of *Tintoretto* (which was formerly Painted by *Guariento*) and fils up all that Front. In the Front over againſt that, within a ſquare of Marble, is an Image of the Holy *Virgin*, holding in her Arms, her little Infant, compaſſed about by four Angels. The Windows of this Hall, look ſome into the Court, and others into the Sea. Near hereunto is the Magazine of the Pallace, which is never opened, but to Foreign Princes, wherein is proviſion of Arms, for fifteen hundred Gentlemen, more or leſs, and 'tis divided into four ſpatious Portals, with the Doors thereof of Cipres Wood, which give a moſt ſweet ſavour. On the other ſide of the Hall of the Great Counſel is beheld the Hall of the Inquiſitors, with many and divers Pictures, amongſt which is a Judgement, drawn by the hand of *Tintoretto*.

Thence deſcending by the Foſcaran Stayers, you enter the Dukes Chappel being the Cathedral Church of S. *Mark*, wch is built with the faireſt and fineſt Marble with great skill, and no leſs expence, whoſe Pavement is compoſed all of little pieces of *Porphiry*, and *Serpentine*, and other pretious Stones after the Moſaick manner, with divers Figures. Among others, there are ſome Figures Effigiated by Commiſſion of *Gionachino Abbat* of *Santo Fiore* (as is the common Fame) by which is preſaged and demonſtrated the great ruine which will fall upon the People of *Italy*, with other ſtrange misfortunes: Where you beheld two Cocks, very boldly to carry away a Fox (wich ſignifies (as ſome will have it) that two *French* Kings ſhould carry away, and force *Lodovico Sforza* out of the Seigniory of *Milan*. And alſo ſome Lyons Large and Fat appear as put in the Water, and ſome others ſet upon the ſhore very lean. Upon the Walls of the fineſt Marble, on the left hand, are two Tables of white Marble, ſomewhat weaved with black, which at their joyning, repreſent a Man, ſo perfectly figured, that 'tis very wonderful to conſider it. Whereof *Albertus Magnus* in a work called *Meteora* (as of a great rarity) makes mention. There are in this ſumptuous Temple (reckoned amongſt the chief of *Europe*, (though not ſo much for its vaſtneſs, as the deſign and pretious materials) thirty ſix Collumnes of the fineſt Marble, which are large two feet Diamiter. The Roof of it is divided into five Cupoloes covered with Lead. From the plain of this Place, to the very Top of the Temple, are the Fronts wrought up in *Moſaicke* work, with Figures in a Field of Gold, and certain little Heads of Pillars, and Juttings out, or Eeves of Marble, upon which are ſet certain Images carved in Marble ſo perfectly, that they ſeem alive. There are alſo above this place on that part, which lies over the great Gate (whereof this Part hath five made of Braſs)

four

four Horſes very Antique of Braſs guilt, of an exaĉt Proportion, and extremely beautiful, which the *Romans* cauſed to be caſt, to put them in the Triumfal Arch of *Nero*, when he Triumphed over the *Parthians*, and they being afterwards tranſported by *Conſtantine* to *Conſtantinople*; from thence (the *Venetians* being thereof become Lords) tranſported them to *Venice*, ſetting them upon the Temple of Saint *Mark*. In the Porch of the ſaid Church, is ſeen a red ſquare Marble Stone, upon which *Alexander* the third ſet his Foot upon the neck of *Frederick* the Emperour, whereon for that reaſon, are engraven theſe words :

Super Aſpidem, & Baſiliſcum ambulabis.

· After which mounting to the Top of the Quire, by certain Steps of the fineſt Stones, you come to the place where the Singers ſtand on the Ghief Feaſt dayes. There upon the great Alter, is the rich and fair Pixe framed of Gold and Silver, bedecked with many pretious Stones, and Perl of an infinite price, which all perſons admire that behold it. This Altar is covered over by one Arch, diſpoſed into the form of a Croſs, adorned with Marble, which the Antients called *Tiberiano*, ſupported with four Pillars of excellent Marble; wherein are carved the Hiſtory of the Old and New Teſtaments. Behind this Altar, ariſe four Pillars of the pureſt *Alablaſter*, five foot in length, tranſparent as Glaſs, placed there for Ornament of the Sacred and Holy Body of Jeſus Chriſt conſecrated or the Euchariſt. In this Church are preſerved with great devotion, many Reliques : and among others the Body of the Evangeliſt, this Republiques Proteĉtor Saint *Mark*, with his Goſpel written by his own hand.

On the right hand of the Temple, in the midſt thereof, is a large and high Gate, wrought all of Moſaique work, on the one ſide wherof ſtands the Effigies of Saint *Dominick*, and on the other that of Saint *Franciſco*, which as 'tis reported, were made by order of the above named *Gionachino* many years before the ſaid Saints came into the world. Within this Gate is kept the moſt rich Treaſure of Saint *Mark* ſo much ſpoken of; wherein are twelve pretious Crowns, with twelve Breſt Plates, all compaſſed about with fine Gold, and garniſhed with many Stones of great value. Among divers others, with *Rubies, Emeralds, Topaſſes, Criſolits*, and other pretious Stones, and Perls of numatchable bigneſs; Two Unicorns Horns of a great length, with a third ſomewhat leſs. Many very large Carbuncles, Veſſels of Gold, Scollops of Agat, and Jaſper Stones of a good bigneſs. One Huge Ruby given this State, by *Domenico Grimani*, a moſt worthy Cardinal. An Emerald hower-glaſs heretofore preſented to this moſt illuſtrious Seigniory, by *Uſcaſſano* King of *Perſia*, with many other pretious things, Veſſels, and Cenſores of Gold, and Silver. There alſo lies the Mitre or Bonnet (as we call it) with which every new Duke is Crowned. The which is traverſed all over with the fineſt Gold, and polliſh't, in whoſe wreathes, are many moſt pretious ſtones; and at the very Top, a Carbuncle of ineſtimable valew; I might alſo ſpeak of the Candle-ſticks, and Challices, with other things of ſuch imminent valew, as may create wonder in the beholders, but would take up too much time and room to deſcribe them in this Abreviation.   D 2   Juſt

Just opposite to this Temple, and distant from it about Eighty Paces, stands the high Steeple, which is 40. Foot square on all sides, and Two Hundred and Thirty high, with an Angel set upon the Top, which like a Weather-cock turning with the Wind to all corners where it blowes, ever hath the Face towards it. All the said Top or upper part thereof, is richly guilt, which presents it to the Eye of such as addresse to *Venice*, (by reason of the reflection of the hot Sun thereon) *Lucidely* shining at a great distance; In the foundation of this Steeple was more expended (as *Sabellico* declares) than in all the other structure. They ascend to the uppermost part of this Steeple, by certain little winding steps within, where a most excellent Prospect discovers it self: as first, the City of *Venice*, divided into six Precincts, consisting of many little Islands, whose Bankes are conjoyned with Bridges, the Streets, the open Places, the Churches, the Monasteries, and other sumptuous structures; Moreover, the small Islands seated round about the City to the number of sixty, with their Monasteries, Churches, Pallaces, and most beautiful Gardens; Upon some of which Islands, are erected many Columnes, by the *Aquleiesi*, the *Vicentini*, the *Opitergini*, *Concordiesi*, *Altinati*, and several other People, who to fly the Fury of *Attila*, King of the *Hunnes*, recovered this Place; gives no small Imbellishment to this View. Between the said Moorish Grounds, now the Streets and the Sea, by Dame Nature is raised a Fence or Bank, to defend the City & the small Islands, against the furious Waves of the Sea, (with which 'tis invironed) Which Fence is Thirty five Miles long, and bends in the shape of a Bow, opening it self in five several Places, for each of which is a Gate, as well to permit Barkes to enter in at them, as to maintain the said Channels full of Water. The profound Havens of *Chioza*, and *Malamocco*, with the Forts built at the Mouth of the said Havens, to keep any Armado or Fleet at a distance; And lastly, the beholding the Mountaines of *Carnia*, and of *Histria*, and on the Right Hand, the *Apenine* Hills, with *Lumbardy*, together with the Famous Hills called *Euganei*, with the mouthes of the Rivers *Adice*, and *Poe*, and behind them the Alpes of *Baviera*, and of the *Gerisons*, alwaies covered with Snow, gives no small satisfaction, nor beauty to his Prospect.

And now we come to the Famous *Piazza*, or broad place of S. *Mark*, whose platform resembles a Carpenters square, at the one end whereof stands the Admirable Church of St. *Mark*, and at the other, That of St. *Geminian*, wrought with excellent Stones, and round the said Place are built fair and sumptuous Houses all of Marble Stone, under which are large open Galleries, wherein are Shops for several Artificers. In this place daily appear an infinite number of Persons, of all Qualities and Countries, in their several Habits, as well for Newes and Discourses, as for Traffick and Merchandize.

At the upper end of the said Place, upon the Channel called *La Giudeca*, are two Pillars admired for their Heigth and Bignefs, which were transported heretofore from *Constantinople*, upon the one whereof, stands a Winged Lyon, the Republick Armes, in token of St. *Marke* their Protector, with this Motto, *Pax tibi Marce Evangelista-ment*; and upon the other, is set the Statue of St. *Theodore*, between which Justice is done upon Traitorous Persons. These were brought

from

from *Greece* to *Venice*, in the time of *Sebastian Giani* the Duke, upon, certain Vessels of burden, together with another of equal Greatness, the which overcomming the Power and Industry of the Workmen labouring to lay it on the Earth, it fell into the Water, where at this time tis to be seen in the Deep: These vast Collumns, were reared by an Engineer of *Lombardy* named *Nicolo Berreterro*, by the strength of great Ropes wet with water, retiring by little and little; who asked no other reward for this his worke, but that it might be Lawful for Dice-Players to play therewhen they pleased without any penalty: This *Piazza* is not intirely one alone, but fower united together. Opposite to the Church are reared three Standards upon three high pieces of Timber which are fastened by Lead cast into the bored holes, they are wrought with signres to denote the liberty of this City and have Brass Pedestalls. On the right side of the Church stands the Clock-house adorned with the Celestial Signs gilt thereon with the Sun and Moons monethly ingress into them, most exactly wrought and painted. Neer the Steeple is a sumptuous Palace built in this Age, after the *Ionick* and *Dorick* fashion, which reaches even to the Church of Sain *Geminian*, which for the excellency of the Marble, Statues, Casements, Cornishes, Frets and other ornaments, together with the most incomparable Architecture, gives not place to any palace of *Italy*. Next is the *Zecca* or *Mint-house* built all of flint Stone, and Iron Barrs, without any manner of Timber. Annexed thereunto Stands the Library, which had its Original from *Petrarca*, and was afterwards aggrandized by the Cardinals *Niceno*, *Alexandro*, and *Grimano*. Lastly, this *Piazza* is rendred so Proud and marvellous, by the Uniformity of Building, and other Imbellishments, that I cannot say all *Europe* affords its like.

　　The Island *Muran*, must next be visited by taking *Gondola*, or *Boat*, which for its Furnaces of Glass is much admired through the World. This Island is distant from *Venice* about a Mile, and was begun to be inhabited by the *Altinati*, and *Opitergini*, for fear of the *Hunnes*. At present 'tis very comely, and resembling *Venice*, as well in the structures, as in the Quantity of Churches, but much more pleasant and delightful, in respect most of the Houses have open and spacious Gardens, set with all sorts of fruitful Trees. Among others, is the Church of Saint *Peter*, with a Monastery belonging to the preaching Fryers, well built, wherein is a famous Library full of good Books.

　　In this Place they make all sorts of Vessels of Glass (called Crystal Glass) whose variety & Workmanship surpass all others of the same materials of the whole world. And the Artizans (except in excellency of the materials) every day find out new Inventions to make them appear more desirable, with works divers from one another. I will not speak of the variety of colours which they give thereunto, because 'tis so marvellous that I imagine it worthy all Peoples sight. They counterfet excellently several things of *Agate*, *Calcidonian*, *Emerald*, and *Hyacinths*, with other pretty Toyes so excellently, that I believe were *Pliny* to be revived, and should behold them, he would (admiring them) much more praise these mens workmanship, and these artificial things, then he does the vessels of Earth made and burned by the People of *Aretini*, or of any other Nation.

Muran.

E　　　　　　　Opposite

Oppofite to the *Piazza* of Saint *Mark*, and about half a mile diftant, is feen the Church of Saint *George*, the Greater, a ftately ftruĉture of Marble.   In which is beheld moft curious Marble, both in the Pavements, and in the Statues, with rich workmanfhip of Silver, and moft fumptuous Sepulchres of Princes.   The Fryers of Saint *Benediĉt* have here a noble Monaftery, wherein are long open Galleries, fpacious Courts, ample eating-Rooms, and fleeping-Chambers, as alfo moft pleafant Gardens, with a worthy Library.

In *Venice* are feventeen Rich Hofpitals, with a great number of wealthy Churches, adorned with the exaĉteft marble Stone; confifting of fixty feven Parifh-Churches fifty fower Convents of Fryers, twenty fix Monafteries of Nunns, eighteen Chapels, fix Schools, kept within the Principal Fryeries or Monafteries. In all which Churches are fifty bodies of Saints, one hundred forty and three Organs,& many Statues made at the coft of the Republick, in remembrance of illuftrious Perfons, which have valiantly fought for her, or done fome other fignal piece of fervice, that is to fay, 165 of Marble, and 23 of Brafs, among which moft worthily prefents it felf, That proud Statue on Horfeback wrought with Gold, of *Bartolomeo Coglione* the moft famous Captain-General of the Venetian Army, dedicated to him by this Republiek, before the Church of Saint *John* and *Paul*, in teftimony of his Fidelity, and Valour.

Moreover, there are fifty fix Tribunals, and ten Gates of Brafs. The Store-Houfe of the *Germans*, which is five hundred and 12 foot in circumference, whofe Front outwards hath many excellent Figures, and inwards two Galleries which go quite round the one above the other, wherein are two hundred Lodging Chambers. There ftand alfo up and down this City, befides what are above mentioned, infinite more Statues, Piĉtures, and glorious Tombes.   At all feaf ns it abounds plentifully with fruits and herbs of all forts, and two hundred feveral forts of Fifh; furthermore there are four-hundred and fifty |bridges of Stone, fourfcore thoufand Gondaloes or Boats, with twice as many Gondaloers or Watermen, with a vaft number of Chanels, among the which the Principal is called the Grand Canale, or Chanel, one hundred and thirty paces in length, and forty in bredth, over which is built that moft artificial Bridge, called the *Rioalto*, being one Arch which conjoynes both the Banks, to be accounted for its heighth, length, and bredth, amongft the moft glorious fabricks of *Europe*; whereon are ereĉted twenty four fhops covered all alike with lead, that is to fay twelve of a fide with magnificent Baluftrades behind.   They afcend this Bridge by three degrees of fteps, that in the midft confifts of fixty fix Steps, and thofe of each fide, of one hundred forty five; to thefe rarities, may be added the infinite concourfe of People.

And to the end we may remove that erroneous opinion that this City was built by Fifhermen; let us obferve what *Caffiodoro*, who was Counfellor, and Secretary of *Theodorick* King of the *Gothes* fpeaks thereof.   *Vos* (faith he) *qui numerofa navigia in ejus confinio poffidetis, & Venetiæ plenæ nobilibus, &c.* which happening in the four hundred ninty and fifth year of our Salvation, and from the building thereof between 80. and 90. years, gives a fair prefumption, that the *Vene-tians,*

tians could not acquire so great reputation, nor less possess so many Vessels on the Sea, had they not been somewhat rich and noble too sometime before.

Your next visit must be to the Arsenal, or Magazine of War of this City, seated on the one side of it towards the two Castles, and *Palace* of the Patriark, which are compassed about with high Walls, and with the Sea. This Arsenal affords but one entrance by one only Gate, and by one only Chanel, where thorow are guided in all the shipping, and 'tis about the quantity of two miles in circuit. Herein generally they make all their works, and engines of War, but most particularly their Charge is to prepare here these 4. Materials for that Service, Timber, Iron, Brass, and Hemp. Of which their charge of Timber-work, they are so provident, (that besides what at first shewes it self to the view) there is under the water a good quantity of Gallies, great and small, Gallefoists, Pinnaces, Brigantines, Masts, Main-yards, Oars, and Rudders, for their Sea vessels. And for the Iron work, Bullets of all sizes, Nayls, Chains, Anchors, with divers Plates of Iron, as likewise for Brass, all sorts of Ordnance, and of all proportions. And lastly, of their Hempen works, all sorts of Shrouds, Sails and Cables. To which several works, continually attend a vast number of Workmen, and excellent Handicraftsmen, who being as it were born in that Place, and from thence obteining their livelihood, Neither delight in any other Place, nor do no other thing, but what there by their several Callings they are directed unto.

Therein are erected most ample Arches, wherein their several Vessels are kept dry, and built, some fully finished, some building, and others repairing. The next Curiosity, is their spatious Halls, full of Arms for defence in *Maritine* service, as great Celades, Cariages, and Breasts; and no less provided of Offensive Weapons, as Pistols, Daggers, Bramble Sithes, Partisans, Javelins, Two Handed Swords, Cross-bows, and Long-bows; Others of those Halls are filled with Artillery, as small and great Muskets, Falcons, whole Cannon, Demicannon, and Quarter Cannon, Sacres, and Culverins. There are some pieces of Atillery which have from Three Barrels to Seaven, which are called (if I err not) the Organs, Engines made more for a certain Greatnesse and Magnificence, than for use and service in War. To say no more, the whole is kept and governed with that order and neatnefs, 'that it doth not onely delight the Beholder, but would satisfie the most insatiable Appetite of gazers, and fill them with a certain spritely and Martial Ardour.

In fine, the Commonwealth hath in this place all sorts of Ammunition of Warr, as well for Land as Sea-service. All Engines for offence, all charges for defence, and lastly, all things whatsoever made ready, either to set in order an Armado for Sea service, or an Army for Land-service, which may be needful. And although from this place (which may properly be called the Work-house and Storehouse of War) they every Day fetch Arms and Ammunition, as well for their force upon the firm Land, as upon the Sea; Yet neverthelefs, by the daily labours of the Artizans, 'tis so restored, that it seems to no more diminish, than the Sea does by the many Rivers that issue

ſue out of it.   Furthermore here is kept the ſtately Galley called the *Bdcentoro*, adorned greatly with Gold and rich carvings, which never goes forth but upon ſolemn Feaſt Dayes, and particularly upon the Day of the Aſcenſion of our Saviour, on which Day, the Prince in great ſtate, with a Train of the principal Senatours enter herein, and being thence rowed to the Port of the two Caſtles near the *Adriatick* Sea, there after certain Ceremonies, the Duke ſolemnly marries the Sea, and caſts therein a Gold Ring, in real aſſurance of this Republicks Dominion thereof.

This Republick allow the Greek Church a full liberty in *Venice*, who uſe as much ceremony in their Religion as the Church of *Rome*, but leſs ſuperſtition.   Nor have the *Jewes* mean privileges, (for provided they alwais wear a red hat to denote the Blood they wiſht and drew upon their own heads when they crucified our Saviour, and withhout which tis Lawfull for any one to kill them) they have as great immunities in all things as the Naturals, and more power than the Common ſort; here alſo they have a Synagogue for every Nation, whereof they have nine in their *Guetta* or Court, which is aſſigned them for their habitation.   Their concourſe hither is from their immunities grown innumerable, which I ſuppoſe may give as great occaſion as any other for this Cities vaſt Traffique whereof ſhe is Miſtreſs in theſe parts, as alſo for the riſe and fall of the Exchange at the pleaſure of her Merchants: in their Bank are managed vaſt ſumes of money, and infinite exchanges dayly made, and yet a very ſmall ſum of money told out or payed through the yeer, ſuch is the Reputation of thoſe eminent Senators who are there the Bankers, where moſt of the Merchants accounts are kept for a ſmall matter; the Ducket de Banco, whereby they compute their greateſt ſums and govern their exchanges, is but an imaginary Coyn, riſing and falling at their pleaſure.   The Citizens rich and poor, wear a black Cap edged with fur on their heads, and are habited commonly with a long black Gown with large ſleeves with a kind of ſkirt to throw over one ſhoulder, and their Collar alwaies open.   Their Ladies did formerly wear their own or a counterfet hair below the ſhoulders trimmed with gemms and flowers, and mounted in their Chippenes (high as a mans legg) they walk between two handmaids to diſtinguiſh themſelves from the Courtezans. (from whom the State for their free trade extract a great exciſe yeerly) who go covered with a white veil of tiffany.   But of late yeers they uſe the french freedome both in habit and converſation much differing from the Italian reſtriction through their Jealouſie.   We had almoſt

 Zuccca. forgot the Iſland of *Zuecca* (diſtant from *Venice* one mile) wherein vaſt Edifices as well for divine worſhip, as for the uſe of the Citizens, with ſtately Gardens diſcover themſelves, among the reſt the Church (*del Redentore*) or of the Redeemer deſerves a place even amongſt the faireſt of *Venice* for its ſplendor and ſumptuouſneſs, being deſigned by *Palladius* the famous Architect, and built by order and at the coſt of the State by a unanimous Vow which they made in the yeer **1576** when they were infected with an extreme plague: Which to denote, over one of the Gates of the right ſide of the ſaid Church, we finde it thus written.

Chriſto

Chriſto Redemptori.

Civitate Gravi Peſtilentia
Liberata,

Senatus ex voto.

Here alſo is ſhewed ſome of the Coyns in Silver, which were ſtamped by Duke *Luigi Mocenigo*, in the Seaventh Year of this Republick.

The Journey from *Venice* to *Milan*, by the Province of *Marca Trivigiana*, and *Lumbardy.*

PADOVA.

TO goe from *Venice* to *Padoua*, firſt they take Boat at *Venice*, and row five Miles upon Sholes in the Gulf of *Venice* to *Lizafuſina*, so called from a Dutch word corrupted : At which place the direct *Lizafuſina.*
courſe of the River *Brent*, was heretofore by the Lords of *Venice* artificially locked up, to the end, that running through thoſe Pools and ſalt Moors, it might not through time and continual running work down the neighbouring Grounds: which to prevent, there was an Engine erected (called *La Rota del Carro*) whereby with excellent Induſtry, the Barkes, with all their Lading and Merchandize, were drawn up and tranſpoſed from out of theſe Pools, or ſalt Moors, into the River, and out of the River in like manner into the Pools; which at this time is taken away, and for ſupply thereof, the water is locked in with four ſeveral Flood-gates, the firſt at *Strà*, the ſecond at *Dolo*, the third at *Mirà*, and the laſt at *Moranzan*. From *Lizafuſina* to *Padoua* they account four Miles, whereby they travel either in Boats, which are drawn up againſt the ſtream of the River, or elſe by Land. On each ſide of which River throughout, appears a large and moſt fertile *Campagna*, with a rich ſoyl, embelliſhed with ſtately and moſt ſumptuous Palaces, and lovely Gardens, and no leſſe beautified with the continual travelling of all ſorts of People to and fro. Firſt they arrive at the Country of *Oriago*, called in Latin *Ora lacus*, becauſe to this place extend the Mooriſh Grounds or ſholes, thence at *Dolo*, and then at *Strà*; Upon the left Hand, ſtands the great Town of *Gambarare*, ſo infinitely populous, that tis almoſt incredible; In the end they attain at *Padoua*.

PADOVA the Learned.

The ancient City of *Padoua*, is ſeated in the Province belonging
F to

to *Venice*, called *Marca Trivigiana*, in the midſt of a ſpacious Plain, having the Sea at Twenty Miles diſtance on the Eaſt and South parts thereof: Towards the Weſt, a large champion Country; And towards the North, the Mountains *Euganei*; It is of a triangular form, invironed with double Walls, and very deep Ditches; The *Venetians* have fortified it very much, by the immenſe Walls and Bulwarks, built by them according to the modern way of Diſcipline and Judgement in Warr.

We need not produce Teſtimony from antient Writers, to prove the Antiquity of this City, nor that it was founded by *Antenor*, Brother of *Priam* King of *Troy*, and that it was denominated heretofore *Pado*, either from *Pò*, or *Patavio* of *Paphlagonia*, becauſe theſe things are notorious to all; As alſo that *Padoua* was Head of the Province of *Venice*, now *Marca Trivigiana*, or *Marquiſate* of *Treves*, and that it was ever Friend, and allied to *Rome* without any kind of ſubjection, being extremely beloved and eſtemed, not leſſe for their Alliance or Parentage, having their joynt Original from the Famous *Troy*, than for the many ſervices and kindneſſe received from it. Nor find we in any Author, That *Padoua* was either ſubjugated, overcome, or moleſted by the *Romans*, but that it alwayes ſtood free from the *Roman* Yoke, and that it aided the Republick on many occaſions; And particularly, at that time when *Rome* was taken by the *Galli Sireni*, in the Warr againſt the *Umbri*, *Boi*, the *Cimbri*, and at ſeveral other times; So that it well merited and obtained the Franchiſe and Liberty of Citizens and Comunalty of *Rome*, and to be inſcribed in the *Fabian* Tribe of *Rome*, without ſending thither new Inhabitants, or making it a Colony, from whence the *Padouans* derived equal voice both Active and Paſſive, and participated all the higheſt degrees of that great Sate; And therefore we read in the Hiſtories of *Rome*, and in thoſe of *Padoua*, That many *Padouan* Houſes transferred themſelves to *Rome*, & as many Roman Houſes to avoid the Civil diſſentions tranſlated themſelves to *Padoua*. We may then conclude it to be no great wonder, that we find in ſo many ancient Writers, and upon ſo many Marble Stones, the Remembrance of ſo many Citizens of *Padoua* that were Roman Conſuls, as *Qninto Attio Capitone*, *Seſto Papinio Alenio*, *L. Arontio Primo*, *L. Stella Poeta*, *L. Arontio Aquila*, *Giulio Lupo*, *L. Giulio Paulo* the Expounder of the Law, *L. Aſcanio Pediano*, *Traſea Peto*, *C. Cecinna Peto*, *Pub. Quartio*, and ſome others. Another *Peto* was deſigned Conſul, and *Peto Honorato* was Corrector of *Italy*, ſo alſo many were Ediles, Prætors, Tribunes, Cenſors, Prieſts, and chief Buſhops. It was then ſo great and powerful, that they uſed to muſter five Hundred Cavaliers or Horſemen, And *Strabo* writes, that they commonly ſent to the wars, one Hundred and twenty Thouſand Foot Souldiers. It maintained it ſelf ever glorious and invincible, until the Barbarous Nations made themſelvs to be felt in *Italy*, for at the time of the Roman Empires declination, *Padoua* alſo indured the ſmart, being by the moſt Potent *Attila* (the Rod of God) wholly ruinated, and caſt down even to the very Foundations; And though after that it was reſtored by *Narſete*, yet was it another time deſtroyed by the *Longobardi*. But afterwards under *Charles* the Great and his Succeſſors, it began to fill it ſelf, and to take ſome ſmall reſtoration. This City

ty was governed at firſt by Conſuls, and after with a *Podeſtà*,
or Provoſt, at ſuch time as it became under the Power of *Eccelli-*
no the Tyrant, who treated it moſt cruelly, which evidently appears;
For at this day, neer the Church of Saint *Auguſtine*, they ſhew a great
Tower, wherein the *Padouans* were impriſoned, tormented and
ſlain, nay the Cruelty of this wicked Tyrant ſo far exceeded, that in
one day in the City of *Verona*, for no other cauſe than his fantaſti-
cal humour, he cauſed twelve thouſand *Padouans* to be Butchered.
Out of the ruines of ſo many noble Palaces deſtroyed by him, he
intended and begun near the Bridge a new Cittadel for his habitation and ſecurity, but he lived not to finiſh above a fourth part,
which is built with walls of a vaſt thickneſs with flint-ſtones ſquared, with a fair Palace and a proud Tower, which in truth is the
moſt beautifull in all *Padoua* (and is poſſeſſed at preſent by *Il Signor*
Conte Giacomo Zabarella.)   Many notable things are extant in this City, but in particular there is a vault under ground which paſſeth
under the River, and goes even to the *Piazza*, to the Palace of the
Captain, and to the other abovenamed Cittadel. After his death
Padoua recovered her Liberty, and became very powerfull, ſo that
ſhe got under her dominion, *Vicenza*, *Verona*, *Trento*, *Treviſo*, *Fel-*
tre, *Belluno*, *Conegliano*, *Ceneda*, *Saravalle*, *Chioza*, and *Baſſano*, with
all their Territories, all the good ground among the *Fennes*, and the
greateſt part of the *Friuli*, and other important places; then the
Carrareſi made themſelves Lords thereof, and kept the power a-
bout one hundred yeers; at laſt the *Venetians* got the poſſeſſion, having ſlain *Franceſco Novello* with all his Children, and extinguiſhed
the principality of the *Carrareſi*. Through this City runs the River
Brent together with the *Bacchiglione*, which dividing it ſelf into many branches gives a great accomodation to the Citizens.   One of
which branches or Arms they have brought to paſs thorow the dike
round about the Walls of the City. It affords in great aboundance all
neceſſaries for livelihood, from whence the Proverb ariſes, *Bolognia*
(*Graſſa*) or wallowes in good cheer, but *Padoua* (*ſurpaſſa*) ſur-paſſeth it.
The bread they make here is the whiteſt of *Italy*; And the wine is by
Plinie accounted amongſt the moſt noble and excellent.   This City
hath about it ſeven gates, many Stone Bridges, five ſpacious *Piazzaes*,
with many beautiful Edifices as well publick as private: Particularly
the Palace uſed for the civil Law is the proudeſt in all *Europe*, if
not in all the World, for ſo much as that it is covered with Lead,
without ſuſtaining either of Pillars or Beams, though its bredth
is eighty ſix foot, and length two hundred fifty ſix.   Which Palace after it had continued a foot 202 yeers being in part ruinated
by fire, the *Venetian* Lords in the yeer 1420 rebuilt with greater ſplendour.   The figure of this Hall is like a Quarry of glaſs with equal
ſides, but not right angled, not for the nearneſs of the Fabrick as
ſome will have it, but becauſe natural reaſon ſhewes, that a man
ſtanding bolt upright is with much more eaſe thrown down than
when he ſtands a little drawn backwards, its ſite is turned to the
fower Quarters of Heaven, ſo that at the Equinoctial the Beams of the
Sun at his riſing entring through the Eaſtern Windowes, beat upon
the Weſtern Windowes, between which is nothing erected to obſtruct it: and ſo upon the contrary. And at the ſolſtice or ſtay of

the Sun, when it can neither go higher nor lower, the Beams enter thorow the Gates on theSouth part, and play upon the oppofite part; in fum, there is neither Gate or any other part without excellent Art and workmanfhip.   The painting of it reprefents the influence of the fuperiour bodies upon the inferiour, divided with the figns of the *Zodiack*, in imitation of that Circle of Gold which ftood in the Sepulcher of *Simandio* King of *Egypt* : In this Painting is to be noted the Antient Habits, and amongft others a Prieft, who holds a Planet upon his back, which antiently they ufed large and of rich ftuff, from whence it took its name. The Inventer of thefe Paintings averreth that this was *Pietro d'Abano* a *Padouan*, who was a moft famous Philofopher and Aftrologer, whom it may well be, fince fo many yeers before paft, that thefe prefent Paintings copyed by the hands of certain *Florentines*, were drawn out from thofe which were preferved in the Antient Palace, by the hand of *Giotto*, and really thefe modern ones are very like to thofe which in the plain *Aftrolobe* defigned by the invention of *Pietro d'Abano* are treated on by *Pierio* in the thirty fecond and thirty ninth book of his hieroglificks.   And if the Antients made fuch a noife and fo much account of the *Obelisk* which in the Field of *Mars* in *Rome* fhewed by his fhadow the length of the Nights and Days, what fhall we fay of this Fabrick, wherein are collected fo many noble fecrets all worthy to be contemplated and admired?

Whofoever hath an appetite in *Padoua* to behold Paintings let them fee the Church of the Confraternity of Saint *Antonio*, where they'l meet Pictures upon boards drawn by *Titian*, and other famous Mafters, the Chapel of Saint *Luke* in the Sanctuary, where may be feen the true effigies of *Fecellino* the Tyrant, as alfo in the Font of the *Domo* or chief Church by the hand of an excellent Lymner.   In the remarkeable Hall of the Lords of *Zabarella Veraria* may be feen pourtrayed the fuft Subjects of this City, as *Antenor* its Founder, *Volufio* the Poet, *T. Livio* the Hiftorian, *Q. Afcanio Pediano* the Grammarian, *C. Caffio* the Tribune, *L. Orontio Stella* the Poet, and *Trafea Peto* the Stoick, both *Roman* confuls, *C. Valerio Flaccho* the Poet, *L. Giulio Paolo* the Lawyer, *Petro d'Abano* the moft famous Philofopher and Aftrologer, *Albetino Muffato* the Poet, Doctor and Knight, *Alberto Verimitano Theclo*, *Marfilio Santo Soffia* an admirable Phyfician, *Marfilio Mainardino* a Philofopher, Aftrologer, and a moft learned Divine, *Bonaventure Peraghino* and *Francifco Zabarella* Cardinals, *Bartolomeo Zabarella* ArchBifhop of *Florence*, and *Giacomo Alvarato* the famous expounder of the Law, with a fair hiftory of the moft Antient times of *Padoua*, and the Genealogie of the Houfe of the *Zabarelli*, with this following fubfcription :

Elogia hæc virorum Illuftrium Patavinorum
Conditorumque Urbis cum Genealogiâ Nobilis
Familiæ Zabarellæ ex Hiftoriis, Cronicifque
Quam breviffimè collecta Joannes Cavafeus fecit,
Scripfit in Pariete Presb. Francifcus Maurus
Pucivigianus cerebrofus, pinxit Gualterius cura
Et impenfa Comitis Julii Zabarellæ ædium

Domini, *Omnes contivanei. MD. XLIX. Idibus Martii.*

In private houses may alfo be found moft excellent curiofities, as with the Family of *Mantoua*, for *Marco Mantoua* a moft emi-nent Lawyer built a fair Palace in the Street of the *Hermits* with a delicious Garden annexed, in the firft Court whereof ftands a great Coloffus of Marble, being the figure of *Hercules*, and above is a ftately Library no lefs replenifhed with Books, excellent Pictures, pour-traits of eminent men of the World, and fingular fculptures, than with collections of Brafs Figures, Marbles, Medals, and o-ther exquifite things both natural and artificial, which with the faid Palace are now poffeffed by Signor *Gafparo Mantoua* Doctor of Phyfick and Nephew of the abovenamed *Marco*.

Luigi Coradino Doctor of Philofophy and of the Laws, hereto-fore Reader of the *Digefts* or Volums of the Civil Law in the *Uni-verfity*, a man of a moft quick wit and polite Learning, an excel-lent difputant, and particularly converfant in antiquities, made a noble collection of Books, Pictures, Sculptures, Medals, antique Brafs and Marble Tablets, and other rarities, which for the moft part are enjoyed by the Signor *Andrea* his Son, Doctor of Philofophy and Phyfick, and Reader in the College, a *Virtuofo*, who conferves them in their Antient Houfe in the Street called *Torecelle*.

Gio Domenico Sala Doctor of Philofophy and Phyfick, moft renow-ned for having been fo many yeers Reader in the *Univerfity*, and for having exercifed his Profeffion of Phyfick with a known reputation, In his Palace which ftands in the Street called *San Lorenzo* hath fet up a Study replenifhed with Books, Pictures, Marbles, Brafs pie-ces, Medals. and other pretious rarities, and in particular he hath there a large and neat Prefs with fhelves all made with Walnut Tree, filled with Veffels of Chriftal, with all the fimple minerals, and other rare and exquifite things, which were collected by the Signor *Conte Giacomo Zabarella*, Doctor, Reader of the College, and Ca-non of *Padoua*, after whofe death coming to the hands of Signor *Bonifacio Zabarella* his Brother, they were by him given to the above-named Signor *Gio: Domenico*, in teftimony of being his great Friend and Ally, as a gift of moft fingular eftimation.

Benedetto Salvatico Knight, a Philofopher, and Phyfician, and chief Reader of the *Univerfity*, a moft fignal perfon, no lefs for his Reading than eminency in Phyfick, hath reftored near the *Domo* or chief Church, his Palace, making there a moft ftately Gallery, gar-dens with Fountains, Voleries, and a thoufand other excellencies, befides his books and Pictures

The Signor *Conte Giacomo Zabarella* Count of *Credazza* and of the Empire, a moft renowned and vituous Perfon, hath fo much labou-red in the ftudy of Hiftory and Antiquities, that meritorioufly by the Learnedft Pens he is ftyled the Reftorer of Antiquity and renewer of things devoured by time, being as well read in the Genealogie of Princes and other Illuftrious Families, a work as may be faid with-out compare; Befides that he hath found out the Invention to bla-fon Coats of Gentility to a great perfection, with the right Li-nage and the equal compartments. The works compofed by him give

with many difcourfes, Orations, Elogies and other workes much
efteemed by the Learned;He hath in the Street called *Coda* the whole
length of his Palace erected a moft noble Library, wherein befides
that there are great Quantities of Books, of Hiftories, of Humanity,
and other Learning all moft choice, fo alfo are there a good number
of Manufcripts in Paper and Parchment, whereof many are fet in
gold with exquifite Limning in Vermillion, many whereof were
never printed, whofe very Originals he is Mafter of: Moreover,
he hath the Chronicles of *Padoua* as well thofe that are in print as in
manufcript; as alfo many of *Venice* and other Cities : And befides
thefe in a Prefs of Nut-Tree of a notable Largenefs and Workmanfhip he hath collected many Marbles, Brafs pieces and other things
natural and Artificial, Antient and Modern, of great value, as alfo
a quantity of antient Medals, and of the later Princes both of
Gold and Silver, and other Metals, which are of a fufficient valew, befides many rare Pictures by the hand of the chief Men of
the paft Ages, and the authentique pourtraies of *Francefco* Cardinal, *Bartolomeo* & *Paulo* Archbifhops, *Orlando* and *Lorenzo* Bifhops, all
of the houfe of *Zabarella*, and likewife of the Counts *Giaccomo* the
elder, *Giulio* and *Giacomo* the Philofopher, and of other eminent
men of his houfe; He alfo preferves the great privileges granted
to his houfe by many Popes, Emperors, Kings and Princes, with
the Key of gold given by *Maffiminian* the firft, Emperor, to the faid
Count *Giacomo* his Anceftors, he likewife preferves many Antient
and notable Seals of his Anceftors, wherewith they ufed to feal the
privileges of thofe Counts, Knights, Doctors, and Notaries which
were created by them, together alfo with many other moft incomparable excellencies both concerning his own Family and many
others.

Monfignior Giacomo Filippo Tomaffini Bifhop of *Citta Nova*, in the
Street called *Ponte de Tadi*, hath his Palace reftored and fignalized
by the Signor *Paulo* his Brother long fince Doctor of Laws and the
firft Advocate of his Age in his Countrey lately deceafed with a
univerfal forrow. This Signor is generally efteemed for a moft virtuous perfon, a Philofopher, a Divine, an Aftrologer, an Hiftorian, and a Humanift, in all which he hath juftified his Judgment
by thofe moft Elegant Books he hath wrote upon all thefe fubjects,
fo much approved by the Virtuous: His Study excels no lefs in
Books, Pictures, Medals and other things of valew, Than in the
fignal Library of the works of the Lawes left him by his faid Brother.

The Signor *Conte Giovanni de Lazara*, Knight of the Order of Saint
Stephen, Son to the Signor *Conte Nicolo* Knight of the fame Order, hath
no lefs honoured his Country by his Nobility and Virtue, than for
his eminency in the knowlege of the Antiquities of it, and many
other Countreys : whereto he hath added a Collection of divers
manu-

msnuſcripts of great eſteem, as alſo a good quantity of Medals and
other things of price, among which the antient Seal of the *Padouan*
Republick (whereof *Scardenone* in the 12 folio takes notice) is greatly valued : Beſides on one ſide of his Palace (which is one of the
faireſt of the City) he hath drawn a Border whereon are ſet the
Pourtraies of many Lords and Princes the Predeceſſors, and Parents
of his Family.

The Signor *Sartorio Orſato* Doctor in Philoſophy and Phyſick, Son of the Signor *Orſato* Knight of Saint *Mark*, an eminent
Subject in his Countrey, is a young Student not leſs read and expert
in Philoſophy and Phyſick than in Hiſtory, Humanity, and Antiquities, and in his brave houſe in the Street of Saint *Franceſco*, hath
made a Collection of the beſt Books and ſquares, with a good
number of Medals, Marbles, braſs pieces and other ſingularities of
great Price : who having compoſed ſeveral works both in Proſe and
verſe, as well in the Latine as Italian Language, to add to the fame and
beauty of this his houſe, collects all the Antiquities of Marble Stone
that can be found and obtayned in this Countrey.

The Signor *Franceſco Orſato* his Parent or Ally having his handſom
ſtructure near the *Piazza Forzate*, is a Gentleman virtuous and of
no leſs noble Spirit, skilfull in the Mathematicks, in *Maretine* Affaires, Hiſtory, and Horſmanſhip, and hath amplified a Study with
Books, Tablets, Medals, Marbles, and Braſs pieces, and other
valuable and Antique Curioſities : Beſides which in his Hall is
drawn round a Friſe, whereto are hung large Tablets made by the
chief Lymners of this Age, with the Hiſtories of the ſeveral illuſtrious
Women in the holy Scripture mentioned.

The Signor *Giovanni Galvano* Doctor of Lawes, Reader in the
ſtudies, and an excellent Diſputant, is meritoriouſly at this time created Protector of the famous Nation of the Germans, being elected
to that degree not ſo much for his ſingular Vertue and Intelligence
in his profeſſion of the Law, and defence in Criminal cauſes, as for his
knowlege in Languages, Humanity, Hiſtory & other the moſt worthy
Studies, as appears by the moſt learned compoſitions made by him,
which demonſtrate his great Wiſdome; which alſo clearly appears
by his skill in Antiquities, and in the Collections made by him of
Books, Tablets, Marbles, braſs pieces and other rare and exquiſite things, wherewith in abundance he hath no leſs beautified his
moſt ſignal Study, than with his Collection of antient Medals, both
of Gold and Silver, and other ſingular Metals of great valew, in
the knowlege whereof moſt Men of this Age will yeeld him a Precedency.

The Signor *Aleſſandro Fſſè* a moſt worthy Patriot, and much honoured in his Countrey, hath in his houſe likewiſe near *Santa Mar-*
garita got together a notable quantity of Medals and antient Seals,
and other rare and eſtimable curioſities. With which we will end
our account of the excellencies of private Houſes.

In the next place are preſented to our view and admiration ſeaven marvellous things which are Temporal, and ſeaven that are
Eccleſiaſtick, beſides many others : For the firſt ſeaven are named
il Pallazzo della Ragione or Hall of Juſtice, the Publick Schools, the
Palace of *Foſcari alla Arena*, the Court or Palace of the Chieftain,

theCaſtle for the *Munition*, the *Ponte* or Bridge *Molino* and *Il Pratto del-la valle* or *Meadow*; And for the Eccleſiaſtick theſe Churches, *Il Domo, Il Santo, Santa Juſtina, Santo Agoſtino, Li Carmini, Li Heremitani,* and *San Franceſco.*

In the *Palazza della Ragione* or Hall of Juſtice abovenamed are ſtanding fair Antiquities, among others is one of that immortal Treaſure of Hiſtory and Antiquity, *Livie*: in whoſe ever-living memory on that ſide of this Hall towards the Weſt, is erected a Sepulchre or Monument with this old inſcription or epitaph added thereunto.

V. F.

T. LIVIVS

LIVIÆ. T. F.

QVARTÆ L.

HALTS

CONCORDIALIS

PATAVI

SIBI ET SVIS

OMNIBVS.

Titus Livius 40. *Imperii Tib. Cæſaris* an°. *vita exceſſit, ætatis vero ſuæ,* LXXVI. and not far diſtant from thence ſtands his Image.

On the right hand of which is erected another Monument with an Image made of the whiteſt Marble of *Sperone, Speroni,* a man of an elevated Ingenuity, as may be known by his works, whichfor the moſt part he hath writ in the *Italian* tongue, with this Inſcription following. *Sperono Speronio ſapientiſſimo, eloquentiſſimoque, opti-mo & viro, & civi, Virtutem, meritaque acta vita ſapientiam, eloquen-tiam declarant ſcripta. Publico decreto. Vrbis quatuor viri* 1589. *& Vr-bis* 2712. Over every Dore of this great Hall (whereof it hath four) is a remembrance of thoſe four moſt famous men who for their Birth challenge this City, and for their virtue have no leſs Illuſtrated this their Countrey than Italy it ſelf with the whole Univerſe. The one is of the abovenamed and not to be too much honoured *Titus Livius,* the words whereof follow.

T. Livius Pat. Hiſtoriarum Lat. nominis facilè princeps, & cujus Lacte-am eloquentiam ætas illa, quæ virtute pariter, ac eruditione florebat, adeo admirata eſt, ut multi Romam non ut Vrbem rerum pulcherrimam, aut Vr-bis, & Orbis Dominum Octavianum, ſed ut hunc Vnum inviſerent, audi-rentque, a Gadibus profecti ſint. Hic res omnes, quas Pop. Rom. pace bel-loque geſſit quatuordecim Decadibus mirabili felicitate complexus, ſibi, ac patriæ gloriam peperit ſempiternam.

Over another Dore.

Paulus Pat. I. C. clariſſimus, hujus Vrbis Decus æternum, Alex. Mam-meæ temp. floruit, Ad Præturam, Præfecturam, Conſulatumque evectus. Cujuſque ſapientiam tanti fecit Juſtinianus Imperator, ut nulla civilis Juris particula hujus legibus non decoretur. Qui ſplendore famæ immortalis ocu-lis poſteritatis admirand. Inſigni imagine hic merito decoratur.

Over the third Dore.

Petrus apponus Pat. Philoſophiæ, Medicinæque ſcientiſſimus. Ob idque Conciliatoris cognomen adeptus. Aſtrologiæ vero adeo peritus, ut in Ma-

gia

giæ suspicionem inciderit, falsoqne de Hærisi postulatus, absolutus suit.
Over the last Dore.

*Albertus Pat. Heremitanæ Religionis Splendor, continentissimæ vitæ,
sumpta Parisiis Insula Magistrali, in Theologia tantum profecit, ut Paulum,
Mosen, Evangelia, ac libros Sanctorum laudatissimè exposuerit. Facundissi-
mus ea ætate concionator. Immortali memoriæ optimo jure datur.*

There is also in this Palace a Marble engraven after this manner.

*Inclyto Alphonso Aragonum Regi, Studiorum Authori, Reïpub. Venetæ
fœderato, Antonio Panormita Legato suo orante, et Matthæo Victurio hujus
Vrbis Prætore constantissimo intercedente, ex historiarum Parente, & T. Liv.
ossibus, quæ hoc tumulo conduntur, Brachium Patavin. cives in munus con-
cessere 1451.*

To conclude with this Palace or Hall of Justice, if considered as
an upper Room, tis the fairest and most spacious of *Christendome*, of
which there is no part but hath some Astronomical secret; tis con-
vered with Lead, and round about goes a stately corridor of Marble.

Near the abovenamed Palace stand the Schools for all Learning,
which is the second Marvel, not only of *Padoua* but of *Europe*,
within is a square Court, the building two stories high one over another, sustained with most fair Pillars; and round about in every corner are the Arms of all such as have been Consuls or Protectors in
that *University*; some in colours only, some in colours and stone, with
their Country, name, and yeer set up, at the *Venetians* charge, to make
famous this Nursery of Learning. The *Anatomick Theater* erected
in those Schools stands above, and is most neatly contrived, and most
commodious both for the Professor & the Spectators. This *University*
of *Padoua* is as it were the Market place of Learning (and much approaches the Academy of *Athens*) To this place from all parts of the
World throng the most eminent in all the liberal sciences, and no
small number of the Nobles as Scholars, not only from all parts of
Italy and its neighbouring Provinces, but from the farthest parts of
the World. In this City are ten Colleges, where are allowed honourable Pensions to many Scholars.

The first College stands in the Street *Santo* called *Prattense*, derive-
ing its name from its Founder *Pileo Conte di Prata*, Cardinal, and Bishop of *Padoua*, in which are appointed 20 Scholars, *Padouans, Venetians, Trivisans,* and *Furlans*, with a Prior or Governor, who
heretofore kept a Coach: The Scholars pensions were 20 Crowns
per Moneth and more, but the Merchants Banke of *Venice* (who u
sually payed them) being of late lessened, at present, besides their
Lodging and Service, they have but ten Crowns by the yeer. The
Cardinal committed the Government thereof to *Francesco Zabarella*
his Nephew, and after his death to the most antient of his house,
and of that of the Family *di Leone*, recommending it also to the care
and overseeing of the successive Bishops of *Padoua*, and to the Pri-
or of the College of the Professors of the Laws.

The second called *Spinello à Ponte Corvo* instituted by *Belforte Spinello* of *Naples*, is governed by the *Priors* of the Masters of Art, & by the
most Antient of the house of Doctors, where are maintained four
Scholars Masters of Arts for five yeers, two *Padouans*, one *Trevisan*,
and another Stranger, each of whose allowance is twenty five Duckats by the yeer.

H

The

The third named *da Rio* built in the ſtreet ſo called, and inſtituted by that Family, conſiſts of 4 Scholars Maſters of Arts, approved by the moſt antient of that family, their ſtay is permitted for 7 yeers, their allowance is, Lodging Rooms, Bread and Wine, with twelve Duckats; and they ought to be of *Padoua* or its Territories.

The Fourth called *del Campione* ſituated in the *borgo di Vignal* is for nine Scholars in the Arts: two *Padouans*, two *Triviſans*, two *Farrareſians*, two *French men*, and one other Foreiner, and for ſeaven yeers, they are allowed Wheat, Wine, Wood, Service, Lodging, and ſome moneys. The Patrone or Maſter is the *Abbot* of Saint *Ciprian* of *Muran*.

The fifth named *Santa Cantarina* is ſubmitted to certain Noble *Venetians*, and hath for Scholars in the Arts 16 who have Corn, Wine, Money, Salt, Lodgings, and Service allowed in a handſome proportion for ſeaven years.

The ſixth dedicated to *Santa Lucia* by the *Breſcians* conteyns 6 Scholars in the ſciences choſen by the Communalty of *Breſcia*, their allowance is 25 Duckats a peece with their Lodging and ſervice defrayed.

The ſeaventh called *Feltrino* founded in the Street *Santo*, is governed by the nobles of the family of *Altini in feltre*, the continuance of the Scholars (who muſt be ſtudents in the Laws) is ſeaven yeers, their number is but two Scholars and one Artiſt, they have for allowance a quantity of Wheat being 16 meaſures for each, and 10 Maſtellaes of Wine with their Lodgings.

The eighth built in the Street *San Leonardo* named *del Ravenna*, is put under the tuition of *Piavano di S. Giulano di Venetia*, & the Scholars have Lodging Rooms, Services, and one Duckat allowed by the yeer for each.

The ninth in the *Viginali* called *Cocho* is for Six Noble *Venetians*, each ones allowance, being Lodging, Service, and 40 Duckats yeerly.

The tenth called *Amulio*, near the *Pratto della vallæ*, is for 12 Scholars Noble *Venetians*, founded by *Marco Antonio Amulio* Cardinal, and every Scholar is allowed, Lodging Rooms, his ſervices are payed, and ſix Duckats by the year.

The third notable and marvellous Temporal Rarity of *Padoua* is the *Piazza* or place caled the *Arena*, which is a noble Court, round about which ſtands the old *Arches*, and *Veſtigia* of a proud *Theatre*, which by the antients was called *Naumachia*, but of later yeers they uſe it to run a Tilt, and for all manner of horſemanſhip, with many other games; the Ladies ſtanding to behold them in the open Caſements of that proud Palace, which ſtands at the head of the Court in a Lunary form, the *Arena* or Court being Oval.

Backwards towards the Wall are gardens filled with Vines and pretious Fruits, as, alſo on that ſide which is towards the Church of the *Hermits* with a ſmall Chapel dedicated to the holy Virgin, which is alſo a *Priorate* of the houſe of *Foſcarie* and belonging to that ſerene Family of *Venice*.

The fourth marvellous objeſt is the Court of the Captain or Governour of the City, where the Proud Palace of the ſaid *Præfeſt*, the Chamberlains and many other Citizens habitations, beſides the

dwel-

dwelling of a world of other People are so contrived that it may
not improperly be called a little Cittadel : This was the Kingly
house of the *Carraresi*, Its Chambers may truly be said to be built
for Princes, with two halls which for their Largeness and Noble-
ness could not be built for other; the one is Called the Hall of *Gi-*
ants, wherein stands the publick Library : here are pourtrayed the
most eminent Subjects of the *Roman* Republick, & of the World, with
a representation of their most famous Acts, by the hand of *Gualterio*
a most eminent Lymner, with their Elegies under each figure, heretofore composed by the most virtuous *Giovanni di Cavazzi* a gentlemā of
Padoua, and inscribed in a signal Character by *Pietro Francesco Tucivi-*
giano called the *Moor*: The Books conteyned in the said Library are
most excellent and in great abundance; The signor *Gio Battista*
Salvatico, Doctor, Knight, and a Gentleman of *Padoua* bequeathed
to it, by his Testament, his Collection of the Books of the Laws of a
great valew. The signor *Giacomo Caino* a Gentleman of *Furlan*
Doctor and Reader in the College hath likewise given to it the Library of *Pompeo Cacino* a Physician his Uncle, of no less esteem; The
signor *Conte Giacomo Zabarella* hath added to it a brave quantity of
Manuscripts, some writ in parchment, others in paper, bound in
Leather Lymned with Vermillion and Gold rarely and exquisitely :
some whereof were never Printed, amongst which are the workes
of Cardinal *Zabarella*, of the Count *Giacomo Zabarella* his Grandfather of Philosophy; of the Count *Francesco* his Father, which are
in rime and prose in the *Tuscan* Tongue very learned, and treating
of many subjects concerning his own Family : Therein also are the
Works of *Cesare Cremonio* the Philosopher, and many other bought
at the Publick cost, and others added there by the Signor *Ottavio Fer-*
rari a Gentleman of *Milan* Reader of Humanity in the Schools, and
the publick Library Keeper, which Library is every day so increased
by the Nobility and others, that tis well hoped within a little time twill arrive to the Reputation of the richest and most famous in the World.

The fifth wonder is the Castle for the *Munition* abovenamed near
the Church of Saint *Agostino*, which was built by the Tyrant *Eccelli-*
lino for his safeguard, wherein he slew so many Noble *Paduoans*, that
he had almost destroyed the whole City: herein are the publick *Gra-*
naries to maintain plenty in the City, and all sorts of Ammunition
for its defence in time of need.

The sixth admirable thing is the *Ponte Molino*; so called from the
thirty wheels of Mills there erected (a most signal Object) and the
five Arches of flint Stone; near which stands a Palace in manner of
a Fortress built with those very Large squared & wrought Stones w^{ch}
were brought from the other ruinated Palaces and Forts by *Eccellino*
the Tyrant, with a Fort and most fayr Tower, in the yeer 1250
And is now possessed by the Count *Giacomo Zabarella*, as is above
said.

The seventh wonderfull Object of *Padoua* is *il Prato della valle* a
Meadow so ample that twould alone contain a great City : It was
antiently called *Campo Marzo*, the field of *Mars*, from the *Martial* exercises there used, and in this place were many Saints beheaded by
the *Pagans*, to such a number that they are wont to say that part

which is compassed by Water was emplastered with the blood of those Martyrs: Here every first *Saturday* of the Moneth is held a free Fayr or Market of all sorts of Cattel and other Creatures, and at the Feast of Saint *Antonio* is a famous Fayr there, which although it happens in the hottest Weather, being there kept for fifteen days in the midest of *June*, and that there are then many thousands of Creatures, yet there is never seen a Fly to molest them.

If to these might be added an eighth Wonder, we would name the Vineyard or Garden of the Knight *Bonifacio Papafava*, situate in the Street called *Vanzo*, where besides a most fair and adorned Palace, you behold many statues of excellent workmanship, and infinite numbers of Cittron and Orange Trees, which forme lovely walks to the Passengers, for beautifying whereof, of those Trees are framed Arches and Prospects to delight the eye; to whose confines is conjoyned a full stream of water brought from the main River by a curious Aqueduct, which being confined to one Gate under the Wall, gives at its utterance a sweet murmur, and with its clear gurgling on every side washes the Foot of the Palace: And the flowry bankes within which the said Rivolet is contained renders the Palace as it were in an Island of so specious delights and pleasant Savours, that what is added by Art to that of Nature may well cause it to be termed the eighth wonder. Hither flock for their Pastime the Ladies and Gallants of *Padoua*, inviteing with them also the Foreiners with their Musick and other Pastimes, where (in the hottest Weather) the shade of the Trees, the Ampleness of the Walks, the pleasantness of the Waters, and the beauty of the site add (to their other joys and delights) a fresh Ayr. And although these beauties shew themselves in perfection, yet that magnanimous Cavalier never ceases to illustrate it (to his no small costs) with greater delights; and by this and his other Gallantries shewes himself to be born of that Family which for its Greatness and Dominion was no less formidable in *Italy*, than renowned in *Europe*. At this present resides here, this Noble Person with his Brother *Scipio Papafava*, Knight of the great Cross of the Order of *Hierusalem*, Prior of *Messina*, and the most worthy Primate of the whole Kingdome of *Sicilia*, together with the virtuous *Roberto* Son of the above named Cavalier *Bonifacio*, young in yeers, but his conditions and practices may challenge the ripest Age, who is the Comendatory Abbot of *Sebinico*, being Doctor of Philosophy, of Divinity & of the Laws, a true Splendor to his Country and Family, being conversant in the Greek, Latine, and Hebrew Tongues, and well known in the Mathematicks, as was testified by the singular experiments of his Ingenuity some Moneths since. There flourishes likewise of this Noble Family at this time a numerous company of Cavaliers and great Subjects, who degrade not from their most famous and Antient Progenitors, of whom to speak but little will diminish from their Fame, and much is not opportune in this place: for their Ordinary dwelling, these Signors have a Palace in the Street *San Francesco Maggiore*, where they have Coppies of exquisite Books in all the Professions, left them by Monsignor *Ubertino Papafava* Bishop of *Adria*, Brother of *Bonifacio*, besides many antient Manuscripts and Authors not yet printed, which relate the Histories of this Family

as

also the old coyning Press of the *Carrarefian* Princes, with other pretious monuments of this House, preferved in the Chamber of Rowles of the said Palace, which may be termed the most large and worth seeing of this City.

And now we come to the Spiritual wonders and Churches of *Padoua*, whereof the first is the *Domo* or Cathedral Church, fituate (near)in the midst of the City. The *Padouans* were converted to the Christian Faith, by the predication of Saint *Prosdocimo* their first Bishopp authorized by Saint *Peter*, who (among others) baptized *Vitaliono* the Chief Man in this City, who therefore built the Church of Saint *Soffia*. *Henry* the fourth Emperor enriched this Cathedral, giving to it twenty feaven rich Canonicats, of so good a revenew that they may be styled so many Bishops; among which are four dignities, that is to say, Arch-priest, Arch.Deacon, The Person that hath charge of the wax, *&c.* And the Deacon; there are twelve under Canons, six Custodi or Rectors, and six *Manfonary* or Houskeepers, and more than 60 other Persons and Clerks belonging to the Chapel, befides the Masters of Grammar and Musick, with many excellent Singers, so that this Clergy exceeds a hundred Persons, and their Revenew above a hundred thousand Duckats by the yeer, which makes it the most noble and Rich of *Italy*: and therefore tis that the Bishop of *Padoua* is styled a little Pope, and his Canons with some reason the Cardinals of *Lombardy*, for that their Chapter is alwaies filled with the Nobility of *Venice*, *Padoua*, and other Cities, whereof so many have ascended to the Miter, and Hatt, that tis worthily called to this day the Seminary of Cardinals and great Prelates.

In this Church (not elfewhere as is pretended)lyes enterred the Wife of *Henry* the fourth, whofe name was *Berta*, as is proved by this antique Infcription.

Præfulis, & Cleri præfenti prædia phano
Donavit Regina jacens hoc marmore Berta
Henrici Regis Patavi, celeberrima quarti
Conjunx tam grandi dono memoranda per ævum.

Under the Chorus within a rich Monument of Marble, lies the Body of Saint *Daniel*, one of the four Tutelars.

Two great Cardinals repofe in this Church, who were both Arch priefts of the fame, that is to say, *Pileo de Pratta*, and *Francefco Zabarella*, with other eminent Perfons.

Pileo Conti di Pratta a Citizen of *Padona* and of *Furlan* was for his vertue created Bishop of *Padoua*, and afterwards Cardinal of Saint *Praffede* by Pope *Gregory* the 11th. and Apoftolick Legate. But in the yeer 1378. the Schifm being rifen between *Urban* the fixth his fucceffor, and *Clement* the Antipope, he was depofed by *Urban*, after whofe death *Bonifacio* the ninth fuceeding, he was again created Cardinal with the Title of the *Tufculan* Bifhop, and Apoftolick Legate, and finally he dyed at *Padoua*, and was buried in this Church in a fublime and most noble Arch with this memorial.

Pileus Pratta Card.
Stirpe Comes Pratæ , præclarus origine, multis
Dotibus infignis , feclo celeberrimus Orbe:
Defunctus ftatuit fic fuprema voluntas,
Hac Cardinalis Pileus tumulatur in urna.

And this Arch was heretofore in the Chapel of the Holyeft, on the right fide of the Chorus, but being neceffitated to make the door of the greater Veftry in that place, it was removed out of that Chapel, and adjoyned to the neareft Wall, in a worthy and eminent Place.

Francefco Zabarella, a Philofopher, Divine, and a fublime Lawyer, was efteemed the Prince of the wife men of the World in his Age, and his works left behinde him prove his defert of that Title: He was a moft Learned man in all the fciences, and of a moft holy Life, for which reafon the *Florentines* and *Padouans* offered him the Epifcopal Dignity, and other Princes not a few eminent Degrees. At laft Pope *John* the 22d. created him Arch-Bifhop of *Florence*, then Cardinal of *SS. Cofmo*, and *Damiano*, in the yeer 1411. and atter that Legate of the Apoftolick Sea, & Præfident of the Council of *Conftanza*; where being earneftly defired and defigned for Pope, he dyed in the 78rh. yeer of his Age, in *Anno* 1477. For whofe Body (tranfported into his Countrey) was erected a moft fayr *Maufeole* a rich Monument, where it repofeth to this day in the Chapel of the Bleffed Virgin, on the left fide of the Chorus, in an Arch of pure white Marble with this Memorial.

Franc. Zabarellæ Flor. Archepis. viro optimo,
Urbi & Orbi gratiffimo, Divini Humanique juris
Interpreti præftantiffimo, in Cardinalium Collegium
Ob fummam fapientiam co.optato, ac eorundem animis
Pontifice prope maximo Io. 22. ejus fuafu abdicato
Ante Martinum V. ob fingularem probitatem in Conftant.
Concilio. Joannes Jacobi viri Clariffimi filius id
Monumentum ponendum curavit. Vixit Annos LXXVIII.
Obiit Coftantiæ 1417.

This Chapel was called of *SS. Pietro*, and *Paulo*, and was acquired and endowed by *Bartol. Zabarella* Arch-bifhop of *Spalatro* for the ufe and name of his Family; who thence are Patrons of it and maintain therein two Chaplains; afterwards it took the name of the Bleffed Virgin, when the Noble *Matron Antonia Zabarella* Sifter to the Cardinal bequeathed to it by her Will that moft holy Image, which was found in her houfe, then placed over the Altar of this Chapel, which Tradition faith was painted by Saint *Luke*: which *Robert King* of *Naples* gave to *Francefco Petrarcha*, by whom twas tranfported to *Padoua*, and left to *Giacomo* the 2. of *Carrara* its Lord. After whofe deceafe it came to *Marfilio* his fecond Son, who gave it in portion with *Fiordilige* his Daughter, Wife of *Pietro Zabarella*, then it came to the hands of the faid *Antonia*, by whom with other gifts twas left to the *Domo*, and is that moft holy Image which in

their

their Proceffions they carry when they would obtein in their greateft neceffity the Divine Affiftance by her Interceffion. In this Chapel are other Epitaphs and Monuments, of the Noble Family of
Zabarella, whofe Original is known to proceed from the moft Antient *Sabatini,* of *Lolonia;* whofe Anceftors came from the *Cornelii,*
Scipioni of Rome; of whom were the moft glorious *Scipio, Cinna,*
and *Sylla* Princes of Rome; with many other Heroes, befides the holy Popes *Pio, Cornelio,* and *Silveftro,* and the Emperours *Balbino,*
Valeriano, Gallieno, Tacito, and *Florian, Celfo,* two *Saturnini* and *Avito,*
and many other Saints and eminent Perfons, in *Bolonia,* of that Family were alfo the Saints, *Hermete, Aggeo, & Caio* Martyrs, il *B. Sa-*
batino A oftolo di S. Francefco, Sabatino Bifhop of *Genoua, Elector* of
Carlo Calvo Emperour, with many other grand Perfons who have
illuftrated and governed that City: Alfo their houfe being fetled in
Padoua by *Calorio Sabbatino* Count and Knight of *Bolognia,* his pofterity were called *Sabarini* and *Sabarelli,* from whence arofe the fir.
name *Zabarella,* of which Family befides the Cardinals abovenamed, there have been *Bartol.* Arch-Bifhop of *Spal.* and *Florence,*
who dyed a defigned Cardinal; *Paolo* Bifhop *Argolicenfe,* and
Arch Bifhop *Parienfe, Orlando* and *Lorenzo,* who dyed with the
name of Bleffed Bifhops, the firft of *Adria,* the fecond of *Afcoli;* five
Arch-Priefts and feaven Canons of *Padoua,* many Doctors, moft famous Readers of the Univerfity in all Ages, famous Counts and
Knights, many valorous Captains, as, *Andrea* General of the *Polen-*
tani, and *Andrea* the fecond, General of the Church, *Giacoma* the
firft made Count and Knight of the *Dragon* by *Sigifmond* the Emperor, & was by the Popes *John* the 22d. *Martin* the 5th. and *Eugenius*
the 4th. conftituted Governor of divers Cities, Senator of *Rome,*
and called by a Bull, Apoftolick Baron.

   Bartol the fecond, Doctor, Knight, and Prætor of divers Cities,
Præfect of *Florence* and *Roman* Senator, who as alfo *Giacopo* the fecond Counfellor and Knight of the Golden Key were by *Maffim.* the
fecond Emperour created Counts, and Knights, to them and to the
eldeft Sons of their pofterity for ever; which was afterwards confirmed to *Ciulio* his Son by *Ferdinand* the fecond, Father of *Giacopo*
the third *Zabarella* the Philofopher; of fuch grand Fame were thefe
perfons; and thefe great men were known to be of this Family befides many others eminent both In Letters and Arms.

   But having mentioned two *Padouan* Cardinals, it feems convenient to me to give fome account of the reft, fince they have adorned
this their Country with fuch a dignity.

   Simone Paltanico was the firft *Padouan* Cardinal, who being a perfon of great Knowlege, and the higheft virtue, merited from Pope
Vrban the 4th. to be created Cardinal of *S. Steffano & Martino* in
the yeer 1261 and afterwards Apoftolick Legate. He dyed in the
yeer 1276. His Family is extinct in *Padoua,* but in honour at *Vicenza*
under the Noble firname of Counts of *Poiana.*

   Tileo de Pratta was the fecond *Padouan* Cardinal, as is abovefaid, of
this Houfe are the Counts of *Portia* in *Friuli.*

   Bonaventura Badoero of the Counts of *Peraga,* was a man of great
Wifdom and goodnefs, and being a *Hermitan* Monk, he read
Philofophy and Divinity in his Schools; who after the other de-

grees aſcended to the Generalſhip, and thence by Pope *Urban* the 6th. in the yeer 1384. was created Cardinal of *S. Cicilia*, and deceaſed five yeers after. Of this Houſe are the *Badoeri*, Noble men of *Venice*, and the *Padoeri* of *Padoua*.

Bartolomeo Oliario the *Minikin*, a famous Philoſopher and Divine, was by the *Florentines* elected for their Paſtor. after which by Pope *Boniface* the ninth he was called to the Cardinalſhip of *S. Prudentiana* in the yeer 1389. and deceaſed 7 yeers after.

Franceſco Zabarella, was the 5th. *Padouan* Cardinal and Arch-Biſhop of *Florence*, as before is related.

Lodavico Mezarota being a Philoſopher and a Phyſician, deſerted that his profeſſion, and put himſelf under the command of *Giovanni Vitelli* General for the holy Church; and behaving himſelf well therein aſcended from one degree unto another, till in the end (after *Vitelli* his death) he was conſtituted his ſucceſſor, and Patriark of *Aquileia*: wherein he made ſuch progreſs as is not to be imagined; let it ſuffice that he reſtored the Church to its Liberty, and delivered the *Florentines* and *Italy*, for which his Noble deeds he was by Pope *Eugenius* the 4th made Cardinal of *S. Lorenzo*, then Biſhop of *Albany*, and Chancellor of the holy Church, he dyed in the yeer 1465: at this day is his Family extinct.

And beſides theſe there were others of this City intended for Cardinals, who being overtaken by death could not poſſeſs that dignity, as *Gabriel Capodeliſta, Aquenſi* an Arch-Biſhop was deſigned Cardinal by Pope *Clement* the 5th, in 1304. *Bartol. Zabarella* Arch-Biſhop of *Florence*, having been Apoſtolick Legate in *Germany*, *France*, and *Spain*, for weighty affairs, with the happy ſucceſs of his Labours, and the great ſatisfaction of Pope *Eugenius* the 4th. was by him deſigned Cardinal, but upon his return, an indiſpoſition ſeiſed him and deprived him of Life in *Sutry*, being but forty ſeaven yeers old, in *Anno noſtræ ſalutis* 1445. *Franceſco Lignamineo* Biſhop of *Ferrara* and Apoſtolick Legate was by Pope *Eugenius* the 9th. deſigned Cardinal, but he was prevented by his death in the yeer 1412. *Antonio Giannotti* a famous Lawyer, Biſhop of *Forli*, and Arch-Biſhop of *Urbin*, was Vice Legate in *France* and *Bologna*, where he dyed at his 65th. yeer, being then by Pope *Clement* the 8th. deſigned Cardinal *Anno* 1591.

In the Palace of the Biſhop theſe things are worth a ſight, The moſt ample dioceſs of *Padoua*, drawn in a large ſquare by *Marco Cornaro* Biſhop of *Padoua* a Prelate worthy of eternal memory, and a great Hall where to the life (as is believed) are drawn the Pictures of 112 Biſhops of this moſt antient and Noble City. The Church of Saint *Antonio* of *Lisbone* merits the ſecond Place amongſt *Padoua*'s fair Churches, as well for the deſign and artifice, as for the pretiouſneſs of the Marbles and other Ornaments. The Roof of this Temple is diſtinguiſhed into ſix marvellous Chapels covered with Lead. Firſt muſt be ſeen the Royal Chapel of this Saint, adorned with the fineſt Marbles, and 12 Noble Collumns, in the nine ſpaces of which Columns between the one and tother, are engraven his Miracles by the moſt rare Sculptors of that Age, ſo well that it renders the ſpectators ſtupified. In the midſt of which Chapel ariſes the Altar of this Saint, and within it lies entered his body. Upon

this

this altar stand seaven Figures of Brass of a just proportion, wrought by *Tytian Apetti*, the excellent sculptor of *Padoua*, Its Roof is adorned with the fairest Frets and figures made of pargetting stuff guilt richly, and its Pavement exactly composed with Marble and Porphyry and checkerwise. This Saint having lived 36 yeers dyed the 13th of *June* 1231, and was canonized by *Gregory the* 9th. in the City of *Spoleto*, in the yeer 1237. On which day in *Padoua* they go in procession carrying his Tongue in a little woodenBoul with great solemnity and superstition; which is accompanyed with all the Fryers of Saint *Francis*, that is to say, by the Conventuals *Capucines*, and those that go uppon woodden Pattens called *Zoccolani*, and with all the Doctors of the Colleges, as well of the Laws, and Physick, as those of Divinity and Philosophy; wherewith they also carry all the Vessels of Silver and other pretious things bestowed upon this their Saint, as also an infinite number of their holy Relique preserved in curious Vessels: Among which are the Figures of ten Saints of pure Silver, 16 rich Chalices, 50 Vessels, 3 whereof are to contayn their Eucharist, many Silver Candlesticks, Lampades, Censores, and 50 Sylver Votaries or pieces dedicated by the vowes of several persons, which are as big as a small Child. Likewise a Shipp furnished with Masts, Sayls and Shrouds, together with a model of the City of *Padoua* both being neatly cast in Silver. In a fayr Reliquiary they preserve the Tongue of the glorious Saint *Anthonio* and in another his under Chap. In others all of Silver guilt framed with most exact workemanshipp, they keep a cloth dipped in the pretious blood (as they say) of our Saviour Jesus-Christ; three thornes of his Crown; some of the wood of his Cross; of the hairs and milk of the blessed Virgin; some of the Blood issuing out of the five wounds given Saint *Francesco*; and many of the Bones and other rare reliques of infinite of their Saints, as may be seen in the Treatise published by Count *Giacomo Zabarella* Præsident and Treasurer of the Venerable Tombe of the glorious Saint *Antonio:* Who (besides the revenue of the Convent wherewith the Fathers are mainteined) possesseth a great Revenue, together with much Silver and other pretious houshouldstuff, all bestowed upon that Saint by Princes, and private Persons, which Wealth is governed by seaven Presidents, vulgarly called the *Signori all'Archa, di San Antonio*; three Ecclesiasticks and 4 Seculars, with a Casheer, who receives the Revenues, and pays the Musicians and other disbursements, which Officers are elected every yeer, and every Six Moneths two of them change. In the Convent is a fayr publick Library, much amplified by the reverend Father *Francesco Zanotti*, an eminent Person of *Padoua*, who alwaies governed his Convent with great prudence as *Guardian*, and his Religious Order whereof he was Provincial: whereto the most reverend Father *Michael Angelo Maniere Guardian* and Provincial also hath added his Industry with great success and evidence of his Prudence, Virtue and Goodness; both whose good Actions have given a great Splendour to the Fame of this most Noble Convent. Near to this said Library is another Room wherein are kept the rare collections of Count *Giacomo Zabarella*, given to the said Saint; which consists of many excellent Books and Manuscripts, and all the Histories (in being) of *Padoua*, *Venice* and other Cities

K   which

which no where elſe are to be found, alſo of Medals, Marbles, braſs Pieces and other notable Antiquities, with the Golden Key, and all his workes, all which being before fully related, are here abbreviated to avoid Prolixity.

Oppoſite to the Altar of Saint *Antonio* is the Chapel of Saint *Felix* the Pope of like *grandezza* : where alſo repoſe his Bones; round about which are hung Pictures excellently wrought by *Giotto*, wherof *Dante*, *Boccacio* and other writers take particular notice : In it are the Tombes of the *Signori Roſſi* and *Lupi* Marqueſes of *Soragna*; and next the Chapel of Saint *Antonio*, with which it maintains like Grandure and Fame, it is the moſt eminent of all; the greater Altar whereof is richly carved in Marble, and hath on the right ſide a Candleſtick of a very great heighth, and wrought with many Figures, & over againſt it an artificial Chorus adorned with lovely Figures carved in wood : In this Church likewiſe are the Sepulchers of *Fulgoſio* of *Marin*, and *Aſcanio Zabarella*, the firſt famous in Letters, the ſecond in Arms; which are erected in the Chapel of Saint *Catherine* appertaining to their Family; in another Tombe lies buried *Andrea Zabarella* with *Montiſia Polenta* his Wife, Daughter of *Bernardino* Signor of *Ravenna*, with many other eminent perſons, which would take up too much room and time to ſpecifie. Before the ſaid Church ſtands a noble Statue of Braſs caſt by *Donato Fiorentino*, and preſented to the State of *Venice*, in memory of the Valour of *Gattamelata da Narni*, who was Captain General of their Armies : whoſe effigies is there erected on Horſeback, and whoſe body with that of his Sons ly buried in the Chapel of Saint *Francis* with two fayr Epitaphs inſcribed over them.

The third eccleſiaſtick excellency of *Padoua*, is the ſumptuous and ample Church of Saint *Juſtina*, where are kept with great devotion the bodies of Saint *Luke* the Evangeliſt; Saint *Matthias* the Apoſtle, of the Innocents, of Saint *Proſdocimo* firſt Biſhop of this City and Province, of *Santa Giuſtina* the Virgin Martyr, of *Giulian* of *Maſſimo* ſecond Biſhop of *Padoua*, of *Vrio* the Conſeſſor, of *Felicita* the Virgin, *Arnaldo* the Abbot; together with an infininte number of Reliques, which they preſerved in a moſt Antient Cemetery called in thoſe days the Pit of Martyrs: there alſo ſtands a ſpeckled ſtone, upon which certain Martyrs were beheaded, another ſtone whereon *San Proſdocimo* celebrated divine ſervice : Herein likewiſe they conſerve the Tablet of the bleſſed Virgin paynted by Saint *Luke*, and with great devotion brought from *Conſtantinople* by the bleſſed *Vrio*. Its Chorus which compaſſeth the high Altar round, is made all of Walnut Tree, and upon it engraven by *Richardo Franceſco* the Hiſtory of the Old and New Teſtament. It hath much Silver Utenſils and pretious veſts; to ſay no more, this Chapel for its ſtructure and beauty, is an incomparable piece; And not a little illuſtrated by that proud and wealthy Monaſtery of Saint *Juſtine* now contiguous with it, which for its ſumptuouſneſs, Grandure, and Riches, may be reckoned one of the Faireſt of *Italy*. On the Walls of the Cloyſters amongſt the Legend ſtories deſigned, they have inſerted hundreds of old inſcriptions, with the draughts of old ſtones and pieces of Urns dug up when the foundation of the Convent was firſt Layed. It hath for revenue 100000. Crowns yeerly. It

keeps

keeps an Abbot with many Fryers of Saint *Benedict* ; And here began the Reformation of that Order, about two hundred yeers since.

The fourth signal, is the Church of Saint *Augustino*, of the Fathers Dominicans : which was first a Temple of *Juno*, wherein the Antient *Padouans* dedicated the spoils of *Cleonimus* the *Spartan*, as saith *T. Livie*. Thence it became the particular Chapel of the *Carraresi*, who there fixed the Sepulchers for their Family. Where also are the Monuments of *Marieta*, Mother of *James King* of *Ciprus*, and *F. Carlota* his Daughter, with many Memorials of other Grand Persons, as well of this City as Strangers ; and in particular of *Pietro da Abano*, near the great Door. It hath a Stately Convent with a fayr Library, where are the Pictures of the chief Fathers of that Order.

The fifth Marvel is the Church of the *Carmelites*, famous for its vast height, and grandure, with one only Arch, and a most high Cupulo; Its Chapels are all of one resemblance, and in great perfection : Herein they keep an Image of the blessed Virgin, who, as they say, showrs down her continued favours upon those that devoutly by her intercession pray for them to God Almighty. In this Church are certain Monuments of the *Naldi*, Famous Captains, and many other Noble Families of *Padoua*.

The Sixth Ecclesiastick wonder, is the Church of *Fremitani*, wherein lies buried *Marco Mantoua*, the famous Doctor of Lawes. Here are the Chapels of the *Cortellieri*, painted by *Giusto* an antient Lymner, and of the *Zabarella*, by the hand of *Montegna*.

The seventh is the Church of Saint *Francesco*, wherein are the Tombes of *Bartolomeo Cavalcante*, *Jeronimo Cagnolo* an excellent, Doctor, and of *Longolio* whereon *Bembo* composed the ensuing Verses.

> *Te Juvenem rapuere Deæ fatalia nentes*
> *Stamina, cum scirent moriturum tempore nullo*
> *Longolio, tibi si canos, seniumque dedissent.*

In the Church *de' Servi*, is enterred *Paolo de Castro* ; and near the Church of *San Lorenzo* stands a pure Marble Chest, erected upon four Columns which is concluded to be the Noble Heroe *Antenors* Tombe, from this Epitaph engraven upon it in old Characters.

> *Inclitus Antenor patriam vox nisa quietem*
> *Transtulit huc Henetum, Dardanidumque fugas,*
> *Expulit Euganeos, Patavinam condidit Urbem.*
> *Quem tenet hic humili marmore cæsa domus.*

In the Church of the *Capucines*, lyes buried Cardinal *Commendone*.

The Chief Families of *Padoua*, and Cavaliers are *Alvorati*, Marquess of *Falcino*, a City of the County of *Bolzonella*; *Lazara* Count of *Paludo* ; *Leoni* Count of *Sanguineto* ; *Obizzi* Marquess of *Orgiano*; *Zabarella* Count of *Credazza* ; *Buzzacarini Capidilista*, *Conti*, *Datti*, *Papafava*, *S. Bonifacii*, and besides those aforenamed, these following, viz. *Ascanio Pediano* the Oratour ; *Aruntio Stella*; *Vallerio Flacco*; *Volusio Poeta*; *Jacomo Zabarella* a most worthy Philosopher ; with many others both valiant and Learned who have much added to the renown of this City.

Between the Church del *Santo* and that of *San Giustina*, lies the Physick Garden filled with simples, and planted in the yeer 1546. at the cost of the Students in Physick and Philosophy, to the end they might the more commodiouſly ſearch into the nature & vertue of every Medicinal Herb : The chief care and cuſtody of this Garden, is alwayes committed to ſome excellent Doctor in Phyſick, who Reads to the Students, the names and nature of every Simple; in the latter times *Melchior Guillandino, Giacomo Antonio Cortuſo,* and *Proſpero Alpino,* three excelling Perſons underwent this charge, but at preſent tis in the hands of the learned *Giovanni Veſſinghio,* or *Weſtlingius,* a Knight and Anatomy Reader in the Univerſity. A man allowed ſo great an eſteem for his excellent knowlege, that he was become the Admiration of this Age, when I was in In honour of *Italy,* whome a woïthy and Noble Perſon of our Nation , being caſually at *Padoua,* at the proceeding of certain Engliſh, to the Degrees of Doctors , and having been an Auditor at ſome of his Lectures, compoſed theſe enſuing Verſes upon the Anatomy.

Edmond Waller Eſpuire.

> *Learned* Weſtlingius *, had we but the Art,*
> *To tell the Treaſures of the nobler part;*
> *And could the Soul's high powers deſcribe as well,*
> *As you, the Palace where that Queen does dwell;*
> *In her Anatomy my Muſe might finde,*
> *Praiſes proportion'd to your knowing minde ;*
> *To whoſe great art and induſtry we owe*
> *That all the wonders of our Frame we know :*
> *For not the inventory, we alone*
> *Of every Nerve, Vein, Artery, and Bone,*
> *Receive from thence, but are inſtructed too*
> *What the wiſe Maker has deſign'd them to :*
> *The great importance of the ſlendreſt ſtring,*
> *And uſe of every (ſeeming uſeleſs) thing :*
> *As if our firſt Creator you had ſeen,*
> *Or had of Counſel with* Prometheus *been,*
> *That all the Plagues which his raſh Brother threw*
> *On wretched Man, might have their Cure from you.*

Ten miles out of *Padoua,* towards the Port of the *Malomocco,* ſtands the Caſtle *Pieve de Sacco,* from which the Biſhop of *Padoua* takes his Title of Count, a little beyond that, ſtands *Polverara* where are bred the largeſt foul, as Cocks and Hens, of all *Italy.* Near which begins, the Sholes or Gulph of *Venice,* between which appears the moſt antient now deſerted Citty of *Adria* which formerly gave the name of *Mare Adriaticum,* to the Sea now called the Golph of *Venice.*

Polverara.

Adria.

Towards the North ſtands the Caſtle *di Campo San Piero,* whence that Noble Family took its name and Original. Between *Padoua* and *Baſſano* is built a Cittadel.

Towards the Weſt is the City *Vicenza;* with the famous Mountains *Euganei,* ſo called in the Greek tongue, for their exceſſive deliciouſneſs; whence the *Padouans* extract great quantities of Medicinal herbs. Which Hils are neither part of the *Alps,* nor part of the *Apenines,* a thing ſcarce credible: than which *Conſtantine Paleologo* ſaid (as *Rodegino* reports) that beſides the Terreſtial Paradice

Euganei.

twas

twas not poſſible the World could afford a place more full of delights.   At five miles diſtance from *Padoua,* are extant the Baths of
Albano, where is to be admir'd the different kinds of Waters: how
out of a vaſt high cavernous Rock ariſes two ſources of Water not
above 2 foot one from the other , of a perfect different nature; the
one whereof encruſts & converts into a hard white ſtone, not only
the Banks by which it runs, but what ever els is caſt into it,in crea-
ſing the ſaide ruſtment of what is thrown in,according to the time
tis left in it, and that which is more,it begets Stone of the ſame nature upon the wheel of a Mill which is turned by its ſtream, which
every Moneth enforces the workemen to beat it off with *Pickaxes* that
their Mill may not be hindred; the Water hereof is never drunk
by any creature, being held very hurtfull; but the other Water
runs upon a light Sand, is much more light in weight than the firſt,
and is divers times drank for ſundry healthfull operatiõs:the people
have dug the Earth in parts round the ſaid Hill, and have found
Sulphure,about the middle part, and at the root of them having
dug towards the *Eaſt* and *South* parts they have found Salt.   *Abano*
at this day is nothing ſo much inhabited as we ought to believe it
was heretofore;by reaſon that upon any digging they often find underground, many Reliques of Antiquity; ſome alſo will have it
that here they ſpun the fineſt Linnen Cloth.   On the other ſide of
Abano ſtands the ſumptuous and rich Monaſtery of *Praia,* with the
black Monks of Saint *Benedict:* and near it the Church of *Santa Ma-*
ria di Monte Ortone. Approaching whereunto is the Convent of the
Fryars Ermitans of Saint *Auguſtine,* called *Scalci,* or without Shoos
in which are ſources of boyling water, and mud,excellent for pains
and ſhrunk ſinews: though the difficulty with which they are
come at, renders them of leſs common uſe than they would be, for
they are a vaſt way in the Earth, and in ſmall quantities too: but
they are of a white colour, and ſtiff as well wrought clay;   not
black and dirty as thoſe which are commonly gotten out of the
adjacent *Montagnone.* They paſs from *Padoua* to *Eſtè* upon the River, and upon the way eſpy the noble Caſtle of *Monſelice,*(environed with moſt pleaſant Hills) alſo the foundations of a ruinated
fortreſs, where they gather infinite numbers of Vipers, for the
compoſing of that ſo much famed *Venice* Treacle: On the left ſide
whereof is the Hill *Arquato Contrada,* much ſpoken of in memory of
Franc Petrarca, whoſe habitation being long there, at length he
gave up the Ghoſt, and was there honourably interred in a ſepulchre of Marble, with this Epitaph enſcribed, which himſelf made,
as followes.

> *Frigida Franciſci, lapis hic, tegt oſſa Petrarcæ,*
> *Suſcipe virgo Parens animam, ſate Virgne parce,*
> *Feſſaque jam terris, cæli requieſcat in Arce.*

    At this day alſo may be ſeen there his Houſe, his Chair, and little
Garden.
    Two miles diſtant from *Arquato* upon a little Hill, is *Cataio,*
a large Town of the Signors *Obici:* thence they come to *Battaglia* a
Pariſh near the River, ſeaven miles after which one arrives at *Eſtè* a
noble Caſtle and ancient: whence that Illuſtrious Family of *Eſtè*
                                          drew

L

drew their Original. Whofe Palace is transformed into a Monaftery by the *Dominican* Fryers. From this Country they extract (befides abundance of all other things for fuftenance) excellent Wines. It contains 100000 Souls, and the publick have 18000 Crowns of yeerly income. There they afcend the Mountain of *Vende*, where is a Monaftery of the Fryers of *Mount Oliveto*, three miles whence ftands another Mountain, where is the rich Abbacy and Monaftery of the Fryers of *Camaldol*. Tenn miles beyond *Efte* is feated the noble Caftle of *Montagnana* nothing inferiour to that of *Efte* neither in Riches nor Civility, where they much trade in Hemp. Eight miles farther is *Lendinara*, a very ftrong Caftle & Town wafhed with the River *Adice*: but the Ayr is a little grofs in the Winter time, it contayns 4000 Souls. Near which is the Caftle *Sanguinedo*, in the Confines between the *Venetians*, and the Duke of *Mantona*: where there is a fayr even way for eighteen miles length. Ifuing out of the gate of *Padona* called *S. Croce*, which leads to *Ferrara*, firft you meet *Confelve* heretofore a Caftle of the Signori *Lazara*, where ftands the moft delitious palace of the Count *Nicholas* of *Lazara*, a magnanimous and generous Knight, wherein *Henry* the third, King of *France* and *Poland* quartered: near it lies the Count *Paludo*, whence the faid Signor derives his Lordfhip: tis a Country Noble and Fertile, is a Convent of the Fathers Hermitans founded by *Giovanni de Lazara*, Knight of *S. Giacomo*, and Lieutenant General of the *Venetian* Cavalrie in the yeer 1574. After which is met *Anguillara*, whereby the *Adice* paffeth. Farther on they go to *Rovigo*, made a City by the Prince or Duke of *Venice* feated, 25 miles from *Padona* and 18 from *Ferara*; It was built out of the Ruines of *Adria*, whence tis not allocated above a mile; tis bathed by an Arm of the *Adice*, where are erected noble dwellings, environed with a deep Ditch or Foffe, which in circuit are about a mile; its Country is moft Fertile, being compaffed about with the 4 Rivers, The *Poe*, the *Adice*, the *Tartaro*, the *Caftagnaro*. And fo it borrowes the name of *Polefine* (which fignifies *Peninfula*, almoft an Ifland) from its length, and the circumvolution of thofe Rivers. Many Illuftrious Perfons have added to the Glory of this their Countrey, as the Cardinal *Roverella*, *Brufoneo* the Poet, *Celio*, the *Riccobuoni*, and *Gio Tomafo Minadoi* a moft learned Phyfician, who wrote the *Perfian Hiftory*, with other famous men. It hath a Church dedicated to Saint *Bellino*, heretofore Bifhop of *Padona*, the Priefts whereof with miraculous fuccefs reftore to health fuch as are bit by mad Dogs, whom they as fuddainly cure as indubitably, with a certain exorcifm, which if malignity proceeded in a natural courfe of Phyfick, would not only require the beft skill but length of time. Whofoever reads the 36th Ch. of the 6th. Book of *Diofc.* and thofe other Tractates writ on that infirmity, may comprehend how great this miracle is. *Mathioli* in the cited fol. of *Diofc.* owned the fuccefs, and willing to deduce it from fome natural caufe, faith, that poffibly thefe Priefts might intermix fome medicinal herb or fecret with that bread which they are wont to blefs for Dog-bitten Mad Perfons: but this may eafily be anfwered, For this Church is governed by two poor Priefts who many times defert it; nor are they of a felected condition; and twere ftrange if fince the time of Saint *Bellino* to this day none fhould arrive

there

therebut he muſt bring that medicinal ſecret with him, Secondly they give but one little morcel of that bleſſed bread to a perſon, and it can ſcarce be imagined enough of the medicine ſhould be conteyned in ſo ſmall a parcel of Bread, for ſo wonderfully a dangerous diſeaſe. Thirdly the Nuns of Saint *Pietro* in *Padona*, have an antient Key which was *San Bellinoes*, which Key heated, and its ſign made on the head of the mad Dogg, he never after that is troubled with the leaſt ſign of madneſs: Which being, tis neceſſarily conluded, and the Phyſicians muſt *per* force confeſs, that tis a pure Miracle wrought by God at the interceſſion of *San Bellino*, who by the inſtigation of certain evil People, was torn in pieces by Doggs, and his glorious Corps layed up in the ſaid Church of *Poleſene.*

Deſiring to go to *Ferrara*, Firſt they take the way *Roſati*, till they arrive at the *Poe*, which paſſing by *Bark*, they reach *Francolino*, a County ſome five miles from *Ferrara*.

VICENZA.

*V*Icenza is now ſeated in the *Marca Trivigiana*, or the Marquiſate of *Treves*, It was built (according to *Livie*, *Juſtine*, and *Paulo Diacono*) by the *Galli Senoni*, who fell down into *Italy* in the Reign of *Tarquinius Priſcus*, in *Rome*, giving the name of *Gallia Ciſalpina*, to that part poſſeſſed by them: But *Strabo*, *Pliny*, and *Polybius* will have it to be founded by the Antient *Tuſcans*, and that it was one of the twelve Cities under their dominion, on this ſide of the *Apenines*, and that it was much encreaſed and amplified by the *Galli Senones*. When afterwards the Cities thereabouts performed good ſervice for Omnipotent *Rome*, at the deſcent of other French men, in the yeer 366. into *Italy*, and at their Aſſayling of *Rome*, *Vicenza* being one of them, in recompence of their aſſiſtance ſo oportunely contributed, was created *Municipal*, a Free City: whence exerciſing their own Laws and Statutes they participated of the honours and dignities of *Rome*; and thence tis we find ſo many of its Citizens iu the Magiſtracy of that grand Republick, among others, *Aulus Cecinna*, the Conſul, was General of the Army of *Vitellius* the Emperour, In whoſe honour (becauſe he ſo much ſurpaſſed the fame of an ordinary Citizen) It will not be impertinent to place here this following antient inſcription.

A. Cæcinnæ Felicis, Viteliani exercit. Imp.
Ob Virtutem, & munus Gladiatorum apud ſe
exhibitum Cremona.

To it was allotted alſo the Title of Republick and City, as is to be ſeen in many antient Marble Stones up and down the Countrey, and twas aſſigned to the Tribe *Menemia*. It was under the protecti. on of *Brutus* and *Cicero*, as appears in his familiar Epiſtles, and in this antient inſcribed memorial:

D. Bruto, & M. Tullio Viris in Senatu
contra Vernas optimè de ſe meritis Vicent.

All the time the Roman Empire continued in its Grandezza, it

            ever

ever followed the victorious Eagle, which decaying, this also suffered much Calamity, and underwent those mutations, which it and all the Cities of *Italy* groaned under with miserable example: Not at all, nevertheless, declining from its antient Vigour and Reputation : Whence it was that the *Longobardi* held it very considerable, and assigned to it, Its own particular Dukes and Counts, Those Governours calling themselves by that Title, for that they continued for life, and to their Heirs *masculines* after them : Of one of whom *Paolo Diacono* makes a noble record in the life of *Leon* the Emperor, which was *Peredeo* Duke of *Vicenza*, who marched to *Ravenna* in assistance to the Pope, and there dyed fighting valiantly for his Holiness.

This City was by *Desiderio* the last King of the *Longobardi* selected amongst all his, to place securely his Son *Aldigerio*, when himself was besiged in *Pavia*, by *Charles* the great; but it avoided not its total destruction.

The Reliques of its antient Theatre, which at this day demonstrate themselves in the Gardens of the *Signori Figasetta*, and *Cnaldi* (wherein both the Kings of the *Longobardi* and those of *France* often sate to behold the publick shewes and Games) And the fragments of the hot Bathes, with the Pilasters for the Aqueducts, give sufficient testimony that it had no defect of whatsoever, either for Ornament or magnificence, other famous Cities use to enjoy. And at that time when *Lotarius* the Emperor endeavoured in *Rome*, in the yeer 825, to reform the occasion of the *Feudes*, and to that end convocated the principal Lawyers of the primary Cities of *Italy*, He also invited the *Vicentine* Counsellors with an honourable testimony of what esteem he had for the City *Vicentia*.

Furthermore when *Ottone* King of *Germanie* (the *Berengarii* being overcome and discomfited) was by the Pope crowned Emperor, he remised the *Italian* Cities in Liberty, granting unto them Power to elect their *Podestà* or chief Governour, and to enjoy their own Laws, among the rest *Vicenza* participated of that so great a gift: Whence forming a *Carrocio* or Chariot which was the Badge of a free City, and acknowleging the Empire with the ordinary Tribute, it lived in the form of a Republick, (although much perplexed with the most cruel factions of its own Citizens) until the yeer 1143. When *Federico Barbarossa* having gathered the utmost of his Power, forced all the Cities of *Italy* into servitude, and destroying *Milan*, in the rest constituted a German *Podestà*

Vicenza endured not long this Tyranny, but united with *Padoua* and *Verona*, they shoke off the yoke, and sent the first Embassadors to the *Milanesi* to offer them assistance, and to perswade them to do the like; and so they concluded the famous League of the Cities of *Lombardy*, by which Colleagues *Barbarossa* (being overcome between *Como* and *Milan*) was driven to the other side of the *Alpes*. Which victory the peace of *Costanza* followed, to the conclusion whereof came also the Orators of *Vicenza*, where they megliorated enough their Cities Condition, and the state of their Liberty, chiefly for that *Henry* the Son and successor of *Federick* confirmed the abovenamed Peace with all the conditions conceded by his Father : All the Embassadors of the Colleagued Cities randezvousing

at

at *Piacenfe*, to that purpofe, where alfo was the Emperor, and *Michael Capra* a *Vicentine* was comiffionated thither for the City of *Bolognia*.

In thofe dayes the Republicks Library flourifhed in this City with infinite côcourfe of Forein Nations, abounding with the moft worthy Profeffors in all the fciences and Arts, which it appears continued to the yeer 1228. In which yeer *Federick* the fecond being exalted to the Empire, an extream Enemy to the Pope and Cities of *Italy*, after many ruines whch he brought on others, in the yeer 1236 burnt and deftroyed *Vicenza*; exercifing his greateft cruelty againft the moft potent Citizens, which reduced it withgreat eafe under the wicked Tyrant *Eccellino*, continuing fo until his death, when waving and debilitated, it by degrees crawled up the fteps of its Antient Liberty; yet not fo ftrongly, but that after 45 yeers it underwent by the Citizens negleĉt, the Signory of the *Scaligeri*, who there governed under the fhadow and name of an Empire: and that title not improperly taken, for that *Can Grande* at that time their head, was a moft valiant and potent Lord.

Vicenza was well treated under their goverment, and many publick Edifices reftored, but the wheele of Fortune running round, and the Line of thofe Lawfull Signors extinĉt, *Antonio* the laft of them and illegitimate, was firft deprived of *Verona*, then of *Vicenza*, by *Gio Galleazze* firft Vifcount of *Milan*, by whom it was held very dear, and fo much honoured for its fidelity, that he made it the Chamber of his Empire.

He dead *Catarina* his Wife diftrufting her own ability to maintain fo great Dominions, by her Letters full of Courtefy, abfolving their Oath of fidelity, gave the *Vicentines* ample Liberty to eleĉt their own Government, who after divers confultations and many folicitations to colleague themfelves with the *Switzers*, and to become one of their Cantons, having at large fupervifed the great calamities of the paffed times, and fearing future miferies, At length the Advice of *Henrico Capra* (a wife and efteemed Citizen of great Intereft both for his many adherents and riches) prevailed to furrender themfelves of their own free accords to the Republick of *Venice*, whofe pleafing Goverment was then become famous through the whole world. Who accepting with all Gratitude this their free offer, confirmed unto them all fuch Jurifdiĉtions, Statutes, & Prerogatives, as they knew how to demand; and in particular the Confularfhip the moft Antient Magiftracy of this City, and received it into proteĉtion, ftyling it the firft Born and moft faithfull City, under whofe Signory it hath ever fince continued, dayly encreafing both their Wealth, and conveniences.

Yet notwithftanding, at the Inroad of *Gieradada*, the State of *Venice*, (though unwillingly) gave way to the Signory of the whole firm Land; by which means *Vicenza* fell into the hands of *Maffiminian* the Emperor, who fent thither *Leonardo Triffino*, to receive poffeffion thereof, as Vicar of the Empire, which he performed there, as alfo in *Padoua*: Who with *Vicentia*, through the great affeĉtion they bore the Republick of *Venice*, and the fingular Prudence of the *Venetian* Senate within fome few yeers after eafily returned to their former Obedience under it.

ThisCity is four miles in circuit, in form like the figure of a Scorpion, & although in former times it had the Reputation of strong, from the double Walls which invironed it; yet tis neither fortified nor capable of Fortification: it being situated at the bottome of a Hill that comands the Town; however (voluntarily living like the Antient *Spartans*) the Citizens profess that the Walls of their Breasts suffice to maintain even to the death their Fidelity to their natural Prince, which preserves it with safety. It is washed by two Rivers *Bacchileone* (by some Latines called also *Meduaco Minore*) and *Rerone Ereteno* before mentioned, together with two other small Brooks, *Astichello* and *Seriola*, which serve them with many conveniences. All which united at a small distance from the City, form a Navigable River as well upwards as downwards, capable of Vessels of a huge burthen, who passing by *Padoua* reach *Venice*, and give the best occasion and reason for the riches of that Countrey.

They account that it with the Burroughs conteyn 40000. Souls, being replenisht with Proud and Stately Palaces, Noble Temples and publick Structures built after the modern Architecture: the Hall of Justice (wherein the Judges assemble to do Justice) for its Antient and modern Structure may be compared with any in *Italy*: Upon the highest Tower raised to a Wonder (which joyns to it) is placed the *Horologe* which serves all the City within, and a mile out of it, most comodiously.

The *Piazza* most capacious for all their Justings and Turnaments, (where morn & even reder themselves the Nobility) is no less adorned with Open Galleries & the Fort of the said Palace, than with a fayr habitation, for the Seignor *Capitano* and the Fabrick of that mount *Piety*, which is so rich that they lend such sums as the poor Citizens require without any Usurie. Besides this (which is called *Piazza Maggiore*) there are five other *Piazzaes* for the publick markets, of Poultry, Grain, Wine, Wood, Hay, Fish, Fruits, and Herbs. And as the Splendidness of the *Vicentians* Spirits is apparent in profane things, so does their Piety and magnificense, no less shine in and towards the Divine worship: For which they number in the City 50. Churches accounted Stately, and beautified with antient and modern Pictures, whereof 14. are *Parochials*, 17. of *Fryers*, and 12. of Nuns, all well furnished with receptacles and other necessaries for subsistence: Among which the *Mendicants* or begging Fryers, by the Charity of the Citizens, have no mean Reliefs. In the Country are also 3. other Monasteries of Nunns, and above 20. of Fryers, besides *Parochials*, which are very ample in the Villages.

They are well stored with Hospitals for the poor of all conditions, having nine, besides the Confraternities and other retreats of Godly persons who wait on works of Charity. In the Cathedral (signal for the good Bishoprick of 12000 Duckats yeerly Revenue) besides other Reliques they keep the bodies of the Martyrs *Carpoforo* and *Leoncio Vicentines*. And in the Church of *Santa Corona* of the Dominican Fryers one of the thorns of the Crown of the Saviour of the World, given in the yeer 1260. by *Lodovico* or *Lewis* the Saint King of *France*, to *Bartolomeo Breganze*, Citizen and Bishop of *Vicenza* It received the Light of the Faith of Christ by the teaching of Saint *Prosdocimo* first Bishop of *Padoua*, Saint *Paul* yet living.

Near

Near the *Domo* ſtands *l'Oratoria de Madonna*, or the Oratory of our Lady, raiſed by thoſe of that confraternity, in imitation of that of *Rome*, which poſſibly in magnificence and beauty it ſurpaſſeth.

Its State under the *Venetian* Dominion is ſuch, as certainly no City under their power hath greater privileges. The *Conſul* the moſt antient Juriſdiction of this City judging all Criminal Offences, and its own Citizens all other civil Cauſes: For which end the Council chuſeth a round of four Doctors and 8 *Laicks*, which change by fours every month. Theſe form the proceſs for Manſlaughter, in their City and Territory, and being ſummoned to meet Morning and Evening, in the Congregation, the Antienteſt of the Doctors aſſuming and ſtating briefly the Caſe, firſt gives his Judgement, after whom all the reſt, from one to the other, and laſt of all the *Podeſtà* who hath but one voyce, pronounce theirs, and the ſentence paſſeth by the Major part of Opinions, whence there is no appeal : And their Juſtice hath been ſo duly adminiſtred, that hitherto the ſupreme Prince never violated nor revoked their Judgement. The ſaid 4. Doctors have alſo their ſeat of Juſtice for Civil Cauſes, whence there is an appeal to one Judge (who is therefore ſtiled the Judge for Appeals) who muſt be of the ſame College, or to the *Podeſta* or his Aſſeſſors, ſo that tis in the will of every perſon to determine his Cauſe before the proper Judges of *Vicentia*.

The Deputies who repreſent the City conſult and order thoſe things which appertain to its honour and the publick good, and have abſolute power in all their Cities Proviſions : who chuſe four of the chief Nobility , called the *Cavalieri di Commun*; who with their Officers overſee the Weights and Meaſures, and that all the orders made for the benefit of the People be duly executed , and in caſe of any defect report it to the Deputies; Theſe Magiſtrates are every yeer created by the council of the 150 Citizens, and alſo are choſen every yeer, whereby to give occaſion to every one to demean himſelf well and to live virtuouſly.

It hath three Colleges, One of the Doctors of Lawes , where none is admitted , that cannot prove himſelf of a houſe of Nobility, of one hundred yeers ſtanding, and Legitimate Iſſue for three Ages, beſides that, he is examined of his knowlege at his entrance, and obliged to proceed Doctor in the Univerſity of *Padoua*. The ſecond is of Phyſicians more modern, and the third of Notaries, moſt antient and reſtrained.

It hath Six thouſand duckets of Income by the yeer, which is expended in repairing the Bridges, Highways, and Palace, maintaining an Ordinary Reſident at *Venice*, and other extraordinary charges. The *Vicentines* delight to go abroad in the World, (an humour ſeldome met with in the *Italians*) as well to learn good breeding, as to provide for their Families : So that returned home they live in all ſplendor and politeneſs, both within and without doors, go richly apparelled, as well Men as Women, and keep many followers; which they may well do, by their abundance of Riches

For which cauſe this City is reputed full of Gentry, and their common Title is, *il Signor Conte*. Nor are they leſs noble in their buildings, both publick and private, than in their garb : for by the induſtry

duftry of *Palladius* a *Vicentine* and reviver of the Roman Architecture, it fhewes it felf moft pompous, and equal to any other
great City: The *Vicentines* are great Lovers of Strangers, liberally entertain with all forts of Regalios, the acquaintance and friends they
take knowlege of in other places, and willingly take the oportuni-
nity to treat any great Prince.

They erected a Theatre by the invention of *Andreo Palladio* the
Renovator of the good and antient Architecture (capable of 5000
perfons in their Seats) as by this infcription appears.

Virtuti ac Genio
Olympior: Academia
Theatrum hoc a fundamentis erexit
Paladio Archit.
Anno. 1584.

The Stage, or Scene, is a ftupendious thing to behold, for the
many Statues and Corinthian Pillars; the Profpective reprefents a
Royal City, where was firft performed, with great Applaufe, and incredible fatisfaction to the whole Province, in the yeer 1585: the reprefentation of *Epidus* Tyrant of *Soffocles*, acted with lordly pomp,
as well in the habits, as mufick, *Chorus*, and illumination of the
Theatre. The Olympick Academy (to whom we owe this work)
ought therefore to be thanked as the receptable of the Mufes, and
all other noble and elevated ingenuities. The *Vicentines* chiefly
have the obligation for this work, to the memory of the Cavalier
Chieregato Governour of all the Militia of the Kindome of *Candy*,
and reftorer of all the antient and good difcipline for the
Infantery.

Befides that Olympick it hath another Academy more modern for
Horfe, founded, by the Count *Oderico Capra* Leader for his Highnefs of
one hundred Men in Arms, not lefs ufefull for the Exercife of the
Youth, than for the manage it gives the Horfes, with much profit to
the Prince in warlike Occurrences, where good Mafters Riders are
well entertained.

Which makes the City be filled with well managed Gennets and
other the beft Horfes of *Lumbardy*. For inftance, view the Stable of
the faid Count *Oderico*, furnifhed with 15. Courfers, of the beft Ra-
ces of *Italy*.

Going out of the Gate, *Del Caftello*, is the *Campo Martio* (made in
imitation of, that antiently in *Rome*, which was for the hunting
of wild Beafts) for the exercifes of the youth, and Souldiery, wate-
red round; whither the Ladies and Gallants refort in the fummer
Evenings to participate the frefh Ayr, which the furrounding Hills
afford. The Arch or entrance into this field will remain as a lafting
monument of *Palladius* who built it. Oppofite hereto is the Garden
of the Count *Leonardo Valmarana*, which is very praife-worthy for
the long and beautifull clofs walk of Citron and Orange Trees, and
plenty of all Fruits, together with the Labyrinth. At the head of
the Burrough ftands the Temple of *San Felice* and *Fortunato* the Martyrs, which fome believe that *Narfitze* built, therein is preferved the
Body of *San Fortunato* and head of *San Felice*, which were lately
found

found in the Cloyster of the Bishop, miraculously in a Chest of Lead, with Letters signifying so much: *viz.* The head of *San Fortunato*, and the Body of *San Felice*, of whose Martyrdom Cardinal *Beronio* makes mention.

A mile further is the *Olmo*, made famous by the overthrow which *Alviano* the *Venetian* General received from *Cardona* and *Prospero Collonna*, Captains of the Spanish Army. Somewhat beyond stands the Castle of *Montecchio*, with the Palace of the *Conti Gualdi* where *Charles* the 5th. Lodged. Whence by *Montebella* they pass to *Verona*, leaving on the right hand the pleasant Valley *Dressina*, with *Valdagno* and *Arcignano*, most populous and trading Villages, where they make Linnen Cloth, not ordinary, neither in quantity, or quality. And on the left hand *Lonigo Podestaria*, which for its white bread and good wine carries the Bell: famed also for the birth of *Nicolo Leoniceno*, a most renowned Physician, and very much endeared by *Hercoles* first Duke of *Ferrara*, near whom he lived and dyed, having long read in that University.

Issuing forth of the Gate *de Monte*, one sees another Arch of *Palladins*, with a most high Stayr case, to the top of *Madonna del Monte* held in high veneration for the continual Miracles wrought at her intercession, and much frequented by the Neighbouring People. A quarter of a mile farther by the River side which is navigable; upon a little Hill(as it were artificially separated from the other, and of a Facil ascent) stands the *Rotonda*, of the Signors Counts, *Oderico* and *Mario Capra* Brothers, so called from the round *Cupola* at the top(or likeness it hath with the *Pantheon* at *Rome*)which covers the Hall of the same Figure: They mount to it by four ample Marble pair of Stayrs, where are four spatious Chambers worth seeing for the fair Columns which seem of an excellent Marble called *Paris*. From each of which one may behold various prospects, from one an *immense campagna*, another the large Theatre and Town, the third mountains over Mountains, the Fourth Land intermixt with Waters, so that the eye rests marveloufly contented. The round of the said Hall garnished with Figures of Plaister of *Paris*, and Pictures and bordered with gold, receives its Light from the Top like the *Pantheon* of *Rome*. The Chambers are all guilt & mingled with Histories of excellent Invention and Pictures drawn by the hand of *Alessandro Maganza* a *Vicentine*, *Palladins* made this his Masterpiece, for tis so contrived that it conteyns Geometrically a Round, a Cross, and a Square: And if in any place the Heavens seem to display their eternal Beauty, more than in other, tis there. They use to say that *Apollo* and the Sisters with their Chorus sojourn there, And that *Bacchus* resides in his deep Sellars; which are so vast, and filled with the best wines, and they with so much liberality and bounty free to all persons, That they must not be passed without a visit: nor the Gardens filled with Citrons and all sorts of outlandish Flowers: all which are splendidly governed and freely shewed to all Strangers with all kind acceptance from the Patrons.

The passage over the Park of *Longara* planted with incomparable fruits by the said Counts, will not appear tedious at your arrival at *Custoza*, beautified with the Acqueducts for wind, which driving the *Fresco* upon the Palaces exceedingly temperate the heat of the

N

Sun

Sun in *Leo*, together with the most cool Wines, kept in those great Cavernes in Snow: whose dry and wholsome Ayr (though as twere congeled) makes them be infinitely frequented in the Summer, as a most singular delight and without a Parallel.

On the right hand of *Custoza* having traversed the Bridge *Bacchiglione* and drawing some miles towards *Padoua*, is seen the Castle of *Montegalda*, formerly an important Frontier against the enemies, but now by the benefit of this Peace become more like to the Castle of *Alcina*, the storehouse for the Munition, being now applyed to conteyn waters for the use of artificial fountains, and the Ditches converted into walks planted with Citron and Orange Trees, whose blossoms afford a most pleasant odour into the Palaces; but not to come to near *Padoua* already so fully visited, let us return by *Custoza* again to *Vicenza*, and in the way thereto leading by the River side, between it and the Mountains behold the *Vicariate Barbattona*, whose Hils called *Alcini* a little hanging and receiving the heat of the Sun at high Noon, afford those delitious wines esteemed only fit for the Palate of an Emperor called *Monte Alcino*.

From *Vicenza* desiring to go to *Ferrara*, they travail by *Poiana* which terminates the confines on that side, where the most Noble Palace of the Count of *Poiana* most worthy of its Builder *Palladius*, and furnished with excellent Pictures, deserves a serious view.

A mile forth of the Gate of Saint *Bartolomeo*, stands the Palace of *Circolo*, appertaining to the Count *Pompeoi Trissino* built after the modern Architecture by his Grandsir *Giovan Ciorgio*, a famous Poet, and no less skilled in this Art, than in all others, as well as the liberal Sciences, which deserves a visit for its compact structure and excellent Invention: whence advancing over a fair plain, one reaches at some miles distance the pleasant Country of *Breganza*, famous for its sweet and flavorous wines.

Turning on the left hand a rough Country conducts one to *Maarostica*, a Seat for a Podesta, and a large Castle, the Country and Birth place of *Angelo Matcaccio*, a most learned Man, and Reader of the Civil Lawes for a long time in *Padoua*, at the same time, *Alessandrio Massaria*, was Chief Reader in Phisick, and of the *Conte de Monte*, both *Vicentines*, and the *Esculapii* of this our Age, and from *Marostica*, at three miles distance, is seated *Bassano*, now out of its Territories, heretofore comprehended in them, and to this day in Spirituals governed by the Bishop of *Vicenza*.

On that part of *Breganze*, which is washed with the *Astico* is Scituated *Lonedo*, and the Palace of the Signory *Conto Alessandro*, and *Girolamo Godi*, built at excessive expence on those Craggy places, whereto ascended (though with much pains and some sweat) tis compared to the Mount of Virtue; for that having gained the Top, there is found what may restore one with such plenty and gentlenefs, that it may be said the Goddefs *Abondantia*, there had emptied her Basket. The Architecture is most exact, the Pictures of excellent hands, the Prospects wonderfull, the Fountains Beautifull and the Cittrons and sweet Flowers for all seasons not despicable, but above all the affablenefs and Civilities with which the *Padroni* treat all Strangers, is most to be admired.

Through the Gate *Santo Croce*, they travel to *Trento*, the Country

try whereto is bounded with a continued Lift of little Hills which afford moft delitious Wines, till arrived at *Schio*, where they mount on very cragged waies.

Schio is a principal Town, Seated at the feet of thofe Mountaines, at 15. miles diftance from the City, filled with Merchandize and Comodities; it conteins five thoufand Souls, a People neat and civil as well as Warlike. It gave birth to *Giovan Paolo Mamsfrone*, who from a private Souldier arofe to the chiefeft honors in Wars, and both he and his Son *Giulio* are not a little famed for their excellent Conduct and valour, in Hiftories.

Through the fame Gate taking the *Strada militare*, at ten miles Journey, prefents it felf *Tiene*, a noble Town, in a moft pleafing fcite, and not a little beautified by the Palace, of the Count *Francefco Porti*, which though built after the antient Architecture is neverthelefs full of Majefty: beautified with fprings of running water, Labyrinths, fpacious Gardens, Citron and Orange Trees, and an Ayr pure and fweet, even to ravifhing admiration.

Two mile farther, upon the raifed Hillock of *Carè*, is lately erected the *Romitorio*, by the Charity and free gifts of the *Peafeants* of *Romiti Camaldolenfi*, whofe fituation with their quotidian induftry and labour, muft foon render the place fuch, and fo beautifull, that it may difpute the Palm with the chief houfes of Religion.

From *Tiovene* a large Town coafting the *Monte fummanno* and the Torrent of *Aftice*, by the confines of *Furni*, one arrives at *Trento*, by a very ill way, only capable of Horfes: at 28 miles end. Along the *Aftico*, (where they take red Trouts,) may be feen thofe Edifices, wherein is made writing paper, the Furnaces and Forges for Iron, and the fawes which being drove by the Waters, faw that Timber and reduce it to forms, which in great abundance grows on thefe Mountains, which alfo ferve for the feeding their Flocks and Herds.

The *Summano* is famed for its rare fimples, and for the Temple of *Mary* the Virgin, which (according to common belief) was heretofore dedicated to the God *Summano*, which Idol being deftroyed by Saint *Profdocimo*, the Temple was confecrated to the Mother of God. Some yeers fince was found there a moft antique Stone engraven with Roman Letters, which by the Learned is intepreted thus. *Palemon Vicentinus Latinæ Linguæ Lumen.* And gives confidence that *Palemon* was buried there, which *Rhemio Palemon* the *Vicentine*, flourifhed in the time of *Auguftus*, in Grammar and Rhetorick, when thofe profeffions, were in much more efteem than at this day, the very Emperours in thofe dayes not difdaining to affift therein.

From *Tiovene* you afcend to the *Sette Communi*, which are feven Villages filled with a great number of moft fierce People dwelling on thofe Mountains, whom one would think created by Nature for a Parapet to the *Vicentines*, againft the incurfions of the *Germans*, Their Language is fo ftrange, that though it approach the *German* as much as it can, yet the fharpnefs of their pronunciation, renders it unintelligible even to the *Germans*; fome think they were the Reliques of the *Gothes*: They enjoy many exemptions for their fidelity to their Prince and the City.

Maximilian, the Emperour, in *February* 1508. attempted by this part to ſurpriſe *Vicenza* with a flying Army deſcending from *Trento*, but the noiſe thereof ſpread, and the *Peaſants* raiſed, by *Girolamo*, and *Chriſtofero Capra*, with others of their Family in *Piedmont*, who having poſſeſſed themſelves of the narrow paſſes of *Aſiago*, and the *Furni* with five hundred Souldiers of their party oppoſed his Army, compelling them with much ſlaughter to a diſhonourable retreat: Their Readineſs and Valour in which action was greatly acknowleged by the *Venetian* Senate,

In Sum, All its Territories are moſt beautifull, the Hills contending with the Valleys, for fertility and goodneſs: The wines (there growing in great Plenty) are eſteemed without compare the beſt of all theſe Countreys, which occaſioned the Proverb, *Vin Vicentin*, *&c.* with that variety of Colour and Taſt (a rare thing) that both Winter and Summer, the moſt delicate Palate may meet its full ſatisfaction: There being Wine ſweet and ſharp, which pleaſe and cut, Aromatick, and Fragrant, Stomachal and brisk, with a hundred other real differences, all moſt digeſtible healthfull and gratefull to the Palate. It produceth Corn of all ſorts, Pears, Apples, and all other Fruits for every Moneth in great abundance.

The *Peaſants* have ſuch infinite numbers of Calves and Kids that they ſupply half *Venice*, whither the conveniency of Water and cariage invites them to vent the ſuperfluities thereof, as alſo their admirable Veniſon, Partridges, Pheaſants, Godwits, Quailes, and Quoiſts; and although their Fſhing is not equal to their Fouling, yet they want not, either red or white Trouts, Lampreys or other Stonefiſh, beſides what certain Lakes afford of excellent ſorts.

They much inrich themſelves by the Craft there much uſed, as well within, as without the City, of making Cotton Clothes, which are eſteemed no leſs for their goodneſs than whiteneſs.

They have likewiſe great quantities of Silk-worms, and therefore tis that their Countrey is ſo well planted with Mulbery-Trees whereof the Worms feed, and thereof they extract at leaſt 500000. Crowns a yeer, diſtributing them to all Merchants that reſort thither for them, which much adds to their Riches; here alſo they fetch Fullers Earth for many uſes into ſeveral Countreys, as alſo the Sand, wherewith at *Venice* they polliſh their Looking Glaſſes.

Trento affords them ſome mines of Silver, and Iron, but much Stone for all ſorts of Structures, ſome whereof for their hardneſe are compared to the Iſtrian Stone, and others for their fineneſs to the Marble of *Carrara*.

The conveniences of Tymber, Stone, Sand, and unſlacked Lime, conſidered with their active and ingenuous Natures, together with the laborfouſneſs of the *Peaſants*, and the beauty and variety of Sites, is that which nouriſheth ſo much the Art and diſcipline in their Workmen of the Architecture of *Palladins*.

Whence *Botero* deſervedly accounts this Province for one of the four moſt delitious and rich Provinces of *Italy*. Its Ayr being ſo pure and healthfull, that they reach great Ages, beſides that this Climat in all Ages hath produced Men eminent, no leſs or Learning than Arms, as appears in the Hiſtories, and enclines the ordinary ſort to a certain Spriteneſs and aptneſs to all occupations and exerciſes.

In

In its Territory, they number one hundred and three score thoufand Souls : which added to them of the City, amounts to two
hundred thoufand, difperfed into 250. Towns and Villages, which
are governed by two *Podefta'es*, and eleven *Vicariats*, Noble *Venetians*,
and Noble *Vicentines*, whofe Jurifdictions, are limited to civil mat-
ters, only : Criminal Caufes being wholly referved to the Confu-
lary.

The Prince draws from *Vicenza*, eighty thoufand Duckats annually without the leaft charge ; and makes the Province to maintain
three thoufand felect, and well difciplined Foot, under four Captains, who alwaies refide at their feveral Quarters, and the City one
thoufand Musketteers: Alfo for the urgent neceffity of War, they
have made a new calculation of fuch perfons as are fit to bear Arms
from 18 yeers old to 20. and they have thereupon enrolled in a Book
the names of 16000. flourifhing brave Youths: Its Territory, is one
hundred and fifty miles in circumference.

Vicenza is diftant from *Padoua* 18. miles, from *Venice* 43. from *Verona*, 30. from *Mantoua*, 50. from *Trent*, 44. from *Trevifo*, 32.

Thus for a conclufion, we may with truth affirm, that reflecting
on their Political State, the ftrength of the City, which confifts not
fo much in the circuit of the Walls, as the Liberty and amplitude
of its Territory, Their riches and the number, Valour, and gallantry, of their People: *Vicenza* will find few Cities equal, and
confequently will find no fmall efteem from a wife Prince.

VERONA The Antient.

Tis the Vulgar *Criticifm* on this name, that fyllabilzed, It comprehends the three firft fyllables of the three head Cities of *Italy Ve
Venetia, Ro Roma, Na Napoli*, others more ftricty interpret that whatecer
may be found in thofe three Cities abounds there. *Verona* is reckoned
amongft the moft Noble Cities of Italy: Built long fince by the *Tofcanes*,
& was one of the twelve, by them cmōanded on this fide the *Apenines*,
The Galli *Cenomani* peopled it having beat out the *Tofcanes*. Its name (as
fome other fay) was taken from an antient Noble Family of the
Tofcanes called *Vera*. It is feated near the Mountains towards the
South, as twere in a plain, and is in form little lefs than a Square : In
the time of *Auguftus Cæfar*, it was much larger, as many induce-
ments make us believe, among others, That tis written they ufed to
fet forth 50000 Souldiers, which appears no great wonder fince
Cornelius Tacitus called *Oftilia*, a Burrough thereof, though now diftant from it 30. miles, we may thence conclude, they numbred
200000. Souls, *Martial* calls her great, and *Strabo* moft great. Its
fituation is very ftrong by Nature, yet the *Venetians* have made it
now accounted impregnable, through the many wonderfull Fortifications of *Baftions*, Bulwarks, Caftles, Towers, Counterfcarpes,
added by them, and the deep and large Dykes, kept full by the River *Adice*.

It hath one Fort in the Plain Country near the River, and two
in the Mountains, the one named *San Felice* the other a more modern, called *San Angelo*: the which guards the Plain, and aptly repels
the furious affaults of any Enemies. It hath five Gates no lefs ftrong
O   than

then adorned with Sculptures, Collumns, Statues, and other fair
Marbles. Besides, in the City are many things from whence may
be gathered. That it hath been a most antient and Noble City: Under the Castle of *San Pietro*, they yet shew the great foundations of a
Theatre with the entire doors of the *Scene*, as also the Signal of that
place which was antiently deputed for the Naval Fights, in that
place, where now is the Orchards of the Fathers Dominicans. In the
Piazza de Bestiani, stands the most antique and great Fabrick, the
Amphitheatre built of square Marble Stones, called by the *Veronei*
the *Arena*. The outward wall, whereof had four fair Rows of Pillars Arches and Windows, composed of four sorts of Architecture,
that is to say, one Dorick, one Ionick, one Corinthian, and one
mixed with good order, being a Structure not less fair than high, as
may be credited from that little part which yet is a foot. The *Barbarous* who sacked *Italy*, disrobed it of all the Marble Stones and Ornaments of the exteriour circuit, even to the foundations wherewith to adorn their other Structures leaving that so Noble work, deprived of all its Majesty; howbeit from those small reliques remaining, one may take a judgement of the grandure and quality of the
rest, as easily, as from the nails may be guessed what creature a
Lyon is, because the Reason and art of Architecture, and circular
proportions make it easily comprehended; that every one of the
said Orders or degrees of the exteriour Wall, had seventy two parts
or as one would say, Arches and as many Pillars; and from the void
places in the third order, which was the Corinthian, one may know
that there were 144. Statues between the Arches, and Pillars; Being
entred at the Porches, which within encompass the whole Fabrick in
three orders, one would wonder at the great number of Stayrs
Steps & waies, which on every side were used by the Spectators to go
in and out without disturbance. Who might altogether (although
a great multitude) mount and descend with great facility and no
trouble by those numberless ways In the midst is the *Arena*, and tis
a noble sight to behold that spatious plain of an Oveal form, 34 per-
ches long, and 22 ½ broad, environed with 42. Seats, which ly *gra-
datim*, one above the other, still extending to the Top, and were capable of 23000. Persons, which might sit there commodiously; under which Seats are the said Steps and wayes. The inward part also was despoiled by the barbarous of all its Marble Seats, though at
present the Citizens of *Verona*, at their proper expence have restored that, and adorned it as formerly, and at certain times use to
shew to the people Games, and huntings, after the Antient custom.
We find not in authentique Histories who founded this Noble Fabrick, but *Torello Saraino*, a *Venetian*, and a most learned man, en-
deavours to prove by many arguments, that the Theatre, and the
Arena, were built under *Cæsar Augustus*, one whereof is that we evidently find in *Suetonius Augustus*, constituted many new Colonies
through *Italy*, and sought to enrich and adorn many of the old, to
which opinion adds, saith a certain Chronicle (as saies *Torello*)
wherein tis written that the *Arena* was built in the twenty second
yeer of the Empire of that *Augustus*; with whom *Ciriaco Anconitano* dis-
agrees but little, who in his *Itinerary* of *Sclavonia* collects many antiquities of *Italy*, and says that the *Arena* of *Verona*, called by him
                                                                    the

the Laberinth, was built in the 39th. yeer of the Empire of *Auguſtus*. But *Magino* the moſt excellent and celebrious Mathematician writes much otherwiſe, for in his deſcription of the *Marquiſate* of *Treeves*, under *Tolemeo*, ſpeaking of *Verona*, he ſaith, that that Amfitheatre which was built by *L. V. Flaminius* in *Anno*. 53. After the building of *Rome*,&c. But let every one believe hereof as he pleaſeth, tis ſufficient that the *Grandezza*, the magnificencie, and nobleneſs of the work gives to underſtand, that it was erected in the moſt flouriſhing days of the *Roman* Empire, the Majeſty, and greatneſs, whereof it much repreſents.

Tis known that a little diſtant thence was the place where the Sword players exerciſed, and to this day are to be ſeen, the footſteps of the Arch Triumphal erected in honour of *C. Marius*, for his victory over the *Cimbrians*, in the Territories of *Verona*, ſome part of the proſpect or Front of the antient *Piazza*, yet remaining, ſhews it to have been of excellent Architecture, Tis ſaid that there was the *Via Emilia*, the *Emilian* Way, which lead to *Rimeni*, *Piacenza*, *Verona*, and to *Aquilegia*, where appears an Arch of Marble, Dedicated to *Jupiter*, who alſo had a Temple on the Hill, the foundations whereof are now extant ruinated by time, but adorned with carved Hierogloſicks.

In the *Via Emilia*, were many four ſquared Arches of Marble, three whereof, we now behold, one of which was built by *Vetruvius* and ſhews 'twas framed with true rules of Architecture. In *Verona* are many other Signes, of Venerable Antiquity, as great Ruins of her Houſes, with many Chambers adorned with figures, compoſed of ſeveral pieces of Stones, of Temples, of Arches, Triumphals, Palaces, Aquiducts, Collumns, Statues, Epitaphs, Medals, of Gold and Silver, Urns and the like, which by the firing that *Attila* King of the *Hunns*, put to it, were loſt and deſtroyed: the aPvements, in ſome places being thereby become twenty foot under ground. This City, hath many ſumptuous Palaces, and among them the Council houſe, or Chamber of Juſtice is the chief, of a ſquare form, with 4. Halls, and one ſquare low Court, wherein there is ſo much room, that they therein do Juſtice, and hold Council at the ſame time, comodiouſly: upon the roof whereof ſtand expoſed to the ayr the Statues of *Cornelius*, *Nepos*, *Emilius*, *Marcus*, old Poets, of *Pliny* the natural Hiſtorian, and *Vetruvius* the Architecture, and in a very high Arch, the Statue of *Hieronimo Facaſtrao*, all which men graced their Mother *Verona* by their ſingular virtues.

Beſides which, there are two Palaces for the Governours and many others eminent enough of particular *Veronians*. They praiſe alſo the great Bell, which is in the high Turret, The *Piazza* frequented by the Merchants; the Burrough where they teazlle waſh and preſs Clothes, and the Field called *Campo Martio*, where they exerciſe the Souldiery. There are alſo other *Piazzaes* for the Markets, and to walk in, one for the Nobility, and another for the Marchants: In the bigger whereof ſtands a Stately Fountain with a Statue repreſenting *Verona*, with a Kingly Diadem at her Feet.

The moſt beautifull River *Adice* runs by *Verona*, which comes juſt from the *Alpes* of *Trent*, and ſends two arms through the Streets of the City for its greater conveniency, by which River they convey to

Verona divers Merchandices from *Germany* and *Venice*. There are many Mills within and without the City, and other Edifices for the *Mecanicks*. They have four Bridges over the *Adice*, all erected with excellent artifice and beauty, one whereof hath two spatious Arches, which give a Noble prospect, *Europe* scarce affording any more polite and truer built.

This City abounds with all things necessary. Their fruits are all delicious, but the Figs *Bardolini* exceed all others. It hath Fish very sweet from the Lake *Garda*, Good Meat from the excellent Pasture, exquisite Wines from the Hills, good Corn from the Vales, and good health from the Ayr, though somewhat piercing. The Merchandize of Cloth and Silk, mantains above 20000. Handicrafts-men.

Verona was under the *Etrurians*, the *Euganei*, the *Heucti*, the *French* and the *Romans*, with whom it was confederated and had voices in the *ballottinges* of *Rome*. The *Romans* never sent a Colony into *Verona*, but it was ascribed to the *Tribu Poblilia*, and the *Veronians* have had many Magistrates in *Rome*. Heretofore 4.Deputies had the clear and mixt government of this City, as the *Roman* Consuls, which 4. were created by the Citizens, together with the other Magistrates: whereof they yet retein some shadow by having Consuls, the wise men, the Counsel of twelve, the hundred and twenty, and the Prefect of the Merchants. Afterwards the *Roman* Empire declining, *Verona* became under the Command of certain barbarous Tyrants, but they being driven out by the *Ostragoths* and they by the *Longobards* who were Lords of it 200. yeers, it was finally freed from their Signory and fell into the power of the successors of *Charles* the great, that is of *Pipin* and *Berengarius*, and others who there made the Seat of their Empire, as *Albano* King of the *Longobardi*, had done formerly.

In the Reign of *Ottone* the First, it again recovered its Liberty; but discords arising among the Citizens, it was opprest by the Tyranny of *Ezzelino*, and the *Scaligiri*, its own Gitizens, who Lorded it for 200. yeers. Last of all being also opprest by others, it voluntarily rendred it self to the power of the *Venetians* who in those daies, were esteemed the Justest of Lords. It was converted to the Christian Faith by *Euperius*, commissionated to preach there from Saint *Peetre*. It had thirty six Bishops Saints, with *S. Zenone* its Protector, to whom *Pipin*Son of Charles the great, dedicated a Church with twelve pounds of gold for yeerly revenue. The greater Church, is a most noble one, and rich with a Chapter of Canons of much authority. In the Church of *S. Anastassia* is a fayr Chapel of *Giano Fresco* a *Genouai* Captain, filled with Marble Statues and his own effigies.

The people of *Verona* are pious, and have alwaies had good Bishops, in particular lately *Augustin Falerio* a most upright Prelate and illustrious Cardinal as he was ever accounted by the most holy Fathers and Docters of the Chvrch. Nor will we forget *Nicolo Hormanetto* Bishop of *Padona*, nor *Giberto*, who was the reformer of many Churches, the first of whom, brought into that Province *Carlo Borromeo* Doctor, and Head of all the holy men, and the most shining Star of the College of Cardinals. Nor that the Churches of *Verona* (before the Conncel of *Trent*) were reformed into that order they still observe
They

They give divine honors to *Lucius* the third Pope, who going to *Verona*, there to call a Council, paſſed into a better Life, and was there interred in the great Church; whence in *Verona* was created *Urban* the third his Succeſſor.

Verona is well peopled, and hath many noble Families: and hath produced ſignal Men in all exerciſes. It had ſome Conſuls in *Rome*: it hath had many holy men and many bleſſed, among which is famous *San Pietro* the Martyr, of the Preaching order, buried in *Milan*, born in the Street of *S. Stefano* in *Verona*, where at preſent may be ſeen the houſe of his Nativity. The *Veronians* have ſharp wits, and are much inclined to Learning, which hath occaſioned that it in every Age hath brought forth Men of excellent eſteem in all ſciences. They were *Veronians* that have their five Statues ſet upon the publick Palace: So alſo was the learned *Scaliger*, for whoſe ſake and his Family (*i Signori della Scala*) is erected in the heart of the City a Stately Marble Tomb, encompaſſed with Iron work, reſembling a Ladder, which that name implies. It hath afforded ſome Women too, ſo well read in the Greek and Latin tongue, and the Sciences, that they have held diſputes with many learned Men, among others *Iſotta Nogarola* was glorious, it hath one Porphyre Tomb of a King of the *Goths*. In ſumm, *Verona* poſſeſſeth all thoſe things that may render a Citty perfect, and its Citizens happy: So that tis no wonder that many Emperors (induced by the beauty of the place) ſpent ſome Moneths of the yeer there, as we read in the codicils of *Juſtinian*, and *Theodoſius*, and that *Alboino*, firſt King of the *Longobards*, and *Pepin* Son of *Charls* the Great, and *Berengarius*, with other Kings; of *Italy*, ſelected it for their own Reſidences; and to the end no ornament might be wanting, inſtituted an Academy for good Letters, and Study of humanity in the houſe of the Signori *Bevilacque*, whereof *Cota* a good Poet of our times ſaies well thus.

Verona, qui te viderit, & non amarit protinus
amore perditiſſimo, is credo ſe ipſum non amat,
caretque amandi ſenſibus; & tollit omnes gratias.

The Territory of *VERONA.*

THe Territory of *Verona*, in our times is about 80. Miles large, from the Confines of *Torbolo*, a Caſtle of *Trent*, towards the *South* to the *Poleſene* of *Rovigo*, and from the *Eaſtern* part from the confines of *Vicentia* to them of *Breſcia*, which are towards the *North* 46. Miles, and 15. miles towards *South-Eaſt*, where it confines with the *Padouan*, tis 30. miles long, a fertile plain. towards the *Northweſt*, it hath 25. miles of mountainous Countrey: Towards *South* and by *Eaſt*, thirty Mils to the *Ferrarian* or *Mantouan* confines, of moſt fertile Countreys, being no leſs pleaſant than fruitfull of whatever can be deſired. It hath Mountains, Hills, Woods, diverſe navigable Rivers, clear fountains, oyl, good Corn, good Wine, Hemp, and great plenty of Fruit, and Trees bearing Apples, more ſweet, freſh, and of longer keeping than any other Country: It hath Fowl, and Fleſh of all ſorts, divers ſorts of Stone, and Chalk, Villages

lages with fair Fabricks, and foundations of antient Towers: In sum it may well be called as fair and happy a Territory as any other, and more than some are.

Going out of the Gate *Vescovato*, turning on the left hand, after having met with many fruitfull Hills, and the ruins of an antient Castle, you come to the Burrough *S. Michael*, which hath a fair Church dedicated to the blessed *Virgin*, wherein they have seen many miricles, and many Paper Mills, being 5. miles from *Verona*, then following the way a little on the right hand, one findes the Baths, helpfull for the Sterility of Women, and to refresh the Reyns, where the Learned *Calderino* was born, who after lived in *Rome*.

Tis reported, that there stood an antient Castle, and that the Church of Saint *Matthew* the Apostle, was a Temple of *Juno*. Opposite whereto upon a Hill is seen, *il Castllo Soave*, built in a lovely site by the *Scaligeri*; a little forwarder is *Monte Forte*, a Town belonging to the *Veronian* Bishoprick, upon the very confines, as on the other side on the confines is the Burrough Saint *Boniface*. On that part which looks towards the *North-East*, are some plains well inhabited. That part looking towards the *South*, begins from the *Porta Nova*, and goes to *Lonico a Cologna*, wherein is nothing remarkable, more than its fertility, and the head of the River *Tartaro*; and on that side towards *Mantoua*, 17. miles distant from *Verona*, is the Island *Scala*, so well replenished with people and goods, that it hath in some sort the face of a City.

Towards the *West*, before *Verona*, lies a Stony untild Champion or Downs, but famous for divers deeds of Arms there, performed by great Captains; Tis said, that *Sabino Giuliano*, who would have gotten the Empire, was there by *Curino Cesare* overthrown and slain, that *Odouacro* King of the *Herlui*, and *Turcillingi*, having by violence obteyned the Kingdome of *Italy*, forcing out *Augustolo*, and therein tyranized some yeers, was in this place discomfited in a Battel of three days, by *Theodorick* King of the *Ostrogoths*; That *Lamberto* Son of *Guidon* King of *Spoleto*, was there overcome with 14000. *Hungarian* Souldiers by *Berengarius*. That some yeers after, by *Cugone Arelatense*, *Arnoldo* Captain of *Baviera*, with a potent Army of *Germans*, was there cut in pieces, whom the *Veronians* first called into *Italy* for King against *Hugone*, and had received into their City as victorious and triumphant. That there likeness was overcome and deprived of his Kingdom the second *Berengarius* by *Rodolfus Borgondus*; and that in antient times in that place were fought many Battels (of no less consequence than obaining or losing of the Kingdom of *Italy*) with various success. But as to what *Biondo* saith, that in that Down *C. Marius*, vanquished the *Germans* and the *Cimbrians*, who made a furious incursion into *Italy*, 'tis very uncertain, because Historians much differ in describing the place where that memorable Act was performed.

Thence one may go to *Villa Franca* and *Sanzeno*, rich Villages confines to the *Mantoua* Territories, but if from those Downs one take towards the *South*, having passed many Villages, you arrive at *Peschiero* a strong Castle, but of ill Ayr, 14. miles from *Verona*, seated on the Banks of the Lake *Garda*, where the River *Menzo* hath its source, and on the left side of the Lake five miles further off (most

ill

ill way) ſtands *Rivoltella*, and two miles onward *Deſenſano*, the confines of *Verona*.

On that part of *Verona*, towards the *North-weſt*, are many Hills
placed in the form of a Theatre, where they are ſtocked with fertile
Vineyards; and ſo much adorned with beautifull Palaces and Gardens, that the proſpect at a diſtance much pleaſeth; within theſe Hils
is the Vale *Paltena*, inhabited and Fertil, and following the plain, appear many and ſtately Palaces, on the banks of the *Adice*, which runs
through that *Campagna*.

At 10. miles diſtance from *Verona* upon the aſcent of certain little Hills, may be beheld the Valley *Pulicella*, repleniſh't with many
Caſtles & great Towns, behind which begin the Mountains of *Trento*,
they ſay that in the ſaid Valley, there are two teats of Stone cut with
a Chizel, which conſtantly diſtill a water, wherewith if a Woman
having loſt her Milk bath her Nipples, it will return in great abundance. Returning to *Verona*, by the *Adice*, on one ſide is the foot of
the Mountain *Baldo*, and many Caſtles and Burroughs: On the other
ſide a plain to *Peſchiera*, and there begin the Mountains which are on
the right hand-ſhore of the Lake: there ſtands *Bardolino*, where thoſe
incomparable Figs grow, whereof *Soliman* Emperor of the *Turks* delighted to diſcourſe of, with the Chriſtian ſlaves, as alſo, *Gardo*,
which gives name to the Lake, and many other Caſtles: In this place
is to be admired, the vaſtneſs of the *Venetians* Minds, who conveyed
over thoſe rough and mountainous places, both Galleys and Ships
armed in all particulars, to fight in the Lake with *Filippo Viſconſe*
Captain of the *Milaneſians*, Mount *Baldo*, whereof ſomewhat is ſpoken
formerly, ought here to be ſet before all the Mounts of *Italy*, being
30. miles in circumference, affording excellent and rare plants, and
ſome veins of Copper.

The Lake *GARDA*.

ANtiently the Caſtle *Benaco*, gave name to this Lake, where now
is *Tuſculano*, but at preſent it takes name from *Gardo* aforenamed.
This Lake from *Peſchiera*, which lies on the *South* of it, is 35. miles
long towards the *North*, and from *Salo*, on the *Weſt* ſhore to *Garda* or
Lacice on the *Eaſt*, is 14. miles broad: It is very tempeſtuous, and
many times raiſes waves as high as Mountains, which at certain ſeaſons of the yeer, makes it dangerous to navigate, and this they believe proceeds from the encloſure of the winds by the Mountains,
hindring by their ſurrounding its iſſuing out, Wherefore *Virgil*
ſaies,

Fluctibus , & fremitu aſſurgens Benace marino.

This Lake affords well-reliſht fiſh, in great plenty, but chiefly
Trouts, Carps, and Eels, whereof *Pliny* ſpeaks at large. Eight miles
from *Peſchiera*, runs a neck of Land into the Lake, two miles long,
which ſeems to divide the Lake. Here antiently was *Sirmione* which
gave birth to *Catullus* the Poet, but now remains nothing but a ſmall
Caſtle, though abounding with all delitiouſneſs. On the ſame ſide
is *Rivoltella*, and *Diſenſano*, a principal Market Town of thoſe parts,

not defective in any thing.   But on the other ſhore there are many
fair Caſtles, among others *Salo* & *Prato di Fame*, where the Biſhops
of *Trent*, *Verona*, and *Breſcia*, may each (ſtanding in his own Dioceſs)
ſhake hands, The Country there is pleaſant, bearing Olivs, Figs,
Pomegranates, Lemons, Citrons, and other fruitfull Trees, which
there flouriſh much, by having the River & Lake on one ſide, and
the Mountains on the other, defending it from blaſting winds, and
affording the reflex of the Sun all day, from its riſe to the ſetting,
which renders it one of the beautifulleſt places of *Italy*. The number
of the People inhabiting this Valley and Lake of *Garda*, ſhall be given in the Deſcription of the Valleys.

BRESCIA.

BReſcia by the *Romans Brixia*, is ſeated 20 miles from *Diſenſano*,
which a direct Road leads unto, but ſomething Stoney. Some
will have it called *Breſcia* from *Britein*, which in the Language of
the *Galli Senones* (the reſtorers of this City) ſignifie rejoycing Trees,
as if the quantity of Fruits wherewith they are yeerly hung, made
them rejoyce. *Livie* and other grave Authors write, that *Breſcia* was
built by the *Galli Senones*, in that age when the Kings commanded in
Rome, and that the *Romans* made themſelves Maſters thereof, after
they had conquered all *Lombardy*. They further ſay, that it alwaies kept
inviolable Faith with the *Roman* People, and particularly in that
calamitous time, when *Hannibal* deſtroyed their Armies. Beſides they
ſay, that it was reduced into a Colony of the *Romans*, after the aſſo-
ciated Warr, together with *Verona*, and the other Cities, on that ſide the
Po, by *Cn. Pompeius Strabo*, Father of *Pompey* the Great, and a little
time after *Cæſar* reckoned the *Breſcians* in the number of the *Roman*
Citizens; under whoſe Empire it continued till its Majeſty was at
the height, when it was no leſs rich than potent, as may eaſily be
conjectured from the many antient Marble Stones, and Statues,
with the inſcriptions and Epitaphs of illuſtrious Perſons, and of
divers famous deeds thereon which ly diſperſed in the City and up
and down its Territory.

Tis ſeated in a plain (at the foot of certain Hills) more long than
broad; although but three miles in circuit, yet well repleniſhed
with dwellings and inhabitants. Its vicinity to the Hills beautifies it
with many Fountains, a commodity which many Cities of *Lombardi*
want. In it are many *Piazz.es*, the greateſt whereof is that where
the publick Palace is erected; which for its fairneſs, may be accounted one of the Nobleſt Edifices of *Italy*. Under which Palace
are fair Porches, with ſhops affording well tempered Belly pieces
of Armour, Swords, Muskets, and other military Arms, which
hath nominated it *Breſcia* the Armed: other ſhops are no leſs furniſhed with the fineſt Linnen cloth, a Commodity by which theſe Citizens acquire great Riches. A ſmall River called *Garcia* paſſeth
thorow the City, which at its iſſuing forth is artificially drawn on
this and that ſide to irrigate their Fields. It hath five Porrs or Gates,
and one impregnable Caſtle, built with Stone upon a Hill. The *Torre de Pallada* is of rare *Tuſcan* work, and therein is the Great Bell of
the City. It heretofore ſuffered much calamity through the Factions

ons and enmity of its Citizens, whose fury was such that proscription and Death to their Enemies, without fyring and destroying their Houses and Goods, but trivally appeased: Which caused it to change in 28. yeers its Soveraign seven times, in the time of *Lewis* the third, and *Otto* Emperors, Its Citizens being much addicted to Arms. Tis a most horrible thing to read the History of *Capriole*, of those calamitous times, representing the great slaughters of the Citizens, with their Proscriptions and Banishments, the sacking, burning, and ruining, of their Habitations, and the desolation of the City; much resembling the times and Actions of *Marius*, and *Scilla* and the *Triumvirate*. At this day tis governed by the *Venetians* with great peace, and such increase of Riches, that its former smart is scarce perceptible. It received the light of the Christian Faith by *Domo* the preaching of *Sant Apollinare*, Bishop of *Ravenna*, in the yeer of our Lord, 119. It hath some fayr Churches, among them the *Domo*, (whose Bishop with a good Revenue hath the Title of Duke, Marquiss, and Count) where a Skie-coloured Cross called *Oro Fiamma*, is much reverenced by the People, who indubitably beleeve it to be the same which appeared to *Constantine* the Emperour fighting against *Maxentius*, The Motto, *in hoc signo Vinces*.

Next is the Church of *Santa Giulia* the Martyr, built by *Desiderius*, King of the *Longobards*, in the yeer 735. adorned with rich Vests *Santa Juliia* and pretious vessels, and honoured with the bodies of many Saints, together with those of *Ansilperga*, the Sister, and *Hermingarda* the Daughter, of that King: which ly in its noble Monastery: wherein two daughters of *Lotario* the first Emperor, one sister of *Charles* the the third, one Daughter of *Berengarus* the Usurper of the Empire, with many other Virgins of Royal blood, have spent their days in the service of God, under the Orders of Saint *Benedict*.

Brescia is well replenished with People, and among them with many noble and illustrious Families, as the *Gambari*, the *Martinengi*, the *Magi*, the *Avogradi*, *Averoldi*, *Luzaghi*, *Emilii* and others. It hath given Birth to many Saints, of whom they name only *San Giovita* and *Faustino*, who suffered Martyrdom for the Faith of Christ, on the Walls towards *Verona*, whereof at this day appear some Marks of it. It hath had thirty Bishops canonized for Saints: Its Territory is so large, spatious, and long, that tis believed, the Bishop thereof hath the Cure of near Eight Hundred Thousand Souls: It abounds with all things necessary for human Sustenance, and the People are reputed of a quick-witted and elegant Ingennity: whereof an elegant Poet writes.

Cælum hilarem, frons læta Urbi, gens nescia fraudis,
Atque modum ignorat divitis uber agri.

The Territory of *BRESCIA.*

THe *Bresciau* Territory, is one hundred miles broad, begining from *Mosa* 15. miles distant from *Mantoua*, and ending at *Dialengo* at the top of *Alcamonica*, and 50. miles long, extending from *Limona* on the Lake *Garda* to the *Orzi Novi*, the Countrey conteyning 450. Towns, Villages, and Castles well peopled, and affording all forts of Corn, Grain, Wine, Oyl, and Fruits: Towards the *Eaft*, on the Road leading to *Verona*, on the right hand, ftand *Gedi*, *Manerbio*, *Calvefano*; *Calcinato*, on the left, the Mountains, *Bredizolo*, *Padengo*, and the Lake, with the fair Town of *Lonato*, 15. miles off *Brefcia*. Towards the *South* by the way of *Cremona*, are feen *Pirola*, and *Afola*, a ftrong Caftle, Iffuing forth the Gate *San Nazario*, towards the *VVeft*, on the right lies *Triviato*, on the left, *Quintiano*, a noble Caftle. This is the way of the *Orzi Novi*, where ftands a ftrong Caftle 20. miles from *Brefcia*, built in *Anno* 1134. Here they vant much of the excellency of their *Linnen* Cloth, near which paifeth the River *Oglio*, which terminates the *Venetians* dominions. And going out of the Gate *S. Giovanni*, you meet the *Torrent Mela*, *Corato* a rich Country, and *Reato* the moft populous Town of the *Brefcian* Territories; a little farther a moft fertile plain, beautified with many Caftles, from the dwelling of the French therein tis called *Francia Carta*, but before you can reach *Palazzolo*, muft be paffed the River *Oglio*, over a ftately Bridge, from whence they enter the Territories of *Bergamo*.

The BRESCIAN Valleys

THis City hath three principal Valleys, the firft called *Valcamonica*, lies towards the *VVeft*, and is bigger than both the other; extending it felf 50. miles towards the *North*, is continued with furrounding Hills, among which, is a running current yeelding good Trouts, which River enters at the head of the Lake *Iffeo*, running through it, and out of it with the fame name, and p ffing through the Playn, many Arms and Branches are drawn from it, to overflow the fields, whereby they become moft productive of Grafs, Hay, Corn, &c. It hath fome minerals of Iron and Copper, Its chief Town is *Brenna*; towards the end, this vale divides it felf in o two parts, one whereof extends to the County of *Tirolo*, the other reaches the valley *Tellina*.

The fecond is the Vale *Troppia*, which takes its commencement 6. miles off the City, and extends it felf 20. miles long to the *North*, circumfcribed with Mountains, and wafhed with the River *Mela*. In fome places tis narrow, and tis moft fruitfull neareft the City: wherein 10. miles off the City, is the rich and Noble Caftle and Town *Cardone*, much talked off, for the good Harquebufes there made: It affords Iron Mine, and that gives caufe of the Ironworks there built.

The laft is the Vale *del Sole* 22. miles long, conjoyned with the other, through which paffeth the River *Chiefe*, which iffues from the Lake *Ifeo*, wafhing it for 10. miles fpace, affording good Fifh, efpecially Trouts; here alfo are fome Ironworks. This Vale divides it felf into many Branches, by many Rivulets; and in many places, is well and neatly planted with Vines and fruitfull Trees: Thefe two laft Vales are in the power of the *Venetians*, and produce Souldiers of great gallantry. The whole *Brefcian* Territory affords neer 800000. Souls, befides what the City it felf contains.

The

The first and shortest way from *BRESCIA* to *MILAN*.

Going out of *Brescia* by the gate *San Giovanni* for *Milan*, are seen *Cocaglio Pontoi*, so called from the similitude of *Ponto Oglio*, the River which washes that Castle Walls: Then *Martinengo*, *Triviglio*, and *Cassano*, much famed for the mortal stroke there received by *Ezzelino* the Tyrant of *Padoua*, from the *Romans*; on the right hand the *Campagna Giare di Adda*, then the Castle *Caravaggio*, head of all the *Giara di Adda*, strong by site and Art, rich and abounding. Here in the yeer 1422. they fable an appearance of the blessed Virgin, where she reposed, they dugg a Well, whose Waters are good for all infirmities, there also, they erected a most stately Church. At *Cassano*, you repass the River *Adda*, then travaling 10. miles, arrive at *Cassina*, the white Hostery, then 10. more to *Milan*, this way from *Brescia* to *Milan*, is accounted 50. miles long.

The second Voyage, but longer, from *BRESCIA* to *MILAN*.

This way is more straight and long, than the other, which they take out of the Gate *San Nazario*, and at 20. miles end arrive at the *Orzi Novi*, whence passing the River *Oglio*, they come to the most noble Castle *Soncino*, where in Winter time they make a certain pleasant Bread with *Almonds*, they also make Latten Candlesticks, the Inhabitants are both Civil and courteous. This Castle is endowed with the Title of a Marquisate, and belongs to the State of *Milan*, over the Gate whereof are set the Arms of *Spain*. In *Soncino*, the Tyrant of *Padoua*, *Ezzelino*, would needs dye, born of *Saxon* blood, and 70. yeers old, who having received a mortal wound in one Knee, from the Army in *Cassano*, would not permit them to dress the wound, nor apply any remedy, where he unhappily and Meritoriously abandoned this Life; five miles farther lies *Romanengo*, and so much more far *Crema*, which on the *East* is washed by the River *Serio*. This *Crema* was antiently one of the four principal Castles of *Italy*, but is at present a City, and an Episcopal Seat, tis placed in an ample plain, fortified with Rampants and Ovals, well enriched, full of civil People, replenisht with Houses, abounding with human necessaries, and under the Government of the *Venetians*. The *Domo*, the *Tower*, the *Piazza*, and the Palace of the *Podesta*, are worth a visit. The *Podesta* which the *Venetians* commissionate thither, governs 46. other places; here the women get well by whitening sowing thread, and weaving of Linnen Cloth. Thence (passing the River *Torno*) 10. miles farther is *Lodi* (*Laus Pomponia* by the *Romans*)

Caravaggio

Cassina

Soncino

Crema

Lodi

a great City on the side of the River *Ada*, famous for the Cheese made there not much inferiour to the *Parmifen*; then *Malignano*, a Caftle honoured with the Title of Marquifate of the Noble Family of the *Medici* at *Milan*, and fo to *Milan*, this way is 62. miles long. All which way is like a Garden, the high-ways ftreight, & Level on both fides whereof, run chanels of Water, on each fide of which are planted Trees, up which run their Vines, and the Fields are fome Meadows, and the reft yeeld plenty of Corn.

The third Journey from B R E S C I A to M I L A N by the way of B E R G A M O.

PArting from *Brefcia* by the Gate *San Ciovanni*, paffing the *Torrent Mela*, are feen the Caftles *Cacaglio*, and *Palazzuolo* afore named, and on the other fide of the River *Oglio*, the Village *Malpaga*, built in a fayr plain by *Bartolemeo Coleone* of *Bergamo*, who there ended his days, at 76. yeers of Age, and was buried in *Bergamo*. In honour of whome for having been the moft valiant and faithfull Captain of the *Venetian* Army, is erected his Statue on Horfeback gilt all over, with a Marble Bafis, before the Church *San Giovanni*, and *Paolo* in *Venice*. On the left hand lies *Orgiano* and *S. Maria* of *Bafella* a Church with a fayr monaftery for preaching Fryers; whence paffing a Noble Bridge over the River *Serio*, you arrive at *Bergamo* 30. miles from *Brefcia*.

BERGAMO.

THe City of *Bergamo*, is fo antient that its founders are not known, yet fome averr they were the *Orobii* which in greek fignifies Inhabitants of the Mountains. *Giovanni Annio* of *Viterba* with *Giovanno Chrifoftomo Zancho*, much labour to demonftrate and prove the Antiquity of *Bergamo*, and wherefore fo named, by many etimologies of the word, as well in Greek, as in Hebrew, and in the end conclude it to be thus called in Hebrew, which in Latin founds, *Inonditorum clypeata civitas, vel Gallorum Regia Urbs, quæ a Græcis Archipolis, a recentioribus autem Latinis tum princeps, tum Ducalis Civitas appellari folet.* And a little further fay. *Igitur Bergomum Regalem veterum Gallorum urbem extitiffe, nomen ipfum manifeftiffime docet.*

Others are of opinion, that twas firft built by the *Tufcans*, and afterwards reftored and enlarged by the *Galli Cenomani*: Its Country towards the *Faft* is plain, fertile, and productive of Fruit· On the North and *Weft*, rugged, Mountainous, and barren. Tis rendred a very ftrong City, by thofe thick walls which inviron it, and thofe bulwarks, and other engins of War, which for its defence againft Enemies the *Venetians* have erected. Tis fmall and feated on the fide of the Mountains. It hath two Burroughs conjoyned with it, where they have raifed ftately edifices as well for Divine worfhip as private Citizens habitations. In one of which is yeerly kept a Fayr which begins on the day of Saint *Bartolemo*, and continues for many

ny days, whither the vaſt quantity of Merchandize invites as much People, as *Italians*, *Germans*, *Grizons*, and *Switzers*: The Ayr is moſt ſerene there, and its Territory produceth ſweet wines, Oyl, and many pleaſant fruits. In ſome places (for want of Land either ſit for tillage or Vines) the people employ themſelves in working Woollen and Linnen Clothes, which they afterwards carry into all parts of *Italy*. Their Language is very ruſtick, but that renders not the People ſo, who are civil and ingenuous, and no leſs diſpoſed to Learning than Trade, whence it took the ſurname of *Bergamo* the witty.

It hath produced many noble Wits, who by their excellent virtues have added to its Luſtre: Whereof were *Alberico di Roſato*, Doctor of Laws, and *Ambrogio Calepino*, whoſe works no ingenuous perſon neglects to have. Fryer *Damiano*, a convertite of the order of Preachers, was a man of ſo great Ingenuity (in cementing pieces of ſeveral woods together, with ſuch artifice, that they have been often miſtaken for Pictures drawn with a pencel.) that his fellow hath not been known herein. Fryer *Pagano* of the ſame Order, gave excellent example of conſtancy at his death given him by the Hereticks. Hence alſo, have iſſued men of great Judgment and Counſel, to govern the Republick, particularly of the Family of *Foreſti*, with many Cardinals, Prelates, and excellent Captains.

The firſt Advancer of the Chriſtian Religion in this City, was Saint *Barnabas*, a Diſciple of Chriſt, in the 25th. yeer of our Salvation; together with *Anatolone* the Greek, and *Caio* the Roman, giving it for Biſhop *Narino* one of its Citizens; who having governed it with great ſanctity of Life and Religion for thirty yeers, deceaſed, and was there interred; whom many holy Biſhops from one to another have ſucceeded.

In the Domo of *Bergamo*, are 25. Bodies of Saints, kept with great devotion. Where near the high Altar ſtands the Sepulchre of *Bartolomeo Colcone*, a famous Captain, and Citizen of it, with his Effigies in Marble, which he cauſed to be cut for him by the Life, the Epitaph whereof follows.

Bartholomeus Colleonus de Andegania virtute immortalitatem adeptus, uſque adeo in re militari ſuit illuſtris, & non modo tunc viventium gloriam longè exceſſerit, ſed etiam poſteris ſpem enim citandi ademerit, ſæpius enim à diverſis Principibus, ac deinceps ab Illuſtriſſimo Veneto Senatu accepto Imperio, Tandem totius Chriſtianorum exercitus ſub Paulo Secundo Pont. Max. delectus ſuit Imperator: Cujus acies quatuordecim annos, ab ejus obitu ſolo jam defuncti Imperatoris, tanquam vivi nomine militantis juſſa, cujus alias contempſerunt.

Obiit Anno Domini 1475. quarto nonas Novembris.

In the Church of Saint *Agoſtino* is the Tomb of Fryer *Ambrogio Calepino*, who with great diligence and induſtry, collected all the Latin words in a form approved by the graveſt writers: whoſe works are known to all the World, being divulged where ever the Latine Tongue is ſpoken.

Bergamo, together with its Burroughs, contains a great number of

Souls : Above it stands the *Capella*, or Chapel, a place strong by its site upon a high Mountain, and by the most impregnable Walls wherewith it was encompassed by *Luchino Visconte* Lord of *Milano* and *Bergamo :* but at this time tis wholly abandoned and half ruinated, being found by experience of little ayd to the City when need required : here at first was layed a foundation for a Monastery for the Order of *S. Dominick*, and a Chapel built, whence called *Capello*.

Bergamo was long time subject to the Roman Empire; after whose fall twas burnt by *Attila*; then it was yoaked to the *Longobardi*, who styled themselves Dukes thereof; then reduced under the power of Kings of *Italy :* and so continued till the daies of *Filippo Turciano*, who became Lord thereof *Anno* 1264. After it was Subjugated by *Luchino* the Viscount. Then *Mastino della Scalla* made himself Lord thereof. By whom some time after twas sold to *Pandolfo Malatesta* for thirty thousand Duckats of Gold. And after it had been some times occupied by the French, of its own accord it gave it self to the *Venetians*, under whom it peaceably reposeth to this day. If farther and more at large any one desires to be satisfied in the history of *Bergamo*, let him read the book entitled, *La Vigna di Bergamo*.

<table><tr><td>

Vale Serina.

Brombana

San Martino

Calepio
Chiusontio
Manca

Como

</td><td>

Serio runs close by *Bergamo*, deriving its source from those Mountains, between which towards the *North* are 6 vales. The first is called *La vale Seriana*, from the River *Serio's* running through it, which is well peopled, who by *Tolomeo* are called *Beccunni*. The second is *Vale Brombana*, so named from its vicinity with the Banks of the River *Brembo*, each of which are extended for thirty miles long. The third is *Vale di San Martino*, 15. miles long. The fourth, *Vale di Calepio*, the fifth, *Vale di Chiusontio*, the sixth, *Val di Manca*; in which between Towns, Villages, and Hamlets, are numbred 200. Inhabited places, of which the chief are *Calepio*, *Lever de Chiusonto*, and *Vertua*, where they make excellent Woollen Clothes. On this side the Territory of *Bergamo* extends it self 28. miles. Upon *Calepio* is the strong Castle *Lenco*, where a Bridge conjoyns both the Banks of *Adda*. On the *West Bergamo* hath the City of *Como*, *Monza*, and the Hills of *Brianza*, towards the *East Brescia*, and towards the *South Crema* with the above-described Places. *Bergamo* is accounted 32. miles from *Milan*, having on the right hand the Rivers *Brembo* which dischargeth it self into the *Adda*, further on, near the *Adda* is the well-fortified Castle of *Trezzo*, reared by *Bernardo* Viscount of *Milan*, *Anno* 1370. together with that artificial Bridge, which on the left hand over the *Adda* discovers it self with the abovenamed Places. At twelve miles distance from *Bergamo* stands *Colonica* a small Village, where imbarking you pass 20: miles in the Water and so arrive at *Milan*.

</td></tr></table>

CREMA.

THe Relation of this City should have been placed between the narrations of *Brescia* and *Bergamo*, where in the second voyage from *Brescia* to *Milan* tis only briefly touched, but the Author having found himself tardy, in omitting an account of this esteemed one of the prime Cities of *Lombardy*, apollogizeth for his placing it here in the end of this Book, and promiseth a reformation in the next impress.   Being

Being then in the City of *Brescia*, and going forth the Gate *San Nazario*, after twenty miles travel you arrive at *Orzi Nuovi* : and having past the River *Oglio* find the Castle *Soncino*: and five miles more forwards meets *Romanengo*, and so many more the City *Crema*, which is situated in the *East* shore of the River *Serio*, by which tis deliciously washed ; it lies in the Centre of fruitfull *Lombardy*, between five illustrious Cities, at thirty miles distance from each, which encompasse it like a Crown, whereof she may be termed the Cross, that is to say, *Milan, Bergamo, Brescia, Cremona,* and *Piacenza,* who affording it what it stands in need of , and expending its superfluities, concur in the rendring it a rich City, tis full of regard, and filled with Merchandize and a haughty self-conceited sort of men, but better illustrated by their gratious and loving Women, who flourish, are free, and most pompous in their array. It is adorned with sumptuous and magnificent Fabricks, among which the most conspicuous are the publick Palace, the *Piazza* and the *Domo* with its Tower (wherein is a large Bell) of fair and open Architecture, with two regardfull Chapels, one dedicated to the blessed Virgin, all over garnished with excellent pictures, the other to Saint *Mark* no less beautified with gilt Images. Two other notable things this Church owns, to wit, that Wooden crucifix, which in *Anno* 1448. was cast into the Fire by a certain man called *Giovanni Alchini,* of the faction of *Gibellina Bergamesca,* which would not burn, but is still preserved with the one side a little singed in a particular Chapel, with great Veneration, the other is a Key of *San Bellino,* which hath the foretold miraculous curing virtue of such as are bit by madd Doggs.

In the same Church are conserved certain trophies of Banners, and a Lanthern of a Gally, taken together with the Gally in a Naval fight against the Turks, by a Preacher of the most noble Family of *Zurly*, during the fight, being set at the head of the Gally. Besides the above named Fabricks and things worth seeing in this City, two Hospitals are valuable. One for the infirm, the other for the decrepit and outcasts : the sacred Mount of Piety is well endowed, and governed with great providence by the publick, to supply the necessities of the City and Country.

There is also a noble Academy for Students, who under the name of *Sospinti*, employ themselves in good exercises with an impulse of generous emulation. Distant a quarter of a mile from the City stands (towards the Castle) a magnificent Temple of great devotion, named *Santa Maria della Croce,* of an admirable Structure, and adorned with many rare Pictures : To this noble and fair City, though Little (as little best corresponds with little) belongs a small but most fertil Territory, washed all over with current and Christalline waters, which affords the City good Fish, as Lobsters, Trouts, Gudgeons, and Eels, and the Country an enriching of their soyl by overflowings, whereby it yeelds great plenty of Corn and Grass, the first whereof they have for their own use and other Cities, and with the second they make incomparable cheese.

But that wherewith it most abounds is Flax, which after made into the finest Drapery is spent all over *Italy*.

In its territories though small, are contained fifty four Villages, and Towns, the chief whereof are, *Monte dine*, *Stanengo*, *Camisano*, *Tetrore*, *Vaiano*, *Bagnelo*, *Madegnano*, being all most populous.

The Original of this City, was taken from its situation, for being invironed then with the three Rivers, *Ada*, *Oglio* and *Serio*, it was very strong, and that strength as is believed invited many noble men of the neighbouring Cities (in the time of the Wars of *Albonio* King of the *Longobards*) to retire themselves thither, and from *Cremete* one of the chief of those Nobles it took its name. For Forty yeers it maintained it self in liberty, but then she with the other Cities of *Italy* suffered shipwrack, being by the *Longobards*, *Frederick Barbarossa* and others, many times, taken, burnt, sacked, and destroyed, and subjugated sometimes to the Emperors, sometimes to the French, and sometimes to the *Germans*. But now tis governed by the most Serene Republick of *Venice* under whom it hath the privilege to keep every yeer a Fair beginning at the end of *September* being frequented with innumerable concourse of People, divers Merchandizes and Commodities, and great store of Cattle of all forts.

It ever was the Mother of illustrious persons, as well learned in all the sciences, as famous Captains, eminent Engineers, Generals of Armies, writers of Histories, as well Moral as Divine, Prelates of the greatest Negotiations, and Cardinals, some whereof have possessed the Pontificial Chayr.

MILAN the great.

Milan was an antient and illustrious City, and for a long time (through its beauty remained an imperial Seat.) Behind its shoulders rise those Mountains which separate *Italy*. Before it is a long and spatious Plain which extending it self above 200. miles, reacheth the Church lands between *Rimio* and *Pesaro* on the one side, and *Istria* and *Osia*, on the other side. Whereof *Polibius* writes thus. There is a plain, between the *Alps* and the *Apennines* of a triangular Form, wherein are pleasant Fields above all the Fields not only of *Italy* but all *Europe*. Of which Triangle, the *Apennines* form one side, the *Alps* another, and the *Adriatick* Sea or Gulf of *Venice* (as it were the basis to the other two) makes up the third side.

And although *Milan* was heretofore a small Town, it was nevertheless much aggrandized and amplified by *Belovese* King of the *Galls*, having environed it with a Wall 24. foot broad, and 64. feet high, which compassed in all the Streets and round of the City: in which Wall were raised 130. Bulwarks, and Towers of immense bigness and heighth, which had six principal Gates. This was effected 270 yeers before *Brenta* King of the *Senoni*, fell down into *Italy*, who threw down and levelled it with the Foundations. But the *Roman* Senate having restored it to its first form and beauty, and being increased in Riches and People, *Attila* King of the *Hunns* descending into *Italy*, ruined it once more.

Afterwards, twas again rebuilt by the Arch-Bishop *Eusebius*, rearing the Wall again, and re-edifying the ruinated Building. And one hundred yeers after, that is in *Anno Salutis* 577. the *Goths* exercised so great cruelty towards the *Milanesi*, that after they had cast

down

down the Walls, and Edifices, they in one day flew thirty thoufand Citizens.

This City was likewife ill treated by *Erimberto* Brother of the King
of *France*, and by *Federick Barbaroffa* the Emperor: who with in
tendment of its perpetual defolation ploughed & fowed it wth. falt,
but being afterwards reconciled to the Citizens, he reftored it to
its former beauty, encompaffing it round with a wall, wherein
were fet out fix principal Gates: At which time, *viz.* in the 1177.
year, the circnit of it was fix miles without the fuburbs, but now
there is a Wall drawn round, which comprehends therein the Suburbs alfo, which was done by *Gonzaga* Lieutenant of the Emperor
Charls the 5th. and is in circumference ten miles; having very deep
Foffes or Ditches, and ten Gates.

This City, before the coming of *Bellovefo*, as is aforefaid, was but
a Town called *Subria* built by the *Tufcans*, then *Bellovefo* coming
from *Gallia*, beat out the *Tufcans*, aggrandized and much beautified
the Town: As to the name *Mediolano*, as formerly called, diverfe
are the opinions, fome fay twas fo called for that it was feated between two Rivers, the *Adda* and the *Tefino*.   Others fay, that name
was impofed on it by *Bellovefo* by the command of the Gods, giving
him to underftand, that he fhould build a City where he fhould find
a Farrowing Sow, half black and half white, with Wool between her
fhoulders: Whence finding fuch a Sow in that place, and eft-eming
it a good augure and præfage, he built it, naming it *Mediolana*, as much
as to fay, *Meza Lana*, or half Wool, in remembrance of which thing
we find in a Marble over the Gate of the Palace of Merchants the
fhape and figure of the faid *Scrofa* or Farrowing Sow.

The *Galls* kept the Dominion of this City, a long time, under *Bellovefo* and his Succeffors, till they were beaten out by the *Romans*,
who fubjected it for a great while to them, under whom it augmented in riches and People, chiefly under the Emperors as well Greek
as Latine; fome whereof much delighted to refide there, invited
thereto by the beauty of the place, and the comodioufnefs of managing the Wars againft the *French* and *Germans*, as neceffity required.
It fo much humoured *Trajan*, the Emperor, that he there built that
proud Palace which to this day retains his memory.

Adrian, *Maffiminian*, *Hercules*, *Filippo* a Chriftian Emperor, *Conftantine*, *Conftanzo*, *Theodofio*, with many other Emperors, dwelt there,
left moft ftately Edifices, and caufed four Wi-draughts or Common
fhores to be dugg, which continue to this day. Afterwards it became
fubject to the *Goths*, and to the *Longobards*, who being driven out
by *Charls* the great, it came under the power of the Emperors.   In
which time *Contado Suevio* being Emperor, it began to take boldnefs
and afpire to Liberty, when Juftice was adminiftred by the Captains
and other Officers elected by the People uniting with them the Primate or Arch-Bifhop of the City, by the Peoples election: In which
time great difcord arifing between the Nobility and Plebeians, and
thereby governing themfelves very ill, they to prevent thofe difor-
ders put themfelves under the power of thofe of *Torre*, afterwards
to the *Vifconti*, who a great fpace kept the Dominion, whom the
Sforzefchi fucceeded, them the *French*, and laft of all the houfe of *Auftria* obtained it, and keep. it to this day in good peace and tranquillity.   S   *Milan*

Milan lies under the sixth Climate or Degree, which affords it a great benignity of the skies, yet the Ayr is somewhat thick. Chanels of water environ both the City and Suburbs, upon which by Barks they conveigh great abundance of goods and provisions of all sorts. In truth tis a wonderfull thing to behold the great plenty of all things, for the life or necessity of Man, which are there, and tis held for certain, that in no other part of *Europe*. there is so great provision for the Belly, nor at less price, than is here: whence the Proverb is taken *Solo in Milano si mangia.* For whereas in other Cities one finds not above three *Piazzaes* at most, where are kept such publick Markets, in *Milan* there are a hundred, whereof 21. are principal, which every fourth day of the week are vastly laden with all sorts of Provisions: For wines they chiefly have *Vernaccie* of *Montferrat*, and the Wines of *Brianza* so much spoken of: Moreover for that it is the Centre of *Lombardi*, hither they transport infinite quantities of Merchandize, from *Germany*, *France*, *Spain*, and *Geneva.*

Tis seated in a wide Plain, having about it green hills, delightfull Meadows, navigable Rivers and Lakes, which furnish them with delicate Fish. In summ, this Country affords in most plentifull measure whatsoever can be desired. Tis so thronged with *Artizans* of all sorts, that the vulgar proverb goes.

Chi volesse rassettare Italia rovinarebbe Milano

But the chief of them are Gold-Smiths, Armourers, Gun-makers, and Weavers, who here exceed in these particulars, and in works of Christal, either *Venice* or any other part of *Italy*; the Nunns work here likewise most exact and neat curiosities in straw works. It abounds likewise with most magnificent and Stately Palaces, among which the stupendious Palace of *Tomaso Marini* (built with so vast expence and Artifice, that whoever beholds it stands amazed) shines like the Moon among the Starrs.

The Castle of *Porta Zobbia*, named among the chief of *Europe*, both for its site, greatness, beauty, and its plenty of Artiglery, Arms, and Ammunition, is so impregnable, that hitherto twas never taken by force, but through failer of provisions and Famine it hath been yeelded up. This Fort may be compared to an indifferent City, for within it are streets, Piazzaes, Palaces, Shops for Gold-Smiths, and all other Trades whatsoever, together with all sorts of Victuals and other provision in time of War, as well as Peace. Immense *Bastions*, with three large profound Dykes, environ it, through which run great Chanels of Water, with a most vast Wall, and spatious Ramparts, under which they walk by a close way made to that purpose. Upon the Battlements and through the Porteholes up and down, are drawn out great Mouths of Cannon, and other pieces of Artiglery set upon Iron Carriages, some whereof shoot Bullets of 800. pound weight, with such force that no obstacle can withstand them; It hath one place to lay up, and dispose the Arms in a Capacious Arcenal, replenisht with infinite Arms of all sorts both for Offence and Defence. The Tower in the midst of it, is of a square form, and is in circuit (not reckoning the Towers which one may

call

call little Forts)200. paces. The whole Caftle or Fort is 1600.paces
in circumference,befides the Trenches. In fine tis accounted by all
Ingineers the faireft and ftrongeft fortification of *Europe*. They unwillingly admit any Stranger to fee the out-works, much lefs the interiour parts.

It abounds with rare and excellent Pictures, among others there
is one upon the Front of a Palace near the Fort, wherein are painted
the Acts of the *Romans*, by the hand of *Trofo da Monza*, fo divinely,
that tis impoffible to add to it. The Images are done fo exact to the
life and fo natural, that all the beholders reft aftonifht, and expect
fpeech from thofe inanimate (but feeming breathing,and moving)
Pictures.

To fay no more, Art here hath overcome Nature. Towards the
Gate *Beatrice*, is the Front of another Palace (of the *Lituadi*) painted
fo rarely well by the hand of *Fremitano*, that it almoft fafcinates the
eyes of the *Afpicients*. And at the Gate *Tofa*, ftands an admirable Statue made to the middle, at the Publick coft, in remembrance of a
Strumpet, who principally caufed *Milan* to gain its Liberty.

Milan from the death of *Bellovefo* continued ever head of the adjacent Countrey, which made the antient Emperors to fend thither a
Lieutenant with title of Count of *Italy*, who alfo was Captain General of the Empire, and remained there with Confular authority,and
Captain of their Armies, that he might bridle the Fury, and fhut
up the paffage from the Inroads into *Italy* of the *Ultramontancous*
People.

Such is the wholfomnefs of the Ayr, the Beauty of the Country,
aud Copioufnefs of fuftenance, that it hath tempted many Princes
(defirous to reft quiet) to make this their Retreat, and *Afylum*, as alfo many other great Men that they might the more commodioufly
apply themfelves to the Study of Learning: Of which were *Virgil*,
Alipius, Saint *Auguftine*, *Hermolao Barbaro*, *Merula*, *Francefco Filelfo*,
Celio Rodigino, *Alexander* the fixth, and *Pious* the fourth Popes. And
although too often this City was thrown down to the very foundations, and at laft furrowed with the plough of the Enemies, yet it
ever revived again, and that with more beauty and Splendor than
at firft, increafing ftill fo much in Riches and People, that it ever
kept a place among the chief Cities of *Italy*.

Near the Church *San Salavdore*, there ftood a proud Palace of the
Emperors, with a Temple dedicated to *Jupiter*, made in emulation
of the *Campidoglio* at *Rome*, and where now the Counfel is kept, was
the Palace for Juftice; where alfo the Proclamations of the Dukes
were accuftomed to be publickly read, and the due punifhments executed on Malefactors. There was alfo a Theatre to prefent Comedies, a place for Horfe-races,and a large Circle where now is *Santa
Maria Maggiore*. The Garden near *San Steffano*, was an Amphitheatre, where they accuftomed to fight Duels. The Church of *San Na-
zarie* was an old Prifon, where they condemned Malefactors to fight
with the wild Beafts there preferved to that end in great number,

The Common Field was then a Theatre, where the young men
exercifed themfelves in taming and manning of Horfes,and fighting.
Where the Cathedral Church is, was a place with Stalls many waies
where they made their Feafts to their Heroes andHoufholdGods.The

Stalls now for the Cattel, then was a pleasant Garden, beautified and planted with many Fruit trees and plants brought from far Countries; great store of odoriferous flowers; Rivolets of Christalline waters, Statues and Sculptures of Marble.   Where the Church of *San Lorenzo* stands now, were the hot Baths of *Maximinian*, *Nero*, and *Nerva*, the Emperors, nothing inferiour to them at *Rome*.

Besides which antiquities, there yet is preserved a stately Armory in the Palace, replenished with most noble Arms, worthy any Prince for the value and fairness, being not onely inlayed with Gold and Silver, but engraven with greatest Cost and Workmanship; where now is the Church *San Lorenzo*, was a Temple dedicated to *Hercu'es*, made in the form of the *Rotunda* at *Rome*, near which were erected 16. Marble Pillars, and upon them a Palace for the Emperours, part whereof was ruined by fire, the rest by time, nothing but the Pillars remaining All this Fabrick was raised by *Maximinian Hercules*, who ordained the Town should be no more called *Milano*, but *Herculeo*.   At one end of those Pillars is this inscription put in.

Imp. Cæsari L. Aurelio vero Aug. Arminiaco Medico Parthico Max.
Trib. Pot. VII. Imp. IIII. Cos. III. PP. Divi Antonini Pii. Divi
Hadriani Nepoti. Divi Trajani Parthici, Pronepoti Divi Nervæ.
Apnepoti
Dec. Dec.

This *Milan* was alwaies a potent City, whence we read that it many times made opposition to the *Romans*, and often fought the *Goths* and other Barbarous People, and also against both the Federicks the first and second Emperours, obtaining a most glorious victory: It subjected to it *Navara*, *Bergamo*, *Pavia*, *Como*, *Lodi*, and *Tortona*, and freed *Genoua* from the hands of the *Moors*, The *Romans* were wont to say.

Qui miseram citius cupiunt effundere vitam,
Mediolanum adeant, gens ea dura nimis.

It was so much prized by the adjacent Countreys (that it being ruined by *Federick Barbarossa* the Emperor) *Cremona*, *Verona*, *Piacenza*, advised how to restore it at their own cost and charges, and in all times twas very populous.

It received the light of the Faith from *S. Barnabas*, sent thither from Saint *Peetre*, who then resided in *Antiochia*, which was in the 46. year after the coming of our Saviour, where he substituted for Bishop *Anatalone* the Greek his Disciple, whom in process of time succeeded many holy Bishops, among others that glorious pillar of the Church Saint *Ambrose* the most renowned Doctour; who finding the Bodies of *San Gervaso* and *Protaso* the Martyrs, caused that Church to be built which is now called *San Ambrogio*. This was the Cathedral Church, where is seen the true effigies of the brazen Serpent made by *Moses*, brought hither by *Theodosius* the Emperor, as also the effigies of *San Bernardo* upon a Pillar, who in this Church said Mass, preached and wrought miracles. Likewise a sumptuous Sepulchre wherein lies *Lewis* the second Emperour, and *Pepin* King
of

of *Italy* both Sons of *Charls* the great, there under the Altar within a deep Pit locked with four Gates of Iron, is kept with great reverence the body of Saint *Ambrose*, and a book writ with his own hand: *Angelberto* of the illuftrious Family of *rufterly* in the time of *Charls* the Great, being Arch-Bifhop. The Emperor gave to this Altar a noble *Pall*, embroidered with Saints and Angels, in 20. feveral Squares, in the midft whereof is the Saviour of the World, as he role from the dead, upon whofe head is a Diamond fet round with gemmes of ineftimable valew. On both fides of which Altar are four other Images of Saints, in the middle is a Crofs. The Vefts are all over befet with many pearls and pretious ftones; behind the Altar is another Crofs of filver two Cubits high, and one & an half broad, where are 23. figures of Saints of embolfed work; This fo ftupencious work coft in thofe days 28000. Scudaes, and is now worth 100000. *Polvinio* the excellent Sculptor of thofe times was the Artificer of it. Saint *Ambrose* ftood at the Gate of this Church, when he excomunicaed *Theodofius* the Emperor, commanding him not to enter therein. Contiguous with it is a noble and ftately Monaftery of the Fryers Celeftines. At the iffuing out of Saint *Ambrogio*, is a poor Chapel in a blind corner with a Well, where Saint *Ambrofs* baptized Saint *Auguftine*: and tis known, that this was the way, which Saint *Auguftine*, and Saint *Ambrose* took hand in hand to give thanks to God in *San Gervafo*, for the holy Baptifm received, finging *Te Devm Lau. damus*, as the Infcription teftifieth.

Hic beatus Ambrofius babtizat Auguftinum, Deodatum, & Alippum, hic beatus Ambrofius incipit te Deum laudamus. Auguftinus fequitur, Te deum confitemur.

The meannefs of the place makes it moft credible to be true, the name of *Carolus Boromæus* a Council of *Trent* Saint, highly cryed up at *Milan*, having too much extinguifht the memory and efteem of that learned Father.

The Church of *Santa Tecla*, is replete with holy Reliques; here refts Saint *Ambrose*, and among other Reliques a Nayl which was fixed and drove through a member of the Body of onr Lord and Saviour Jefus Chrift into the Wooden Crofs whereon he was crucifyed, by the wicked Jewes, wch. was beftowed on it by *Theodofius* the Emperor: This is the antienteft Temple of *Milan*, and was firft confecrated to the Saviour, after to the Virgin *Mary*, and laftly to *Tecla*, but antiently many yeers before the coming of the Meffiias, they fay there ftood a moft famous Temple of *Minerva*, where (as *Polybius* averrs) this goddefs was adored and reverenced with the greateft and moft particular devotion, whence many fuppofe this Ciry took its name, for that in the antient Celtique and German tongues *Magdalant* fignifies the Land or Country of a Virgin, which opinion is likewife confimed by *Andrea Alciato I. C.* A veritable Author in all the fciences, who in his Emblems writ this Epigram.

T

Quam

*Quam Mediolanum ſacram dixere puellæ
Terram, nam vetus hoc Gallica lingua ſonat,
Culta^c Minerva ſuit, nunc eſt, ubi nomine Tecla
Mutato, Matris Virginis ante Domum.*

Santa Maria della Scala, was founded by *Regina*, Wife of the *Viſconte:* and enjoyned to be ſo called, becauſe ſhe deſcended from the Family of the *Scalaes* of *Verona.* It ſtands where was antiently the Palace of the *Turriani:* And where the Church of Saint *Dionigeis* ſtood in old time a Dragon, which then greatly afflicted the Country and deſtroyed many, at laſt he was ſlain by *Umberto Angiere,* who was thereupon created *Viſcont.*

There are two Chapels in the Church of Saint *Mark,* in one whereof is the moſt excellent Pictures of *Lomazzo,* containing in one the Apoſtles, Prophets, Sibils, and many other pourtraies: In the other the fall of *Simon Magus* from Heaven, which it repreſent, as moſt horrible ſpectacle.

The Church of *San Nazario,* contains certain proud Tombs of the illuſtrious Lords, the *Trivultii* chiefly that of *Giacomo,* of whom may be truly ſaid: He that never was quiet lies ſtill here: Near this Church they ſhew a red ſtone, which they term the holy Stone, wherein are cut the victories, and trophies which Saint *Ambroſe* glo riouſly obtained upon the *Arrians,* in memory whereof, to him was erected a Statue at the Gate *Tico.* The Church of *S. Fedele,* is admirable, no leſs for its beauty, than for the Architecture of *Pellegrino.*

The Church of *San Paola* and *San Barnabas,* for the Nuns is moſt noble, where was firſt founded the Order of the reformed Prieſts of the beheaded *Saint John:* They have one rare croſs cut by *Bramantino.*

The Church of *Santa Roſa,* is for the preaching Fryers, who have the keeping of the holy *Roſarie.*

In the magnificent Temple of *San Gottardo,* are excellently drawn the effigies of the *Viſconte,* where ly buried *Azzone Viſconte,* and *Gio Maria* the ſecond Duke. Its beautified with a ſtupendious Belfry, and a fair Garden.

The Church of Saint *Euſtorgio* the Biſhop, ſhewes a ſtately and ſumptuous Sepulcher, wherein ly the bones of *San Pietro* the Martyr. A rich Tabernacle where is kept the head of Saint *Euſtorgio,* and the Tomb of the three *Magi,* with this inſcription. *Sepulchrum Trium Magorum,* where lay the Bodies of thoſe *Magi,* which were brought hither by Saint *Euſtorgio,* in *Anno* 330. when he came laſt out of the *Eaſt;* but many yeers after, this City being deſtroyed by *Fedrick Barbaroſſa,* in *Anno* 1163. Theſe Bodies were conveyed to *Colonia Agrippina* by *Rodolphns* the Arch-Biſhop, now they keep in that Sepulcher, the Body of *Euſtorgio* with many reliques of other Saints, Martyrd there for the Faith of Chriſt· Here alſo are kept the Aſhes of many noble *Milaneſians, inter alia* of *Matteo Viſconte* firſt Duke of *Milan,* and of *Gio Merula* a moſt Learned Man, who was interred with geeat pomp in the time of *Ludovico Sforza,* with this Epitaph on his Tomb.

Vixi

Vixi aliis inter spinas mundique procellas.
Nunc sospes cœlo Merula vivo mihi.

Over the Gate of the Convent of the preaching Fryers (from whom many excellent *Theologians* have issued) is placed the Pulpit, wherein Saint *Petre* the Martyr being preaching to the People at noon day in *Midsummer*, obtained by his Merits and the instance of his Prayers, that a Cloud hung over the Auditors in manner of an *Umbrella* preserving them from that intollerable heat; near the said Church gusheth out the fountain of Saint *Barnabas*, where though an unpolished place, he baptized and said Mass, of which water, who drinks is immediatly delivered from the malignity of any Feaver.

The Temple of *S. Lorenzo*, formerly dedicated to *Herode*, was much more sumptuous than the abovenamed Churches, which in the yeer 1085. being in great part burnt, received great damage in the Mosaick of Gold, and in the destruction of many Brass figures about the Pillars.

The royal Church of Saint *Aquilino* founded by *Placida*, Sister of *Honorius* the Emperor, and wife to *Constantine*, shewes on its Front fair Marble Colums, and within as noble Pillars of Porphiry. In the Church of *Stephano* was slain with many stabs the Duke *Galeazzo Maria Sforzo*. In *S. Giovanni* lies the Tomb of *Barnabo Visconte* Prince of *Milan*.

The Church of *S. Statiro* and *Celso*, is proud of the excelling *Genius* and Architecture of *Bramante*, the Limner of *Urbin*, in many works he wrought there; The Front of that of Saint *Mary*, of its excellent Statues wrought with so much art, that all conclude it impossible to equal them: and that of the Peace or Pace of its rare painting of the history of the blessed Virgin and her Father by the hand of *Gaudentius*, and moreover the Virgin her self painted by *Marco Uglono* the Painter, which stand near the Cross, and lively expresseth a real sorrow.

In the Church of Saint *Francis*, is a Tablet of the conception, together with Saint *Gio*, the Baptist, a Child adoring our Lord, so well done by the hand of *Vincio*, that they cannot be paralleled. In the Church *della Passione*, is a stupendious piece of the celebration of the last Supper, where is truly represented the amazement of the Apostles, by *Christofero Cibo*.

In the Church *delle Gratie*, founded by *Germano Rusca*, and aggrandized by *Ludovico Sforza*, is painted in a Tablet the Picture of our Lord crowned with Thorns, by *Titian* the worthy of eternal memory, about the Cupula are Angels formed by *Gaudentius*, whose vestments are rarely wrought, and in another place Sain *Paul* painted, writing and contemplating, Herein lies buried *Beatrice* the Dutches, so well beloved by *Ludovico* her Husband, that he vowed never to sit at table again at eating, and lived so a yeer about: One Epitaph over the Gate of the Cloysters, artificially made, shall be here inserted.

Infelix partus, amissa ante vita, quàm in lucem ederet, infelicior, quod
matri moriens vitam ademi, & parentem conserte sua orbavi; in
tam

tam adverso fato, hoc solum mihi potest jucundum esse, quod Divi pa-
rentes ne Ludovicus & Beatrix Mediolanen.   Duces gennere, 1497.
tertio Non. Iunuarii.

In this Church lies *Giovanni Simonetta*, who wrote the history of
the *Sforzeschi*, and *Giulio Camillo* a most Learned Man, whose Epi
taph, placed on another door of the Cloysters, followes

Iulio Camillo Viro ad omnia omnium scientiarum sensa mirificam eruenda,
& ad scientias ipsam in suum ordinem aptè constituendas natura mirè
facto, qui apud Dominicum Saulium Idibus Maii 1544. repentino
mortuus concidit. Dominicus Saulius amico desideratissimo posuit.

Which Church is possessed by the preaching Fathers, with a
stately Convent, to be reckoned one of the chief of *Europe*, for larg-
ness and beauty of building and the number of the learned and best
Fathers, which that Order enjoys, where they shew in a refectory
the Picture of our Saviour with the Apostles at the last supper,
drawn by *Leonardo Vinci* with such vivacity and Spirit that they seem
to move, and be sensible of the passions of Love, Sorrow, Joy, admiration, Suspition, *&c.* particularly in the Face of *Judas* one sees
exprest that Treason, which he had conceived in his mind; *Leonardo*
Vinci, having compleated all the Apostles, not wanting more to its
finishing than the visage of our Saviour, it happened that he could
never accomplish it, because he had exprest so great beauty and
glory in the Faces of Saint *James* the greater and the less, that he had
left no possibility for his fancy to draw any thing beyond them:
Whence pondring the impossibility of the thing, he resolved to consult with *Bernardo Zenale* another worthy Painter of those times; who
its reported made him this answer This Picture hath one Errour
which God only can rectifie, for tis not imaginable that thou or any
other Painter in the World can express more grace and Majesty, than
thou hast presented in the one and t'other *James*, wherefore leave it
as tis; *Lonardo* did so, as appears at this day, yet not so demonstra-
ble, because time hath in part defaced the glory of those Faces. There
also are the effigies of *Lodovico, Beatrice*, and both their Sons afterwards Dukes, *Massiminiano*, and *Francesco*. In the Church of *S. Vit-*
torie of the Fryers of the Mount of Olives, is seen a Saint *George*,
giving death to the Serpent, wrought by *Raffael* of *Urbino*.

The great aud sumptuous *Domo* or Cathedral, was founded with
infinite expence by the Duke *Giovan Galeazzo*, built with such industry, that for its greatness and Architecture, the pretiousness of
the Marbles and workmanship, few Temples of the World can be
paralleled unto it. Tis all of white Marble, and about it are 500.
Statues of the same. Its length from East to West is 250. Cubits, and
breadth 130. It hath six Cupolaes, one 80. cubits high, two 50. a-
nother forty, and the others 30. The four Pilastres of the greater
Cupola are 32 cubis distant one from t'other; It hath three propor-
tionated Isles with five gates in the front; the Casements, and Arches are of a Pyramid form, the Iron Bars which sustain this great
work, are so hugely bigg, that the Architectors of *Charles* the fifth
beholding them from the ground were amazed at them; Among the
other

other Statues, there are two moſt ſtupedious, the one of *Adam*, the other of *S. Bartolomeo*flleaed, divinely carved by *Chriſtopher Cibo*, in one of which may be clearly diſcerned the whole Anatomy of Man, which is unparalleld. It hath two great Organs, in one of which ſtands *David* the Prophet, playing on the Symbal before t he Ark, wrought with great artifice by *Gioſeſſo* of *Monza*. It hath two noble Veſtries, wherein they preſerve their Veſtments, rich Ornaments, and Veſſels given them by Arch-Biſhops, and Dukes, with many reliques of Saints. It hath beſides a ſtately *Chorus*, where the Dukes of *Milan* are intombed, and before the great Altar ſtands the Grave of Cardinal *Carlo Borromeo*, whoſe ſanctity of Life, and the form of good living, preſcribed by him to others, hath raiſed this opinion, that his Soul aſcended immediately out of his Body into Heaven : In another part is the Tomb of *Giacomo Medici*, Marques of *Melignano*, a Captain of great valour, and his ſtatue with h is natural Viſage, and Military habit in Braſs, made by *Leone Aretino*. In thisChurch they reverently keep alſo one of the Nayls wherewith our Saviour was nayled to the Croſs, given by *Theodoſius* the Emperor.

Among the other pious places, is the great Hoſpital of *Milan*, praiſable, ſeated in an Iſland, and invironed with Columns, and Porches, tis 600. rods about, 150. of a ſide ; Tis divided into four moſt capacious appartments, having underneath many little Shops made on purpoſe for the workers, employed for the uſe of the Hoſpitals: In the middle walk are 112. Beds for ſick perſons, all hung with Curtains, equally diſtant one from another, and accommodated in ſuch manner, that at the ſaying of Maſs all may hear. Its revenue is 50000. Crowns, ſomtimes exceeds 90000. Crow n s per. *Ann*. It maintains 4000. Souls, and for its noble Structure may be fit for the greateſt Prince.Five miles out of *Milan* on the Road of *Como*, is the *Lazuretto* of Saint *George*, (for the infected of the Plague) which edifice is four-ſquared, 1800 yards in circuit, round it runs a Channel ; and within it are infinite beds with ſufficient proviſion of all neceſſaries.

In this City are many Noble, Lordly, and magnificent Families, among others the Ancient houſe of the *Puſturley*, the *Turriani*, who came from *Valle Saſſino*, and ſometime governed here, from this Family came *Matteo Turriano*, who being Captain for *Conradus* the ſecond Emperour, in *Arabia* againſt the *Moors*, was taken Priſoner, and Martyrd for the Faith of Chriſt. The *Viſconti*, as ſome ſay, were deſcended from the *Trojani*, who built *Angiera*, near the Lake *Maggiore*, which City they long poſſeſſed, when being the moſt potent Family in *Lombardy*, *Matteo Viſconte* was conſtituted imperial Vicar of *Milan*, and all *Lombardy*, and permitted to carry the Eagle in his enſignes. Others ſay this Family had its original from the Kings of the *Longobards*, Be it as twill, twelve Princes of the *Viſconti* held the dominion of *Milan* 170. years Under Duke *John Galleazzo*, it commanded 29. Cities beſides *Lombardy*, among others *Genoua*, *Bologna*, *Piſa*, *Belluno*, and *Trento*. From the illuſtrious Family of *Sforzaes* have deſcended ſix Dukes of *Milan*, Cardinals, Queens, and one Empreſs. And beſides the aforenamed, the Families of the *Trivultii*, *Biraghi*, *Medici*, *Ruſchi*, *Mezenti*, *Bezzozzi*, and others are of *Milan*.

U

It

It produced 4. Popes, *Urban* the third, *Celestine* the fourth, *Pius* the fourth, and *Gregory* the 14th. Two Emperors, *Didius Julianus*, and *Maximinianus Herculeus*, who built the *Hercolean* hot Baths, and here in *Milan* deposed and quit the Emperial *Diademmes*; as also *Virginius Rufus*, thrice Consul, with many Cardinals, Bishops, Saints, with eminent Scholars in all ages, as *Salvio Giuliano*, Grandsire to *Giuliano* the Emperor, *Paulo Eleazarno*, *Gioan Lignano*, *Giasone del Maino*, *Filippo Deno*, *Andrea Alciato*, *Marco Massimo* the Historian, and Astrologer, *Cecilio* the *Comick* Poet, the Cardinal *Paulo Emilio Sfrondato* Nephew of Pope *Gregory* the 14. a person worthy of much praise, for his goodness and integrity of life.

The Arch Bishop of *Milan* hath the Title of Prince, and hath a long time enjoyed the primacy thereof: Its Jurisdiction extended it self heretofore to *Genoua*, *Bologno*, and some parts of *Sicilia*, and proceeded from its riches and pride, to that rashness, that for 200. years it withdrew it self from the *Roman* Bishops, but *Carlo Borromeo* hath taken off much of that obliquy, by the splendour he hath given to that Arch-Bishoprick by his holy conversation, whom Cardinal *Federick* his Nephew succeeded, a worthy imitator of his Uncle.

Before a Palace near the *Forta Lodivica*, is an Altar of Marble Stones, where on one side is carved *Diana Luci fera* (as *Cicero* calls her) with a burning Torch, as *Lucillus* writes in his Satyrs.

——Et Regyna videbis
Mænia, tum Liparas, facelinæ templa Dianæ.

For this Godess was in this manner adored in the Island, *Lipari*, and at its Feet is a Blood-hound with the eyes towards the Goddess, on the other side is *Apollo Medico*, leaning on a Tripode, with a Bow in his right hand, and a quiver of arrows hanging at his shoulder, near his feet a Scepter, and the Serpent *Pitone*, who is therefore called by the Poets *Pitio*, & *Citaredio*, before the said Altar may be read this inscription.

Æsculapio & Hygiæ
Sacrum
C. Oppius. G. L. Leonas
VI. Vir. & Aug.
Honoratus. In Tribu.
GL. Patrum, & liberum
Clientium. & Adcensus
Patroni. Sanctissimis
Communicipibus suis. DD.
Quorum. Dedicatione
Singulis Decurionibus
*III. Augustalibus. *II. Et
Colonis. Cenam. Dedit
L. D. D. D.

There are in *Milan* 11. Collegiat Churches, 71. Parochials, 30. Convents of Fryers, and 8 of Regulars, 36. Monasteries of Nuns, 32. Confraternities or Fryeries, which with diverse others amount to 238. Churches, with 120. Schools, where Boys are instructed in Christian Doctrine and other Learning.

It

It hath therefore worthily attributed to it the name of *Milan* the great, and the estimation of one of the four great Cities of *Italy*, that is, *Roma*, *Venetia*, *Milano*, *Napoli*, and *Antonio Callo* reckons it one of the ten greatest of *Europe*, it well may be accounted and taken for the greatest of any *Metropolis* in a Dutchy.

Going forth of the Gate *Camasina*, towards the North, and the Mountains, at 25. miles distance one arrives at *Como*, which rea affords nothing worthy observation, but the Town *Berfalina*, where Saint *Peetro* the Martyr was slain by the *Hereticks*, and in that place where he wrote the 12. Articles of Faith, with his blood, there is a Grott where they continually digg Earth, and yet it appears no hollow; Over that place they pretend likewise to see a great splendour, which God sheweth for the glory of that holy Body there inhumanly slain.

COMO.

Como is a City famous for the genteelness of her Citizens and flourishing Muse of *Paolo Giovo*, is seated in a Plain environed with Mountains, and near the Lake *Lario* or *Como*, within which and opposite to *Como* is a small Town built as it twere in a Peninsula, and at the lower end thereof stands a Palace, where the abovenamed, *Paolo*, had embellished a Library with a noble collection of Books, and the pourtrays of the most illustrious persons, as is expressed in his books called *gli. Elogii*, but at present there remains nothing of it more than certain pictures upon the Walls, The Images, Books, Robes of *Prete Janni* King of *Æthiopia*, the Bowes and other Arms of the *Antipodes*, with many other curiosities not elsewhere to be found, and of good valew, are removed thence to the Palace of the *Giovii*; within *Como* in the *Dome* or Cathedral Church on the left hand is erected the sumptuons Tombe of *Benedetto Giovo* the famous writer, in the City likewise may be read many epitaphs and writings, testifying their antiquity and constant fidelity to the *Roman* Common-Wealth.

The Lake *Como*, is 36. miles long, and somewhat more than three miles broad, upon which (when calm) the Citizens in their boats recreate themselves, near the end stands the Fountain of *Pliny*, and *Belacio*, a Palace of the *Signori Spondati*, invironed with spatious Gardens, which are adorned with fair Arbours, and the Walls clothed with Gessamines, Roses, Rosemary, and other sweets, together with some Woods of Juneper Trees, which harbour all sorts of Birds.

Ten Miles distant from *Milan*, and between it and *Como*, stands the stately Castle *Monza*, which is washed by the River *Lambro*, It was amplified by *Thedorick* first King of the *Goths*, and *Teodolina* the Queen, there erected a magnificent Temple dedicated to Saint *John* the Baptist, endowing it with great riches, among others with a Saphyr of inestimable price, a Brood Hen and Chickens of Gold, and many other vessels of Gold, therein also are preserved many reliques in Vessels, given to it by *San Gregory*.

Then appears *Somasca* upon the Mountains, a Town often named for the Original of the Religious order of the regular Priests of *Somasca*; a little more forward, you see (near the Banks of the Lake

Como the impregnable Castle *Leaco*, whence you passe by water to *Como*, and then advancing a little farther, the Traveller cometh to the Country of the *Grizons*, through which runs the River *Adda*.

On the left hand of *Monza*, rise the Mountains of *Bianza*, which afford most excellent Wines, and three miles distant from *Monza* on the right hand lies a well-manured *Campagna*, wherein *Francesco Secundo Sforza*, defeated the French Army, commanded by *Lotrecco*, where after the death of many thousand Souldiers, on both sides, he obtained a glorious victory. On this side also (before the arrival at the River *Varo*, the boundary of *Italy*, appears the small River *Martesana*, an Arm of the *Adda*, which runs under the *Gorgongiola*, over which stands a Bridge, whence they descend to *Milan*, and thus we have described the places on the Eastern Part.

Issuing out of the Gate of *Milan*, *Vercella*, towards the West, you meet the compleat Town *Ro*, near by which, passeth an Arm of the *Tesino* to *Milan*, on the other side of which Rivolet, is *Enfalaro* with many other Castles, whence taking the right-hand way, you arrive at the *Lago Maggiore*, at the very source of the River *Tesino*, which goes to *Pavia*, near which stands *Angiera* whence the *Signori d' Angiera*, now Viscounts, take their rise. Then at 17. miles distance from *Milan* upon a Mountain, (being as twere one of the Boundaries to the Lake) appears the devout Temple of *Santa Maria del Monte*, whither resort great concourse of People, to obtain their requests from God at the intercession of the blessed Virgin *Mary*. Then passing the *Tesino*, you find *Viglebia*, a new small City but fair, where stands the magnificent Palace called the *Sforzesca*, so named from *Lodovico Sforza*, Duke of *Milan*, who built and gave it to the Religious Order of the Dominican Fryers, who to this day possess it.

From whence on the right hand way, lies *Novarra*, and the Country *Lemellina*, and on the left hand, the Castle *Mortarra*, heretofore called the fayr Wood, but afterwards from the great slaughter of the *Longobards*, there made by *Charles* the great, fighting with *Desiderius* their King, it was named *Mortara*. On the same side also is the Castle *Valese*, and the Town *Varalle* under the Mountains, where in burnt Earth is effigiated the Sepulchre of our Saviour, with all the mysteries of his passion in divers little Chapels, to which much Application is made with great reverence by the neighbouring Peoples near which begins the Loke *Laguno*, and the Country of the *Grizons*.

The Journey from *MILAN* to

PAVIA.

BEtween *Milan* and *Pavia* stands the most noble Monastery of *Certosa*, built by *Giovanno Galeazzo Visconte*, first Duke of *Milan*, endowed with a great Revenue, in whose Temple himself lies buried, in a stately Marble Tombe, wherein is erected his Statue with his lively effigies, and inscribed a curious Epitaph, containing his famous notable Deeds, which Church hath many wonderfull Statues

tues, Sculptures, and Pictures|, fair Chapels, with Altars enriched with Gold, and pretious Stones, and a Vestry replete with Vests, and Vessels of Gold, and Silver of good valew, and many Reliqus of Saints.

Near which Monastery is a Park, invironed with a Wall of twenty miles square, wherein are plowed Lands, Meadows, and Woods, and therein are preserved great quantity of Wilde Beasts, for the Chase, as Hares, Roe-Bucks, Stags, Fallow-Deer, with other Creatures, which was imparked by the same *Galeazzo*, but is in some places fallen to the ground. Here *Francesco* the first King of *France*, encamped his Army, when he besieged *Pavia*, in the year of our Salvation 1525. at which time himself with the King of *Navarre*, and many prime Barons of *France*, were taken Prisoners by *Monsignors*, of *Lonato*, and *Barbone*, Captains of the Army of *Charls* the fifth Emperour.

PAVIA.

*P*Avia according to *Pliny* was built by the *Levi*, and *Marini*, a People of *Liguria*, not far from the *Poe*: But *Entropius* and *Paulus Diaconus* will have it to be founded by the *Insubri* and *Boii*, after the Declension of of the Roman Empire, to whom twas for some time subject. It was subjugated afterwards to *Attila* King of the *Hunns*, then to *Odoacro*, King of the *Heruli*, who having taken it by force, sacked it, burnt it, and levelled the Walls with the Earth: Then it became under the power of the *Longobardi*, who there fixing the Regal Seat, raised many sumptuous Edifices, as saies *Paolo Diacono*, among others, the Monastery of *Santa Chiara*, was built by *Partarito*, the Church of *Santa Maria della Pertiche*, by *Theodolinda* the Queen, the Monastery of *S. Pietro in Cielo Aureo*, by *Lutruprando* the King, who brought thither from *Sardigna*, the venerable Corps of Saint *Augustine*, there yet kept in a well-polisht Tombe of Marble, with great reverence, with many other Structures, which for brevity sake are passed over; here also, one may see the Castle built by *Giovan Galeazzo Visconte*, and also that antique brass Statue on Horseback, called *Regisole*, which many conjecture to be made for *Antonius*, from the Lineaments of the Face add Beard.

There were 22. Kings of the *Longobardi*, and they reigned 202. yeers, whose Nobles much adorned this City, making her the Regal Seat, and Mistris of their Provinces·

It hath produced many illustrious men, among other *Giovan* the XVIII. Pope, and *Tesore Baccaria*, Abbot of *Vall Ambroso*, Martyred in *Florence*. It hath many noble Edifices. chiefly that Tower wherein the great *Boetius* quitted this mortal veil. It is seated in a well tilled Vale near the *Appenine* Hills, and the River *Tesino*, over which was carried a stately Bridge by the Duke *Galleazzo Visconte*.

This City *Pavia*, as well in the forenamed Battel in 1525. as in several others before and since in latter times, when the *French* undertook invasions into Italy and beseiged it, hath fatally proved the overthrow of their Armies, the loss of theirdesigns, and the Ruine of their Interest in that Country.

In this City was instituted a famous University, not much inferi-

X

our

our to that of *Paris*, by the Emperour *Charles* the Great, whose zeal to amplifie the Christian Religion, caused him to send thither learned *Theologians*, to teach publiquely the true Doctrine, as also other eminent Doctors well read in all the Sciences, who were much encouraged to repair thither by their large Stipends and his signal favours; *Giacone* the so much celebrated Doctor, among others, spent many years in this Academy, also *Baldo*, having here read for some time, dyed, and lies interred in the Convent of the Fryers *Franciscans*, and tis conceived that the sereneness of the Ayr, so much sharpens the *Genius* of the Students, that it hath thence acquired the name of a glorious University.

The Faith of Christ was first preached and taught to the *Pavians* by the blessed *Sirus* of *Aquleia*, at the same time that the Apostle Saint *Peter* taught in *Rome*, from which time to this day they have constantl profest the same.

Its Citizens coveting their own Liberty, presented themselvs to *Philip* Arch-Bishop of *Ravenna* Legate of the Roman Church, in the yeer of Christ 1259. whereby they were long time kept under the Apostolick Sea, no less in Spirituals than Temporals, which the more evidently appears by the Oath which the *Podesta* and other Magistrates solemnly took at their ingression into their several Offices, precisely in this form.

> *Ego Potestas, vel Consul Justitiæ Papiæ, &c. Ad honorem Dei, & Virginis Mariæ, ad honorem & reverentiam S. R. Ecclesiæ, & Serenis. DD. Ludovici Romanorum Regis, & Civitatis Papiæ bonum statum juro ad Sancta Dei Evangelia, corporaliter tactis scripturis, quod sum & ero fidelis S. R. Ecclesiæ, & Rom. Imperii.*

The Emperour *Charles* the great, taking a Journey into *France*, left for his Lieutenants in this City, the *Languschi*, principal Gentlemen of *Pavia*, with the title of Vicars, which constitution the succeeding Emperoors successively approved, till the time of *Fedrick Barbarossa*, who granted them power to elect their own Consuls to govern the City, whence it was that at the Treaty and Peace made by the said *Frederick* with the People of *Lumbardy*, this City there interven'd as free, and not subject to any others.

The *Pavians* (after, the expiration of the 280. years wherein the Emperors enjoyed her) elected *Gio Galeazzo Visconte*, for Count of *Pavia*, under which capacity the Princes *Visconte*, and *Sforzeschi* successively possessed it, as doth now the King of *Spain*, to whom they surrendred themselves with another title and jurisdiction, to shew that this City holding themselves not at all subject to the Dutchy of *Milan*, but Muncipal, they might be acknowlged particularly as Counts of the Roman Empire.

No City in *Lombardy* can better extinguish any Novelties or Uprores than this of *Pavia*, and its Territory, which with the environing Rivers give limits to and divides the *Milaneses*, *Novareses* and other People of the hilly Countries, from the *Genoveses*, *Tortoneses* and those of *Bobio Alexandria*, and *Casal*, so that those several People can neither make league nor unite at their own pleasures without the consent of the Citizens of *Pavia*, which is duly called the Fatal Gate and

and Key of *Lombardy*, from its dominion over the Rivers *Poe*, and *Tef-fino*, and from its oportune fite, being empowred to give or deny paffage to or from either fides and fhores of thofe Rive .

Hence we may go by Boat on the *Tefino* to *Piacenza* or *Cremona*. But journying by Land, you leave on the right hand the Caftle *Vichiera*, *Tortona*, *Alleffandria*, *Montferrate*, and then *Piedmont*.

The Journey from *MILAN* to *BOLOGNA*

by the *VIA EMILIA*, afterwards

to *FLORENCE*, and Laftly

to *ROME*.

INtending to travel from *Milan* to *Rome*, you muft proceed out at the *Roman* Gate, and after fome fpace towards *Lodi*, you meet on the right hand in the Territory of *Milan*, the rich and famous Monaftery of *Chiaravalle*, to which the Abbot *Manfredo Archinto*, among other Farms, gave the great Vineyard *Pilaftrello*, which was formerly called the Vineyard of the Poor; for that the wine there collected and thereof made, was ufually difpenc'd among the Poor, being to that end preferved in one entire Veffel, the greateft in the World, which contayned 600. meafures, (each of which held about three gallons) was conjoyned with great Beams, and encompaffed with large Hoops, which when empty, hath for its grandure, been held a worthy object to many People, and to fome Princes, Kings, and Emperors, among which was *Charles* the fifth who difdained not to enter therein. Somewhat further from whence in the Territory of *Pavia* lies the Town *Landiciano*, and at tenn miles diftant from *Lodi* the noble and rich Caftle, *Meregnana*, and clofe by it runneth the River *Lambro*, which brings to it delight, and all forts of provifions; near it is the place where *Francis* the firft King of *France* flew 16000. Switzers, by whofe deaths *Maffimilian Sforza* happened to lofe his Seignory and liberty; thence fix miles ftands the Caftle *S. Angelo*, wafhed by the *Lambro*, where every *Wednefday*, is kept a fayr Market; thence three miles you fee the place where antiently ftood *Lodi* the Old. On the left of this fair way lies *Cremona*, and other places, whereof we have formerly treated in the voyage from *Brefcia*, to *Milan*; on all fides, you behold this Country abounding with Fruit and manured with Vineyards.

X 2

LODI

LODI.

THis City was founded by *Frederick Barbaroſſa*, three miles diſtant from the old *Lodi*, at whoſe foundation laying, the
ſaid *Federick* with himſelf brought all his Princes, and endowed it
with many privileges, which (under the ſhadow of the Empire) preſerved it a long time in Liberty. Afterwards it choſe for its Lords
the *Veſtarini*, its own Citizens, and in the end ſubmitted to the Dukes
of *Milan*. The old *Lodi* was called antientiy *Laus Pompeia*, for that
it was reſtored by *Pompeius Strabo*, Father of *Pompey* the great, and
this new *Lodi* was made a City by *Corrado* the ſecond, Emperour, at
the requeſt of *Frimberto*, Arch-Biſhop of *Milan*, and though at his
inſtance yet it no way abated the envy reigning in the breaſts of the
Milaneſi, for they in the yeer 1158, under *Uſſi*, for the great hatred
between them, deſtroyed it, being not at all ſatisfyed with their
throwing down of the Walls, and driving away the Inhabitants, untill they had inforced the Citizens to live in villages ſeparate one
from another, at ſuch diſtance that they might not aſſemble nor
take Counſel how to reſtore their unhappy Country, prohibiting
them traffick, and ſale of any thing, or to joyn in allyance, under
penalty of loſing their patrimony, and baniſhment; into the like
puniſhment fell ſuch of them as went out of the place they were confined to, under which miſery and ſervitude they continued for 49.
yeers. But the *Milaneſi*, were ſeverely chaſtized for this their cruelty, by God the juſt Judge. Their City *Milan* being not long after
ſacked and burnt by *Frederick* the Emperor.

This City ſituate in a plain, is of two miles compaſs and a round
form, having a pleaſant and fertile Territory environing it,
which produceth all ſorts of Grain, delicious Wines, and lovely
Fruis: The Paſture, and Meadows, are alwaies in a flouriſhing green,
being well preſerved (from the ſcorching heat) by the overflowing
of the Waters, which for that conveniency are conveyed in 4. or 5.
Chanels, one above another almoſt to a wonder, and ſo much to
their advantage that they mow their Meadows 4. or 5. times a yeer,
which with their paſture affords them ſo much milk as is incredible
to ſuch as have not ſeen it, wherewith they make abundance of Cheeſe
and ſome of them weigh 500. weight, here alſo they dry with ſalt
thoſe ſavory Calves Tongues, ſo much admired every where.

It hath many Rivers, and they afford excellent Fiſh, particularly
moſt delicate Eels, The City contains 12000. Souls, and many noble Families, among others that of the *Veſtarini* who a long time Reigned over it: It hath alſo given Birth to many Perſons, no leſs eminent in Letters than Arms.

It received the light of the Chriſtian Faith, from the preaching of
Saint *Barnabas*, at the time when *Milan* was therewith enlightned. *S.*
Baſſano, was Biſhop of this City, to whom a Church therein is de-
dicate, enriched with ſacerdotal habits, embroideries of Gold, and
Jewels, Cups, Croſſes, Cenſors, and other valewable Veſſels. Tis
waſhed with the River *Adda*, over which there is raiſed a Bridge of
Wood, ſix miles off which, is the rich Abbacy of *Borgheto*, and ſix
miles

miles thence ſtands mount *Columbano*, much celebrated for the delicate Wines, and fruit; on the left hand of the *Strada Ricca*, lies the
Town *Samalia*, with an Hoſpital, and the Abbacy of the Fryers of
Saint *Gyralamo*, a little farther ly *Lorleſco*, and *Puſturlingo*, built by the
noble *Puſterli* of *Milan*, whence (croſſing the River by Boat) about
a mile lies *Piacenza*.

PIACENZA.

SOme will have this City to take its name from the Pleaſantneſs of
its ſite, and the beauty of its buildings, nor have we any other
Original for *Piacenza:* Tis ſeated near the *Poe*, in a delightfull place,
having a flouriſhing *Champagne*, and fruitfull Hills, The firſt yielding plenty of Corn, and other things, for humane ſuſtenance, the
later incomparable Wines, delicate Fruits, and Oyl: The Meadows,
(alwaies green, by reaſon of the artificial flowing from the ſurrounding Rivers) are continually ſtocked with great herds of Cattel,
whence they extract that cheeſe which for its goodneſs is ſo much
cryed up through *Enrope*, that when they would commend any
Cheeſe, they call it of *Piacentia*; It affords alſo certain ſprings of ſalt
water, (from which with fire they extract the whiteſt ſalt) and ſome
Mines of Iron, and Woods filled with Creatures for the Chaſe.

It was reduced into a Colony of the Romans, together with *Cremona*, in the 350th. yeer after the building of *Rome*, by their ex-
pulſion of the French out of that Country, as *Livy* ſaies, who of it
makes an honourable mention in divers places, as well as divers o-
ther Hiſtorians, whence tis gathered, that twas very flouriſhing in
the time of the *Romans*, ſince when it hath ſuffered many calamities,
more by civil than forein invaſions: In the 70th. year after the Nativity of our Saviour, when *Vitellius* waged War againſt *Otho*, the
Amphitheatre ſtanding without its Wall was burnt, which made *Si-
lio* to ſay *Quaſſata Placentia bello*.

It is embelliſhed with noble ſtructures: As the antient Fountain
erected by *Auguſtus Cæſar*, the ſumptuous Church of *Santa Maria* the
Virgin, the Church of *Santo Antonio* the Martyr, the fair Church
of *S. Giovanni* officiated by the Fryers of *S. Dominick*, and that of *San
Siſto*, with a worthy Monaſtery, but above all is reſplendent the
Temple of *Sant Auguſtino*, attended by the canonical Regulars, which
at firſt was compaſſed about with a weak Wall, but afterwards ſo
well fortifyed with ſtrong Walls and a Fort built of Stone, that it
acquired a place among the ſtrong holds of *Italy*: The City is four
miles compaſs, and the Ditches add one mile more, and is waſhed
by the Rivers *Trebia* and *Poe*; after it had a long time enjoyed its liberty, it became ſubject to the *Scotti*, *Turriani*, the *Landi*, the Dukes
of *Milan*, the *French*, the *Romans*, the holy Church, but at preſent it remains in peace under the *Signori Farneſi*.

Pliny drawes a concluſion of the goodneſs and temperature of the
Ayr, from the old age the Inhabitants arrive to, who writes that in
his time, one of its Citizens lived to be 120. yeers old, and in its
Territory were ſix perſons, who were 110. yeers old a peece, and one
that was aged 140. yeers. The City contains 18000. Souls, whereof 2000. religious, many noble Families of great name flouriſh
there

there at this day, at the *Scotia*, *Landa*, and *Ansusciola*, who possess many Castles and Jurisdictions: Among many other illustrious and vertuous persons, it gave birth to *T. Tinca* the old fluent Oratour, and to Pope *Gregory* the tenth, who dyed in *Arezzo* in *Tuscany* where many signes appeared of his great merits.

Going out of *Piacenza*, towards the East and North appears the mouth of the River *Trebia*, much spoken of by Historians, for the overthrow of the Roman Army, given by *Hannibal*, but afore it stands the Church of Saint *Antonio*, where the six Souldiers were miraculously burnt by fire, who blasphemed his name. Then you see *Stradella* and the Castle of Saint *Giovanni* and *Vichiera*. On the left ly the *Apenine* Hills, among which stands enclosed the City *Bobio* thirty miles from *Piacentia* where *Teodolenda* Queen of the *Longobardi*, built a rich and sumptuous Monastery, at the request of *San Colombano*, assigning it great possessions for susteining the *Monks* who served God, from which Monastery have issued thirty two Saints.

At *Piacenza* begins the *Emilian* Way, called *Via Emilia*, according to *Livy*, which was set out by *Emilius* the Consul, and extends it self from thence to *Rimini*, towards the South. On the right appears most sharp Mountains, wherein are built fair Castles, Towns, and Villages, but none of moment, except *Corte Maegiore*, belonging to the *Pallavicini*, and *Arquato*, much named for the sweet Wines there produced. On the left hand of the *Emilian* Way, stands *Cremona*, whither you may go also by Water from *Piacenza* upon the *Poe*: Between *Piacenza* and *Cremona* at 12. miles distance on the *Via Emilia*, appears the Castle *Fiorenzola*, called *Fidentia*, by *Tolomeo*, and likewise *Livy*, writing in his 88th. Book, that *Silla* forced *Carbone* out of *Italy*, having overthrown his Army at *Chinso*, *Faenza*, and *Fidentia*. Here is that famous Abbacy, where with royal and splendid provision, *Pietro Antonio* the Abbot, received *Francis* the first King of *France*, *Charls the* 5th. Emperour, and *Paulus Tertius* the Pope; more forward stands the *Burgo* Saint *Donnino*, fortifyed with new Forts, and created a City lately at the instance of *Ranuccio Farnese*, Duke of *Parma*, Having repassed the *Poe*, you arrive at the River *Tarro*, whence to *Parma* is four miles, with a continued course of the *Appenines* on the right hand.

PARMA.

THis City is rich and adorned with stately Edifices, illustrious Families and many Inhabitants. It hath a delightfull and fruitfull Territory, yielding Corn, Fruit, Oyl, Wine, and Cheese known through the World, which hath acquired it a place among the rich and noble Cities of *Italy*.

Tis seated on the *Via Emilia* in a plain at five miles distance from the *Apenines*, between which and the Suburb on the West, passeth the River *Parma*, over which is raised a Bridge of carved Stone conjoyning both the Banks: Tis not known whether this River took its name from the City, or the City from the River, no antient Author making mention of it, but *Livy*, *Polibius*, and *Cicero* with other grave Writers, speak honourably of the City. It was made a Colony for the Romans together with *Modena*, as *Livy* averrs, in his 39th.
Book

Book in thefe words.　*Fodem anno Mutina & Parma Coloniæ Romano-rum Civium funt deductæ bina millia hominum in agrum, qui proximè Boio-rum, ante Tufchorum fucrat, Octona jugera Parmæ, quina Mutinæ accepe-runt.*

Its People are fayr, and of as noble and fpritefull Genius, difpofed not only for Government of the Republick, but alfo to Letters and Arms. It hath a fayr and large Campagna, which nourifhing immenfe numbers of fheep, affords them plenty of fine Wool, whereof *Marti-al* faies,

Tondet & innumeros Gallica Parma greges.

and in another place.

Velleribus primis Apulia, Parma fecundis
Nobilis, Altinum tértia laudat ovis.

Its Ayr is fo temperate, that *Pliny* faies in the time of *Vefpafian,* there were two men 123. yeers old each. The *Campagnia* is fo fpati-ous that all behold it with wonder, where ftands a Palace for the Dukes, embellifhed with Gardens and Fountains.

It was fubject to the Roman Empire, till the decay thereof, when it recovered its liberty in the yeer of our Lord 1248. it was ftraightly befieged by *Frederick Barbaroffa,* determining not to depart thence, till he had deftroyed it, which refolution caufed him to build a City near it, called *Vittoria,* 800 els long, and 600. broad, with eight Gates, and large dykes, but this his defign was prevented by a fal-ley of the *Parmezans,* who affayling his Army overthrew it, and de-ftroyed *Vittoria.*

The *Domo* of Cathedral Church is fayr and fumptuous, having many Canons and other Priefts to officiate : In the Church of *San Gi-ovanni,* dwell the Fryers of Saint *Benedict:* In the Church *Steccata* is ftately Architecture, lovely Pictures and Images: In the Church of the *Cupucines,* lies buried *Aleffandro Farnefe* the invincible Cap-tain and *Madama Maria* his devout Confort. Every Church hath fome works of *Parmegianino* and *Corregio,* the famous Painters.

In *Parma* are the noble Families of the *Pallavicini, Torelli, Roffi, Gi-berti, Sanvitali,* with others.

It hath produced men eminent in Learning, Virtue and Arms, as *Caffio* the Poet, *Macrobio* a worthy Writer, with others; It is fub-ject to the moft ferene houfe of the *Farnefi,* who have therein raifed many ftately Fabricks, and lately the Duke *Ranuccio* erected a School for all the general fciences; drawing thither by his large Stipends, the moft eminent Doctors of *Italy.*

It is four miles in circuit, and contains 22. thoufand Souls.

Forth of *Parma* towards the North is *Colorno* a well-governed Caftle, with other fair places, and towards the South, having paffed the River *Taro* and travelled 35. miles you meet *Borgo* a noble Caftle of the Dukes of *Parma,* from which Country befides great plenty of all neceffaries for humane fuftenance, they gather fometimes a hun-dred thoufand bufhels of Chefnuts, and when leaft 50. thoufand. It alfo produceth Men difpofed to Letters, Arms, and Merchandize,

Colorno

Borgo

Y 2

it

it ſtands in the midſt of the *Apenine* Hills being ſurrounded with them, and hath 23. Towns under it. More forward is *Pentremoli* a fayr Town, twelve miles further is the ſtrong Fort called *la val di Mugello*, then *Bardo* and *Campiano*, where the River *Taro* takes its ſource, and paſſeth at three miles diſtance by *Borgo*.

Traveling on the *Via Emilia*, from *Parma*, at the foot of the *Apenines*, appears the Town and Caſtle *Chiarngolo*, whereof the illuſtrious Family of the *Torelli* hold the Government, then in the plain Country *Montechio*, and *San Ilario*, ſeated on the banks of the River *Lenza*, over which the Counteſs *Matilda*, with great expence, built a Bridge of burnt Brick, then keeping the *Emilian* Way for 15. miles you arive at *Reggio*.

REGGIO.

THis City is built on the *Via Emilia*, and named *Regium Lepidi*, by *Strabo*, *Cicero*, *Cornelius Tacitus* and other writers: By whom it was built, is not certainly known, many contending that *Marius Lepidus* one of the *Triumvirate*, (who divided the Roman Empire) was its firſt founder, others that it was built long before his time, but by him made a Colony.

This City being deſtroyed by the *Goths*, under *Alarico* their King, Its Citizens were conſtrayned to abandon it, and fly to more ſecure places, till the *Longobardi* were overcome and driven out of *Italy* by *Charls* the Great, when the Citizens returning by degrees to their deſolate City, began to reſtore it, and immure it with a ſtrong Wall. It was governed by it ſelf for ſome time in liberty after the manner of the other Cities of *Italy*, then twas governed by others, till it delivered it ſelf into the hands of the Marqueſs of *Eſte*.

Tis a noble City, well peopled, and abounding with all things, although the ayr is not very good. It hath fair and large ſtreets with ſumptuous Structures, as the magnificent Church of *S. Proſpero*, Biſhop of this City, where his Corps are devoutly kept, which hath a plentifull revenue, and is adorned with excellent Pictures, but particularly with ſome drawn by *Coreggio*, worthy of eternal memory: In the Walls of the Orchard of the *R. R. P. P. de ſervi*, was lately diſcovered an Image of the holy Virgin, where God doth many favours to ſuch have recourſe unto him through her merits. The City contains many noble Families, as the *Canoſſi*, *Manfredi*, *Fogliani*, and *Seſſi*, who poſſeſs great Lordſhips and Caſtles.

Near unto *Reggio*, ſtand certain Hills, who are no leſs beautifyed with Towns and Villages than delicate Vines and fruit Trees. Towards *Parma* one ſees the Caſtle (ſtrengthned by its ſite) where *Matilda* the Counteſs preſerved Pope *Gregory* the ſeventh, from the ſnares of the Emperor *Henry* the fourth Enemy of the *Roman* Church, who afterwards repenting himſelf for that his crime, from thence went on his naked feet and with his bare Head in the midſt of Winter through Ice and Snow to the ſaid Pope, to obtain pardon for his offence, whom his Holneſs courteouſly received and pardoned, a remarkable inſtance of what power that Dignity heretofore was. At this day the moſt noble Family of *Canoſſa* are Maſters of this Caſtle and the others ſurrounding it, from which a little diſtance ſtands

the

Bardo

the Caſtles and other places of the *Signori Monfredo.*

Keeping the way of the Mountains, you arrive at the Countrey of *Groſſignana*, where ſtands Caſtle *Novo*, which hath formerly given birth to many illuſtrious perſons, and in our days to *Giulio Urbano* Doctor and Apoſtolick *Prothonotary*, who for his excellent doctrine was much eſteemed by the Princes, and Cardinals of the Court of *Rome*, who af ter he had long exerciſed the Office of Vicar General for Cardinal *Luiga Cornaro* Biſhop of *Padoua*, with grear praiſe in th at quality, deceaſed in the yeer 1592. leaving an excellent exa mple to all mortals. Whoſe Brother *Urban*, gave no leſs ſplendour to his Country, being Captain of the *Militia* for the *Venetians*. At preſent lives *Filippo Urbano*, their worthy Nephew, a Canon of the *Domo* or Cathedral Church of *Padoua*.

Returning to the *Via Emilia* you meet the Caſtle *Scandiano*, honoured with the title of a Marqueſate, ſubject to the *Signori Tieni*, noble *Vicentines*, on the left hand lies the Caſtle *Roldo*, belonging to the Family *Seſſi* a feudatorie of the Emperour, Saint *Martino*, *Gonzaga*, and *Nuvilara*.

Between *Modena* and *Reggio*, near the River *Lenza*, ſtands *Correggio*, a well-governed and honourable Caſtle, and well peopled, it was created a City by the Empire, and appertains to the moſt illuſtrious Family *Correggio*, formerly great in *Padova*, and called *Giberto*, from which heretofore iſſued a Cardinal, at this time *Girolamo Bernero*, of the preaching Order gives great honour to this Country, who was aſſumed to a Cardinalſhip by *Siſto Quinto*, High Biſhop, for his incomparable virtue and goodneſs of Life, who continues a prudent lover of the virtuous, and a great Zealot for the Chriſtian Religion. Then where the River *Lecchia* cuts in ſunder the *Emilian* way, ſtands the ſtrong Caſtle *Rubiera*, with a well-made Bulwark, environed with Hills, whence travailing in a large Road, you arive at *Modena*.

MODENA.

THis noble City was reduced into a Colony of the *Romans* together with *Parma*, in the 570th. yeer after the building of *Rome*, as *Livy* and other Hiſtorians write, who in ſeveral places make there, of honourable mention, which teſtifies that in that time it was rich and powerfull, and this is alſo confirmed by the many inſcriptions and antient Marbles which are extant up and down the ſame. It was enough illuſtrated by that notable battel which was fought near it, when *Hirtio* and *Panſa* were Conſuls of *Rome*, the conſequence whereof was the Loſs of the *Senates* authority, and the peoples liberty, for then *Mar. Antonius* beſieged *Brutus* in this City, who by the aſſiſtance of *C. Octavius Cæſar*, obtained the victory againſt the ſaid *Antonius*. Afterwards it ſuffered many ruines from the Barbarous, as Saint *Ambroſe* mentions, that he ſaw it with the other adjacent Places upon the *Via Emilia*, thrown down and deſtroyed. It was layed waſte by the *Goths*, and *Longobards*, who afterwards being driven out by the Emperour *Charls* the great, and he having eſtabliſhed his Son *Pipin* King of *Italy*, the Sons of the Citizens of *Modena* aſſembled themſelves together from their ſecure retirements, and took counſel how to rebuild this City, which in procefs of time they effected as is now feen, fomewhat diftant from the antient *Modena*, as *Leandro* more at large difcourfeth.

The City is fmall, of an orbicular form, & feated in a plain abounding with fruits, and delicate Wines. The Dukes of *Eftè*, *Alfonfo* the fecond greatly amplified this City, and raifed fair edifices. In the *domo* they devoutly preferve rhe bones of *S. Giminiano*, its Bifhop, for whofe merits God delivered many poffeffed with Devils. Tis full of noble and ingenuous People, whence not only many famous Captains, Counts and Marquefes, have proceeded, but alfo many Cardinals, Bifhops, and other prelates, with moft learned men, of whom are *Sadoleto* and *Segonio*, whofe works are of note to all. It continued a long time in liberty, as did the other Cities of *Lumbardy*, but is at prefent fubject to the Dukes of *Eftè*, who by their conftant refidence much ennoble and enrich it, they here Make Vizards and Targets, much efteemed through *Italy*.

Forth of *Modena* towards the South under the *Appenines* ftands *Formegine*, *Spezzano*, and ten miles off it, *Saffulo*, a noble and civil Caftle, with a fumptuous Palace of the Family of *Pia*, wafhed by the River *Secchia*, where ftands a fair Church dedicated to the bleffed Virgine, whither refort infinite People to obtain Graces. Upon the faid Mountain are many other Villages and Hamlets, which alfo may be feen on that part of *Modena* towards the Eaft.

Thefe Caftles heretofore fubject to feveral Lords, and particularly to them of *Monte*, who were then very potent in thefe Countreys, and poffeffed all the placs in the *Graffignana*, which confines with *Bologna*, and among them *Seftola*, aed *Fanano*. Then going Weftward you fee the *Alpes* of *San Pelligrino*, and the Caftle *Aquario* famous for its Baths. After turning to the South, by thefe Mountains runs the *Tyrrehene* Sea; fomewhat further near *Bologna*, on the Banks of the River *Panaro*, appears Caftle *Vetro*, and *Spilimberto*, of the *Signori Rangori*, whence four miles you finde *Vignola* a Town honoured with a Marquifate, fubject to the *Signori Boncompagio*, which Town confines with the *Bolognian* territories.

Towards the North is feated *Correggio*, at 12. miles diftance, thence and fomewhat further the moft noble Caftle or rather Imperial City *Carpi*, which may very well be paralleld to many Cities, both for the great and ingenuous People, and the fupeifluity of all things neceffary. It hath the title of a Principality, and was a long time enjoyed by the *Signori Pii*, but is at prefent By the Duke of *Modena*.

On the Eaftern part of *Modena*, is a Chanel upon which you may be conveied eight miles by Boat, unto *Finale*, then paffing on the *Panaro*, and entring the *Poe*, they go to *Terrara*, upon the River *Pinaro*, where the Chanel runs into it, ftand *Bon Porto*, and *San Felice*, praifed for good Wines.

Along the *Via Emilia*, 3 miles diftant from *Modena*, paffeth the River *Panaro*, near which are the confines between the *Modonefi*, and the *Bolognefi*, in which place *Claudius* the Conful copeing with the Enemies, took 15000. Prifoners, and 700. *Liguri*, moreover in the fame place *Rotari* King of the *Longobardi*, routed the *Roman* Army, and flew feven thoufand of them.

There

There alfo the Army of the *Modonefi* being difcomfited by the *Bo-lognefi, Enzo* King of *Sardegna,* Son of *Frderick,* the fecond, was ta: ken Prifoner. On the other fide of the *Panaro,* is *Novantola,* with an antient and noble Monaftery founded by *Anfelino,* Kinfman of *Aftolfo* King of the *Longobards,* having been a worthy Captain in their Army, and there quitting this World, created himfelf Captain of a thoufand *Monkes,* endowing the place with ftore of Goods and Revenues, about the yeer of our Salvation 780. It was afterwards reftored by the Countefs *Matilda,* and is inhabited by many *Monks,* who have Jurifdiction as far as *Spain,* wherein are kept the body of Saint *Adrian* the Pope, and fome part of S. *Silvefter,* with many o-ther Reliques, and fome antient Books, particularly the Breviary of the faid *Matilda.*

Near the *Via Emilia,* between *Bologna* and *Novantola,* ftands S. *Aga-ta,* a Caftle built be *Barbaroffa* the Emperor, and *Crevalcore* formerly called *Allegra Cuore* where twice the Armies of *Bernabo Vifconte* Lord of *Milan,* were overthrown. Then one comes to *San Giovanni,* a Countrey yeelding Wheat and other Grains. On the left fide of the *Emilian* Way, are feen *Caftiglione,* and *Cafile Franco,* 15. miles from *Bologna,* in which Territory was lately raifed an inexpugnable Fort, by Pope *Urban* the 8th. from whofe name tis denominated *Urbano.* Near which is the *Foro de Galli,* where *Irtio* and *Panfa,* the *Roman* Confuls fighting with *M. Antonius,* obtained a glorious Victory, but with it their mortal wounds whereof they both dyed in the fame place: Then appear *Piumanio, Bazano,* and *Crepellano,* pleafant Ca-ftles, feated on thofe little Hills, at the Feet of the *Apenines.*

On the left fide of the *Emilian* Way five miles diftant from *Bologna,* is the River *Lavino,* and *Ghironda,* which joyning togeher encom-pafs *Forcelli,* in a triangular form at one miles diftant from the *Via Emilia,* where *Octavianus, Marcus Antonius,* and *Marcus Lepidus,* par-ted the Monarchy between themfelves, which *Forcelli* feems now a *Peninfula,* though it may be perceived to have been an Ifland; af-terwards thefe two Rivers throw themfelves into the *Poe:* About a mile before you arrive at *Bologna,* there is a very long Bridge, built of Stone, which reacheth from the one fide of the River to the other whence to *Bologna* is an eafiy mile.

BOLOGNA la *Graffa* or *BOLONIA* the Fatt.

Bologna was antiently head of the 12. Cities which the *Tufcans* poffeffed on that fide of the *Apenines,* who being driven out by the *French,* and the *French* by rhe *Romans,* it became a Colony of the *Romans,* who fent thither 3000. men to inhabit. After the *Romans* it was fubjected to the *Grecians,* the *Longobards,* and to the *Efarcato* of *Ravenna.* Afterwards recovered liberty like the other Ci-ties of *Lumbardi,* at which rime the wicked factions of the *Lamber-tazzi,* and *Geremei* arofe, and reduced it to great mifery and fervi-tude, which their fufferings caufed them to recommend themfelvs to the *Roman* chief Bifhop. Afterwards to the *Pepoli, Vifconti, Bentivo-gli,* and finally it wholly put it felf under the wings of the Pope, who now enjoys it with peace.

It is fituated at the Foot of the *Apenines* in the midft of the *Via Emi-*

lia,

lia., placed according to *Ptolomeo* in the 6th. Climate, at 33. degrees and a half, having the ſaid *Apenines* on the South, the *Via Emilia* or *Roman* Way, on the Eaſt, and the pleaſant and fertile *Campagna* leading to *Ferrara*, and *Venetia* on the North; At its beginning twas formed a ſmall City, according to the accuſtomed manner of the Ancients, with two only Gates, the one towards *Rome*, the other towards *Lumbardi*. Afterwards in the time of *Gratian* the Emperour, they adjoyned two other Gates, and at the reſtauration, which *San Petronio* made (after the deſtruction by *Theodoſius*) they made 9. Gates, as ſome ſay, 12. as others, where now are extant certain little Turrets called *Turroſetti:* At laſt enlarged as at this day, the ſaid Gates were made twelve, and was ſo much encreaſed, that certain yeers paſt being meaſured within the Walls, Its circuit was found to be 5. miles in length two miles want a quarter, and in bredth one mile, from the Port *S. Mammola*, to the Port *Galliera*.

It is formed in the ſimilitude of a Ship, more long than broad, at one ſide ſhewing the figure of a Prow, and at the other that of a Poop having in the midſt the moſt high Tower *Aſinelli*, which repreſents the main Maſt, the Tower *Gariſenna* the Scale, and the other ſmall Towers, the Shrouds to the eye of the beholder. Within it is no manner of fortification, the Citizens having caſt down thoſe that were, who confiding in their own valour and prudence, content themſelves with a ſingle Brick-Wall, which encompaſſes it; near it runs the River *Savona*, and through it the *Reno*, which ſerves for tranſportation of Merchandiz from *Ferrara*.

That *Bologna* abounds with all things is known to all, whereby they give it the ſtile of Fatt: Its Fields are fair and large, producing all ſorts of Corn, and Wines of the beſt ſorts in *Italy*, with all kinds of Fruits, particularly Olives, ſo bigg and ſweet, that they give not place to them of *Spain*; it hath alſo Woods for Foul, and Beaſts of Chaſe, and notwithſtanding there be few Lakes, yet tis plentifully ſerved with fiſh from *Comacchio* and *Argenta:*

Here (to maintain their Epithite of *Bologna la graſſa*) they make thoſe famous Salſages, which for their excellency are eſteemed a coſtly diſh through the World, as alſo a Conſerve of Quince and Sugar called *gelo* or gelly, fit for the Table of a Prince. They here alſo work with great Art, Sheaths for Knives of boyled Leather, and fair Harquebuſes, and Flacks or Bottels. They have great numbers of Silk-Worms, from whoſe labour they extract quantity of Silk, whereof they make Sarcenet, Velvet, and other Silks, in ſuch plenty, as that they not only ſupply all *Italy* therewith, but *England* and the Low Countreys.

Its Territory affords many Quarries of white Stones, and great ſtore of Hemp and Flax, ſome minerals of Allum, with medicinal Fountains both hot and cold.

It hath but one *Piazza*, which yet for its largeneſs, may be ſaid to be three conjoyned, in the midſt whereof ſtands a ſumptuous marble Fountain, whereon ſtands a Brazen *Neptune*, made by *Giovanni Bologna*, a Flemiſh Sculptor, in very much excellency, whence guſheth a moſt clear ſtream of Water. It hath a general uniformity of building, having ſtraight and ſpatious Streets, and on each ſide of them before the Houſes Arches, of the ſame Structure, where the
Citi-

Citizens recreate themfelves without fear of the fcorching Sun, or the dripping Rains. There is one fpatious Garden of the *Poeti*, & another of the *Pafelli*. Near the Church of S. *Giacomo*, where now appear a good fpace of old rinesu, was formerly a regal Palace of the *Bentivogli*, (while they were Lords of *Bolonia*) whofe Majefty and Magnificence is treated on by *Beroaldo*.

Tis adorned with fuperb and fpatious Edifices, as well for divine worfhip as private ufe; Among others the Popes Palace, over the gate whereof is the Statue of a Pope in Brafs, and that of the *Campeggi*, (where in the time of *Giulio Terzo*, the Council of the *Pepoli* and *Malvezzi* met) are of fuch grandure, that any Prince may be received there. The Palace which fronts the Church *San Petromio*, was built by the *Bolonians*, for a prifon for *Enzo* King of *Sardegna*, where he lived, and at the coft of the publick was royally entertained for twenty yeers, till his death.

Furthermore the Citizens Houfes are beautified with Vefts and other things, to the pride of any others of *Italy*, and their Sellars fo deep under ground that they apprehend no Earth-quake; The Tower *Afinelli*, fo named from the founders, and *Garifenda* fo called from its pendency downwards, difcover the great ingenuity of the Architector.

Its principal Temples are, that of *San Pietro* the feat of the Bifhop, where ly many Cardinals, Bifhops, and other learned Doctors, with many Reliques of Saints, Pictures, Sculptures, and Ornaments of gold and Silver of high valew. The *Domo* which ftands on the *Piazza*, dedicate to *San Petronio*, Bifhop and Protector of the City, is fo great and magnificent, that few Churches are equal to it; here *Charls* the 5th. received from Pope *Clement* the 7th. the Crown of the Empire: The Church of Saint *Francis* is well built, where Pope *Alexander* the 5th. a *Bolonian* lies buried, and *Odoffredo* and *Accurfio*, two great Lights of the Civil Law; then the magnificent Monaftery of *San Salvidore*, and the noble and rich Nunnery *del Corpo di Chrifti*, where lies enterred the bleffed *Catharine*, who was a Nun therein, whofe nails upon the hands and feet grow as if fhe were living: The Church of *San Giacomo*, with its Chapel built by *Giovanni fecundo Bentivoglio*, was a work only for a King, wherein lies the faid *Bentivoglio*, with many of his defcendants, fome of the *Malvezzi*, and other illuftrious perfons, with many Reliques of Saints, guarded in a rich and ftately Altar by Cardinal *Poggio*.

The Church of S. *Martin*, where repofe the bones of *Beroaldo* and *Alexandro Achellini* the Philofopher. The Church of *San Giovanni*, entombes an image of *Cecilia* the Virgin Martyr, painted by the divine *Rafael* of *Urban*, the afhes of the bleffed *Elena*, and *Carlo Raino* a famous Doctor of Laws, four of thefe Churches Canons have been Bifhops of *Bologna*.

The Church of Saint *Stephen* the *Proto*-Martyr, is fumptuous built by S. *Petronio*, where among other Reliques they fhew the Afhes of *S. Vitale, Agricola & Petronio*. The Church of Saint *Benedict*, enclofeth is the Body of *San Proculo* the Martyr, and the Cel wherein *Gratian* compofed his Decretals. In the Church of Saint *Domenick*, in whofe Quyer is rarely effigiated the old and new Teftaments, here lies *Enzo* King of *Sardegna* in a proud Tombe, and many famous Doctors of

A a

Civil

Civil Laws, and Physick, as also *Tadeo* and *Giacomo* *Pepoli*, who some
time were Lords of *Bolonia* at the high Altar may be seen many Reliques of Saints, of which are the body of *San Domenick*, on whose
Tomb are layed more than 300. Figures of Gold and Silver, and
one of the Thorns of the Crown of our Saviour, with the Bible written by the hand of *Ffdras*, in the Hebrew Tongue, in white parchment ; here reposes also the Body of *San Domenick* the Patriark,
and institutor of that Order , with many other stately Tombs, Candlesticks, Lamps, Censers, and other Ornaments. This Church hath
a noble Convent , with many Cloysters, and Dormitories for the
Fryers, and a large Refectory excellently painted , and one of the
largest Cellars of *Italy*; therein is likewise a Cemetory wherein to
bury the Fryers. And an excellent Library, scarce any equal, none
better to be found , kept and encreafed dayly by the Fathers with
great diligence, and here fits the Inquisition. In this Convent dwell
one hundred and fifty Religious, and here they keep the publique
Studies of the Sciences, which hath occasioned principally that five
Popes, many Cardinals, Bishops, and holy Fathers have proceeded
hence, among which were *San Pietro* the Martyr, *San Ramundo & Egi-
dir Fofcararni* Bishop of *Modena*, who behaved himself prudently and
learnedly at the Council of *Trent*.

The first Bishop of *Bologna* was *SanZama*, who in the 270th-yeer after
Christ first preached the Faith here, *Dionifius* being then Pope, whom
71 have succeeded of good Doctrine and holy conversation, of whom
nine are Canonized, and two held for Saints.

Moreover from this excellent Country have Issued 6. Martyrs, 13.
Confessors, 14. Men Saints, and 7. Women. It hath 179. Churches,
that is 33. for the Company of *Laicks*, 3. Abbacies, 2. Prepositors,
2. for the Regular Priests, 24. for the Fryers, 23. Monasteries for
Nuns, 10. Hospitals, 5. Priorates, 2. Collegiate Churches, and
the *Domo*, which is consecrate to Saint *Peter*, and giveth the title of
Prince to its Bishop, with a great Revenew, with many other Churches which are either Parochials or Oratories.

The Univerfity was placed in *Bologna* , by *Theodofius* the Emperor,
in the yeer of our Lord 425. and much amplified afterwards by
Charles the great , and *Lotario* the Emperor; the first Reader of the
Civil Laws here was *Irnerio*, induced thither by the said *Lotario*, fince
when many wise and well-read men in all sciences have proceeded
hence; in the time of *Giovan Andrea* the Splendour of the Canon Law
and *Azone* the Fountain of the civil Law, we read there were ten
thoufand Students in this City.   *Azone* faies *Legalium ftudiorum fem-
per Monarchiam tenuit Bononia*, hence tis that *Gregory* the 9th. directed
his decretals to the Univerfity of *Bolonia* and *Boniface* the 8th. *Sifto* ,
and *Giovanni* the 24th. the Book of the *Clementines*.

The Fabrick of the Univerfity is very proud, with a large Hall and
fpatious Courts. In the City are many Colleges for several Nations, and
to fpeak its praifes in one word, tis a moft happy Univerfity, and merits that Character which all men give it, *viz.*

Bononia docet, & Bononia mater Studiorum.

The City contains 80000. Souls , among them many noble Families, with many titled, as Dukes, Marquefes, Counts, Captains of War,
befides infinite Scholars.   Its

Its Riches are great and equally divided among the Citizens, whence tis that they alwaies preferved a good reputation. It fought with *Federick Barbaroffa*, and took his Son *Fnzo* Prifoner, maintaining him fplendidly for 22. yeers. It fubjugated more than once, *Forli, Imola, Faenza, Cefena, Cervia*, and other places. It glorioufly maintained a War againft the *Venetians*, for 3. yeers together, with an Army of forty thoufand men, and had fome Families very potent, as may appear by that of the *Lambertazzi*, who being banifhed with all its followers, out of *Bologna*, in the yeer 1274. they fay that what with Men, Women, and Servants, they who by that decree went out, amounted to the number of fifteen thoufand perfons.

The Burroughs and Suburbs of *BOLONIA*.

FOrth of *Bolonia*, towards the Weft, at the Foot of the Mountains, is the Church of *San Giofeffo*, and the Monaftery of the *Certonifi*. Upon the top of the Mountain *Guardia*, is reverenced an Image of the bleffed Virgin drawn by the hand of *S. Luke*. Out of the Gate towards the *Emilian* Way, there is a noble Monaftery of the Crutched Fryers, and towards the South the Church *Mifericordia*, where refide the reverend Fryers of Saint *Auguftine*. Out of the Gate *San Mammolo*, is a Monaftery of the Jefuites, and upon the hill is the miraculous *Madonna del Monte*, a Church of the Benedictine Fryars, where are the natural effigies of *Baffarione* and *Nicholo Perotto*.

Towards the Eaft is the Church of *San Vittore*, placed among the Hills, where *Bartolo* the moft learned Doctor, refided 3. yeers as it were unknown, near which are ftately Palaces. Without the City alfo ftands *San Michelle in bofco*, upon a hill, with a rich and proud Monaftery. The Church is garnifhed with fair Colums, Statues, and Sculptures of Marble, and fumptuous Altars with rare pictures, the Quire with excellent Land skips, there is a ftately Library, & refectory with excellent Pictures drawn by *Vafari* among, them the effigies of *Clement* the 7th. in the Cloyfter lies buried *Antonio di Butrio*, a Doctor of Laws, and *Ramazzotto*, a valourous Captain in the Wars. Its apportments are excellent Architecture, and its gardens moft delitious, from which Monaftery, befides the City and Territory of *Bolonia*, you have a full profpect of the pleafant Country of *Lumbardy* fo much commended by *Polibius*, in the fecond book of his hiftories, as alfo of thofe Snowy hills the Alps, which appear like Clouds, the Adriatic Sea, and the mouth of the *Poe*, which runs into the Sea by many branches, and likewife of *Mantoua, Ferrara, Imola, Mirandola*, and other furrounding places, which feem as fo many fair Rofes and flowers difperfed over thofe Fields.

· The Teritory of *BOLOGNA*.

TRavailing out of *Bologna*, South-Weft, you meet with the moft antient Monaftery or Priorate of *Santa Maria del Renu*, whence have proceeded 2 Popes, with many Cardinals, Bifhops, Saints, and other Religious. Then turning on the left hand towards the *Apenines*, and keeping the River *Reno*, on the right, you arrive at the Bridge *Cafalecchio*, a little farther you fee the *Chiefa*, which is a

Wall traverfing the *Reno* from fide to fide, to force the Water down
a Chanel, cut artificially to *Bologna*, for the driving certain Engines
and Mils for grindidg Corn, for making Veffels of Copper, and Arms
for War, for beating of Spices, and Galnuts, for twifting of
Silks, for burnifhing of Arms, and for edging of divers Inftruments,
for making of Paper, sawing of Planks, and divers other Myfteries,
and in the end to convey the Barks to *Malelbergo*, and thence on the
Poe, to *Ferrara*. Then you enter the Vale *Reno*, between the River
and the Hills, which is moft productive of all Grains and Fruits, in
which Valley ftands the magnificent Palace of the *Roffi*, a Palace for
its capacioufnefs and delights fit to lodge an Emperor; on the Hill
near it is the Town *Coloffina*, wch. before you can afcend you muft pafs
under a Rock by a way cut thorow with Iron, on the left hand beholding a prodigious hollow, through which the *Reni* paffeth. Then
you find *Panico*, a Town a long time poffeffed by the Family of *Panico*, which at this day is wholly extinct. More forward one difcovers
a fair Plain called *Mifano*, and in it certain foot-fteps of Edifices,
and other Antiquities, purfuing which way you arrive at the Town
Vergata, the feat of the Captain who hath Jurifdiction over the Inhabitants of the adjacent Villages, and is diftant 15. miles from *Eoloni-
a*. Whence travailing on the right hand, fhew themfelves *Cefio*, *Barg-
hi*, and *Caftlighone*, Caftles of the *Signori Pepoli*, near whereto are
the confines of the *Florentine* Territories, but on the right hand a-
long the Banks of the *Reno*, are the Baths of *Porretta*, where from
Rocks gufh out hot Waters very medicinal, whofe virtue is mani-
fefted to all by the Proverb which faies *Chi beve l'acqua della Borretta,
ò che lo fpazza, ò che lo netta*, thence taking the right-handway, you
enter the *Graffignana*, treated of diffufely before.

Taking the Way through the Gate *Galliera*, towards *Ferrara*, you
meet *Corticella*, then puffing the Bridge over the *Reno* you fee *San
Georgio* a Caftle ten miles off *Bologna*, where leaving the Caftles *Cen-
to* and *Pieve*, on the left, appears *Poggio*, appertaining to the noble
Family *Lambertini*, intending then for *Ferrara* you muft keep the direct
Road.

On the right hand of which Way near the *Canale*, lies *Bentivoglio*,
a fumptuous Palace with a Tower in the midft of a ftrong Fort,
whence fayling down the *Canale* in Boats, called *Sandoli*, one paffeth
by *Malalbergo*, an Inn infamous by name and Deeds, *Bottifredi* a Tavern, *Minerbo* a Town, and *Butrio* a Caftle, whofe Countrey affords
plenty of Hemp, which for its length and ftrength is much efteemed at *Venice*, and by them ufed for Cordage for their Veffels. Near
the *Emilian* way, towards the Eaft, ftand *Molinella* a Palace, *Bolonia-
li Valti*, a Village, *Medicina* a Caftle, and *Ricardina* a Town, between
which was fought that fharp battail by the Army of *Bartlomeo Cogliono*
againft that of *Galeazzo Sforza* Son of the Duke *Francefco*, wherein the
faid *Bartolomeo*, remained Conqueror, and near hereto, lies the Valley
Argenta, and the Caftle *Guelfo*, where begin the Territories of *Imola*.

On the *Via Emilia* towards *Romagna*, five miles off *Bologna* on the
right hand lie moft pleafant Hills, beautified with Palaces, Gardens
and Fruit Trees, and fome Woods of Juneper the harbour of much
Foul, which Hills afford the fweeteft and largeft Olives of *Italy*, not
at all inferiour to them of *Spain*. Near wch. lies the Way leading to *Florence*

rence. **Near the** *Emilian* **Way also runs the River** *Savena,* **over which is built a Bridge of Brick, not far from which are discovered the ruines of another stately Bridge, which was raised at the cost of the Countess** *Matilda.* **On the right hand appear the feet of the** *Apeniues,* **with some Hills embellished with Towns and Villages. On the left is a good and fertile Plain, and the Road to** *Ferrara,* **and on one side of the** *Emilian* **Way, are the Ruines of the Antient City** *Quaterna,* **which was destroyed by the** *Bolonians,* **in the yeer 385. after a long Battail, and on the other side is the Castle** *Butrio,* **ten miles off which you finde the River** *Selero,* **over which is a Bridge of stone; near which stands the Castle** *San Pietro,* **built by the** *Bolonians,* **whose Fields afford plenty of Grain, Flax, and Fruit, and the Ferry no less gain ; on the right hand of** *Selero,* **stands** *Dozza,* **a Castle endowed with the title of a Count, belonging to the Family** *Campeggi* **in** *Bolonia,* **and** *Paradello* **a Convent of the Fryers of the third order of** *San Francesco,* **called** *Minimi,* **built with wonderfull cost and Artifice by Pope** *Giulius* **the second, tis thence to** *Imolo* **a mile**

Having perused all the Territory of *Bologna,* **nothing remains but the number of People, which what in the Territories with the Cities and Burroughs amount to 207797. Souls.**

Quaterna

San Pietro

Dozza

The Gests or Journies from *BOLOGNA* to *FLORENCE, SIENNA,* and *ROME*

TO go to *Florence,* you must travail South-East, out of the Gate *S. Steffano,* through a pleasant, and fertile Country, wherein rise some Hills, and having gone ten miles, you arrive at *Pianora,* a Town filled with Hosteries, then at *Loiano,* among the sharp Hills, somewhat farther lies *Scara,* a place much honoured by its Countryman *Romasciato,* a famous Souldier, *Petra Mala, & Fiorenzuola,* a new Castle built by the *Florentines:* Thence after passing the River, you must gain the top of the *Apenines* through a rough and laborious way having no repose in all that Straight three miles passage, till the arival at a little Hostery at the very top, on the left hand of which passage lies a profound Vally, so deep and so horrid, that it many times turns the brain of the Traveller to behold it, & hath occasioned some those in staggering whimses, to fall down to their inevitable ruine. Descending from whence you attain *Scarperia,* so called from its site, on the slopeness of the *Apenines,* whence the eye may behold the lovely places of *Tuscany:* Finally having travalled fifty miles from *Bologna* you reach *Florence.*

Pianora

Scarao

Scarperia

Fiorenza la Bella. FLORENCE *the Fair.*

FLorence doth not boast it self much of antiquity, being founded but an inconsiderable time before the Triumvirate, & divers are the opinions about its building, some will have it built by the *Fiesolani,* who considering the difficulty & sharpness of the ascent, & descent of the Mountain whereon *Fiesole* was built, by little and little abandoned *Fiesole,* and built their habitations in the plain near the Banks of *Ar-*

B b

no,

no. Others ſay by the *Fluentines* who here dwelt. As to its name, it was called *Florence,* either from its ſo great felicity, in the ſuddainneſs of its increaſe, like a Flower to its perfect beauty, or for that it was made a Colony to *Rome,* the Flower of the World. Tis ſeated in a plain, and is cut through in two parts by the River *Arno.* Tis compaſſed on the Eaſt and Northparts, in the likeneſs of a half Theatre by pleaſant Hills, and on the Weſt it hath a glorious Plain, extending it ſelf forty miles broad, placed between *Arezzo & Piſa,* aud is ſecured from the force of the Enemy by the *Apenines;* tis five miles in compaſs, and rather of a long than circular Form. Heretofore it had 4 principal Gates, and 4 Poſternes, when alſo it had 62. Towers the habitations of Gentlemen. Afterwards it was in great part deſtroyed by *Attila* King of the *Goths,* who ſlew ſome of the Citizens. After which the Walls were caſt down by the *Fieſolani,* and the barbarous, which moleſtations, enforced the Citizens to quit it and retreat to adjacent Caſtles, and ſo it remained wholy deprived of inhabitants till the year of the Incarnation of our Lord 802. When *Charles* the great from his Crownation as Emperor at *Rome,* returning for *France,* ſtayed there ſome daies, and the place being agreable to him he gave beginning to the Walls, and therein erected 150 Towers, one hundred braces or Yards in the heighth, and enjoyned all the diſperſed Citizens to re-inhabit it; from that time it augmented daily, and was governed in Liberty, being (for all that) many times infinitely perplexed with the wicked Factions of the *Neri* and *Bianchi,* the *Guelfi,* and *Gibellini.*

Antiently their Government was thus. They created two Conſuls for one year, giving them a Senate of one hundred Fathers wiſe men, afterwards this Order changed, and ten Citizens elected calling them *Antiani,* which order was alſo ſeveral times changed, through the differences between the Gentlemen and Citizens, and the Citizens and common people.

The Citizens by their Ingenuity heaped up much Riches, and that made their pride ſo great, that the one would not give place to the other. It ſubdued many Ciities of *Tuſcany* and *Romagna,* particularly *Piſa* a potent Republick is at preſent under one ſole Prince with it.

The ſereneſs and goodneſs of the Ayr generates many good Wits there, and their Ingenuity procures great Riches. It is divided (as aforeſaid) by the *Arno,* over which are built four magnificent Bridges. It hath plenty of all things; from the environing Hills, Plains, and the navigable River. It ſtands as it were in the heart of *Italy,* is the conſtant reſidence of its Prince, and its people are ſo induſtrious that there is ſcarce a Merchandizing City in the World without ſome *Florentine* Merchants, which gave occaſion to Pope *Boniface* the XI. to ſay that the *Florentines* were the 5th. Element; no City in *Europe* (except *Rome*) produced more Architectors, Painters, and Sculptors than this, whence tis that it abounds with admirable Palaces, Temples, Pictures, and Statues, upon one of the Bridges is the Gold-SmithsStreet, upon another of ſtately ſtructure the ſeaſons of the year, in Marble. Oppoſite to this ſtands a Column of an immenſe bigneſs, and upon the top thereof a Statue of Juſtice in Porphire, which *Coſmus* the firſt great Duke raiſed as a Trophe in that place, for that walking for paſtime, the newes there firſt reached him of the great

Victo-

Victory which the Marquefs *Marignano*, obtayned over *Pietro Strozzi*, in the yeer 1555 and with it *Sienna*, near it is the *Palazzo de Strozzi*, no lefs to be admired for the immenfity of its Fabricks, than for its rude Architecture. Here on the right lies the Merchants vault fupported with fayr Pillars, and before it a Brafen Bore, cafting forth Water; ftrait on is the *Piazza Maggiore*, or great place, in the midft whereof is the Statue of *Cofmus* the great Duke on Horfe back in Brafs with this infcription on each fide of the *Bafis*.

Cofmo Medici Magno, Etruriæ Duci Primo, Pio, Felici, Invicto, Ju-fto, Clementi, Sacræ Militiæ, Pacifque in Etruria Authori, Patri, & Principi Optimo, Ferdinandus F. Mag. Dux, Mag. Dux I.I.I. erexit. An. C IC. IC L X X X X I V.

behind this,

Profligatis hoftibus, in deditionem acceptis Senenfibus.   Plenis liberis Sen. Fl. Suffragiis Dux Patriæ renunciatur.
Ob. Zelam Religionis præcipuumque Juftitiæ Studium.

Between which Horfe and the *Piazzo Vecchio*, is a Fountain, and ronnd about its Laver the Family of *Neptune*, with his Colofs of Marble in the midft; bore up by fourHorfes, the whole not to be paralleld, much lefs excelled by humane Art.

The Porch in the fame *Piazza* is remarkeable for its Arch and Statues, one whereof is of *Judith* in Brafs, and in another ftone are pourtrayed three perfons, in feveral poftures, cut all out of the fame ftone reprefenting the Rape of the *Sabines*.

Oppofite unto the *Piazza* ftands the Royal Palace of the Duke, at the entrance into which, ftands a Coloffus of *David*, made by *Michael Angelo*, and another of *Hercules* treading on *Cacus*; within is a ftately Coutt fet about with Pillars of *Corinthian* Work, and over them painted the famous deeds of *Cofmus* the great Duke and all the places fubject unto that *Dutchy*, above them is a fpatious Hall with divers Statues, among them one of Pope *Leo* the tenth, another of Pope *Clement* the feventh, both of the Family of the *Medicies*, from whence the Dukes Gallery invites a view, in the lower ftory whereof fit the Courts of Juftice, with an Arcade to walke in, on each fide above are the fhops of the Dukes *Artifans*, In the uppermoft part are preferved as many wonders as things, fome to be admired for their richnefs, rarity, and Art, others for their antiquity, On each fide of the Gallery are placed above 80. Statues, among them that of the Idol brought from the Temple of *Apollo* at *Delphos* with this verfe on the Pideftal.

Ut potui huc veni Delpis & fratre relicto,

And that of *Scipio Africanus*, holding up his Gown under his Arm are moft admirable, over the Statues hang the Pictures of the moft famous Scholars and Souldiers of the modern times.

At the right handof this Gallery are feveral Stanzaes of Curiofities which none can behold without aftonifhment at the richnefs and variety of obferveable things.   Bb 2   In

In the firſt Room, ſtands the Tabernacle or Al
Lawrence Chapel, all of choice Marble, compacted
pretious ſtones of an ineſtimable valew.

In the ſecond is a Table with flowers and Bird
Colours of pretious Stones, with a Cabinet of 20
valew within which is the paſſion of our Saviour wit
ſtles all carved in Amber.

In the third is a Cabinet with *Calcidon* Pillars fi
Medals of Gold, and round about infinite other na
al curioſities, amongſt them the Nayl turned half
chimy, and the Emperors head cut on a Turquoiſe
nut; next is the Armory, and therein the habits a
Arms of ſeveral Ages and People, amongſt them t
habit, *Hannibals* Head-piece, and *Charlemains* Sword
a Magnet which attracts & ſupports fourſcore poun

In the laſt, is the curious Turnery of Ivory, and
tal Alablaſter, and in the Gardrobe are 12. Cubbar
and a ſervice of Maſſie Gold, and a Saddle emb
with Pearls and Diamonds, which with many oth
rioſities (a theme copious enough for a volume) d
of this Prince equal with any Kings in Chriſtendom

From the ſaid Gallery is a Corridor or private p
an admirable braſs Statue of *Perſeus*) to the prou
the other ſide of the River, where the Duke keep
Front is very Majeſtique, towards the baſis of D
midſt *Ionick*, in the uppermoſt *Corinthian*. In th
with Statues, and a Magnet of a prodigious greatn
Fountain. Its Gardens are moſt ſpatious, embelliſ
Walks, Labirynths, Fountains, wherein are Swans
Hares, and all other recreative Creatures. It alſ
wherein his Highneſs maintains all ſorts of Savage
ſeveral Stanzaes, as Lyons, Bears, Wolves, Ty
according to their ſeveral ſpecies there breed, and
order that all reſorting beholders are aſtoniſht at it.

The Streets are large, long, and ſtrait; paved wi
each ſide of them are many ſtately Palaces, bedec
tues, Fountains, &c. by which with its other ſing
City acquired the Surname of *Florence* the fayr.

The Chnrches are ſo much beautifyed, with th
tectture, Sculpture, Picture, and other Curioſities, th
ſcribe them particularly muſt write a volume, y
Temple *Santa Maria del Fiore*, muſt not be paſſed
Filino and *Giotto*, two excellent men in Limning
ly buried. Therein are the twelve Apoſtles cut in M
excellent Sculptors of that Age. The ſtupendiou
with the pieces of *Vaſari* and *Zucharo*, famous pai
Francesco Brunelesco at that heighth is ſo large that t
top will contain 16. perſons, the Steeple is all bui
rable Marble ſtones and garniſhed with Statues, v
famous Statuaries in emulation one of another. Be
the *Babtiſtery* built in an *Octogon*, antiently the
herein ſtands that Egregious Veſſel or Font of pretio

they baptize their Infants, whose four Gates of Brass are esteemed without their equal. Herein *Baldeffar Goffa* once Pope of *Rome* (depofed from the *Papacy*, at the Council of *Coftanza*) lies buried in an artificial Sepulcher of Brafs made by *Donatello*, with his effigies and these Letters. *Balthafar Coffa, olim Joannes vigefimus tertius.*

The noble Temple *Santa Maria Novella*, for its marvellous Structure may be compared to any other of *Italy*, which *Michael Angelo* was wont to call his *Venus*.

Among its other notable things appears the Sepulchre of the Patriarchs of *Conftantinople* who fubfcribed to the Council celebrated under *Eugenius* the fourth, near to which Church adjoyns the fumptuous Monaftery for the Fryers, wherein were celebrated certain feffions of A general Council, in the prefence of the Latin and Greek Church, the Pope, the Emperor and four Patriarkes.

The Mirrour of Art and wonder of this Age Saint *Laurence* Chapel is fo glorious, that who enters muft imagine himfelf in fome place above terreftrial, which is overlayed with fine polifht Stones, of all colours upon Earth dugg up within the Dukes Territories, twas built by *Cufmo Medici*, and in the midft of this Church ftands his Sepulchre with this Epitaph, *Decreto, publico, Patri Patriæ*, with many other fumptuous tombs, therein alfo is a Library (not defpicable) founded by Pope *Clement* the 7th. the Church *Santa Croce* hath a moft ftately Pulpit, in it is the fumptuous Sepulchre of *Leonardo Aretino*, and the Temple of *Michael Angelo Bonorota*, made by his own hand. Over his Urn ftand thofe three Arts he was fo renowned for; bewailing the lofs of their Patron. Herein alfo is a fayr Organ, fet up at the charge of *Cofmus* the great Duke, the very manufacture whereof coft 4000. Crowns. The Church *Santo Spirito*, is built with the ftrict rules of Architure, and fupported by vaft long Columns of Stone, and hath a fair Cloyfter for the *Jacobins*, which was painted by the *Greeks*, before the *Italians* knew that Art. The graceful Fabrick of the *Monaftery* of Saint *Mark*, hath a gracefull Chapel for the *Signori Salviati*, wherein is the Tombe of Saint *Antonio* Arch-Bifhop of *Florence*, and there one may read this Epitaph of *Ficus Mirandola* an eminent Scholar.

> *Joannes jacet hic Mirandula, cætera n orunt*
> *Et Tagus, & Ganges forfan, & Antipodes,*

The *Annunciade*, is a place of great Devotion, whither every feafon refort infinite people to a *Madenna*, drawn by the hand of Saint *Luke*, tis a magnificent Temple filled with ornaments of Gold and Silver Statues, gemmes and other rich gifts, it hath a fumptuous Monaftery, and in it a fair Library and Stndy. There are many fayr Churches which for brevity fake are omitted. It hath 37. Hofpitals, 44. Parifh Churches, 12 Priorates, 54. Monafteries of Nunns, 24 of Fryers, with other Confraternities of Children in great number, whence as alfo from the infinite number of Fryers of all Orders in this City, we may collect, that the *Florentines* are more enclined to Religion, than any other People of *Italy*.

This renowned Country hath been the Birth-place of many excellent Ingenuities, who have not onely been a glory to it, but to all

C c

Italy. Some whereof follow Saint *Antonio*, Arch-bishop of *Florence*, St.*Gionan Gualbarto*, St.*Andrea Carmelitano*, St *Filippo de Servi*, with others, who have either instituted new Religious Orders, or reformed the old. Four Popes, *Leon* the 10th. *Clement* the 7th. *Leon* the 11th. of the Family of the *Medici*, and *Clement* the 8th. of the house of *Aldobrandini*, with many other Cardinals, Bishops and other Prelates of the Court of *Rome*, many excellent Captains in War, among them *Pietro Strozzi*, grand Marshal of *France*. And infinite Persons excelling in Letters, as *Dante, Petrarca, Bocacccio, Cavalcante, Beniviedi, Politiano, Crinito, Ficino, Palmerio, Paffavanti, Cino del Garbo*, a Physician, *Macchiavel Accucfir, Gloffatori, Donato Acciaivolo*. And for Painters, Sculptors, and Architectors, it hath produced so many, that we may say those Arts are to them proper and connatural. It hath two Accademies, one for Painting, the other for the vulgar Tongue, whereof the *Florentines* are heads and Masters. We must not omit one good Argument of their state Abilities, which was that at one instant in the time of Pope *Boniface* the 9th. there resided 13. *Florentines*, as Embassadors from divers Princes at *Rome*. It hath several noble Families, whereof some are gone into *France*, where they dwell with Titles and Principalities, others to *Venice*, and others to *Rome*, who all live in honour. The City contains 85. thousand Souls.

For eight miles round about the City, there seems another *Florence* so full are the Fields speckled with Country Seats, some for publick use, as the sumptuous Monastery called the *Abbacy* of *Fiefole*, founded by *Cofmo Medici*, the Monastery of Saint *Domenick*, which yet retains the Episcopal Seat, one walk of Pyne Trees two mile long, and another of Ciprefes leading to *Pioggio*, with many more. And others for private as *Pratolino*, much spoken of, which *Francefco* the great Duke built, adorning it with Palaces, Statues, Pictures, and Fountains, so well contrived and difposed that tis worthily esteemed one of the pleafant places of *Italy*.

Two miles forth of *Florence* at the Foot of the *Apenines*, appears some Footsteps of the ancient City *Fiefole*, where formerly the South-fayers, and fortune-tellers inhabited. It was antiently of that power, that it gave affiftance to *Stilicone*, the *Roman* Captain, for the destruction of the *Goths*, whereof were then flain above one hundred thoufand. The premifes confidered, we may conclude there is no Province in *Italy* more furnifht with delightfull and well-peopled Cities, than that of the Great Duke, whofe Anceftors by uniting the States of three Republicks together, to wit, *Pifa, Florence*, and *Siena*, doth now entirely poffefs all *Tufcany*, the nobler part of *Italy*, his Revenue exceeds 100000. pound *fterl. per. Annum*.

SCARPERIA.

ON the way which leads to *Bologna* ftands *Scarperia*, being 16 miles from *Florence*, noted for Knives, Cizers, and other such like things, there made. And among those Mountains lies the moft fruitfull *Mugello*, Whofe Inhabitants, are called *Mugellini*. Here *Cofmus* retreated for his delight, when he was folemnly ftyled Duke of *Florence*, commanding a Fort and Palace to be built and environed them within a fpatious Wall, wherein he kept wilde beafts for the Chafe.

More

More forwards lies the Way to *Faenza*, and *Romagna*, near it begins the *Crefentino*, contained between the *Ronta* and *Arno*, reaching to *Arezzo*, well peopled and very fertile. And from the higeft Mountains, you may look down into the Vally *Ombrofe* where *Giovanni Gualberto* a *Florentine*, gave beginning to the Order named *Religione di Valle Ambrofa*, in the yeer of our Lord 1070. and alfo into *Umbria*.

On the North-Eaft part lies the Palace *Poggio*, of the great Dukes, a houfe fwarming with Statues, and rarities, and a Park for Beafts of Chafe, where is alfo a *Fortezza*. And oppofite to it lies the noble Caftle *Prato* accounted one of the firft four of *Italy*, here they make bread white as Snow, and here they keep with great devotion the Garter of the Virgin *Mary*, a little more near the *Apenines*, is *Monte Murlo*, much fpoken of for the taking thofe *Florentines*, which fled out of *Florence*, and there embodied, by *Aleffandro Vitelli*, Captain for *Cofmus* the Duke, which fecured his Principality.

PISTOIA.

AFter which, entring a lovely Plain, you meet the City *Piftoia*, twenty miles off *Florence*, which though little, is neatly compact and rich, and would have been better, had it not much groned under the factions of its own Citizens. Twenty miles of *Piftoia* ftands *Lucca*, which governs it felf in Liberty, and by the ftrength of its Wall, the Richnefs of Trade, and the Induftry of its own Citizens, maintains it felf well with all things neceflary, 'tis an antient City, and was made a Colony of the *Romans*. *Defiderius* the King built its ftrong Walls which with its fite enabled it to endure a fix moneths fiege by *Narfetes*; towards the Sea, ftand yet the footfteps of the Temple of *Hercules*, the River *Serchio*, runs clofe by *Lucca*, whence the famous baths of *Italy* are ten miles diftant.

Out of *Florence* towards the Weft in that fpatious Plain, ftands the Caftles *Empoli*, and *Fucecchio*, there is alfo a Lake of that name, as alfo *San Miniato al Todefco*, fo called for that 'twas built by certain *Germans* under *Defiderius* their King,

PISA.

COafting the River *Arno*, you attain *Pifa*, an antient City built long before *Rome* by the *Grecians*, and was one of the 12 Cities of *Tufcany*, it was powerfull at Sea, and obtained many victories againft the *Genovefi*, it fubdued *Cartagine*, conquered the Ifland of *Sardegna*, and delivered its King Prifoner to the Pope. It recovered *Palermo* in *Sicilia* out of the hands of the *Sarazens* who had long enjoyed it, it flew the *Sarazen* King of *Majorca*, It fent 40 Galleys in affiftance to *Almerico*, King of *Jerufalem*; againft the *Sarazens*, who poffeffed *Alexandria*. It greatly affifted the Popes in their adverfity. It was fo potent, happy, and rich, that Saint *Thomafo* treating of the four things, reckons it among the four moft potent Cities of *Italy*. But from that time that at the inftance and requeft of *Frederick Barbaroffa*, it captivated fo many Prelates of the *Romifh* Church, & two Cardinals which came from *France* to the *Lateranian* Council, it only decayed

Lucca

Cc 2
from

from bad to worſe, till it loſt Liberty and Power, yet in proceſs of
time by the reſidence of the Knights of *S. Stefano*, and the Univerſity,
it recovered and ſtill preſerves the Countenance of an honourable
City, *Plato* will have it well ſituated, being four miles then (now
eight)from the Sea, ſo that tis not placed upon the Sea ſhore, but near
it, not upon the Mountains but near them, in a Plain juſt ſo divided from the royal River *Arno*, as *Plato* fancies his City. Tis endowed with four things which create wonder, the Church of ſaint *John*,
the *Domo*, the Steeple, and *Campo ſanto*, which was raiſed with that
very holy Earth, which they brought home in their Galleys, when
50 of them were ſent to aſſiſt the Emperor in the recovery of the holy Land. On one ſide of it lies *Lucca*, on the other *Livorgeo*, or
Ligorne.   Twas deſtroyed by the *Florentines* in the yeer 1509.

Intending from *Florence* to *Siena*, you muſt go out at the *Porta Ro-*
mana, through which *Charles* the fifth entred after his Victory in *A-*
frick, and ſo paſſing by the Monaſtery *Certoſini*, attain *Caſſano*, *Taver-*
nelli, and *Staggia*, by a direct way, having pleaſant hills and fruitfull Valleys, on each ſide. In the way appears the Caſtle *Certaldo*, the
Birth-place of *Giovani Boccaccio*, the Prince of *Tuſcan* Poets, who dyed in the 62. yeer of his Age in the yeer of our Lord 1375. and was interred   in a Marble Tombe in the *Domo* of *Certaldo* with this Epitaph.

> *Hac ſub mole jacent cineres, ac oſſa Joannis.*
> *Mens ſedet ante Deum meritis ornata laborum*
> *Mortalis vitæ genitor Boccaccius illi*
> *Patria Certaldum, ſtudium ſuit alma Poeſis.*

Somewhat further ſtands the Bourg Saint *Geminiano*, famous for
its good wine *Vernace*. Tis adorned with fair Churches, noble Palaces, illuſtrious perſons, and a gentle people, built by *Deſiderius* King
of the *Longobardi*. Weſtward from which lies the antique City *Vol-*
terra, which was founded 100. yeers before the firing of *Troy*, and
500. before the building of *Rome*, tis built on a hill, the aſcent to
whoſe top is 3 miles, its Walls are of ſquared ſtones, 6 foot long, layed
& cemented without Mortar, It hath five gates & before each a Fountain of clear water & within them two other ſtately Fountains with
many antiet ſtatues & on thē old Epitaphs, it hath a rich Territory, is
ſubject to the great Duke, it produced *Perſio* the poet, and divers other
wits, beyond it lies the Sea. On its left hand lies *Anciſa* the Country
of St. *Francis* the Patriark, *Fighine* and other good places.

AREZZO.

TRavailing towards the Eaſt, you meet *Arezzo*, accounted one
of the antient twelve. The *Aretines* contributed 30000. Crowns
as many Celades with other Kinds of Weapons to the *Romans*, and
120000. buſhels of Wheat to furniſh the *Armada* of 40 Galleys, which
was to convoy *Scipio* againſt the *Carthaginians*.   It hath ſuffered many and many calamities, but with the government of *Coſmus* the
great Duke, it began to take breath and reſtore it ſelf. *Pliny* ſaies
their Veſſels of Earth were in his time eſteemed the beſt of *Italy*. *San*
Donato its Biſhop was there Martyred in the time of *Valentinian*
the Emperor, who baptized *L. Zembio* the Tribune, and then endowed

dow ed the Church of *Arezzo* wherein lies buried *S. Lorenzo* and *Pellegrino*, brothers and Martyrs, and *Gregory* the 10th. chief Bishop; the house of *Petrark*, is yet to be seen; there begins the State of the Church. On the direct way to *Siena*, stands *Poggibonzi*, a place noted for the perfumed Tobacco compoſed there, which the *Italians* take as profuſely in powder as the *Engliſh* in pipes, as alſo *Aſcia*, and near it *Siena*.

Peggibonzi

SIENA   Paolo V.

THis City was named *Siena*, from the *Galli Senoni*, who reſided there under *Brennus* their Captain, and built it on the back of the hill *Tuffo*, twas made a Colony by the *Romans*, and afterwards underwent the ſame miſery with the other Cities of *Tuſcanie*, In proceſs of time it recovered liberty, and therewith its former emulation with *Florence*, againſt whom it fought and obtained a glorious victory, after which it became ſubject to the *Petrarci*, its own Citizens, whome diſcarding it continued a free State till the yeer 1555. when the great Duke recovered it. Its ayr is very good and wholeſome. Its Inhabitants very courteous, who profeſs and ſpeak the purity of the *Italian* Language. without the *Porta Romana*, the City appears with a great deal of Majeſty, being beautifyed by the many Towers raiſed in honour of ſuch perſons as performed ſome eminent ſervice for the Common-Wealth, among theſe Towers (which yet retein the memory of its former freedome) that of *Mangio*, ſurpaſſeth for heighth, which though founded in the bottom of the *Piazza* out tops all the City, and ſerves for a Clock-houſe; from its top is an incomparable proſpect to the confines of *Tuſcany*; at the foot of this hideous ſtructure is a Marble Chapel to which adjoyns the Senate houſe built by the *Goths*, at one end whereof ſtands a column bearing *Remus* and *Romulus* ſucking a Wolfe in Braſs, the Arms of this City: Its *Piazza* lies in the heart of the City, ſo formed, that whoſoever paſſeth over it muſt be ſeen by all: In the midſt of it is a Marble Fountain whence iſſues ſweet Water out of the Wolves mouth: The whole City is paved with Brick: The houſes are for the moſt part built of Brick *alla Moderna*, the chiefeſt is that proud Palace built of ſquared ſtones by the Pope *Pius* the ſecond and the Arch-Biſhop, who is of the Family of the *Picolomenies*,

Among its Churches the *Domo* dedicated to the Virgin *Mary* is worth noting, for though in compariſon of others in *Italy* it be but ſmall, yet for the pains and charges which it muſt have coſt, tis inferiour to none, being both without and within of black and white Marble. The Facade is admirably garniſhed with Statues, about the inſide are the heads of all the Popes. The Pulpit is an unparallel'd piece, beſet with figures of Marble; but its ſingularity lies in the Pavement, wherein many parts of the ſacred hiſtory are ſo lively repreſented in ſeveral colours of Marble, that no pencil can come near it, though many Maſters take pattern from thoſe figures in ſtones: In it is a Chapel, wherein is kept the Arm of Saint *John* Baptiſt given to a Pope by the King of *Peloponeſus*.

In The royal Church of Saint *Domenick* in *Campo Regio*, is kept the head of *Santa Caterina* of *Siena*, and many Bodies of Saints, and near to it stands the Hospital where Pilgrims may have their full refreshment for several daies, wherein is remarkeable the diligence of the Attendants, in satisfying the Appetites & necessities of the poor and infirm; in the Chapel lies the Founder *B. Suforius*, as yet uncorrupted though nine hundred yeers since he dyed.

The Walls of *Siena* are of an exceeding compass yet but slight stocked with caper Trees, that Fruit growing best in Morter.

The City was reduced to the Faith of Christ by *S. Anfano* a *Roman* Citizen, who was afterwards beheaded; It particularly hath a great devotion to *Santa Maria* the Mother of God, as appears by the Motto round their Common Seal.

Salve Virgo, Senam Veterum, quæ cernis amænam.

Many illustrious Men hath this City afforded, as Saint *Fernard* the restorer of the Order of *Minorites*, the blessed *Giovanni Colombino* first Institutor of the Jesuites Order, Saint *Ambrogio de' Bianconi*, the Institutor of the Canons Regulars and of the Monks of Mount *Olivet*. Four Popes, as *Alexander* the third, who by his pious life and exceeding patience overcame four Anti-Popes, set up against him by *Frederick Barbaroffa*, *Pius* the first, and *Pius* the second of the Family *Picolomini*, and *Paolo Quinto* of the *Borghefi*, with many Cardinals, Bishops, Prelates, and Doctors, in all the Sciences most famous.

The Countrey about *Siena* is filled with all sorts of great Chase, so that Wilde Bore and other Venison in its season is commonly sold in Butchers shops. Its Territory is very pleasant and fruitfull, and in a word the City is one of the principal in *Italy*.

Mount Olivet

On the left hand at twelve miles distance Mount *Oliveto* discovers it self, much spoken of for the order of white Fryers of *Oliveto* taking its rise there, whereon is built a sumptuous Abbacy, and therein dwell a vast number of Monks devoted to the service of God, whence (the river also being past) you finde *San Querico*, so called from a Church dedicated to that Saint, and *Radicofano*, where *Defiderius* King of the *Longobardi* built a strong Fort, and the great Duke another, to whom they are now subject; here ends the patrimony which the Countess *Matilda* consigned the Church, whereof *Viterbo* is head. Between *San Quirico* and the Banks of the River *Orica*, stands the City *Pienza*, the Countrey of Pope *Pius* the second, and so called from his name. Further upon a high and rough Mountain stands *Chiufi*, one of the twelve Cities of *Tufcany*, where *Porfenna* King of the *Tufcans*, was buried, who there built a Labyrinth, wherein who entred without a clew of thread, was certainly buried; at present this City is depopulated.

Radicofano

Pienza

Chiufe

Monte Pulciano

Somewhat farther towards the North is *Monte Pulciano*, a City not very antient, but populous and rich; seated in a delightfull Country abounding with all things desireable. It gave birth to *Marcellus* the second chief Roman Bishop, and Cardinal *Bellarmine*, who wrote acutely upon the disputed controversies of all the Heresies; beyond which are many delightfull places.

On the other side of the Road which goes from *Quirico* near the River *Arbia*, are the Baths of *Petriolo*, and the mouth of the River *Affo*, near which are many fayr Bourgs, and the *Maremma* of *Siena*,

wherein

wherein is the City *Groffetto*, in the Jurifdiction of *Siena*, well fortified by the great Duke, and *Montamata*, where are great plenty of Acorns, and grain to dy Scarlet; under thefe Mountains lies the Bourg *Santo Fiore*, much honoured by the illuftrious houfe of the *Sforzaes*, where they have a Stately Palace, together with large poffeffions and Lands for hunting and other paftimes.

The Traveller is many times obliged to pafs the River *Paglia* in this Journey, which fometimes is dangerous, on the other fide of which lies *Aquapendente*, (fo called from its fite, on the hanging of a hill, and by it runs a rapid ftream) *San Lorenzo*, and *Bolfena* a good Town built out of the ruines of the antient City named *Urbs vulfimenfium*, then accounted one of the twelve chief ones of *Etruria*. Its Territory is very fertile, as may appear by the *Olive* Trees bearing in the firft yeer planting according to *Pliny*: Here they reverenced the Body of the Virgin *San Chriftina*, who being caft into the *Paglia*, for the faith, thence returned without the leaft hurt, leaving the track and impreffion of her Foot on the ground, which appears to this day; here alfo happened the great miracle of the confecrated hoaft, which being in the hands of the Prieft, (who doubted the truth of it) of a fuddain bled extreamly, and fo all bloody was carried to *Orvieto*, where with great honour tis preferved in the *Domo*; in the River is an Ifland delightfome and fertile, and a little Church *Maufcolum* or burying place of the *Farnefi*; here the prudent and religious Queen *Amalafunta* was wickedly flain, at the command of *Theodato* King of the *Oftrogoths*, whofe gravity and fweetnefs of fpeech was fuch, that arguing with condemned perfons on death, fhe fo much convinced them of the good, that they little feared the punifhment of it.

On the left fide of the faid Lake is *Orvieto*, *Cagnarea*, and *Tevere* all Cities. On the right the City *Soana*, the birth place of Pope *Gregory* the 7th. at prefent almoft uninhabited, *Petigliano*, and *Farnefo*, appertainning to the noble Family of *Farnefi* in *Rome*; fomewhat further is the City *Caftro*, of the faid *Farnefies*, fo furrounded with Rocks and Cavernes, that it appears to the Enterers rather an obfcure Den for wilde beafts, than habitations for Men.

From whence walking towards the Sea, you finde *Orbello*, *Talamoni*, *Monte Argentaro*, and *Port Ercole*, all ftately places fubject to the King of *Spain*. On whofe right-hand they fhew the noble Caftle *Tufcanello*, fubject to the *See* of *Rome*, fo antient, that (if it be permitted to beleeve them) they fay it was built by *Askanius* Son of *Eneas*, and upon one of the ports appears an old Marble with an Epitaph carved thereon, fhewing his Original and defcent. As alfo the City *Cornetto*, by the antient *Tufcans* dedicated to *Pan*, whofe ftately antique Walls, fhew it to have been an honourable City; Pope *Gregory* the fifth was born there, *Giovanni Vitalefco* a Cardinal, and Father *Mutio* a Jefuite, with many other famous Men; feaven miles off *Cornetto* ftands *Civita Vecchia* on the Sea fhore, a fortified Port.

On the left hand of the *Via Regia*, lies *Horti*, an antient City which is the *Tufcan* boundarie.

Further off is *Tevere*, and the Lake *Bafanello*, in Latine, *Lacus Vadimonis*, and hereabouts ftands *Baffanello Caftello*, *Magliano*, *Civita Caftellana*, *Galefe*, and the *Via Flaminia*, which leads from *Rimini* to *Rome*.

In the way from *Bolsena* to *Rome*, is the Grove *Monte Fiascone*, where the Antients with great ceremony and solemnity were wont to sacrifice to the Goddess *Giunone*, near which stands the old City *Monte Fiascone*, which was a long time besieged by *Camillus*, who was not able to reduce it, for the strength of its site. Its Territory yeelds *Moscatella.*

Monte Fiascone being passed, you enter a large and pleasant Plain, in which stands *Viterbo*, antiently called *Vetulania*, but *Desiderius* the King having inclosed it, *Longhola Tuffa*, and *Turrenna*, within one Wall, by his *Edict*, yet to be read in a white Marble Table in the Palace of *Viterbo*, commanded it to be called *Viterbo*; tis head of the Church Patrimony, and behind it lies *Monte Cimeno*. Tis adorned with stately Edifices, amongst which the *Domo* is famous, where four Popes ly buried, *John* the 21. *Alexander* the 4th. *Adrian* the 5th. and *Clement* the 4th. and the Church *Santa Rosa*, wherein that Saints body is kept entire, & an admirable Fountain, casting out great quantity of water. This City was a long time subject to the *Vecchi* and *Gotti*, its Citizens, who driven out, it submitted to the Pope. Tis well inhabited with a civil people, and abounds with Corn, Oyl, Wine, and Fruits; in its Territory are eleven Rivers, which store it with excellent Fish. It wants not Baths of warm water, among the rest those of *Bolicano* are named for their Miraculous virtue. A mile forth the City stands the Church *Quierria* dedicate to the Virgin *Maria*; finally it hath afforded Men of excelling Judgements.

From this City you ascend the Mountain *Viterbo*, called *Mons Cyminus* by the Latins, upon which is the Castle *Canepina*; near thereto stood formerly the Castle *Corito*, built by *Corito* King of *Tuscany*, whose foundations yet remain, there also was then a thick and terrible Wood, through which none durst pass, no more than the *Calidonian* or *Hercinian* Wood, but at present the Trees are cut and a way comodiously layed out. At the Foot of this Mountain towards the South, is the Lake *Vico*, in Latin called *Lacus Cyminus*, near it stands the Village *Viro*, and the Castle *Soriano*, where there was an inexpugnable Fort, whence for 60, yeers the *Brittons* Souldiers could not be expelled.

Pursuing the way towards *Rome*, you finde *Ronciglione*, which hath a lovely Fountain, and *Caprinica*, inhabited by 500. Families; beyond which lies *Sutri* an antient City, built (as is believed) by the *Pelasgi* a *Grecian* people, before *Saturnus* came into *Italy*. The *Romans* taking the advantage of this City, assaulted the *Tuscans* and overcame an Army of 60: thosand *Tuscans Spoletines* and *Ombri*: Its ill ayr renders it near uninhabited. Beyond *Ronciglione* lies *Caprarola*, a Castle of the *Farnlfies*, where whatever can be desired for Recreation is competently provided for, by Cardinal *Alexandro Farnese.*

Not far distanr from it is *Civita* a City now of smal importance, though antiently because they would not assist the *Romans* (then afflicted by *Hannibal*) we find them by the *Romans* condemned *al Doppio.*

Passing on the *Via Regia*, one meets *Rosolo* a Bourg adjacent to a Lake of immense profundity, & two miles beyond it *Campagnana*, and upon the same way a standing Pool, where was *Cremera* a Castle built by the *Fabii* and destroyed by the *Vesenti*, here were slain in one day
by

by the said *Vesenti*, 500. Servants, and 300. persons of that Family, for having privatly complotted an insurrection for their Country *Rome* against them, one Childe sleeping in a Cradle escaped and became the restorer of the *Fabii* in *Rome*. More forward stands the Town *Baccano*, and the Wood called *Bosco di Baccano*, which was lately a harbour for *Assassinates* and other people disposed to ill, whence it grew into a proverb when we would advise any one to stand upon his, guard to say. *Perche siamo nel Bosco de Baccano*, but through the vigilance and care of the late Popes, tis almost a secured passage.

On the right-hand stands *Anguillara* a Town of much Fame, whose Lords having behaved themselves gallantly have acquired to themselves and Country eternal honour. The *Signori Orsini* possesse it, and *Bracciano*, which is entitled a Dutchy. From the aforenamed Lake runs the River *Arone*, whence the Romans convey by pipes the water they called *Sabatina*, from the Lakes name *Sabatina*. Towards the Sea lies the Monastery *Santo Severa*, made now a Fort, and *Ceri* a Castle upon the shore. On the left-hand of the *Via Regia*, lies the *Via Flaminea*, and six miles beyond *Beccano Ijola*, then *Storta*, two Towns, and thence tis seaven miles to *Rome*. One may also travail from *Bologna* to *Rome*, on the *Via Emilia*, and so pass *Imola*, *Faenza*, *Forli*, *Cesena*, and *Rimini*.

IMOLA.

Imola called in Latine *Forum Cornelii*, enjoyes a good Ayr, a fruitful Territory, a commodious situation for all things, *Narsetes* in the yeer of Christ, 550. destroyed it, but *Dasone* second King of the *Longobardi*, restored it, and called it *Imola*, *Galeazzo Sforza*, Son of *Francis* Duke of *Milan* possessed it, and gave it in Dowry to *Girolamo Riario Savonese*, in *Anno* 1473. some time after twas taken forcibly by *Cesar Borgia*, Son of Pope *Alexander* the 6th. finally (after several other Lords) it became under the power of the Church, who yet keep it in peace. *Martial* the famous Poet, resided here for some time, as may be drawn from his verses, and many Illustrious persons were born here.

COTIGNOLA.

BEtween *Imola* and *Faenza*, stands *Cotignola*, a Castle small, but strong, near the River *Senio*, encompassed with thick Walls, and profound Dikes; the Castle was built by the *Forlevesi*, and *Faentini*, but the Walls and Ditches by *Giovanni Aguto*, Captain and Standard-bearer to the *Roman* Church, to whom twas given by Pope *Gregory* the 11th. It was the Birth-place of *Sforza*, *Attendolo*, the first of the *Sforzescan* Family, who wrought himself at a Pickax, and yet in less than one hundred yeers his line and Family, hath yeelded one Empress, many Queens, Marqueses, Dukes, Counts, Captains, Bishops, Arch-Bishops, Cardinals, and other eminent persons.

FAENZA.

*F*Aenza is divided by the River *Lamone*, which passeth between the Bourg and the City, where there is a strong bridge of Stone, which conjoyns the City with the Bourg, and the *Via Emilia*. Tis ancient, and the first Founders are unknown; it enjoys a serene healthfull Ayr, a fertile Territory, and a people good-natured and lovers of their Country. Here they make the best and finest Vessels of Earth of all *Italy*. It hath produced men eminent in all the Sciences. It was several times destroyed by *Totila* King of the *Goths*, *Frederick Barbarossa*, and by a Captain of the *Brittones*, but *Frederick* the second Nephew of the first, built that Fort, cast down and levelled the Walls in rhe yeer 1240. which now are seen, for that by their fidelity to the Church, they gave him great difficulty to take it: The *Manfredi* then got it, and rebuilt the Walls, from them the *Bolonians* took it, from them *Mainardo Pagano*, its Citizen, a great Captain, and from him the *Venetians*, from whom after the rout, they received at *Giarad' Adda* by *Lewis* the 12th. King of *France*, it returned again to the devotion of the Church, under whome it hath ever since continued.

BRISIGELLA.

*T*His Town is seated in part on a Plain, and in part on the side of a hill, it hath two Forts, the one on the East called the Tower, where with the touch of a Bell they give notice how many Horses enter, the other on the West, both set at the outmost part of the Town. It hath two Fountains, the Water of the one so sweet and light, that none is accounted better, the other so gross and heavy, that they give it not to their Beasts, but account it only fit for cooling their Wine, and cleansing and dying their silks, which shine more here than elsewhere, and that is attributed to the crudity of this water. Its Territory is called *la Valle d' Amone* from the River so named, which having its sourse from the top of the *Alps* of *Florence* with little water in a short course driving Mills, runs thorow the Valley to *Faenza*.

This Valley and Territory contains 49. Villages, every one having its own Parish, and a sufficient allowance for its Pastors. The Farmers are rich and civil, they muster 800. Men, who are well exercised youth, and the best armed of any in the Ecclesiastick State. Which Villages are all contained under the name *Bresigella*.

The said Valley is so fertile in Wine, Oyl, Corn and other necessaries, that though there be 18000. Souls, yet one yeers crop affords sustenance enough for all them for two yeers, were it not exported into other Countreys.

It hath one noble Palace belonging to the *Signori Spadi*, which hath all the commodities of Church, Fishponds, Fountains, Gardens, Vineyards, Wood for Foul, Conservatories for Snow, with all sorts of trees of exquisite fruit, Citrons, Lemons, Oranges, Pynes, and other delights that may be required, & this is alwaies so well accommodated with all necessaries for the Kitchin, houshold-stuff, and
Plate

Plate, that whenever any Prince or Embaſſador arrives, they need not tranſport thither the leaſt thing, there is one Oake which five men cannot brace.

This Town hath one eminent Collegiate for the Prelates; every Wedneſday they keep here a Market, ſo great for all things, that it attracts infinite People, for which they pay no toll. It flouriſhed in Arms two Ages paſt, through the nobility, generoſity, and Valour of the Family of *Naldi*, the ſtatues of *Vicenſo* and *Dioniſio Naldi*, are in *Venice* erected. And in Religion and Learning, by many famous Men.

The Voyage or Journey from *MILAN* to *CREMONA*, to *MANTOVA*, to *FERRARA*, and to *RIMINI*.

IF you would ſee the places, diſtant from the *Via Emilia*, when you are arrived at *Lodi*, you muſt go towards the *Adda* Eaſtward, and at twelve miles diſtance meet *Caſtiglone*, and ſee Caſtle *Novo*, and *Pizzichotone*, a famed Place, for that *Francis* the firſt King of *France*, being taken Priſoner, by the Imperialiſts, under *Pavia*, was reteined there, till by Order of the Emperor *Charls* the fifth, they embarked him at *Genoua* for *Spain*, hence tis but 15. mile to *Cremona*, all good and direct even way.

CREMONA the Faithfull.

CRemona is built on the banks of the *Poe*, in the 7th. Climat, on the Weſt parts of *Italy*, tis eight miles in circuit, environed with Walls Baſtions, and Ditches, and hath one Cittadel on the Eaſt part, the moſt ſtupendious, ſtrong and formidable work in all *Italy*. Its firſt Founders are not known, but their judgements approved for its good Ayr. It was a good Colony of the *Romans*, and alwaies maintained ſuch fidelity to its Princes, that among the Cities of *Italy* it merited the ſurname of faithfull. In the time of the Triumvirate of *Auguſtus*, *Antony*, and *Lepidus*, it ſuffered much miſery, its Territories being divided alſo among the Souldiers, whoſe neighbourhood to *Mantoua*, made it participate in miſery, and cauſed *Virgil* to lament in his 9th. Ecloge, *Mantoua vel miſeræ nimium vicina Cremonæ*.

Cornelius Tacitus relates its then wofull ſufferings. Afterwards in *Anno* 630. it was all caſt down by the *Gothes*, *Longobards* and Slaves and 600. yeers, after that deſtroyed by *Frederick Barbaroſſa*, and depopulated. But afterwards it was reſtored and amplified, and governed in liberty, till through civil diſcords *Vberto Palavicino* got the dominion, who driven out, certain leſſer Lords kept it in ſervitude, as now *Cavadabo*, now the *Ponzoni*, now the *Fonduli*, now the

Viſconti, whoever of them was conqueror got it , and with the conquered it alwaies ſuffered. Alſo the *Venetians*, *French*, and *Sforzeſchi* had it by Arms, but now the King of *Spain* reigns in it, and maintains in great tranquillity.

Sigiſmond the Emperor to gratifie *Gabrino Fondalio*, granted it licenſe for a publique Univerſity, with all ſuch privileges, immunities and exemptions, as thoſe of *Paris* or *Bologna*, enjoyed.

The ordinary buildings are ſo great, that they may be termed Palaces, reared with great expenſe and excellent Architecture. It hath broad ſtreets, with Orchards, Gardens, and Mills as well within as without the City, a Chanel for driving them being brought from the River thorow the City.

It hath one Tower ſo high that it is reckoned among the wonders of *Europe*, which was built in the yeer 1284. Upon it at one inſtant were, Pope *John* the 22th. *Sigiſmoud* the Emperor, with *Gabrino Fondulio*, Lord of the City, who afterwards was ſad at the heart , that he had not precipitated the Emperour and Pope to eternalize his memory, as did *Heroſtrato*, who only to commemorate his name gave fire to and burnt that ſtupendnous Temple of *Diana*, built in *Epheſus* at the common charge of all the Potentates of *Aſia*, in two hundred yeers. It hath a Cathedral with a good Revenue, and many other ſtately Churches, wherein are kept many Reliques of Saints , and much riches, ſeveral Hoſpitals and other pious places.

The Families of *Cremona*, are for the moſt part deſcended from the *Romans*, who there made a Colony, others from the veterane ſouldiers, who for reward of their Labours had houſes & Lands there aſſigned them, and others from the *Goths*, *Longobardi*, *French*, *Germans*, and other people of *Italy*; it hath given birth to many eminent *Eccleſiaſticks*, Lawyers, Phyſicians, Souldiers, and Poets. The people are of an induſtrious and accute wit, and have invented ſeveral ſorts of Stuffs, Silks and Clothes, and make excellent Swords.

Without the Gate *Puleſelia*, ſtands the Church *San Guglielmo*, where is a large Pond which did formerly contain troubled and ſtinking water, but *San Domenick* and *Francis*, who dwelt there, making the ſign of theCroſs over it, they were thereby miraculouſly converted into clear aud ſweet waters.

Near the *Porta San Michaele*, ſtood a Temple dedicate to the Goddeſs *Februa*, whereof nought appears now. Cloſe by the Walls runs the noble River *Oglio*. On its Weſt part lies nhe Territory of *Lodi*, on the North *Bergamo* and *Breſcia*, on the Eaſt *Mantoua*, and on the South *Piacenza*.

Between Towns and Hamlets this City poſſeſſeth 41. places, and all its Country round about is a plain planted with trees in excellent order with Vines clinging to them, and moſt productive of all grains herbage and other neceſſaries.

Piadona

From *Cremona* to *Mantoua*, leads a direct even road, and upon or near it lye *Piadena*, the Country of *Bartolomeo Platina*, cloſe by which paſſeth the *Oglio*, *Caneſdo*, where the *Oglio* ſpends it ſelf in the *Poe*, the Caſtles *Aſola*, and *Acquanegria*, *Bozzolo* a Town, and *San Martino* where *Scipion Gonzaga* the Splendor of the College of Cardinals lies buried. Then the River paſſed which croſſeth the Road, you leave

Gazuolo

the Bourg *Marcheria*, and *Gazuolo*, where there is a ſumptuous and

royal

royal Palace of the *Gonzaghi*, whose also are the 3 Castles, from *Gazu-olo*, to *Mantoua* twelve miles.

But the way from *Cremona* to *Mantona*, on the left side of the *Poe* lies thus, first to the Town *San Giovanni*, and *Ricardo*, then to *Ponzono*, *Gusnola*, and *Casal Maggiore*, and then to *Sabioneda*, an imperial City, very fair and stately, a draught whereof was taken by order of the Duke *Vespasiano*. Beyond which lies *Viadona*, and *Pomponesco*, where lies the passe over the *Poe*, whence tis eight mile to *Mantoua*, in the way are *Montecchio*, a mannor of the *Palavicini*, *Colorno* under the *Parmesans*, the Castle *Bresegello* of the Dokes of *Estè*, formerly a City, but destroyed by the *Lougobardi*, whose King *Alboino* there, slew *Totila* King of the *Gothes*, and by that victory made himself Lord of *Italy*, *Gonzaga*, where the Duke of *Mantoua* hath a noble Palace, *Reggio*, *Huolara*, *Luzzara*, and *Guastallo* entitled with a Principality, thence to *Borgo Forte*, and so to *Mantoua*.

MANTOVA

For its antiquity gives place to no City of *Italy*, being founded not only before *Rome*, but before the destruction of *Troy*, (which happened according to *Eusebius*, Saint *Jerome* and others, 430. yeers before the building of *Rome*) *Leandro Alberti*, shewes that *Mantoua* was built 1183. yeers before the coming of our Lord into the flesh. And as it was more antient than the rest, so was its Original more noble, being founded by *Ocno Bianoro*, the most antient King of *Tuscany*, who was Son of *Tiberino* King of *Tuscany*, and *Manto Tebena* his Queen, and so called it *Mantoua* from the name of his Mother. It was first inhabited by three noble people, the *Tebani*, *Veneti*, and *Toscani*, as *Virgil* the Prince of Poets celebrating the noblenes of this his Country testifies in his 10. book of his *Æneades*.

Ille etiam patriis agmenciet Ocnus ab oris
Fatidicæ Manthus, & Tusci filius amnis,
Qui muros, matrisque dedit tibi Mantoua nomen.
Mantoua Dives avis, sed non genus omnibus unum.
Gens illi triplex, populi sub gente quaterni
Ipsa caput populis Tusco de sanguine vires.

Tis seated among the Marishes created by the River *Mencio*, is strong by nature and art, large and well built, adorned with sumptuous Palaces and fair Churches, noble Piazzaes, spatious recreative places, and direct streets. Tis a merchandizing City, and copious of all trading through the conveniency of the waters. The people are of an acute genius, and not less disposed to Learning, Arms, and all Sciences, than to Traffick and Merchandizing.

In the Church of the reverend Fathers of Saint *Domenick*, is the Tomb of *Giovanni de Medici*, Father of *Cosmus* great Duke of *Tuscany*, where may be read this Epitaph.

Joannes Medices hic situs est inusitatæ virtutis
*   Dux, qui ad Mincium tormento ictus, Italiæ*
*   fato, potius quam suo cecidit. 1526.*

In the Church of the *Carmelites* lies *Batista Spagnuolo*, General of that order, with this Epitaph.

Reverend. P. Magister Baptiste Mantuanus Carmelita, Theologus, Philosophus, Poeta, & Orator Clarissimus, Latinæ, Græcæ, & Hebraicæ linguæ peritissimus.

In the sumptuous Temple Saint *Andrea*, is some of the pretious bloud of our Lord, and the body of *San Longino* the Martyr, *Montigna Padouano* lies likewise buried here with this Inscription.

Ossa Andreæ Mantiniæ famosissimi Pictoris cum duobus filiis in sepulchro per Andream Mantiniam nepotem ex filio constructo.

And underneath are these two verses.

Esse parem hunc noris, si non præponis Apelli,
    Enea Mantiniæ, qui simulacra vides.

In the *Duomo* (where the Ingenuity of *Giulio Romano* a famous Architector hath expatiated it selt) lies the entire body of *San Anselmo* Bishop of *Lucca*. In *San Egidio*, lies *Bernardo Tasso*.

Mantoua hath eight Gates, is in compass four miles, hath in it 50. thousand Souls, and the aforesaid Lake or Marish, lies 20. miles round it, near it is the Royal Palace of *Te*, built by *Giulio Romano*.

Five miles off *Mantoua* West-ward, stands a Temple dedicate to the Virgine *Mary*, filled with presents, and vows, wherein lies the body of *Baldassar Castiglione* in a fayr Tomb.

St. Benedict

Twelve miles distant from it South-ward, is the magnificent and sumptuous Monastery of Saint *Benedict*, seated in a Plain near the *Poe*, which was built by *Boniface, Marquess* of *Mantoua*, Count of *Conossa*, and Uncle of *Matilda*, in the yeer of our Saviour 984. which for its Magnificense, Riches, and sumptuousnefs of building, and what more imports, for its observance in Religion, antecedes all the other Monasteries of *Italy* The Fryers *Benedictines* have possessed it for 200 yeers, from whom have issued many Religious, filled with sanctity, good doctrine, and grave customs. Its possessions traverse a great space of ground, and from the privileges of Pope *Pasquale* the second, we may collect they had dominion in spirituals and temporals, over the Towns *Guernelo* and *Quistello*, with 38. parish Churches in the Diocess of *Mantoua, Luca, Bologna, Ferrara, Parma, Malamocco, & Chioza*, The most illustrious Countess *Matilda*, (whom none comes near for her signal benefits conferred on the *Roman* Church)being 69. yeers old here finisht her days, in the yeer 1161. and was layed in a Marble Sepulchre in the Chapel of the blessed Virgin, which being opened 320. yeers after, her body was found unperisht and untouched, her Effigies upon a Mare (like unto a man) stands upon her Tombe, in a long red Gown, and a Pomgranade in her hand, where among her other Epitaphs, this old one may be read.

Stirpe, opibus, forma, gestis, & nomine quondam
Inclyta Mathildus, hic jacet astra tenens.

In that part of the Monaftery where now is the common Kitchin below, and Graneries above, was the Palace of *Matilda*; It hath as much Land as 382. yoke of Oxen can till. It hath a Rampart goes round a great part of its Lands about, 7 miles long, which coft in raifing above 27000. Crowns], which in *Anno* 1560. was made in a few moneths to ftop the inundations of the *Poe*.

Two miles beyond *Mantoua* at the mouth of the River *Mincio*, which iffues from the Lake, and goes to *Ferrara*, ftands the Bourge *Ande* now called *Pietole*, where *Virgil* was born, beyond that *Hoftia*, and *Roveredo*, and then *Lago Scuro*; where you imbark for *Venice* ; hence after three miles travail you arrive at *Ferrara*.

FERRARA.

THis City is feated on the Banks of the *Poe*, which wafheth it on the Eaft & South part, tis garnifhed with ftately and fump tuous ftructures, and fpatious and noble Piazzies which was firft paved with brick, by the Marquefs *Lionello*, filled with noble Families and rich Citizens, and tis moreover famous for the Univerfity here eftablifhed by the Emperor *Frederick* the fecond, in defpight of the *Bolonians*. And although this City cannot boaft its antiquity from the *Trojans*, *Grecians* or *Romans* (being not a thoufand yeers fince twas walled by order of the Emperor *Mauritius*) yet through the diligence and love of its Princes, tis fo increafed in Edifices and Riches, that it hath deferved a place amongft the chief Cities of *Italy*, which increafe happened under the Illuftrious Family of *Efte*, *Giulio Cefar della Scala* a famous Poet commends *Ferrara* thus.

Inclyta quæ patulo fruitur Ferraria cœlo,
  Reginas rerum limine ditat aquas ;
Aurea nobilitat, ftudiorum nobilis ocii
  Ingenia, audaci pectora prompta majus,
Magnanimique Duces, genus alto è fanguine Divum.

And this fhall fuffice touching *Ferraras* antiquity, which in the yeer 1598. came into the power and patrimony of *S. Petre*, by the induftry and pains of Pope *Clement* the eighth.

In the *Duomo* lies Pope *Urban* the 8th. in a fumptuous Marble monument, near which one may read of the learned Man *Gregorio Geraldo*, what enfues, *viz.*

Quid hofpes adftas? tymbion
Vides Gyraldi Lilii,
Fortunæ utramque paginam
Qui pertulit, fed peffime

Est usus, altera nihil
Opte ferente Apolline.
Nil scire refert amplius
Tua aut sua, in tuam rem abi.
Lil. Greg. Giraldus Frothon. Apostol. mortalitatis memor
Anno 72. V. S. P. Cur. 1550.

In the Church of Laint *Domenick,* near the Gate, is a stately Tomb with this inscription.

D. M.

Nicolao Leoniceno Vicentino, qui sibi Ferrariam patriam maluit, ubi an-
nos 60. Italos, & provinciales magna celebritate Græcè, & Latinè
instituit, continua serie apud Principes Estenses magno in honore ha-
bitus, Vnus omnium magis pectore, quam lingua philosophiam profes-
sus rerum naturæ abditissimarum experientissimus, qui primus herba-
riam bene desitam, & sylvam rei medicæ injuria temporum negli-
genter habitam in dispositionem magna ope mortalium revocavit, in
barbaros conditores pertinaciter stylum perstrinxit, & studio verita-
tis, cum omni antiquitate acerrimè depugnavit, annos natus sex &
nonaginta, cum jam æternis monumentis in arcem immortalitatis sibi
gradum fecisset, homo esse desiit Alphonsus Estensis, Dux Tertius, &
S. P. Q. Ferrariens. benemerito posuere, sexto idus Junii. M. D.
XXIV, Bonaventura Pistopholo grato ipsius discipulo pocurante.

In the noble Church of the *Benedictines*, upon a Column of the Prince of *Italian* Poets, may be read thus.

Ludovico Areosto Poetæ Patritio Ferrariensi Augustinus Mustus tanto vi-
ro, ac de se bene meren. Tumulum, & Effigiem marmoream, ære pro-
prio P. C. Anno salutis M. D. LXXXIII. Alphonso Secondo Duce,
vixit annos 56. obiit anno sal. 1533. 8. Idus Junii.

And a little below, that of the composition of *Lorenzo Frizoli.*

Hic Areostus situs est, qui comico,
Aures sparsit Teatri Urbanos sale
Satyraque mores strinxit, acer improbos
Heroa culto, qui ferentem carmine,
Ducumque curas cecinit, ac prælia
Vales corona dignus unus triplici,
Cui trina constant: quæ fuere vatibus
Gratiis, Latinis, vixque Hetruscis Singula.

In the Cloyster of the *Carmelites* stands a Marble Tablet with a memorial of *Alanardo* thus.

Jo. Manardo Ferrariensi viro uni omnium integerr. ac sanctis. Philosopho,
& Medic. doctis. qui ann. P. M. LX. continenter tum docendo, &
scribendo, tum innocentis. medendo omnem medicinam ex arce bona-
rum literar. fædè prolapsam, & in barbar. potestatem, ac ditio-
nem redactam prostratis, ac profligatis hostium copiis identidem, ut

Hydra

*H)dra renascentibus in antiquum priſtinumque ſtatum, ac nitorem
ſtituit. Lauream omnium bonorum conſenſu adeptus IIII. & LXX.
ann. agens omnibus omnium ordinum ſui deſiderium relinquens hu-
miliſc hoc ſarcophago condi juſſit.
Julia Maranda uxor. mæſtiſs. quod ab eo optabat poſuit
Hæc brevis exuvias magni capit urna Manardi
　　Nam virtus latè docta per ora volat.
Mens pia cum ſuperis cæli colit aurea templa
　　Hinc hoſpes vitæ ſint documenta tuæ.
M. D. XXXVI. Men. Mart.*

The Journy from *FERRARA* to *VENICE*.

CHIOZA.

PArting from *Ferrara* five miles upon the *Poe*, ſtands *Francolino*,
where embarking, and paſſing by the ſeveral Towns *Ronigo*, *Ta-
poza*, *Corbola*, and *Arriano*, you embark on the Sea, near the *Porte Goro*, whence ceaſting the Land North-ward, you ſhall arrive at *Chioza* a City which hath a good Port, The people conſiſt for the moſt
part of Mariners Fiſhermen, and good Gardiners. *Chioza* is famous for
the deeds of Arms performed there between the *Genoveſi*, and the
Venetians and was much increaſed by the people of *Eſte* and *Monſelice*,
who fled thither to to ſave themſelves at the inroade of the *Hunns* In
the time of *Ordelaſo Faliero*, Duke of *Venice*, the Biſhoprick of the
City *Malimacco*, (overflowed by the Sea) was tranſferred thither, and
for that cauſe twas created a City. On the Eaſt part of *Chioza* in the
Sea lies a Ridge of Sand in the Sea in the nature of a Rampart
poſe to oppoſe the fury of the *Adriatick* Sea, 30 miles long from
South to North. Tis almoſt incredible what vaſt quantities of Comodities are extracted from it to *Venice*, which are there produced
by the ingenuity of the Gardiners, the fertility of the Soyl, and the
natural Orchards full of greens whereof and of gardens it moſt conſiſts, which are ordered exactly well. From *Chioza* ſayling Southward
you ſe *Ancona*, *Peſaro*, *Rimini*, *Ceſenna*, and *Ravenna*, but going by
Land, diſcover many Ports, as *Goro*, *Bebe*, *Volano*, *Magnavacea*, *Pri-
mano*, and *Brondolo*.

From *Chioza* to *Venice* are 20. miles, in which ſpace ſtands *Malomocco*, an Iſland heretofore enobled by the Duke of *Venice* his Reſidence, there is the *Porto Malomocco*, which through its profundity
is rendered dangerous. And alſo *Poveggia*, now an uninhabited Iſland,
but at the firſt *Venetians* planting, well-peopled, in it ſtill remains
a miraculous Crucifix, together with many other ſmall Iſlands, Monaſteries, Hoſpitals, Orchards, and Gardens, between which lies the
moſt noble City *Venice*, who ſcarce finds a Parallel.

The Journy from *FERRARA* to *RAVENNA*, and to *RIMINI*.

IN the Suburbs of *Ferrara* towards *Oſtro* the *Poe* being paſt by a
certain long Bridge of Wood, ſtands the Church of S. *Gregorio*,

wherein the Body of *S. Maurelio* firſt Biſhop of *Ferrara*, is carefully layed up.   Here the *Poe* parts with a great Arm, which having bathed the great Level, runs by *Mejaro, Mejarino*, and other places into the Adriatick Sea; But the greater Chanel runs Southward, and at 8. miles diſtance hath on its Banks the Bourg *Argenta*, ſo named from from the quantity of Sylver which every ſo many yeers, it payed to the Church of *Ravenna*, on its right hand are many deep Trenches filled with good fiſh.

Three miles beyond *Argenta* ſtood *Baſtia*, a Fort (now demoliſhed) where the Armies of Pope *Giulius* the ſecond, and *Alphonſo* firſt Duke of *Ferrara*, fought a ſharp Battail. Ten miles beyond it lies *Lugo* a noble Town, *Bagnac avollo*, a Bourg, and *Cotignana* the native Country of the *Sforzeſchan* Princes, *Babiano, Mazolino, Imola*, and *Faenza* with others.

On the left ſide of the *Poe*, are fertile Fields, and a Palace of the Prince of *Eſte*, ſo large and well furniſhed, that it may give a reception to a great King. In this neighbourhood were antiently twelve large Towns : whoſe inhabitants by one unanimous conſent built *Ferrara*.

Purſuing the *Poe* for twenty miles, lye many fayr and pleaſant Towns, as *Longaſtino* and *Filo*, ſo called for that there the *Poe*, runs for ſix miles as ſtrait as a thred or line. *San Alberto*, and *Priniaro* where the *Poe* runs into the Sea, from *Sant Alberto* looking Northward you may ſee *Comacchio*, near the Sea ſhore, with a Lake or ſtanding Pool round it, wherein they take vaſt quantities of Mullets, and Eeles, ſome weighing 30. pound, *Comacchio* was antiently a famous City, but now tis near deſtroyed by the waters, hereabouts alſo lies the Abbacy of *Pompoſa*. On the left of Saint *Albergo*, are Fenny Fields, wherein to this day may be ſeen the *Foſſa Meſſanitia*, made by our *Anceſtors*, but now tis a narrow Chanel to navigate to *Ravenna*, in ſmall Barks, it formerly run 50. miles navigable, and was called *Paduſa*.

RAVENNA.

THis City is more memorable for its antiquity than fair building being firſt built by the *Theſſalonians*, who being perplexed and moleſted by the *Ombrians*, and *Sabines*, voluntarily gave it them up, and returned into *Greece*, but the *Ombrians* were thence driven by the *French*, and they by the *Romans*, under whom it remained till they with the *Heruli* took the Country *Odoacre*, but then they were driven out by the *Oſtrogoths*, under *Theodorick* their King, who made it his Regal Seat, under whom it remained 70. yeers, and then they were beaten out by *Narſete*, Præfect of *Juſtinian* the Emperor, under the Title of *Exarchi*, after whom 17. more *Exarchi* governed it 170. yeers, who were all that time held in continual skirmiſhes with the *Longobardi*, who were called into *Italy* by *Narſete*, againſt the ſaid Emperour of *Conſtantinople*. For *Narſete* being accuſed to *Giuſtino*, Succeſſor to *Juſtinian*, for ſome crime, whereat *Giuſtino* was offended which backed with the inſtigation of the Emperours wife, cauſed the Emperour to ſend another to be *Exarche* in his Room, who being exaſperated againſt the Emperour for it, invited in the

Longo-

Longobardi againſt the Empire, by whoſe hands the *Exarcate* of *Italy* was extinct. This *Exarche* was in the nature of a King, having plenary Juriſdiction in all things without appeal: *Aſtolfo* ſome time after being overcome by *Pipino* King of the *French*, gave up *Ravenna* to the Church of *Rome*, but *Deſiderius* ſucceſſor to *Aſtolfo*, not regarding his Faith after the retreat of *Pipin* with the *French* Army, poſſeſſed himſelf again of *Ravenna* and other Towns, but the Emperour *Charles* the Great returning into *Italy* with the *French* Army, overcame and took him Priſoner, when the *Longobardi* were forced to quit *Italy* altogether, ſo that it hath ſuffered many diſgraces, and was afterwards ſacked by the *French*, and deſtroyed by civil diſcord.

Strabo ſaies that in his time *Ravenna* ſtood upon certain Piles driven into the *Fennes*, and that the water paſſed under it, ſo that no coming was to it but by Bridges or Boats, and when the waters were high, then the people were forced to get up into the upper Rooms, yet for all that twas healthfull, as *Alexandria* in *Ægypt*, but now the Waters are ſo dryed up that the *Fenns* are become Excellent Meadows, Paſtures, and Corn Grouuds, many Hiſtorians agree that twas much beautified by *Auguſtus Cæſar*, accommodating it with a great Bridge, and erecting the high Tower called *Faro*, where he encamped an Army for defence of the Gulfs and lodged the Souldiers in the midſt of the City, in a form like a Caſtle, which afterwards was called the *Fortezza* of *Ravenna*, it had another Fort called *Ceſarea*, with Walls and Baſtions, which ſtrongly fortifyed the Port of *Ravenna*, but at preſent neither the Ports nor Forts appear, only ſome certain old Churches and Monaſteries of little moment. On the *Porta Sperioſa*, for its ſtructure, and good Marble called *Aureı*, is this Title.

TI. CLAVDIVS. DRVSI. F. CÆSAR.
AVG. GERMANICVS. PONT. MAX. TR.
POT. COS. II. DES. III. IMP. III. P. P. DEDIT.

Whence tis ſuppoſed that the Emperour *Claudius* fortifyed *Ravenna* with Walls and a new Port, *Biondo* affirms, that *Ravenna* was amplified by *Placida Galla*, ſiſter of *Arcadio*, and *Honorius* the Emperours, and by her Sons *Valentiniano*, and *Tiberio*, alſo *Theodrick* King of the *Goths*, beautified it with ſtately edifices, and enriched it with the ſpoil of the other Provinces, as appears by thoſe Churches, Palaces, & other ſtructures raiſed by him and his ſucceſſors, and yet extant.

In *Ravenna* near the *Piazza Santa Maria* ſtands a great *Convent*, and in it the magnificent Tombe of *Dante Algieri*, erected to him by *Bernardo Bembo* the *Venetian Podeſta* in *Ravenna*, with this Inſcription by the ſaid *Bembo*.

> *Exiguo tumulo Danthes, hic ſorte jacebas*
> *Squallenti nulli cognito pene ſitu,*
> *At nunc marmoreo ſubnixus conderis arcu,*
> *Omnibus & cultu ſplendidiore nites,*

Nimirum Bembus Mufis incenfus Hetrufcis
Hoc tibi, quem in primi hæ coluere, didit.

And with this other Infcription which the faid *Dante* near his death compofed.

Jura Monarchiæ, fuperos Phlegetonta, lacufque
Luftrando cecini, voluerunt Fata quoufque
Sed qua pars ceffet meliorib. hofpita caftris,
Actorumque fuum petiit fælicior aftris,
Hic claudor Danthes patriis extortis ab oris,
Quem genuit parui Florentia mater amoris.

The biggeft Church of *Ravenna*, is the Arch-Bifhops, upon whofe high Altar was formerly fuftained a maffy Silver heaven or canopy on four Pillars, which was worth 30000. Crowns, with excellent ornaments wrought with Gold, all which were taken away by the facriligious people of *Lewis* the 12th. King of *France*, when without any difference he facked this City, for which they afterwards received from the moft high condigne punifhment, being moft of them cut in pieces, or forced to leap into the *Poe*, or *Tefino*, where they drowned themfelves. In a Semicircular Chapel, are Limned thofe firft Arch-Bifhops of *Ravenna* (elected by the fhewing of a Dove) in Mofaick work, a fair piece, whofe election was after this manner. *Sant Apollinare* (believed one of the 72 Difciples of Chrift, then afcended into Heaven,)departing from *Antiochia*, with Saint Petertogo to *Rome*,had in his paffage taught the Chriftian Faith at *Ravenna*, and afterwards ftayed there to govern it,whom none of the Difciples by him left judged themfelves fit to fucceedto govern thatChurch where fore all of them together withdrew themfelves into a Temple to praytoGod to demonftrate to wch of them it would pleafe hisDivine Majefty to commit that care,whereat the holy Spirit in the form of a Dove defcended upon the head of one, who was underftood by it to be elected by God to that Dignity, after which manner eleaven Arch-Bifhops were fucceffively chofen. And the Cafement,whereat the Dove entred is yet apparent though half fhut, over the Arch of the high Altar in the Church of *Spirito Santo* in this City, in which Church on the left hand is a heap of Bricks, near which in a Corner ftood *Severus* a mean perfon and a fimple Man, upon whofe head the holy Spirit defcended vifible to all, he being the laft of the eleaven.

Tis worth ones pains to view the Church of Saint *Apollinare*, called the golden heaven, built moft fumptuoufly by *Theodorick*, King of the *Oftrogoths*,it hath two ranks of moft noble greatColumns,brought hither by that King from *Conftantinople*, and is garnifhed with many pretious Marbles, extracted from *Rome*, and other places of *Italy*, and alfo fome other Churches.

In *Ravenna* are many antiquities, Epitaphs, and antient Memorials, whofe Letters and words require a Univerfity of Interpreters. The ruines of a ftately Palace(fuppofed King *Theoricks*)appear yet in the midft of its Fountain is a ftatue of *Hercules Horarius*, not elfewhere found. *Hercules* ftands like an *Atlas*, bending with his left knee as ready to rife, who with his two hands elevated and his head

together

together fupports a Solar *Horologe*, whereon the fhadow of the needle
from the Sun fhewes the houre of the day. A like ftatue of *Hercules*
was found in *Rome* in the Vineyard of *Steffano del Buffalo*, which inftead of the *Horologe* fupported a round Globe with the Celeftial
Signs, diftinctly figured, but this difference is not of any great moment, nearly weighing the Signification of the thing for the knowlege of the hour arofe from the obfervation of the Celeftial motion,
and tis the Sun diftinguifhes the hour, who by his annual courfe vi-
fites the whole Cirk of the Firmament, which hath caufed fome to
conjecture, that *Hercules* fignifies the Sun, and that the 12 labours
counted as of a Mans, is the Ingrefs of the Sun through the twelve
Signs in the circuit of the skies, whereby the Sun of it felfcafts forth
its beams, perfuing which Opinion, mifterioufly though with fomewhat accult fenfe they apply to the fun all the other Fables of *Hercules*, which are two tedious here to be applyed, let it fuffice to have
fpoken fo much to the purpofe, of that ftatue, to roufe up our youth
into a more near Scrutiny of the fenfe of the Fables of the antients,
from the knowlege wherein may be extracted many natural fecrets,
hid under thofe their fayings and Fables.

Before *Ravenna* ftands a moft antient round Church of the bleffed
Virgin, being fo fair and large, that the inward circle is 25. foot in
diametre: The walls are finely wrought, and all the pavement is
layed with fmall ftones of various colours, difpofed into divers pleafing figures after the Mofaick work, the Roof is of one fquared entire hard ftone, hollowed, in the midft whereof is the *Cupola*, whereby the light penetrates, tis fcarce imaginable how or by what Art fo
great a ftone could be mounted fo high, nor where had the Edge or
Plate on the Walls at top as near as can be gueffed are about 35 foot
in circuit, above the faid Edge on the top four fair Collumns in former times fufteyned the noble Sepulchre of *Theodorick* King of the
Oftrogothes, of Porphire, fpecled with white, being one entire ftone
eight foot long, and four foot high, with a cover of Brafs figured
and wrought to admiration with gold and other garnifhments, which
Tombe tis fuppofed *Amalefunta* his Daughter erected, but in the time
of the *French* war, the wicked Souldiers of *Lewis* the 12th. King of
France, with hopes of fome great booty within, drew it down and
broke it, whereof fome Reliques yet remain.

Three miles forth the City in the way to *Forli*, runs the River
Ronco, on the Bank whereof ftands a Crofs of ftone, in teftimony
that in the year 1512. *Gaftone de Fois* Captain of the *French* Army,
there obtained a victory with the lofs of his own life, for that being
too fiercly bent againft his enemies. he advanced two forward with
very few in full fpeed of his Horfe, and of a fudden was dead, in
which battail dyed that day eighteen thoufand Souldiers, between
French, *Spaniards*, *Italians*, *Germans* and *Switzers*.

H

CER-

CERVIA.

NEar *Ravenna* lies that notable Wood called *Pigneda*, from the infinite number of Pyne trees there growing, whose Fruit supply all *Italy*. Some miles beyond which stands *Cervia*, a City, but ill peopled by reason of the malignant ayr , all whose Inhabitants are such as get a livelyhood by making Salt, with Saltwater dryed in the Sun , whereof they make such quantity, that white Salt lies in Mountains. In it is nought worth noting, unless the model of so old a City, built meerly for necessity. The Cathedral Church , although it hath a good revenue , seemes but a Church of a Villa near it lies a Tomb of Marble, in form of a Pyramide , with two lovely Children carved at the foot of it. After it had been under several Lords in *Anno* 1527. it became a part of the Church Patrimony and so continues.

Whence you must passe the River *Savio* in whose Port *Cæsar Octavianus* prepared a great *Armada*, and then to the River *Pistatello* formerly called *Rubicone*, famous not only for that the *Romans* made it the bound of two Provinces, calling the one towards *Rome*, *Italia*, and the other towards the *Alpes* , *Gallia Cisalpina*, and commanded that no Commander of what quality soever, should presume to pass that River towards *Rome* with armed Souldiers ; but also for that *Julius Cæsar* afterwards (against the determination of the Senate and people of *Rome*) conducted his Army over that River towards *Rome*, where he first consulted by reason of the dangerous consequence might ensue so rash a Deed, and in the end resolved and passed saying , *Eatur quo Deorum ostenta, & inimicorum iniquitas vocant, Jacta sit alea :* and upon his demurr , there he saw certain Birds fly , called *Augurii* which (to his Judgement) seemed to invite him to transport those Souldiers he had commanded in *France*, to commence a War against *Rome* his Mother and Country.

Travailing from *Ravenna* to *Rimini*, on one hand lies the Sea, and on the other fertile and pleasant Fields, the *Via Flaminia*, and *Alpes*, at whose Feet stands the stately City *Forli*.

FORLI.

TIs believed, that (after *Asdrubal* was slain by the *Roman* Consul *Livio Salinatore* then united with *Claudius Nero*) certain old Souldiers built a Castle and called it *Livio*, in honour of the said *Livius* the Consul, a mile and halfe's distance from where *Forli* now stands, but because in the *Via Maestra*, there was a fair Town wherein they made their Mart for Merchandize, and Seat of Judicature, for that cause called *Foro*, they say that the Inhabitants of *Livio*, after some time coufidering that twas more comodious to inhabite the said Town than their Castle *Livio*, agreed with the Townes-men to cohabite together , and accordingly by Common consent, with leave of *Augustas* , which was easily obtained through the mediation of *Livia* his confort, and *Cornelio Gallo a Liviese*, they conjoyned those two names, *Foro* and *Livio*, and for brevity called the place *Forli*, which in Latine by the name clearly appears being called *forum Livii*,

Livii, which union was made in the time that our Lord Christ was being on the Earth, and 208. yeers after, the first foundation of the Castle *Livio*, *Forli* is placed between the Rivers *Ronco* and *Montone*, enjoyes a delicate ayr with a most fertile Country, in Wines, Oyls, Corn, and Fruit together with Coriander, feed, Annifeed, Cuminfeed, and Woad in great abundance.

The men of *Forli* are for the most part gallant beyond meafure, and retains the martial difpofition of their firft Founders. It was a long time fubject to the *Romans*, after them to the *Bolonians*, and becaufe four *Bolonians* banifhed out of *Bolonia*, were courteoufly entertained in *Forli*, the *Bolonians* raifed a great Army againft them, but in a Battail received fuch an overthrow by the *Forlefi*, that they never could raife their heads after it, whereby the *Bolonians* power being abated. the *Forlefi* yielded themfelves up to the *Roman* Church, from whome afterwards revolting *Martin* the 4th. difmantled it, and threw down the Walls, configning it to the Family *Monfredi*, from whom it paffed to the *Ordelafi*, who again Walled it round, but *Siftus* the 4th. gave it to *Giorlamo Biario Savonefe*, whom *Cæfar Borgia* Son of *Alexander the* 6th. expelled and and took it by force of Arms, but at laft in the time of *Giulius* the fecond, it again returned to the Church under whom to this day, it continnes in peace and fidelity, it hath yielded many learned and brave men, as *Guidon Bonato*, *Rainiero*, *Biondi*, and others.

BRITTONORO.

ABove *Forli* ftands *Brittonoro*, called in Latine *Forum Trijarinorum*, this City is built upon a hill, and above it hath a ftrong Fort fatal to *Frederick* the fecond, it was a Town, but created a City at the inftance of *Egidius Carrilla* a *Spanifh* Cardinal, and Legate of *Italy*, who having deftroyed *Forlimpopoli*, transferred thence his Epifcopal Seat, to *Brittonoro*, in *Anno* 137 . it participates a moft happy Ayr, and rich Country, in Olives, Figgs, Vynes, Fruitful Trees, and good Waters. It hath one place erected intentionally for a profpect, where you have a full view of the Adriatick Sea, of *Dalmatia, Croatia, Venetia*, and all *Romagna*, at one inftant; *Barbaroffa* the Emperor, at the inftance of Pope *Alexander* the third, being reconciled to the *Venetians*, for this beautiful profpects fake requefted *Brittonora*, of the Pope for his habitation, but the Pope perpending the conftant fidelity of this People to the Sea of *Rome*, prevayled with the Emperor by fair words, not to take from the Churches government, a place that in all occafions had demonftrated fo fincere a Faith to it, and fo it continued under it till *Alexander* the 6th. configned it to *Cæfar Borgio*, his Son, after whom the civil difcords had almoft deftroyed it,

its Inhabitants being fo prone to Arms that they know not how to live in Peace, Finally *Clement* the feaventh, configned it to the Family *Pii*, who yet enjoy it.

FORIMPOPOLI.

A Mile and halfe from *Brittonoro*, on the *Via Emilia* ftand *Forlimpo-poli*, called in Latine *Forum Popilii*, which is one of the four Fori recorded in *Pliny*, on the *Via Emilia*. T was a City, but in the year 700. *Vitaliano* being Pope, *Griomaldo* King of the *Longobardi*, fecretly entred it on the Sabbath day, when all the People with the Bifhop were at Divine Service, and flew all the Males and Females, which done he facked the City, and levelled it with the ground. It was afterwards renewed by the *Forlinefi*, and again deftroyed by *Egiddio Carilla* the Popes Legate dwelling in *Avignone*, who in the yeer 1370. plowed it and fowed it with falt for its utter extirpation, transferring the Epifcopal Seat to *Brittonoro* as afore'aid, twenty yeers after which *Sinibaldo Ordelafo* Lord of *Forli*, repaired it, and built the formidable Caftle now there. It enjoyes a good ayr, fertile Fields, and a great Ferry affording ample profit. *Bofello* a moft holy man of of ftupenduous miracles, was its Bifhop, in the Catalogue of Saints, whofe holy bones now lye in the Church called *Santa Lucia*, *Antonel lo Armuzzo* with his Sons *Meleagro*, and *Brunoro*, much honoured this Country, who by his Genius and ftrength from a mean perfon acquired the dignity of being Captain, of the Popes Cavalry.

SARSINA.

NEar *Forlumpopoli* is feated the City *Sarfino*, at the foot of the *Appenines*, whofe Citizens furnifhed 20000. Armed Souldiers in fupply to the *Romans* againft the *French*, when they made a moft furious eruption over the *Alpes* into *Italy*, Its ayr is healthfull, and Territory abounds with Olivs ; Vines and other fruitful Trees. It continued a long time under *Malatefti*, but when *Rimini* became fubject to the Church *Sarfina* yeelded with it afterwards, *Leo* the 10th. beftowed it on the houfe of *Pii*, this City gave birth to *Vicino* Bifhop of *Liguria* a moft holy man, and famous for working miracles, which property his body (lying in the Cathedral Church) yet retains, in operation over fuch perfous as were oppreffed with evil fpirits lye expelling them. As alfo to *Plautus* that antient and famous *Comick* Latin Poet, who (tis commonly held for truth) wrought here at the Bake-houfe, as a Baker for a lively-hood, and when he had any fpare time, he compofed his Comedies, and fold them, the better to fupply his neceffities. Which Opinion *Eufebius* alfo confirms.

CESENA.

CEfena lies at the foot of a Hill near the River *Savio*, which fo rapidly runs by it down from the *Apenines* that it overflows and infefts, many grounds, before it runs into the Sea. This City hath a ftrong Cittadel upon the hill adjoyning to the heart of the City by means of a Pyle, built by *Frederick* the fecond Emperor now near ruined. Tis worth ones pains to fee the Church, where on the roof hangs a piece of a poudered Hog, nayled to it in remembrance of a

Mira-

Miracle wrought thus. San *Pietro* the Martyr, caused the Convent
of Saint *Domenick* to be built, in the time of whose strncture, craving
Almes for the Love of God, it happened that this piece of the Pou-
dred Hoggs flesh was bestowed on him, whereof he gave and fed the
Workemen and Labourers till the said Convent was finished, and
still there remained that which now hangs up there, for that what
ever the Saint cut off, grew & increased day by day in the same manner
and quantity, as in its first state, as if it had not been at all touched or
diminished. It abounds with excellent wines and all other necessaries.
Its original is not known, yet twas ever and is still well peopled. It
was under the Emperors, the Church, the *Bolonians*, the *Ordolasi*,
Mighardo di Suffenna, and the *Malatesti*, the last of whom *Mala testo No-*
vella, collected a stately Library, not now so despicable also to be passed without a view, in the Monastery of Saint *Fraucis*, who surrendred the City to the Church from whom twas wrested by *Cæsar Bor-*
gio called Duke *Valentino* Son of *Alexander* the 6th. and from him it
once more returned in obedtence to the Church, and so continued
in quiet ever since; on the Mount near it is a Church called *Maria del*
Monte Cefena, where the *Benedictines* serve.

R I M I N I.

THe number of Antiquities through this City shew it very antient: Twas beautifyed divers times by *Augustus Cæsar*, and the
succeeding Emperors, with sumptuous Fabricks, whereof the reliques
yet remaining give a sufficient testimony many Historians relate, that
twas made a Colony of the *Romans* before the first *Punick* War, together with *Bencvento*, *Publius Sempronius Sofo*, and *Appius Claudius*, Son
of the Blind, being Consuls, which was 485 yeers after the foundation of *Rome*. After which twas held and inhabited by the *Romans*,
as a *Fortezza* in those Confines against the *French*, and there most of
the *Roman* Commanders (designed with Armies to forein Countries)
were wont to make their Rendezvous, signifying to their People,
what day they should there render themselves, as *Livy* more plainly sets down. Twas called *Rimini* from the River *Rimini* which
washes it. The *Picenti* first justly held it, but they were overcome by *Appius Claudius* who triumphed for it, and dilated the Empire from *Esino*, or *Fiumesino* to the River *Piffatello*. Tis seated in a
most fertile Plain, having on the East and West parts of it excellent
plow-Lands, on the South great plenty of Gardens, Orchards, Olive-
Woods, and Vineyards upon the hills of the *Apenine* Mountains,
and on the North the *Adriatick* Sea, all which as twere in emulation
strive which shall exceed the other in affording of necessaries and de-
licacies of all sorts to its Inhabitants.

Tis a comodious and fair City, replenished with structures *alla Mo-*
derna, in the *Piazza* is a glorious fountain sprouting sweet and clear
waters through several pipes. Towards the Sea are some Reliques of a
stately Theatre; over the River *Arimino* stands a Bridge built with
large square Marble stones by *Augustus*, which conjoins the *Via Flami-*
nia, to the *Via Emilia*, and the City to the Suburb, which is 200. foot
long in 5. Arches, and 15. broad, whose sides are wrought in *Dorick*
structure, upon one of which is inscribed the Titles of *Augustus Cæ-*
sar, and on another those of *Tiberius Cæsar*, whence we compute

this Bridge was finiſhed 778. yeers after the foundation of *Rome,* *C. Calviſius,* and *Gn. Lentulus* than Conſuls, being begun by *Auguſtus* (who much laboured to beautify and accomodate the *Via Flaminia* ſparing no coſt) and finiſhed in the daies of *Tiberius*. Some part of the old Port appears yet but ſo inconſiderable, that it can onely receive ſmall boats. But how great and magnificent this hath been, may be collected from that proud and ſtupendious ſtructure, the Church *San Franceſco,* which was built by *Sigiſmond Malteſta,* Prince of this City, with the Marble Stones haled out of the old Port.

At the *Porta Orientale,* leading to *Peſaro,* is a fair Marble Arch, erected there in honour of *Auguſtus Cæſar,* when having been ſeaven times Conſul, he was elected for the eighth, he having fortified and adorned (by commiſſion of the Senate, and Will of the People of *Rome*) the five chief Roads of *Italy,* as may be gueſſed, from thoſe few legible fragments of carved Letters yet remaining, whereby it appears that the *Via Flaminia,* was of great conſideration, *Auguſt us* having aſſumed to himſelf the care of accommodating that Road from *Rome* to *Rimini* (as *Suetonicus* recounts) and given the charge of accommodating the reſt to certain illuſtrious Men, with order to diſpoſe what ever ſpoiles they took from the Enemies, to that purpoſe. For a memorial of which publique benefit, are yet extant certain moneys or medals of Gold then ſtamped with the Effigies of *Auguſtus,* with his titles on the one ſide, and on the other an Arch with two Doors elevated over a Way, on the top whereof ſits Victory driving a triumphal Chariot, with theſe words, *Quod viæ munitæ ſint,* which words declare the occaſion of that great honour done to *Cæſar* was for his care and coſt in amending the high Waies & publick Roads. Of which Arch now wholly deſtroyed, many Reliques ly on the *Via Flaminia* even to *Rome*.

But the ſhorteſt way to *Rome,* is to go over the Hills which ly South-ward from *Rimini,* where ſtands the Caſtle *Fiore,* to paſs the River *Iſauro,* thirty miles whence is *Vrbino,* and eight miles more is *Acqualagna,* there to enter the *Via Flaminia,* and travail to *Vmbria.* In the *Via Flaminia,* on the right hand upon a Hill is *Verucchio,* the firſt habitation of the *Malateſta,* to whom it was given) by *Otho* the Emperor, and higher in the Mountains is the Bourg *S. Martino,* in in Latine *Acer Mons,* a noble rich and well-peopled Place, which hath ever preſerved it ſelf in full Liberty, nor was it ever conquered, which at a diſtance looks like a confuſed heap of Mountains, without way or means to aſcend to. On the ſame way 15. miles off *Rimini* begins the Plain, which reaches without obſtacle of hill to the *Alpi Cottie,* which divide *Italy* from *France,* this Plain is very ſpatious and fertile in all things, filled with Towns and Villages on all ſides. In view whereof lies *Poggio,* Imperial, at whoſe foundatian *Frederick* the third Emperor layed the firſt ſtone, where the Pictures of all the line of *Auſteria,* are excellently delineated.

PESARO.

This City was built by the *Romans* 119. yeers before the coming of Chriſt, near the River *Iſaurus,* whence with little alteration it took its name. Its Walls and Bulwarks were begun by *Franceſco*

Maria del Rovere,& finished by *Guidi Baldo*,his Son;tis beautifyed with stately structures for divine,publick and private Use, worth a view. Without theCity is built thePrincesPalace.In *Pesaro* they hold certain Fairs whither resort Merchants from farr Countries,but in regard the Port is stopped so that none but small Boats may enter, they carry their Merchandize on Asses and Mules. Twas made a Colony of the Romans 569. yeers after the foundation of *Rome*,*Claudius Pulchrus* and *Lucius Porticus Licinus* being then Consuls, and among the rest sent thither to inhabit was *L. Acius* the excellent Tragick Poet, born of Father and Mother that were *Libertines*. *Plutark* (in the life of *Antonius*)records this City to have received much damage by a Cleft or falling in of the Earth , after that *M. Antony* had a second time conducted *Romans* to inhabite there , which was a short time before that Warr,awherein himself with *Cleopatra* wereovercome by *Augustus*.   At the Palace of the Governour is a Magazine furnished with excellent and various Arms.

From *Pesaro* you must go to *Fano*, and along the shore to *Senigalia*. Near the *Porta* of *Rimini* is a Bridge over the River*Foglia*,which is the Confines of the Provinces of *Marca d'Ancona* and *Romagna*.   On the way appears *Novellara Monte Abate,Monte Barucio*,and 15.other Towns *Pesaro* yeelds such store of the best Figgs that they are there dryed to transport over Italy, and are accounted better than those from *Sclavonia*.

FANO.

THis City was so denominated from the Temple of Fortune here erected,which in Latine is called *Fanum*. It stands on the *Via Flaminia*, in a good Soyl, which yeelds all sorts of Corn , Wine , and Oyl, in great plenty. Many say *Augustus Cæsar* made it a Colony,conducting thither *Roman* People to inhabit , at that time when he(as *Suetonius* writes)drew out of *Rome* 28. Colonies, and *Pomponius Mela* saies,that from the name of *Julia Cæsare*,twas called *Giulio Fanestre*,as may be also collected from certain old inscriptions there extant.From the Reliques of the old Walls, and from the Arch placed over the Gate by which you enter coming from *Rome* on the *Via Flaminia*,may be drawn , that twas begirt with Walls by *Augustus*, and restored afterwards by *Costantio*, and *Costanto*, Sonns of the great *Constantine*.

The said Arch remained entire till the time of Pope *Pius* the second, and was made with great Art, carved with figures and Letters, but was destroyed by the Artillery in the War against the *Farnese*, though for its remembrance a draught of it was take n and carved on the Walls of the Church *S. Michiele*, at their common charge,whereof,nor of any thing else of antiquity does ought entire appear.

In its neighbourhood beyond the River *Metauro* , are some places famous for theDeeds of Arms there performed.For *M. Livius*,*Salinato* &*Claud. Nerone* Consuls overcame and slew *Asdrubal* Brother of *Hannibal* the *Carthaginian* , on the Banks of the River, which made *Hannibal* despair of maintaining Carthage against the *Romans*, seeing the head of his Brother carried at the head of the *Roman* Army for his view whereby to render him cowardly. Somewhat beyond which place is the Field where *Totila* King of the Goths was overcome by *Narſete Evenucho*, the firſt *Exarck* and Legate of *Juſtinian* the Emperor, which victory wholly freed *Italy* from the Government or rather Tyranny of the *Gothes*, for that *Totila* being mortally wounded fled thence to the *Apenines* (as *Procopius* in his third Book of the *Gothick* hiſtory relates) and there dyed.

The Voyage or Journey from *FANO* to *FVLIGNO* by the *VIA EMILIA*

FOSSVMBRVNO.

TRavaling Weſtward from *Fano* appear many villages among the Mountains, and then taking the *Via Flaminia* Southward on the right-hand ſhore of the River *Metauro*, you arrive at *Foſſumbruno*, a City placed as twere in the midſt of the Plain between the Hill and the River. Its Frabricks are modern, by reaſon that the old were wholly caſt down by the *Gothes* or *Longobardi*, In the biggeſt Church remain ſome old Inſcriptions, denoting its antiquity; from which City purſuing the Journey you muſt paſs the River *Metauro* by a woodden Bridge, then entring the *Via Flaminia*, on each ſide paſſing by pleaſant and fertile Fields, you reach the River *Candiano*, near which lies the Hill *Aſdrubal*, ſo denominated from the overthrow there given *Aſdrubal* by the abovenamed Conſuls. Whence the *Via Flaminia*, was paved by *Auguſtus* to *Rome*, half a miles length whereof was cut thorow a ſtony Rock with a Chizel, which is twelve paces broad, tis called *Forlo*, Then were certain Letters inſcribed, which age hath worn out, yet their ſenſe remains, *viz.* That that noble and & laborious, work was performed by *Titus Veſpaſian*, *Candiano* runs for three miles along the Hills, which paſſed, lies a Plain, and 10. miles thence is *Acqualagna*, where dyed *Totila*, King of the *Gothes* overcome by *Narſete* as aforeſaid, beyond which is the City *Cagli*, and the Bourg *Cariano*, built out of the Ruines of the City *Lucerla*, heretofore ſtanding where now the Bridge is, but deſtroyed by *Narſete*, when the perfidious *Elenterio*, arrogating to himſelf the Title of Emperor was diſcomfited, beyond which is the heigth of the *Alps* which terminate the Province of *Ancona*, and *Senigaglia*, *Sigello* and *Galdo*.

NOCERA.

LAſtly upon one of the *Apenines*, ſtands *Nocera*, heretofore famous for the Earthen Veſſels there curiouſly made, now for the Abundance of the Wine called *Muſcatello*, at the foot of the Mountain whereon *Nocera* ſtands, is the Valley *Trinia*, ſo named from the
River

River *Trinia*, wherof *Silius* speaksthus, *Triniæque ingloriushumor*, calling it unworthy among Rivers, for not being navigable. The way thorow which Valley is very dangerous, beacufe of the neceffity to wade feveral times through the River, where fometimes the poor Travellers are bemired, by reafon that in the bottom there is a moft ftiff mudd, whereby they are oft drowned through their Ignorance of certain Whirl-pools, covered with mudd, not eafily to be avoided but by fuch as are well skilled in the paffage. The faid vale is 12 miles long, and in it is *Foligno*.

The Journy from *FANA* to *FOLIGNO* and *ROME*, by a better but longer Way.

BEeyond *Fano* upon the *Adriatick* Sea, is *Sinigaglia* a famous and antient City, firft called *Sena*, from the *Senoni* who built it. When the *Senoni* were driven out by the *Romans*, they made it a Colony together with *Caftro* and *Hadria*, *Dolabella* being Conful, about the time that *Italy* was extended beyond the River *Efe*, and the Dutchy of *Spoleto* added to it. *Titus Livius* in his 27th. book affures us that *M. Livius Salinatorus* the Conful quartered in *Senigaglia* when *Asdrubal* was not above half a mile diftant, overlooking all *Italy* and raifing in it great terror, when *C. Nerone Collegne* of *Livy*, withdrawing himfelf from *Bafilocata*, with a flying Army of 6000. Foot and 1000. Horfe, by a nights march, conjoyned himfelf with *Livy*, and the next morn the two Confuls cut in pieces the Army of *Afdrubal*, and flew the faid Captain, while he defigned to fly over the *Metauro*, as afore declared.

ANCONA.

TIs a famous noble rich City, and hath the moft eminent Port in all *Italy*: whence the Merchants out of *Sclavonia*, *Greece*, *Dalmatia*, and all *Europe* frequent it. All Writers agree it had its foundation from the *Siracufany*, flying from the Tyrany of *Dionifius*, 'Tis likely it became a Colony of the *Romans*, 485. yeers after *Romes* building when the *Marchiani* were overcome by *Publius Sempronius*, the Conful, and the Confines of *Italy* enlarged. For then twas neceffary to place *Roman* People on thofe boundaries. It took its name from *Ancon* in Greek which fignifies an Elbow, in which form is its Port and Harbour a fecure Station for Ships. Many Writers, worthy belief) fay, that in the time of the *Roman* Empire twas a renowned City aed well Inhabited for the conveniency of the Harbour, and nobly reftored by *Trajan* the Emperor with incredible expence, whereof fome Reliques remain.

It hath fair Fabricks, rich Merchandize, bufinefs, and People in good number. 'Tis environed with Walls and Bulworks, there erected at the charge of the Popes to enable it with reſiſtance againſt invaſions a good part of the Walls are yet of Marble, antiently twas all of Marble, the Port hath ſtrong Pillars to faſten ſhipping to, and convenient deſcents to the Water, as alſo ſtrong Cranes ior removing Goods into, and out of the Veſſels. Some Medals are yet extant ſtamped in honour of *Trajane* with the form of that Port, & a *Neptune* Crowned in water before the Mouth of the Porte, with the Rudder of a ſhip in his right-hand, and a Dolphin near. It hath two chains wherewith they ſhut up the entrance, therein are at all times Ships and Galleys of all ſorts. There is an Arch moſt ſtately, raiſed in honour of *Trajane*, in gratefull acknowledgment of that publick benefit, his reſtoring the Porte, by the Senate and People of *Rome*, which Arch although diſpoiled of thoſe Ornaments, it formerly had, yet (like the Picture of a fair Woman) it attracts the eyes of the beholders raiſing wonder in them, moving the Fancy to conſider the Art, beauty and proportion of that Piece, from the great ſquares of Marble and degrees yet to be ſeen, on all ſides ſhewing a moſt proportionate and beautifull appearance.

'Tis of no ſmall conſideration: That all the *S*tatues and other Ornaments, are carved into, or inlaid in thoſe great ſquare ſtones, and not fixed outwardly, which Squares too are ſo cloſe connexed that tis impoſſible to put in the point of a Knife between them, but looks as if twere one entire Rock, which ſhewes the skill and Art of the Artificer. On it is inſcribed as follows.

IMP. CÆSARI. DIVI. NERVÆ. F. NERVÆ.
TRAIANO. OPTIMO. AVG. GERMANIC. DA-
CI. CO. PONT. MAX. TR. POT. XIX. IMP.
IX. COS. VI. P. P. PROVIDENTISSIMO:
PRINCIPI. SENATVS. P. Q. R. QVOD. AC.
GESSVM. ITALIÆ. HOC. ETIAM. ADDITO.
EX. PECVNIA. SVA.
PORTV. TVTIOREM. NAVIGANTIBVS. RED-
DIDERIT.

On the Right-hand.

PLOTINÆ. AVG.
CONIVGI, AVG.

On the Left-hand.

DIVÆ. MARCINÆ.
SORORI. AVG.

Thereby we ſee that Divine honours were then given to *Trajan* and his Siſter.

'Tis not ill ſpent time neither to aſcend the Mount *Ancona*, and behold its Rarities, which is the promontory *Cumero*, where firſt is the antient Cathedral Church Saint *Ciriaro*, of admirable Architecture, and curious Marbles, in its Veſtry are infinite Reliques of Saints, and offirings of great valew preſented for devotion. One may gather from
                                                           ſome

some verses of *Iuvenal* that not far distant was dedicate a Temple to
Venus but no thing now remains of it. From that heigth may be seen
a large space of Sea, the bending of the Port, the placing of the City
and the lite of the Promontory it self, so con-joyned with the *Appenines*, that some say it appears their head, but others more rationally its Arm, reaching hence to Mount *Angelo*, all along ashore of
the *Adriatick* Sea. As also many near Cities, Caltles, and Burges, as
Sirolo celebrious for the good Wine called *Anconitana*, by *Pliny, Orbino,*
Osimo, and others.

Upon a Mount near the River *Musone*, stands *Cingola* a Castle built
by *Titus Labienus*, out of the many robaries committed by him, while
he was Embaffador of *C. Cæfar* and *Proconful in Gallia* in that long War.
The shape of which Castle we finde engraven upon certain pieces of
silver and gold with his Titles, of whose so great Riches, *Cicero Sili-*
us, Valerius, Alax. and *Dion.* speake scornfully invectively, and bitter-
ly, but now to our Voyage.

The holy house of *LORETO*.

Fifteen miles being paffed you finde placed upon a hill the famous
Church of the Virgin *Maria de Loreto*, visited from all partsof the
World by *Pilgrims*, either through penance enjoyned thereto, or their
own vows or devotion, Tis called *Loreto*, for that in antient timeftood
near it a Wood of Laurels. Some will have, that in the same place *viz* the
Mout, stood the Castle *Cupra* of the *Tuscans* with the antique Temple of
Juno Caprana now tis a Town but yet envroned with Walls, Ditches,
Fortreffes, and Arms in readinefs, to defend it felf from the violence
and snares of the *Corfari*, banisht Persons, Robers and other wicked Men, whereby the Inhabitants live securely and are well provi-
in all things for the receit of ftrangers. 'Tis a moft ftately Church,
built with squared Stones of excellent Marble of great coft, in the
midft whereof the *Pilgrims* visite that moft holy Chamber of the Virgin *Mary* with a great devotion, which is compaffed in with a furrounding square of Marbles engraven and wrought with figures of
admirable artifice, but so placed that it toucheth not the Walls thereof in any part, and tis credibly held, that those Walls within which
the Queen of Heaven was born and brought up, ought not to be more
wrought or adorned by human induftry. This Chamber was brought
hither from *Paleftina* by *Angells*, and he is pronounced an Infidel
that doubts thereof. having so many grave Authors and dayly Miracles to prove it.

The great quantity of Tablets, Offerings, and Prefents, hung upon the Walls, Pillars, and Cornifhes of the Church, at the firft entrance will raife a certain pronefs to honour the place in the moft ob-
durat heart. There it clearly appears how great and infpeakable figns
the moft great God fhewes of his Power for the Salvation of human
kind, by granting all the prayers of fuch as with a devout and fincere
heart feek him, &c.

The infinite Miracles wrought there, fhew that God will be fought
in one place more than another, in the Church hang many pourtraies
of human mifery (as in a theatre) which notwithftanding our merci-
full God conduceth to a good end, as particularly by divers acci-
dents by Water, evil Times, Shipwracks, Thunderbolts Earthquakes

Deſtructions, Precipitous falls, braking of bones, Sickneſſes, diſeaſes, Plague, Slaughters, Robberies, Priſons, Torments, hunger, Want, and many others, which a hundred tongues can hardly explicate as *Virgil* ſaith.

With which afflictionsGod is pleaſed to exerciſe his Children, to expreſſe his Clemency more than his Juſtice, that by it we may more truly prepare our hearts and our Souls worthy for his habitation,and for our eternal bliſs.

In this Church are many rare and pretious gifts of ſeveral Princes, dedicated to the Virgin *Mary*, in the Veſtry are kept the Veſts, Veſſels of Gold and Silver and other Riches of immenſe valew, and about the Chnrch are many Tablets of Verſes in praiſe of the Church.

The Nobleneſs and Magnificence of the Church of LORETO, compendiouſly drawn out of the ſive Books of *Floratio Torſellino* a Jeſuiſt.

ALthough no day paſſeth wherein theCel of the holyVirgin isnot viſitedbymany ſtrangers,aswell*Poles,Spaniards,Germans,Portugals,* & other *Oltramontaneous* and *Oltramarine* Nations as *Italians*)yet there are two ſeaſons in the yeer, when there is exceeding concourſe to wit, Spring and Autumn. In the Spring begins the Solemnity, the day of the Conception of our Lord, and in Autumn the day of the birth of our Lady, and each ſolemnity continues for 3. Moneths, wherein each day the houſe of *Loreto* is repaired to by great multitudes of people,the greater part whereof go in companies with their Enſignes, having carryed before them a Crucifix with the Images of Saints. Every Company hath its own governors & Prieſts who ſing, & the *Donatives* offered follow, which are of more or leſſe valew according to the qnality of the Perſons and their Devotions, which method of going&ſinging praiers& praiſes toGod,excites great piety in the Pilgrims,and people who follow (though not in order) in infinite multitudes. When at a diſtance the Companies begin to ſee the Church (which is ſeated on a hill above the Fields) they internally are moved to devotion, and caſt themſelves upon theground weeping for joy, ſaluting the Mother of God,and then purſue their journey, ſome renting their garments and putting on ſackcloth, others beating themſelves, and being beaten by others with many ſtripes on the nakedſhoulders.Inthe mean time thePrieſts ofLoreto,go to meet theſeCompanies, introducing them into the Church,with ſolemn muſick, Trumpets,and Bells, when they approach the dore the Companies again fall flat on the ground ſaluting the Virgin from the bottome of their hearts, with ſuch zeal, that the beholders are moved to tears.   Ar-

Arrived at the Chamber of the Virgin, which shines most clear by
the many lights brought in their hands, they contemplate the Effigies of the *Madonna*, with such Piety, Tears, Sighs, and humility,
as is wonderfull, and many affix them selves so much to consider the
place and Actions which the Mother of Christ there performed, that
were they not driven out by other companies who overtake them,
they would never remove thence, but such as come from far Countreys, not being able to preserve the order of Companies, resort
thither in the best manner they can, the most part if not all communicate there, and leave their offerings at the Altar, but the most precious offerings are consigned to the deputies, whose charge is to set
them and the givers names down in a Book, for perpetual remembrance. The Altar erected by the Apostles, and the effigies of the
Virgin *Mary*, are alwaies clothed from time to time with sumptuous
garments, aud ornaments of great valew both in Gold and
Jemms.

  The Church is alwaies full with wax lights and Lamps burning,
resounding with musick and Organs, but what more imports tis filled
with the Spirit of God, which terrifies the bad, rejoices the good, heals
the infirm, and works stupendious miracles. The number of the
Pilgrims at *Faster* useth to be 12000. and at the *Penticost* and nativity
of the Virgin not much inferiour if not more, there hath been the day
of the said Nativity in our times, and the day following above two
hundred thousand Persons which hath necessitated the intendents,
to make a rail round about the Cel whereby to exclude and admit
whom they think fit, that they may not be opprest by Multitude.
Moreover because in all times the Companies of Souldiers intending for the Wars resort thither first to confess and communicate, the
Road is so well accommodated with Inns and houses of Reception,
that any Person though delicate and weak, may make the journey
on foot, besides that the continual concourse of fresh companies to
and fro, renders the way less heavy; this convenience invited *M.
Antonio Colonna* (not to speak of others) a famous, rich, and great
Commander, to take that Journey on foot. These Companies having seen the countenance of the Virgin, rejoyce spiritually, and commonly acknowlege they have gathered great benefit from the Pilgri-
mage though difficult. Were it not too long & difficult twere worth
ones pains to recount the vowes there made, and rendred to God,
how many there escape out of the mire of Sin, how many are there
loosed from the intricate tyes of carnal and forbidden pleasures, how
many there lay down their hatred and old envy, how many men almost desperate to do more good, and bound already to the Gates of
hell by compact between them and the Divel, yet there deliver themselves from the Enemy, and recover a state of Salvation; finally, as
the Soul is more pretious than the Body, so the Miracles of the blessed Virgin of *Loreto* wrought for the Soul, are more than those that
are for the Body, so that to discourse more at large the things touched here, were a desire to measure and confine the divine power by
humane frailty. Which to avoid, tis better to let it alone, than un-
dertaking it to rest unsatisfied, and although for the most part Fame
surpasseth the thing spoken of; yet whoever hath seen *Loreto*, must
confess Fame could not speak so much of it and its glory as he there
saw and contemplated.   L l   The

The remarkable and wonderfull
Site of the Houſe of
LORETO.

TIs credibly reported, that the houſe of the bleſſed Virgin leaving (of its own accord) *Galilea*, firſt went into *Dolmatia*
and there ſtopped in a Wood of *Marchiano*, whence it went into a
Mountain belonging to two Brothers who were at diſcord, but to
remain there for a time, God having determinated that it ſhould ſtay
where now it ſtands, and we hope will ever continue if ſome ſins
of the adjcent People make not the place unworthy and tis preſu-
med that ſince it came from *Galilee* and the mount becauſe the ſins of
the People there made it unworthy, ſo the knowlege the Virgin had
of the quality of this People made her tranſmit her habitation hither
and the often mutations of the places makes it evident to all, that
this is the true *Stanza* or Cell of the bleſſed Virgin departed from
Galilea.

It arrived in this Province in *Italy*, in the yeer 1295. and in leſſe
than a yeer changed its place of ſtay three times though but within
compaſſe of a mile, but who will conſider its now aboade muſt find
that the wit of man could not invent a better.

P.Battiſta Mantouano Viccar General of the *Carmelites* (among other
grave Authers)to whom this houſe was firſt given in cuſtody before
it left *Galilee*) averrs the trnth of the former relations: Societies of
Prieſts, that are *Linguiſts* have it now in government whereby to be
the better able to take the confeſſions of all Nations and give ab-
ſolutions, &c.

RECANATI.

FRom *Loreto* the way leads to *Recanati,* a new City built out of the
Reliques of the old *Helvia Ricina*, whereof ſome will have *Mace-*
rata to be built alſo, which *Helvia* was once magnificently repaired
by *Helvio*, many of its old foundations and the baſes of an Amphitheatre yet appear upon the Road. From *Loreto* to *Recanati*, is three
mile of very rough Way, over Mountains. In it is held a publick
fair every yeer in September, in the great Church lies Pope *Gregory*
the 12th. who in the Council of *Conſtanza* renounced the Papacy,
tis ſeated on the top of a high and ſpatious Mountain environed
with the *Apenines*, *Gingolo*, the Sea, and ſome other little Hills. Beyond which is a plain, in it, *San Severino*, heretofore a Bourg, but
made a City by Pope *Sixtus quintus*, *Mathelica* and *Fabriano*, famous
for the Pure writing paper there made, and then *Gamerino*, a well fortified place abounding no leſs in Riches than People. It alwaies
aſſiſted

aſſiſted the *Romans*, aud hath produced many emminent Men. Through the Vale *Camerino,* you may go to *Foligno* and *Spoleto.*

MACERATA.

KEEping the direct Way thorow the Mountains you meet *Mace-rata,* famous for greatneſſe and beauty, and the moſt noble City of the *Marchiano.* In it is a College of Lawyers, called the *Rota,* deputed to hear Cauſes, and the Reſidence of the Governors of all the Province, Two great Cauſes for its full peopling: About it ly ſeveral Bourgs, Caſtles, and Towns, as *Tolentino*, where they reverence the reliques of *San Nicolo,* of the *Auguſtine* Order, who there lived holily: *Montalto, Fermo, Aſcolo,* and *Scravalle,* beyond which lies *Santa Anatolia,* whence through a Valley lies the way to *San Foligno,* which is two days journy from *Loreto.*

FOLIGNO.

THe *Longobardi,* having deſtroyed *Foro Flaminio*, the Inhabitants out of its Ruines built *Foligno.* The City is rich in Merchandize, ſmall but pleaſant, it hath a goodly porte, whence the Citizens repelled the aſſaults of the *Longobardi,* the Cities *Perugia* and *Aſſiſia* are Weſtward twenty miles from *Foligno.*

All along the *Flaminian* Way, ly moſt flouriſhing Fields, planted with all ſorts of Fruits, Vines, Gardens, Olive-Trees,& Almonds, praiſed to the skies, by *Propertius Virgil,* and other Poets.

On the right hand lies *Mevania,* the Countrey of *Propertius* and its Territory, which produceth large Bulls and Oxen, on the left was the Antient Temple of *Metuſca,* near it is the Source of the River *Clitumnus,* iſſuing wirh a clear and plentifull head of Water, enough to water the Fields of *Bertagna,* which at its ſecond ſtage, had the name of a God given it by the blind Gentiles, to whom tis believed the neighbouring Temple of Marble (now antique yet noble) was dedicate in old time. Tis made in that form (which *Vitruvius* writing of the order of Temples, teaches that thoſe of Fountains, *Nimphes, Venus, Flora,* and *Proſerpina.* ought to have, to wit to have ſome ſimilitude with their Gods) and hath in the Ornaments of the outſide leaves of Bears-foot, and Holm tree, which demonſtrate the fruitfulneſs of *Clitumnus,* which the Antients obſerved, ſo fatned the adjacent Paſtures, that thereby the Herds of Cattel grew very great, and (*Pliny, Lucan,* and *Servius* the Commentator of *Virgil*) averr that thoſe Cattel drinking of the water of *Clitumnus* became white.

Out of theſe Herds the *Roman* Conquerors uſed to ſelect the moſt fair, and in their triumphs to ſacrifice them for a happy Augury to the victory brought with them. The ſame alſo were led by the Emperors, (which triumphed) with their horns guilt, and bathed with the water of this River, unto the *Campidoglio,* and there ſacrificed to *Jove* and other Gods, which made the *Spoletini* to honour *Clitumnus* as a God, and to it were dedicated by the antients, Temples and Groves, as may be collected from *Propertius* in theſe words.

Qua formofa fuo Clitumnus flumina Luco
Integer, & niveos abluit unda boves.

Virgil the Prince of Poets in the fecond of his *Gorgicks*, fpeaking politely of the praife of *Italy*, faith thus.

Hinc albi Clitumne greges & maxima taurus
Victima fæpe tuo perfufi flumine facro
Romanos ad templa Deum duxere triumphos.

Silius alfo touches upon this conceipt in the *Carthaginian* War in few
words to wit

Et lavit ingentem perfufum flumine facro
Clitumnus taurum.

SPOLETO.

IN the fame day the Traveller may go from *Foligno*, to *Spoleto*, a fplendid City deficient in nothing, the Refidence of the *Longobardi* Princes now ennobled by the Title of the Duke of *Ombra*, antiently twas a
ftrong *Roman* Colony fo made by *Litius*, and reduced by the *Romans*,
when they had overthrown the *Ombri*, in the Confulate of *C. Claudius Centone*, and *Marius Sempronius Tuditanus*. Which Colony (after
the *Romans* had received the Rout near *Trafineno*) was fo bold as to
withftand *Hannibal* the Conqueror, and taught him to gather what
vaft ftrength the *Roman* Empire was of from the power of one fole
Colony, by forceing him to turn tayl, & retreat after the loffe of many
men into the *Marchiana*. The old broken ftructures fhew that it flourifhed greatly in the *Romans* time. One may yet fee the Palace of *Theodorick* King of *Goths*, deftroyed by the *Goths* but rebuilt by *Narfete*
Captain for *Juftinian* the Emperor. The Temple of Concord, the
foundation of a Theatre and of ftately Aquiducts.

TERNI.

THe following day through the Valley *Strattura* (clofed in by
Hills, Rocks, and cliffs of the *Apenines*) you reach *Terni* called
Iteranna by the Antients from its inclofure between the branches of
the River *Nera*. The old Ruins of the Edifices fhew it to have been
in all things greater than at prefent, and within memory tis known
much decay came to it by inteftine hatred and civil difcords.
Many antient Marble Infcriptions fhew that twas a free City of
the *Romans*, but at what time it received the title of a free City, and
the Prerogative of *Roman Denizenfhip*, is not certainly known. *Pighius* obferves from a great Marble ftone fixed in the Walls of the Cathedral Church, that twas built 544. yeers before the Confulate of
C. Domitius Enobarbus, and *M. Camillus Scribonianus*, who were Confuls 624. yeers after the foundation of Rome, and that facrifice was
made in *Terni*, to the health of Liberty, and the *Genius* of the City,
to

to gratifie *Tiberius Cæsar*, who then elevated himself from the feet of *Seianus*: The said *Pighius* deduceth thus much from the Title on the said Marble, and in his Annales of the Senate and People of *Rome* sets it down more distinctly: we conclude from the whole that twas built 80. yeers after *Rome*, under *Numa*, and then obtained its title of a Municipal City. The Territory of *Terni* through the site, and the usefullnesse of the sweet Waters, is all of a fat soyl being exposed to a benign Sun, which in some part appologizeth for what *Pliny* saies, to wit, that the Meadows are mowed 4 times in a yeer, and afterwards fed, besides that Turnips have there lately grown of 30. pound weight (whereof four makes an Asses Load) and *Pliny* saies 40. pound weight.

NARNI.

KEEping the *Via Flaminia*, you arrive at *Narni*, placed on a rough Hill of difficult ascent, at the foot whereof runs the River *Nera*, roaring through the breakings of the Rocks, wherewith it encounters; *Livy* and *Stephano Gramatico*, derive the name of the City from that of the River, and *Martial* in the 7th. book of his Epigrames describes it thus.

> *Narnia sulphureo, quam gurgite candidus amnis*
> *Circuit ancipiti vix adeunda jugo.*

The same *Livy* affirms, that the City was first called *Nequino*, and the Inhabitants thence *Nequinati*, when subdued by the *Romans*, from the paultry and wicked customes of the People, but afterwards the *Roman* Colony despising that name, called it *Narni* from the Rivers name.

The Triumphs in the *Campidoglio* set forth that the *Nequinati* were confederate with the *Sanniti*, and with them overcome by *M. Petinus* the Consul, who therefor triumphed in the 454th. yeer of *Rome*, and then made a Colony as aforesaid.

Now the Cities form is long, and fair in Fabricks, and plentifully supplyed from its near *Campagna*, though in the memory of our Ancestors, and since it hath been much turmoyled with troubles and Warrs. Without *Narni* over the River are wonderfull great Arches of a Bridge, which did conjoyn two high and precipitous Mountains between which the River passed, some believe this Bridge was built by *Augustus* with the spoils of the *Siacambri*, and *Procopius* affirms it, adding that more eminent Arches were never seen, the Reliques now appearing demonstrate it the work of a flourishing Empire, and of excessive expence, *Martial* tis supposed speaks herof in these words.

> *Sed jam parce mihi, nec abutere Narnia Quinto,*
> *Perpetuo liceat sic tibi ponte frui.*

The stones of this Bridge are cemented with Iron and Lead, one Arch now to be seen is 200. foot broad and 150. foot high, under which tis said is buried great Treasure.

A stream is brought into the City which passeth for 15. miles under most high Mountains, and supplies three brass fountains; there is also a water of *Narni* called *carestia* or Famine, because it never appears but the yeer before some great famin, as it happened in *Anno* 1589. it yields also many healthfull waters.

Forty miles off *Narni* to go in the way to *Rome* is a Mountainous Rock, through which the Way is cut with Chizels 30. foot deep and 15 broad, beyond which is pleasant way to *Ottricoli* a mile from *Tevere*.

Passing by the antiquities of the *Via Flaminia* and the vast ruines of *Ottricoli*, you come to *Tevere*, beholding by the way great Reliques of publick structures, as Temples, Baths, Aqueducts, Conservatories of water, a Theatre and Amphitheatre, which testify the grandezza and magnificence of that municipal City, while the *Roman* Empire flourished.

Two inscriptions of statues dedicate to the Father and Daughter by the publick, make appear that they built those Baths at their own expence, and then gave them to the publique, both which are inscribed on Marble as followeth.

L. Iulio L. F. Pal.	*Juliæ Lucillæ*
Iuliano.	*L. Julii. Juliani. Fil*
IIII. Vir. Æd.	*Patroni municipi*
III. 1: D.	*Cujus. Pater*
IIII. Vir Quin que	*Termas Ocricula-*
Quinq; 11. Dast	*nis a Solo. Etructas*
Patrono	*Sua. Pecunia. Dona-*
Municipi	*vit*
Plebs. Ob. Merita	*Dcc Aug. Plebs*
L. D. D. D.	*L. D. D. D.*

Whence you passe by the Town *Tevere* near the stone Bridge built by *Augustus*, which Bridge was so great, that with its ruines it turned and hindred the course of the River, thence coasting the foot of the Mountain *Soratte*, at night you lodge at *Rignano*.

Pope *Clement* the 8th. commanded (imitating *Augustus*) to his great costs and no less glory, this Bridge to be repaired; here terminated the Burroughs of *Rome* in the time of the Emperour *Aurelianus*; and we read that in former times *Rome* was 150. miles in circuit; and that while *Constantine* reigned, the Walls and buildings from *Tevere* to *Rome* were so thick, that who was but seldome conversant there took it for the City of *Rome*. The River being past you meet *Borgheto*, the City *Castellan*, and *Caprarola*, and farther on is the Bridge *Milvio* or *Mole*, where God shewed to *Constantine* a Cross with these words, *In hoc signo vinces*, with which encouragement *Constantine* fought and overcame *Maxentius* the Tyrant, by which Bridge one passeth the *Tevere* or *Tiber*, and so arrives to the Suburbs of *Rome*, entring the *Porta Flaminia*, now called *Porta del Popolo*.

LUC-

LVCCA.

THis City glories, in the univerfal agreement of all Authors, that tis one of the moft antient of *Italy*, and they that fpeak of its lateft Original attribute it to *Lucchio Lucumone Lacrte* of *Tufcany*, who reigned 46. yeers after the foundation of *Rome*. from whom fome fay it took its name *Lucca*, but fome others averr twas built long before that time, even by the *Grecians* before the deftruction of *Troy*. It alwaies was for its ftrength and power of much confideration: and that made *C. Cempronius* after the overthrow he received from *Hannibal* at *Trebbia*, and the leffe fortunate day fought before *Piacenza* to recover *Lucca*, with the remnant of his Army as to a place that ycelded afecure retreat; and the valorous *Narfete*, who for the Emperour *Juftinian*, freed *Italy* of the *Goths*, could not have gained it with his 7 Moneths tedious and moft rigorous fiege, had he not by a certain wile and cunning perfwaded or rather intreated theCitizens to deliver their City of their own accord and with their own terms. Its Seignors or Lords have fo well added to its former ftrength, that no City in *Italy* comes near it, for it hath eleaven ftrong Bulworks in leffe than 3. miles circuit, and a vaft wall, with works within, upon which the Trees planted, the pleafant and fertile hills furrounding it, and the ftately Palaces in the heart of it renders it a moft delightfull City.

Strabo reports the *Romans* often raifed there many foot Souldiers and fome Horfe, and *Gafper Sardo* writes that at the Naval fight bethe Chriftians and *Sarazens* in *anno* 1179. *Lucca* had feaven Galleys, under the command of *Nino delli Obezi* its Citizen, a valiant Captain, who was alfo Lieutenant of thofe of the Church in the fame Fleet, when they obtained immortal fame in that Victory, and in 1303. the *Lucchefi* colleagued with the *Florentines* againft the *Piftoiefi*, and of the 16000. foot and 1600. Horfe, then in the Army, the *Lucchefi* had 10000. Foot, and 600. Horfe.

This City was beloved, and held in great efteem by the *Romans* conceding to it, the fo much coveted privilege of a municipal City, and making it a Colony.

We read in particular, that (at the needfull repairing of *Rome*) C. *Cæfar* paffed a winter there with two hundred Senators. whereof were *Pompey* and *Crafus*, who here complotted and conftituted the firft Triumvirate. Near the Church of Saint *Auguftine*, are fome Reliques of a noble Temple dedicate to *Saturn*, with the foot-fteps of an Amphitheatre, infallible teftimonies of its Grandure.

In the time that *Tufcany* with the reft of *Italy* divided into 12 Governments was under the *Longobardi*, *Lucca* was the appointed, refidence for the Regent of *Tufcany*, where (as fuch) *Defiderius* refided, when in *anno* 577. he was created King of the *Longobardi*. Afterwards twas governed by Marquefes, who alfo refided there as in the *Metropolis* of that Province, where the *Marchefe Adalberto* dwelt with infinite Splendour, and fo nobly in *anno* 902. received there *Lewis* the Emperour, that he admiring the Kingly magnificence and greatneffe wherein the *Marchefe* lived, faid to one of his Intimats, that truly (abftracting from the Title) he faw not wherein the *Mar-*

chefe

Marquess was inferiour to him. Among the, Marqueses of *Tuscany*, *Bonilf du Lucca* for his great Riches, his own valour and merits, was so much renowned, that he obtained for his wife, *Beatrice* Daughter of *Corradus* the second, and Sister of *Henry* the third, whose Issue *La Contessa Matilda*, in a short course of time, remained Heiress and Lady of this and many other Cities of *Italy*, and at her death bequeathed the Ciry *Ferrara* and that state which is called the Patrimony of Saint *Peter* to the *Roman* Church, by her last Will and Testament, which is yet preserved in *Lucca*.

Afterwards *Lucca* began to relish the beloved fruits of its antient Liberty, and in the yeer 1288. obtained a confirmation of it from the Emperour *Rodolphus*, in which times being chiefly ruled by the *Guelfan* Faction, it was a long time preserved in good amity, and confederate with the *Florentine* Republique. Wherefore in *Anno* 1304. when the *Florentine* Republique was much perplexed by the Factions *Bianchi*, and *Neri*, the *Lucchesi* were requested by the *Florentines* to aid them, in repressing their tumultuous and confused Government, and when absolute power was given to the *Lucchesi* over all *Florence*, from *Lucca* were sent some of the most prudent Citizens, accompanied with 9000. Souldiers, the most part horse: Who being suddainly arrived, settled their guards up and down the City as they pleased, and as if the City *Florence* had been absolutely under their Dominion: which done, they took in hand the government, and with the entire satisfaction of that Republique, in sixteen days, they quieted the tumults and Factions, and established the form of the Government for the future.

Some time after the which *Lucca* was governed by *Ugoccione* and by *Castruccio* its Citizen, an excellent Captain, who with his own single valour kept the neighbouring Common-wealth in continual fear and suspicion, and finally after it had undergon for severall yeers through adverse fortune, the tyranny of divers Governours, its Usurpers; It reobtained for a certain sum of mony its former Liberty, from *Charls* the 4th. which (except from the yeer 1400. to 1430. when twas usurped by *Paolo Gnsinigi* its Citizen) it hath ever since enjoyed most happily, and doth at present rejoice therein, and live in great tranquillity yet under the protection of the Catholick King, and with such security, that those Gentlemen to whom the Government of the Republique is committed, neither watch at, nor take care for any thing more than the publique good, and Union of all its Citizens, the two principal and necessary Foundations, for the maintenance of the Republique. Its administration and Government is an *Oligarchy*.

This City is replenisht with many good and Artfull Structures, and a great number of stately Churches; Among which Its Cathedral, dedicate to Saint *Martin*, retains the chief prerogative. This Church hath been much adorned and favoured by the Popes, and first by *Alexander* the second, who in the yeer of our Lord 1070. (as we read in *Baronius*) was pleased to take upon himself the pains to consecrate it, then *Urban* the sixth in anno 1382. there celebrated *Mass* the night of the Nativity of our Lord, and honoured the chief standard bearer, with the reading the Epistle by his order. The Bishop and Canons are endowed with great Privileges: being allowed the use
of

of the Archiepiscopal Ornaments, that is a Cross and Pall : and the Canons are faculted to bear the Priests cope, and purple Sattin robes, and the Mitre of white Sattin, *More Cardinalium,* and the Bishop is so great, that the Canons acknowledge no other Superiour but the Apostolick Sea.

 Among the many graces wherewith this Church is favoured by the most high God, some may especially be considered; first that *Lucca* was the first City of *Tuscany*, that (as *Fr. Leandro* and others recount) received the light of the holy faith, which happened in the 44th. yeer of our Salvation, by the means of Saint *Paulino Antiocheno*, the Disciple of Saint *Peter*, crowned a Martyr upon the hill *S. Juliano*, by *Anozino* President in *Pisa*. Secondly, that in the time of *Charles* the Great, with most singular favour it obtained the holy Countenance or Visage, (*Volto Santo*) formed and placed miraculously by a divine hand, on rhe venerable Statue of the Saviour of the World : framed by *Nichodemus* his Disciple, when he stood as 'twere bereaved of senses, with consulting to form the head with such perfection as might give honour to the Statue.

 In it lie the bodies of *S. Paolino, Rigolo* and *Frediano.* Its principal Protectors, with those of 53. other Saints, whereof 14. were *Lucchesi.* In the yeer 1588. was found here a Miraculous Image of our Lady, through whose mediation God hath here done wonderfull graces to the faithfull of divers Nations. It hath afforded Popes, Cardinals, Lords, and famous Captains in great numbers with exquisite Sholars: whereof one must be mentioned, to wit Fryer *Panigni*, having so great a renown through all parts of the world for his elaborate and exact Translation of the holy Scripture out of the Hebrew into the Latin Tongue, whom we will set alone though many others in several Sciences, Qualities, and Honours might be well remembred with him. Many noble Families quitted this their Countrey, either to avoid the plagues, or tyrannies of Usurpers, and retreated to *Venice* and *Genoua*, where some of them are in that honour as to be admitted Partners in the government of those States as if originally of those Republiques.

 The Territories of *Lucca* are small, but through the Industry of the Inhabitants, most fertile and abounding in all things, and so well peopled, that they have eighteen thousand Men enrolled in the Militia, besides those of the City : In them lies those so health, affording Bathes, celebrated by many Historians and other writers, whither annually resort from all parts infinite infirm and Lame Persons, who for the most part return comforted and recovered : In the way whereunto they pass two Bridges over the River *Serchio*, whose Arches are so large that they are wonderfull to the beholders : And tis certain all *Europe* cannot shew two Bridges so noble and fair.

 Many other remarkable things might be inserted of this most noble City and its State, but to avoid prolixity, and pursue the stile begun, the more curious are referred to the particular writers who treat thereof most copiously.

GENOVA.

THis City is head of the Province *Liguria*, situate on the Sea shore at the foot of very high Mountains which though sterile by nature by the Inhabitants industry are become most fertile and produce most necessaries besides those delights which ly on the South part of it. Its ayr is good, though somewhat enclineing to hot and dry tis built in part upon hills and in part upon a Plain or Level. On the Maritine part Westward, It hath a Port may well merit the name of the most importent of *Italy*. It enjoyes the Treasure of Liberty, and is governed in form of a Republique, all its state being content with that form, knowing that to the obedient Life Henour and Goods, under that government are in no hazard. It stands between two Rivers the one on the East 70. miles long, the other on the West a 100. In the River on the *Levant* about 6. miles from the City is the comely Town of *Nervi*, which plentifully stores it with Fruits and Flowers all the Winter. Tis Mistress and sole Governess of the Island of *Corsica*, whence in time of need they can advance a good quantity of Souldiers not inferiour in Arms or Valour to any other Nation. The People of *Corsia* most willingly yeelding them Obedience, for their protection, and that costs them but a quarter of a Crown annually for each fire, and some other incensible tax. Every two yeers the Republique sends thither a Governour and the other Lawgivers and Judges, who haviug finished their Offices, are arraigned by two Gentlemen impowred thither to that effect, who without any trouble to the subject, do them justice against any Governour or Judge at their own doors, who hath done them wrong. Which rule they also observe through all other parts of their state. On all part of the City are infinite pleasant Gardens and Pallaces beautified with all that Art can add to them or Riches procure their Structures being *alla Moderna* though somewhat high in most parts by reason that the City is but small, so that they are necessitated to make the best use of their Room which renders the streets in most places narrow and in some a little obscure. Though one street may be well termed the Mistress of the World called *Strada Nova*, being spatious, long, even, and on each side embellished with most stately Marble Pallaces, the fairest whereof belongs to the Duke of *Oria*. It hath a most spatious Port in form of a Theatre compassed in with noble Structures, which though defended by a most magnificent Mole (judged the greatest in Christendome) yet is when the South and Southwest Winds blow very tempestuous. Opposite to it is a *Pharos* bearing a Lanthern (for light to ships in the night time) of an extraoadinary bigness. *Darsina* is a haven to it also, which is a sure retreat for Galleys and shipping at all seasons: The Galleys being there layed up in their several classis. For publick Edifices it hath the Merchants Hall. The publick Granaries the Dukes Pallace with the Armory of 30000. Men. And their Churches which though (in respect of others of *Italy*) they have not so much Beauty, that once seen they yeeld a *Gusto* to a second view, yet for their polisht Marble and inward Ornaments, were they placed any where but in *Italy* might well merit a larger Account. In
Saint

Saint *Lorenzo* theCathedralChurch is shewed to Persons of quality an
Emerald of ineftible price: as alfo the fumptuous Chapel of *San Gio
Battifta,* wherein they adore his Afhes.

Who delights to fee Pictures of greatMaifters muft repair to thePa-
lace of Prince *D'Ora,* reaching from the bottom of the fhore to the
top of the Mountains, divided into three Gardens. In the fii ft whereof theTerrafes andPorticues bore up one above another with Marble
Pillars, the Fountain of Eagles, and the Family of *Neptune* are very
magnificent. On one fide of which is that famous Cage of Iron work
of fo vaft extent, that it enclofeth a wood of Cypres and other
Trees: The other two are filled with Grotts Orange Trees, and other
delights. And who is curious to fee Statues and Pictures, may repair
with fredome to the Pallaces of the Signori *Giuftiniano, Pallavicino,
Horatio, Chiavari,* and *Giovan, Caclo Doria;* who have collections of
fuch Rarities of fo great valew, as is fcarce to be believed a Treafure
for a private Man. Two Stautes which *Giuftiniano* hath for their incomparable and Price deferve particuler mention, to wit, an antient
Cupid of Maible fleeping, and an antique head with a body to it,
efteemed moft rare antiquities.

Religion fo flourifhes in *Genoua,* that they may (with thanks to
God)fay that tis there in the higth of Glory.

It contains about a hundred thoufand Souls more or lefs: out of
which in all Ages have proceeded Eminent Sholars and Souldiers.

Which fhall end the relation here with this fhort Addition, that
whofoever for delight fees *Genoua,* muft repair thither in the begining
of Summer, who for profit or Merchandize may take their own conveniency. To take a perfect view, and a full profpect of the City, in
a calm and ferene day you muft embark in a fmall Boat, and eloign
on the Sea the diftance of an ordinary Sight, where the City feems
fo to be united with the Burroughs, and both fo conjoyned afford fo
fair an Object, as muft be confeft to be a moft beautifull and noble
Profpective.

And who would behold *Genoua* from a high place, muft afcend
the Steeple of the Church of *S. Benigno,* and the *Pharos* where the
Lanthorn ftands.

In the Church of Saint *John* the *Baptift* among its other Reliques,
they pretend to have the heads of Saint *Laurence,* and Saint *Sebaftian*
the Martyr, the Arms of Saint *Matthew* and Saint *Theodore* the Martyr
and the right hand of Saint *James* the lefs, together with a certain veffel of *Calcidonian* ftone, beftowed on this Church by Pope Innocent
the 8th. which they fay to be the fame difh wherein the Daughter
of *Herodias* brought in the head of Saint *John Baptift* to her Mother.
In the fame Church lies the body of *S. Siri,* or rather *Sylus,* the third
Bifhop of this City, under the high altar with this Epitaph.

*Hic, recubat Sylus facro baptifmate dictus,
Cujus terra levis Florida menbra premi.*

wherewith this Book concludes.

the end of the firft Book.

LVCCA
MALTE
S. CROCE IN GIERVSALEM
S. SEBASTIANO

THE
HISTORY
OF
ITALY,

BEING

A Compendious DESCRIPTION
OF
ROME

THE
Miſtreſs of the WORLD, with an Account
of all particulars therein worth Obſervation
as well Divine as Humane.

The Second PART.

Ammianus Marcellinus in the 14th. Book of his Hiſtory ſpeaks
after this manner of *ROME*.

T is not a little wonder that Virtue and Fortune (whom the
world conclude almoſt at perpetual diſcord) ſhould accord together in that inſtant of time, when *Rome* for its
agrandizing, had ſo much need of their united force. By
which their conjoyned ſtrengths, *Rome* augmented her Empire to
that Greatneſs, that ſhe ſubjugated the whole World. Tis worth
conſidering the Paralell between her and a Childe : Who in its firſt
                              O   Infancy

Infancy creeps, when she began to be built and peopled : then it ac-
quires vigour & strength, for Adolescential Exercises, so she then warred only with her neighbours, but when arrived to more full strength
is employed in Manly disputes: So she when arived to be 300. yeers
old, and increased both in vigour and People, began to pass Mountains and Seas, pursuing Warr into the farthest Countreys, where
she obtained and brought home innumerable Victories and Triumphs from the Barbarous and wilde Nations : In the end, having
made infinite noble Attempts, and acquired whatever upon Earth
through Valour was to be obtained (as twere arrived to mature Age)
she begun to acquiesce, whereby the better to enjoy those good benefits and Advantages, which she had then provided for: Comitting the Troubles of Government to the Emperors (as to her Natural Children) for her better and more pleasing repose: At which time
although the People participated of that publique Ease and Profit,
and the Souldiery moved not for her further advancement: yet such
was the Care of her Greatness : that the *Roman* Majesty was no less
Reverenced than feared.

Virgil in praise of *Rome* wrote these Verses.

Ipse Lupæ fulvo nutricis tegmine lætus
Romulus, Assaraci quem sanguinis Ilia Mater
Eduxit, genti Mavortia condidit olim
Mænia . Romanosque suo de nomine dixit.
Illius auspiciis rerum pulcherrima Roma
Imperium terris, animos æquavit Olimpo,
Septemque una sibi muro circumdedit Arces :
Felix prole virûm: qualis Berecinthia Mater
Invehitur curru Phrygias turrita per Urbes,
Læta Deûm partu, centum complexa ne potes
Omnes cælicolas, omnes supera alta tenentes.
Hanc olim Indiginæ Fauni, Nimphæque tenebant :
Gensque virûm truncis, & duro robore nata,
Quæ duo disjectis tenuerunt oppida muris :
Hanc Janus pater, hanc Saturnus condidit Urbem.
Janiculum Huic, illi fuerat Saturnia nomen.

And *Ovid* surnamed *Naso* composed these of *Rome.*

Crescendo formam mutavit Martia Roma,
Appenini genæ, quæ proxima Tibridis undis
Mole sub ingenti posuit fundamina rerum,
Quanta nec est, nec erit, nec visa prioribus annis.
Hanc alii proceres per sæcula longa potentem,
Sed dominam rerum de Sanguine natus Juli
Effecit, quo, quum tellus suit usa, fruuntur
Ætherea sedes, cælumque sit exitus illi.

Who saith also in another place:

Hîc ubi nunc Roma est, olim fuit ardua sylva
Tantaque res paucis pascua bobus erat.

In

In another.

Gentibus est aliis, tellus data limite certo,
Romanæ spatium est urbis, & orbis idem.

Divers other testimonies and Declarations of the Magnificence
of *Rome* were writ by *Ausonius Claudianus*, *Rutilius Numantianus*,
old Authors, and by *Julius Cæsar Scaliger*, *Faustus Sabeus* a *Brescian*,
and other modern writers, which for brevity sake are here omitted
but without comitting an unpardonable fault, we must not leave
out these elegant verses of *Marcus Antonius Flaminius*, viz.

Antiquum revocat decus
Divûm Roma domus, & caput Urbium.
Vertex nobilis Imperî:
Mater magnanimûm Roma Quiritium.
Fortunata per Oppida
Cornu fundit opes Copia divite,
Virtuti suus est honos,
Et legum timor, & prisca redit fides.

Nor these of *M. Valerius Martialis.*

Terrarum Dea, gentiumque Roma,
Cui par est nihil, & nihil secundum.

The praise of *R O M E* written by *S T E F A N O PIGHIO.*

ROME the Glorious is replenisht with stupendious Structures, as well publique, appertaining to the Popes, as private, belonging to Cardinals and Princes, who at this time frequent
that City. The Gardens behind the *Vatican* called *Belvedere*, from
their beauty and pleasantness, are no less estimable: In which Pope
Sistus quartus, erected a noble Palace without regard to his expence,
foe it might be excellently carved, painted, guilt, and embellish't
with rare figures, thereby to make it a Kingly Receptacle for entertainment of such eminent Princes and Lords, as should repair to
Rome : Before the Front of that Pallace where the Pope resides, is a
most stately Porticue composed in the form of a Theater, raised
some steps above the Earth, and garnished with many marble Statues: and on the western part is another Porticue which stands between the one and the other Palace, (*Belveder* being near the
Popes Palace) and will be when finish't according to the design, a
most stately Piece and of great value.
But of greater wonder are those footsteps and marks of old *Rome*
which seem rather the works of Gyants than of ordinary men: al-
O o 2   though

though(compared to what twas)much inferiour by the great fallings and decayes of Towers, and Walls in divers places , where stood formerly publique Edifices. *Martial* in most elegant Verse sets the Theater of *Titus Vespacian*, before the seaven wonders of the World: and not unworthily, since to this day , it creates admiration in all judicious Men, by its prodigious Structure. Who admires not the *Pantheon*, or the *Circalean*, *Dioclefian*, and *Constantinian* Baths, which Fabricks are built with rare art, and so great that they seem Castles and Towns : Or the vast number of Arches, Triumphals, Collumns, Sculptures of whole Armies figured to the Life: Pyramids, and Obelisks , of so vast bigness, that who would transport one of them must build a ship large and strong enough to float and sail laden with a Mountain. What shall we say of the great entire Statues, of the *Castori* on Horseback? of the great bodies of Rivers prostrate on the ground ? of so many brass Statues and Vessels capacious to bath in? or of those Marble Tablets and Pillars with hundreds of other excellencies. Each of which are worthy of , and would fill up a particular volume if worthily described.

The Gardens of *Belvedere*, contain some Statues of white Marble far bigger than the body of a Man, as of *Apollo*, of *Hercules*, of *Venus*, of *Mercury*, of the *Genius* of the *Prince*, thought by some to be of *Anthony*, of *Adrian* the Emperor, of a Nymph leaning near a River, judged by some to be *Cleopatra*, and of *Laocoon* the Trojan with his two Sons, enveloped in the twistings of the Serpents, a piece much applauded by *Pliny*, cut out of one entire Stone, which that it might receive as excelling shapes, and forms as could be carved by industry or Art, *Agesandro*, *Polidoro* , and *Asenodoro* , three rare *Rodian* Sculptors applyed their joynt Industry, study, & pains: This curious Sculpture, was preserved by miracle of Fortune, at the destruction of the Palace of *Titus Vespasian* the Emperour, as also of the River *Tevere*, or *Tyber* with the Wolfe giving suck to *Romulus* and *Remus* carved out of one tire Stone, and likewise the great *Nilus* leaning on a *Sphinx* , on the heigth whereof stand sixteen Children, denoting the sixteen Cubits of the increase of that River, observed by the *Ægyptians* , and every one of those Children is in such manner figured, that it excellently describes the effect, which at that rise and increase it wrought on the Land of *Ægypt* sa, for example, the sixteenth Child is placed upon a shoulder of the River, with a basket of flowers and fruits upon its head, and this Child signifies that the increase of the River, to the sixteenth Cubit, enriches the Earth to the production of great plenty of Fruit and brings gladness to it. The 15th, signifies that all is secure and well , and the 14th. brings joyfulness, but all the other increases under 14. are unhappy and miserable as *Pliny* observes in the ninth Chapter of his fifth Book of Natural Histories ; and moreover some Creatures which are only proper to that Countrey with its plants, called *Calamo* a Cane, *Colo Cassia* *Ægyptian* Bean, and *Papiro* called Papir Reed, whereof they were wont to make great leaves to write on, & thereof was the first paper made, & thence as is supposed was that name borrowed which are no where to be found out of *Ægypt*, no more than the Monsters to wit , *Hippotami* or the Sea Horse, whose Feet are like an Ox , back and mayn like a Horse, tusks like a Boar, with a long winding tayl. *Ichneu-*
moni

moni, the *Indian* or *Ægyptian* Ratt, whose property is to creep into the Crocodiles Mouth when he gapeth, to eat his Bowels and so kill him : *Trochili*, a Sea-foul friend to the Crocodil, somewhat like to a wagtail, or Sea Wood.cock : *Ibidi* the black stork, a Bird in *Ægypt*, which hath stiff Leggs, and a long Bill, wherewith when its sick, it adminiftreth it self a Glifter of Sea Water, *Sciachi*, Land Crocodiles: *Crocodrili*, Sea Crocodiles, which can only move the upper Jaw or Chaps. And also the pourtraits of the *Terrofiti*, a generation of *Pigmies* or dwarfs inceffant Men, perpetual Enemies of the Crocodiles, whereof *Pliny* in the 25th. Chapter of his eighth Book of Natural Hiftories treats at large. together with many other fingular Statues in the faid gardens of *Belvedere*, which when seen, thorowly examined, and underftood by intelligent Perfons, yeeld them great delight and fatisfaction.

In the Bath of Pope *Pius* the 4th. is a work of great efteem, being an Ocean cut out of the faireft Marble. The Antients thought the Ocean to be Prince of the Waters, and Father of all things, a Friend to *Prometheus*; And that by means of the humidity and liquidnefs of the Waters, all things feem to generate from Seeds with the affiftance of the Heavens: therefore they believed that every thing received Life from Water, with the favourable friendfhip of the temperat *Genius* of the Cæleftial Bodies. This figure hath the Body covered with a thin vail, whereby they would fignifie, that the Sea fhrouds the Heavens with Clouds of its own vapours, meaning by the Sea, the whole generation of waters, and they denote the Earths being covered with plants by theHairs beard and ordinary skinns beingall figured by the leaves of divers tender Plants. It hath two horns placed upon the Forehead. Firft becaufe the Sea provoked by the winds roars like a Bull; and fecondly becaufe the Sea is governed by the Moons motion, which they called *Cornuta*, thirdly, becaufe the Sea is called Father of Fountains and Rivers, which they figured *Cornuti* or horned. In its right hand is put the Rudder of a Ship, in token that the Waters (by means of the Ships being guided by thefe Rudders) are furrowed as beft likes the Pilot, of which Comodity they feigned *Prometheus* to be the Inventor, they have placed it upon a *Maritine Monfter*, to demonftrate that the Sea is generator of many wonderfull Monfters : One of which to the purpofe is feen in *Rome* in the Antique marble fphere of *Atlas* placed among the celeftial fignes, upon this very occafion : Tis faid that *Andromada* contending for beauty with the Nymphs of the Sea, being overcome, was by them given to this Monfter, which devoured her, out of whofe body(flain on the fhore of *Perfeus* who would have faved that Virgin) there iffued fo much blood, that it dyed the Sea red, whence that Sea was afterwards called *Citreo* or the Red Sea, for all which the *Citreo* is not that gulfe, which is vulgarly called the red Sea, but is that part of the Ocean affianced to the Gulph, which wafhes *Arabia* on the South, but now to our relation of *Rome*.

The firft and cheif part whereof to be vifited through devotion, are the 7. principal Churches, and then the others in their order : wherein are preferved infinite reliques of Saints, and fome remarkable Ones of the holy Jefus our Lord and Saviour as the the Towel of *Santa Veronica* with the effigies of Chrift, the Speer of *Longinus* wherewith he was run into the Breaft. One of thofe Nayls, wherewith our Lord was nayled to the Crofs. One of thofe thirty pence, which as the price of Treafon were given to *Judas* the Traitor by the wicked Jews, all which you are obliged particularly to fearch out as exceeding fingularities not elfewhere to be found.

Of *ROME* the Old, and *ROME* the New,

and of its admirable Excellencies.

ROME formerly the Emprefs of the World cannot be enough praifed: Her power was fo great, her Riches fo immenfe, her fubjects fo innumerable, her Territories and Dominions fo vaft: That well might Saint *Hierome* (in his three wifhes for intermixing that concerning her with fo divine things) be pardonable, which three wifhes were, To have feen our Saviour in the flefh, to have heard Saint *Paul* preach, and to have feen *Rome* in her Glory: which had fo fpread her felf over the whole Earth that a perfect *Idea* of her cannot be comprehended, and muft needs have been the happieft fight that mortal eye could attain to. But when confidered what fhe was, and how fince devoured by fire by the infatiable *Nero*, and how pillaged facked and thoufands of mifchiefs done her by the Barbarous, at the decay of the *Roman* Empire; One may well wonder how the new *Rome*, fhonld be even emulous to exceed the Old: Being at this day the Queen of Cities, the Flower of *Italy*, and as one may fay an Epitome of the whole Earth. She is the Lodging for all Nations. The theatre of the beft Ingenuities of the World, the Habitation of vertue, of Empire, of dignity, of Fortune, The Native Countrey of the Laws, and of all People derivatively, the Fountain of Inftruction, the Head of Religion, the Rule of Juftice, and finally the Original of infinite bleffings, although the Hereticks, Enemies of the truth, will not confefs it, as this Author is pleafed to term thofe of the Reformed Religion.

A Better nor more concife defcription of the glory and deftruction of *Rome* the Old cannot be given than is in thefe two Verfes out of an elegant Poet an Englifh Man.

Roma fuit quondam Terræ, Regina Marifque,
At nunc nec Terras, nec Mare Roma regit.

The fame Poet likewife with noe lefs elegancy defcribes the Grandeur and Eminency of *Rome* the New, under the Popes in thefe two enfuing Verfes.

Roma fuit quondam Terræ Regina Marifque,
Nunc mare nunc Terras, amplius illa regit.

Rome

Rome is scituate in a Countrey sterile enough, and is subject to the Sea, the Winds, and an obscure thick Ayr.

The Circumference of *Rome*, when in her greatest splendour was fifty miles, but now (though not much inferiour comparing her Ecclesiasticks and her immediate possessions with her former Empire) she exceeds not thirteen miles in circuit: In those days she had twenty eight spatious principal Streets, which yet may be traced out and their names with great certainty set down, to wit.

La Via

Appia.	*Latina.*	*Labicana.*
Tiberina.	*Nomentana.*	*Campana.*
Præneftina.	*Cimina.*	*Setina.*
Quintia.	*Valeria.*	*Oftienfe.*
Flaminia.	*Tormenfe.*	*Tretoriana.*
Tiburtina.	*Laurentia.*	*Ardeatina.*
Cornelia.	*Claudia.*	*Caffia.*
Collatina.	*Gallicana.*	*Janiculenfe.*
Solaria.	*Emilia.*	*Trionfale.*
Aurelia.		

With these were others of name, that is to say *L'alta Sommita*, upon the *Monte Cavallo*, now called *Quirinale*, near the *Campo Martio*, *Via Lata*, *La Suburra* near *San Pietro* in *Vincula*. *La Nova* by the Bathes of *Antonius*, *La Trionfale* near the *Porta Vaticana*, *La Vitellia* contiguous with *San Pietro* in *Montorio*. that is at the *Gianiculo*, *La Deta* in the *Campo Martio*, *La Fornicata* near to the *Flaminia*.

The Antient and Famous Gates of ROME are 15.

LA *Flaminia*, called now *Porta del Popolo*, the Gate of the People, La *Gabiofa*, now *di fan Methodio*. La *Collatina*, now *Princiana*, La *Ferentina*, now *Latina*, La *Quirinale*, now called *Agonia*, La *Capena*, now *di fan Paolo*, or *Oftienfe*, La *Tiburtina*, now shut up. La *Tortuenfe*, now *Porta Ripa* L'*Esquilina* now *di fan Lorenza*, L'*Aurelia*, now *di fan Paneratio*. La *Nevia*, now *Porta Maggiore*, La *Fontinale*, now *Settimiana*, La *Celimontana*, now *di Sti Giovanni*, La *Vaticana*, which lyes on the shore of the River *Tevere*. *Tyber*.

Moreover the Burroughs have these ensuing Gates, which were latelier made than those above named; to wit, *Porte di Caftello*, de *Cavalli Leggieri*, l'*Angelica*, la *Pertufa*, & *di fan Spirito*, now the Triumfale, by which the Countrey Men were not permitted to enter.

The Hills comprehended within the Walls of *Rome* are ten *viz.*

Il *Capitolino*, or *Tarpeio*, upon which were standing in the time of *Tarquin* more than Sixty Temples, between great and small with most high Towers, twas compassed with a Wall, and then called the dwelling of the Gods.   P p 2   Il

Il Palatino, or *Pallazzo Maggiore,* all hollowed underneath; This at present is filled with gardens and the ruines of old structures, where stood formerly many noble Fabricks, as the Pallace of the Emperors, the great house of *Angustus,* of *Cicero,* of *Hortensius,* and of *Cataline,* but now in lieu thereof is the stately and spatious Garden of the *Farnezes.*

L'Aventino now called *Santa Sabina,* upon which was the first dwelling of the Christian Popes.

Il Celio, which rise where now stands the Church *Laterinense,* and *Santa Croce,* of *Jerusalem,* in the place of many signal Temples of the Gentiles, and fair Aqueducts.

L'Esquelino, where stands now Saint *Pietro in Vincola:* in the stead of the houses of *Virgil,* of *Propertius,* and the gardens of of *Mecenas.*

Il Viminale, where stands now in lieu of the old House of *Crassus,* The Churches of *Santa Prudentia,* and of *San Lorenzo* in *Palesperna.*

Il Quirinale, now called *Monte Cavallo,* where antiently flourished the Palace and Gardens of *Salustius* and the Houses of *Catullus* and *Aquilius.*

Which said seven Hills were those antient Hills in *Rome,* whence she was denominated *Settigemina.* Afterwards upon divers occasions these following were added.

Il Colle de gli hortuli, or *Pincio,* called vulgarly *di Santa Trinità* upon which formerly stood a Temple of the Sun: where now is that round Fabrick, and deep well.

Il Vaticano, where now stands the Church of Saint *Pietro* and the Pallace of the Pope.

Il Gianicolo, called *Montorio,* where the Churches of *San Onofrio,* and Saint *Pietro di Montorio* now stand.

Il Testacco, which is no other than great heaps of broken pieces of potters Vessels, the Street and residence of those Handicrafts Men being there, they cast those broken pieces which were of no use, into that place which raised this Hill, which Hill or heap rather of broken Vessels is near the *Porta Ostiense,* and near it the famous Sepulcher of *Cicero.*

CHURCHES.

IN *ROME* are above 300. Churches all much frequented, but of them, seaven are more particularly visited through devotion: To wit, *San Pietro nel Vaticano, San Paolo* in the *Via Ostiense, S. Maria maggiore* in the *Via Esquilina, San Sebastiano* without the Gate *Capena* or *S. Sebastiano, San Giovanni Lateranense* in *Monte Celio, Santa Croce,* in *Hierusalem,* in *Monte Celio, San Lorenzo* without the *Porta Esquilina,* called *San Lorenzo* vulgarly.

These five following Churches are beautifyed with noble Brass Gates *San Pietro nel Vaticano, Santa Maria Rotonda, Santo Adriano* antiently the Temple of *Saturn, Santi Cosma,* and *Damiane* (formerly the Temple of *Castor* and *Pollux,* and *San Paolo* in the *Via Ostiense.*

In *Rome* are five principle Church yards or Burying places the first of which lies near Saint *Agnese,* the second near Saint *Pancratio,* the third by Saint *Sebastiano,* the fourth by *San Lorenzo,* the fifth by

San

San Priscella, besides which and many other smaller burying places of such primitive Christians as were martyred or dyed (to this day held in great Veneration) there are above twenty even now without the City.

In it are many Hospitals so well provided that possibly they may be reckoned the most worthy object of the modern Excellencies in *Rome,* whereof some are Common for all Nations and all persons as *L'Hospitale di San Spirito* in the *Vatican: San Gioanni, Laterano,* in *Monte Celio, San Giacomo di Augusta,* in *Valle Martia, Santa Maria della, Consolatione in Velabro,* and *Santo Antonio, in Esquilino,* into any of which the infirm of all Countreys with great love and diligence are received governed and taken care of for their perfect ease and cure of their diseases.

The Hospitals deputed to particular Nations are these. The Hospital of *Santa Maria dell'Annima,* for the *Germans* and *Flemings, San Lodovico* for the *French: San Giacomo* for the *Spaniards: San Tomaso* for the *English: San Pietro* for the *Hungarians, Santa Brigida* for the *Swedes San Giovanni,* and *San Andrea,* for the *Dutch, San Giovanni Battista* for the *Florentines, San Giovanni Battista* near the Banks of the *Tyber,* for the *Genovefes,* instituted and endowed by *Media dusto Cicala,* besides many houses both for poor and Orfanes, of which no particular Catalogue is set down, least filling the volume with the less considerable, we leave not space for the more observable things in *Rome.*

In the Popes Palace called the *Vatican* are the Libraries: The one contains selected choice books alwaies shut up. The other two filled with Latin and Greek Books, written by the Pen in parchment, are as much open: and free to any students for two hours in the day, which were furnished by Pope *Nicholas* the 5th. And now there is a new one collected by Pope *Sistus* the 5th. The Inscriptions, Pictures and Verses of which were made publique by the judicious Pen of *Angelo Rocca,* Bishop of *Tagasta.*

Some other Libraries in *Rome* are worthy notice, to wit, that of *Santa Maria del Popolo.* Of *Santa Maria sopra la Minerva.* Of *Santo Agostino,* of *Vallicola,* of Saint *Andrea,* and of the *Jesuists* Colledge: besides three others which at the siege and sacking of *Rome:* were robbed or burnt.

The Popes Gardens, where Persons of Quality have free ingress together with the houses and Gardens of the Cardinals and other noble Persons of *Rome* yeeld ample solace and recreation to the Lovers of Antiquity by their great varieties in those particulars.

These Pallaces omitting many others deserve a serious and timely visit, to wit, that of the Family of the *Conservadori nel Campi doglio,* of the *Massini,* of the *Rusali,* of the *Rucellai;* of the *Furnesi,* of the *Colonne* the *Mattei, Cevoli,* and *Borghesi,* together with the Pallace *Latterenense* royally repaired by Pope *Sistus* the 5th.

The City *Rome* was antiently divided into nineteen Præcincts or Wards, whereof at present remain but these 14. *de Monti, della Colanna; del Ponte; del Arenula, della Rogola, della Pigna, del Capitello di Transtevere di .:.... del Campo Martio, di Sant Eustachio, di Sant Angelo, della Ripa, del Borgo.*

The six stone Bridges built over the *Tevere* or *Tyber,* are these *Ponte Molle* or *Milvio,* two miles distant from the City, without the *Por-*

ta del Popolo. Ponte _Angelo_ or _Elio_ antiently. _Ponte G
Pope _Siftus_. _Ponte_ Saint _Bartolemeo_ or _Coftio_. _Ponte A
Palatino,_ and _Ponte dei quatro Capi_ formerly called
fo there was one more called _Sublicio,_ whofe Pyles
near the _Aventine_ hills: and another called Trium
appear at _San Spirito._

The Waters wherewith the City is fupplyed
virgine which runs through the _Campo Martio,_ the
cholas the 5th. _l'Alfietina_ reftored by _Innocent_ the 8tl
La Salonia canducted at the coft of _Pius_ the 4th. be
others waters were conveyed by _Gregory_ the 13th.
ent times.

The Piazzaes in _Rome_ are many but thofe of moft
are _La Piazza Vaticana, La Navona , La Giudea_ and I

The new Porticues, or open Galleries which ar
three, _viz :_ That _della Benedittione:_ That in the _Va
ting the Piazza and the _Cerridore_ towards _Belvedere._

The Piazza or market place for Fifh, ftands now
time it was.

That for the Hoggs, Oxen, Cows, Sheep, &c.
was the _Foro Romano._

The Bakers have four Piazzaes, and conjoyned
Shambles: in the _Piazza Novana,_ every _Wednefda_
Market.

The Hills are very little inhabited the ruines of
dring the Ayr fo unwholfome, as to be only fit for
yards, not dwelling Houfes.

Pope _Siftus_ the 5th caufed many fair ftreets to be
The refiding Palace of the Pope ftands contiguou
of Saint _Pietro,_ wherein are contained many ftupe
the Chapel of Pope _Siftus,_ the _Paulina,_ replenifht
pictures of _Michael Angelo , Bonarota_ a _Florentine,_ fo
and exact, that twere the glory of this age to finc
ter could approach then in art or Similitude.   F
Holinefs hath Retreats for the Summer as one near
ther near _Santa Maria Maggiore,_ a third near the _Fo_
the moft favoured and therefore moft ordinary re
Cavallo, heretofore called _Quirinale._

The Palaces of the Cardinals are difperft up ar
as aforefaid.   The houfes of the Citizens are not
in Structure, Antiquities, Pictures and other noble l
Fountains. The Caftle Saint _Angelo,_ or _Mole d'Adrian_
Cittadel, alwaies furnifhed with all warlike provi
folemnize great Feafts and Holy dayes three times
the difcharging of all the great Guns, and Firewor
Feftival day of _San Pietro & Paolo,_ the fecond is
ally on the day whereon the immediate Pope is fel
tifical Chair, the third on the day the faid immec
ned: The Guard of which Caftle is committed
Quality: who is underftood to have compleate
Government at 7 yeers end : and is then comonly
Cardinals Cap, or fome thoufands of Crowns.

The Aqueducts of the old Romans with their conferves for waters were many : but that of *Acqua Claûdia,* was compofed with fo much Art, and at fo vaft expence, that but only to repair and reftore it to its antient form coft five hundred and fixty Talents befides which there was, *l'acqua Martia, Aleff andrina, Giulia, Augufta, Sabbatina, Appia, Traiana, Tepula, Alfietina, di Mercurio, della, Virgine, del'Aniene* the old, and *Antoniane* the new, and others : together with infinite Baths, as *le Anliane, le Variane, le Titiane, le Gordiane, le Novatiane, le Agrippine, le Alexandrine, le Manliane, le Dioclefiane, le Deciane,* & thofe Bathes appropriate to *Trajan, Philip Adrian, Nero, Severus, Conftantine, Farnus, Domitian* and *Probus* with many others.

The Piazzaes alfo in thofe days were divers, a *Sla Romana,* that of the *Piftory.* of *Cæfar,* of *Nerva,* of *Trajan,* of *Auguftus,* of *Saluftus,* of *Dioclefian,* of *Enobarbus.* and the *Efquilina,* with thofe particularly ufed for Herbs, Beafts, Fifh, Sheep, Hoggs, Bakers, for the Countrey market people, and the *Tranfitoria.*

The Triumphal Arches which are moft famous follow, of *Romulus,* of *Claudius,* of *Titus Vefpafian,* of *Conftantine,* of *Lucius, Settimius Severus,* of *Domitian,* of *Trajan,* of *Fabianus,* of *Gordianus,* of *Galienus,* of *Tiberius, Theodofius* and *Camillus.*

The Amphitheatres named were thefe, that of *Stafilius Taurus,* of *Claudius,* and that of *Titus Vefpafian,* which was capacious, enough for one hundred and fifty thoufand perfons. The Theatres thefe, that of *Scaurus, Pompejus, Marcellus, Balbus,* and *Caligula.*

The *Circi* or Show places in *Rome* were *Il Maffimo, l'Agonio, Il Flaminio,* that of *Nero,* and that of *Alexandre.*

The memorable Porticues or open Galleries Denomminations, enfue, *Il Pompeio, Il Corinthio, della Concordia, della Libertà, di Augufto, di Severo, di Panteo, di Metello, di Conftantino, di Q Catullo, del Foro, di Augufto, di Trajano, di Livia, del circo Maffino, di Nettuno, di Quirino, di Mercurio, di Venere Cricina, di Ottavio, Julia,* and that called *Tribunale Aurelio.*

The famous Collumnes were, *Lo Roftrata, la Lattaria, la Bellica, la Menia,* thofe of *Trajan,* of *Cæfar,* of *Antonius pius,* and thofe in the Porticue of *Concordia.*

The *Piramides* thefe, one in the *Circo maximo,* one in the *Campo Martio,* one in the *Maufeolo* or rich Tombe of *Auguftus,* one of the Sun of the *Araceli,* of the Moon, of the holy Trinity, of the *Vatican,* of Saint *Petre,* and of *San Mauro,* which flankes the *Roman* Colledge.

In *Rome* were three Coloffus, one of *Nero,* another of *Apollo,* a third of *Mars* and two other Pyramides one of *C Celtius,* another of *Scipio.*

Alfo fome places called *Naumachie,* appointed for Naval Fights, as large as the *Circus Maximus,* and were called of *Domitian, Nero,* and *Cæfar.* The proud Fabricks named *Settezonii* were two, the one of *Severus,* which Pope *Sextus* the 5th. caufed to be overwhelmed, the other of *Titus.*

Some Horfes were erected compofed of feveral Materials, as of *Marcus Aurelius,* of *Antoninus,* in the *Campidoglio* of *Domitianus,* of *L. Verus, Trajanus, Cæfar. Conftantinus,* of *Fidia,* and of *Prafitelle,* in the *Quirinale,* or *Monte Cavallo.*

                                    The

The Names of such as have writ of the Famous things in *ROME*.

THese following Authors have wrote of the City *ROME*. *P. Vittore* wrote of the Parts of the City; *Aristides sosista* in Greek an Oration in praise of *Rome*; but the more modern are *Giusto Lipsio, Lucio Fauno, Bartolameo Marliano*, lately set forth with Prints *Lodovico Demonciosi*, in a Book intitled *Gallus hospes de Urbe*, printed at *Rome*: *Poggio a Florentine, Fabriccio Varriano, Flavio Biondo, Rafael Volaterrano, Francesco, Albertini, Rucellai, Sorlio, Giacomo Boissardo, Mauro Andrea Fulvio, Rosino, Panuino, Vuolfango Lazio*.

Of the modern state and greatness of *Rome* under the Popes *Flavio, Biondo Thomaso Bosio Eugubino*, and *Thomaso Stapletono* an *English* Man, have at large discoursed.

Of the seven Churches of *Rome, Onofrio Panuino*, (who wrote also of the burying places) *M. Attilio Serrano*, and *Pompeio Augonio* the *Roman* Library keeper in the vulgar Tongue, and of the other Churches *Lorenzo Schradero Sassone* in the second Book of his Memorials of *Italy*.

Of the times and impresses of the Consuls and Emperors, *Cassiodore* a *Roman* Senator, *Marcellino, Vettor Tanunense, Gioanni Cuspiniano, Carlo Sigonio Onofrio Panuino, Stefano Pighio*, whose History is beautified with figures, and *Uberto Golizio*, who did the same with the Meddals.

Passing by the Antient Greek and Latine Authors. These ensuing have wrote the Histories of the *Roman* Emperours, *viz. Plutark, Dion, Herodian, Julianus Cæsar, Ammianus, Lampridius, Spartianus, Aurelius, Victorius*, with others who have been often reprinted. Also the Images of those Emperours were treated of and published by *Uberto, Glotzio, Hiperbolita, Giacomo, Strada Mantoano, Sebastiano, Orizo*, and others, moreover the Images of the said Emperours and their wives were stamped in Copper by *Levino Hulsio Gandavese* in *Spire*. Furthermore the Lives of the Emperours were set forth in Verse by *Ausonio Borgidolense, Gia, Micillo*, and *Orsino Velio*.

Of the Columnes of *Rome, Pietro Giacone Alfonso Chianone* and *Pietro Gallesino*, the one of the *Rostrata*, or Pulpit bedecked with beaks of Ships, in the *Campidoglio*, the second of that of *Trajan*, the third of that of *Antoninus*.

Of the Acqueducts and Waters entring *Rome*, *Sesto Julio Frontino, Aldus Manutius*, and *Giovanni Servilio* of the *Acqua Virgine* wrote *Duca* the *Roman Legist*: Of the increase and Augmentation of the *Tyber Lodovico Gomesio* and *Giacomo Castiglione*.

Of the Magistrates of *Rome, Pamponeo Leto, Andrea Dominico Flano* whose works are erroneously attributed to *Fenestela Carlo Sigonio Giovanni Bosino* in his seventh Book of the *Roman* Antiquities, and *Giachimo Perionio* of the Provinces *Marian Scoto*, and *Guido Pancirolo.*

Of the Senate, *Aulo Gellio, Giovanni Zamosio*, Great Chanfellor of *Polonia*, and *Paul Manutius*.

Of

Of the *Comitia,* or Assemblies of the People for electing Officers, *Nicolo Grucchio, Carlo Sigonio,* and *Giovanni Rosino* in his 6th Book of the *Roman* Antiquities.

Of the Judges, *Valerius Maximus,* in his 7th. Book and *Giovanni Rosino* in his 7th. Book of the Antiquities of *Rome.*

Of the High Priests. *Andrea Dominico Flacco, Pomponeo Leto,* and *Rosino* aforenamed.

Of the times of their Festivals, and of their Games, *Ovidius Naso, Lidius Geraldus, Rosinus* and *Josephus Scaliger* in his Book, *De Temporum emendatione.*

Of the *Triclinia,* or Supping Parlours, or their Banquets and manner of sitting at Table, *Pietro Chiacon Toletano, Fulvio Orsino* a *Roman: Ramusio, De quæsitis per Epistolam,* and *Andrea Baccio, De vini Natura.*

Of the sharp pointed Steeple erected by *Sixtus* the 5th. *Pietro Angelo Barba, Pietro Galesino, Michel Mercator,* and *Giovanni Servilio.*

Of the Theatre, and Amphitheatres *Justus Lipsius,* and *Giovanni Servilio,* in his first Book of the wonderfull works of the Antient.

Of the *Roman Militia,* *Polibius, Justus Lipsius, Giovanni Antonio Valerino, Giovanni Servilio* in 30. *lib. De mirandis Carlo sigonio,* and *Giovanni Rosino.*

Of the Provinces *Sextus Rufus* in his Breviary; and *Carlo Sigonius,* of the Colonies *Sextus Julius Frontinus, Onofrio Panuino,* and *Carlo Sigonio.*

Of the Ciphers or Figures of the Antient, *Valerius Probus* the Author of that tenth Book added to *Valerius Maximus* of the *Roman* surnames, whereof also *Sigonius* hath writ, *Panuinus* and others.

Of the antiquity of the Edifices, and the ruines of *Rome,* *Carolus Sigonius* in his Book *De antiquo Jure Civium Romanorum. Paulus Minutius,* who wrote also of the Laws of *Rome,* as did *Antonius Agostinus* and others.

The Figures of *Romes* Antiquities were stamped in Brass by *Antonio Salamanca* and others. The Tablets in brass likewise by *Onofrio Panuino* and others: The Statues in *Rome,* were published by *Giovanni Giacomo Boissardo* and others. The Images of the illustrious Persons were taken from the Marble figures and printed by *Achille Statio,* a *Portuguese,* and *Theodore Galleo,* by whom also were set forth the lively Visages of the modern illustrious *Italians,* as also of the nine learned Greeks, who being taken at *Constantinople,* first brought the Greek letters into *Italy* and afterwards conveyed the same into *Gallia* and those parts beyond the *Alpes.*

The old Inscriptions on Marble and other stones in *Rome* and elsewhere, were divulged by *Pietro Appiano, Maritino Smetio, Fulvio Orsino* and divers others. The Epitaphs on Christians Tombs are collected by *Lorenzo Scradero* a *Saxon,* and by *Chitreus* in his Book of delight in travails.

Of the *Roman* wonders *Ubertus Glothzius* hath wrote an ample Book, which also comprehends the Inscriptions and meddals of *Apulia,* and *Sicilia, Sebastiano Erizzo* and others.

The Lives of the *Roman* Chief Bishops and Popes were made publick by *Bartholomeo, Platina Papiro. Maxone* and others: whom we

must

muſt not read without great circumſpection *Panuino* hath likewiſe
preſented to common view all their Images taken by the life.

Of the Cardinals, their times, and appurtenances, *Onofrius Panu-*
inus Alfonſo Chiaccone a *Spaniard* and others have wrote, and *Theodorus*
Gallus in *Anvers*, engraved the Images and Elogies of twelve Cardinals.

Of the ſeaven Churches of *ROME*, which are moſt viſited, and more richly fraught with Indul- gencies and Priviledges than the Reſt.

THE Moddel of the Temples of *Rome* vary according to the
different times and humours of Men ; ſometimes building
them Round, without Collumnes, without traverſing, and without Caſements, leaving in the Covering an open hole or *Cupola* for
the light to enter in at. Of this ſort is the *Rotonda* of *Rome*, a Church
worthy conſideration for the Architecture. Which ſome times our
Anceſtors made in an Orbicular forme, but with rowes of Pillars
diverſly placed, as is *San Stefano*, in *Monte Celio*, heretofore the Temple of *Juno*, and that of *Coſtanza* or *Conſtantina* in the *Via nomentina*,
without the *Porta Viminale*, which tis thought was antiently the
Temple of *Bacchus*. Sometimes they uſed to build their Temples
Square, with one or two Bankes or Pillars, as now appear *S.Giovan-*
ni Latcranenſe in *Monte Celio*, *San Paolo* in the *Via Oſtienſe*, *Sant Agneſe*
without the Walls. And other times they formed them by entreſſing
or joyning the Pillars together at Top, near to which juſt under the
Roof they fixed their littleCaſements, wch. were more or leſs according to the proportion of the Structure : of which Sort are many in
Rome, with ſtately Frontiſpieces, ſome of them being adorned with
Columns of pretious and divers coloured Marble, and many others
whoſe Pavement are wrought in figures with little pieces of Marble
alla Moiſaca.

The Firſt of the Seaven principal Churches of *ROME* called *Santa Croce*, in *HIERVSALEM*.

THis Church is the firſt and chief in devotion, ſeated in *Monte*
Celio, nobly built by *Helena* Mother of the Emperour *Conſtantine*
the Great: In it are 20. Collumnes, and two fair tombs of black, red,
and white Marble : the covering of the High Altar is ſuſtained
by 4 Marble Pillars. One inſcription there to be read, ſhewes that
the ground or earth (the Foundation or Floor thereof) is the true
holy

holy Earth brought from *Jerufalem.* Tis believed this was the *Afylum* or Sanctuary in the life time of *Romulus*, and that *Tullius Hoftili-
us* afterwards enlarged the City to the faid *Afylum.* Tis obfervable
that in the fame place, where Impunity for evil works was afforded
to Malefactors under the firft Founders of *Rome*; under the Chrifti-
Religion, Our Lord God is pleafed to grant remiffion of our
Sins.

In this Church is the Tombe of Pope *Benedict* the 7th. with an
Epitaph in verfe : and of *Francefco Guigone* a famous Sculptor. More
of this Church will be fpoken in the fecond dayes Journey.

The Second Church of the Saints, *F A B I-*
A NO and *S E B A S T I A N O.*

THis Church ftands in the *Via Appia*, built with plain work in a
long form, the pavement Marble, contiguous with a fair Monaftery now deferted. Herein were at firft repofed the Bodies of St.
Peter, and St. *Paul.* The High Altar is fuftained with four Marble
Pillars, and is raifed with Stone, as are moft Altars in *Rome.* Under
an Iron grate, lyes the Body of St. *Stephen* the Pope a Martyr, and of
45. other bleffed Popes, with the Reliques of above 74 thoufand
Martyrs And for that this Church is fo far diftant. The Pope grants
that inftead of vifiting it in the extream hot weather, The People
fhould repair to *Santa Maria del Popolo* for their Indulgencies. Of this
Church more will be faid in the voyage of the fecond day to the *Via
Appia.* And of *Santa Maria del Popolo*, in the Catalogue of Churches.

The third Church named *San G I O V A N N I*
del L A T E R A N O.

THis may be called the Chief amongft the feaven principal
Churches, having been formerly the Abode of the Popes in
Monte Celio, and *Sixtus* the 5th. though in vain, reedified that Pontifical Palace even from the very foundations, wherein was frequent-
ly celebrated the famous fynod called *Synodo Lateranenze* in *Rome.*
The *Roman* Emperours ufed to receive the golden Crown in this
Church. Its pavement is wrought with lovely Marble, and Its
Roof richly carved and guilt. It hath many Reliques of Saints, as
the heads of St. *Peter* and St. *Paul*, the Veft of St. *Stephen* bloudy and
torne by thofe Stones caft at him, and divers other things worthy
veneration : Of which the Bulls of Pope *Sixtus quartus*, and of Pope
Gregory cutt in Marble, affirm the Veritie. This Church was repaired in many places by *Nicholas* the 4th. in the yeer 1291, the teftimony whereof yet remains in the Front. Tis reported, That its
Collumnes were tranfported by *Vefpatian* from *Jerufalem* to *Rome.*

This is one of the five Patriarchal Churches.

The *Baptistary* is conjoyned to the said Church, wherein *Constantine* the Emperour was baptized by the Pope St. *Sylvester*. Into one of the Chappels whereof dedicated to St. *John Baptist*, no Woman is permitted to enter under pain of Excomunication, in memorial that One Woman was cause of the death of St. *John Baptist*, who first published Baptism. The Collumnes of Porphyr therein standing, being rubbed with ones hand, smell as sweet as any Violet, they were brought from *Pilates* House, together with one of its Gates, and the Collumne whereon the Cock stood, who by his thrice crowing put St. *Peter* in mind of the words of our Saviour. In Saint *John* they preserved the Ark of the old Testament, the Rod of *Aaron*, the Ladder brought from the Palace of *Pilate*, whereto Christ was bound when whipt with rods, the drops of whose blood yet appear on it. The stone whereon the *Jews* cast lots, with other notable things, particularly treated on by the Authors aforenamed. These things are publickly shewed to Pilgrims. the Epitaphs of Pope *Sylvester* the second, and of *Antonio Cardinale Porthogese*, are legible in verse, as also of *Lorenzo Valle*, a Canon of this Church who deceased 50 yeers old in *Anno*. 1465. In whose commendation this Elogy was sett up.

> *Laurens Valla jacet, Romanæ gloria linguæ.*
> *Primus enim docuit, quâ decet arte loqui.*

Here is the *Porta Santa*, which at the beginning of the yeer of Jubilee the Popes use to set open. In the Voyage of the second day other things will be mentioned of this Church.

The third Church named *SAN LORENZO* without the *PORTA ESQUILINA*.

THis large Church is sustained by 36 Marble Pillars, and connexed with it is the Monastery of the Canon Regulars of St. *Austin*, which is called *di san Salvadore*. Here is one of those places under ground (as St. *Sebastiano*) wherein are layed many of the bones of Martyrs brought from the *Cemeterio Ciriaco*, and here are the Reliques of *San Lorenzo*, among which is the stone, whereon that blessed St. being taken off the Gridiron was placed, and expired, which stone is covered with an Iron Grate. On the left side of the high Altar, stands the Tombe of *Eustachius* Nephew of Pope *Innocent* the 4th whereon are carved some fair statues, as 'twere actually endeavouring to bring a Lambe to the Sacrifice. This was one of the five Patriarchal Churches, and will be farther spoken of in the Voyage of the second day:

The

The Fifth of the principal Churches called *SANTA MARIA MAGGIORE nel MONTE ESQUILINO.*

THis in respect of the other Churches is small but polite, 312. foot long, and 112. broad, Its pavement is wrought with Figures in *Mosaick* work, and the Roof guilt. In it is one Altar of Porphyr, and a Tomb of Porphyr wherein lies *Giovanni Patricio,* who built this Church. In a Vault under ground is kept the Crib or Manger wherein our Saviour was layed at his Birth, often visited, with Masses and Prayers, for which end *Sixtus quintus,* there built a glorious Chappel, deputing to it Clerkes, who ought there continually to attend for divine Worship.

Here are engraven the works of Pope *Pius* the 5th. for the service & propagation of the Christian Religion, in perpetual remembrance of so good a Pastor: whose Body he ordered also should be put in an honourable Tombe on the one side, and his own to be placed on the other side, when it should please the Lord to call him to himself. On the right side of the high Altar lies the body of Pope *Nicholas* the 4th. near whose Tomb stands an Image of the blessed Virgin painted by Saint *Luke.* Here also is the Sepulchre of *San Girolame.* And here ly buried *Alberto* and *Giovanni Normando. Platina* who wrote compleatly the lives of the Popes. *Lucco Gaurico* a famous Mathematician and Bishop of *Cività. Francesco Toledo* a Jesuit; *Zforfeschi* d.t *Santa Fiera* and *i Cesis,* three Cardinals. Upon the Pillars are some antient Pictures of such as undertook the Argument for the Catholick Faith against the Hereticks (who condemned images) when that point was disputed in the Councel. Before this Church *Sixtus Quintus* reared an Obelisk, which is the least of the four in *Rome,* and is without *Hieroglyphick* notes, as that before Saint *Giovanni Laterano* hath. On the back part of this Church is erected a Marble Collump, not so great as neat, in memory of the Absolution which *Henry* fourth King of *France* and *Navarre,* obtayned from *Clement* the eighth in *Ann.* 1593. This was one of the five Patriarchall Churches, and will be further treated of in the third dayes Journey.

S s

The

The Sixth of the Principal Churches, called *SAN PAOLO NELLA VIA OSTIENSE*.

THis is the faireſt and biggeſt Church of *Rome* being 120 paces long and 85 broad built by *Conſtantine* the great, & ſuſtained (as may be ſaid) by a Grove of ſtately Pillars.

Tis paved with Marble. Many Inſcriptions are there placed and publiſhed by orhers. One moſt remarkable is this. *P. P. P. R. R. R. S. S. S. F. F. F.*

The Venerable *Bede* being at that time moſt learned was conſulted and deſired to reſolve the ſignification of thoſe Letters, which he thus explained.

> *Pater Patriæ Perfectus*
> *Regnum Romæ Ruit*
> *Secum Sublatâ Sapientiâ*
> *Ferro, Flamma, Fame.*

The High Altar is ſupported by four Porphyr Pillars expoſeing to publique view the Image on the Crucifix, which ſpake to St. Brigide while ſhe prayed : as the Inſcription declares, and the Bull verifies. Here alſo are ſtupendiouſly expreſſed in *Moſaick* work, the Imagea of Chriſt, of Saint *Peter*, Saint *Paul*, and Saint *Andrew*, ſo lively that words ſeem to iſſue out of their mouths, together with all the Inſtruments of the Paſſion and death of our Saviour. This Church was nobly reſtored and beautified by *Clement* the 8th. an excellent Pope: In the Braſen gates, are figured divers holy hiſtories Greek and Latin; From the inſcriptions tis gathered, that theſe gates were placed there, by *Pantaleon*, Conſul in the time of *Alexander the* 4th. This was one of the five Patriarchal Churches. In it are the Sepultures of ſome Popes, as of *Giovanni* who dyed in *anno* 1472. and *Pietro Leone* and the memorials of *Julius* the third *Gregory* the 13th. and *Clement* the 8th. who opened the *Porta Santa*, in the yeer of Jubile. This Church is at preſent governed by the Fryers of the Order of St. *Benedict*. Here is the Chappel of St. *Paul* in good part reſtored by *Alexandro Farneſe*, a Cardinal in *anno* 1582. In the Veſtry are many Reliques of Saints, the Collumnes whereon St. *Paul* was decapitated, and a ſtone wch. they uſually faſtened to the Feet of the Martyrs for their greater torment. In the Chapel of *Porta Celi*, are the reliques of 2203 Perſons martyred by *Nero*. whence at a ſmall diſtance is the *Tre Fontane*, or three Fountains, the place of Saint *Pauls* Martyrdome (fully reſtored and beautifyed by *Clement* the 8th.) whoſe head being cut off, took three leaps, and at each Leap, a ſpring aroſe and ſtill runs with clear waters.

The

The Seaventh of the Principal Churches of *ROME*, called *S. PIETRO* in *VATICANO*.

FOR Beauty, fumptuoufnefs, Artifice, and Worth; not only *Rome* but the whole world yeelds this meritorioufly a precedency to all other Churches, efpecially in that part built in later times, to which *Sixtus* the 5th. added a noble *Cupolo*, wherein are figured the Celeftial *Hierarchy* in pieces of Mofaick, that the beholders believe them painted. And *Gregory* the 13th. as glorious a Chappel in honour of Saint *Gregorie Nazianzene*, wherein he was buried. Without doubt it is the moft perfect model of decent Magnificence in the World, there being an anfwerable uniformity within and without. And may juftly be compared (if not faid to furpafs) the Temple of *Diana* in *Ephefus*, formerly accounted one of the feaven wonders of the world: burnt by *Heroftratus* who by that horrid Act fought rather to perpetuate his name than to ly unremembred in his Grave. The Old Church had 24 collumnes of fo various coloured Marble, as are not matchable, which were taken from the adjacent Sepulchre of *Adrian* the Emperour, who was moft exquifite in all his works. Thofe other Pillars in the Chappel of the holy Sacrament and thofe that fupport the *Volto Santo*, that is the Towel of *Veronica*, with fome others, were tranfported from *Jerufalem* into *Italy* by *Titus Vefpafianus* and taken out of the Temple and Palace of *Solomon*, after that the *Jews* were wholly overcome and their faid City deftroyed. The top is all of fquares, *Levati* as they call it, like the *Pantheon*, in the Center of the Church ftands the great Altar, all of folid Brafs, in fuch ftupendious pillars that each weighs 25000. pound and is of fo incomparable workemanfhip that no Cathedral but St. *Peters* is fit to entertain it. Herein is the Sepulchre of the Emperour *Otho* the fecond, buried in *anno* 1486. in porphirie: A greater porphyre ftone then this *Italy* affords not, except that of *Santa Maria Rotonda*, the Sepulture of *Theodorick* King of the *Oftrogothes*. This was one of the five Patriarchal Churches, and the old part was built by the Emperour *Conftantine* the great, who caufed it be fuftained by Pillars: But Pope *Julius* the fecond in *anno* 1507 was the Founder of the new part, himfelf laying the firft ftone of the foundation with his own hands in the prefence of thirty five Cadinals, *Bramante*, of *Urbin*, was the Inventor of the Model, which *Michael Angelo*, *Bonarota* the *Florentine*, afterwards added to and corrected.

Antonio Fiorentino, by order of *Eugenius* the 4th. made the gate of Brafs, with the figures of Chrift, the bleffed Virgine, of Saint *Peter*, and *St Paul*. In the holy week every yeer they fhew here the Vifage of Chrift, called *Volto Santo*, impreffed on the Towel of *Veronica*. There is one Figure of the Virgine *Mary* holding Chrift dead in her lap the work of *Michael Angelo*, whofe alfo is that moft excellent

Ss 2 Picture

Picture of universal Judgment, placed in the Popes Chappel. On the Eastern part of the Church hangs the Pinnace of St. *Peter*, in Mosaick work by *Giotto Fiorentino*. In the Chorus stands the Tombe of Pope *Sixtus* the fourth, all of Brass, and on the top lies his Figure represented sleeping, with Vertue on both sides, and round it the Sciences, that is *Theologie*, Philosophy, and the liberal arts with his Inscription, The work of *Antonius Palladius*, in *anno* 148 2. Herein also besides those of the first Martyrs *Lyno*, *Cleto* and others, are the graves and Tombs of many Popes to wit, of *Innocent* the 8th. in Brass. of *Pius* the 2d. a *Siennois* & *Pius* the 3 Son of a Sister of *Pius* the 2. Of *Marcellus* the 2 who lived in the *Pontificacy* but 22. dayes. *Julius* the third, all without Inscriptions. These following have all Epitaphs in verse: As *Nicolas* the 5th. *Eugenius* the 4th. *Urban* the 6th. *Adrian* the 1st. *Gregory* the 4th. and 5th. *Foniface* the 8th. *Paul* the 3d. whose Brass Tomb stands in the new part. *Innocent* the 4th. *Urban* the 7th. *Gregory* the 13th. and 14th. and also *Balbo* the most learned in the Greek, and Cardinal *dalla Porta*.

Who desires more ample satisfaction in the particulars of the 7 principal Churches of *Rome*, shall find it in the diligent writings of *Onofrius Panuinus*, and *Attilius Serranus*, in the Latin tongue, and of *Pompeio Ugonio* in the Italian. Let this compendious description, content the curious in this study here, who for more light are referred to the Authors above named. Now lets pass to the other Churches and memorable places.

A Catalogue of the Churches of *ROME*, set down Alphabetically with the Epitaphs most worthy noting therein extant.

A *Santo Adriano tribus Foris*, was a Temple first dedicated to *Saturn* in *foro Romano*, then to *Nerva* the Emperour, and lastly to St. *Adrian* when Cardinal *Gio Bellaio*, repaired it.

Santo Agapeto near *San Lorenzo*.

Santa Agata a Church of the *Gothes* under the *Viminale*. Here stand the Figures of *Diana* and of *Peace*, to whom 'tis believed twas dedicated. Before the Gate are figured certain Children with the *pretexta* on, which was a Gown edged about with purple silk, that the Noble mens Children of *Rome* wore till of the age of seaven yeers, who sit on seats as if at School.

In it likewise is the Tomb of *Giovanni Lascaro* with two Greek Epitaphs.

Santa Agnese, in the *Borgo de Parione*, or the *Via nomentana*, a Church built with stately stones, beautifyed with 26 marble Collumnes and a descent of 32 steps. Near it stood formerly a Monastery now fallen

to

to the ground, firſt deſerted for the intemperate Ayr. In it was layed the body of St. *Agneſe anno* 1141. Its Porticue was built by Cardinal *Julius* Nephew of *Sixtus* the 4th. Near this ſtands a Church dedicated by *Alexander* the 4th. *S. Coſtanza* Daughter of *Conſtantine* the
Emperour: Which was formerly dedicated to *Bacchus*, as is collected
from a Porphyr Tomb yet remaining there, upon which are carved
certain Children treading of grapes. Its form is round; It hath
24 Marble Pillars, and is politely wrought *alla Moſaica*.

Sant' Alberto nell'Eſquillie.

Sant' Aleſſio nell'Aventino, formerly the Temple of *Hercules* a Conquerour. In this Church is preſerved the pair of Staiers, under
which in his Fathers houſe, that Saint lived unknown for ſome time
In it likewiſe *Vicenza* Cardinal *Gonzaga* lies buried.

Sant' Ambroſio, of *Maſina* in *Rome* or the high ſtreet of *Sant' Angelo*,
and another of the ſame in *Campo Martio*.

Sant' Anaſtaſia at the foot of Mount *Palatine*, in the Street *Harenula*: This was a Temple of *Fqueſtrian Neptune*, whom they alſo ſtyled
Conſcio, for that they believed him a God knowing of ſecrets.

Santo Anaſtaſio, in the ſtreet *Ardeatine*, near to *Tre Fontana* the
three Fountains.

Santo Andrea della colonna, in the ſtreet *Trevio de Ania* near the Palace of the *Savelli. Dalla Tavenula* between the hills *Celio*, and *Eſquilino
Delle Fratte dalle Barche*, on the Banks of the *Tyber. Degli Orſi*, in the
Harenula. In *Montucna*, at the foot of the *Capitolino*. In *Nazareno*
in the *Harenula*. In *Paliura* in the *Palatino*. In *Portogallo*. In
ſtatera, at the Foot of the *Capitolino*. In *Tranſtevere* in the *Vaticano*,
in *Piazzo Siena*, which hath a rich Chapel of the *Ruſellai*. *Santo Angelo nel Foro Eovare* in the Fiſh market, heretofore a Temple of *Mercury* in *Dioclefians* hott Baths; was dedicated by *Pius* the 4th. to the
bleſſed Virgin and the Angels, near it is a Cloyſter for the *Carthuſi-
an* Fryers ſupported by 100. Pillars. In it lies buried the ſaid *Pius*
the 4th. *Bocca, Scorbellone: Franceſco Alciato*: and *ſimonetto* Cardinal *S. Angelo*, of *Mozarella nel Monte Giordano*.

Santa Anna, in the *Flaminian Circe*, and under the *Viminale*.

Sant' Antonio in *Portogallo. Di Padona*, in the *Valle Martia. Nel Eſquilino*, where at the feſtival of Saint *Anthony*, they drive all their Beaſts
and Sheep up near to the Altar, that they may afterwards be pro-
tected againſt the danger of Diſeaſes and Wolves. Near to it ſtands
the Hoſpital reſtored by *Pius* the 4th. a *Millaneſe*.

Santo Apollinare, formerly the Temple of *Apollo*, *Julius* the third
joyned to it the Colledge of the *Germans*. Near it ſtood the houſe of
Mark Antony the triumvir.

Li ſanti Apoſtoli XII. in *Trivio*, here reſide the Fryers *Conventuals* of
Saint *Francis*: The Inſcription on a Marble ſtone aſſures us, twas
built by *Conſtantine* the Great, afterwards ruined by the Hereticks,
and then reſtored by *Pelagius* and *Giovanni* the Popes. Wherein are
the Graves and Tombs of the great Cardinal *Niceno Beſſarione*, the
Tuſculan Biſhop, and *Conſtantinopolitan* Patriark. Of Cardinal *Pietro Savoneſe*. Of *Bartolomeo, Cameriero Beneventano*, the Divine and
Lawyer. Of *Cornelius Muſſus* Biſhop of *Bittonto* the Prince of Preachers *Li Santi Apoſtoli* XII. in the *Vatican*.

Santo Auguſtino in Campo Martio a convent of the *Auſtin* Fryers,

T t 2

Herein

Herein lies the body of *Santa Monica* the Mother of Saint *Auſtin* a Father and Doctor of the Church with theſe Verſes.

Hic Auguſtini ſanctam venerare parentem,
Votaque fer tumulo quo jacet illa ſacro.
Quo quondam grato, toti nunc Monica mundo
Succurrat, precibus preſtet opemque ſuis.

This Saint *Auſtin* was Biſhop of *Hippo* in *Alexandria*, a man of a moſt profound wit, and learning, and of a moſt holy and religious life. And theſe *Auſtine* Fryers obſerve his inſtitutes of life living in comon, ſerving God day and night, and are tyed by the vows of poverty, Chaſtity and Obedience. The Cardinals *Burdegalenſe* and *Verallo* ly buried in this Church.

Santa Bibiana in *Monte Aventino*. Here ſtood the Baths of *Anthony*, and the Palace of *Licinius*.

Santa Barbara in the high Street *Pigna* was formerly a Temple of *Venus* in the *Pompeyan* Theatre.

San Bartolomeo of the Iſland in *Tranſtevere*, was heretofore a Temple of *Jupiter*, or as ſome ſay of *Æſculapius*. Now is there a Convent of *Franciſcans* called *Zoccolanti*, from their going on wooden pattons and an ancient Inſcription in ſtone to the God *Semone Sanco*, here alſo lyes the body of Saint *Bartholomew*.

San Baſilio, in the *Foro di Nerva*.

San Benedetto, in the *Piazza Catinara*, and in the *Piazza Madama*.

San Bernardo near the Pillar, and Baths of *Trajan* the Emperour.

San Biagio, in the *Campo Martio*, *della Tinta*, on the Bank of *Tiber*. Here ſtood the Temple of *Neptune*, wherein ſuch as were delivered from Shipwrack, uſed to hang up a Tablet with the ſtory of their danger and manner of deliverance painted and deſcribed in it: *Dell Anello* in the Road *Pigna della Foſſa*, as you come from the *Eſquiline*, *delle Coltre* in the *Campitello*.

Santa Bibiana, in the *Eſquilie*.

San Bonifacio in *Aventino*, at preſent called *Sant' Aleſſio*.

Santa Brigide in the Street *Harenula*.

Santa Cecilia in *Tranſtevere* for Nuns. In this Church is the body of this holy Virgin with many other bodies of Saints, honoured with great devotion, and tranſlated from *Campo Martio*, by Cardinal *Paulo Emilio Sfondrato* Nephew of *Gregory* the 14th.

San Ceſario in the Road *di Ripa*, excellently repaired by Pope *Clement* the 8th.

La Chieſa de' Cartuſiani, or *Carthuſians*, which is called *Santa Maria delli Angeli*.

Santa Catharina, in the *Flaminian Circ*, now *delli Funari della Rota* and *il Borgo Novo*.

San Celſo, near the Bridge, *Caſtello* in *Banchi*.

San Criſogonio in *Tranſtevere*: wherein ſtands the Tomb and Epitaph of *Girolamo Alexandro* a moſt learned Doctor, and of *David Uviliano*, or *Evelyn* an Engliſh Oratour.

Santo Clemente in *Monte Celio*: here lies the body of Pope *Clement* the Martyr, conveighed to *Rome* from *Cherſona* a City of *Pontus*: as as alſo of Cardinal *Vincenſo Laureo*.

Santa

Santa Coſtanza, in the Street *Nomentana*, This is conjectured to have been a Temple of *Bacchus*, for a Monument yet appearing of Porphyr ſtone.

Santi Coſino and *Damiano*, in the *Via ſacra*, ſo called for that the South-ſayers uſed to paſs that way; This was formerly the Temple of *Romulus* and *Remus*. In it are the Tombs of *Creſcentius*, and *Grudone Piſano*, with the Epitaphs in verſe.

San Coſmo, under the *Gianicolo*. Antiently the Temple dedicated to Fortune:

Santa Elizabetta in *Parione*.

Santa Eufemia in *Eſquilie*.

Santo Euſtachio near the *Rotonda*, was formerly a Temple of the good ———. ....

San Franceſco at the Foot of *Gianicolo*, Herein is the ſepulchre of *Pandolfus* Count of *Anguillarie*, who when 100. yeers old became a *Franciſcan* Fryer.

San Gregorio, in *Velabro*.

San Gregorio, at the head of the *Ponte fabritio*, and in *Monte Celio*, formerly a Monaſtery of the *Germans* and *Flemings*, but now of Fryers. Here ſtood antiently the houſe of *San Gregory* the firſt Pope, and here they yet ſhew the Table, whereat he dayly fed a great number of poor Perſons, as in his life wrote by *Giovani Diacone* is ſet forth & here lies Cardinal *Lomelino* a *Genoveſe* Many Epitaphs of *Florentines* are here ſet up, and of *Edoardo Carno*, and *Roberto Peramo* two Engliſh Knights both Lawyers, who being driven out of their Countrey for defending the Catholick Religion, came to *Rome* to finiſh their days in the peace of the Lord: As alſo of *Antonio Valle* of *Barcellona*, And of one *Statius* a Poet, who wrote with *Virgil*, as may be collected from this Epitaph.

> *Statius hic Situs eſt, juvenem quem Cipris Ademit*
> *Præcocem Æneæ carmine quod prenteret,*
> *Statio, Statio F. Dulciſs.*
> *Chriſtophora M. Pientiſs. P.*
> *Vixit. Ann. XXXIII.*

San Girolamo, near the *Corte Savella*, here the *Oratoriani*, a Religious Order, inſtituted with great piety by Saint *Philippus Nerius* a *Florentine* Prieſt in the laſt age; who from this Oratory of St. *Hierome* took their name, for that it was the place frequented by them for their exerciſes of Catechiſing and preaching. whoſe number is greatly increaſed by his Diſciples

San Giacomo in *Circo Flaminio*: This is an Hoſpital for *Spaniards*, divers Epitaphs of which Nation are there inſcribed, with the memorials of *Bartolomeo Cuevio* the Cardinal, and of *Bernardino*, Biſhop of *Cordova*. In it is the Pourtray of *Pietro Ciocconio*, a Prieſt of *Toledo*, who had moſt happy ſucceſs to his labour in amending the Books of holy and prophane writers *Degli incurabili. Scoſſa cavallo*

San Giovanni Battiſta in *Monte Celio*. *San Giovanni Evangeliſta* before the *Porta Latina*, in *Monte Celio*, formerly a Temple of *Diana*, *San Giovanni Colivita* in the *Iſola*: ſuppoſed an antient Temple of *Æſculapius Nel Ponte in Monte Celio*; *Nel Laterano*, one of the ſeaven principal Churches before ſpoken of. In *Dola*, upon *Monte Celio*. *Nell'Oglio* before the *Porta latina*. *Del Mercatello al Campidoglio*, *De Malua*

...na in Tranftavere. Della Pigna, in the high Street *Pigna*.

San Giovanni & Paulo nel Monto Celio, with two Lyons before the Door. The one holding a Boy between his Teeth, and the other a Man, in it is one Sepulchre of porphyr ftone. Here antiently was the *Curia Hoftilia*.

San Giofeffo in the ftreet *Pigna*.

San Giuliano in the *Efquilino*.

Sant'*Juo* in the *Campo Martio* appertaining to the *Biertoni*.

San Lorenzo near a Fifh Market, *Nel Viminale. Nel Gianicolo*, antiently a Temple of *Juno Lucina*, here lyes Cardinal *Francefco Gonzaga*. In *Fonte nella Valle Efquilina*. In *Miranda* in the *Foro Romano*. In *Palifpirna* on the hill *Viminale*, wherein is infcribed an Epitaph of Cardinal *Cuglielmo Sirleto*, the moft quaint in the Greek language, here ftood the Palace of *Decius* the Emperour. In *Damafo*, in the *Pigna* : where are expofed the Epitaphs of *Annibal Caro*, the moft elegant in the *Tufcan* language. Of *Giacomo Fabia* of *Parma*. Of *Pietro Marfa*. Of *Giulio Sadoleto, Girolamo Ferraro* and other illuftrious men. To this Fabrick were brought the Marbles fculptures and other ornaments of the *Arco Gordiano*.

San Leonardo in Carine. In *Olfeo*. In *Septifolio*. In *Efquilino*, and *S. Leonardo Vecchio* among the obfcure fhops, on the bankes of the *Tyber* in the *Longara*.

Santa Lucia, in the Palace : heretofore the Temple of *Apollo Palatino Nelle Botteghe* obfcure. In old time the Temple of *Hercules*, and of the Mufes.

San Lodovico near *Novanna*, the Church of the French Nation adorned with the Epitaphs of the moft Noble Perfons of *France*.

Santa Maria Egittiaca formerly the Temple of *Fortuna virilis*, wherein (as is fuppofed) then ftood the *Bucca Veritatis*, a marble ftatue fet up by the *Romans*, for the tryal of Chaftity, with a wide mouth and great lips: A daughter of *Volateranus Regulus* to prove her Virginity unpolluted (being accufed for that crime) put her hand in its mouth and withdrew it without hurt: another Damofel making the fame tryal, being unchaft, had her right hand bit off by the Statue. *Santa Maria del animam Parione*, a ftately Church wherein the *Germans*, and *Flemings* refide and affift the neceffitous Pilgrimes of thofe Nations. In it is an Image of the Virgine *Mary* with thefe Verfes.

Partus, & integritas difcordes tempore longo
Virginis in gremio fœdera pacis habent.

On the left hand of the great Altar ftands a Sepulchre of *Adrian* the 4th. (made by Cardinal *Eutcefora*) who was the only perfon that could fay he had created another Pope in his own life time. On the right the coftly Tombe of *Carlo* Prince of *Cleves*, who dyed in the yeer of *Jubilee* 1575 the 13th. of February with the univerfal forrow of all good men, but chiefly of *Gregorie* the 13th. *Stephano Pighio*, wrote his life with that learned Book entitled *Ercole Prodicio* with the Epitaphs of *Francefco Forefto, Giovanni Rofeto* and other noble and excellent men.

Santa Maria in *Araceli*, on the *Capitolino*, formerly a Temple of *Jupiter*

Jupiter Ferenius, now a Convent of the *Zoccolanti*, or *Francifcans*, In it are many antient Epitaphs: and an Altar fupported by four lovely Pillars, Tis the Church for the Senate and People of *Rome*, embellifhed with the ornaments of the Temple of *Quirinus*: and is afcended unto by one hundred twenty four fteps.

Santa Maria Aventina, on the hill *Aventino* formerly the Temple of the *Dea bona*, or good Goddefs. Here may be read the lamentation of a woman flain by her Husband. *Santa Maria de' Cacabary in Pigna Santa Maria in campo fanto*, in the Vally *Vaticano*, wherein fome Epitaphs are legible.

Santa Maria nel Campidoglio, antiently the Temple of *Jupiter Capitolinus Nella Capella* beyond the *Tevere* or *Tyber*. In *Candelorio*, in the ftreet Saint *Angelo, della concettione*, the Conception, in *Monte Celio. Nel Velabro*, formerly a Temple of *Hercules*. In *Dominica*, on Mount *Celio*, where were the Aqueducts of *Caracalla*. *Nel Efquilino*, in *circo Flaminio*, in times paft the Temple of *Ifis*, In *corte* under the *Campidoglio Liberatione dell'inferno*, fometime a Temple of *Jupiter Stator* in *foro Romano. Di Loreto Delle Febre* in old time the Temple o. *Mars*, *Della Confolatione* and *Della Gratie*, where formerly ftood the Temple of *Vefta* between the *Capitolinum* and *Palatinum*, there the *Veftal* Virgins guarded the facred Fire, and the *Palladium*, which was a woodden Image of Pillars with rouling Eyes, brought by *Æneas* from *Troy* (when fired) into *Italy* with his other houfhold Gods, and was by him fnatched out of the fired Temple.

Santa Maria fopra Minerva fo called for that this was a Temple of *Minerva*, at prefent the Fathers *Dominicans* poffefs it, and a Colledge for *Theology* founded by the Bifhop of *Cutcha*. In it are the Tombes and Epitaphs of *Leo* the 10th. and *Paul* the 4th. with many others among which the Chief are of *Pietro Bembo*, of *Giovanni Morone* who was thirteen feveral times *Legatus a Latere* for the Pope, and Prefident of the Councel of *Trent*, and of *Giovanni Torrecremata*, who bequeathed a large Revenue for mariage Portions for Virgins, which are folemnized yeerly in the Popes prefence on the Feftival of the *Annunciation*, In it alfo are the afhes of *Egidio Fofcari*, Bifhop of *Modena*, who in the Councel of *Trent* was ftyled the Greater Light: Of *Sylvefter Aldobrandino*, Father of *Clement* the 8th. of *Giovanni Annio*, the Hiftorian and of many other eminent Fathers: As alfo the body of *Santa Catarina* of *Siena*, and the Epitaph of *Guglielmo Durando*, Bifhop of *Numata*, who compofed a Book entitled, *Rationale Divinorum Officiorum*, with other volumes of the Law.

In the faid Temple was erected the firft Fryery of the *fancto facramento* by *Thomafo Stella* a Preacher: and *Michael Angelo Buonarota* was the inventor of the Tabernacle for keeping the confecrated Eucharift. Before the Door of the Church ftand the Tombes of *Tomafo di Vio*, and *Giovanni Badia* Cardinals and of *Paulo Manutio* the Elegant, who for all his Fame, ran the fame Fate with Pompey the Great, who living filled the world with his glory, and dead no Epitaph nor memorial remains of him, but we find there this Epitaph of *Raphael Stantio* a Painter of *Urbin*, though much lefs renowned than the preceding.

Uu

Hic

Hic ſitus eſt Raphael timuit quo ſoſpite vinci
Rerum magna parens, & moriente, mori.
Patria Roma fuit, Gens Portia, nomen Julus
Mars puerum inſtituit, Mors Juvenem rapuit.

Santa Maria de'Miracoli in *Monte Gordiano Di Monterone*, in the ſtreet St. *Euſtachio Di Mont ferrato* the Church of the *Catalonians*, in *Monticelli* , in the *Heremula Della Navicella*, in *Monte Celio, Nova*, in the *Foro Romano* formerly a Temple of the Sun and Moon, now enjoyed by the Monks of *Mount Olivet*. *Annonciata* the Colledge of the Jeſuiſts. *Della Pace*, the dwelling of the Canon Regulars, therein ſtand a Tomb of *Marco Muſuro* a Learned Candiot with this Epitaph.

Muſure, ò manſure parum, properata tuliſti
Præmia, namque cito tradita, rapta cito,

Antonius Amiternus Marco Muſuro Cretenſi, creElæ
diligentiæ Gramatico, & raræ felicitatis poetæ, poſuit.

Here are the Tombs of *Capa ferro*, and *Mignanello* Cardinals, and this Epitaph of *Julius Saturnus*

Patris eram quondam ſpes, & ſolamen Julus
Nunc Deſiderium mortuus & lacrimæ

Santa Maria delle Paline, in the *Via Appia* formerly a Temple of *Saturn* and *Opes* where they ſhew a ſaphyr brought from Heaven by the Angels, wherein the Virgines Image was cut as they ſay by the life in Heaven.

Santa Maria del Popolo near the *Porta Flaminia* , before which Pope *Sixtus* the 5th. erected an Obeliſk. Tis a *Convent* of the *Auſtine* Fryers the Popes give licenſe for the People to pay their devotions here while violent heats continue inſtead of Saint *Sebaſtian* which ſtands a good diſtance without the Walls. In it are many fair Chapels, and Tombs of many Cardinals particularly of *Hermolao Barbaro* Patriark of *Aquileia* with this Epitaph.

Barbariem Hermolaos Latio qui depulit omnem
Barbarus hic ſitus eſt, utraque lingua gemit
Urbs Venetum vitam, mortem dedit inclyta Roma
Non potuit naſci clarius, atque mori.

On the ground this ſad complaint of one that dyed upon an inconſiderable hurt may be read

Hoſpes diſce novum mortis genus ; improba felis
Cum trahitur, digitum mordet, & intereo.

Santa Maria di Portogallo at the end of the Suburbs. In *Puſturla*. In *publicolis*, near the Palace of the *Signoro Santa Croce. Al Preſepe.* *Santa Maria Rotonda*, ſo called from its orbicular form. A Temple for-

formerly dedicated to all the Gods, and to their Mother, and built in a round figure, to the end the Gods might not fall out for precedency of place, for that they feigned their Gods would not give place to one another. *Thermes* refusing it to *Jupiter*. Now this Church is confecrated to the bleffed Virgin and all the Saints. Tis a moft noble Fabrick, built by *Vefpatianus Agrippa*, who was three times Conful, as by the Infcription appears. This by the moft skilfull *Artizans* in Architecture, and chiefly by *Lodovicus Domontiorius*, in his book intitled: *Gallus Hofpes in Urbe*, is held for an *Idea*, Example and Pattern of true Architecture : Tis of a crofs figure as broad as high : the Roof was formerly covered with Sylver plates, but *Conftantine* the Nephew of *Heraclius*, took them with the other ornaments of the City away, inftead whereof *Martin* the 7th, overlayed it with Lead: It hath but one window, which is at the very top, and admits as much light as is neceffary : in antient time it had 7 fteps of Afcent into it, now it hath eleven of defcent, a good argument to what heighth this City is raifed by its ruines. Its noble Porticue is fuftained, by four great pillars, with beams and Gates of Brafs. The Great Altar is oppofite to the Door. On the wall appears the head of the Mother of God. The afcent to the Top is by 100 fteps. Before the Church ftands a great Veffel of *Numidian* Marble, fquare at top but bellyed like a Bee-hive. Near which were two Lyons with *Ægyptian* Letters, and a round Veffel of the fame Marble. In it is the fubfequent Epitaph of *Tadeo Zaccaro*, a Painter, contemporary with *Raphael d'Urbino*, the Prince of the Painters of later Ages, who we formerly faid, lyes buried in *Santa Maria fopra Minerva.*

> *Magna quod in magno timuit Raphaele, per-æque*
> *Thadæo in magno pertimuit genitrix.*

Santa Maria Scala Cæli, without the *Porta Oftienfe*, where 10000: Perfons were Martyred : tis called *Scala Cæli*, becaufe St. *Bernard* there praying for the Souls of the dead, had an appearance of a Ladder from the Earth to heaven, upon which he faw fome Souls afcend into Paradife. *Del Sole* under *Monte Tarpeio della Strada* near the *Portico Corinthio*, and the *Campidoglio* now denominated *Del nome di Giefu* A noble Church built by Cardinal *Aleffandro Farnefe*, for the Jefuits, wherein himfelf is interred. In *Tranftevere.* Here in the time of *Anguftus* gufhed out in a common Inn a fpring or fource of Oyl, which continued running for one whole day, prefaging that a fhort time after Chrift the fource and fountain of Mercy fhould be born, Here was a Church built in honour of the Virgin *Mary* by St. *Peter*, which by fucceeding High Bifhops was adorned with excellent Pictures, and enriched divers times with gold and filver and encreafed in bignefs to what it now appears. In it are the Sepulchres of *Staniflao* Bifhop of *Varma* who was that *Polack* Cardinal Præfect of the *Tridentine* Councel and the fcourge of the Hereticks.

Of Cardinal *Campeggio*, and *Altemps* a man of great Difpatch. *Tranfportina* in *Borgo* in old time the Temple of *Adrian* the Emperour, wherein St. *Peter* and St *Paul* were fcourged. In *Via Lata* the Church of the Fathers Servients, where under ground many Trophees and Triumphumphal Images have been found.   In it lyes buried Cardinal *Vitello-tio Vitelli:* Here St. *Luke* wrote the Acts of the Apostles, *Acta Apostolorum :* and this was the place where St. *Paul* prayed.   *Del Trivio,* which Church was restored by *Belisarius* great Captain ' for *Justinian* the Emperour, as appears by an inscription on a stone, here lyes *Luigi Cornaro,* and others, it appertains to the *Padri Croicchieri,* the crutched Fryers.

Santa *Maria* in *Vinea* in the descent from *Monte Tarpeio.* In *Via delle Virgini,* amplifyed by *Pietro Donato* a Cardinal therein enterred, where also *San Philippo Nerio,* accounted one of the Saints of Pope *Gregory* the 15 his Family, setled his order of Oratories, which was a true School for well living.

Santa *Maria Magdalena,* in the stree *Colonna,* Between the Hill *Santa Trinita,* and the *Tyber.   Nel Quirinale,* where is a Monastery of Nuns governed by the *Predicatory,* instituted by *Maddalena Orsina.*

San *Mauro* in the midst of the Jesuits Colledge: Near this Church is an Obelisk which though small, appears glorious through the Hierogliphicks carved on it, here lies *Pietro Giglio* a great Schollar who dyed *anno* 1555 whose Tombe *Georgio* Cardinal of *Armignac* caused to be built as to his familiar friend.

San *Marcello nella Via Lata,* was a Temple of *Isis,* in it are the Fryers Servients, in it are buried the Cardinals *Mercurio, Dandino,* and *Bonuccio.*

San *Marco,* wherein lies *Francesco Pisani* a *Venetian* Cardinal.

San *Martino* of the Carmelites in *Monte Esquilino,* where Cardinal *Diomede Caraffa* is buried.

Santa *Martina* in the *Foro Romano,* antiently a Temple of *Mars Ultor.*

Santa *Margarita* at the Foot of the *Esquilino.*

San *Matteo* in *Esquilino,* possessed now by the *Austin* Fryers, but formerly by the crutched Fryers, which Church is supposed to be the house of their first Founder Saint *Cletus* the first Pope, for that tis seated in the *Borgo Patritio,* where he was born : which having consecrated he gave to his Disciples and Children for the service of God.

San *Michael in Borgo.*

Santi *Nereo & Archielo* near the Baths of *Antonius,* formerly a Temple of *Isis* in the *Via Appia.*

San *Nicolo* in *Agone.* In *Archemoni. A capo le Cose. Degli Arcioni.* In *Carcere a Ripa* formerly the publique prison. In *Calcaria* near which was the *Portico Corinthio.*

Sant'*Onofrio* in *Gianicolo,* where lyes Cardinal *Madruccio,* who dyed the day of his creation, Cardinal *Lodovico* Madruzzi, Nephew of the first Cardinal *Sega,* a *Bolonian,* and *Tasso* the excellent Poet.

San *Pancratio in Gianicolo,* wherein is a Pulpit of neat fair porphyr, & underneath it are *Grottos* filled with the bodies of Martyrs: Herein lies Cardinal *Dersonese,* and near it was slain *Bourbon* the enemy of God.

San *Pantaleone* in *Sebucca* formerly a Temple dedicated to the Goddess *Tellus,* and to *Pasquinus.*

San

San Paolo in *Regola* in the street *Harenula.*

San Pietro & Marcellino, heretofore the Temple of *Quietas.*

San Pietro in carcere. This was the *Tulliane* prison, whereof *Saluſt* makes mention in *Catalines* conſpiracy. *Diodate* in the *Via Piamenſe, Montorio* in the *Gianicolo :* A fair Church and well adorned, wherein is the fair Chapel of *Bradamante,* endowed by *Ferdinand* King of *Spain,* near it ſtands a Convent of Obſervants of Saint *Francis* Order of this ſociety died *anno* 1597 Fryer *Angelo* a learned *Spaniard,* who wrote a great Volume upon the Symbol or Creed of the twelve A-poſtles. In it are ſeveral pieces of *Raphael d'Urbino,* and *Sebaſtia-no Venetiano,* two famous Painters, and ſeveral Tombs. *San Pietro Domine quo vadis,* in the *Via appia Rotonda,* this Church was ſo called becauſe Saint *Peter,* flying perſecution, Chriſt appeared to him, of whom Saint *Peter* demanded whither he was going in theſe words *Domine quo vadis?* to whom Chriſt anſwered I am going to *Rome,* that I may there be once more crucified : from which words St. *Peter* took courage, and returned to *Rome,* where he was afterwards cru-cified, and his head ſet on high. *S. Pietro* in *vincula;* where the Chains wherewith Saint *Peter* was bound in *Jeruſalem* and in *Rome,* are ſanctimoniouſly preſerved, as alſo the Bodies of the *Maccabei* and a part of the Croſs of *Sant Andrea,* whoſe head is kept iu *San Pietro* in the *Vatican,* being ſent by an Emperour of *Conſtantinople* to the Pope, and the reſt of his Body is in the Kingdom of *Naples :* This Church hath one ſtupendious Altar : and braſen Doors, wherein the paſſions of Saint *Peter* are excellently repreſented : Under the Sepulchre of Pope *Giulio* the ſecond lies a moſt fair ſtatue of *Moyſes* the Captain of the *Hebrews,* the workmanſhip of *Michael Angelo,* of *Florence.* Many other memorable things are ſhewed in this Church. In the Convent is a Palme tree which alone in *Rome* produceth ſea-ſonable and ripe Fruit : Here lies buried the Cardinals *Nicolo Cuſano, Sadoleto,* and *Rovero,* the walls preſent ſome inſcriptions of the old Gentiles. Some other things will be related of this Church in the third dayes Journey.

San Peregrina alla porta pertura, whence that *Burge* takes name.

Santa Proſſede in the *Eſquilino* built by Pope *Paſquale* the 1 ſt. where-in ſtands the Pillar to which our Saviour was bound when ſcourged, conveighed from the Eaſtern parts by Cardinal *Giovanni Colonna:* and here Saint *Peter* dwelt. At the Altar are ſix Pillars of Porphyr and two of black Marble with white ſpots. In it are many bodies of Saints repoſed, and in the midſt is a hollow with a grate over it, wherein *Praſcede* ſqueazed the blood of the Martyrs, which he had ſucked up with ſpunges in divers places : About 400. yeers agoe the Monks of *Valle Umbroſa* reſided here.

Santa Priſca in Monte Aventino, antiently a Temple dedicated to *Hercules.*

Santa Prudentiana in the *Viminale :* here they ſhew that ſtone upon which the bloudy Hoſt appeared, while a Prieſt miſdoubted the ho-ly Sacrament at the Altar. This is the moſt antient Church of *Rome* and ſaid to be the place where Saint *Peter* celebrated Maſs : here ly the bodies of 3000. Martyrs and a venerable Veſſel for their blood. The *penitentiary Dominicans* inhabite there : and the Monks of Saint *Bernard.* Cardinal *Gaetano* a noble *Roman,* who built a ſtately Chapel

Xx

in

in it, and Cardinal *Radzivil Limano* (a good patriot of the Catholick Religion though born of Heretick parents) ly buried there.

Q   *Santi Quaranta Martini*, commended by Saint *Baffilia* in a sermon.

Santi Quatro Coronati in *Monte Celio*.

Santi Quirico & Giulita in the Suburbs.

R   *San Rocco nella Martia*.

S. *Rufina* beyond the *Tyber*, and at Saint *Giovanni Laterano*.

S   *Santa Sabina* in *Monte Aventino*, the first Residence of the Popes, is now of the *Dominican* Fryers : here they shew the stone which the Devil in vain cast at Saint *Dominick* with intention to kill him, before the Door of this Church stands the greatest Urn of one stone in *Rome*. Here they keep the Reliques of Pope *Alexander* of *Quentius* and *Theodulus* the Martyrs: Of *Sabina and Seroffia* the Virgin all Martyred under *Adrian* the Emperour *anno Christi* 133. and here layed up by *Fugenius* the 4th. *anno* 822. who is likewise enterred here with an Epitaph in heroick verse, as are the Cardinals *Bartano* and *Tiano*, Here grows yet a Pomgranat tree planted by Saint *Dominick* with the affiftance of *San Giacinto*, which the *Romans* through devotion defpoil of all Leaves and Fruit the first day of Lent, the Pope and Prelates coveting of its Leaves which they wear. Here Saint *Dominick* gave the first Rife to his Order, and vefted *San Giacinto* in his Religious Order and habite, where he had many Vifions of Angels.

Santo Sabba Abbate in *Aventino*; where arifeth a stately great Sepulchre, believed to be of *Titus Vefpafian*.

San Salvadore del Campo in the *Strada Giulia*, *Di Laurane* in *Monte Afelie Di Copelle* in the Precinct *Colonna del Lauro*, near *Monte Giordino*, which belongs to the noble Family *Orfini*, who with the *Maltei* ly there buried. *Dal Portico* under the *Rupe Tarpeia*. In *Maffime*, a Temple first dedicated to *Jove, Minerva*, and *Juno* ly M. *Pulvilius Statera*. dedicated to *Saturn* in the *Campi doglio, Delle Stufe Della Pietra*, a Tem. ple of the Goddess *Piety* in old time. *De Pedemonte*. *Delle tre Imagini*.

San Spirito in *Vaticano* beyond *Tiber*, where stands that rich Hofpital fo worthy confideration where Cardinal *Remnano Francefco* is enterred.

San Sebaftiano and *Fabiano:* of which is said in the defcription of the 7 principal Churches.

San Sergio & Bacco in the *Campidoglio* formerly a Temple of Concord.

San Simeone in the high ftreet *Ponte ·*

San Sifto in the *Pifcina inferna* of old Temple of Vertue and Honour. Here in Saint *Dominick* raifed a defunct, named *Napuleone* from the dead: and wrote many other miracles: Here the first Nuns congregated, from a general feparation over *Rome*: but they were tranflated into a more falubrious Ayr. It being extream nau feous.

San Stanifliao, A Church of the *Polanders*.

San Stephano of the *Hungarians*. *Rotondo in Monte Celio*, formerly a Temple of *Faunus*, but now a Colledge of the *Germans*, round which is drawd the Triumphes of the holy Martyres, *Nel foro Boario*. A temple of the Goddess *Vefta*, In *Via Giulia*. In *Silice, Dell Frullo* near the Porticue of *Anthony*.   *San*

Santa Susanna, *in Monte Quirinale:* where stands a fair Brasen Cistern and Vessel filled with holy water.

San Silvestro in *Colonna   A Santiquaro. Nel Quirinale* dedicated by *Clement* the 7th. *anno* 1524: wherein the Cardinals *Rebiba, Antonio Caraffa*, and *Francesco Cornaro* ly buried. Beyond the *Tyber* near the Arch of *Domitian.*

San Tomasa in *Monte Celio nel Rione Harenula, nella Via Julia* in *Pari-one.*

San Theodoro at the foot of *Monte Palatino* antiently the Temple of *Romulus* and *Remus* or as others say of *Pan and Bacchus.*

Santa Trinita de monti, built by *Lewis* the 11th. King of *France* by the Council of Saint *Francis*, appertains to the *Minimes* who are near all *French*. In it are buried *Rodolfo Pio: Crasso* and *Bellay* Cardinals: *Lucretia della Rovere* Niece to *Giulius* the second, and *Marco Moreto* a most eloquent Oratour with this Epitaph.

> *Hic Marci caros cineres Roma inclyta servat*
> *Quos patria optasset Gallia habere sinu.*
> *Stat colle hortorum tumulus, stat proximus asiris.*
> *Quæ propius puro contigit ille animo.*
> *Tu sacros larices lacrimis asperge Viator.*
> *Et dic, heu lingua hic fulmina fracta jacent:*

Santa Trinita of the *English*. This is a Colledge of *English* Catholicks, whence divers have been transmitted into *England*, who were there martyred by the (*ut aiunt,*) Hereticks. Herein lies Cardinal *Allen* who took a voluntary banishment from his own Countrey: and employed the rest of his days in great Labour and pains in defence of the Catholick Faith.

San Trisone near *Sant Agostino.*

San Valentino in the *Circo Flaminio.*

San Vitale in the *Quirinale*, lately repaired and now governed by the Jesuits.

San Vito nel Rione del Ponte wherein lyes *Carlo Visconte* a Cardinal.

The Officers of the Popes Palace,

THe Popes Court exceeding that of any other Christian Prince his Officers also be many. Which is governed with such Order. That not only the meaner persons but also the Cardinals (whose dignity is equal to that of Kings) travel not forth the City without licence first obtained.

The number of Cardinals is not præfixt, but left to the will of the Pope: forty of them at least, being alwaies obliged to reside in *Rome* : where also many Arch Bishops and Bishops are constantly present.

In the Popes family are the persons under written.

A Uditori di rota.	A Uditors of the Roll 12.
A Chierici di Camera.	A Clerks of the Chamber 7.
Auditor di Camera.	Auditor of the Chamber 1.
Comiffario di Camera.	Comiffary of the Chamber 1.
Maeftro del facro Pallazzo.	Controuler of the holy Palace 1.
Comiffario Generale del fanto Officio.	The General Commiffary of the holy Office. 1.
Reggente del Cancellaria.	The Ruler of the Chancery: 1.
Protonotorii Apoftolici.	Apoftolick Prothonotaries 7.
Subdiaconi.	Subdeacons. 6.
Accoliti.	Refolute Men 8.
Secretarii Apoftolici.	Apoftolick fecretaries 8.
Corretto di Cancellaria.	The Punifher for the Chancery 1.
Summifta.	A Summift 1.
De Confueti.	Obfervers of the Rules 1.
Abbreviatori minori.	Lefs Abbreviators 12.
Cufto di de Cancellaria.	Keeper of the Chancery 1.
Secretorio delle Cedole.	Secretary of the Docquets 1.
Hoftiario di Cancellaria.	The Hoftia keeper of the Chancery 1.
Scritttori Apoftolici.	Apoftolick writers 101
Camierieri Apoftolici.	Apoftolick Grooms of the Chamber 60.
Scudieri Vivandieri Apoftolici.	Querries of the ftable or Vianders. 140.
Cavalieri di St. Pietro.	Knights of St. *Peter* 400.
Cavalieri di St. Paulo.	Knights of St. *Paul* 22.
Scrittori di Brevi.	Writers of Briefs 81.
Procuratori di Penitentiaria.	Proctors of the Office Penitentiaria 24.
Scrittori di Penitentiaria.	Writers in the office Penitentiaria 29.
Correttori di Piombo.	The ftampers of the Leaden Seal 104
Correttorio di Penitentiaria.	The Stampers of the Office Penitentiaria 11.
Solicitatori.	Purfevants 100.
Correttori del Archivio.	Overfeers of the Arches or fpiritual Court 10.
Scrittori del Archivio.	Writers in the Arches or fpiritual Court 10.
Secretarii delle Bolle Salaciate.	Secretary of the Penfionary Buls 8
Regiftratori del ifteffe Bolle.	Regifters of the faid Bulls 4
Maeftri delle Bolle Regiftrate.	Mafters of the regiftred Bulls 4

Notaro

Auditore delle contradette.	Hearers of differences	14.
Maestri delle Suppliche.	Masters of Requests	4.
Chierici delle suppliche.	Clerks of the Requests	6.
Notari della Camera Apostolica.	Notaries of the Apostolick Chamber	9.
Scrittori del Registro delle supliche.	Writers in the Registry of Requests.	20.
Notari del Auditor della Camera.	Notaries for the Auditor of the Chamber	10.
Notari di Rota.	Notaries of the Rouls	48.
Notari del Vicario del Papa.	Notaries of the Popes Viccar	4.
Notari del Governatore civile.	Notaries of the civil Magistrat	11.
Notaro de maleficii.	Notary of Offences	1.
Notaro di Cancellaria.	Notary of the Chancery	1.
Presidenti di Ripa.	Presidents of the Bench	141.
Portionarii.	Partakers	612.
Corsori.	Apparitors	19.
Servatori d'Arme.	Keepers of the Arms	24.
Verghe Rosse.	Red Rodds	24.
Catene nel Sacro Pallazzo.	Chains in the sacred Pallace.	71.
Porte di ferro.	Gates of Iron	25.
Gavalli leggieri communemente.	Light horses comonly 100 or 200.	
Bombardieri.	Gunners	300.

Switzers, or *Germans* for guarding the Gates of the Popes Pallace, of whom 200. or 300. alwaies keep Sentinel.

Pope *Gregory* the 13th. in tenn yeers of his Enjoyment of the Pontifical Chair instituted nineteen Seminaries or Colledges for all Nations in *Rome,* for the benefit and propagation of the Catholick Faith and for reception, as well as Instruction of such as abandon their own Countreys by reason of persecutions.

To which are since added 7 more instituted by *Clement* the 8th. and others.

Of the Obelisks. Columnes and Aqueducts of *ROME.*

THe Obelisks restored erected and transferred by Pope *Sixtus* the 5th. of glorious memory with incredible expence, by the workmanship of the Inginier *Domenico Fontana,* and consecrated to the most holy Cross are these.

The Obelisk of *Tiberius Cæsar* standing now in the Piazza of St. Peter in *Vaticano:* in the second yeer of his inauguration, *anno Dom.* 1586.

That of *Augustus Cæsar* brought from Ægypt, and translated from *San Rocco* to *Santa Maria Maggiore* is not engraven nor carved at all.

                    That

That which was consecrate to the Sun transferred from *Circo Maſſimo*, (where it lay on the ground) to *San Giovanni* in *Laterano*, is carved with *Ægyptian* characters, and was reared the third year of his Papacy; *Auguſtus* took it from its place in *Ægypt* & conveyed it vpon the *Nilo* into *Alexandria*, where imbarquing it, he sent it by sea for adornment of *Rome*, which he sought to imbellish in all things possible: which his endeavour and coſt caused him once to vaunt, that he found *Rome* all of Brick, but left it of Marble

That dedicated to the Sun by *Auguſtus* in *Circo Maximo*, being drawn out of the Ruines among which twas buried, was tranſlated with infinite expence to the *porta Flaminia* and railed before the Church *S Maria del Popolo*

Besides the abovenamed, divers other Obelisks and Pyramides are yet extant in *Rome*, but all of ſmall value, except that which was newly erected in the *Piazza Novana* by Innocent the X which is admirable.

We gather from the writers of Antiquity that formerly there were many more Obelisks in *Rome* then at preſent appear. *Pliny* the time of *Veſpaſian* names many of them. *Ammianus Marcellinus* the contemporary with *Julian* the Emperour sets down more, but *P. Victor* commemorates to the number of 42. treating of the leſs. *Andrea Fulvius*, *Pietrus*, *Angelus*, *Burgeus Figafetta*, and *Michael Mercato*, in the latine and vulgar tongue give thereof moſt ample accounts.

Auguſtus Cæſar tranſmitted two Obelisks from *Ægypt* to *Rome*, at the time he overcame *Marc Anthony* and *Cleopatra*, and *Publius Victor*, reckons ſeaven more conveighed thither afterwards. One whereof was placed in the Gardens of *Saluſtius*, which took up all the ſpace and the vale from the Church *Santa Suſanna* to the *Porta Collina*: This (they ſay) was conſecrated to the Moon, and carved with *Egyptian* Characters, What vaſt Veſſels were built for conveighing theſe *Pliny* and *Ammianus* diſcourſe at large, and one they ſay had 300 mariners in her. Now let us ſpeak of thoſe Obelisks that are marked with *Ægyptian* Characters: That of Saint *Peter* and *Santa Maria maggiore* being without ſuch.

The Obelisk before Saint *Giovanni Laterano*, all over engraved with Hieroglyphicks was brought as aforeſaid by *Conſtantine* the great out of *Ægypt* into *Alexandria* and erected in *Conſtantinople*, and thence by *Conſtantius* his ſon in an immenſe Galley wherein were 300 Rowers at the Oar, to *Rome* and by him placed in the *Circo Maximo*: which *Sixtus* the 5th. anno 1588 with incredible expence removed to Saint *Giovanni Laterano* where the Popes uſed formerly to inhabit. A ſecond he removed from the *Circo Maſſimo* to *Santa Maria Maggiore* formerly Conſecrated to the Sun.

The third in the Vineyard of the great Duke of *Tuſcany*, filled with Hyerogliphicks: tis but ſmall but tis thought ſtood in the *Campo Martio*, in the time of *Tarquine* the proud.

The fourth leſs than the former was transferred from the *Campidoglio*, by *Ciriaco Mattei*, and ſtands in the Vineyard of the *Mattæi* who had it of the gift of the Senat and people of *Rome*: this hath ſome ſmall Images on the top only; the others all over.

There is another lying in the *Via Appia*, near the Sepulchre of *Cæcilia Metella* broke in 3 ſeveral pieces: which (tis much admired)

that

that Pope *Sixtus* the 5th. did not erect as well as the rest: nor is it to be believed but that he would have done it, had not death interrupted this and his other designes. One other smaller Obelisk stands near the Jesuits Colledge.

Tis admirable that upon all those Hierogls. & Obelisks the sign of the Cross is figured: which might happen, either for that the *Ægyptians* through some mistery honoured the Cross, or for that they might have had some relation touching it from their Ancestors, and yet without knowing the signification. At the time when by the Emperour *Theodosius* his command all the Idols of *Ægypt* were destroyed, On the Breast of *Serapis* was found the sign of the Cross, whereof the signification being enquired into, the Priests skilled in the sacred misteries of the *Ægyptians* declared, that they understood by it the Life to come after death here: which could not portend other, than the eternal beatitude whereto our Saviour by his death on the Cross opened the way. Thus *Socrates* the writer of the Ecclesiastick Histories in his 5th. Book 27th. Chap. recounts, as also do *Ruffino, Georgio Cedreno,* and *Suida,* in their writings. We must observe that the punishment by the Cross in those dayes common to Malefactors was taken away by *Constantine* the Emperour a true Christian, through his Reverence of our Saviours death: who in lieu thereof constituted the Gallows, as divers Authors relate: Which Emperour also prohibited by a severe Law, the conculcating any Cross upon the Earth Let thus much serve touching the Obelisks of *Rome,* if the Reader be curious to search into those in *Constantinople* and other places (the discourse whereof is not to our purpose) let him peruse the treatises of *Michael Mercato, Pietro Bellonio,* and *Pietro Gillio,* upon this subject.

In *Rome* also are 3 famous Collumnes: one Called *Rostrata* in the *Campidoglio* erected by C. *Duilio,* after the *Carthaginians* were overcome in the *Punick* War. Another of *Trajan,* which *Sixtus* the fifth dedicated to St, *Peter:* and that of *Anthony* which the same Pope consecrated to Saint *Paul* in *anno* 1580.

The A Q U E D U C T S.

TIBERIUS *Cæsar* conveighed the *Acqua* Virgin into the City but the works falling to decay Pope *Nicholas* the 5 in the yeer of Christ 1554. and the seaventh of his Papacy restored it to its first beauty as by the Inscription at the *Fontana di Trevi* appears.

Sixtus the 5th: brought the *Acqua Felice* into the City, calling it *Felice* from his own name before he was advanced to the Pontifical Chair: Other Popes have likewise layed and restored other waters for the Citizens conveniency and delight.

A Guide or Direction for the most convenient view of the Antiquities of ROME.

WE will begin from the *Vatican*, chiefly in favour of those who come from *Tuscany* to *Rome*, entring by the *Porta Vaticata*, near the Castle Saint *Angelo*. Here ly the Meadowes and fields of *Quintius* or as others say of *Pincius* at this day called *Prata* a lovely and pleasant place, whither the youth usually resort for Recreation.

The *Porta Elia*, called vulgarly *di Castello* leads to *Adrians* Mole, A vast Pile which he raised for the burying place for himself and the *Antonini*, being large and strong, but at present better accomodated than in his time, for that the Popes have made it a Fortress for their own retreat and security, in time of imminent danger of Enemies, to which a long Gallery under Ground leads from the Palace of St. *Peter*, for their more convenient and safe passage. Heretofore One *Cresentius* made himself Lord of it by force of Arms and of the City also: but at present the Popes possess it, and cal it *Castel* St. *Angelo*, from the Marble statue of an Angel with a sword in his hand sett on the top of it, which *Alexander* the 7th. augmented and fortified in ample manner as by the Inscription on the Bridge may be understood. In it are kept the three millions of Gold, which may not be imployed on any use but defence of the Apostolick state in point of Arms. The Marbles, Collumnes, and Statues formerly there, were conveighed to the *Vatican*, and placed in the Church of Saint *Peter*, and the Papal Palace, and nothing of Antiquity left behind but the structure, and two heads, the one of *Adrian* the Emperour armed, the other of *Pallas*, with some inscriptions on the walls, which notwithstanding, tis yet most worthy observation. Here stands the *Ponte* or Bridge *Elio*, so called for that *Elius Adrianus* the Emperour built it for his Sepulchre: but at present tis called *Ponte di Castello*, on either side of it stand the statues of. the Apostles Saint *Peter* and Saint *Paul*, wrought with excelling Workman·ship under Pope *Clement* the 7th. at the time that the *Tyber* grown beyond its usual limits, overflowed to the great devastation of the City and this Bridge in *anno* 1530. Being upon this Bridge, you may see opposite to you the Hospital of *Santo Spirito*, and the Ruines of the triumphal Bridge, which was so denominated, for that over it were lead the Pompes of Triumphs as the way to the *Campidoglio*.

All that part of the *Vatican* hill between the Bridge and the Palace is now called *Borgo*, but was formerly named *la selva* because before the time of Pope *Alexander* the second the *Vatican* Grove grew there, wherein was erected a Pyramide for the Sepulchre of *Scipio Affricanus*, whereof some reliques may yet be seen in that part of the

Tem-

Temple called *Paradiso*; as the great Pyne Apple, and Peacok of Brafs guilt.

In the *Borgo*, almoft all the Edifices are ftately and noble, and in particular thefe following : The Palace of the Cardinal of *Cefis* at the gate of Saint *Onofrio*, whofe firft Court is full of Statues and infcriptions, the particulars whereof are printed and publifhed: in it is an Effigies of the *Amazon Hippolito* infinitely applauded, being the workmanfhip of *Michael Angelo*, the Prince of Sculptors, another of *Apollo*, a third of a *Sabyn* Woman, no whit inferiour to that of the *Amazon*, had it Arms proportionable.

In the garden ftands a ftatue of *Bacchus* upon a Pediftol : A Veffel of Brafs with a *Faunus*, a *Neptune*, aud an *Apollo*, holding a Harp in his hand : An Image of *Agrippa*, the Daughter of *Marcus Agrippa* Another of *Julia* the Daughter of *Auguftus Cæfar*, a Pallas armed, and *Herma* defloured. On the right hand appears a fountain with 22 Circles about it of Marble ftone, on which ftand the ftatues of *A faunus, Jupiter Hammon, Pompey* the Great, *Demofthenes*, *Spenfippus* the Philofopher, who was thought to be the Son of a Sifter of *Plato*. In profpective from the Gate may be feen *Rome* triumphing for the overcoming of *Dacia*, fitting on a Throne with a Murrion on her head and a Branch of Laurel in her hand, with *Dacia* placed near it, in a mourning pofture and Habit; round it are Trophees, as Arms of the Barbarous, two conquered Kings in *Numidian* Marble, bigger than ordinary men, two ftatues of two of the *Parcæ*: and two *Sphinxes* of the fame Marble.

Contiguous with it ftands a round Fabrick called the *Antiquario*, from the many Antiquities contained in it: On the Front is fixed a Vifage of *Jupiter*, in porphyr ftone, and an effigies of *Poppea* the wife of *Otho* the Emperour: above which ftand five ftatues, That is of *Pallas, Ceres, Victoria, Copia, and Diana*. Within are feen the Statue of *Somnus*, or of *Quies*, or as others will have it of *Æfculapius* with Poppy in his hands, and an Image of a *Sabine* Lady. In the gate on the left hand appears a Vifage of *Jove*, as bigg as a Gyants, on the right another of *Hercules*, and in the midft a third of *Pallas*. And under that of *Hercules*, a *Satyre*, who blows a Shepheards pipe of feaven Reeds: a neater piece of work then which is fcarfe to be feen, which is attributed to *Scopa*. Under that of *Jove*, a head of *Pyrrhus* King of the Epirotes with a *Leda* and a *Cupid*. The *Satyr*, and the *Leda* are moft compleat ftatues. In it are the heads alfo of *Portia, Cato, Jupiter, Ganimed, Diana, Neptune*, with a moft antient *Ægyptian* Image called the head of *Aftrate* Mother of *Ofarides*, or as others will of *Ope*, or *Cibele* the Mother of the Gods.

Near the gate ftand two ftatues, one on the left hand of *Aries Fiffus* of moft white Marble, with thefe words on the Bafis, *Secura Simplicitas*. The other on the right hand of *Leone*, with thefe words upon the bafis, *Innoxia Fortitudo*. Near which ftands the Emperour, *Heliogabulus*, clothed at his full length, with certain antique Ceremonies in the facrifices engraven on the Bafis: Upon another Image of an Emperour triumphing drawn by four horfes, ftands a *Simia* an Ape cut in *Æthiopick* Marble in the form the *Ægyptians* ufed to worfhip it. In the Hall is a head of *Bacchus* of red ftone, with a *Neptune* over it, drawn in a Chariot by four horfes, and two ftatues of the Goddefs *Pomona*.　　　Z z　　　The

The study of the Cardinal hath its pavement wrought in figure with small stones : and in it are many heads of illustrious *Romans*, as of *Scipio*, *Africanus*, *Marcus Cato*, *M Antonius* the triumvir, *Julius*, *Cæsar*, *Septimius*, *Severus*, *L Sylla*, *C Nero*, *Julia Mammea*; *M. Antonius Caracalla*, *Adrianus*, *Macrinus*, *Cleopatra*, *Fauſtina*, and *Sabina*, As also a Library furnished no less with Books of Antient than modern Authors, In the withdrawing Chambers are Gems and pretious stones, so well wrought that they best speak themselves, therein also are *Scipio Naſica*, *Brutus*, *Adrianus Imperator*, a sleeping *Cupid*, and a Child, with divers other vaine things so rare and curious, and rich, that did *Rome* afford no other Palace than this, you will say when seen, you could not better dispose your time and travel then to behold it; And that it alone deserve the pains of a Journey thither.

The Popes Pallace.

ON the Top of the *Vatican* Hill stands that proud Pallace of the Popes, which like a large City is capable of three Kings and all their followers: here the Popes (induced thereto from the beauty of the scite, and temperature of the Ayr) for the most part make their dwelling, having deserted their former on the *Laterano*. The first thing here to be viewed is the Chapel of *Sixtus*, which for its grandeur and beauty may be paralleld to any other great and noble Church: in it the Card inals assemble themselves for election of the Pope, and call themselves the Conclave, upon the high Altar whereof is that noble Picture representing the Universal Judgment, painted by *Michael Angelo*, a Piece so generally applauded, that it's held invaluable, for its exellency, and unimitable by all succeding Artists, though divers and those the best attempt it dayly : Near it is the *Capella Paolina*, painted by the same hand: whence the way lies into the Gardens called *Belvedere*, The fair sight both for their infinite beauty and the prospect of the most part of *Rome*, in it are many foreign rare plants. Herein stands the statue of the *Tyber* foxes connexed with a wolf which gave suck to *Remus* and *Romulus*; The *Nyle* upon a *Sphinx* with 17. Children denoting the increases of that River with its effects upon *Ægypt*, with several monsters & strong creatures proper only to that River : which statue was heretofore found near Saint *Stephens* Church, and being thence conveighed into those gardens, is there presented to publique view for that general approbation of excellency which is meritoriously given it.

On the walls of the said *Belvedere* are moreover 12 several deformed Creatures set up, which are carved out of the politest Marble : And in certain Corners and Nooks stands a shape of *Antinoo*, cut in the whitest Marble of singular Artifice and in this form by the command of *Adrian* the Emperour, who deputed divine sacerdotal honours with Temples, whose memory alsothat he might perpetuate, he built a City in *Ægypt* calling it from his name *Antinopoli*, On the right hand is the River *Arno* in the shape of a Man lying along, diffusing water from his Tomb, with *Cleopatra* on his left hand leaning on her

right

right hand. In the second Armory ſtands *Venus Ericina* prepared to come out of a Bath. In the third is the ſame *Venus* playing with *Cupid* and this Inſcription.

Veneri Fœlici Sacrum Saluſtia Helpis D. D.

Near it is a *Bacchus armeleſs,* and that Trunk of *Hercules,* pronounced by *Michael Angelo,* to be the moſt compleat ſtatue of *Rome,* the name of *Apollo* as ſculptor is inſcribed on it, as alſo two other Caraſſes the one of a Lady the other of *Mercury,* and an Arch of Marble, wherein is figured the Chaſe of *Meleager* found in the *Vatican* Vineyard, appertaining to his Sanctity.

In the fourth Armory in the *Cants* ſtands a ſtatue of the Emperor *Commodus* in the habit and ſhape of *Hercules,* holding a Child on his Arm, whoſe humour was to be ſo figured and called as hiſtorians report. In the fifth *Apollo Pitheo,* with a Serpent at his feet, and a *Carcaſe* having a piece of Cloth upon one Arm, a Bow and Arrows in his hand, and all over naked. In the ſixth is *Laocoon* with his two Sons enveloped by two Dragons as *Virgil* writes the ſtory, all of one Marble ſtone: This Piece was eſteemed by *Michael Angelo* the Miracle of Sculpture: and before his time by *Pliny* who ſaies that, 'twas wrought by *Ageſanero Poliodoro,* and *Athenodoro* the principal Sculptors of their times, and preſerved in the Palace of *Titus Veſpaſianus* and found in his ſeaven Halls. Some ſpace from which lies *Cleopatra* ready to give up the Ghoſt, of ſo exact workmanſhip and polite Marble, that underneath the Marble Garments which ſeem to lie over the whole body, the Limbs and ſhape of the perſon, do perfectly appear. In the ſame Palace and Gardens which are five, ſome in Terrace, others low, beſide the aforenamed not a few nor mean Veſſels and ſtatues preſent themſelves as gratefull Objects to the Viſitants thereof: As to paſs by others a Fountain made after a ruſtick manner, round which ſtand feigned Gods and Sea Monſters, very well repreſented: Together with the Images of Pope *Paulus* the 2 and the Emperor *Charls* the 5th. drawn by the hand of *Michael Angelo,* and a ſtatue of one of the Curiatii, which is a fair one, and ſtands where the *Switzers* keep their Guard.

In the Armory, are Arms and all accompliſhments for 35000. men horſe and foot, and over the door of it is this Motto

Urbanus VIII. Literis arma, Armis Literas.

In the *Conſtantine* Hall, to paſs over the other things which are infinite, are painted ſeveral picturs drawn by the principal Painters in all Ages, chiefly the Battel fought at the *Ponte Milvio,* and the victory obtained there by *Conſtantine,* againſt *Maxentius,* the work of *Raphael Stantio* of *Urbin.*

In the Gallery Pope *Gregory* the 13th. for the benefit of the Popes to his great coſt, cauſed all the Provinces Regions and Chief Cities of the whole World, to be artificially and exactly lymned annexing to each Province in a ſweet ſtyle its *Encomion.*

This Pallace was begun by *Nicholas* the third, augmented by his ſucceſſors, finiſhed by *Julius* the ſecond & *Leo* the 10th. garniſhed and

　　　　　　　　　　beauti-

beautified with Pictures and other Ornaments, by *Sixtus* the 5th, and *Clement* the 8th. so that at this day it remains a stately Receptacle for his holiness, and a worthy object for all Forreigners.

Of the Church of Saint *Peter*, on the *VATICANO*

THis hath meritoriously its place among the seaven Principal and the Library Churches of *Rome*, and will therefore require breifer account here, Tis the most famous and splendid of *Rome*. On that part which is ascended by steps, is a Pillar erected, compassed about with Iron barrs, and this inscription on it.

Hæc est illa Columna, in qua Dominus noster Jesus Christus apocliatus, dum populo prædicabat, & Deo Patri in Templo preces effundebat, adhærendo stabat, quæ una cum aliis undecim hîc circumstantibus de Salomonis templo in triumphum hujus Basilicæ hîc locata fuit.

In this Temple is likewise preserved the head of Saint *Andrew* the Apostle, and the spear which was run into the side of our Saviour, when he hung upon the Cross: It was sent as a gratefull present to Pope Innocent the 8th. by the *Turkish* Emperour: Here also is the *Porta Sancta,* which is never opened but in the yeer of *Jubile*, and that finished is shut again. Which shall suffice to avoid Repetition.

To the Church of Saint *Peter* is joyned the little Church of *Santa Petronilla*, formerly a Temple of *Apollo*, as that of *Santa Maria della febre* was of *Mars*. in the Piazza of Saint *Peter* stands the Obelisk translated thither from the Circ of *Nero* in the yeer 1586. at the Instance and cost of *Sixtus* the 5th. where it lay in neglectfull obscurity, in old times called the Obelisk of *Cæsar*, and under it were then laid the Ashes of *Julius Cæsar*; *Dominico Fontana* was the Engineer. Its heighth is 170 foot besides the Basis which is 37 foot more on the bottom tis 12 foot broad and at top 8. It weighs without the Basis 956148. pound the Instruments prepared for its removall and erecting weighed 1031824. pound. The Removal of it we must needs conclude so admirable as to deserve a place among the great wonders of the Antients, if we despise it not (as is usual) for that twas modern.

The Circ and *Naumachia*, the place for sea battails of *Nero* were near herunto, where they made their sportive recreations in barques upon the water, and cruelly cast those that confessed the name of Christ, to be devoured by wilde beasts.

The *Borgo* hath five gates, to wit, *L'Elia* at the Castle Saint *Angelo*, That of Saint *Peter* under the Popes Gardens, *La Pertusa* on the highest

eſt part of the hill. *La Vacina*, at the Palace of the *Ceſis*, and the *Trionſale*, now called of *Santo ſpirito*, near which *bourbon* received a ſhot which occaſioned his death, and the ſurrender of *Rome* to the Emperor *Charls* the 5th.

The Hoſpital of *San Spirito*, was firſt inſtituted by *Innocent* the 3d. afterwards aggrandized by *Sixtus* the 4th, In it they govern with no leſs honour than love the foreign Infirm perſons: ſo that many rich Men diſdain not to retire themſelves thither for the government of the ſick and infirm, and thereto imploy their skill and time though at their own charges, not having their own proper houſes in *Rome*.

Of the Hill *Gianicolo*, now called *Montorio*.

THe Hill *Janiculus* is now called *Montorio quaſi mons aureus*, or the goulden Mount: near it lies the Circ of *Julius Cæſar*, where appear ſome fragments of the Sepulchre of *Numa Pompilius*, which yet demonſtrate 'twas no great Fabrick: a certain aſſurance, that Ambition had not then in thoſe times any great place in *Rome*.

Montorio is ſo called for the ſparkling of the ſand there; Where ſtands a Church of Saint *Peter*, and a round Fabrick wrought excellently *Dorick* wiſe, the deſign of *Bramante*. At the high Altar of the ſaid Church is a Marble ſtone whereon Chriſt was figured by *Raphael* of *Urbin*. On the right hand at the entrance into the Church Chriſt is rarely painted upon the Wall being whipt, by *Baſtiano the Venetian* called *del Piombo*. Here ſtands the Tombe which *Julius* the third cauſed to be built for himſelf then living, where for all that he had not the happineſs to lye (dead) but was buried in a mean place in the *Vatican*.

The Gate of Saint *Pancratio*, was formerly called *Aureliana*, or *Settimiana*, for that it was repaired by *Septimius Severus*, who near it erected an Altar and certain Baths: without this gate you ſee an Aqueduct not very high, through which ran the waters of the Lake *Alſetino*, into the Baths of *Severus*, of *Filippus*, and into the *Naumachia*, the place for Sea Fights of *Auguſtus*.

Where now ſtands the Temple of *Santa Maria* in *Tranſtevere*, was formerly a *Taberna Meritoria*, or a *Locanda* as they now term it being a place for letting out Chambers: There ſtood alſo a Temple of *Æſculapius* for the deceaſed, to whom (becauſe they believed him a God alwaies regarding and aſſiſting to their healths) the infirm had recourſe, and ſacrificed.

The *Naumachia*, was a place purpoſely ſet apart for the preparing all things neceſſary for Naval fights. This place is at preſent called *à Ripà*, in *Rome*, where the Veſſels are ſteered by *Oſtia* into the City; beſides in antient time in the *Naumachia*, they often preſented certain Warlike and Naval ſports for the Solace of the Princes and multitude.

The *Ponte Aurelio*, or *Gianicolo* conjoins the part *Tranſteverina*, or beyond the *Tyber* to the City, but being broken in the civil War 'twas afterwards called *Ponte Rotto*: At laſt being reedified by *Sixtus* the 4th. to that magnificence it now appears in, it took the name of *Ponte Sixto*. In the midst of the *Naumachia* rise the reliques of the *Ponte Sublicio*, upon which *Horatius* alone in the War against the *Tuscans* sustained the assaults of the Enemies till such time as the *Romans* could break down the said Bridge near the Gate, by which means the Enemies were obstructed in their hoped for entrance into the City. *Æmilius Lepidus* caused it afterwards to be built of stone : From a top this Bridge the Emperour *Heliogabulus* the Monster of Nature and Mankind having a stone hung about his Neck, was cast down into the *Tyber*.

Near hereunto ly the Fields *Mutii*, given to *Mutius Scævola*, by the publick, for the noble Act he performed in the presence of *Porsenna* King of the *Tuscans*.

At the Port of *Ripa*, *Leon* the 4th. built two Towers to hinder the inroads of the *Sarazens*, who often by *Ostia* run up the *Tyber*. Then *Borgo* was called *Citta Leonina*; *Alexander* the 4th. named it *Borgia*, and added to it good increase of all things.

L'Isola Tiberina, is believed to have rise and beginning in the time of *Tarquin* the proud, 'tis not very broad but a quarter of a mile long and was consecrated to *Æsculapius*: In it is at this day a Church dedicated to *San Bartolomeo*, At the point of the Island you may see the form of that Ship, wherein the Serpent *Epidaurus* was conveighed into the City, which form was sometime since exposed to view by the inundation of the *Tyber*.

In the gardens of Cardinal *Farneze*, beyond the *Tyber* are divers *Venuses* of the whitest Marble, and several Pyles, on which are figured Men, Lyons, Women, the nine Muses, Satyrs and other things, and a broken pillar with a Greek inscription very memorable which was brought from *Tivoli*.

The Bridge *Cescio* or *Esquilino* conjoines the part beyond the *Tyber* to the Island; 'twas built by *Valentianus* and *Valens* Emperors, and is now called *Ponte* Saint *Bartolomeo* from that Church which stands in the Island contiguous with it? In the same Island stands the Church of *San Giovanni Battista*, which formerly was the Temple of *Jupiter*, and in the uppermost part of it yet appear the ruines of a Temple of *Faunus*, which was reduced to that sad condition by the Inundation of the River.

The Bridge *Fabricio*, called also *Tarpeio*, connexeth the Island with the City, passing through the midst of *Marcellus* his Theatre, 'tis at this time called *Ponte dai quatro capi*, from certain statues there reared, each of which hath four faces and heads.

The Theatre of *Marcellus* was built by *Augustus Cæsar*, at the Bridge *Fabricio*, in honour of *Marcellus* the Son of his Sister *Octavia*,) capacious for eighty thousand persons) to which structure that she might add the more lustre as in remembrance of her said Son *Marcellus*, the said *Octavia* compleated a most admirable & well furnished Library of Books of all sorts and sciences. This Theatre the House of *Savelli* at present possess: The said *Augustus* raised also the Banqueting house called *Octavio* in honour of his said Sister *Octavia*, part whereof yet is on foot, in the midst of the said Theatre, where are some shops of Goldsmiths now, but was formerly much more beautified by many rare statues, as among others with a Satyr, the work of *Praxitelle*,

Prafitelle, the nine Mufes of *Timarchide*, and the Image of *Juno*, now placed in the Manfion of *Julius* the third in the *Via Flaminia*; *Cæfar Germanicus* illuftrated the faid Banqueting Houfe, with the addition of a ftately Temple, dedicated to *Speranza* and Hope, towards the Piaza *Montanara*, to which was conjoined the Temple of *Aurora*, much renowned among the Antients the very Footfteps whereof time and misfortune have razed out.

The Houfe of *Savelli*,(in the Theatre of *Marcellus*,) poffefs a moft rare piece, being a Lyon cut in Marble, with three Men Armed and prepared to fight him, together with many other Marble Tablets: And a garden very delicious, wherein are feveral Pyles, whereon the Labours of *Hercules* are engraven, and divers Statues of Men and pieces of *Mercury*.

. *San Nicolo* in *Carcere*, formerly was the Prifon for the common people, but for that a Daughter expreffed fo much Piety to her Father there bound in chains as to nourifh him many dayes with the milk from her own breafts, *Attilia Gabrione*, raifed there a Temple dedicating it to *Piety*.

Santo Andrea in *Mentuzza*, was in old times a Temple confecrated to *Juno Matura* by *Cornelius* the Conful, under the *Campidoglio*.

You may fee the broken Bridge of *Santa Maria Tranfteverina*, or *Ægittiaca*, fo named from the Neighbouring Church; which was formerly called *Ponte Senatorio* and *Palatino*, for that the Senators paffed over that Bridge in religious manner to the *Janicolo*, to confult the Books of the Sybills, and thence returned to the Court of the Emperours.

The Houfe of *Pilat* placed near the *Ponte Senatorio* fabuloufly by the Vulgar, if we make a narrower infpection, and contemplate the moft high ruine there appearing, muft needs have been the *Sudatoria Laconica*, or hot Baths. The *Foro Olitorio*, is the *Piazza Montonora*, where *Evander* erected an Altar in honour of *Nicoftrata Carmenta* his mother.

The Church of *Sancta Maria Ægittiaca*, formerly the Temple of *Fortuna Virilis*, remains almoft intire and unblemifhed having a long row of high Pillars on both fides. Some report it to have been confecrated to *Pudicitia Matronalis*, and that therein was the *Bucca Veritatis*, which is efteemed a fabulous ftory, and that ample round porphyr ftone ftanding before the Greek Schools, which they fay was the *Bucca veritatis*, conld be applyed to no other ufe then for a Chanel or receipt of waters, as in divers other ftones of the like form up and down the City ufed to the like occafions is moft plainly apparent.

In the houfe of the *Serlupi* in the Fifhftreet, they fhew a moft compleat piece, being the head of the Emperour *Vefpafian* as big as a Gyants, cut in white Marble.

In the next houfe appertaining to the *Delfini*, are the heads of *Lucius Verus*, and *Marcus Aurelius*, of *Bacchus*, of a Child laughing, and of fix others with fome Urns, and ftones with remarkable infcriptions.

Of the place where the *Afylum*, or fanctuary for refuge ftood, there is no Certainty becaufe fome place it in this part, others in the

Campidoglio, wherefore no ampler account can be given of it, upon a certain foundation.

San Stephano Rotondo, which denomination it borrowed from the form of the Fabrick, stands by *Santa Maria Ægittiaca*, 'twas built by *Numa Pompilius*, and consecrated to *Vesta*: tis sustained on every part by *Corinthian* Pillars, aud receaves the light from the top, as doth the *Pantheon*.

La Rupe Tarpeia, lies on the utmost part of the *Campidoglio*, being a vast *præcipice*, opposite to the Church *Santa Maria Egittiaca*, *Manlius Capitolinus* being found guilty of an intention to Master *Rome* and become its Tyrant, was at the comand of the Senate præcipitated from this Rock. Some say, that *Ovids* house stood among those ruins which are near the Church *Santa Maria della Consolatione*, others that it was in *Eurgo Georgio*, near the *Porta Carmentale*, at the Foot of the *Capitol*, where also *Valerius Amerinus* dwelt, and *Opis* and *Saturnus* had Temples.

The Temple of *Vesta* built by *Romulus* between the *Capitolinum* and the *Palatinum*, stood where now is the Church *dalle Gratie* or *dalle Consolatione*, wherein the Vestal Virgins kept the holy and perpetual Fire, and the *Palladium*, with the Domestick houshold Gods brought by *Æneas*, *from Troy* into *Italy*, but the said Temple being burning, the *Palladium* which was a wooden Image of *Pallas* with roling eyes was snatched out of the Fire and translated into *Velia*, where now is *Santa Andrea* in *Palata*.

The *Foro Boario*, took its name either for that there they sold their Bulls, or because *Evander* having received the Bulls of *Gerion* consecrated that place for perpetual remembrance of that Victory, Adjacent to the Temple of Saint *George*, in *Velabro* stands a fair Arch all of Marble, beautified with excellent figures of Sacrifices, erected in former times by the Goldsmiths and Merchants in honour of the Emperors, *Septimius Severus*, and *Marcus Aurelius*. And contiguous with this Arch stood the Temple of *Janus Quadrifrons*: four squ-red and in e very front a large Gate, and 12. Nooks, wherein tis believed they set up twelve statues, representing 12 Months. The *Romans* sacrificed to *Janus* as Prince or President of the sacrifices, calling him also *Vertumnus*. Many Temples in *Rome* were dedicated to this God, among which that chiefly flourished which *Numa* built at the *Porta Carmentale* near the Theatre of *Marcellus* which had two Gates only, and they stood alwaies open in time of warr, and shut in times of Peace. Historians report these Gates to be three times only lockt up: The first by *Numa* the Founder, the second by *Titus Manlius* the Consul. The third by *Augustus Cæsar*, when he had wholly overcome *M. Antonius*: *Suetonius* reports that twas a fourth time shut by *Nero*, which is proved by certain Coynes of the said Emperor yet extant, with these words on the one side. *Pace Populo Romano Ubique, Porta Janum Clausit:* Now this Temple is consecrated to *Santa Catherina*.

Il Velabro, where stands *Santo Georgio* in *Velabro*, was so denominated for this cause: When the *Tyber* overflowed and covered the face of the Earth, they could not pass into the *Aventinum*, from one bank to the other unless in Boats, for their passage wherein they payed a certain piece of money, which in Latin signifies a Booth, those boats being covered over.

Santa

Santa Maria in *Cosmodin,* is called *Schola Græca,* perhaps for that in former times t was enjoyed by Greeks. They fable, that here Saint *Augustin* taught, and that here was another *Bucca Veritatis.* Annexed to this Church towards the Tyber stood a Temple of *Hercules Victor,* the reliques whereof shew its form to have been round, t was destroyed by Pope *Sixtus* the fourth. They report that Flyes never entred into this Temple, *Hercules* by Prayer to *Myagrum* the God of Flyes, having obtained this favour, for that being about to sacrifice to *Jupiter,* the Flyes molested the sacrifice: Nor Doggs, Because the same *Hercules* affixed his Club to the Door of the Temple, which so terrified the Doggs (it having an innate Virtue to fright Doggs) that they durst not approach the Gates: Neither Women Servants or made Free could assist to the holy Exercises in this Temple, And only freemen and the Sons of Freemen had admission thereunto.

The Great Altar erected by *Hercules* stood near the *Schola Græca,* and by it *Æmilius* built the Temple of *Pudicitia Patritia,* wherein when *Virginia* entred, being her self noble but the Wife of a *Plebeian,* she was cast out by the other Matrons, whereat being offended she raised another Temple in *Borgo Longo,* to *Pudicitia Plebeia,* which caused a great *Feud* in the *Patritian* Matrons, but neither of the one nor the other does any footsteps now remain.

Monte Aventino. hath been ever counted infamous and inauspicious, for the contest there happening between *Romulus* and *Remus* wherein the last was slain. *Ancus Martius* the 4th. King of the *Romans* granted it to the *Sabines* for their habitation, but others write that it began to be inhabited only in the daies of *Claudius* the Emperor: tis now called by its old name *Mons Aventinus.*

The Church of *Santa Sabina,* standing on the top of the *Aventino* antiently dedicated to *Diana,* was built by *Ancus Martius,* or as others say by *Servius Tullius. Servius* the sixth King of the *Romans* was Son of a Servant or slave, wherefore he commanded that there every year on the 13th. of *August* a solemn Feast should be kept for the Slaves, on which day of their solemnity their Masters should not command them. Here *Honorius* the 4th. dwelt, and *Pius* the fifth erected there some stately Fabricks, to which *Girolamo Bernerio* called the Cardinal of *Ascoli,* added others with a Chappel. This Cardinal was of the Order of the preaching Fryers, and for that cause hath been a loving Patron to that Order.

The Church of *Santa Maria dell' Aventino,* was a Temple consecrated to *Dea Bona,* not far from which stood the House of *Julius Cæsar :* whence *Calphurnia,* the wife of *Cæsar* proceeded among the other Matrons to the said Temple to the Nocturnal duties performed to the said Goddess, when *Clodius* inamoured of her, habiting himself in the garment of a Woman, conveighed himself in amongst them, all men being prohibited admission to those duties: Who being no less ignorant of the place than of the Ceremonies, wandred too and fro in search of his Friend *Calphurnia,* and by that means was discovered by a certain Maid. Upon the *Aventino, Hercules Victor* had a Temple, which is now called the Church of *Santi Alexii.*

Bbb

The

The Hott Houses or Bathes which stood upon the *AVENTINO*.

THe Hot houses or Bathes of *Decius* the Emperour called *Deci-ane*, were near *Santa prisca*, formerly a Temple of *Hercules*, whereof as of the ensuing great ruines yet remain: Those called *Variane* stood near Saint *Alexius*. And those of *Trajan*, with his Palace on the farthest part of the *Aventino* in the Vineyard of *Francisci Albertini*, a *Roman* Citizen.

The *Remoria*, yet retains its antient name. 'Twas held an inauspicious place because in the bloud of *Remus* was unhappily begun the City: who was there slain by a wicked man with a Pickax at the command of *Romulus*, and interred in the same place. the *Via Remoria* extends it self from the *Circo Maximo* over the top of the *Aventino* just to that Fabrick of Pope *Paul* the 3d. wherewith he fortified the City.

Here stands the Sepulchre of *Cacus*, of whom they make mention in the Fables of *Hercules*, which is a sharp broken stone in the midst of the Church *Santa Maria Aventina*, where also was antiently a Temple of *Hercules*.

At this *Præcipice*, were the *Furcæ Gemoniæ*, to which Malefactors were dragged with Iron hooks, and there inhumanely slain, hither the Emperour *Vitellius*, with an Iron hook fixed under his Chin, and his Cloths torn of to his Buttocks was dragged, and slain by the command of *Vespasian*, for having put to death *Sabinus*, *Vespasians* Brother.

The *Porta Trigemina* though very antient, remains yet almost entire at the Foot of the *Aventino* near the *Tyber* in the Vineyard, to which the Baths of *Trajan* are annexed.

This Gate was called *Trigemina*, from the three twin Brothers, called *Horatii*, who marched out at that Gate, when they went to fight for the Liberty of their Countrey, against the three Brothers *Curatii Albani*, which *Albani* being slain with two of the twin Brothers *Horatii*, the third returned triumphant.

The *Dioclesian* Granaries of the *Roman* people were repaired and augmented by *Dioclesian* the Emperor, from whom they took their name. They stood between the *Tyber* and the *Monte Testaceo*, they consisted of 150 several apartments, and their ruines appear like a Fortress in the Vineyard of *Julio Cesarino* a *Roman*.

Monte Testaceo stands near them, which was raised by the pieces of Potters Vessels, there cast by the Potters whose streets were there, which place was assigned for that use that they might not throw them into the *Tyber*, for fear of stopping the current and diverting the stream to their greater damage, nor cast them into the Fields to obstruct the fertility thereof. Whence it grew to the heigth of
160 foot

160 foot and two miles in compafs Some,(but foolifhly,)call it *Monte di ogni Terra*, ridiculoufly fabling their conjectures, that this Mount was raifed by the Veffels of feveral Nations wherein they brought their Tributes to *Rome*, which Veffels they fay they were commanded to caft in that place in perpetual remembrance of that their fubjection. In old time the *Circus Olimpicus* comprehended all that fpace which the *Monte Teftaceo*, takes up now

The Pyramid of *C. Ceftius Septemvirs* or the feventh of the Epicures or gluttons, remains yet entire neare the *Porta Oftienfe*, within the City Walls,being built with white Marble,in great fquare ftones and although the Infcription names only *C. Ceftius*, yet tis believed to have been the common burying place of all the *Septemviri Epuloni* whofe charge was to fee that the Feafts, the Banquets, the folemnities, and facrifices of the Gods were ftrictly obferved.

La Porta Oftienfe, (now named *di San Paulo*) was built by *Ancus Martius*, and called *Oftienfe*, becaufe through it lies the way to *Oftia*. Without which gate ftands the Church dedicated to *Sancto Paulo* a moft fplendid Church, one of the feaven principal of *Rome*, and much frequented by the people. Therein ftand four rankes of vaft Marble Collumnes which fupport it. They are excellently wrought in *Dorick, Ionick, Attick,* and *Corinthian* works,nor is there any Church in *Rome* Replenifht with fo many Pillars, nor garnifhed with fo polite and exquifite Marble ftones, which were tranflated from the two *Porta's Oftienfes* The one of *Nero*, the other of *Antoninus*.Somewhat beyond which ftands another Church, called the *Tre Fontane*, An antient Temple before whofe portal rife many pretious Pillars of Porphyr ftone, which fhine with various Colours: within are fhewed three fources of Fountains, whofe waters are efteemed holy and falutiferous for many infirmities, they believe, thefe Fountains to fpring miraculoufly at and ever fince the time that Saint *Pauls* head was cut off by the command of *Nero* the Emperour in that place.

The Vifitation of the aforenamed particulars, being exactly performed will be fufficient for the firft day.

The fecond dayes Journey in perufing the noted things of *ROME.*

ENtring from *Borgo* into the City by the Bridge *Caftello*, you meet a way which divides it felf in two, on the right hand towards the *Tyber* goes the *Strada Julia,*in which the houfe of the *Cevali* ftands worthy a view,and in the other ftreet near the *Banchi,*is the houfe of the Cardinal *Sforza,*replenifht with Antiquities, noble Pictures,and a Library of Greek Manufcripts.

Alla Pace in the houfe of *Lancellotto Lancellotti,* a Gentleman, are many rare antiquities.   Bbb 2   At

At the end of the *Parione* are the ample houses *Arianæ*, in whose Angle is seated That Statue of *Pasquin*, the most famous of all that City yea of all the World. This some suppose to be made for *Hercules*, others for *Alexander* the great: but there is no certainty of either, though it appear the workemankip of some rare Artist.

In former times they were wont to load this Image with Libels a-against the Princes, Cardinals and famous Men, and noble Matrons and sometimes against the Pope: but now left off because of the severe prohibitions, since when though they dare not fix them to the *Pasquino*, yet still they vent their reproofs and scandals under some other specious pretence, publishing them some other way by the name of *Pasquinata. Antonio Tibaldeo* a *Ferrarian*, being no less learned than Venerable, reports this story of this statue: That there was in *Rome* a certain Taylour well known in his trade and good at his occupation, called *Pasquino*, whose shop stood in this street : this man was well customed by *Prelates, Courtezans* and other people, who resorted to him for their Rayments, This Taylor employed great number of journeymen, who like vile persons spent all the day their tongues freely speaking ill of this & that person not sparing any, taking occasion from what they observed in those persons which resorted to their shop; the constant custome of slandering in that shop made it become ridiculous even to the persons offended, esteeming those rascals unworthy of any credit, and so no other regard was had to it. Whence it came to pass afterwards, that if any person would defame another he did it under covert of Master *Pasquino*, saying he had heard say so in his shop, which relation caused all the Interessed persons in that reproach, not to make any more account of it. This reverent gentleman *Pasquino* being dead, it happened that in paving the street, this statue was found half buried and broken near his shop, which because twas incomodious for the passage to leave it there, they erected just at the shop of Master *Pasquino* whence the back-biters (taking a good occasion) reported that Master *Pasquino*, was returned again and not having courage enough to own the abuses they put upon others, they used to fasten their Scrolls to that statue: presuming, that as twas lawfull for *Marco pasquino* to speak any thing, so by means of this statue they might scandalize others with such things, as in the light and bare faced they durst not own. This Custome continued long till at last twas prohibited with severe penalties.

Near hereto is the great Pallace of the Chancery, built by the *Travertini*, in a square form with the stones translated from the Amphitheater of *Titus Vespasianus*, which was called *Coliseum*, which Theatre the Popes would not permit to be wholly destroyed, but left some part in its first Lustre, that by it might appear the splendour of the whole, as a testimony of the magnificence of the *Roman* Empire. In it stands one great Image of *Bacchus*, wrought by *Michael Angelo Bonarota*, at his first arrival at *Rome*, when he sought to depress the Fame of *Raphael Sanctius* of *Urbin*, which he brought inferiour to his own reputation by his Art and policy. Two other great statues one of *Ceres*, and the other of *Opes* as is believed. And on the upper part are fixed certain heads, as of *Antonius Pius, Septimius Severus, Titus, Domitianus Augustus*, and *Geta* the Emperours, of a *Sabin*

Woman

Woman. of *Pyrrhus* King of the *Epirots* of *Cupid* and a Sword Play-
er.

Thence not far diftant ftands the Piazza *del Duca*, wherein is the
faireft Pallace in *Rome*, built with exceffive coft by Pope *Paul* the 3d
a *Farnezian*, It abounds with fo many antiquities that to fpeak diftinctly of them, would fill up a volume : we will therefore pafs
briefly over them, as now they remain, many things having been
changed in later times.

For the Architecture tis enough to fay *Michael Angelo Bonarota*, had
a chief part therein, and for the Materials, better could not be had
then were employed in it, which were brought from the Amphitheatre : As to the ftatues,

Two of *Hercules* ftand in the Court, famous for their workmanfhip and antiquity, the leffer whereof is moft commended; One of
Jupiter Tonante, with two immenfe fword players, the one having
the Scabbard of his fword hanging at his fhoulder, and with his right
foot kicks the Target, the murrion, and the ground, the other holds
behind him a boy dead in his hand : But that which furpaffeth all
ftatues is the *Tauro Farnefe*, a Bull with five perfons bigger than the
natural, cut to wonder, out of one ftone by *Apollonius* and *Taurifcus*
of *Rhodes*, whence twas conveighed and placed in *Antoninus* his Bath
where about one hundred years fince twas dugg up as entire as if
made but yefterday, and now ftands in this Pallace aftonifhing all
that behold it.

In the afcent on the ftayers, you fee one ftatue of the *Tyber*, another of *Oceanus*, and at the top of two barbarous prifoners in their old
habits.

In the Rooms above, who delights in Pictures and Sculpture will
meet enough to occupy his whole fancy. As the Pictures of *Francefco*
Salviati, and *Tadeo Zucchero*, both which are much applauded, drawn
as if they were taking the frefh ayr : And in a Gallery which is as
noble as well painted by the Brothers *Carazzi Bolonia*, painters of
great Fame, you will find many antient heads of fignal perfons as of
Lyfia, *Euripides*, *Solon*, *Socrates*, *Diogenes*, *Genone*, *Poffidonio*, and *Se-*
neca, with the noble ftatues of *Ganimede*, *Antinoo*, of *Bacchus*; fome
fair Veffels, and the ftatues of *Meleager*, which deferves a name by it
felf for its great price, being efteemed worth five thoufand Crowns
then which no ftatue in *Rome* is more entire. No People under the
Sun give fo great prices for ftatues as the *Romans* : all which are fo
ftudious of thofe kind of Ornaments, that in acquiring them, they
emuloufly ftrive which fhall exceed in coft or curiofity. In one Chamber they fhew the Duke *Alexander* of glorious memory, having under his feet the River *Scalda* or *Scelda*, with *Flanders* kneeling before
him, and behind Victory crowning him, all which ftatues are cut out
of one Marble ftone, bigger than the Life. There alfo are three doggs
caft rarely in Brafs. The *Bibliotheque* of this Pallace, the Meddals and
carved Toyes, are moft famous things, but the Pictures of *Raphael*,
and *Titian* are incomparable, nor are the Limnings leffe admirable:

Oppofite to the *Farnefi* live the heirs of *Monfignior d'Acquigno*, in
whofe houfe are divers infcriptions, an *Adonis*, a *Venus* of four thoufand
Crowns price, a *Diana* begirt with a Quiver of Arrowes a Bow in

ber hand like a huntreſs, and a ſtatue of *Bon Evento* holding a looking glaſſe in the right hand, and in the left a Garland of Ears of Corn an abſolute Piece, wrought by *Praxitelis*.

Adjacent to the *Campo di Fiore*, ſtands the Palace of the Cardinal *Capo di Ferro*, much leſs than the *Farneſian* Pallace, but in ſplendor and Architecture no whit inferiour. In the Frontiſpiece is painted the ſpring time : The Preſident of the ſpring is *Venus*, (which was drawn to the ſimilitude of the Body of *Livia Columna*, a moſt beautiful Princeſs) & whatever is there repreſented is amorous: The Complexion of the men is ſanguine, and all are marked with the Element of Ayr. So in the other fronts, are expreſſed the complexions Choller, Melancholy, and Phlegme, the Elements Fire, Water, and Earth, the ſeaſons Summer, Autumne, and Winter, and the Præſiding Gods, *Mars*, *Saturn*, and *Janus*, which are moſt abſolutely performed, and were the work of *Michael Angelo*, with whom this Cardinal contracted a moſt intimate Friendſhip; and being no leſs liberal than Ingenious obtained of him, what ever ſo rare an Artiſt could poſſibly invent, among the reſt a ſecret conclave wherein many things are expreſt with the higheſt Art and perfection.

The houſe of the *Orſini*, in the *Campo di Fiore*, which was raiſed out of the ruines of the *Pompeyan* Theatre, is embelliſht with many good ſtatues in the Courts.

The Temple of Saint *Angelo* in *Peſcaria*, was formerly of *Juno Regina*, which being burnt, was reſtored by *Septimius Severus* and *Marcus Aurelius* the Emperors, as the old Title there to be read verifies : near which are ſome of the Pillars taken from the *Portico* of *Septimius Severus* dedicated to *Mercury*.

At the Tower *Citrangole*, ſtands the houſe of the heirs of *Gentile Delfino*, which Gentleman had more meddals than any other Perſon in *Rome*, and his Garden filled with inſcriptions: In them ſtands a Statue of *Canopo* placed in the form of a Water Pott, before whoſe breaſt they have prepoſed a Tablet filled with *Hierogliphick* letters, by which 'tis believed the ſecret Myſteries of the Sacrifices are delivered : In *Parione* at the houſe of the *Maximi* may be ſeen a *Coloſſus*, which vulgarly is thought to be the ſtatue of *Pyrrhus* King of the *Epirots* armed, bought a long time ſince by the *Maximi* of *Angelo* for two thouſand Crowns as alſo a Marble head of *Julius Cæſar*, with many other things worthy conſideration.

In the houſe of the *Leni alla Ciambella*, are many noble ſtatues lately brought thither from the *Porta di S. Baſtiano*, to wit an *Adonis*, a *Venus*, a *Satyr*, and many excellent heads, where in an old Pile was found an entire purple Garment with ſome rings and other notable things. Near which ſtands the houſe of Cardinal *Paravicino*, a Signor of neble Qualities, who much delights in Pictures, whereof and thoſe good too he hath not a few. Contiguous with which ſtands the houſe of the *Vallei*, wherein was erected a ſquare Marble ſtone, with a *Solar Horoſcope*, and the *Zodiack* ſignes, where the dayes and howers of every Moneth were denoted, and whatever the Antients were wont to obſerve as well in the ſacrifices of the Gods, as in the Countrey affairs, as fully as our Calenders now expreſs them: but this with divers other Rarities, by the inſtability of its Patrons, were amoved, and ſuch as they left remaining (for what reaſon we gueſs not) obſcured.

On

On the Afcent of the *Campidoglio* dwels *il Signor Lelio Pafqualino*, a Canon of *Santa Maria Maggiore*, a Gentleman of polite learning, and exquifite manners, where the ftudious of Antiquities are freely ad-mitted to glutt themfelves with the moft curious things in *Rome*, as felect Meddals, rare carved works, Implements, and *Habiliments* of Antiquity in great number. In fumm in his houfe are a Treafure of thofe things, and he hath obferved in this kind more than a man can poffibly behold in one day: if he be refolved to publifh his ob-fervations for the pnblick good of the *Ingeniofi*, tis certain that a pure and naked index of the Antiquities which he hath collected, would alone advance the ftudious of good Letters no lefs in facred then Profane Learning.

On the left hand of the *Campidoglio*, ra ifes it felf a Temple and the Monaftery of the *Francifcans* called *Araceli*, to which they afcend by 124 marble fteps diftinguifhed into five degrees: The Temple is fupported by two ranks of Marble Pillar s on both fides, then which the world affords not a more fumptuous, the *Vatican* fet apart: This Temple in old time was dedicated to *Jovi Feretrio* by *Romulus* after the *Sabyn* warr, becaufe in that place *Jupiter* gave affiftance to the King then oppreffed with the violence of his Enemies. On the left hand upon the third Pillar is engraven thefe words *A Cubiculo Au-guftorum*, and in other places of the Church, are two ftatues of *Conftantine* and *Maximinian*, and at the two horfes of *Caftori* fet at the top of the fteps, is reprefented a fair profpective from the en-trance to the inward part.

In the *Piazza* of the *Campidoglio*, ftands a great ftatue of *Marcus Au-relius Antoninus*, or as others think of *Lucius Verus*, of *Septimius*, of *Metellus* on horfeback, twas transferred hither from *San Gio Latera-no*, by order of Pope *Paul* the third a *Farnefian*.

Near the Pallace rife great ftatues of Rivers, to wit of the *Nyle*, with a *Sphinx* under it, of the *Tygre*, with a *Tyger* near, both having their heads bedecked with flowers brought from the River, and a-nother great ftatue, by fome thought to reprefent the *Rhene* a River of *Germany*, by others to be an Image of *Jupiter Panarius*, becaufe the *Romans* freed themfelves from the fiege of the *French* by cafting bread into their Tents: This Statue is called *Marforio*, and by means of it they ufe to anfwer to the flaunders of *Pafqui-no*.

Upon a collateral ftayer, Cafe ftands a Columne called *Milliaria* upon which are engraven two infcriptions the one of *Vefpafian* the o-ther of *Nero* Emperours.

In the *Pallazzo dei Conferuatori* are many things worth a view, among others a lyon holdnig a horfe with his teeth, whofe miraculous work-manfhip *Mic. Angelo* was wont to cry up to the skies. Near it appears a moft antient Tombe at the afcent upon the fteps, and a Pillar poin-ted with Iron with its infcription, (according to the manner of thofe antient times) of *C. Duilio*, in honour of whom (having overthrown the *Carthaginians*) this was erected. Hereof many Authors make mention. Beyond which are certain tablets engraven, with the Tri-umph of *Aurelius*, and a facrifice made by him, and at the entrance of the Gate are carved in Marble the Meafures or fcannings of the Greek and *Roman* Foot: by which you behold an old ftatue belie-

Ccc 2

ved

ved falfly of *Marius* in a gown. In the hall of the *Confervatori* ftands a *Hercules* in brafs guilt, with his Club in the right hand, and one of the *Hefperian* apples in the left, this was found in the *Foro Boario* in the ruines of the *Ara Maxima*, A Satyr of Marble with the legs of a Goat bound to a Tree: a Statue of Brafs upon a Marble Pillar of *Juno* fitting picking a thorn out of her foot. With another figure ofbrafs of a wolfe, giving fuck to *Romulus* and *Remus*. This was formerly kept in the *Cornicio*, near the *Ruminale*, whence twas firft, tranflatedto *S Giovanni Laterano*, and thence to the *Campidoglio*: Both thefe Figures having a general applaufe from all beholders.

Being entred into the Hall of the faid Pallace, you behold the lofty feats (fo famous through the world) of the Magiftrates and the *Roman* Triumphs: Thefe were tranflated hither from the Court where they were found by Commiffion of *Paul* the 3d. that they might be viwed and confidered: Upon the fubject of thofe feats now fomewhat decayed and broken through Age, Cardinal *Michele Silvio* compofed certain fmooth verfes there to be read, Where alfo you find an honourable memorial in marble of the deeds of the moft illuftrious *Alexander Farnefe*, Son of *Ottavio* Duke of *Parma*, whofe ftatue ftands in the fame place, as alfo that of *M Antonio Colonna*, who together with *Giovanni d'Auftria*, obtained a glorious victory on the Sea againft the *Turks* in the *Curfolari*: Together with fome great ftatues of Popes, in a fitting pofture as twere giving Benediction to the People as of *Leo* the 10th. *Gregory* the 13th. *Sixtus* the 5th. all well defervers of the Chriftian Republique; and other things giving delight to the Spectator.

In the paffage from the *Campidoglio*, to the *Rupe Tarpeia* in view of the *Piazza Montanara*, ftood the Temple of *Jovis Optimi Maximi*, which was the largeft Temple of *Rome*, built by *Tarquinius Prifcus*, and adorned & inriched by *Tarquinius Superbus*, with the expence of forty thoufandpound of Silver.

The Defcent from the *Campidoglio* or, Capitoll.

FRom the *Campidoglio* or *Capitol*, you go down into the *Foro Romano*, which is the fpace of ground from the Arch of *Septimius* to the Church of *Santa Maria Nuova*. At the foot of the *Campidoglio*, you find the Triumphal Arch of *L. Septimius Severus* entire, faving that fome part is under ground, the Earth being raifed by vaft ruines of ftructures: it hath Infcriptions on both fides, with the Warlike Expeditions made by that Emperor by Sea and Land. Here *Camillus* built a Temple & dedicated it to the Goddefs *Concordia*, when he had reconciled the Common people to the Senate, whofe alfo was that of *Juno Moneta*, afcended by one hundred fteps: 'Twas called *Junone Moneta*, becaufe it præmonifhed, and advifed *Romans*,

with

with an intelligible voice, that the *Galli Senones*, were coming upon them. Those eight Collumnes there now being, on whose Capitols are inscribed these words *Senatus Populusque Romanus incendio consumptum, restituit*; are the Reliques of the said Temple of *Concordia*, wherein the Senate frequently assembled, and made their oraisons.

On the left part of the descent from the *Campidoglio*, lies the place called *Sanlto Pietro* in *Carcere*, consecrated by his holiness *San Silvestro* to *San Pietro*, because he was there taken bound and imprisoned, where a Feast was wont heretofore to be solemnized the first day of *August* in remembrance of the Chains wherewith Saint *Peter* was bound which was translated afterwards to *San Pietro* in *Vincula*, in *Monte Esquilie*, the Prisons were first built there by *Ancus Martius*, to which *Servius Tullius* annexed the Vaults or Sellers under ground called *Tulliani Carceres*, wherein (as *Salust* writes) those were strangled who had given in their names to *Catalines* conspiracy.

The Church of *Santa Martina* (in whose angle the *Colossus of Marforii* lies) was formerly consecrate to *Mars Ultor* the Revenger. *Augustus* built and dedicated it after the *Philippensian* Warr in *Pharsalia*: some say, That in this Church was the secret place where the Acts of the Senate were kept. In it is a Title made in the times of *Theodosius* and *Honorius* the Emperors.

Next unto it is the Church of *Santo Adriano*, antiently the Temple of *Saturn*, built or rather restored by *Mannlio Planco*, being first dedicated by *Minutio* & *Sempronio* the Consuls: This was the Exchequer of *Rome*, wherein the publique Treasury was preserved as we read that in the time of *Scipio Emilianus* it had in it eleaven thousand pound weight of pure gold, and ninety two thousand pound weight of silver, beside an infinite quantity of coyned moneys. Here also the *Tabulæ Elephantinæ* were layed up, wherein the numbers of the 35 tribes of *Rome*, were recorded: as also the *Military* Ensignes, the Decrees of the Senate, the publick Acts, with the spoils of the Provinces and conquered Nations.

'Tis supposed that *Santa Maria Liberatrice*, was a Temple dedicated to *Venus Generatrix*, It stands at the Foot of the *Palatine*, those three hollow Pillars some believe to be those before the foot of the *Ponte aureo* of *Caligula*, which was supported by 80 Pillars, made with incredible cost, over which they passed from the Pallace to the Capitoll.

The Pillar at *Santa Maria Liberatrice*, is one of those upon which was placed the golden Statue by *Domitian*, near which stood the Statue of the River *Rhene*, now called *Marsorio* and is in the *Campidoglio*, Erected by *Domitian* for that that Emperor triumphed over the *Germans*.

Near it was the Temple of *Concord*, with that of *Julius Cæsar* on its right hand, and that of *Paulus Æmilius* on its left hand, whose structure cost nine hundred thousand Crowns.

Those high wals which are beheld at the Foot of the *Palatine* are part of the *Rostri Nuovi*, which were so called for that there they setled the *Rostra* or stemm of their Galleys: here now is the Vineyard of Cardinal *Farnese*. There *Cicero* frequently made his O-

D d d

rations

rations, there the Fathers assembled and made Laws, and there the head and hand of *Cicero* (which wrote his Philippick Orations) were fixed to a Spear by command of *Antonius* the Triumvir, whose dishonourable deeds are therein declaimed against. The *Rostri Vecchie*, were in the *Corte Hostilia*, near the place of the Council which touched the Church *Santa Maria Nuova*, which place is called *Comitia* as much as to say a place to retire themselves together in : for here the senate and People of *Rome* assembled to treat of the affairs of the the Common-Wealth : and there is built now the holy house of *Sancta Maria de inferno*.

The Temple of *San Lorenzo* in *Miranda*, stands in the ruines of the Temple of *Faustina* and of *Antonio*, where we find this Inscription *Divo Antonino, & Divæ Faustinæ S. C.* As also twelve fair Pillars, near which stood the Arch of *Fabius*, and the covering of the Palace, which was called *Libone*.

The Piazza of *Julius Cæsar*, extended from the Temple *Faustina* to that of *Santa Maria* but at the Piazza of *Augustus* the Church of *Santo Adriano*, in *Trefori*, is conjoyned with it, And in that of *Augustus*, were certain Porticues and in them statues of illustrious Men set up by *Augustus* who lived in the house of *Livia*, in the *Via Sacra*. The Temple of *Santi Cosmo* and *Damiano*, was antiently dedicated to *Castor* and *Pollux* which some alledge without foundation to be the Temple of *Romulus* and *Remus*.

The Temple of Peace, begun by *Claudius* and finished by *Vespasian*, was most magnificent and stately, of whose most high structure some reliques yet remain not far from the Church of *Santa Maria Nova*, and one Pillar yet entire, the highest and biggest of all *Rome* In the gardens of *Santa Maria Nova*, appear yet two high round courses of two antient Temples of the Sun and Moon, which some will have to be of *Isis* & *Serapis*. There *Tatius* built a Temple to *Vulcan*, and in that quarter *Æsculapius* also had a Temple, and *Concordia*, built by *Fulvius* in *anno* 303. after the erecting of the Capitol : Out of which Temple of *Concordia*, tis thought *Vespasian* afterwards raised that of Peace, translating to it moreover many ornaments from the Temple of *Solomon*, after he had destroyed *Jerusalem*.

Not far distant from the *Via sacra*, stands the Marble Arch of *Titus Vespasian*, wherein are carved the pomp of the Triumph, and the spoyls brought from *Jerusalem* at the overthrow of the *Jewes*, as the Ark of the Covenant the Candlestick for the seaven Lights, The Table whereon they set the bread of the Proposition or shewbread The Table of the ten Commandements delivered by God to *Moses*, and the sacred Vessels all of pure gold, used in the sacrifices by the *Hebrews*, besides which the Triumphal Chariot of the Emperor is carved thereon with this Inscription.

Senatus Populusque Romanus Divo Tito,
Divi Vespatiani F. Vespasiano Augusto.

The *Foro* or Court *di Nerva* is also called *Transitorio*, or the passage because through it they passed into the *Foro Romano*, and in that of *Augusto*, where stands the *Arco di Noe*, so called corruptly by the Vulgar

gar ftood the noble Picture *di Nerva,* where in Fret work are thefe
words.	Imperator *Nerva Cæfar Auguftus* Pont. *Tib.* Pont. *II.* Imp. *II*
Procons. The Fragments of this Arch are yet extant between the
Church Saint *Bafilio,* & the Tower for the Militia. Near it rifeth a certain fquare ftructure called by the vulgar *Studiolo di Virgilio,* & they ridiculoufly fable, That the Poet was hung out of it by a certain whore
for a fpectacle to the People one whole day. Which to revenge *Vir-*
gil (Who ftudied the Magick Art) effected that the Fire in the whole
City was extinguifhed, and all the people forced to give fire to their
Candles and Lights at the flames which were raifed fer fhaming of
the Strumpets. This fable is painted every where but without an Author: Nor is it likely any fuch thing could happen to that great *Vir*
gil, who for his continency was called *Parthenius.* If any thing in
this Fable be true I fuppofe twas writ of fome other *Virgil* a Magician
by whom the *Neapolitanes* fpeak alfo many things to have been performed; among others that by the Magick Art he hollowed the
Mountain *Pofylipum* and made it penetrable, the Sepulchre of *Virgil* is
erected near this famous Cavern.

Near the Temple of Peace is that of the *Santi Cofmo* and *Damiano,*
which was the Court of *Romulus,* where the Senate congregated
when they had any important affair to confult about: It was wholly burnt, when they burned the body of *Publius Claudius,* flain by *T.*
Annione Milone, with the *Bafilica Portia* near it, which *Marco Portio*
Catone the Cenfor reared a top of the houfe of *Mevio.* There was alfo
another Court in *MonteCelio,* where now ftands the Church confecrated to *Santo Gregori.*

MONTE PALATINO.

THis Hill was inhabited many yeers before the building of *Rome*
and there when at its greateft fplendour, did the Emperors
and other, great Perfonages for a long time refide, but now tis overwhelmed with Ruines, and fo great a Devaftation, that tis the moft
uninhabited Place of *Rome:* befides its Defert uncouthnefs and
Thorns, affording nothing of good more than a little Church of Saint
Nicholo, fome Cottages, and a Vineyard of Cardinal *Farnefe.* Thereon of old ftood thefe ftately Temples following to wit, one dedicate to *Vittoria* built by *C. Pofthunius* the Ædile, Another to *Apollo,* wch
being deftroyed, was afterwards reftored by *Auguftus Cæfar,* to grea-
er beauty, with the addition of that Porticue, whofe reliques yet
remain more entire than any other in *Rome,* a third to the *Penati*
brought thither by *Æneas,* and honoured with much reverence:

Others to the Gods *Lari,* to *Faith,* to *Jove Victorius,* to *Heliogaba-*
lus, to *Orco* and many other Gods, of whofe Temples not any imaginable *Veftigia* are now extant: And thofe magnificent Palaces of the
Cæfars, Tarquinius Prifcus the King, of *Cicero* who bought his Pallace
of *Craffus* for 50 thoufand Crowns: of *Marcus Flaccus* which ftood
neer that which was bought by *Cicero,* whereof *Q. Catullus* made a
great Lodge.

That part of the *Palatino* which lies towards the Arch of *T. Vefpaf-*
an, is called *Germano,* from the Twyn Brothers *Romulus* and *Remus,*

there brought up by _Fauſtulus_ the Shepheard whoſe habitation was in that place: the ſpace from thence to the Arch of _Conſtantine_ the Great was called _Vela_, for that there the Shepheards dwelt, whoſe cuſtome was to fleece or pluck the Wool from off the ſheep (whence they were called in Latin _Vellera_, Fleeces of Wool) before the way of ſhearing was invented.

Towards _Santa Maria Nova_, _Sçaurus_ had a noble Palace with an Open gallery ſupported with Pillars forty foot high without the baſes or capitol.

The great Palace _Gregoſtaci_, was ſo denominated, for that there they uſually entertained the Embaſſadors of divers Nations: Here _Quintus Flaminius_ dedicated a ſtatue to _Concordia_, when he had reconciled the People to the Senate, or rather the Senate to the People. The Church _Sant'Andrea_, in _Pallaria_, is the old Temple, wherein the _Palladium_ and _Penati_, which _Æneas_ brought with him from _Troy_ into _Italy_ were at firſt placed, but afterwards tranſported into the Temple of _Veſta_, and the charge of them committed to the Veſtal Virgins. Near it ſtood the houſe of _Valerius Publicola_, which for ſome ſuſpicion raiſed among the People, they levelled with the ground in one night.

On that part of the _Palatine_ towards _Monte Celio_, ſtood a Temple of _Cibele_ called alſo _Dindimene_ and _Ope_, The Iinage of which Goddeſs was tranſlated from _Ida_ a Place in _Phrygia_ to _Rome_, and reverenced with great devotion. On that part reſpecting the _Aventino_, was the houſe wherein _Auguſtus Cæſar_ was born, whoſe ruins yet ariſe to a vaſt altitude: to which was adjoyned a Temple of _Apollo_, upon whoſe top was fixed a golden Chariot of the Sun, of which ſome fragments are yet in being, as alſo a Library, called _Palatina_: Wherein ſtood a ſtatue of _Apollo_, as Maſter of the _Chorus_ among the Muſes raiſed 50...... the noble work of _Scopa_, It may be conjectured that the Baths of _Palatini_ lay in the Vinyard of _Thomaſo Fædra_, a _Roman_ Gentleman towards the _Arco Maſſimo_, approaching which were the _Curia_ of the _Salii_, and _Auguri_, with other Fabricks, into theſe Baths by an Aqueduct, rann a ſtream of the _Aqua Claudia_.

At the foot of Mount _Palatine_, to wit at the Pillars of the Gallery of _Caligula_, is a round Fabrick, being the Church _S. Theodoſius_, which was at firſt built and conſecrated to _Jupiter ſtator_, by _Romulus_, about the time of the _Sabyn_ warr; when the _Romans_ turned tail, and running away, were by the entreaties of _Romulus_ perſwaded to face their Enemies, and receive Victory, ſome ſay that this was not the Temple of _Jupiter Stator_, but that it was the ruins of the old Court which ſtood near the Temple of _Concordia_.

Leaving the Temple of _Janus Quadrifrons_, and the _Foro Boario_, in the deſcent to the _Circo Maximo_, you meet a hollow place into which out of certain Pipes run copious waters, where the Women waſh their Linnen; tis ſaid that here were the Fountains of the Nimph _Junturna_ in _Velabro_, now called _Fonti S. Georgii_. The Vault which appears contiguous with a great Arched common Shoar, was built by _Tarquin_, for reception of the Channels and Filth of the Citty, with a commodious conveyance thence into the _Tyber_. Which Arch was ſo ample, that a Cart and Horſes might conveniently paſſe

tho-

thorow it. We read that the Cenſors ſometime ſould the Filth of this Vault and ſink for the fatning the Fields about, to certain perſons for 600000. Crowns, which when twas told the Emperor, he anſwered.

Odor Lucri bonus ex re qualibet.

Now tis called *Chiaviea,* Cloſe by which lies the *Lago Curtio,* a Lake ſo denominated from *Curtius* who threw himſelf and horſe armed præcipitouſly into that *Vorago*, or opening of the Earth, that he might avert the peſtilential Ayr exhaling out of it, which infeſted *Rome* with a great contagion. There alſo grew the Grove of *Numa Pompilius,* wherein he ſpoke and treated with the *Nimphe Ægeria,* from whom he learned the Ceremonies of the Sacrifices, and where twas unlawfull for any one to ſpit. In this place the Aſhes of the *Galli Senones* were layed up, now tis called *Dolioli,* from the *Dolia* or earthen Veſſels, wherein they put the Aſhes of the ſlain, to be buried.

The *CIRCO MASSIMO,*

OF all the Ornaments of the *Circo Maximo* ſcarce any thing is to be ſeen, more than the entire circumſcription of the place whereby its amplitude is diſcerned: It lies between the *palatino,* and the *Aventino*, and is about half a mile long and three Acres broad which ſome ſay was capable of 260 thouſand men, others reſtrain it to one hundred and fifty thouſand. Here *Romulus* firſt ſet forth the *Conſaulian Games* to the God *Conſo,* after the rape of the *Sabyn* Women. *Tarquinius Priſcus* deſigned and *Tarquinius Snperbus* built the place, for the celebration of the *Circenſian* games, and other Solaces for the People, which *Auguſtus* adorned, *Caius* amplified, *Trojan* repaired and augmented the Fabrick, and *Heliogabalus* paved it. At preſent tis all about in Gardens, but ſome ſteps and roofs of little cels remain, which are ſuppoſed to have been the Offices of the Actors in the Games, or of ſuch as uttered beer and other neceſſaries, to the People reſorting to the ſhews. Others think them to haue be en the ſtews wherein the Whores dwelt, expoſing their bodies to ſale for gaine. *Neptune* had a Temple conjoined with this Circ, whereof ſome ruines are yet to be ſeen incruſted with Fiſh ſhels. Where the Church of *S. Anaſtatia* ſtands, were erected two Obelisks, the one of which being 132 foot long without the baſes, was tranſlated by *Sixtus* the 5th. to the *Vatican,* the other was 88. foot high. *Auguſtus* tranſported both out of *Ægypt,* for adorning the Circ: wherein alſo was the *Naumachia* for exerciſing Sea-fights: a place now conſiſting of boggs and Reeds: where alſo part of thoſe waters flowed which by an Aqueduct were conveighed into the Circ, called *Aquæ Claudiæ.*

On the left hand riſes the *Moles,* or vaſt Fabrick of *Septimius Severus* called *Settizonio,* from its ſeaven floors, than which no ſtructure in *Rome* was higher. The Emperor raiſed it to that altitude, that it

E e e

might

might be Obvious to such as sayled out of *Africk* into *Italy*: who seeing it, should adore his Ashes layed up at the very top of it, because himself was an *African* by birth. Of which immense Edifice three Rafters now only continue, which through long antiquity seeming to nod, and threaten destruction, *Sixtus* the 5th. caused to be levelled with the foundation to the great dissatisfaction of the *Roman* people. One part of the Title Legible was this.

Trib. Pont. VI. Cons. fortunatissimus nobilissimus.

The *VIA APPIA*.

THe *Via Appia* takes its beginning at the Arch Triumphal of *Constantine*, and leading by the *Settizonio* of *Severus*, conductes one to the Baths of *Antoninus*, whence it passed by the *Porta Capena*, to the ruins of *Alba Longa*, and thence to *Brindesi*. Blind *Appius* the Senator gave name to it, paving it with most hard stone to *Capua*, thence *Cæsar* prolonged it, but *Trajan* repaired, enlarged and compleated it, its reliques are yet to be discerned, at *Rome*, *Piperno* and *Monte Cincello*. but that part of the *Via Appia*, which leads from the Baths of *Antoninus* to the *Porta Capena*, is called the *Via Nova*, all which was paved by *Antoninus Caracalla*, when he built his Baths, then which (except *Dioclesians*) none in *Rome*, are more perfect. In these Baths stand Pillars of *Serpentine* stone, and great Bathing places cut out of Marble: they were placed near the Church *San Sisto*, in the *Aventino*, and to them was adjoyned a Temple of *Isis*, where now is the Church *de i Santo Nereo* and *Archiole*: along the *Via Appia* rose many Temples of Gods, whereof no fragments are now extant.

The *Porta Capena*, was so named from *Capena*, a City near *Alba Longa*, the way whereunto lay through this gate, which was also called *Camæna* from the Temple of *Camænæ*, that is to say the *Muses* which was but a little eloigned from it : It was also called Triumphal because through it, the *Scipioes* entred the City triumphing, and likewise *Charls* the 5th. the Emperor, entred by the same into *Rome*, (*Paul* the third then reigning,) when he came from his *Victory* over the *Africans*, At this day tis called *Porta S. Sebastiani*, from the Church consecrated to the same Saint, which is two miles distant from the gate near the *Cæmetery*, of *Calixtus*. On each side of this way ly magnificent Sepulchres, in great number, yet almost entire, as also the footsteps of Many Temples, though not exactly discernable.

Here also remains a certain round Fabrick, judged to be the Sepulchre of the *Ceteghi*, for in the titles may be read on both sides the name of the Family of *Cetega*, and not far from the City is seen the River *Almone*, which running into *Rome*, commixes with the *Tyber* under the *Aventino*.

That high round *Mole* on the right hand proves it self to have been the Sepulchre of the *Scipio's* by the inscriptions upon it. On the

the left hand as you leave the *Via Appia* you meet the Church *Domine quo vadis*, the hiſtory whereof is related before. The adjacent Fabrick is ſuppoſed to be the Sepulchre of the *Lucilli*, here, a s under diuers others are certain Vaults digg'd, and they divided in ſeveral for the comodious diſpoſal of the Veſſels and Urns con taining the Aſhes of the Defunct. The Brick wall is thought to be part of the Temple of *Faunus* and *Sylvanus*.

On the right hand of the Church Saint *Sebaſtiano*, ſtands an entire Temple but diſpoiled of its ornaments, formerly dedicated to *Apollo*, into which the Shepherds to preſerve their Flocks, from the heats of the day, and incomodities of the nights do often drive them.

About forty paces farther in the adjacent fields, amongſt thorns and brambles, in an obſcure place, is a *ſubterranean Cavern.* whoſe entrance through the heaps of ſtones is difficultly found, but when entred, you behold Vaults built with good Art, on each ſide of which are long repoſitories, wherein the bodies of deceaſed Chriſtians, whom twas not lawfull to bury ſolemnly or openly were repoſed. In theſe Cavernes were the primitive Chriſtians wont to conceal themſelves, to fly the Emperors raging perſecutions, now called *Stanze de Chriſtiani.*

In the Temple of Saint *Sebaſtiano*, they deſcend by certain ſteps into the Caves under ground, which are called *Catecombe.* Wherein in old time the Chriſtians for fear of Tyrants uſually lay hid : in theſe tis reported that forty Popes ſuffered Martyrdome, and with them one hundred ſeventy four thouſand Chriſtians, as by the Inſcription over the ingreſs clearly appears. The place is adored with the higheſt devotion, and its profundity and Darkneſs creates no ſmall fear. Tis not poſſible to find the way in without Torches and Lights, nor ſafe to go too & fro in the ſeveral diviſions(which are like a Labyrinth)without a good guide, Tis called *Cæmiterio, di Califto,* Among the Reliques in this Church they ſhew the Prints or Footſteps of the Feet of Chriſt upon a ſtone, which they ſay were there left by Chriſt at his aſcenſion into Heaven in the preſence of his Diſciples. Many other things are writ hereof by *Onofrius*, and others.

On the ſide of this Church is found a vaſt round Temple ſupported by one hundred Marble Pillars conſecrated to *Mars Gradivus* by *Sylla* while he was *Ædile*, in it Audience was given to the Embaſſadors of Enemies, by the Senate, to prevent their ingreſs into the City, leaſt they ſhould make advantages of their admiſſion as *Eſpials*; they report the greater part of this Temple at the prayers of the Pope Saint *Stephen*, to have fallen down, when by the command of *Galienus*, he was there compelled to ſacrifice to *Mars*: Near hereto they preſerved the Stone *Manale*, which when the *Romans* would obtain Rain they ſolemnly brought in proceſſion into the Citty

Beyond that upon the *Via Appia*, riſes the Walls of a ſquare Caſtle very entire : which ſome believe to have been *Sinveſſa*, others *Pametia*, but the moſt to be credited averr it to be the *Stanza* or abiding place of the *Prætorian* Souldiers, within theſe walls is a ſpatious Concave.

Here on all ſides ly huge Sepulchres, ſome built in a ſquare, others in a round, a third ſort in a Pyramid form, either with brick or Marble,

ble whoſe inſcriptions demonſtrate . that they were erected for the *Metelli*, Among which a great ſtructure in a round form ſeems the moſt conſpicuous, being raiſed with ſquared white marble ſtones to the bigneſs of a Tower, hollow within and open at top, ſo that ſtanding below one may ſee the skies : Its walls are about 24. foot thick, in whoſe circuit are interwoven the heads of Bulls and Oxen cleared of the skin and fleſh, as in their ſacrifices they uſed them, between the garlands of Leaves and Flowers. The heads amount to the number of 200. Sacrificed to the God *Capo de Boi*, and the Antiquaries will have, that at the famous Sepulchre of *Cecilia Metella* a double *Hecatombe* was performed. At the Foot of the neighbouring Hill, if you pronounce a whole heroick verſe, an admirable Eccho returns it whole, and articulately for the moſt part, and confuſed otherwhiles eight times anſwered : In no place is heard ſo rare an Eccho, which is ſaid to be excited by artifice, that at the Funeral of this *Cæcilia Metella*, the ejaculations of the weepers and the funeral houlings might immenſely be mnltiplyed , while that double *Hecatombe* was celebrating, and the Funeſt duties performed in honour of that Matron.

In the next depreſſed place, ly the mighty ruines of the *Circo Hipodromo*, The ſtructure hereof is attributed to *Baſſiano Caracalla* raiſed in the Place where *Tiberius* the Emperor, built the Stables for the *Prætorian* bands: here the Souldiers exerciſed themſelves in running, riding, and driving Chariots.

In the midſt of the *Area*, lie certain ſignes of the places whence the horſes ruſhed out to their courſes, as alſo of Baſes , Statues, Altars, and meets or bounds for the Courſes; round it are many pictures, in the midſt lies an Obelisk of ſpeckled ſtone called *Granito*, flat upon the ground broken in three pieces; carved all over with *Hieroglyphicks*, branches with Leaves and animals. Tis ſuppoſed that *Sixtus* the 5th. would have reared this as he did others had not death ſhortned his days.

Above the Circ riſeth an entire Temple four ſquared, with Pillars, and Corridores before it : Which as is ſuppoſed was dedicated to the *Dio Ridicolo*, uppon this occaſion : *Hannibal* having ſlain 40 thouſand Romans at the battail of *Cannæ*, marched with his victorious Army to the ſiege of *Rome*, and pitched his Camp in that very place : where a diffuſed Laughter being heard over his Camp it cauſed a prodigious fear, and that made him raiſe the Siege and retreat to the *Terra di Lavoro* : which had he obſtinatly continued ſome time longer, (having created ſuch a conſternation in the Citizens)he had undoubtedly taken *Rome* with ſmall difficulty : but as *Livy* ſaies an *Affrican* told *Hannibal*, He knew how to obtain but not how to make uſe of Victory. Thus was *Rome* delivered from *Hannibal*: and the *Romans* in commemoration of ſo great a benefit received from the God of Laughter, conſecrated that Temple to the *Dio Ridicoloſo*.

Hence you muſt return by three miles journey back to *Rome*, and arrived at the walls enter by the *Porta Latina*, near whereto is the Church *S. Giovanni* where tis ſaid the ſame Saint was caſt into boyling oyl by the command of *Domitian*, for which a feaſt is alwaies ſolemnized in *May*, thence follow the ſtreet to the *Porta Gabioſa*, ſo
called

called, for that intending for the Citty *Gaba*, you muſt march out of it, where the *Via Roma* connexeth with the *Preneſtina:* as ſometimes the *Via Appia* unites with the *Latina*.

MONTE CELIO.

Leaving the Wall on the right hand of the *Porta Gabioſa*, you aſcend *Monte Celio*, wch runs along by the wall to the *Porta Maggiore*. This Hill was antiently called *Querquetulano*, from the multitude of Oaks growing thereon, before the *Tuſcans* inhabited it : to whom licence was given to dwell in the Bourg *Toſco*, becauſe they marched under their Captain *Cloche Vibenna*, to the aſſiſtance of the *Romans* againſt their Enemies. On this Hill at this day reſts no Antique thing of moment, more than the infinite ruines of Fabricks. One part of it is named *Celiolo*, where ſtands a Church of *Santo Giovanni Evangeliſta*, called *ante Portam Latinam*, which was antiently a Temple ſacred to *Diana*. On the top of the *Celio*, is a round Church dedicated to *S. Stefano*, by Pope *Simplicio*, from being a Temple of *Faunus*, whoſe antiquity threatning deſtruction, *Nicholas* the fifth repaired it, and *Gregory* the thirteenth beautifyed it with Pictures of Martyrs and Saints.

Curia Hoſtilia ſtood where now is *Santi Giovanni* and *Paulo* towards the *Settizonio* of *Severus*, built by *Tullius Hoſtilius*, different from that in the *Foro Romano*, Here the Senate aſſembled for ſtate affairs.

The Church of *S. Maria* in *Domenica* is ſeated towards the *Aventino*, and was reſtored by *Leo* the 10th. here antiently ſtood the Dwellings of the *Albani*, and near them the Aqueduct for the *Aqua Claudia*, in the Arch whereof are engraven theſe words *P. Corn R. F. Dolabella, Coſ. C. Junius C. P. Silanus Flamen Martial. Ex S. C. Faciundum curaverunt. Idemque Probaverunt.*

By the ſame Aqueduct ſtands a great Fabrick as a conſervatory of the Waters.

The *Caſtra Peregrina* ſtood in old time where the Church of *Santi quatro Coronati*, was built by Pope *Honorius*, and reſtored by *Paſchal* the ſecond. In thoſe Caſtles they uſed to rendezvouz and accommodate the People for Sea affairs, which *Auguſtus* uſed to keep in the ordinary Fleet at *Niſeno*. Between the *Porta Gabiuſa*, and *Celimontana* abound great ruines of the Palace of *Conſtantine* the great (called now *S. Giovanni*) by which may be comprehended the magnificent ſtate and ſplendor of that Emperor.

San Giovanni in Laterano keeps its antient name built by *Conſtantine* the Great at the inſtance of Pope *Sylveſter* formerly the Seat of the *Roman Pontifices* at firſt called *Romæ Epiſcopi* Biſhops of *Rome*, but afterwards (induced thereunto by the pleaſantneſs of the *Vatican* Hills) they tranſlated their habitation thither, building a renowned Palace near St. *Peters* Church.

Near the ſaid Church ſtands *Il Battiſterio di Conſtantino*: of an orbicular form ſuſtained by 8. porphyr Pillars : Report ſaith that *Conſtantine* the Great labouring under a Leaproſie, at the perſwaſions of

F ff

his

his Phisicians resolved to bath himself in the blood of Infants, and for that intent erected this sumptuous structure: but being admonished in a dream to bath himself in holy water in the name of Jesus Christ the true God, whom *Helena* his Mother worshipped, the Emperor obeyed the Celestial admonition, and was baptized in that porphyr Font now in the said Temple: For the truth hereof the Reader is desired to consult his own thought: It not being likely, that so magnificent a structure should be built and intended for perpetrating that notorious crime, which should rather be kept close and tacitely concealed, than published with such vain ostentation; besides that Historians say he was baptized by the *Nichomedian* Bishop, when he arrived in *Asia*, *Boisardo* thinks that the said *Battisterio* was rather the Bath to the *Lateran* Pallace and the Form of the Fabrick induceth him and others to the same belief: But however it was tis most certain that *Constantine* the great, having profest the Christian Religion, was baptized in this Church and the same *Babtistary* tis shewed to this day, and all converts to the Christian Religion, are there still baptized. On the right hand of it are certain holy chappels, and therein preserved many pretious Marbles and some Pillars conveyed hither from *Jerusalem*.

At the entrance of the Church *San Giovanni Laterano*, stand many sumptuous Tombs of Popes, and Altars wrought excellently with Marble, upon the high Altar is the last supper of Christ ingraven in silver of great value, set up by *Clement* the seaventh, who also raised, the great rich Organ, and that stately Vestry for the use of the Church.

Before the *Chorus* were four hollow brasen Pillars of *Corinthian* work, which tis said were brought from *Jerusalem* full of the holy Earth where our Saviour was enterred, others say that *Sylla* fetched them from *Athens*, and others that *Augustus* caused them to be cast in *Rome* of the Beaks of the Galleys taken in the *Actiack* battail and in memorial applyed to the Temple of *Jupiter Capitolino*. Furthermore others say that *Vespasian* translated them with the other spoils from *Jerusalem*. Of late, *Clement* the 8th. caused them to be guilt over, and placed them on the high Altar, with a brass Scutcheon guilt and affixed to them, wherein his Arms are engraven.

Before *Sixtus* the 5th. reedified from the foundations the *Lateranian* Palace, there was a great hall, where the Pope with the *Ecclesiastical* Synod of Cardinals and Arch-bishops rendred themselves when they were to manage any substantial business. Those three great marble Collumnes were shipped from the Palace in *Jerusalem*, here the *Lateranensial* counsels were solemnized with the assistance of the whole Clergy.

The *Scala Sancta*, contained 28 stairs which stood in *Pilats* House the which Christ ascended when he was whipped, are transferred by the Pope into another place where Christians frequent them and for devotion creep up them upon their knees kissing them.

Here were two porphyr chairs, whereof the Enemies of the Catholick Faith recount certain shamefull Fables which have been sufficiently confuted by Cardinal *Bellarmine*, in his first Tome of the controversies of the *Roman* Bishop, as also the story of Pope *Joan* whom the story saies to be *John* the 7th: who succeeded *Leo* the 4th. confuted

futed by the said Cardinal and *Onofrius*, and lately by *Florimondo Rô-
mondo* in *French*,

The Pillar of white Marble placed in the wall, and divided in two
is thought to be broken miraculously at the death of Christ, when
the Veyl of the Temple rent.

Sancta Sanctorum is a Chappel held in great veneration, the ingress
therein is forbidden to women : In it are kept the Ark of the Covenant, the rod of *Aaron*, the Table whereon Christs last supper was
celebrated : of the sacred *Manna*, the Navil string and præpuce of
Christ, a Vyal of Christs blood, some thorns of his Crown, one
whole Nail wherewith he was fastened to the Cross. The Snaffle of
Constantine the great his Horse, which was made of the two nayls
which pierced his feet, the fourth was placed in the Emperors golden Diademe. In the same place are likewise shewed many Reliques which are regarded by the *Romans* with huge Devotion: here
is to be observed that the old pictures of the Greeks, and *Gregory*,
Bishop of *Turona* shew, that Christ was fastened to the Cross, with
two nails in his feet and a little table under.

Somewhat distant from *S. Giovanni*, stands a Gate of the City called
now by the same name, but antiently *Celimontana* from Moupt *Celio*
Hence the *Via Campagna* takes its beginning leading to the *Campagna*
called *Terra di Lavoro* from its sterility : Forth the City it joines
with the *Latina*.

On the back part of *Monte Celio*, lyes the Church *Santa Croce di
Jerusalem*, one of the seaven chief, formerly sacrate to *Venus* and *Cupid*, In it is kept a part of the Lords Cross, and the title of the Cross
writ in three languages, one of the thirty pence, which *Judas* the
Traitor received for betraying Christ, a Thorn of the Crown, with
other sacred Reliques.

Here under the Earth *Helena* the mother of *Constantine* built a Chappel, wherein Women are permitted entrance only upon the 20th.
of *March*, to the Monastery of this Temple is adjoyned an Amphitheatre, somewhat less but more antient than the *Coliseo*, which
was edificated by *Statilius Taurus*, in the reign of *Augustus* : but twas
for the most part destroyed by Pope *Paul* the 3d. for reparation of
the Monastery. On one side of *Santa Croce* appear yet some ruines of
the *Basilica Sessariana*, near the Walls.

The Arches which enter the City by *Porta Nevia*, and pass over the
top of the *Celio*, to the *Aventino*, were the Arches for the Aqueduct of
the *Claudian* water: and were the highest and longest of *Rome*, *Claudius*
conveighed this water from forty miles off into the City; Some of
this water run into the Palace, some into the *Campidoglio*, but the
greatest part to the *Aventino* : The said *Porta Nevia*, was also called
Nevia, and *Santa Croce* and was built in an Arch Triumphal, which
demonstrates the Majesty and grandeur of the work.

Near the *Aqueduct* for the *Aqua Claudia* towards *Monte Celio*, stands
the Hospital S. *Giovanni* being both wealthy and comodious for receipt of infirm and sick Persons, abounding in all sorts of Phisical
ingredients, Physicians, Apothecaries, Surgeons, attendants, and
whatever els can conduce to the good of the Patients: This conveniency hath in all ages induced many Princes and other Persons of
quality and riches, when their Maladies require, to make this Hospi-

tal their abode, though they lye there at their own expence. In the Court of it are Sepultures of divers sorts. Baths with sculptures of Satyrs and different Actions: The battail of the *Amazones*: The Chafe of *Meleager* and other fair objects.

The Temple of S. *Clement* Pargetted with various coloured Marble, hath divers old inscriptions, many figures of the sacred instruments used in the divine services by the Popes as also in the Sacrifices by the Priests of the Gentiles and the Southfayers.

In the return you meet that stupendious and admirable Mole the Amphitheatre, called vulgarly *Colifeo* from the *Coloffean* statue of 120 foot high, which *Nero* erected. The altitude of this Amphitheatre was such, and the structure so compact, that *Rome* afforded nothing more stately. 'Twas eleaven yeers continued labour for thirty thoufand Slaves, and capable of eighty feaven thoufand men, who might conveniently difpofe thefelves in the furroundingSeats for beholding the Playes there yeerly exhibited.

The houfe of *Nero* occupying all that fpace between the Hils *Palatino* and *Celio*, reached to the *Efquilie*, fo ample that it had more the face and femblance of a City, than of a fingle houfe, within were comprehended Fields, Lakes, Woods, and a Gallery of a mile long, with three ranks of Pillars, many of its Chambers were guilt and adorned with gems: and the Temple dedicated to *Fortuna Seia*, had in it an Image of the fame Goddefle of tranfparent Marble.

On the left hand ftands the Arch Triumphal of *Conftantine* the Great, as yet whole and perfect with all his victories and statues carved on it. This Arch was erected in honour of that Emperor by the *Romans* after he had overcome at *Ponte Milvio*, *Maxentius*, who had tyrannically oppreffed *Rome* and *Italy*. At prefent they manage horfes in the *Colifeo*. And near it rifes a proud Fabrick in form of a Pyramid, which was called *La Meta Sudante*, for that thence iffued Streams of water, whereof fuch as had difpofed themfelves in the Amphitheatre to fee the fports, had given them to fatisfie their thirfts when defired by any. Thus ends the fecond dayes Journey.

The third dayes Journey of
ROME.

L Eaving the Caftle Saint *Angelo* on the right hand of the *Torre Sanguina*, paffing through the ftreet *Orfo*, where it divides you find the houfe of *Bildo Ferratino* in the frontifpiece whereof ftands a ftatue of *Galba the* Emperor with other figures.

In the Palace of the Duke of *Altemps*, they fhew many monuments of Antiquity, Epitaphs, Infcriptions, and Reliques which wonderfully delight the eyes of skilfull Artifts, and ingenious Men,
among

among others the ſtatue of *Seneca*, the Philoſopher and the Veſtry and Chapel of the Duke, clear demonſtrations of the piety and religion of the Patrones. Near it ſtands the houſe of Cardinal *Gaetano* containing ſome rare Antique ſtatues.

Towards *Navova* is the Church of S. *Apollinare* formerly the Temple of *Apollo*, and behind it the Church of Saint *Auguſtine*, where the Tombe of *Sant a Monica* his Mother is ſhewed with her Reliques.

That ſpatious Court before the Palace of the Dutcheſs of *Parma*, corruptly called *Piazza Navona*, was formerly the *Circo Agonale*, wherin they exhibited the *Agonalian* fights and games inſtituted by *Numa Pompilius* in honour of *Janus*. *Nero* augmented this Circ, and ſo did *Alexander* the Son of *Manca*, who erected alſo near it a Palace and the famous *Alexandrian* Hot baths. Hereabouts alſo *Nero* and *Adrian* had their Baths, but the continued edifices there have loſt the very foundations of the old ſtructures.

In the houſe of the Biſhops of *Saula*, is ſhewed the Head of M.*Tullius Cicero*, in that of *Alexander Ruffino*, the Image of *Julius Cæſar* Armed, like a *Coloſſus*, with his thighs neatly harneſſed after the oldfaſhion, and opoſite to it, another of the ſame heighth, and veſts of *Octavius Cæſar*. Then which ſtatues, *Rome* ſcarce affords any thing of better workmanſhip.

Thoſe round and high Arches which riſe in that place called the *Ciambella*, are reliques of the Bathes of *M. Agrippa:* near which *Nero* built others, whoſe Fragments ſhew themſelves behind S. *Euſtachio*.

M. Agrippa Built the *Pantheon* near his Bathes in honour of all the Gods, a Temple to be admired for the Architecture and wealth, the moſt antient, entire, and ſplendid of any at this day extant in *Rome* He built it orbicular, that Preeminence of Place might create no quarrels among the Gods. Others ſay he dedicated it to Ope, and *Cibele*, as mother of the Gods, and Miſtreſs of the Earth. Afterwards the Popes conſecrated it to the Bleſſed Virgin and all the Saints. It hath no windowes, being in lieu thereof ſupplyed with light from a great Open ſpace at top, the rain water driving there through is received into a large braſs Veſſel at the bottom, which in old time was covered with plates of ſilver but *Conſtantine* the Nephew of *Heraclius* took away that with the other ornaments of the City; antiently twas aſcended to by 7 ſteps, but now who enters it muſt deſcend 18. ſteps, whereby appears how vaſt are the heaps of ruines. An inſcription of very long Letters teſtifie that Severus, and M. *Antonius* repaired the *Pantheon*: then threatning a ruine. Herein lies *Raphael of Urbin*, the Prince of Painters: And before it ſtands a large Veſſel of Porphyr admirable for the grandeur and curioſity of workmanſhip, one like to which is extant in *Santa Maria Maggiore* under the Crucifix.

Near it *Santa Maria della Minerva*, ſo called from its firſt dedication to *Minerva* preſents it ſelf; where the *Dominican* Fryers inhabit: which hath nothing of antiquity more than the Walls and ſome old Inſcriptions. Here lies the Cardinals, *Pietro Bembo*, and *Tomaſo Gaetano*, learned men of their time: and *Santa Caterina* of *Siena*.

A great arch now old, rude, and diveſted of all its ornaments, ſtood

G g g

ſtood near it, called *Camiliano*, which they think to be built by *Camillus*, but falſly, for thoſe kind of works were firſt ſet a foot in the reigns of the Emperors: ſometime ſince, this Arch was by li. cence of Pope *Clement* the 8th. pulled down by Cardinal *Salviano*, who with thoſe ſtones amplified his own adjacent Palace, near this Arch lay a foot of a *Coloſſus* very great, which is ſuppoſed to be transferred to the *Campidoglio*, where tis now obvious.

In the houſe of *Paulus de Caſtro*, is ſeen the head of *Socrates*, with his whole breaſt, and many other things which will recreate the ſpectator: In the Palace of *S. Marca* in the *Via Lata*, there, is ſuch another Veſſel of Marble as is at *San Salvatore del Lauro*, taken out of the Baths of *Agrippa* and a ſtatue of *Fauna* or as others ſay of the good Goddeſs.

All thoſe things wherewith of old the Court of *Nerva* was garniſhed, are either by age decayed, or tranſlated to ſome other place tis called alſo *Foro Tranſitorio*, becauſe over it they walked to go to the *Foro Auguſto* and *Romano*, for which reaſon that Church is called *S. Adriano* in *trefori*. here ſtood likewiſe the Palace of the ſaid Emperor whoſe ruines were removed elſewhere.

Here alſo lies the *Foro Trajano*, between the *Campidoglio*, the *Quirinale*, and the *Foro Auguſto*, this was environed with a magnificent gallery ſuſtained with noble pillars, whereof *Apolliodorus* was Architector and adorned with ſtatues, Images, and a triumphal Marble Arch, of all which nought remains, except two of the Pillars at *Santa Maria di Loreto*. And one Collumne ſpread over within with Cockle ſhells, which demonſtrates the ſplendor and Majeſty of the Emperors; tis 128 foot high beſides the baſes, which is 12. foot more: tis raiſed by 24 ſtones only, but they ſo vaſt, that it appears the work of Gyants, every one of thoſe ſtones hath eight ſtayers by which they get up inwardly to the top, which are enlightned by 44 Caſements. Round it are carved the noble Acts of *Cæſar Trajano* in the *Dacian* Warr. No part of the world can boaſt a work more admirable, or more magnificent. 'Twas erected in honour of that good Emperor, who was not ſo fortunate as to ſee it finiſhed, for being detained in the *Parthick* warr, upon his return a flux of blood ſeized him in the City of *Soria*, in *Seleucia*, whereof he dyed his body was brought to *Rome*, and his bones incloſed in a Pile, placed on the top of the Columne.

In this *Foro di Trajano*, ſtand the Churches of Saint *Silveſter*, *S. Biaſio*, Sant *Martino*, placed there by *S. Marco* the firſt Pope. *Boniface* the 8th. erected there 3 Towers, called now, *Le Militie*, chiefly that in the midſt, where *Trajan* uſed to quarter his Souldiers.

Above it lies the the Vineyard of Cardinal *Pietro Aldobrandino*, meriting a view, wherein beſides the Fountains and Sources of waters which form many ſtreams, you may ſee ſome old noble Marbles among others *Harpocrate* a Child, wrought by an exquiſite hand, and an old painted picture, found ſome yeers ſince retaining the beauty of its colours: a wonder to believe, ſince it is ſo antient, and ſo long lay hid in a *grotto* near *S. Maria Maggiore*.

IL MONTE ESQUILINO.

AT the *Foro di Nerva* begins the Suburb, which extended to the *Tiburtina* dividing the *Esquilie*, the Vale between the *Esquilie*, and the *Viminale* they name *Vico Patricio*, becauſe many *Patritii* that is to ſay Nobles dwelt in that part.

L'Esquilie, was ſo called becauſe in the time of *Romulus* the Sentinels were placed there, this hill is ſevered from the *Celio*, by the *Via Lavicana* from the *Viminale* by the *Vico Patritio*. The *Via Tiburtina*, as aboveſaid (croſſeth it in the midſt which way aſcends from the Suburb to the *Porta Nevia*, but before it comes to the trophees of *Marius* tis cut in two, the right hand way leads towards *San Giovanni Latcrano*, conjoyning with the *Lavicana*, the left goes to the *Porta di San Lorenzo* by the name of *Preneſtina*.

In the *Via Tiburtina*, is the Arch of *Galienus* the Emperor called *San Vito* from the neighbouring Temple. Here was the *Macello Lanieno*, the Market for all eating things.

The Temple of *Iſis*, now of *Santa Maria Maggiore*, conſiſts of exquiſite ſtructure, adorned with gold and rare Marbles and ſuſtained by *Ionick* Pillars. Here *Santo Hieronimo*, lies enterred and here they ſhew an Image of the Virgin, painted (as is credited) by St. *Luke* the Evangeliſt, Near it ſtands the Church of S. *Lucia*, and that of S. *Pudentiana* here of old ſtood a wood ſacred to *Juno* reverenced with great but blind zeal.

In the Church of S. *Praſſede*, are many inſcriptions, and the Pillar (to which our Lord being bound) was whipped, this they ſay was brought from *Jeruſalem*. In *San Pietro in Vincula* are many admirable things, among others the Tombes of *Julius* the ſecond whereon *Moſes* is engraven by *Buonorota*, a work excelling moſt of the Antient, of Cardinal *Sadoleto*, and Cardinal *di Tucino*.

Thence you go to the Church *de quaranta Martiri*, from whence by the *Via Labicano* to S. *Clement* the *Eſquilie* extended it ſelf, and was there called *Carine*.

Near Saint *Pietro* in *Vincula*, are ſome *ſubterranean* edifices, the remains of *Veſpaſians* Baths, called the *Sette Sale*, being deſigned for keeping the waters requiſite to the Baths, in them was found that ſtatue of *Laocoon* now tranſlated to the *Vatican*, which gives ſuch admiration to all aſpicients. The Church of S. *Maria ne' Monti*, was built by Pope *Symachus*, in the decayes of *Adrians* Baths: the place being thence denominated at this day *Adrianello*.

At the Church *d'Santi Giuliano* and *Euſebio*, elates it ſelf a huge Fabrick of brick work, wherein were the receptacles of the *Aqua Martia*: on the upper part whereof are figured the Trophees of *Marius* that is a heap of ſpoils and Arms bound to the body of a Tree placed there in honour of *Marius* for his expedition againſt the *Cimbrians* which things being afterwards torn down by *Sylla* in the civil war, were reſtored again by *C, Cæſar* to their former luſtre, and yet remain in the *Campidoglio*. Behind the Trophees in that Vineyard appear great ruines of the Emperor *Gordianus* his Baths near which the said Emperor raised a stupendious Palace which had two hundred Pillars in a double Rank. But hereof no more but high walls appear. All its Ornaments and Pillars, being thence translated for beautifying other Palaces.

From these Baths the way on the right hand called *Labicana* goes to *Porta Maggiore*, or *Sante Croce*, antiently *Nevia*. Between this Gate and that of *San Lorenzo*, near the walls rise vast ruines of the Temple dedicated to the name of *Caius*, and *Lucius* the Nephews of *Augustus* and built by him, one arched roof yet may be seen called *Gallucio* as of *Caio* and *Lucio*.

Near it was the Palace of *Licino*, where now *S. Sabina* stands, there placed by Pope *Simplex*, contiguous with which Pallace was the place called *Orso Pileato*, from a Bears figure there.

By the gate *Esquilina*, *San Lorenzo* or *Tiburtina*, by all which names tis frequently called: stands the Church *San Lorenzo*, built by *Constantine* the great in honour of that Martyr replenished with antiquities, but especially the instruments used in the sacrifices are carved on inembossed work, by this Gate also enters the Aqueduct by which the *Aqua Martia* is conveighed into the City, first raised by *Q. Martius*, afterwards consumed by Age restored by *M. Agrippa*.

This water was brought from 35. miles off the City, and ran into *Dioclesians* Baths, and the adjacent places, twas very healthfull, and therefore chiefly accomodated for the drink of the People.

On the other side of this Gate entered the *Acque Tepola & Julia*: the one was conveighed six miles the other eleaven from without the City. To these joyned the *Aniene* which ran from *Tivoli* 20. miles distance. Over the *Aniene* stands the *Ponte Mammeo*, so named from *Mammea* the Mother of *Alexander Severus* the Emperor, by whom twas repaired, from this Gate the *Via Prenestina* reached to *Præneste*, and the *Labicana* to *Labi*.

That part of the *Esquilie* near *San Lorenzo in Fonte*, was named *Virbo Clivio*, which was the Grove *Fugatale* where *Servius Tullius* dwelt and there lies the *Vico Ciprio*, called also *Scelerato*, for that *Tullius* was there slain by his Son in Law, over whose dead body his own Daughter commanded her Coachman to drive her Chariot. This *Vico*, or Town extended to *Busta Gallica*, where the *Galli Senoni* or the French were slain, burnt and buried by *Camillus*: now this place s denominated *Porto Gallo*, where the Church Saint *Andrea :* is built On the top of this *Vico Scelerato Cassius* had his Palace afterwards dedicated to the Goddess *Tellura* now to Saint *Pantaleon*. near *Santa Agna* at the foot of the *Viminale* stood a Temple of *Silvano*, whose decays yet appear.

IL COLLE VIMINALE.

THe hill *Viminale* is next to the *Esquilino*, and runs along by the Walls: twas so named from a famous Temple dedicated to *Jupiter Viminale*: whence also the contiguous Gate took the name *Viminale* and *Nomentana*, from the way leading to *Nomento*, which is now called *S. Agnese* from the Church of that name near it, which was formerly dedicated to *Bacchus*, therein is an old porphyr Arch the greatest now extant in *Rome*, whereon are engraven Boyes gathering Grapes: which some call the Sepulchre of *Bacchus*, but erroneously.

In the *Via Nomentana* a little farther is the *Ponte Nomentano* built by *Narsetes* the Eunuch under *Justinian* the Emperor, as the inscription testifies. *Nero* the Emperour, between the *Porta Suburbana*, and *Salaria*, had *Suburbano* a singular edifice, which he gave to a Freed Man who fearing a publique punishment by a poynard thrust into his brest and the help of *Sporo* another freed Man slew himself: some ruines of this Fabrick yet remain.

Porta Querquetulana is now a Church near which appear square wals the Remains of the Castle deputed for the Souldiers stations apointed for the Emperors guards.

On the *Viminale*, are seen the Baths of *Dioclesian*, of an admired Vastness and sumptuosity, which though much decayed, are yet the most entire in *Rome*, 'Tis said that forty thousand Christians were in a servile manner turmoyled for fourteen yeers in the structure hereof. *Dioclesian* and *Maximinian* began them, but *Constantine* and *Massiminian*, compleated them now called *Alle Terme*, where appears a certain place made for receit of the waters employed in those Baths, called *Bacco di terme*; *Dioclesian* adjoined a Palace to them, whose ruines manifestly shew themselves. And here was that celebrious Library called *Ulpa*, where the *Elephantine* books were disposed.

On the right hand of these Baths, are the Gardens formerly appertaining to Cardinal *Bellay*, but now to the Monks of the order of Saint *Bernard*, to whose industry the ingenious owe the Invention and designes made by wind. And on their left hand, stands the Church of *Santa Susanna*, in old time the Temple of *Quirinus*. In this place they believe *Romulus* (being præascended into Heaven) appeared to *Proculus Julius* then returning from *Alba*, for which cause the Senate consecrated a Temple and attributed to him divine honours. Here also (*ut aiunt*) *Romulus* frequently descended and communicated divers things to *Alba*.

The foundations of the *Olympiade* Baths yet continue near *S. Lorenzo* in *Pane & Perna*, vulgarly named *Pamiperna* where *Decius* the Emperors Pallace stood.

The Church *S. Prudentia*, was built by *Pius* the fourth, at the request of *Santa Prascede* his Sister, where likewise appear the walls of the Baths *Novati*. And the ruines of the Baths of *Agrippina* the Mother of *Nero*, are yet extant by the Church *S. Vitalis*.

H h h

In

In *San Lorenzo* in *Proserpina* shewes it self a great Marble Stone reverenced with great adoration and religion, whereon (*ut aiunt*) the roasted body of *San Lorenzo*, was repo'ed after his death: here lies buried Cardinal *Cirketo* the delight of the Learned of our times.

Beyond the Church S. *Susanna* by the *Via Quirinale* lay heretofore the gardens of *Rodolfo*, Cardinal *Carpente*, then which, no part of *Italy* nay *Naples* it self (where are the most excelling) afforded more delicious. In it were 134 statues engraven with divers artificial figures and other admirable curiosities so well disposed, that no Fancy could reach that Paradise, nor ocular view scarce apprehend its glory, to say no more this garden was an Embleme of that Cardinal its Patron the son of *Alberto Fio* Prince of *Carpi*, for as that exceeded most, so his knowledge in antiquities and Learning was admired by all, he wrote learnedly against *Erasmus*.

IL COLLE QVRINALE or MONTE CAVALLO.

THis hill was so demonstrated from the Name *Quiri* or *Curi*, a Family of the *Sabines* who marching among others under *Statius* their Captain, to reside at *Rome*, inhabited this hill, now called *Monte Cavalli*, from the artificial horses there yet visible. 'Tis divided from the *Viminale* by that way which conducts to the *Porta S. Agnese*. Upon *Monte Cavallo* where were the Vineyards of the Cardinal of *Estè* now stands a Palace of the Popes admirable for the Grottoes, walks, Arbors, and artificial Fountains. The chief was the work of Pope *Clement* the 8th. whereon is wrote the history of *Moses* in *Mosaique* work. Here stand some old statues of the Mules, and here you may hear one of those Organes, called of old *Hydraulici*, because they sounded by force of the Waters. You ascend this Fountain by some steps, upon the ballostres whereof stand certain Vessels which spout out water very high, which in their fall present divers figures before it lies ample fishponds with a Circle of Plain trees wch. afford a thick and lovely shade, in fine such is the the Variety of Marbles, the excellency and fairness of the statues the diversity of the Inscriptions, the beauty of the walks, the pleasantness of the Fountains, and the shade of the Groves in these pontifical Vineyards, That the studious may find here fit objects for their Observations The Curious for their admiration, and the Lovers of Solitude for their deportment and retreats. Hence a little distant lies the Vineyard of *Octavio* Cardinal *Bandini*, well kept and worthy a view. And at the four fountains the Palace of the *Mattei*, which hath some fair statues as well antient as modern.

Round about which lye several other Vineyards and Gardens, as of the *Teatini*, of the *Colonna's* and of *Patriarca Biondo*, near which
.is

is the Church Saint *Andrea*, repaired by the *Jesuites*, where the B. *Stanislao Kostka*, a *Polach*, lies buried who there acomplished his days.

Upon this Mount stand two Colloffus or statues as twere of Gyants holding two wild horses by a Bridle cut in Marble, upon whose pilaster we read, that they were the work of *Phidia*, and *Prasitelle*, from which horses tis called *Monte Cavallo*. And the report goes that *Tiridates* King of the *Armenians*, presented them to *Nero*, who (that he might entertain that stranger King worthily and according to the *Roman* splendor) caused *Pompeyes* Theatre (where he exhibited the Games for that Kings Solace and recreation) in three days to be layed all over with silver Plates : Which magnificence the King did not so much admire (knowing well that in *Rome* were heaped up the riches of the world) as the diligence and ingenuity of the workmen, that in so short a time could perfect so noble ingenious a work, which in him created astonishment.

Here the *Benedictine* Fryers had a comodious habitation: which some time since they surrendred to the Apostolick Chamber, opposite whereto is a Pontifical Palace, built by *Sixtus* the 5th. for their cool retreat in hot weather; whence somewhat, in the *Vigna* of the *Colonnesi*, raiseth it self the *Frontispiece* of *Neros* Pallace, vulgarly called *Frontone di Nerone*, Hence *Nero* beheld the Fire which was by his own incendiaries kindled in the City of *Rome* which afterwards he imputed to the Christians, that by this Calumny he might draw them into hatred with the Senate and People of *Rome*, and by a publick edict commanded, that as many as were apprehended, confessing Christ for God should be burnt and excarnified in *Neros* gardens which Persecution continued three days.

On the other part of the *Quirinale*, are many Arches, Cels, & caves of different workmanship under ground, the Reliques of the Emperor *Constantines* Baths of hot waters. And thence looking towards the Suburbs, you behold an old Temple in the gardens of the *Bartolini*, made ov all and wrought with divers shapes of Fishes and other Ornaments which was dedicated to *Neptune*.

Near hereto is the place vulgarly called *Bagnanapoli*, that is *Bagni di Paulo*, because they were made by *Paulus Æmilius*: The Monastery of the Nuns of Saint *Benedict* built by Pope *Pius* the 5th. and the Palace of the *Conti*, rise out of the ruins of those Baths, whereof to this day some small fragments are extant. The Tower *de Conti*, was raised by *Innocent* the 3d. and that of the *Militie* by *Boniface* the 8th.

On this part of the *Quirinale*, stood the house of the *Cornelii*, called now *Vico di Cornelii*, and *S. Salvatore de Cornelii*, a Temple sacred of old to *Saturn* and *Bacchus*.

From the Church S. *Salvatore*, to the *Porta di san Agnese*, reacheth the Street called *Alta Semita*, on the right hand whereof near *San Vitale*, stood the house of *Pomponius Atticus*, with a wood. Hereby also was the *Suburra Piana*, and at the foot of the *Viminale* a Temple of *Silvanus*:

Upon the top of the *Quirinale*, stood a Temple consecrated to *Apollo*, and *Clara*, two small Temples of *Jupiter* and *Juno*, and the old Capitol, of these structures scarce any reliques appear, here now is the

Monastery of the Nuns of Saint *Domenick*, and the Church of *Santa Maria Magdalena*.

Near *San Susanna*, stood the Court and house of *Salust*, which place is now corruptly called *Callostrico* : his fair gardens took up all that space between the *Porta Salaria* and *la Pinciana*, in the midst whereof stood a small Obelisk carved with Hyeroglyphicks, dedicated to *Luna*, since amoved.

In the descent from the *Quirinale*, towards the *Foro* of *Nerva* a high Tower presents it self, which is vulgarly called *Torre Mezza*, which tis believed was one part of the house of *Mæcenas*, adjoyning whereunto were his delicious Gardens, whereto *Augustus Cæsar* frequently withdrew himself from his more weighty affairs to recreate himself with his Friend, and to revive his toyled Spirits. Others believe it to be a part of the Temple dedicated by *Marcus Aurelius* to the Sunne.

The Fourth dayes Journey of ROME.

FRom the Bourg taking the way over *Fonte Elio*, you up against the streams of the Tyber meet the Church *San Biasio*, at *Ripetta*, which is supposed to have been the Temple of *Neptune*, amplified by *Adrian* the Emperor : here such as had escaped any remarkable shipwrack, hung up Tablets containing the particulars of their deliverance and their vows for it to the God of the Sea.

In the *Valle Martia*, by the Church of *San Rocco* stands the *Mauseolo*, of *Augustus* being a Sepulchre erected by *Octavius* for himself and she successors of the *Cæsarian* Family, out of the ruins and with the Materials of that Amphitheatre (which he destroyed)that *Julius Cesar* built there;its Circuit is yet entire divided into a figure four square lozinged. In this *Mauseolo*, stands a *Matrona* holding a *Cornucopia* with Fruit, and an *Æsculapius* as bigg as a Gyant with a Serpent.

In this *Mauseolo*, were also heretofore two Obelisks of *Granito*, 42 foot high.

The Circ of *Julius Cæsar*, extended from this *Mauseolo* to the foot of the neighbouring Mountain, *Augustus* had a Palace opposite to it, with a stately Gallery, and had here consecrated a Grove to the Gods of Hell,reaching from the Church *Santa Maria del Popolo* to S. *Trinita*.

Some say that *Marcellus* his Sepulchre was contiguous with this *Mauseolo*, and shew its very *Track* : which *Boisardo*, believes rather to belong to the *Mauseolo*,and not a distinct Edifice.

Augustus also had made a place called *Naumachia* for Naval Diversions in the lower part of the *Valle Martia*, (looking towards the

Hill

Hill *Santa Trinita* which *Domitian* restored being decayed through antiquity, and called it after his own name, placing near it a Temple to the Family *Flavia:* where now Saint *Silvestro* stands.

The *Valle Martia* was so denominated, because twas the lowest Gate of the *Campo Martio*, and extended from the *Tyber* to the hills *Santa Trinita*, and from the Piazza of *Domitian* in the *Via Flaminia* to the *Porta Flaminia*.

The *Via Flaminia* took its name from *Flaminius* the Consul, who paved it after the conquest of the *Genovesi* now tis called the *Corso:* for that at some time of the yeer, boys and certain animals run here striving who shall arrive first at the end of the course. This way goes from the *Porta Flaminia* (called heretofore *Flumentana* from its vicinity to the Tyber but at this day *Porta del popolo*) to *Pesaro*, and to *Rimini*. Near this way lye many gardens filled with inscriptions, chiefly those of Cardinal *Lovisio*, *Justiniano*, *Gallo*, *Altemps* and others.

By this Way Pope *Julius* the third accomodated a Vineyard with such ornaments, as for cost and magnificence surpassed all others in *Rome*, and as an Inscription attests, conducted to the publik way a Fountain for the benefit of all persons, wherein tis scarce to be judged which ought most to be applauded, the ingenuity of the Artificers, or the sumptuousnefs and splendour of the *Roman* Chief Bishops.

Beyond this lies *Ponte Molli*, where the Tyrant *Maxentius* was overcome by *Constantine* the Great: which Tyrant that he might not be carried alive in the Triumphs of *Constantine* cast himself headlong off the Bridge into the *Tyber*. Afterwards in honour of *Constantine* was erected the Triumphal Arch between the *Colifeo* and the *Settizonio* of *Severus*.

Returned into the City by the *Porta Flaminia* you find the Arch of *Domitian*, called *di Portogallo*, because in that quarter the Embassador of *Portugall* resided. Tis also called *Tripoli*, a rude and incompact structure, having nothing of moment in it more than the statue of *Domitian*, which some too will not have to be his, but the statue and Arch of *Claudius* the Emperor.

The Church of Saint *Lorenzo*, in *Lucina*, was sacred to *Juno Lucina*, and yet retains its old name, here of old, breeding women and such as lay in Childbed, after the birth used to pay their vows, because by the good will of the Goddefs, not only themselves were preserved in that great peril, but the Life of their tender Infants.

In the street *de Condotti*, in the house of the *Bosii*, some notable and old inscriptions are extant. In the Palace of the Spanifh Embassador a fair and Copious Fountain. In that of *Dionigio Octaviano Sada*, (who translated the old Dialogues of *D. Antonio Augustino*, into *Italian*,) a good number of rare things in this kind. In that of the *Ruzzelai*, a Gallery filled with old statues of rare artifice, and in the Court, a very large brazen horse. And in that of the Cardinal *Desa*, now building, we assure our selves of rare Architecture and great Curiosities.

The *Campo Martio* heretofore without the City, fils that plain between the *Quirinale*, the *Ponte di Sifto*, and the *Tevere* or *Tyber*, here the youthexerciſed themſelves inMilitary diſcipline,and here they hold their Council for creating of Magiſtrates.

Between *Santa Maria del Popolo*, and the *Porta Flaminia*, is ſeen an O-beliſk, filled with Hieroglyphicks, and *Ægiptian Letters* : which *Pliny* writes, to be one hundred and ten foot long, and to contain on it the interpretation of the *Ægyptian* Philoſophy. *Auguſtus Cæſar* cauſed it to be transferred from *Hieropoli* to *Rome*, with two others, which he placed in the *Circus Maximus*. On the Pedeſtal is this Inſcription. *Cæſar. Divi. F. Aug. Pont. Max. Imp. X. J. Cos. XI. Trib. Pot. XIV. Ægypto in Poteſtatem.* P. R. *redactâ Soli Donum dedit.*

The houſe of *Antonino Paleozo*, affords an excellent ſtatue of a horſe and ſome heads, as of *Druſus*, of *Julia* the Daughter of *Auguſtus*, of *Goleria*, of *Fauſtina Giovene*, the wife of *Marcus Aurelius*, of *Adrian*, of *Brutus*, *Domitian*, *Galba*, *Sabina*, *Hercules*, *Bacchus*, *Sylvanus*, and *Mercury* : And likewiſe the Triumph of *Tiberius Cæſar*, cut lively in one Marble ſtone. And that of *Giacomo Giacovazzo*, not a few excellent ſtatues in Marble and Braſs, and other Curioſities.

Antoninus Pius, in that part of the *Campo Martio*, called *Piazza di Sciarra*, erected a hollow Columne with winding ſtairs,and 56.Caſements to give Light within to them : being 175 foot high, ſome ſay it is raiſed with 28 ſtones only,but in this tis not ſo clearly diſcernable as in that of *Trajano*, for that the ſtayers being broke tis not aſcendable. On the ſuperficies of it are wrought the Acts of *Antoninus* with excellent ſculpture of figures, from this,that place is denominated *Piazza Colonna*.

Thoſe eleaven high Pillars, which are ſeen erected at the Church of Saint *Stephano*, in *Truglio*, are the reliques of that open Gallery which *Antoninus Pius* built conjoyned,to his Palace in his Court:as far diſtant from this Church as the *Rotonda*.

Between the Collumne of *Antoninus* and the Fountain of *Acque Virgine*, were the *Septa* of the *CampoMartio*,ſo called for that they were encloſed with ſeveral thick Plancks, in which the *Roman* People aſſembled when they gave their ſuffrages for Election of the Magiſtrates.They were alſo called *Ovili* for their ſimilitude to a Sheepfold here the *Roman* Tribes aſſembled in Council.

That Hill,between *San Lorenzo* in *Colonna*, and the abovenamed Column, called *Monte Acitorio*: took its name from the Latine words *Mons Citatorum*, where every Tribe Se'paratim, rendred themſelvs after they had given their ſuffrages in the *Septa*. On the ſame Hill ſtood a publique Palace, for receipt of Embaſſadors from Enemies who were not licenced to enter the City nor dwell in *Græcoſtaſi*, which lay between the Counſel and the *Roſtri*, in the *Piazza Romana*, Cardinal *Santa Severina* ſo much ſpoken of by the Hereticks, a man of great prudence, and an example for poſterity,erected his Palace on this Hill.

Not far from hence is the Fountain of *AqueVirgine*, conveighed by a loud depreſſed Aqueduct over the *Porta Collina*, the Hill *Santa Trinita*,and through the *Campo Martio* now called *Fontana di Trevi*,we read in the inſcription that *Nicolo* the 5th. reſtored it.And this alone of all the waters (which with ſo great coſts, and ſuch ſumptuous

Aque-

Aqueducts, the antient Princes brought into *Rome*)remains standing
for the publique Benefit.

From the *Serraglio,* or *Septa* of the *Roman* people began the *Strada coperta,* wherein stood heretofore a Temple of *Neptune* and the Amphitheatre of *Claudius* now wholly destroyed.

At the *Acque Virgine* was a Temple dedicated to *Giuturna* Sister of *Turno* King of the *Rutoli,* accounted one of the *Napee* or Nimphes keeping among flowers, and the Countrey goddess, who as the Heathens believed assisted to the fertility of the Earth.

In the house of *Angelio Colorio da Giesi,* now appertaining to the *Farnesi,* are seen many statues, and inscriptions, and one Arch of the stone *Tivoli,* joyning to the *Acque Virgine,* having this Inscription. *T. Claudius Drus. F. Cæsar Augustus.* In the Fountain under the statue of a Nymph now removed are found these verses.

> *Hujus Nympha loci sacri custodia Fonti*
> *Dormio, dum blandæ sentio murmur aquæ*
> *Parce meum quisquis tangis cava marmora somnum*
> *Rumpere, sive bibes, sive lavare jaces.*

Pompeio Naro possesseth two statues which were found in his Vineyard, the one of *Hercules* the other of *Venus.*

⁂⁂⁂⁂⁂⁂⁂⁂⁂⁂⁂⁂⁂⁂⁂⁂⁂⁂⁂⁂⁂⁂⁂⁂⁂⁂⁂⁂⁂⁂⁂⁂⁂⁂⁂

IL COLLE de gli HORTICELLI, now *di SANTA TRINITA.*

THis Hill extends from *San Silvestro* to the *Porta Pinciana* or *Collina* along by the Walls of the City, but some draw it out to the *Porta Flaminia.* The Gate and Hill took their name from *Pincius* the Senator, whose magnificent Palace stood here, and the footsteps of it are yet visible; at the walls of the City upon this Hill was the Sepulchre of the *Domitian* Family : here likewise *Nero* was buried.   On the top of this hill remains an Arch or roof which formerly was part of the Temple of the Sun, near whereto lies an obelisk of *Thasian* stone with this inscription. *Soli Sacrum.*

The Church *Santa Trinita,* now occupied by the Minime Fryars, was built by *Lewis* the XIth. King of *France,* wherein are some Tombes of Cardinals, as of *Antonio Moreto,* and Cardinal *di Carpi.*

At the *Porta Collina* near *Santa Susanna, Salustius* (as aforesaid) had most pleasant gardens, and a splendid dwelling, whose ruines yet appear in the Vale leading to *Salara:* Here stood an Obelisk (now translated elsewhere) sacred to the Moon, engraven with *Ægyptian* Hyeroglyphicks. The place is yet vulgarly called *Salostrico.*

The *Campo Scelerato,* or the *Via Scelerata* (where the deflowred Vestal Virgines were buried alive) compleated all that space, from the *Porta Collina* under the house and gardens of *Saluſtius* to the *Porta Salaria*.

Without the *Porta Salaria*, called alſo *Quirinale Collina* and *Agonale* lye the ruines of the Temple of *Venus Erycina*, whoſe Feaſt was celebrated with ſolemn ceremonies by chaſt Matrons, in the month of *Auguſt*, to the Image of *Venus Ver ecordia*, which Goddeſs was ſuppoſed to render the Husbands placable and benevolent to their wives: in this Temple they likewiſe celebrated the *Agonalian* games, whence t was named *Agonale*.

Three miles without the City over the *Aniene*, ſtands an entire Bridge, which a long inſcription ſhews to have been built by *Narſetes*, tis ſaid that *Hannibal* being on this Bridge vexed with a vehement rain, raiſed the ſiege of *Rome*, removed his Camp and departed.

A little below which, the *Tyber* commixeth with the River *Aniene*, and here *Torquatus* overcame that *French Gyant*, from whoſe neck he took that golden neck chain, which (becauſe in Latine called *Torques*) gave him the ſurname of *Torquatus*. Tis worth obſervation, that the Water drawn out of the *Tyber*, above the City towards the Sea, maintains it ſelf wholeſome, and clean for many yeers, which comes to paſs from the mixture of the River *Aniene* with the *Tyber* , The water of the *Aniene* being thick and polluted with *Nitre*, which preſerves it and occaſions that it cannot putrify without difficulty: and the inhabitants along the *Tybers* banks above where the *Aniene* commixeth with the *Tyber*, mingle the waters of the one with the other, that they may laſt ſweet a long time: although they have been neceſſitated to take them up ſingly and ſeparately. In the gravel of the *Aniene*, they find ſeveral little ſtones in divers forms after the ſimilitude of *Comfits*, ſome round ſome long, ſome little and ſome great, ſo that one would believe they found Almonds, Fennel, Anniſeed, Coriander, and Cinamon Comfits. Of which ſmall ſtones they uſually gather a good heap on the bankſide, to couſen the ſpectators with, and they are therefore called *Confetti di Tivoli*.

Titus Celius the *Patrician* recounts, that in former times a body of a man who was ſlain and caſt into the *Aniene*, was found ſtuck faſt to the root of a Tree under water, which it happened, in proceſs of time, (being without putrefaction) was converted into ſtone, without looſing its ſhape: which ſtony body ſo found he ſaies he ſaw with his proper eyes.

At the *Porta Salaria* are ſhewed the Reliques of an antique Temple, conſecrated to Honour, and of the houſe *Suburbano* of *Nero*, wherein by the aſſiſtance of *Sporo* the *Libertine*, the Emperor *Nero* thruſt a dagger under his nipple, and therewith ſlew himſelf, that he might not fall into the hands of the Senate, then requiring him to puniſhment.

Within the City near the Vale between the hills *Santa Trinita*, and *Quirinale* ſtands the Church *San Nicolo de Archemontis*, ſo named for that the *Foro* or *Piazza*, of *Archemorio* was in that place.

Under the Vineyard of the late Cardinal *Dapi* are certain Chambers and obſcure vaults continued in a long Order: which ſome will have to have been a Tavern, others had rather aſſign them to the uſe of the ſtrumpets for their occupation in the time of the *Floralian*

games

games : which were celebrated in the *Circo Floræ.*

At the Church *de'dodeci Apoſtoli*, you find a Lyon in Marble, an incomparable piece, and in the houſe of *Colonna*, a Marble ſtatue of *Meliſſe* a Lady, as the inſcription declares.

Many other Palaces and houſes of the Cardinals, Nobles, and wealthy Citizens of *Rome*, are plentifully fraught with other Antiquities and excellent Collections of Gold, Silver, and Braſs coynes emboſſed works in divers Metals of ingenious Artiſts. *Onyexes*, *Corneols*, or *Sardonian* Gemmes, *Cornelians*, *Amethiſts*, *Topazes*, *berryls*, *Carbuncles*, *Jacinths*, *Saphirs*, and *Chriſtals* ingraven and cut with the heads of Gods, Emperors, illuſtrious and noble Men, divers Creatures, Hearbs, and Trees, containing alſo divers emblemes, which were heretofore commonly expoſed to the view of ſtrangers by their Patrones : but of later yeers the malignity of this depraved Age hath ſo ill gratified thoſe perſons for their Kindneſs, by many injuries received from ſuch their free admiſſion, that now unleſs recommended by ſome friend to ſome particular perſon in *Rome*, or contracting a Friendſhip through long familiarity : tis not eaſie for a ſtranger to obtain an inſpection of thoſe pretious Curioſities.

Of the Cœmiteries and of the Burying places of *R O M E*, collected out of *H O N O F R I O P A N V I N O.*

THE *Cemeterio Oſtriano*, three miles without the City in the *Via Salaria*, is thought to be the moſt antient of *Rome*, for that Saint *Peter* the Apoſtle in that place adminiſtred the Sacrament of Baptiſm.

The *Protonotario* of the *Roman* Church in his third Chapter of the Acts of Pope *Liberio*, ſpeaks of it in this manner. A little diſtant from the *Cemetrio di Novella*, three miles without the City lay in the *Via Salaria*, the *Cemiterio Oſtriano*, where the Apoſtle Saint *Peter* Baptized.

The *Cemiterio Vaticano* was placed on the *Via Trionfale* near the Temple of *Apollo*, and the Circ of *Nero*, in the Gardens of *Nero* where now the Church of Saint *Peter* ſtands : which beſides the Tombs of Chriſtians had in it alſo a Font for holy Baptiſme, which for the moſt part was not in others.

Seaven miles diſtant from *Rome* was the *Cemiterio* called *ad Nimphas*, in *Severus* his poſſeſſion on the *Via Nomentana*, where the holy Martyres bodies were enterred. As Pope *Alexanders*, *&c.*

Two miles without the City was the *Cemeterio vecchio*, amplified by the *B. Caliſtus* the Pope, from whom alſo it took a name. Herein were certain *ſubterranean* places called *Catacombe*, and in them a deep Pit, wherein the bodies of the Apoſtles *Peter* and *Paul* were layed.

Kkk

Near

Near to the *Cemiterio, di San Califto,* was that of *San Sotero,* and in the fame quarter lay that of *San Zeferino* the Pope contiguous with the *Catecombe* and that of *San Califto.*

The *Cemeterio* of *Calepodio Prete,* was two miles forth the *Porta Gianicolefe* in the *Via Aurelia,* near *San Pancratio.*

That of *Treteftato Prete* in the *Via Appia,* where Pope *Urban* was buried.

That of *Santo Partiano Papa* near to *Santi Abdon* and *Sennen.*

That of *Ciriaco* in the poffeffion of *Veriani* near the Church *San Lorenzo* without the Wall.

That of *Lucina* in the *Via Aurelia,* forth the Gate *San Pancratio.*

That of *Aproniano* in the *Via Latina* not far from the City, where *Santa Eugenia* was buried.

That of *San Felice* the Pope, a mile without *Rome* on the *Via Aurelia,* adjoined to that of *Calepodio.*

That of *Prifcilla,* called alfo *Marcello,* from the Pope *Marcellus* in the *Via Vecchia,* three miles forth the City, was dedicated by the faid Pope *Marcellus.*

That of *San Timoteo* in the *Via Oftienfe* is comprehended now in the Church of *San Paulo.*

That of *Novella* three miles off *Rome* in the *Via Salaria.*

That of *Balbina* between the *Via Appia,* and *Ardeatina,* near the Church of *San Marco* the Pope, was named alfo *San Marco* from the faid Popes name.

That of *San Giulio* the Pope in the *Via Flaminia* near the Church *San Valentino* without the Cities Walls. This alfo may be feen in the Vineyard of the *Heremitanes* of St. *Auguftino.*

That of *San Giulio* the Pope in the *Via Aurelia.*

That of *San Giulio* the Pope in the *Via Portuenfe.*

That of *San Damafo,* between the *Via Ardeatina,* and the *Appia.*

That of *Sant Anaftatio* the Pope within the City in the *Efquiline* præcincts in the Bourg *Orfo,* near *Santa Bibiana.* The *Orfo* was near the *Porta Taurina,* in the *Via Tiburtina* by the Palace of *Licinus.*

That of S. *Hermete,* or *Domitilla,* appointed by Pope *Pelagius* in the *Via Ardeatina.*

That of *San Nicomede,* in the *Via Ardeatina* feaven miles off *Rome.*

That of *San Agnefe* in the *Via Nomentana.*

That of *S Felicita* in the *Via Salaria.*

That of the *Giordani,* where *Aleffandro* was buried.

That of *Santi Nereo* and *Archielo* in the *Via Ardeatina,* two miles forth the City.

That of S. *Felice* and *Adauto* in the *Via Oftienfe* two miles without *Rome.*

That of *Santi Tibullio* and *Valeriano* in the *Labicana,* three miles without *Rome.*

That of *Santi Pietro* and *Marcellino* in the *Via Labicana,* near the Church *Santa Helena.*

That of *Santi Marco* and *Marcelliano* in the *Via Ardeatina.*

That

That of S. *Giannario* reftored by Pope *Gregory* the 3d.
That of *Santa Petronilla*, adorned by Pope *Gregorio*.
That of *Santa Agata à Girolo* in the *Via Aurelia*.
That of *Orfo* at *Portenza*.
The *Cemeterio Cardino* in the *Via Latina*.
That *tra'due Lauri* at S. *Helena*.
That of S. *Ciriaco* in the *Via Oftienfe*.
But we muft obferve, that *Aftolfo* King of the *Longobardi* tearing up
out of the earth about *Rome* the bodies of many Saints , deftroyed
alfo their *Cemeterii* or burying places. and that the Popes Paolo and
Pafchale, repofed within the City, in the Churches of S Stefano, S. *Silveftro*, and S, Prafcede , many bodies of Saints then lying
in thofe *Cemeterii* which were ruinated and layed waft. And that the
Chriftians were buried in the *Cemeterii* within Tombes and Sepulchres of Marble, or of brick, and of thofe Sepulchres fome were hereditary, others beftowed in gift, and that at laft places were affigned
particularly for the Sepulture of Chriftians to wit Church-
yards, &c.

The *Roman* fixed ftations, granted by feveral Popes
to divers Churches of Saints, with great pri-
viledges and Indulgencies.

THe firft Sunday of the *Ad-
vent* is celebrated at *Santa
Maria Maggiore.*

The fecond at S. *Croce di Jerufalem.*

The third at S. *Pietro.*

The *Wednefday* of that feafon
at *St. Maria Maggiore.*

The *Fryday* at the *Dodeci Apofto-
li.*

The *Saturday* at S. *Pietro.*

The Vigils of the Nativity at
S. *Maria Maggiore.*

In the firft Mafs of the Nativity at *Santa Maria Maggiore al Pre-
fepio.*

In the fecond Mafs at S. *An-
aftafia.*

In the the third at S. *Maria
Maggiore.*

On St. *Stephens* day at S. *Stefano nel Monte Celio.*

On St. *John* the Apoftles day at
S. *Maria Maggiore.*

The Feaft of the Innocents at
S. *Paolo.*

The day of the Circumcifion
of our Lord at *Santa Maria* beyond the *Tyber.*

The day of the *Epiphany* or
Twelfe day after Chriftmafs at S.
Pietro.

The *Septuageffima Sunday* at S.
Lorenzo without the Walls.

The *Sexageffima Sunday* at S.
Paolo.

The *Quinquageffima* at Santo
Pietro.

The firft day of the *Quadrages-
fima* or Lent at *Santa Sabina.*

The fecond at S. *Gregorio.*

The third at *San Giovanni* and
Paolo.

The *Saturday* at S. *Trifone.*

The first _Sunday_ of Lent at _S. Giovanni Laterano._

The _Munday_ at _San Pietro_ in _Vincola._

The _Tuesday_ at _Santa Anastasia._

The _Wednesday_ at _Santa Maria Maggiore._

The _Thursday_ of Lent at _S. Lorenzo_ in _Panisperna._

The _Fryday_ at the _Santi Dodeci Apostoli._

The _Satturday_ at _Santo Pietro._

The second _Sunday_ of Lent at _S. Maria_ in _Domenica._

The _Munday_ at _San Clemente._

The _Tuesday_ at _Santa Sabina_

The _Wednesday_ at _Santa Cecilia._

The _Thursday_ at _Santa Maria_ in _Transtevere._

The _Friday_ at _San Vitale._

The _Satturday_ at the _Santi Marcellino_ and _Pietro._

The third _Sunday_ of Lent at _S. Lorenzo,_ without the Walls.

The _Munday_ at _San Marco._

The _Tuesday_ at _Santa Potentiana._

The _Wednesday_ at _San Sisto._

The _Thursday_ at the _Santi Cosmo_ and _Damiano._

The _Fridry_ at _S, Lorenzo_ in _Lucina._

The _Saturday_ at _Santi Susanna._

The Fourth _Sunday_ of Lent at _Santa Croce_ in _Jerusalem._

The _Munday_ at the _Santi quatro Coronati._

The _Tuesday_ at _San Lorenzo_ in _Damaso._

The _Wednesday_ at _San Paolo._

The _Thursday_ at the _Santi Silvestro_ and _Martino._

The _Friday_ at _Santo Eusebio._

The _Satturday_ at _San Nicolo_ in _Carcere._

The fifth Sunday in Lent called the Passion Sunday at _San Pietro._

The Munday at _San Grisogono._

The Tuesday at _San Quirico._

The Wednesday at _Santo Marcello,_

The _Thursday_ at _Santo Apollinare._

The Friday at _S. Stephano_ in _Monte Celio._

The Satturday at _San Giovanni_ before the _Porta Latina._

The Palme _Sunday_ at _San Giovanni Laterano._

The _Munday_ at _San Prascede._

The _Tuesday_ at _Santa Prisca._

The _Wednesday_ at _Santa Prisca._

The holy _Thursday_ at _San Giovanni Laterano._

The good _Fryday_ called _Parasceve_ at _Santa Croce_ in _Hierusalem._

The _Satturday_ at _San Giovanni Laterano._

Easter day or the _Sunday_ of the Resurrection of our Lord at _Santa Maria Maggiore._

The _Munday_ at _San Pietro._

The _Tuesday_ at _San Paolo._

The _Wednesday_ at _San Lorenzo_ without the Walls.

The thursday at the _Santi Dodeci Apostoli._

The _Friday_ at _Santa Maria Rotonda._

The _Saturday_ before the Octave called _Sabato_ in _Albis,_ at _San Giovanni Laterano._

The _Sunday_ of the _Octave_ from Easter day called _Domenica_ in _Albis_ at _San Pancratio._

The Feast of the Ascention at _San Pietro._

The Vigil of the Pentecost at _San Giovanni Laterano._

The Pentecost _Sunday_ at _San Pietro._

The _Munday_ at _San Pietro_ in _Vincola._

The _Tuesday_ at _Santa Anastasia._

The _Wednesday_ at _Santa Maria Maggiore._

The _Thursday_ at _San Lorenzo_ without the Walls.

The _Friday_ at the Santi _Dodeci Apostoli._

And the _Saturday_ of this week of Penticost at _San Pietro._

The

The *Wednesday* of the Feasts in   The *Friday* at the *Dodeci Apost-*
September at *Santa Maria Maggi-*   *oli.*
ore.   The *Satturday* at *San Pietro.*

Besides which there are other stations for every Feast of those Saints
Apostles, Martyrs, Confessors, or Virgines to whom any Church
is dedicated in *Rome*, and for |the most part those Churches on the
daies of their Feasts are visited with a multitude of People, his S.
himself often celebrating Masse or at least being then present, atended
by a great number of Cardinals and Prelates.

Of the *Vatican* Library of the Pope.

THe *Vatican* Library of the Pope is every day frequented by learned Men, and meritoriously for that it is filled with the most
antient books in all the Professions, 'as well Greek, Latine, and Hebrew as other Languages writtten with the pen in Parchment
And ,tis certainly to be admired, that those Popes under so many
disgraces, negociations, Foreign and civil Wars and sackings of
Rome, should still apply their chiefest study and pain in heaping together Books, and preserving those collections.

  Sixtus the 5th in our time beautified and aggrandized it wonderfully adjoining to it a noble Fabrick, and causing most excellent pictures to be drawn about it: Which *Guglielmo Bianco* a *French* Man
praiseth in a singular Poem: and Fryer *Angelo Rocca* by way of History treates of it diffusely. As also *Onofrio Panuino* of the same Order.

  Many great Scholars have only desired favour from the Pope as
to publish an Index of the Greek and Latine Books extant in that
Library, that by this means recourse might be had to *Rome* from all
parts both for the enlightning and correcting Authors, who have
been altogether unseen, or are els printed full of errors. This the
noble City *Augusta* permitted, and by that publique Index set forth
invited all to go thither for comparing the uncorrected for their a-
mendment. How many bookes have *Francis* the first and *Henry* the second Kings of *France* sent forth to light. How many benefits
have the Republique of Scholars had from the Grand Duke of *Tusca-
nies* Bibliotheque: and how much more advantage would all the
world receive from such an Index of the Pontifical Library, which is
of splendidly royal.

  Other Libraries there are also in *Rome*, as that of the Capitol. That
which appertained to the Cardinal *Sirleto* now to Cardinal *Colonna*,
valeued at 20000. Crownes: That of the Family of *Sforza*, and that
of the *Farnesi*, abounding with Greek Authors.

  We pass by many Libraries of private persons no less replenished
with rare Books as that of *Fulvio Orsino*. That of *Aldo Manutio* (who
passed to a better life at green yeers)consisting of 80.thousandBooks.
We must observe though, that *Fulvio Orsino* in the yeer 1600.added
his to the Library of the Pope. And that *Ascanio Colonna* (never e-

nough to be praifed)bought that of *Sirleto* for 14 thoufand Crownes deputing to it intelligentKeeperswith honeft ftipends,that it may rather dayly increafe, then at all diminifh.

The great Duke of *Florence* his noble Library is known to have good numbers of Greek Books, and that of *Urbino*, of Mathematical Writers. That of the *Malatefti* is in *Cefena* in the *Minorites* Convent. In *Bologna* that of the preaching Fathers. In *Venice* that of the Republique. In *Padoua* is that of *Gio Vicenzo Pinello* famous enough: but lets return to the *Libraria Vaticana*.

'Tis certainly concluded that the Gentiles ufually preferved their Booksin the publiqueLibraries as well as private,&tis no lefs evident that the Catholick Church from Chrifts time to ours had alwaies in divers places facred Libraries to advantage ftudents: wherefore St. *Auguftine* in the Narration which he makes, *De perfecutione Arrianorum inEcclefia Alexandrina* faies,that in the Chriftian Churches there were Libraries,and that with the greateft care they preferved theirBooks: and accufeth the impiety of the*Arrians* amongft other things for their taking away and burning the Books of the Church.Saint *Jerome* likewife makes mention of the fame Libraries. when writing to *Pamachius* by his Books againft *Jovinianus* he faiesthat he kept in the ChurchesLibraries *Eufebius* alfo in his 119 Book at the 11 Chapter writeth, that the Church had holy Books in the Oratories, and that in *Dioclefians* dayes,(to the end the name of Chriftian might be wholly extinguifhed) the Oratories were overthrowen , and the books burnt nor does there want conjectures hereof from the holy Scripture for that Saint *Paul* writing to *Timothy*, commands him to tranfport with himfelf his Books to *Rome*, chiefly thofe in 'parchment: and in the firft to the*Corinthians*,he teftifies that in the*Corinthian* Churches,they ufed to read the Prophetick books.*Eufebius* in his 5 book of the Ecclefiaftical hiftory at the 10th. Chapter faies, that the Apoftle Saint *Bartholomew* going to prea ch the gofpel to the *Indians*, left there the Gofpel of Saint *Matthew* writ by his own hand: Which very copy, *Origene* afterwards found in the *Indies*, and from thence carryed it (as Saint *Jerome*averrs) to *Alexandria*, when he alfo brought from the Eaft the Canonical books of the old Teftament. Laftly the Hebrews diligently conferved their facred books, and on every Sabbath read the Books of *Mofes* in their Synagogues wherefore tis reafonable enough to believe , that the Chriftians have alwaies obferved their rule,of diligentlycopying and preferving the prophetick books thofe of the Apoftles and thofe of the Evangelifts: But the places where thefe books were layed up, were not alwaies called by the fame name, but fometimes *Archivium* a Treafury of *Rolls*,*fcrinium* a Coffer where evidences were kept, *Bibliotheca* or *Libraria* a Bibliotheque or Library as in feveral Authors appears.

Then indubitably they ufed to lay up in places deputed to that purpofe the Memorials of greateft importance , the Books of the Bible of the old and new Teftament,and the Books of the holy Fathers; many whereof written by their ownAuthors throughthismeanshave reached our times,and will continue to future Ages if God fopleafe,

And becaufe the collecting and conferving thofe books, required a great expence as well in writers, as Inquifitors, and confervators,therefore the richeft Chriftians comonly contribnted every one

fome

ſome proportion and part, as a common ſtock for theChurch to have the ſame effected.

And in particular we have great obligation to the Emperor *Conſtantine* the Great, who (as *Euſebius* recounts in his third Book of his life) without regard to the vaſt expence, made it his buſineſs to collect and ſecure the ſacred Books, which in the times of the perſecutions the Gentiles had wholy diſperſed.

After which the gathering, keeping, and chooſing Books, was particularly the charge of the Biſhops and Prieſts, for which end they were wont to maintain Notaries, Stationers, and Women exerciſed and skilled in writing, as may be gathered from the life of *Ambroſius* and of *Origene*. Among all other Collectors of Books *Pantenius* the Maſter of the *Alexandrian* School is eſteemed the moſt diligent: likewiſe *Pamſilo* the Prieſt and Martyr (as *Euſebius* relates) inſtituted and governed with great induſtry a fair Library, placing there the Books of *Origene* and ſuch other good Books as he could get written by the hand: of which *Cæſarean* Library St. *Jerom* againſt *Rufinus* takes notice. Furthermore *Alexander* the Biſhop of *Jeruſalem* got together a good quantity of Books, as of *Betillus*, *Hippolitus*, *Caius* and other Eccleſiaſtical writers, and with them compoſed a worthy Library, as *Fuſebius* teſtifies, who alſo confeſſeth himſelf to have been aſſiſted by the ſaid *Alexander* in his own Eccleſiaſtical Hiſtory.

And not to omit the diligence of ſome of later times in the like work, lets remember, that Pope *Clement* the firſt, ſucceſſor to St. *Peter*, who wrote many Epiſtles profitable to the *Roman* Church, deputed ſeaven Scriveners in the ſeaven præcincts of *Rome*, who were maintained out of theChurches Revenne for no other thing then diligently to ſearch out and write the Acts of the martyrs. And *Anicetus* the Pope made it his buſineſs to find out a ſecure place for the laying up the lives of the Martyrs wrote by thoſe Scriveners. Pope *Fabianus* ordained ſeaven Deacons, for ſuperviſors to thoſe Notaries, to take the better care in executing the charge of collecting and true recital of the Martirs lives: Of which Scriveners the Actions of the *Roman* Councel under *Silveſter*, give good teſtimony Pope *Julius* ſucceſſor to *Marcus* who followed *Sil.* determined that the ſaid Notaries abovenamed ſhould diligently gather together, whatever appertained to the amplifying, and fortifiing of the holy Catholick Faith, & that all the things by them writ ſhould be reviſed by the *Primicerio*, or chief, created to that purpoſe, who afterwards was to place and keep in the Church what he had approved.

Pope *Hilary* was the firſt (known) that built a Library, who erected two near, the Founts of the *Laterano*, wherein (for that in thoſe times there were but few Books, and they at great price becauſe wholly written by the hand) he cauſed the writings of the *Roman* Church, the decretal Epiſtles of Popes, the Actions of the Counſels, the recantations and opinions of the Hereticks, and the Books of the holy Fathers, to be layed up and preſerved for the publique uſe of the Chriſtians.

But to return to our purpoſe of the *Vatican* Library: we muſt know that beſide the abovenamed Libraries, the Popes uſed ſo great diligence in collecting books, as they put together one greater than the two former in the Popes Palace on the *Laterano*, which remained there about one thouſand yeers, till *Clement* the 5th. tranſlating the Apoſtolick Sea into *France*, with it carryed the ſaid Library in the *Laterano* to *Avignon* in *France*, which continued there about 120 yeers, till the difference was appeaſed between the Catholicks. Pope *Martin* the 5th. cauſed the ſaid Library to be reconveyed ro *Rome*, placing it in the *Vatican*, where his *S.* had then choſen and ſetled his Reſidence: where they were diſpoſed confuſedly without any order, and a good part loſt. Whereto *Sixtus* the 4th. having regard, & it appearing to him inſupportable, that ſo great a quantity of books ſhould go to ruine through ill government, he built a place on pur. poſe for them adorning it by all poſſible means, placing them me. thodically, and adding ſuch other Books as he could come by, and or- dered the Officers deputed to that end, to govern them with diligence, endowing it with a hundred Crowns a yeer in perpetuity, being the donative which the Colledge of writers of the Pontifical Letters was uſed to make the Popes yeerly, and this was beſtowed on the Library Keepers for their diligence and pains. This then is the *Vatican* Library, filled with the moſt choiſe Books that could be had a great part written in parchment with the pen: others printed: and their number exceeds ſix thouſand books.

Antiently the Preſident of this Library was called *Librario*, then *Cancellario*, whoſe office was to collect with diligence not only the Books, but alſo to copy the Bulls, the Popes decrees, the Acts and Conſtitutions of the Synods, and to keep every thing exactly, becauſe it appeared convenient, that the *Cancellario* or as he is now called the Secretary of the Pope, ſhould have the managing and preſerving of the Books, the Library being in thoſe dayes as twere the Office of the Secretary or Chancery: but in our times the Offices of the Chancery and of the Library are divided.

They uſed to elect Men of the greateſt knowledge and of good life for Preſidents of the Library as *Anaſtaſius* in the Life of Pope *Gregory* the ſecond relates, which *Gregory* he ſaies was firſt Preſident there who being ſent to *Conſtantinople* by Pope *Conſtantine* to the Emperor *Juſtinian* the ſecond, and being queſtioned by him he anſwered learnedly: and the Bibliothecary in the life of the ſaid *Gregory* the ſecond ſaies that he was from a boy brought up in the *Lateranian* palace, and being made Deacon by Pope *Sergius* took upon him the charge of the Library. at laſt *Sixtus* the 4th. on the 10 day of *July* 1475. being the ſixth of his Papacy, created a perpetual Keeper to the *Vatican* Library inveſting him in that Office by his Bull.

Bartolomeo Platina of *Cremona* the Apoſtolick writer, and familiar of *Sixtus* the fourth was the firſt preſident to the *Vatican* Library, for which ſervice he had 10 Crowns *per* Month for his maintenance, beſides proviſion for his own Table with 3 ſervants and one horſe, and the ordinary Vails, which the popes uſually allowed to their Familiants, as Wood, Salt, Oyl, Vinegar, Candles, Brooms, and other the like things.

Bartolomeo Manfredo a *Bolonian* Doctor of the Canons was by *Sixtus* the 4th. *annno.* 1481: in the 11th of his Popedome elected to that Charge in lieu of the deceaſed *Platina.* This *Manfredo* was a Familiar acquaintance of the Popes, and wonderfully learned. And to add ſplendor to this Office the Pope ordained that the Preſidents of the

Library

Library for the future fhould be the firft Squires of the Roman Popes
for ever, and fhould receive the accuftomed honors and profits: firft
giving fecurity to the Apoftolick Chamber of ten thoufand Duckats,
and taking an Oath to keep faithfully and diligently the Library. After *Manfredo* thefe following were fucceffively created.

Chriftophoro Perfona a Roman *Prior* of *Santa Balbina* in *anno* 1484.

Giovanni Gionifii a *Venetian in anno* 1487.

A *Spaniard* who was Arch-deacon of *Barcellona* in *anno* 1492. Poffibly this was that *Girolamo Paolo Cathalano* Canon of *Barcellona* Doctor of both Laws, who was *Chamberlain* of *Alexander* the fixth, whofe
books fet forth and communicated the Practife of the *Roman* Chancery, printed *anno* 1493. being the fecond of the third *Alexander*.

Giovanni Fonfalia a Spaniard Bifhop of *Iteran*, in *anno* 1493.

Volaterano Arch Bifhop of *Ragufa anno* 1505.

Tomafo Ingeranni, or *Fedra Volaterano anno* 1510.

Filippo Beroaldo a Bolonian 1516.

Zenobio Azziaiolo a *Florentine* of the preaching order 1518.

Girolamo Alexandro dell Mota Arch Bifhop *Brundufian* Cardinal 1537.

Auguftino Stenco Eugubino Bifhop of *Chiama*.

Marcello Cervino of *Monte Pulciano* Prieft, Cardinal of the holy crofs
in *Jerufalem*, was created by *Paul* the third. He would not accept the
ftipend, nor the four fportule or Fees ufually given to the Prefidents
of the Library but diftributed thofe emoluments to the two Latin
Correctors, and to him whofe charge was to find out and place the
Books.

Roberto de Nobili of *Monte Pulciano* Dean Cardinal, with the Title
of *Santa Maria* in *Dominica* was created by *Paul* the fourth *anno*
1555.

Alfonfo Caraffa Dean Cardinal of *Santa Maria* in *Dominica*, created
by *Paul* the fourth Anno 1558.

Marc Antonio Amulio Prieft Cardinal a *Venetian* Anno 1565.

Guglielmo Sirleto Prieft Cardinal of *Calabria* the 20th day of May
Anno 1582.

Antonio Caraffa. Prieft Cardinal, with the Title of *San Giovanni* and
Paulo a Neapolitan Anno 1585.

Guglielmo Alano Prieft Cardinal an Englifh man, created by *Clement*
the 8th. Anno 1591.

Marc Antonio Colonna Bifhop Cardinal, created by the fame *Clement*
Anno 1594.

Antonio Saulio Prieft Cardinal created by the fame *Clement* Anno
1597.

And becaufe twas impofible for one fingle perfon to give fufficient attendance to the government of fo many Books the fame *Sixtus*
the fourth gave to the Prefident of the Library, two other perpetual Keepers, perfons of good Faith, and diligence to affift in that
charge, allowing to each 3 crowns falary *per* Moneth, and his Dyet,
and the other abovenamed perquifits, as alfo for one fervant. The
firft of which were *Giovanni Caldelli* a Clerk of Lyons, and *Pietro Demetrio* of *Luca*, who was Reader in the Popes common Hall, created
the 10th yeer of *Sixtus* his papacy; the firft the 29th. of, *April* the fecond the firft of *May. Demetrio* being dead, *Julius* the fecond, the

sixth of *July* in the eighth yeer of his *Pontificacy* created *Lorenzo Parmenio* priest of the Chamber. This pope the 23d of *August* in the first yeer of of his Popedome granted a Load of Charcoals weekly to the said Keepers, but now for the whole yeer is allowed but 24 Load only: In the yeer 1535. *Fausto Sabeo* a *Brescian* Poet and *Nicolo Magiorano Hidronteno* succeeded these, the latter of whom being created Bishop of *Matancpoli* him succeeded *Guglielmo Sirleto*, and him his Brother *Girolamo Sirleto*, *Federigo Ronaldo Valneaſe* being created prothonotary followed *Sabeo*, and *Marin Ronaldo* Brother of the said *Federigo* succeeded to *Girolamo Sirleto*.

Furthermore the same *Sixtus* (that nothing might be wanting to the compleating the splendor of the pontifical Library) created three with the denomination of exquisite writers, the one in Greek a second in Latin, a third in Hebrew, with their Dyet, and four crowns a moneth, but *Paulus* the fourth doubled the greek salary and added two other Greek writers, and one Latin, to the one of which Greek writers and to the Latin he assigned five Crowns by the Moneth, and two Sportule, which is a certain Fee payed to the Pope or Saint *Peter*, by every perſon that got the better in any suite in Law, but to the other Greek he assigned two *Sportule* and four Crowns only. He likewise ordained one Binder with provision of foure Crowns.

Lastly *Marcello Corvino*. President of the Library instituted two Correctors and Revisors of the Latin Books, between whom he divided the benefits accruing to the Presidents denying to retain them to himself as aforetold, and gave two sportule to each, being the four due to himself as president, assigning a Salary of five Crowns to the one and four to the other and the tenth Crown which remained to him of the ten crowne by the Moneth assigned to the presidents he deputed that for him whom *Paul* the 4th had instituted for sweeper, to whom the regalies were not granted. The first Latin Correctors were *Gabriel Faerno* of *Cremona Nicolo Maggiorano*, to whom *Pius* the 4th. added a Greek Corrector, giving to each of them ten Crowns of gold by the Moneth.

CHAP. XI.

Of the Ceremony in kissing the feet
of the *Roman* Bishop.

CHAP. XI.

Taken out of *GIOSEFFO STEPHANO* Bishop of *ORIOLANO.*

Wherein is shewed, that for good reasons the *Pope* wears a Cross upon his Shoe or Slipper, and the *Christian People* kiss his Feet.

AMong the many things the Popes had given them to bear and carry for ensignes of Glory and dignity by the Emperor *Constantine* the Great, with which for long time together they have gone adorned, ware a pair of Slippers made of the whitest linnen cloth for the Ornament of their Feet. (which Slippers we may name Pumpes for their being so apted to the Feet) whereof we read an especial memorial in the Acts of *San Silvestre*, for that the Emperor *Constantine* commanded that the Popes of *Rome* should cloth their Feet with the purest Linnen, in imitation of the high Priests and antient Prophets, who we read in the fifth Book of *Herodian* were thus vested. And tis most certain, that the Sandals or slippers of the *Roman* Bishop are alwaies bedecked with some singular Ornament, differing from those which ordinary Bishops wear at the celebration of their Mass, otherwise how could the blessed *Antidius* near *Segeberto* in *Anno* 418 distinguish the Pope by the slippers he had on, nor could that have happened, if those of the Pope had not had a peculiar Mark differing from those of the Bishops. *San Bernardo* in his forty second Epistle declares that the slippers are a part of those Ensignes which the Popes are obliged to wear at the solemnizing of Mass.

The same thing also is averred by *Innocenzo* III. in his first Book *de Divinis Officiis*, in the 24th Chapter. *Ivo Cornatense*, in the 76th. Epistle, and in his speech *de significatione Indumentorum. Rabano* in his first Book the 22d. Chapter *Durando* in his third Book the 28th. Chapter and many others.

And although the *Roman* High Priests antiently used this sort of Shooing with the whitest Linnen, we must nevertheless, confess, that now the Custome is changed, and in lieu thereof are worne a certain red sort of shooing, with a cross wrought on them the occasion of which mutation may be attributed partly to the reverence of the People, and partly to the consideration of the Popes person.

Wherein will be manifested the humility of the Pope, who knowing all Persons prone to the kissing of his Feet, desired to have the sign

of

of the Croſs fixed thereon, to the end that ſo much honour might be payed to the moſt holy ſign of the Croſs rather than to his own proper perſon: And that his Holineſs would alſo reduce into the minds of the faithfull which kiſs his feet, the paſſion and death of our Saviour.   With great Judgment then, moſt honeſt intention and good end, have they introduced this wearing the ſigne of the Croſs upon the popes Sandals, ſince that the kiſſing of the croſs is an Act of the Reverence born to it, uſed in the moſt holy Church antiently, whoſe cuſtom it was in that manner to reverence not only the holy Croſſe, but alſo the holy Images of Chriſt and of the Saints, the Viſage and heads of which Images the faithfull of old accuſtomed to approach, in token of reſpect and honour, as *Niceforus* in his ſeaventeenth Book the 25th. Chapter recounts, and *Zonara* in the third tome of the Life of *Theodoſilo*.

The ſublime Enſigne of the *Romans* made in manner of the Croſs of the Saviour, which was wont to be born before *Conſtantine* the Emperor, and was adored by the Senate and the Souldiery, is called *Laboria*, perchance for that in Latine it ſignifies Labour, to wit for that that bleſſed Enſigne put the Souldiers in good heart and remembrance, when they were near toyled with fighting, or for that they bore up that Enſign when they marched, or els for that they muſtred the Souldiers under that Banner to ſignifie to them the pains they muſt take under it, as *Paolo Diacono*, relates in the 11th. of his Hiſtory, and *Nicolo Prinio* in the conſults of the *Burgari*, at the 7th. Chap and 23. *Paolino Nolano* demonſtrates very clearly in the 42d. Epiſtle, the Cuſtome, which was, that the princes and great Lords kiſſed the Croſs, ſubmitting to it all the Banners of their glory, and worldly Majeſty.

Nor have they born this Reverence to the Croſs alone, but alſo to all the Inſtruments of the Paſſion of our Lord, as *Sant Ambroſius* in a diſcourſe he makes of the death of *Theodoſius*, averreth, touching one of the Nayls which was pierced through the Feet of our Saviour. To come then to the other Head, wherefore we judge it convenient the change of the white ſlippers or ſandals, for ſlippers or ſandals with the Croſs wrought on them; we ſay that herein the Popes have endeavoured to demonſtrate expreſly the Image of the Apoſtolick charge becauſe they havinng received a charge to teach to all the world, and to preach the Goſpel, have likewiſe adorned their feet with the ſigne of peace and of the Goſpel: that ſo they may walk perfect through the World in vertue of the ſigne of the croſſe. *Iſaiah* the Prophet ſaith thus, Beautifull are the Feet of thoſe who preach Peace, and publiſh good tidings, as if that forſeeing this Uſage, he ſhould wonder, how the heads of the Chriſtian People ſhould find out ſo convenient an ornament to put upon their Feet, ſo that the Nations beholding them ſhould not only remain full of gladneſſe for the good newes which they had heard from them; but ſhould alſo perceive a certain content for having ſeen them all beautifull, all adorned, and ſignalized to the very feet with the figure of the holy Croſs. Becauſe tis uſual to weigh in qualified perſons, all their Actions, all their words, all their Veſtments and habits to their very feet; and ſo the Bridegroom praiſing his Spouſe in the *Canticles*, ſets down as a great concern, that having

fair

fair shoes she walked graciously.   *Tertullian* in his Book of the habits
of women, puts a difference between *Culto* Neatness, and *Ornamen-
to*,Ornament,saying that neatness consists in the quality of the Vests
as of Gold, Silver,and the like habiliments, but that Ornament consists in the disposition of the parts of that body which wears it. Then
the *Roman* Bishops, who reconcile and make Peace by way of their
Letters and Ministers to all Nations to the great astonishment of all,
have obtained and pursued the one and the other of the aforenamed
parts, that is to say Neatness and Ornament.

Furthermore the sign of the Cross is made on the forehead and
Breasts of the faithfull, to the end that as *Augustine* saith upon the
30th *Psalm*, they may not fear to confess the faith,and having overcome the Devil, they may carry the Banner of their Victory in their
forehead, therefore also is the same signe worne upon the feet of the
Pope ,that he by that sign may be directed in that good way through
which he is to lead all the People of God,thereby to shew unto the
Pope, that to him was given this holy priviledge to be our guide by
means of the Cross: wherein(saith Saint *Austin* in the 10th Sermon
de Sanctis Tom 10) are contained all the Mysteries and all the Sacra-
me nts, he fortifies (as we may say) his feet with the Cross, to the
end that he shewing the way and we walking in it,none may wander
from good thoughts. It may also be said that the Pope bears a Cross
upon his feet, that in all persecutions and dangers all his people may
recur securely to his Feet, where remedy may be had to overcome
the difficulties, and doctrine to oppresse heresies if need require, as
tis written in *Deutronomy* at the 33d. Chapter, *Qui appropinquat pe-
dibus accepit de doctrina ejus.* Weighing all which considerations,with
their foundation in the passion of Christ, very rationally have the
Popes placed this signe upon their feet,to evidence these mysterious
significations.   Which is so antient and firm, that in the old Images we see no Pope drawn or carved who hath not also the cross upon his Feet: from which considerations it appears manifestly, that
the perverse and wicked Hereticks of our times are in a great error,
for expressing their dislike of the Popes wearing a Cross upon his
feet, saying that tis an undervaluation and want of due reverence
payed to the Cross.

For answer whereunto by their favour: Is it not true (that as
Cirillus in 3. *Tomo contra Julianum* saies) the old usage was to paint
Crosses on the entrances into houses, and that (as *Nazianzenus* in his
oration against the same saies)on the garments of the Souldiers were
signed Crosses come from heaven, and that the Church to succor
dying persons with spiritual help, used to mark their feet with the
signe of the Cross, and that twas usual to mark the bodies of beasts
with the Cross, as saies *Sainctus Severus de Morbibus bono:* and *San
Chrysostome*, in his demonstration *Quod Deus sit homo.* Did they not
mark the houses, the publick places,the Vests, the Armories, and finally divers other usual things with the Cross, as *Leoncio Cipriottio* a-
gainst the Jews declares, to the end that in every place and in every action, we may rub up our drowsie memories with the passion of
Christ our Lord : And shall we afterwards say, that it expresseth little reverence to the Cross in placing it upon the feet of Christs Vicar, by which we not only are minded of the passion of our Saviour

N n n   when

when we behold it, but intend that thereby is signified, that we ought not alone to submit to the Cross, and tread down all worldly passions, which to the purpose are expressed in Scripture with the name of feet, but also for the Love of the passion of Christ to esteem at nought what ever happens under the Moon. The which cannot be so well signified, by placing the Cross in any other places but on the Feet of the Pope, to kiss which all the faithfull strivingly run together.

GIOVANNI STEPHANO to the purpose of the Exaltation of the Pope speaks after this manner.

The Reason wherefore they carry his Holiness upon Mens Shoulders

TIs not from the purpose to say somewhat of the Lifting up of the Pope, since that all old Authors when they speak of the Creation of any King or Emperour, say that he was elevated and it may be that *Claudianus* speaks to this sense.

Sed mox cum solita miles te voce levasset.

Nor was this the custom of the Barbarous Nations only, but even of the Romans themselves who having chosen any One for their Emperor, lifted him on high, and carryed him upon their Shoulders: so saies *Ammianus Marcellinus* in his 22 book speaking of *Julianus* made Emperor by the Souldiers of *France*; so sets forth *Cornelius Tacitus* in his 20 book and the same likewise speaks *Cassiodorus* of the Goths in his 20th Book *Variacum Epist.* 31. This custom *Adon* of *Vienna* manifests in the sons of *Clotharus*: *Julianus Capitolinus* speaking of the *Giordani*: and *Herodian* in his seventh book treating of the same. In which time, they did not only exalt the *Roman* Princes as aforesaid, and Princes of other Nations, but likewise the præfects of the City whom to honour the more they usually drew up and down the streets in a *Caroach* with an officer going before, who proclaimed, that the præfect came; and this is clearly demonstrated by *Siniachus* in his first book & *Cassiodorus* in his 6th. from 24. But the *Roman* Bishops who from God have chief authority over the eternal way, for demonstration of their dignity, were wont to be conveighed through the City in a certain Chariot, honestly, or meanly clothed, as *Ammianus Marcellinus*, in his 27th book avers in his conceipt of *Damascus* and *Urcisinus* to this point in that time when *Pretestatus* put on the *Pretesta* (which was a Robe the chief Magistrate of *Rome* wore when they sate in Majesty) being then designed Consul: he preposed the Bishoprick of the Christians to the Consulship of the *Roman* people, and was wont to say to *San Damascus* the Pope (as *San Girolamus* also relates in his Epistle to *Pammachius*
chius

chius)make me Bishop of *Rome*, and I will soon make my self a Christian, from which words we may comprehend, that even in those
daies the Pontifical dignity moved the minds of the principal and
greatest persons being that the Consulacy was a dignity to which all
others gave place, as in more Epistles *Cassiodorus* shews in the 10th.
book and *Protestatus* so he might have been high Bishop of the Christians would not only have deserted his old false Religion, but also
Consulship.

That it was the manner of the antient Priests to pass in Coaches
for greater reputation, *Tacitus* in his 12th book clearly proves,
who speaking of *Agrippina*, saies, That shee (to agrandize her reputation this way) was drawn to the *Campidoglio* in a Caroach a thing
then only permitted to the Priests and holy Druides for their dignity. This custom was likewise used by the Virgins (as may be collected from the first book of *Artimedorus*, his Positions) and chiefly
of the Vestals, who were carryed in Litters, attended by many servants with great Pomp, as Saint *Ambrose* relates in his first Epistle to
Valentinian.

But the *Romon* Bishops, besides the Chariot and Coach wherein
they publiquely passed through the City, had also a supportable Chair
wherein being sate it was carryed upon the shoulders of Men deputed to that service, and who lived upon that profession which is manifest enough, not only from that place of *Duo.iio*, where he saies,
that in the fifth Synod, was placed the Chair or Throne of the Apostolick confession, but also more clearly from the most antient *Roman* Order written before *Gelasius* the Popes time, wherein we finde
expressions to this sence *viz.*

When the Pope is entred into the Church, he does not instantly
advance to the Altar, but first goes into the Vestry sustained by Deacons, who received & assisted him, while he descended from his Chair
and to that effect the said Order several times relates the Ceremony
of placing the Pope in the Chair, when he was to take any Journey
and to sustain him by the Arms in descent from the Chair, being arrived at the place where he resolved to stay.

In which words is also to be observed, that the said Order calls this
Pontifical Chair in Latin *Sellare*, which properly signifies a Majestick Throne made for dignity , it being a Chair wrought with Art
and proportionable thereto.

As to the Popes being born up by hands, 'tis easily manifested,
that he was so supported not only at his descent from the Chair, but
also upon several other occasions when not at all in the Chair, which
is proved by the examples of many Popes : As *Stephen* the second
(saies *Palatina*, and *Francesco Giovanetto* in the 90th. Chapter was carried upon shoulders in the Church of *Constantine*, and then in the *Laterano* and *Adrian* the second was so born up in the *Laterano*
by the Clergy and by the chief of the Nobility the Comunalty then
contending with the Clergy and Nobility for that honourable
Office, as appears in the descriptions the 63d. Chapter, which begins. *Cum Adrianus Secundus, &c.* And *Gregory* the ninth was
so sustained in the *Laterano* , laded with Gemmes and Gold.

At which custome none ought to wonder , since so long before
prophesied by *Esaiah* in the 49th Chapter be these words. *Et ef-*

ferent filios tuos in Ulnis & filias ſuper humeros portabunt, in our Engliſh Tranſlation tis thus rendred.

And they ſhall bring thy Sons in their Arms, and thy Daughters ſhall be carryed upon their ſhoulders.

The occaſion for which cuſtome proceeds from the great reverence wherewith the Princes of the World ought to obſerve the Preſidents of the Church, which Princes ought not to omit any convenient honour due to the Church, and ſo conſequently to the head thereof. It ſtands with good reaſon too, that the Pope ſhould be born up on high, to the end that on the one ſide he may the better ſee and beſtow his Benediction on the People comitted to him, and that the People may on the other ſide behold their Head, acknowledging him for Gods Vicar, and thence fortifie themſelves in the confeſſion of the Catholick Faith.

The ſame *P I G H I O* ſpeaks of the Coronation of the Pope in this ſence.

ALL Princes for demonſtration of the Majeſty of Empire have worn a golden Crown. *David* who reigned before *Homer* and before all the antient writers at this day extant, had ſuch a Crown as is proved in the 12th. Chapter of the ſecond Book of Kings, the which he took to himſelf from one of the Cities of the *Ammonites* by him overcome in warr, which who deſires may read in the words of the cited Text. *Ciaſſare* King of the *Medes* (as ſaies *Zonara*, in the firſt Tome) ſent a certain beautifull Daughter of his own to *Cyrus* with a golden Crown upon her head, and with the whole province of *Media* for Dowry. The *Romans* triumphing carryed a Crown of Gold, as *Golliote* relates, which might ſeem improperly and erroneouſly declared, in reſpect all hiſtorians write that the Emperors Triumphing were crowned with Lawrel, if *Tertullian* did not remove this doubt in his Tract entituled *De Corona Militis*, and *Pliny* in his 21ſt. Book the third Chapter ſaies, that the Radiant Crowns were compoſed with Leaves of Gold and ſilver. *Zonara* in the ſecond Tome deſcribing the Pompe of a Triumph ſaies: that while triumphing they carryed two Crowns, one was placed on the head of the Emperor, which was of Lawrel, the other which was of Gold and enterwoven with pretious ſtones, was born up over the head of the Emperour by the hands of a publique Miniſter, who ſtood upon the ſame Chariot whereof *Juvenal* ſpeaks in the tenth Satyr, ſaying.

> *Tantum orbem, quanto cervix non ſufficit ulla,*
> *Quippe tenet ſudans, hanc publicus, & ſibi Conſul*
> *Ne placeat, curru ſervus Portatur eodem.*

And

And *Valerius Paterculus*, faies that this Crown of Gold, was of the colour of a Rain-bow, to demonſtrate the ſigne of a certain Divinity, (ſpeaking of *Auguſtus Cæſar Octavius* in his ſecond Book. As alſo ot the ſame make clear mention, calling it *Radiante*, and *Lucide*, *Suetoninus*, in the life of *Auguſtus* the 44th Chapter. *Pliny* in his *Panegyrick*, the unknown Author in the *Panegyrick* dedicated to *Maximilianus* and *Latinus Peccatus* in *Panegyrick*, whoſe words would take up too much room to ſet down here.

Moreover *Ammianus Marcellinus* in the 17th. book treating of the ſharp pointed Pyramids, faies that they were wont to place Crowns on the heads of ſtatues: which he again confirms in the 24th Book, from which teſtimonies *Lazius* collects in his 9th. Book of Commentaries of the *Roman* Republique, that our Predeceſſors derived the cuſtome of placing on the heads of the Images of Saints in the Churches, Crowns figured in the form ot the raies of the Sun, chiefly for that thoſe images being adorned with ſuch Crownes, ſeemed to have, I know not what kind of ſplendour and Divinity: which reaſon, though it be not, altogether from the purpoſe, yet tis not altogether to be, maintained: for that we rather think, that this uſage and cuſtome had its original from that ſplendour which hath been often ſeen miraculouſly, to ſhine on the heads ot the Saints: Being that (as *Abdias* in the 5th. Book, and *Euſebius* in the ſecond of his Hiſtories relate) the Apoſtles were often overſhadowed with ſuch a Light, as human eye could not behold them, as of old fell out to *Moſes*, whoſe Face (when he had had that near conference with God) did ſhine ſo bright, that *Aaron* and the children of *Iſrael*, were afraid to come near him, as is recorded in the 34th Chapter of *Exodus*.

To return then to our ſubject. The *Perſian* Kings had a Crown to be worn on their heads which *Zonara* ſets down in greek by its proper name, which can neither be commodiouſly expreſſed either in Latin or vulgar tongue: and it was a capital offence among the *Perſians* for any one to put the Kings Crown upon his head as *Dion Chryſoſtomus* denotes in his firſt oration *De libertate & ſervitute*. Likewiſe the prieſts of the Gentiles wore a crown upon their heads, for demonſtration of that repute which appertained to the ſplendidneſs and maintenance of their Sacerdotal office: whence the Antients were ſtupified, at a ſuddain view of the great Prieſt of the *Comani*, to whom (as *Strabo* writes) was granted the firſt honour next the King, and to wear a Royal Crown. Beſides in *Emeſa* a City of *Phœnicia*, the Prieſts went clad with a long robe, having a Crown of pretious ſtones of various colours in token of Majeſty upon their heads. Which Ornament *Antoninus* being made Emperor of the *Romans*, by the multitude, the Souldiery and the Prieſts of the Sun, would not part with again, as *Herodianus* in *libro quinto* clearly proves: and ſo afterwards the Emperors of *Conſtantinople* triumphing, elected rhis ornament, which was called by a proper name as we read in the life ot *Baſilius Porfirogenitus. Triumphum duxit tiara tecta; quam illi tuphum appellant*, although ſome modern Authors call it *Calipera*, as faies *Niceforus Gregorius* in *libro ſexto*.

Our Biſhops then having two royal Dignities, to wit the ſpiritual and temporal, deſervedly wear a double crown, as *Innocent* the third in his third sermon *De coronatione Pontificis*, confirms, saying that the Pope bears the Mitre in token of the spiritual power, and the Crown in testimony of the Temporal, both which are conferred upon him by God omnipotent, King of Kings and Lord of Lords.

But let us examine a little whether the Mitre, and the Crown, are Ornaments adapted to the Ecclesiastical customs.

The mitre by *Snidas* is called the swathe or Fillet of the head, bound about with gold and silver as *Brissonius* explains: and *Eusebius* in his second book, the first Chapter, calls it a shelter; with which Saint *James* the Apostle called the Brother of our Lord, was suddainly adorned, when by the Apostles he was chosen and consecrated Bishop of *Jerusalem*: which Ornament, although it took beginning with *Aaron* Priest of the Hebrew Law, is nevertheless received into the Christian Church, to the end that therewith the Bishops of all Nations may be adorned. *Policrates Ephesinus* wore the Mitre (as *Eusebius* in the 31st Chapter of the third Book relates) as Priest of *Ephesus*: and likewise the other Priests wore almost all the Ornaments of the antient Priests, as the Robe, and the Mitre, that they might appear the more adorned and majestick saies *Eusebius* in his Book; whereof *Amalarius*, *Rabanus*, and others the gravest Authors treat more amply.

What we have spoken touching the Mitre is without contradiction, and is held for truth by the consent of many and sundry Nations, but what is to be spoken touching a Kingdome, and a Royal Crown, is not so perspicuous to all, wherefore to our best power we will endeavour to manifest the same.

Then first is to be observed, that tis the common opinion of all, that this sort of Ornament upon the head of the Pope had its original from the Emperor *Constantine* the Great, as appears in the Acts of *San Silvestre* the Pope: the same opinion is also embraced by all other *Roman* Bishops, as by *Leo* the ninth in the 13. chapter of his Epistle against the presumption of *Michaele*, and *Innocent* the third in his first Sermon of the blessed *Silvester*, confirms That *Constantine* the great at his departure from *Rome* to *Constantinople*, would have bestowed his own Crown upon *San Silvester*, which he refused, but in lieu thereof put a covering upon his head entirely circular, and a little after *Innocent* follows in words to this sence: And for this cause the *Roman Bishop*, in testimony of Empire, wears a Regal crown called in Latin *Regnum*, and in testimony of his Pontificacy he wears a Mitre, which is most convenient, for him in all times and places universally, because the spiritual power hath been ever esteemed for the Prior, more worthy and more great then the Temporal. And reason will yeeld, that *San Silvester* would not wear that Crown, but such a one as only covered the Temples, in respect his head was shaven as the Popes ought to be. Which shaving gave good reason that twas not decent to wear such a Diadem, but rather that circular covering which he chose named properly *Tiara Phrygia*, whereof *Juvenal* speaks in his sixth satyr saying.

Et Phrygia vestitur bucca tiara.

Which Ornament may be supposed to be borrowed either from

Phrygia or *Phœnicia*, as we pleafe, becaufe the *Phrigians* had their
original from the *Phœnicians.* And that this was given the Pope by the
Emperor *Conftantine* the great, is moft evident in the Acts of *San Silvefter*, where the Emperor reckons up thofe things, that he had beftowed on the Pope, and being come to this, gives it the name *Phry-
ginm*, as t was its proper name; but in refpect t was not manifeft to
all, what thing *Phrygium* denoted, he explains himfelf in the fence
by us fet down, faying

et Phrygium nempe tegmen capitis five Mitram.

This particular required fo much explanation, for that *Theodorus
Balfamones*, confounding the fignification of *Phrygium*, by joining it
with the fubfequent *Lorum*, which imports a perfect different thing
hath caufed many to erre in beleeving that *Phrygium* and *Lorum* put
together do denote *Pallinm*, the Cope which Arch-Bifhops wear by
the conceffion of the higheft Bifhop. But t is not convenient for us to
dwell longer upon the difpute, let the intelligent read the latin *Itinerary* in this place, where they'l meet an ample difcourfe upon the fig-
nifications of thefe words.

Other authors will have, that this Crown came not from *Conftantine* but from *Clodoveo*, as they labour to draw from *Segeberto* under the yeer of our Lord 550. who fpeaks to this fence, *Clodovveus*
the King received from *Anaftafius* the Emperor, the Codicils of the
Confulacy, a Crown of Gold with Jewels, and the red garment, and
on that day he was called Conful and King, but the fame King fent
to Saint Peter at *Rome* the Crown of Gold with the Jewels, the Royal Enfigne, which is called *Regnum*.

Armonius alfo confirms in his firft book the 24th. Chapter, that
from *Clodoveus* the Pope had the Crown: and *Anaftafius* the Library
Keeper under Pope *Hormifda*, teftifies that Saint *Peter* received
many gifts: In whom I have read, that in the yeer 776 that *Philip*
the firft Pope and *Conftantine* the fecond Pope were both confecrated in *San Peters* Church (but we muft obferve that the antient Authors under the word confecration underftand alfo the ceremony of
coronation) for that when they fay, that *Charles* the great was confecrated Emperor, they alfo by it underftand he was Crowned,
whence we may draw, that the Coronation of the Pope, had its
rife in long fince paft times, fince that in the yeer 683. under *Agathone* the firft, and *Benedict* the fecond, was raifed the cuftome of giving moneys at the coronation of the Pope, and of expecting the
authority of the Emperor. *Eugenius* the fecond was crowned the
22d. of *May* in the yeer 824. *Benedict* in the yeer 855. *Formofus*
the firft in 891. But after *Clement* which happened in *anno* 1044. all
fucceeding Popes were crowned as (*Panuinus* obferves) in fuch a manner, as by it from that time forwards, the Prophecy of *Ifaiah* in
the fixty firft Chapter may be well known to be fulfilled, where
he faies as our Englifh Tranflation renders it: *For he hath clothed
me with the garments of Salvatio, he hath covered me with the
Robe of Righteoufneffe, as a Bridegroom decketh himfelf with ornaments*: The *Italian* faies, they (meaning the Priefts) are crowned
as Bridegroom; after that the Pope is elevated to this fupreme dig-

O o o 2   nity

nity, he wears the garments of eternal peace, and a Crown upon his head: This is that Son of *Eliachim* spoken of from God by *Isaiah* the Prophet in the 22d. Chapter, to whom even at that time God promised the Robe the Crown and the Key, as you may read in the 20. 21, 22, 23, and 24. verses of that Chapter and so forwards: The Crown is an Ensigne of Empire, the Robe is a signe of familiar government, the which things are found in their excellency in our Pope. So in the 14th Chapter of the *Revelation* of Saint *John*, at the 14th verse tis said that Christ (named the Son of man) appeared sitting on a white cloud, adorned with a golden Crown upon his head. And in the 19th. of the *Revelations* about the 11th. verse tis said, that the same Word of God appeared upon a white horse, with many Regal Crowns upon his head and all his Friends, as may be read in the subsequent verses.

For this occasion principally were these significations by Crowns to wit that Christ through his Wisdom (signified by the figure of a Crown of Gold) hath obtained victory over all Creatures, and subjected them to his Dominion. So likewise the *Roman* Bishop who is ouer all Nations, who hath brought all the People under his authority, (by the *consignation* and power of God) deservedly puts on the covering of his head three Crowns, thereby demonstrating that in glory, Authority, and great works, he surpasseth all the other Kings and Princes of the world.

After so many fore-passed Popes, *Paulus the* second created in the yeer 8465. of the noble *Venetian* Family *Barbi*, as he was of a fair aspect and great Spirit, so he took great care to adorn the papal Mitre, with pretious Jewels and curious workmanship. Lastly let us advertise the Reader that in those breifs written by *Cæsar Costni* in the third chapter of the first book of his various doubts deceives himself, where he would maintain that the Popes bearing a Mitre with three Crowns proceeds from those mysterious significations by him alleaged, when indeed there is no necessity of them and let thus much suffice.

Of the holy yeer of Jubile which is celebrated in *ROME* every twenty fifth year.

The Narration of *P. M. GIROLAMO da CAPUGNANO* of the preaching Order. Extracted from the Book of the Holy Yeer.

CHAP. XII.

GOD granted to the *Jewes* divine benefits indeed, whereupon afterwards that Nation boasted, saying, That his divine Majesty had not treated other People after that manner: But those graces which the Church our Mother hath received from the good-

ness

nefs of God do far furpafs and exceed the Benefits beftowed upon
the Hebrew People : For that the Lord that fhe might be clean and
adorned in his fight, gave the blood of his only Son to wafh her, and
the Treafure of his Wifdome to beautifie her.　Among the other benefits conferred on the Hebrew Synagogue, that of the yeer of Jubile was moft excellent, called moft holy, for that it was the yeer of
remiffion and of the commencement of all things, which the Omnipotent God ordained to be from 50 to 50 yeers. The like grace being due to our Church the Spoufe of Chrift (though with a different
end, for that the Synagogue attended only to temporal affairs, and
the holy Church to fpirituals fingly) by divine difpofition fhe
thought convenient to ordain alfo the yeer of Jubile, though at
firft only from 100. yeers to 100. yeers. perhaps to draw to
good ufe, the antient diabolick cuftom of the celebration
of the fecular Games', which to this end were celebrated every
hundredth yeer in *Rome,* with a preceding general invitation from
Cryers, who proclaimed through the ftreets come to the games, the
which none ever faw fince, nor fhall again : which drew into the
City of *Rome* infinite People of all Nations for the fervice of the devil: And all thofe Nations fince the inftitution of the yeer of Jubile, render themfelves at *Rome* though with much better reafon *viz.*
to ferve the true God, for the falvation of their own fouls : nor
ought our pains feem ftrange to any, for what is faid concerning the
mutation of evil into good, becaufe that not only in this, but in
divers other occafions the holy Church hath had this aime, to confecrate that to God, which the foolifh generations had before time
dedicated to Satan, as may be feen in divers Temples of *Rome,*
now dedicated to the true Lord, and his Saints, which were formerly the Temples of Idols ufed for the diftribution of candles, and to
make their Feafts, as in *San Pietro* in *Vincola,* the firft of *Auguft,* the
firft of thofe ceremonies was made in *Rome,* in honour of *Februa*
by the *Romans* taken for a Goddefs, the other in memory of the triumph of *Auguftus Cæfar.* We find that *Boniface* the 9th. in the yeer
1300. publifhed the yeer of Jubile by his Bull, wherein he declares
as a Reftorer rather then an Inventor or inftitutor of this yeer :
And tis no wonder, that we find no firm teftimony of its inftitution
before that time, becaufe the Church hath had fo many perfecuti-
ons, and fo great toiles, that tis a miracle that any antient Memorials are preferved rather then a wonder that fome are loft. At that
time then, the Pope in writing divulged this yeer, conceding entire
and plenary remiffion of offences and punifhments every hundredth
yeer, which number of (Centum) one hundred, bears alfo a certain
fenfe of returning to good from evil, as is fully proved b y *Girolamus* and *Beda,* principal Ecclefiaftical writers.

Clement the fixth at the Inftance of the *Romans* reduced Jubile to
every fiftieth yeer, chiefly for that the life of man is fo fhort, that very few arrive to one hundred yeers, and for that in the number *quin-
quaginta* fifty, are contained many myfteries pertinent to the Chriftian Religion ; but principally it fignifies remiffion and pardon, the
proper effect of the Jubile . Moreover the Jewifh fynagogue had
its Jubile every 50. yeers, fo that if for no other reafon, at leaftwife
that the Synagogue might not appear richer then the Church twas

fit, that ſhe ſhould likewiſe have a Jubile every fifty yeers.

Urban the ſixth reduced it to thirty three yeers for the increaſe of the Church treaſure, afterwards to be diſpoſed of by Saint *Peter* and his ſucceſſors on the like occaſions.   But laſt of all *Paul* the ſecond reduced it to every 25th yeer, and ſo *Sixtus* the fourth his ſucceſſor obſerved it, as in like manner have all following Popes done. The which we muſt believe was made for many conſiderations, and chiefly for theſe, for that the world as it grows old becomes worſe both in quantity and quality of Life; ſo that through the thouſand dangers which alwaies threaten life, and through the infinite Sins wherein many Creatures are involved, it hath appeared good to reduce the time of Remiſſion to a ſhorter time, whereby to offer frequent invitations to all, to accept the ſpiritual Medicine of Redemption of ſo great vertue) and to fly the works of iniquity.

As to what appertains to the name, tis to be obſerved, that it may be called in Latin *Jobileus & Iobileus*, of which the laſt is leaſt uſed, notwithſtanding that by the vulgar, tis more frequently called *Giubileo* than otherwiſe : This word is not derived from *Giubilo*, which ſignifies Mirth and content (although in truth it ought to be a yeer of rejoycing) but from the hebrew word *Jobel*, wich is as much as to ſay a Trumpet or Sacbut, for that the Iſraelites the ſeventh month before the fiftieth yeer uſed to proclaim the yeer of Jubile with the ſound of Trumpets : furthermore the Hebrew word *Jobel* alſo ſignifies remiſſion and beginning, the proper actions for the yeer of Jubile, for then the *Jews* remitted all debts, and returned all things to their firſt ſtate.

The Pope cannot concede greater indulgences, then thoſe which are granted in the yeer of Jubile, for then they open the treaſury of the Church, and beſtow on every one as much as is abſolutely neceſſary for him, pardoning to him ſins and penances, as well impoſed as not impoſed, freeing of him wholly and abſolutely from purgatory, yea although he ſhould have forgottē his mortal ſins in his confeſſion or that he ſhould not have confeſſed the Venial ſins (for tis not of neceſſity to make cōfeſſion of Venial ſins although ſuch muſt ſuffer pains in purgatory for them, if they be not in ſome way cancelled in this world) in ſuch manner, that the ſoul that in that time ſhall part from the body, doth inſtantly fly to enjoyment of the felicity of Paradiſe.

Our Jubile hath certain ſimilitudes with that of the Jewes, for that they proclaimed the yeer before, ſo do we ours : That they publiſhed in the Piazzaes, we ours in the Churches: that they with Trumpets, we ours with the voice of the Preachers : In that they left the Land unmanured, ours by the merits of Chriſt and his Saints ſupplies our Labour : in that Servants became free, in ours we acquire ſpiritual liberty with pardon of ſins and penances, in that they redeemed their Credits, in ours we receive pardon for our offences : in that ſould poſſeſſions returned to their firſt Patrons, in ours our crimes being cancelled the power and virtue of the ſoul is vivified : in that baniſhed perſons returned to their Countrey, and in ours, who departs this life, immediately aſcends to the heavenly Countrey.

Boniface

Boniface the eighth opened the doors of the Church *Vaticano*, and beſtowed moſt ample indulgence s of all ſins; *Clement* the ſixth , added the doors of the Church *Lateranenſe*, ordaining as is above declared.   *Paulus* the ſecond afterwards added *Santa Maria Maggiore* and *San Paolo*, in the *Via Oſtienſe*, for viſitation. *Gregory* the 13th. in *anno* 1575. ordained, that who would participate the grace of the Jubile , ſhould firſt communicate in the yeer of Jubile : all plenary indulgences are underſtood to be ſuſpended with certain mutations of words, of which the Authors treating on the Jubile, ſpeak to that purpoſe.

The Hebrews procl aimed their Jubile the 10th day of the ſeventh moneth of the forty and ninth yeer .   Ours , we publiſh on *Aſcention* day in the yeer preceding the twenty fifth yeer, upon two pulpits in the Church *San Pietro*, reading the Popes Bull in Latin and the vulgar.

We begin our Jubile , on the Vigil of the birth day of our Lord in the evening, when the Pope with great ſolemnity opens the door of the Church *San Pietro*, which at all other times ſtands continually walled up : and he cauſeth the Lords Cardinals at the ſame time in the ſame manner, to open the doors of the other deputed Churches , all which doors (the yeer ended) are again ſhut up.

In the holy yeer, that is to ſay the Jubile, reſort ſo great concourſe of People from all Countreys to *Rome*, that hiſtorian s write, that at the time of the Jubile of Pope *Boniface* , *Rome* was ſo full of people, that one could hardly paſs in the City, thongh ſo great: and in the yeer 1505. the feet of *Gregory* the thirteenth, in one morning were kiſſed by thirteen thouſand perſons. *Clement* the 8th. in *anno* 1600. would needs waſh the feet of divers Prelates, and other poor ſtrangers come to the Jubile: and the moſt illuſtrious Cardinals among which were *Montalto* and *Farneſe* expreſſed great charity and homility to poor pilgrims.

That tis convenient to celebrate the Jubile in *Rome*, rather then any other City is maintained by pregnant reaſons: *Rome* is the moſt worthy and noble of all other Cities and we therefore underſtand when we name *Citta* or City, without any other appellation, that it muſt be *Rome*. She hath had the Empire, is the head, the Miſtris, and a compendium of the World. She is full of Riches : hath beauty in her Scite, her Country, fertility of ſoyl, great comodiouſneſs from the Navigation of the *Tyber* , and the proximity of the Sea. She is the common Countrey of all, and in her are of all Nations, and every people may there find a proper Church for their own Nation, as in deed moſt Countreys have.   There Religion flouriſheth more than elſewhere as appears by the infinite Prieſts and Fryers, which there at leaſtwiſe in their diuine duties, if not continually praiſe the Lord and pray for all.   There the Churches are much viſited , the Poor releived, the virgins married , and many other pious works performed worthy of perpetual memory. She is a City of ſingular ſanctity, and in her are placed the moſt noted things appertaining to our Religion as the Manger wherein our Lord was layed at his birth, the ſwadling clothes, the Cradle, the garment, the Coronation Robe, the Crown of thorns , the Nailes, the Iron of the Launce, the croſs and the Title of Chriſt. In it are bodies of Apoſtles, of Martyrs,

of Confessors, of Virgins, and infinite Reliques of Saints. She is
the seat of the Pope, who is Prince of the Church, Vicar of God,
Pastor of all, who when abroad, is beheld, admired and adored by
all, every one seeking to kiss his Feet, wondring at the *grandezza* of
the Cardinals, the gravity of the Bishops and the multitude of the
Priests. A treasury of Indulgencies in *Rome* lye continually exposed
to whomsoever needs them, where in former times the Christians
were persecuted and more cruelly intreated then in any other
place. And finally the Faith of the *Romans* was and is such, that e-
ven in the Apostles times, it was preached through the world, that
is to say in that part only then styled *Roman* before twas Christianiz'd
Rome, then (which in greek imports strength, in hebrew Greatness)
being the most worthy place of the whole world, with good reason
in her and not elsewhere, ought the Jubile to be celebrated.

The Narration of *STEPHANO PIG-HIO* touching those military Ensignes, which the *Pope* useth to bestow on temporal Princes.

CHAP. XIII.

THE *Roman* Bishop useth to bestow great honour on Princes,
which for all that doth seldom happen, from the rarity of
the occasions for which they are sought. This custom was
most antient, begun with the foundation of the holy scripture in
the history of the *Maccabees* (part of our *Apocrypha*) as we read in the
15th. Chapter of the second book of *Maccabees*: That *Judas* the
Captain of the Israelite Army before he came to battail against *Nicanor*, saw in a Vision *Onias* the high Priest, holding up his hands
towards Heaven, and praying for the whole people of the Jews: and
Jeremias the Prophet giving unto him the said *Judas* a sword of gold
exhorting him to give battail in these words: Take this holy sword
a gift from God, wherewith thou shalt wound thy adversaries,
wherewith *Judas* being comforted, drew to battail on the sabbath
against the Enemies, and behaved himself so well, that he slew
not less then thirty five thousand Men, with *Nicanor* their Captain
and so remained victorious. Hence then proceeds the custome, that
the *Roman* high Priest every yeer, the night before the Nativity, before he begins the Duties, blesseth and consecrateth a sword, with
the scabbard, the belt, and the pummel of gold, and a hat placed on
the top of it, not made after the common sort, of Felt, but of the
finest blew silk, with the whitest Ermine skinns round about it,
and a Crown of gold enterwoven all over and set out with Jewels of
good value. This is a noble donative wch. the Pope provides only of
that night, to bestow it upon some Christian Prince, who either hath
done or is to undertake some notable impress for the Christian Religion

gion : nor is this without myſteries, but hath many, the which every Chriſtian Prince ought to know, and conſider.

The *Roman Rivale* teacheth us, that the ſword ſo conſecrated,
tipifies the infinite power of God, which is in the eternal word,
wherewith God hath created all things : Which word on that night
put on human fleſh, and to which the Father Eternal gave all Power,
as himſelf declared about the time of his Aſcention into heaven, and
then conſigned it to Saint Peter, and to his ſucceſſors, whoſe duty
tis to govern that holy Church then newly by him inſtituted, and
conſecrated with his own blood, againſt which hell ſhould not pre-
vail: Commanding that they ſhould teach all thoſe things which
were learned from him, and to invite and intreat, all Nations
(through Baptiſm and the Goſpel) to enter this new City, out of
which there is no ſalvation, and in which they muſt obey the Laws
of the divine Empire. Who is not ſurprized with conſideration of
the diſpenſations of God, in the divine Majeſties election of this City *Rome*, for the head and bulwark of the Chriſtian Republique,
which was upon the point at that time Head and Lady of the whole
world. Whence Saint *Peter* the Governour of the firſt Church was
deſtinated to this Province, and twas commanded to him, that the
Croſs ſhould Triumph in the *Campidoglio*, to the end that thereby and
thence the light of eternal truth might with the more facility be
diſperſed into all parts.

By the ſword then thus conſecrated is denoted that Empire, and
that ſupreme power of government upon Earth, which Chriſt left
to Saint *Peter* his Vicar, and to his ſucceſſors; and that the *Roman*
Biſhop ought to be acknowledged for the head of Chriſtianity,
whom, all thoſe that tender their own ſalvation, ought to obey and
ſerve in ſpirituals for the love of Chriſt.

Furthermore that ſword ſignifies, what prudence, and Juſtice, e-
very Prince ought to obſerve, and becauſe the ſharp point wounds
where tis thruſt on by the hand, therefore the handle of this ſword
is adorned with gold, a metal which amongſt the Antients impor-
ted Wiſdom, whereby the Prince ought to learn, that near his hands
wiſdome muſt have her ſeate, that ſo he may not tranſact any thing
raſhly, nor without due conſideration. Gold hath been taken for the
ſymbol of Wiſdome, from her ſimilitude in Excellency, for as the
one ſurpaſſeth and maſtereth all metals in goodneſs and value, ſo
Prudence or Wiſdome, as we may ſay, ſurpaſſeth and overcometh
all other things, And this cauſed *Solomon* in his proverbs to make
his exhortation ſaying, My Son poſſeſs thou Wiſdome, which is
better than Gold, and get thou Prudence, for this is more pretious
than Silver, Saint John in the *Apocalyps* calleth wiſdome enflamed
Gold, which penetrates the breaſt with the ardour of the holy Spirit. The *Magi* offered Gold to Chriſt then an Infant, and the *Egyp-
tians* were deſpoyled of their Gold by the, *Iſraelites*, the one and the
other thereby ſignifying, Wiſdome in a miſtical ſence; and twas ſo
in truth ſpoken literally as our hiſtories relate *Plato* (whoſe doctrine
did not much diſagree from the Chriſtian) often compares Wiſdome
and the Beauty of the mind to pure gold. Finally the Aunt and
Gryphen of *India* ſignified no other thing wch. *Animals* (as antiquity
feigned) got together as much gold as poſſibly they could and after-

wards kept it with diligence: even so Wisdome is not to be had
without labour, and noblenesse of mind; the Aunt here being an
embleme of a laborious Creature, and the Gryffen (feigned to proceed from the copulation of an Eagle and a Lyon) here represents
the greatness of mind. Whence the same antients wisely and properly dedicated the Aunt and the Gryffen to *Apollo* the God of wisdome.

Moreover the sword signifies the Tongue, the best and worst
member in Man, as it happens to be imployed : and therefore the
antient said ,that evil spoken men carryed a sword in their mouth :
and *Diogenes* the Cynick, seeing a fair young man to speak dishone-
stly, sayed to him, art thou not ashamed, to draw a sword of Lead
out of an ivory scabbard? and in *Isaiah* we read *Posuit os meum quasi
gladium acutum* : and Christ in the Gospel saies, *Non veni pacem mit-
tere sed gladium*, where we see, that by the sword is intended the
word preached from God ; and so in other places of Scripture under the name word, is comprehended the tongue or the sword
wherefore aptly also to our purpose it may receive the same signification, the Pope giving to understand to Princes, that they in particular ought to have their tongue and speech adorned with Gold,
that is to say clothed with wisdom and prudence, with which sword
they ought to separate the good thoughts from the bad, and by their
wise counsels to penetrate and see into the very hearts of o-
thers.

To this misterious sword the holy Pope adjoyns a belt interwoven with gold, which even of old was a sign of Majesty and military
dignity: well then may the Prince (on whom tis bestowed) apprehend the exhortation by it given him, to demean himself well for
the holy Church against all factions.

The Hat, which is the covering of the head, the most noble part
of man, is an Ensigne of nobility and liberty, which hat also antiently was wont to be made in the form of a half sphere, as twere
one part of a great egg divided just in the midst, but in later times
our modern ar ificers not apprehending the significations, or willing
to fructifie humours, make it after another fashion. Its round form
putting us in minde of Heaven, by which we are covered, and ad-
viseth the Prince, to direct all his actions to the glory of God, and
the benefit of his soul, for whose eternal dwelling were the Heavens
made: the celestiel colour of the said hat denotes the same
thing.

The white colour of the skins and the Pearl, signifies that sincerity and purity of the mind wherewith the Prince ought to be endowed, to the end he may in the end accomplish a concomitance
with those most sacred minds, the wch to that time he hath or ought
to have endeavoured to imitate with all clearness of conscience. The
Colour white, hath been alwaies esteemed gratefull to the Almighty, being a mark of Inocency & therfore from great antiquity all men
in the duty of sacrifice used to cloth themselves therwith; *Pythagoras*
his sentence is, that every white thing is good. Fully in his second
book *De legibus* saies, that white is very agreeable to God. We might
also bring testimonies to this purpose from *Cicero* and others, but to
what end should we search prophane authors: since Christ himself

in

in his glorious Transfiguration made himself obvious to many, clo.
thed with rayments white as snow: and the Angels also who were
at the sepulchre of our Lord the morning of his resurrection day,
when the women went to seek after the most holy body, presented
themselves in white garments: from the above specified records the
Prince is advised of the nature of that Animal the Ermine, off which
those skins are taken, for the Ermine is infinitly neat, and enemie to
filthiness and durt, in so much that the mouth of their Cave being
environed by the hunters with dirt, they do rather expose themselvs
to be taken then to run for their escape through dirt to defile themselves.

All which things then advise us. That God does expect in us,
Cleaness of heart, sincerity of tongue, wisedom of mind, elevation
of the understanding and prudence in our actions. whereof his Ho-
linesse by that beatified sword adorned in the aforecited manner, in-
tends to give the Prince a continual remembrance, that in goodness
and works he ought to surpasse all other sort of people in an eminent degree, begin by the omnipotent God in the government of
the world made so much superiour to all other People.

The Prince at the reception of this gift, kneels down, and the
Pope then gives it him, exhorting him by many expressions to be a
good souldier of Christ: Then the Prince acknowledging the Pope
as Vicar of God returns his thanks in Latin, swearing that he will
not lay any thing more to heart, then a correspondence by his actions, with the desire of his holiness, and all other Christian Princes:
afterwards he delivers the Sword to his most noble and chief Mini-
ster who bears it before the Crofs while the Pope goes out of the Vestry: At last, having had a congratulation from the Cardinals and
Embassadors, and taken leave, the Prince with the sword born up
before him, being accompanyed by the Governor: of the Castle,
Saint *Angelo*, by the Comptrolor of the Pallace, by all the Nobility,
by the Pontifical Family, and the *Palatine* Court, with great Pomp
and the sounding of Trumpets and noise of Drumms, he marcheth
out of the Palace by the military Porticue, thus attended to his own
Dwelling.

Of the increases of the *TYBER.*

CHAP. XIV.

ON the 9th. day of *November* in the yeer 1379. the *Tyber* rise
three braces or yards, and the mark of it may be seen at *Santa
Maria Della Minerva.*

In 1422. on Saint *Andrews* day under Pope *Martin* it rose above a
brace and halfe.

In 1476. the eighth of *January* a little above the Channell
Shores.

In 1495. in *December* being the third yeer of the Papacy of *Alexander* the ſixth, it augmented thirteen foot, and a little after in *Leo* the 10ths time ſomewhat more.

In 1530. Under *Clement* the 7th. on the 8th and 9th. dayes of *October* it encreaſed twenty four feet, the mark of it appears at Saint *Euſtachio*, upon a wall in the midſt of *Santa Maria del Popolo*, and in Caſtle Saint *Angelo*, where the Governor *Guidon de Medici* then cauſed a ſignal to be made of it.

In 1542. it roſe, and of that riſe *Maria Molza* ſpeaks elegantly.

In 1589. the 24th. of *December*, in the 7th. yeer of *Clement* the VIII. it roſe with ſo vaſt a deſtruction to the City *Rome*, that there remains no memorial of the like: at which time the Pope was but juſt returned from *Ferrara*, being then lately received and reſtored to the Apoſtolick Chair. Whence we may receive for truth this maxime, that ſorrow & wailing are the ſubſequents of Joy. The Pope had enough to do for all the following yeer, to repair the ſtructreus which by that inundation were ruinated, and to reſtore *Rome* to a convenient condition againſt the yeer of Jubile, which happened in *anno.* 1600. The curious are referred to the tracts of *Lodovico Geneſio* and *Giacomo Caſtiglione.*

Touching the preſerving ones health in *ROME*.

UPON this ſubject wrote *Aleſandrio Petronio* a *Roman* Phiſition and *Marſilio Cognato* of *Verona*, a Phiſicion alſo at *Rome*, in his book of obſerving a rule in diet, in the four books of his divers lectures, and others alſo to be found in *Rome* alſo: *Girolamo Mercurio*, ſpeaks ſomethings of it in his various readings.

The air of *Rome is thick*, and ill tempered, wherefore you ought to abſtain from walking abroad, at ſuch times as the Sun does not ſubtelize it, that the sky is not ſerene; that is early in morn, or els late at night, or when the weather is diſturbed or foggy.

In the Church *Santa Maria della Minerva*, you may read theſe verſes to the purpoſe of preſerving health in *Rome*.

Enecat inſolitos reſidentes peſſimus aer
Romanus, ſolitos non bene gratus habet.
Hîc tu quo vivas, lux ſeptima det medicinam,
Abſit odor fædus, ſitque labor levior.
Pelle famem frigus, fructus, ſemurque relinque
Nec placeat gelido fonte levare ſitim.

Romes evil air the ſtranger kills
Brings to its Natives unwelcome ills

Who'l live the feaventh day Physick muft
Nor noyfome fmells, nor labour truft
Hunger and Cold, avoid, Fruit and *Venus* fly
Cold water drink not though nere fo dry.

The Wines drunk in *R O M E.*

They drink in *Rome* the beft wines, as hereafter followeth.

Vin greco di Somma, the beft white, growes in the *Terra di Lavoro* in the *Monte Vefuvio.* named *di Somma,*from the Caftle *Somma*, which ftands at the foot of it.

Chiarello a brisk white wine from *Naples.*
Latino a mean wine from *Naples.*
Afprino a white wine from *Naples,*which is ftiptick, or as we may fay *aftringent. Mazzacani*, a fmall white Wine from *Naples.*
D'Ifchia, the beft *Greek* wine, this Ifland is under *Naples.*
Salerno white and red.
Sanfeveren white and red both good,
Corfo d'Elba, a ftrong white.
Corfo di Brada a grofs white.
Corfo di Loda a heady white.
From the *River* of *Genoua*, white and red,
Gilefe, white and red, fmall, and wholfome.
Ponte Reali, from *Genoua*, white, fmall and healthfull.
Mofcatello di Sardia of a deep colour, fmall, and wholefome.
Vindellia Tata from the *Genouefes,*fmal and wholefome.
Lacrima, the beft red.
Romanefco, fmall white, of divers taftes.
Albano white and red.
De Paolo, indifferent white.
*Di Francia,*moderate red.
Salino, mean white and red from *Tivoli,*and *Velletri.*
From *Segno* moderate.
Magnaguerra, the beft red.
*Caftle Gandolfo,*the beft white.
Della Riccia, the beft white, but fmall, made *Refpife* wine.
Malvafia, from *Candia.*
Mofcatello, the beft and moft excelling wine of *Italy.*

Of the divers forts and kindes of wine fome *Italian* Phyficians have alfo written : to wit *Giacomo Prefetto Netino* printed in *Venice* in *anno* 1559. *Gio Battifta Confalonieri* of *Verona*, printed in *Bafilea* 1539. *Andrea Baccio* ftampt in *Rome* in the yeer 1597'

And now, not recollecting any thing more to be fpoken of to the purpofe of this fmall tract, concerning *Rome*, we will make a conclufion with certain verfes writ in praife of her,that we may obferve the fame method we began with, in our difcourfe of *Rome* to wit her due comendations.

R r r   Verfes

Verses composed by Faustus Sabeus *a* Brescian *in praise of* ROME.

ENCOMION.

Martia progenies, quæ montibus excitat urbem,
Civibus & ditat, conjugibusque beat.
Tutaturque armis, Patribus dat jura vocatis.
Jam repetit cælum Post data jura Jovi.
De nihilo imperium ut strueres, te hac Romulæ causa.
Gignit, alit, servat, Mars, Lupa, Tibris aqua.

Encomion Julii Cæsaris Scaligeri.

Vos, septemgemini, cælestia Pignora, montes,
Vosque trumphali mænia structa manu,
Testor, adeste, audite sacri commercia cautes,
Et Latios animos in mea vota date,
Vobis dicturus meritis illustribus urbes,
Has ego Primitias, primaque sacra fero
Qui te unam laudant, omnes comprenderit, orbem
Non urbem, qui te noverit, ille canet.

The End of the Second Part.

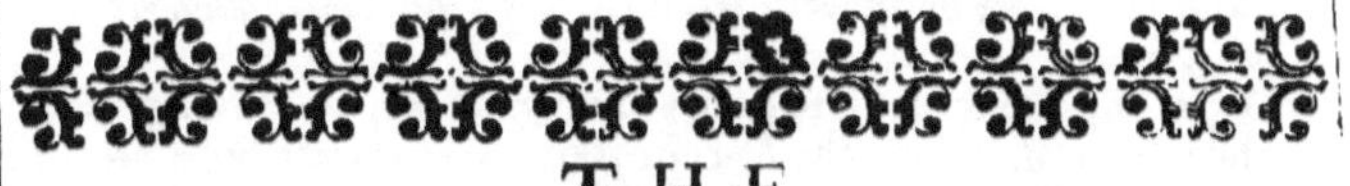

THE
HISTORY
OF
ITALY,

CONTAINING

The VOYAGES and JOURNEYS

FROM

ROME
TO
NAPLES,

The Third PART.

From *NAPLES* to *POZZUOLO*,
With the Return to TIVOLI.

Ravailing from *Rome* by the *Via Latina*, to *Marino*, you pafs between great ruins of many famous Villages, the which were no lefs rich then numeroufly difperft over the *Tufculan Champaigne* and the *Apenine* Hill during the flourifhing age of the *Roman* Empire: and hence tis that the old Town *Mariana*, will derive her Original name from the Caftle *Marino*, On the right hand whereof, lyes near the *villa Luculliana* of the *Licinij*, & the *Villa Murentana*, famous for the *Tufculane* quefions of *Marcus Tullius Cicero*, His immortal teftimony of Morality and Learning : At this day tis called *Frafcati*, and is diftant from *Rome* twelve miles : in this circuit you may, alfo behold the Ville or Manor Houfes of the *Portii*, and of many other the prime Persons of the *Roman* Republick, whom we finde recorded by *Strabo*, *Pliny*, *Seneca*, *Plutarch*, and other writers.

Departing thence turn towards the *Strada Appia*, leaving *Veletri* on the left hand, where the Anceftors of *Augustus* were born, and on the right hand *Aricia*, now called *Ricia*, and *Lo Specchio*, or the looking glafs of *Diana Tremorenfe*, as *Servius* calls the Lake near that Caftle, which Lake is confecrated to *Diana Tourica*, together with the wood famous for the fiction of *Acteon*, and a Temple named *Artimifio* by *Strabo*. Heretofore this was a famous place for the old, but barbarous Religion, inftituted in that place by *Orene* and *Iphegene*, to wit the cuftom of the *Scythians*, the facrificing with humane blood: Here was that Temple, whither the Fugitives brought from *Tauri* the Image of *Diana* hid in a pyle of wood, whence in *Italy* they give the Surname of *Fafcilede* and *Fafcelina*, to *Diana*: but of this fuperftition fhall we with better conveniency treat in another place.

Purfue the Journey juft to the *Pontine* Fens, where at a little diftance, lye the *Tres Tabernæ* or three Taverns the famous Hoftery on the *Via Appia* mentioned in the 28th. Chapter of the *Acts*: which are diftant from *Arelia* eleaven miles and from *Rome* thirty three, as is clearly demonftrated by the antient *Roman Itineraries*, and the very diftance of the places: they are indifferent entire, being built as the other Fabricks of the Romans of great ftones and bricks in fquares. Saint *Luke* writes in the Acts of the Apoftles that certain Brothers yet Frefh men (as we call them at *Oxford*) in the Faith of Chrift, left *Rome* and came to meet Saint *Paul* as far as the *Tres Tabernæ*, at fuch time as he was tranfmitted as a criminal Perfon with a guard of Souldiers from *Judea* to *Rome* by *Portius Feftus* the Precurator. Thence leaving the *Strada* or ftreet *Appia*, (as it may be called from the former beauty, teftified by the ruines of Houfes and Tombs, &c. on each fide) carried through the *Pontine Fens* with vaft expence though now wholly obftructed and impaffable, through the waters of the *Fens*, the ruine of ftructures and fall of Bridges, you are neceffitated to take a long journey, by the *Volfci*, the foot of the *Apenines*, the craggy and fharp Rocks of Mountains to *Terracina*. You fhall fee *Setia* on the left hand, celebrated by the old Poets for the goodnefs of the wines, and going more onward you leave behind you in the plain the walls of *Priverno* deftroyed by the *Germans* and *Brittons*, as *Eionda* teftifies: where in the circumfpection remember that *Camilla* exercifed the Empire of the *Volfci*. Thence paffing by *Priverno Novello* now *Piperno* fcituate in the adjacent Mountain, round which runs the River *Amafceno*, you may behold before your eyes, though at fome diftance, the Coafts of the *Mediterranian* Sea, and fome *Promontories*, which feem as it were disjoyned from the *Terra firma*, the firm Land, of old full of famous Caftles, and now little leffe then wholly abandoned. There will appear to you, in what fcite *Æneas* built *Lavinium* in thofe dayes, and where the City *Laurentum* ftood near the facred Fountain, and the Lake of *Æneas* or of *Jove Indigete*. Furthermore, there is demonftrable, where ftood *Ardea* the City of King *Turnus*, and *Antium* the head of the *Volfci*, together with the famous Temple of Fortune, and where *Aftura*,

infamous

infamous (that we may not call it famous) for the death of *Marcus Tullius Cicero,* the Dictator, so active and famous.

Thence also will your eyes meet the situation of the house of *Circe* the Sorceress, celebrated in the fictions of Poets, of old an Illand, now a most high *Promontory,* placed upon certain Rocks over the Sea conjoyned to the *Terra firma,* by the Plashes of water, and *Peanish* hills, full of woods and Trees, where Fame saies that *Circe* the most beautifull Daughter of the Sun transformed her guests into beasts and Cattel by her Magick Art (which if not credible) let's beleeve she did it by her whorish Art.

Strabo saies, that in the time of *Augustus* here was apparent a Temple of *Circe,* an Altar of *Minerva,* and that Goblet which *Ulysses* made use of, when his companions were metamorphosed into beasts as *Homer* in his verses declares. They assert commonly that in truth the mountain abounds with various plants of occult vertue and with infinite rare herbes, and that thence this Fable had its Original. For the relaters of Natural causes averr, that *Circe.* Κιρκαι, in Greek, signifies the revolving of the Sun, through whose heat, and the reflex of the Summer Raies, the plants and animated things receive vigour, and mutation. Thence then departing, you must passe through the humid and large *Pontine Campagna,* : which is divided in the midst by the *Strada Appia Regina,* (the Queen of streets as we may call it,) from the *Mauseoli,* the Sepulchres, Temples, Villages, and Palaces, wherewith twas once proudly adorned on both sides, now only miserable reliques of its former lustre lying dejectedly and dispersedly in the waters.

TARRACINA.

WAS an antient Colony of the *Romans,* and first of the *Volsci,* twas first called *Anxur,* or *Ansure,* as most suppose in the greek Language, from a certain place sacred to *Jupiter* called *Ansure* the most famous and most antient; which they say the *Spartans* built in that very place, in the same form, as is that of the *Dea Feronia,* in the *Pontine* Fields, built by the *Sircei,* and *Rutili,* who through the rigidness of *Lycurgus* his Laws deserted their Countrey, and after long voyages fixed their abode in the maritime confines of *Italy,* as *Dionysius Halicarnasseus* in his second book of Antiquities sets forth: *Virgil* also makes mention of such a name in the eighth of his *Æneides* standing on the *Circean* Mountain in these verses.

Circiumque jugum queis Jupiter Anxurus oris Præsidet.

Upon which *Servius* in his *Comentary* gives the derivation of *Anxur* in these words, *Circa tractum Campaniæ, colebatur puer Jupiter, qui Anxurus dicebatur, quasi,* Ανυ ξυρυ, *id est sine novacula, because that Jupiter imberbis was there worshipt :* and he saies in another place, *Feroniam Junonem virginem ait existimatam fuisse, veluti Jovem Anxurum, vel sine novacula, et perinde non abrasum ; qui coleretur Tarracinæ, quæ etiam Anxurum aliquando dicta fuit.* And I remember my self to

have

have seen a marble Altar dedicated by vow to *Jove*, a childe, as its antient inscription testifyed.

Strabo writes, that the *Græcians* called her by another name to wit *Trachina*, as much as to say sharp, from the greek word Τραχινα being seated on a sharp and stony mounta in; from which word it seems likely the *Romans* took the name *Tarracina* as is evident by some anique inscriptions: for all which, according to this form I conceive we ought to correct whatever word we meet with differing from this as we find in the fourth of *Titus Livius*. *Anxur fuit quæ nunc Tarracinæ sunt, urbs prona, paludes*: He seems to have in his mind the sharp and stony *Horatian* Countrey, when he so gratiously describes this very voyage of the *Strada Appia* in the second book,

> *Ora manusque tua lavimus Feronia lympha,*
> *Millia tum pransi tria repsimus atque subimus.*
> *Impositum saxis late candentibus Anxur.*

Tarracina is scituate three miles off the Temple of *Feronia* in the *Circean* Promontory, in the *Strada Appia*; which heretofore as *Solinus* testifies, was environed by the Sea, now a populous though small Countrey : whereof that part towards the Sea is fertile and pleasant, of old most adorned and pompous, through the gardens Palaces and possessions of the *Romans*, who were rich and potent, whereof some Reliques and ruines lye scattered here and there, as also some footsteps of that famous Port which *Antoninus Pius* restored with so vast expence. A part also of the Temple of *Jupiter Imberbis* yet stands in the Walls of the *Dome*, as the vast Marbles and pieces of Pillars witness; before it are some old inscriptions with a Pillar to *Theodorick* for having dryed the Fens and renewed the way as by this appears.

> *Inclyta Gothorum Regis monumenta vetusta*
> *Anxurei hoc oculis exposuere loco.*

The *Strada Appia* is compacted of solid stones and even all the way to *Fondi*, which may well entertain the Pilgrim with its marvellous structure, and the consideration of its old Fragments, and above all where tis cut out of most hard millstones, and reduced to a direct plain by chizels of Iron even to the Promontory of *Tarracina*. The Spectator rests stupid at the eveness of the straight way for foot Passengers, at the length of the stones, some being little lesse than 20 paces long and three broad, adorned with ridges or cuts for the drynesse of the way for passengers, and at every ten foot are stones raised for the more easy getting up on horsback or into Cart. Who is not astonisht at the solid wall of the same white Rock, whereon are distinguishable every ten foots distance, and the great number of those ten feet described and easily to be seen? Who is not pleased with the design of those characters so well made, and with so good proportion : and who is not amazed to see those Tombes and Marbles on the waies, of old adorned with triumphs of enemies now deprived wholly of all their fair habiliments? By these ways it seemed good to the antients to propagate the majesty, and au

thority

thority of the *Roman* Empire through the world, and to cause
by those vast Labours and cost their greatness and power to be feared by Forraign Chiefs and Embassadors repairing from beyond the Seas and the *Alpes* to *Rome*; that they might be Astonisht
with the Ornaments of *Italy* and *Rome*. All which things represent
to the present age the vastness of the Fabricks in past times, though
now appearing little less than deformed.

FONDI.

FOND I is but a small Castle, but placed in an admirable scite,
in the plain of the *Strada Appia*, and is as we may say, risen out
of the ruines of the antient perfection of Towns, which bore the
same name, whereof some Fragments yet appear in the adjacent
Fens near the Lake *Fondano*. To speak of it with authority take
these verses of a certain *German* Poet.

> *Collibus hinc, atque inde Lacu, simul æquore cinctum.*
> *Citria cui florent hortis è littore Myrti*
> *Hesperidum decus, et benevolentia culta Diones:*

In our times this Castle received a foul disgrace from the hands of
Hariadeno Barbarossa Captain of the Turkish *Armada*, who by a suddain inroad took it, leading away all the Souldiers and Inhabitants
sacking the Castle, prophaning the Churches, and arrived at his
Gallies clapt all his prisoners into Chains.

The *Strada Appia* is the largest, and was the famousest among the o-
ther twenty eight streets or ways of note, which took beginning at
Rome, and was called the Queen of streets: because that by it passed
to *Rome* such as came triumphing from the East. *Appio Claudio* made it
as far as *Capua*, and *Caligula* caused it to be paved with square stones,
and lastly *Trajane* renewed and restored it to *Brandizzo*, beautifying it on each side with a green hedge of Laurels, Bayes, Pomgranats,
and Mastick trees: pursuing this way before arrival at *Fondi* you
meet the *Mons Cæcubus*, noted amongst the antients for the good wine
it bore as *Martial* saith.

> *Cæcuba Fundanis generosa coquntur ahenis.*

And leaving *Fondi* for *Gaeta*, in the way you see the *Villa Formiana* famous for *Cicero's* slaughter, and the Castle *Itri*, scituate among
certain hills, most fruitfull in Figs, Olives, and other fruit. *Mola*
of old called *Formia Formosa* from the gardens, lies thirty stades
thence; a stade being 125 paces, eight whereof make an English
mile. Thence three miles taking the right hand you arrive at *Gaeta*, which Country, although all along it be but a bank, is so well
cultivated, and so lovely adorned, that it may not only fascinate
and entertain the eyes of the Traveller, but may be said like that
in the Fable, The residence of the Nymphs, being in truth infinitely pleasant, and delightfull: on the right hand of it you have the
prospect of the Sea, on the left, Flowers, Greens and Trees, which

being on this and that side bathed by the murmuring Rivolets, afford a most excellent favour for refreshing the Travellors wearied senses

GAETA.

Virgil speaks in honour of *GAETA* or *CAJETA* in these verses.

Tu quoque littoribus nostris Æneia nutrix
Æternam moriens famam Cajeta dedisti.

GAETA enjoyeth a Port and a Fort, which heretofore *Ferdinando* King of the *Arragonians* founded in a Corner of the *Promontory* towards the East, having then driven the *French* out of the Kingdome of *Naples:* within our memory the Emperor *Charls* the 5th. added to it the neighbouring rock, conjoyning it by a bridge, which may be drawn up at pleasure, to the rock that is highest, and so redoubled the buildings, augmenting its strength, with Towers and ramparts, and enclosing the whole mountain, joyned it to the City by Ditches and Walls: from which Towers (such is their contrivance) the Port and the City though lying much lower, receive a perfect defence and protection: being alwaies guarded with a good garison of *Spanish* Souldiers: nor is any person permitted to enter, neither stranger Townesman or Country man.

The City therefore may be well esteemed secure, since so well provided for by art, with all those Forts bulwarks, &c. and by nature, by its own scituation, having contiguous with it, that *Promontory* as twere hanging over it, and almost round it the waters of the Sea, being as twere in a *Peninsula*, having but a narrow *Isthmus* to come to it by Land, excellently defended by a bridge, a Gate, a Fort, and the Sea waters on each side.

The *Promontory* shews it self with two Heads, on that side regarding the *Mediterranean*, lies the City on the plainest and levelled part, on the other Cliffs, Rocks, and Præcipices which extend into the Sea; tis open from top to bottom, occasioned by a great earthquake, and that a long time since, such many times happening in these parts of Italy. The old Poets and Prophets sometimes called *Neptune, Ennosigæo,* and *Sisittone,* for that as they feigned he turned upside down the foundations of the mountains with his *Trident.* The Inhabitants and neighbouring people in boats with great devotion row into that wide space, and religiously reverence the place: for that they certainly believe that mountain was thus cleft in sunder by an earthquake, at the time our Redeemer Jesus Christ suffered upon the Cross for the salvation of mankind: as in the holy Gospel we find it written, that at that time the Mountains, and stones were rent in sunder. in the midst of the opening of this mountain, stands a Church and a very rich Monastery dedicated to the most sacred and great Trinity, built with the alms of devout souls, you may there see a vast stone, so fallen from the top of the mountain
that

that it may be said to be sustained by a miracle between the broken walls of the opening, where it begins to narrow. There *Ferdinand* King of *Arragonia*, erected a fair Chappel, dedicating it to the *S. S. Trinita*, which appears as in the Sea, and they go to it from the monastery by a way made with hands in the rupture of the Mountain: the broken stones on one side, and the hollowed places whence they fell on the other, when torn out by the earthquake, afford an enticing object.

Among other things there worth a view, is a shrine made by *Charls* of *Bourbon*, a famous, though wicked Captain of later times; who in the bloody assault and sack of *Rome* dyed of a wound from a gunshot: The bones of this bad man, are enclosed in a chest or coffin of wood covered with black silk, and are obvious at the first entrance of the Castle in an eminent place: under it may be read this Epitaph.

> *Francia mi dia la luche*
> *Espanna m'es fuerzo, y ventura*
> *Roma mi dia la muerte*
> *Gaeta la Sepoltura.*

Englished thus by *Jo. Raymond* Gent.

> *France* gave me breath
> *Spain* strength to arms did call
> *Rome* gave me death
> *Gaeta* Burial.

But to study brevity, I have deliberated to run over those things only, which may afford some fruit in reading and learning to the Ingenious.

IN the upper part of the Temple or great Church they shew all the pretious gifts and ornaments of that magnificent house, wherein the Episcopal seat was at first placed, after the burning and destruction of the neighbouring *Formia*, bestowed on it by the cruel hands of the *Saracens*. Out of whose ruines was drawn that huge *Bacchical Crater* or Boul, which holds many of those measures of wine which are called *Crati* or *runnelets* tis made of the whitest marble and is now applyed to the use of a Font for holy Baptism. *Corona Pighio* reports, not to have seen a Vessel (of that sort) more fair nor perfect: in it are most artificial greek Carvings, so well wrought that the sculptor (to shew his own satisfaction) engraved his proper name: the greek letters engraven shew *Salpion* an *Athenian* to be the Author: as appears by this.

Ttt   ΣΑΛΠΙΩΝ

ΣΑΛΠΙΩΝ
ΑΘΗΝΑΙΟΣ
ΕΠΟΙΗΣΕ

The Vessel is engraven with excellent designe and grace, and in it is figured *Dionysius*, he that had two mothers (as the Poets say) & was of the nature of fire: whom *Mercury* by commission from *Jupiter* imediately upon his birth took and caried to *Leucotea* the sister of his mother: they feign, that this *Dionysius* or *Bacchus*, was begotten by *Jupiter* on *Semele*, who being ambitious of equal honour with *Juno*, requested of *Jupiter* to accompany her in his divine Majesty, wherefore *Jove* attended by his lightning and thunder came to her, but she not able to endure his presence, fell forth with in travail, & was delivered of this Son before full maturity, and dyed; and some as foolishly feign, that *Jupiter* cut a hole in his thigh, and put the child in there till the full time of his birth. *Orpheus*, *Pausanias* & *Ovidius* call her *Matuta* or *Nysa* (the more antient poets *Ino*) who they say gave the first suck to *Bacchus* a boy, who grown to more bigness, was delivered to the *Nymphes* to be brought up: whereof *Ovid* in the third of his *Metamorphosis* speaks thus

> *Furtum illum primis Ino matertera cunis*
> *Educat, inde datum Nymphæ Nyseides antris*
> *Occuluere suis lactisque alimenta dedere.*

Here then may she be seen in the habit of a Matron sitting upon a rock, receiving the boy brought her by *Mercury* into her arms, swathing him, and hiding him in her breasts, the Satyrs and Hobgoblins dancing round in the mean time to the sound of a Tabour and pipe. Of which fable who would relate all the mysteries, should have enough to do; wherefore we will reserve it with many other things to be met with in this voyage to a more opportune place, all which the diligent Inquisitor of antiquity *Corona Pighio*, hath communicated to us.

At *Gaeta* I will quit the pains of climing up the top of this high Promontory, to be enabled to see and measure the *Mausoleum* of *L. Manutius Plancus* the Orator, a Pupil of *Ciceroes*.

From which a Chronologer may collect, it is of neare sixteen hundred yeers standing, and built in the time of *Augustus Cæsar*: which for its entirenesse on every side of the sea seems a miracle, the people now call it *Torre Orlandina*, the reward of the rusticknesse of posterity, who little regarding the antiquity of history, originate the works and famous deeds of their ancestors, at their own times, and attribute them to whom they please. This Fabrick is of an orbicular form, and seems to be made of the same architect, as is that of *Metellus* the Son of *Quintus Creticus* in the *Strada Appia*: being composed of two rounds or circles of solid wall, the outmost whereof built with great square stones contains in the diameter 28 paces or 84 foot whence may be deduced the great largenesse of the Sepulchre, by reducing the Line of the Diametre into a Circle: nor does the heighth seem lesse, for as much as the eye can judge of measure: being rai-
secl

sed by 27 stones placed one above another, of a foot and half in thicknesse, on the top of which is layed a Crown, figured out of the raies or battlements of the walls, pompously adorned with the enemies armes and spoiles.

At the entrance of the gate is a space of seven foot wide, made out of the inward Circle, all small manufacture of bricks, and conjoined with the walls without, with a high Arch; and that inclosed by other high Arches reprefents in the middle of the *Mauseolum* the form of a round Temple, which hath foure large receptacles for preserving of statues. The inward walls seem to be pargetted most neatly like marble, giving a lustre so shining and white that it seems like glass, and tis supposed that the reflection of the snow which is beaten in, redoubles the light: there being no other entrance for any then at the door, which of it selfe annot sufficiently enlighten the place: over the door may be plainly read the title of *Lucius Plancus* the Orator, with an elogie of his enterprises, as fairely engraven as if writ on a Tablet: whereof take the exact copy drawn out by *Corona Pighio*, the best corrected of any other.

L. Munatius L. F. L. N. L. Pren.
Plancus. Cos. Cens. Imp. Iter. V I I. Vir.
Ep. L, Triumph. Ex. Rœtis Ædem Saturni
Fecit de manibus Agros Divisit In Italiæ
Beneventi in Gallia Deduxit Colonias.
Lugdunum & Rauticam.

From whence with certainty we collect the age of this *Mauseolum*, for from the Offices and Magistracies administred by *L. Plancus* nominated in this writing, we conclude it must be built fifteen or sixteen yeers before the birth of our Lord Christ; and from our Annals of Magistrates it appears, that he was last of all Censor 25 yeers after his Consulacy and that he dyed in that dignity the yeer of *Romes* Rise seaven hundred & thirty one. And therefore may we assuredly believe that the Title making mention of his Censorship this Fabrick was finished a little after his death and this inscription set up in honour of him, for a memorial of his high dignity and other noble impresses. Thus much shall suffice touching the *Mauseolum* of *Plancus. Strabo* writes that the *Lacedemonians* who came in old time to inhabite there, called this Promontory *Gaeta* from its Obliquity, by which term all other things of a crooked nature, were called in the *Spartan* tongue, to wit αἰτία αἰτία and this gave denomination to the Castle: to the like purpose likewise we read that the antients termed any Dike or whirlepoole, occasioned by earthquake *caiaza*. Some say that the *Trojan Armada* burnt it selfe in the port of *Gaeta*, and that twas therefore called *Apo tou caicin* which signifies to burn: but be it as twill, the better part of antient writers believe with *Virgil* the Prince of Poets, who sings, that *Æneas* returned from hell named the place *Gaeta* and was there buried, from whence by opinion of the antients twas ever esteemed a most antique place.

You may with delight here have the prospect of *Capua*, the Countreys *Falerna, Stellata*, and *Leborina*, the most beautiful parts of Italy, whose hills are plentifully fraught with good wines, whence who delight to drink well and to be intoxicated, fetch from far these wines for the celebration of that *gusto*; and here the antients were wont to say, an important combate was fought between the Father *Liberio* the Finder of wine, and *Ceres* the Goddesse who was the Daughter of *Saturnus* and *Ope* and wife of *Osyris* King of Ægypt, whom the *Greeks* suppose to have first invented the sowing of wheat and barley, which before grew wilde among other herbs, &c.

The *Gaetan* port for its amplitude & antiquity is famous among authors, being well fortifyed by its proper scite and nature against all stormy winds from its neighbouring mountains, and the Countrey about it. *Giulio Cap't*, placeth the Ports of *Gaeta* and *Terracina*, among the other publique great and noble Acts of *Antonio Pio Augusto*, as if formed by him.

Taking the *Strada Appia* between *Mola* and *Suessa*, you will meet some grand structures of Sepulchres of the antients, but laid waft, and among other that which is shewed for the sepulchre of *Marcus Tullius Cicero*, being supposed to be the same by *Giovanni Pontano*, in whose time they say, a piece of *Ciceroes* Epitaph was there found. Yet *Corona Pighio* will not believe, that Sepulchre can be so antient: tis built orbicular, covered at top by bricks, which are supported by a pillar standing in the midst: on the right hand of it lies the port, whence certain stone steps conduct up to the Room above, which are filled with thorns and bushes: it takes name from the Dukes Palace standing opposite to it.

SVESSA.

THis City merits a most peculiar view, being no less famous for its antiquity, then the frequent recordation of antient writers: in her (as *Dionysius Halicarnasseus* writes in his 5th. Book) the *Pemetini* retired themselves, when driven out of their Country *Pometia*, destroyed by *Tarquinius Priscus* King of the *Romans*, whence it began to be called *Suessa* and now *Sessa*, it was also named *Suessa* by the *Aurunci* (as *Livy* testifies) who being overcome by *Titus Manlius* the Consul, aiding their adversaries the *Sidicini*, recovered this place with their wives and Children: This City is scituate in the *Campagna Pestina* near the *Monte Massico* on the *Strada Appia*, in a pleasant fertile & Country: and was esteemed for being the principal City of the *Volsci*, as well as for being a Confine to the *Romans*: twas made a Colony about 440. yeers after the birth of *Rome* as may be collected from *Livy*, though *Velius* writes, that people were sent thither and a Colony made three yeers after *Luceria*: it groaned under frequent losses, and important destructions, both in the *Carthaginian* war, and in the civil Factions: but afterwards from these misfortunes rousing it self, it flourished under the Emperors, chiefly under *Adrian* and *Antonini Pii*, as we draw from the Titles of Statues, from the Elogies, and inscriptions on Marble Tablets, **extant** in divers places thereabouts.

On the right hand of the Church of the Preaching Fryers, stands
the

the tombe of wood of *Augustinus Nisus* a most learned Philosopher of his times.

Looking towards the Sea, on the right hand you may observe populous places yet but villages, excellently cultivated, which are called the *Casali di sessa*.

At twelve miles distance from *Mola* you meet the River *Liris*, in its descent from the *Apenines*, and passage to the Sea, pleasantly irrigating the neighbouring Meadows.

In these *Marius* hid himself in his flight from *Sylla*, here also lies the *Torre di Francolesse*, where *Hannibal* being besieged by *Fabius Maximus*, escap't through that famous *stratagem* of making his enemies drunk: these Meadowes were esteemed by the *Romans* as highly as any under their dominions, as may be easily comprehended from *Cicero*, who magnifies beyond measure the *Strada Herculatea*, calling it a way of great delights and Riches; contiguous lies the *Monte Cæcubo*, famous for being the producer of so generous wine, and for having such celebrious Fens near; which very much pleased *Flaccus* when he praised the *Attick* victory of *Augustus* in these verses.

> *Quando repostum Cecubum, ad festas dapes*
> *Victore lætus Cæsare,*
> *Tecum sub alta (sic Jovi gratum) domo*
> *Beate Mæcenas bibam?*

This River *Liris* terminated old *Latium*, which passed, you came into the Meadows *Minturna* afore specified, where you may see the *Monte Massico and Falerno*, *Sinvessa* and *Minturna* and divers others places, whose description you'l meet with under *Scotio*, in the mean time behold *Capua*.

CAPVA.

Capua of old the head of the *Champain*, then was stigmatized with the Character of great arrogancy and wilful obstinacy as a-among others may be collected from *Marcus Tullius*, who speaking against *Publius Rullus*, Protests, that the *Campani* the inhabitants of the Plain or *Champain*, are haughty minded and proud of the goodness of their Fields, the quantity of fruits, the wholesome air and beauty of their City; From which abundance sprung that foolish request which the *Campani* made, to wit that one of the Consuls might be chosen out of *Capua*; whose delights were such, that they overcame and enervated the army of *Hannibal*; before his arrival there, invincible and powerfull above all others: *Cicero* calls *Capua* the Seate of pride, and mansion of delights, and saies that it creates in the people such customes as if they proceded from the principal of generation, when it may be rather supposed they happen from the nature and air of the place, and custom of living and eating, and hence it falls out for the most part, that the *genius* of the place generates inhabitants like it self.

The new *Capua* is scituate on the banks of the river *Vulturnus*, two miles diſtant from the old *Capua*, the delight of *Hannibal*, and *Paragon* with *Rome* and *Carthage*; where the ruines of Theatres, Acqueducts, Temples, Porticoes, Baths, Palaces, and other Structures ſhew its former magnificence: there alſo may be ſeen many great *ſubterranean* vaults and conſervatories for water, and pieces of vaſt columns, ſufficient teſtimonies of the power and pride of the old *Capua*, although the new adjacent City hath drawn thence a great part of thoſe infinite reliques. *Strabo* will have *Capua* to be named from the *Champain*, and *Publius Maro* likewiſe, who calls the City *Campana* as alſo *Tullius* and *Livius*, its Citizens and the other inhabitants *Campani*, from their manuring great Fields, in that happy plain of *Campania*, now *Terra di Lavore*, which moſt Authors as well modern as old, extol for the moſt fruitful plat of earth in the Univerſe: in a word twas the ſubject of *Virgils* Georgicks. Yet the Poets *Maro, Lucan, Silius* and other ſings, that the *Capi Trojani* companions of *Æneas* gave to it Inhabitants, walls, and denomination.

Of her were firſt Patrones, the *Opici*, and the *Anſoni*, and afterwards the *Oſci* a *Tuſcan* People, from whom twas called *Oſca*, as *Strabo* writes: theſe latter were driven out by the *Cumani*. and they by the *Tuſcans*, who augmenting her power by adding eleven other Cities, made her the *Metropolis*, and as *Livy* writes called her *Volturno* from the approaching Rivers name. At laſt the *Romans* finding her potent, a neighbour, and in the heart of *Italy*, a perpetual enemie, and no leſs emulous of their Empire then *Carthage* it ſelf, terrible and fierce through the friendſhip and company of *Hannibal*, reduced her under their dominion by raiſing many Forts about her, beſieging her to Famine, and the ſlaughter of all her Counſellors, and then they ſould all the Citizens and other people together with the *Campana*, forbidding for the future the City to have any head or publique aſſembly, Magiſtrates Counſel or other footſteps or honour of republique: and commanded that her Palaces ſhould be raiſed, that ſhe ſhould be an habitation for husbandmen only; and frequented by none but libertines, Factors, and other the viler ſort of artizans. In this deplorable condition lay *Capua* above one hundred and thirty yeers, and her Champain *Campania*, was the *Romans* publick to the time of the Conſulſhip of C. *Cæſar*, who by the favour of the *Julian* Law, made againſt the will of the Senate and nobility, conſigned his part by one and one to his Souldiers, and firſt ſurrounding her with walls, made her a Colony, as appears from the Fragments of *Julio Frontino*; when as from a reſurrection ſhe began and continued to flouriſh under the Emperors in the power of the *Romans*, till ſhe was taken and deſtroyed by *Genſericus* King of the *Vandals*, who driven out by the *Oſtrogoths*, they poſſeſſed her, and they expelled by *Narſete*, he reſtored her, but at laſt ſhe was again ruinated and wholly deſtroyed by the *Longobardi*, But tis not known in what time this new *Capua* riſe out of the ruines of the old, nor by whom tranſplanted at two miles diſtance; although moſt likely, that the Citizens driven away and diſperſed by force, and through fear of the barbarous at laſt retired themſelves thither, and *pian piano* by little and little out of the ruines of the abandoned *Capua* founded their new habitations: the new *Capua* lying on the banks of the *Volturnus* is now a great and powerfull City whereof *Julius Cæſar Scaliger*

liger the Poet fings, no leffe biteing than obfcure in thefe verfes.

> *I lammea fi valeat fuperare fuperbia faftum,*
> *Pinguem luxuriam deliciofus amor,*
> *Hoc mollem pinges Capuam, Capuæque colonos,*
> *Et quæ alijs vifa eft, nec fibi meta fuit.*

Capua was the *Metropolis* of eleven famous Cities in *Campagna*, which as alfo *Carthage*, and *Corinth*, *Cicero* efteemed fo potent and rich, as that he thought, either able to fuftain the greatneffe of the *Roman* Empire : *Hannibal* writing of her to the *Carthaginians* faies that after *Rome* fhe had the fecond place in *Italy*.

AVERSA.

THe *Road to Averfa* lies through the *Campagna Stellata*, and thence by the *Leborina*, *Pandolfus Collenutio* the writer of the *Neapolitan* hiftory affirms th it twas at firft called *Adverfa* for this reafon, becaufe the *Normanni*, having planted and fortified their quarters in the ruines of old *Attella* againft *Capua* and *Naples*, founded in the midft of the way the beginning of this City, to the end that from fo convenient a place they might abate the force of two fuch potent Cities.

Having paffed the River *Liris*, you go through *Campania*, the which as well in its abundance of Fruit Corn wine and oyl, as in the frequenzy, pleafantneffe and largeneſs of the *Champain*, far furpaffeth all the other provinces of *Italy* : tis a Land which voluntarily receives the Iron, and permits not it felf to be broke up in vain, but feems ftudioufly willing to afford the Labourer the greateft ufury; tis named *Terra di Lavoro*, and *La Campagna*, and all the way from *Capua* to *Averfa*, with good reafon was called by *Pliny, Leborina quafi Laborina*, a Field in *Campania*, where the ftubble of the Corn is fo great, that the People do burn it inftead of wood, as we have it in *Coopers* Dictionary. It hath had alfo the attribute of happy too, which was never given to any other province of the world except to *Arabia* in the *Orient:* Tis therefore no wonder, that the *Cumani*, the *Opici*, the *Tofcani*, the *Samniti*, and laftly the *Romans*, could not defpife fo great riches and plenty of all things. In particular the *Pianura Stellata*, is fo fat and fertile, that with good reafon it holds the chief place in *Italy* for abundance of all forts of fruits; which the inhabitants call *Campagna Stellata*, from that propitioufneſs of the ftars it enjoyes : *Cicero* in his orations, ftiles it the moft beautifull *Champain* of the whole world. Hence they fetch their Victuals for the *Roman* armies, and this, *Cæfar* (who then prepared his way to the Empire by gifts) divided amongft twenty thoufand *Roman* Citizens. Here the *Samniti* to the number of three hundred and fixteen thouf nd were cut in pieces by *Lucius Vetturius* and *Appius Claudius Roman* Captains. Here they make *Macheroni* in excellency, a fort of eating, compofed of pieces of paft boiled in water and put into a difh with butter, fpice, and grated cheefe upon them : and here properly grows the *Vino Afprino*, which is drunk

U u u 2

at

it *Rome* with so much *gusto* in the great heats.

ATTELLA DE GLIOSCI.

THe old *Attella* was a Castle built by the most antient people of *Osci* tis a famous Castle, and celebrated by all for the Satyrick, lascivious, ridiculous and sharp stories there rehearsed and thence stiled *Attellane*: which afterwards with their facetiousnesse acquired such authority, that from the mumming place of that Castle, they mounted even the *Roman* Theatres : at present both the Land and Towns can boast of nought save some Gentlemens and Lords Palaces there lately erected, more of of it will be spoken under some *Mediterranean* places.

NAPOLI. NAPLES.

AFter eight miles travailing from *Attella*, you arrive at *Naples*, where in every corner as well within as without the City you behold as well beautifull places , as proud Palaces, made with great art and infinite expence . This City is maritimate on the *Mediteranean* shore, and spreadeth it self into a large circuit : scituate among most pleasant hills lying on the north and east parts;and on the south and west parts the Sea: from whose port, without the least impediment, in a serene season , may be clearly seen the two promontories *Miseno* and *Minerva* : as also the Islands *Capreas* the delight of *Tiberius*,*Ischia*, and *Prochyte*, of old so much celebrated by *Srabo Virgil* and other Authors, who unanimously agree that the neighbouring people the *Cumani* built it: and that twas called *Parthenope* from one of the *Syrens* there interred. They write, thatafterwards she was transplanted by the said founders, for that seeming to them to flourish too much , and to increase from the fecundity of the soyl, they feared she might one day get the possession and into the room of their adjacent *Mother Cuma*; for which fact they relate that the *Cumani* groaing under a most heavy pestilence, were advertized by theOracle that the means to pacifie that great affliction and disgrace, was for them to reedifie the City, and annually to honour with sacrifices the Sepulchre of the Goddesse *Parthenope*: wherefore she was restored and rebuilt and thence tis inferred shee was called *Napoli*, by a greek word: there are also others and divers opinions about this matter: as *Licofrone Calscidese*, who in his *Alessandria* calls *Napoli mano di Falero*, and *Isaac Tzetze*, adjoines his interpretation, that *Falerus* the Tyrant of *Sicilia* bu lt *Naples* in *Italy*, and that because he cruelly tormented and slew its strangers of what sort soever, thence the story grew, that the *Syren Parthenope* dyed there, and that to her was erected a Tombe, and she there reverenced and annually adored with sacrifices under the Title of a Goddesse in form of a Bird. And we certainly know , that therefore the *Syrens* were adored as Goddesses among the tutelary Gods

of

the placeby the *Campani* over all that tract of *Magna Grecia*, and this
in the flower of the *Roman* Empire: I remember furthermore that
(many yeers since) I saw in *Naples* the *Syren* carved together with
Ebone and *Sebeto*, tutelary Gods of the *Neapolitans* upon a round
marble Altar, which is now placed in the receptacle of the fountain water, lying on the extremity of the *Mole* in the port of *Naples*;
besides which said opinions, there are of those (as *Diodorus Siculus*
and *Oppianus*) who hold that *Naples* was built by *Hercules*: and *Oppianus* in particular alluding to the name of the City in his poeme of
hunting, calls *Naples* the new Camp of *Hercules*. In fine all writers
concur in this, that she is a most antient City, and was famous before *Rome*, flourishing among the most illustrious greek Cities of *Italy*
for the *Pythagorean* philosophy. Afterwards the *Roman* Empire sprea-
ding it self over *Italy*, because she most forwardly submitted her
self to it, whilst they were in agitation to subject *Campania*, the *Romans* received her among the other free and confederate Cities: and
Livy affirms as well as many other Authors, that she from that time
constantly continued her Friendship, and observed that Faith which
at the first she had given to the *Romans*: Furthermore the affaires of
the Republique being reduced to a bad state in the sixth yeer of the
Carthaginian war, she not only resolved not to withdraw it self from
the *Romans*, in despight of the near lying *Capua* and the other rebel-
liousCities, but also as the said *Livy* relates, sent Embassadors to *Rome*,
and by them would have presented as an Act of Liberality and Noblenesse, to the Senate then in Court, forty Goblets of Gold of great
weight, and therewith offered force, riches, and in sum all whatever
their Ancestors had left them in said assistance and defence of the
Empire and City of *Rome* : To which Embassadors then with all
demonstration of courtesy were returned great thanks, and only
one of those Goblets retained, and that also weighed the least of
them : wherefore for her great and constant fidelity was
she ever esteemed, held and honoured among the free and
Confederate Cities of *Italy*, as well in the times of the Consuls as
under the Emperors, she (*Capua* being opprest, subdued and reduced to the servitude of the *Præfectura*) augmented sufficiently, and
most happily enjoyed for a long time the fruits of her fidelity. Hither
as *Strabo* instructs us, the youth to intend their studies, and many
ancient men to enjoy quiet and tranquility of mind, were wont to
retire themselves from *Rome*, as to the purpose *Silius Italicus*,
and before him *Horatius Flaccus* to the same sung, saying

> *Nunc molles urbi ritus, atque hospita Musis*
> *Otia, & exemptum curis gravioribus ævum.*

Italy affords not a place enjoying so milde and benigne a heaven
as *Naples*, having a double spring yeerly in flowers, which the surrounding Fields produce plentifully as also great variety of Fruits,
and those the most prized; participating no small quantity of fountains, and springs, and of healthfull and good waters : to say no
more tis scarce to be believed a natural thing but wonderfull how
infinite is their abundance? and therefore with good reason may
she be called the Paradise of *Italy*, which particulars have chiefly
XXX

been

been the inviting argument for so many Emperours, Kings, Princes and ingenuous Persons, to make their frequent applications and residence here, and to this day tis reckoned the third City of *Italy*, and the delights which nature hath allowed this place are so great, that meritoriously, is sheltust with so many proud Palaces and stately houses of Princes and other Grandees, who reside in them the most part of the yeer.   Tis most perspicuous and known to all, that *Titus Livius* the *Padouan* Historian, *Q. Horatius Flaccus*, *Statius Papinius*, *Claudius Claudianus* all famous Poets, *Annius Seneca* the Philosopher, and infinite others, who have rendred themselves immortal by their wits, and learned writings, retired to *Naples* for their better and more due attention to their studies. We read furthermore that *P. Virgilius Maro*, lived most sweetly for a long space in *Naples*, and there composed his *Georgicks*, as at the end of his fourth book may be collected.

Illo Virgilium me tempore dulcis alebat
Parthenope studiis florentem ignobilis ori.

He dying in *Brindesi* commanded that his body should be hither conveighed and buried in *Naples*, as we learn from divers testimonies of old Poets.   *Servius* his Comentator writes, that *Virgils* Sepulchre lies two miles distant from *Naples* in the way of *Pozznolo* near the gurge of that *subterranean* cave, the famous Grot under *Pausilipus*, now the Inhabitants shew the place in the gardens of *San Severinus*; over the door of the garden is this inscription.

Maronis Urnam

Cum adjacente Monticulo, extensaque ad Cryptam Planitie.
Modiorum trium cum dimidio circiter, Urbano V I I I. annuente &c.
Renovanda Mem. Praesentis Concessionis singulis X X V I I I annis
in actis Cur. Archiepiscopalis.

Virgils Tombe is built in a *Rotunda* or *Cupola*, about five paces long: on the inside, the walls are of brick in square after the *Roman* way: the outside of massive stone, covered over with bushes and among them, three or four bay trees(an immortal testimony of the Prince of Poets there interred) shoot forth about a mans heighth, round it lye scattered ruines testifying its formers beauty: in the Rock just opposite to the entrance, where his known Epitaph of *Mantua me genuit* was, that being decayed, is placed a Marble stone with these Verses.

S T A I S I i Gencovius.

1 5.   89.   *Qui*

Qui Cineres ? Tumuli hæc vestigia , conditur olim
Illehoc , qui cecinit Pascua ,rura , Duces,

Can. Rec. MDLIIII.

What duft lies here ? this Heap protects his Hearfe
Who whil'ome Warbled Fields, Farms, Fights in Verfe.

The *Crypta Neapolitana* a perfect figne of the *Roman* magnificence
is the Rocky mountain *Pausilipus ,* cut thorough; very high fpatious and well paved, fo that for the fpace of a mile , two Coaches
may go on front under ground.

From the garden of *San Severinus* you may fee the houfe of *Attius*
Sincerus Sannallarius the Poet emulous of *Virgil :* which by his teftament was made a Monaftery , whofe Church is called *Della Beate*
Virgine , therein ftands a marble Sepulchre car ved with great induftry : on the one fide is *Orpheus* or *Apollo,*on the other the *Sybil,* or the
Mufe wrought of white marble , and here read this *Epigram* of Cardinal *Pietro Bembo.*

Da facro cineri Folres, hic ille Maroni
Sincerus Mufa proximus, ut tumulo

Vixit annos 72. Obiit anno 1530.

To return to *Naples :* tis a City at this time no leffe famous for
the nobility and magnificence of herCitizens & inhabitants,then for
the vaft expence , and for the beauty of the ftructures of all forts :
for that the Governors of the Emperor *Charls* the 5th and after
them of *Philip* King of *Spain,*of later yeers Prefidents or Viceroyes,
in the Kingdome of *Nap'es ,* have wonderfully enlarged and forti'
fied her with a new wall, bulwark, Ditches, Towers, Caftles;in fo
much that fhe is now almoft invincible. She is furthermore full of
regard for the many and magnificent Churches, Colledges, Courts
Palaces of Princes and other great Men , as alfo for many old reliques of antient houfes, Epitaphs, Statues, Sepulchres,Collumns,
Altars, Marbles with moft artificial and fair engravings , and other
things , which to recite would take up too much Room here.

Among the reft, any one may meet content in the grand ruines
of the *Quadrate* Temple of *Caftori* which though the fire hath con-
fumed for the moft part, yet appears before it a part of a moft beautifull porticue , with fix prime Pillars of Marble with their cornifhes yet a foot, of *Corinthian* architecture , wonderfull for their
vaftnefs, and the art they are wrought with : they have for Capitols, fome *Cefti,* Iron Clubs (ufed among the *Grecian* wreftlers) to
which were tyed with leather ftraps or dryed Sinews , balls or
bullets of lead, which in their Olimpick games, they ufe to hurl
or caft : which with the Foliage and revolts reprefent a becoming
covering; and on the Frife , to which the Rafters are fixed, may
be read a greek infcription,which clearly manifefts,that this was the
Temple of the *Caftori,* and that the Greek language was in ufe a-

mong

mong the *Neapolitans*, when the Roman Empire flourished: which is also confirmed by the characters by the vast expence of the whole work, & by the exquisit perfectiõ of the art, in the *Timpano* or triangular Frontispiece of the roof: upon these Collumnes were carved many images of the Gods, which the Flames and Age have for the most part consumed. On the Treslel was figured an *Apollo*, & on one & the other side of it, lies Earth and Water in the form they are usually figured, that is in form of a body half raised up, half lying along, naked to the Navil: Earth hath the right hand, holding in its left the horn of the *Copia*, the rest cannot be discerned, being too much broken and ruinated.

The Churches of our Religion, are there in excellent order and rich, as well as many: and so well placed, as pleasant flowers for beautifying a Garden. For example the Church of *S. Chiara*, enjoying a great and fair monastery, was very magnificently built by *Santia* the *Spanish* Queen, and wife of King *Roberto*, who by others is named *Agnese*: which the antient Kings of the noble house of *Durazzo* have made famous with their sumptuous Tombes: and in *San Domenico*, is the Sepulchre of *Alfonso* the first, and of many other Kings, Queens, and Princes; and what is more important, the Image of that Crucifix which spake unto *San Tomaso d'Aquino*, these words: *Tomaso tu hai scritto bene di me:Thomas* thou hast written well of me: and that of *Oliveto*: so also in other Churches, you may see many proud depositories and memorials of the *Kings of Spain*, of the Heroes and other Princes, with statues of Marble as if natural. In the Church of *San Giovanni dalla Carboniera* is the Sepulchre of King *Roberto*, whose praises were writ by all learned men, among the rest by *Petrarcha* and *Boccaccio*. In that of *S. Maria Nova*, lye interred the bones of *Odetto Foix* named *Lotrecce*: and of *Pietro Namarro*, of *Consalvo Ferrando Cordovese*, and in the most religious Tabernace of *San Giannuacio*, are preserved many holy reliques of Saints. Where once in the yeer at least they shew one by one, all those worthy objects: as bones of Saints and other Reliques enclosed in gold and Silver with pretious stones, with the pretious gifts bestowed by Kings and Princes, and other things. Among which with great reverence, is the head of *S. Giannuario*, Bishop of *Pozzuolo* the Martyr; and his bloud stil remaining in a glass vial, though dryed and become hard through time: which vial when brought to the Altar is set near the head of the Martyr, on the Corner of the *Chorus*: and the blood (to admiratiõn) begins to become liquid and to boyl as new wine in the must, as hath been annually observed and seen by all, not without great stupour. Thence you go to the *Annunciata*, a Church famous through the great devotion there exercised, and rich through the many offerings made to it: as also for many reliques of Saints of importance, among others two small bodies of a foot and half long, yet entire, covered with the skins of innocent Children slain by *Herode* the King, at the time our Saviour was born in *Bethlehem*, the wound of one is in the head, the other in the breast.

Contiguous with which lies an hospital, built like a spatious Castle, wherein are maintained as their condition, age, and health require, two thousand souls: therein are also brought up children of

the

the poorer fort, more than eight hundred, between orphane and expofed infants as well males as females: inftructed in letters and art, according to their inclination till they become great. 'Tis a pleafure to fee and obferve their feveral diligent exercifes and works: and this cuftome of Chriftian Charity is certainly very comodious, which as *Corona Pighius* obferves, refembles *Platoes* Republique in part, and imitates that Economical government of the Apes, defcribed by *Xenofonte*, and by *Virgil* the Prince of Poets, defcribed and depainted fo well to the fimilitude of *Platoes* City.

Caftle *Nuovo*, the name is new although built more then 300 yeers fince by the Brother of *San Lodovico*, King of France, who was *Charls* the firft King of *Naples* and Count of *Anjou*, to the end he might thence aid the City and the Port againft the maritimate inroads of enemies. *Alfonfus* the fift of this name, King of the *Arragonians*, reftored it within our memory, after he had expelled the French, and fubdued the Kingdom; and fo well fortifyed it, that tis now held one of the ftrongeft Forts of *Italy*: more efpecially fince the laft Kings, the Emperor *Charls* the 5th. and *Philip* his Son comvpleatly furnifhed it, and all the other Forts of this City, with victuals, good fouldiers, and all other neceffaries and engines of war to keep off the Enemy.

In the midft of this large Caftle, ftands the pompous Palace of the governors, furnifhed with royal and moft lovely houfhold-ftuff wherein the King or Emperor may find a comodious receipt for all his Court: ftrangers are aftonifht at the engines of war, the Artillery, the great quantity of Iron Bullets, the murrions inlayed with gold and Silver, the Shields, the fwords, the Launces, and the other preparation for war there continually preferved. and that admiration becomes much leffened, at the view of the faid palace fo richly laden with tapiftry of filk interwoven with Jewels and gold, the engraving, the ftatues, pictures and the other noble furniture.

Thence you may fee the Caftle *Del'ovo*, fo named for that the fhelf which there inlargeth it felf to the fimilitude of an Ifland, retains an oval form. *Collanutius* writes that this Fort was built by *William* the third a *Norman*, and thence called *Normannica*, which afterwards *Alfonfus* the firft King of the *Arragonians*, repaired and beautifyed in many things: tis faid that the antient called this by a greek word *Miagra*, either from a falutatiferous plant there growing, or from the fite and quality of the place, or for that twas difficult to efcape out of it: This Mole is like an artificial ftreet cafting it felf into the Sea, whither all the gentry in the evening refort for the benefit of the *Frefco*.

The Townefmen fhew one after another Grottes hollowed under the fhelf, alfo fome old memorials erected upon Cliffs, and great quantity of Arms of different fafhions.

Afterwards pafs into the Court of the Palace by the Gulf of the Sea called by *Strabo* and *Tazza, della forma*; and if you would learn the difcipline and labour of the *Galleots* you muft view in the paffage, the near fhores, the Iflands and Promontories round about, as *Lifeno, Procrite, Patecufa, Capreta, Herculaneo*, and *Atheneo* or *Minervio*, which as *Pliny* relates was the refidence of the *Syrens*, and that

Y y y

gave

gave denomination to the Promontory: and here as *Strabo* records, *Ulysses* consecrated a Temple to *Minerva*, for his deliverance from the crafty wiles of the *Syrens*.

For the most part 40 galleys lye in this Port, besides other vessels to discover and do other service: which Port is very large, and as well as is possible defended against fortune with a large bank; which for the space of 500. foot runs from the shore into the Sea in form of a bended arm : and the whole length and bredth made of huge pieces of squared stones.

There gusheth out at one end of the Mole a fountain of sweet water, conveighed thither through the midst of the said Bank; this fountain hath much marble under it, wherein the water is received, the name is drawn from a Latin word, the foundations are known to have been layed by *Charls* the second the *French* King above two hundred and eighty yeers ago: which *Alfonsus* the first a *Spaniard*, amplified with all magnificence afterwards as well as many other publique edifices within the City : this fancy also *Charls* the 5th. Emperor, and *Philip* his Son took up, in augmenting, fortifying and furnishing the same for its commodity and ornament, without respect to the expence.

Hither the mariners in little boats row persons to see the Galleys and the life of the slaves with their arts, who from the want of bread learn to speak with the words of the Poet *Perseus*, *Venter Magister*, &c. and sitting, exercise themselves ; together with the munition and naval preparations for war : here in a little time may be learnt the mariners art, with their manner of living, wherewith they keep their bodies in health, and the offices and charges of the Presidents of the Vessels: thence you go to see the denoted stables of the King, where are kept and managed whole heards of beautifull and valuable horses, where some Princes are always to be found, beholding with attention and delight, their swift course, their wheelings, and turnings, made in as little room, and with as much art as is possible, their curvets and leaps of all four performed excellently at the nod of the switch of the Rider.

Thence you go to the Castle *Santermo*, on the top of the near mountain, very strong, looking on and defending, the City, the shore Port and Islands in the Sea: King *Robert* Son of *Charls* the second built it 250 yeers agoe, adding to it such strength and defences as render it little lesse than inexpugnable, the Emperor *Charls* the first and *Philip* his Son some years since enlarged the *Guasto*, conjoyning it with the City, and increasing the structures in the inward space with new walls and new forts.

On the top of the Hill you meet a most fair and rich Temple with a stately Monastery possessed by the *Carthusians*; In which Monastery if you can obtain so much favour from the Monks (who lovingly receive forraigners and shew their Monasterie) you will meet an ample satisfaction in the view of the Monks chamber in a corner of the Monastery : where you have as great delight as *Italy* affords : for on the right hand is presented to your view, the prospect of the Sea, as large as the eye can reach, the Islands *Enarea*, *Caprea*, and *Prochite* and opposite the manured places of *Pausilipo*, the gulf of *Surrenio*, the streight of *Surrentano*, some Cities and many Burroughs :
On

On the left hand the Field *Holana*, very large, and the mountain *Vesuvius* as high; then looking downwards, you behold *Naples*, which, whither to be styled the miracle of art or nature is disputable, since there you may see, have and enjoy, what ever is esteemed pleasing or sweet.

In the voyage see the garden of *Gacia di Toleda*, kept in as good order as any, twas made with vast expence, and with as many curses; (being with the sweat and blood of enforced galley slaves, reduced to that perfection it now retains) in the time that his Father *Pietro di Toledo*, continued Lord of the City and Kingdom, under the benevolent aspect of the Emperour *Charles* the 5th.

Nor is it a mean pleasure, to view the places surrounding the City worth the seeing, especially in a good season: the which are in that fertile plain, near the Sea in pleasant scites very pompous; and adorned by the nobles with magnificent Edifices and fair gardens, well kept, and enriched: which have such plenty of Fountains, grottoes made by art, and Fishponds adorned with Curral, mother of Perle, and Fish shels of all sorts, as the beauty is almost impossible to be ghessed at, as also of Porticues, walks, vaults covered with Leaves and Flowers of divers sorts, Roses, pomegranates, collumnes and Lodges beautifyed with pictures, statues, and marbles of antiquity, and among those Lodges those of the *Marques di vico*, and the other Princes, placed on the strond near the *Vesuvius*, are very famous: as also the *Villa* of *Bernardino Martizano* adorned with many reliques of of antiquity; *Poggio Reale*, a vast Palace, built heretofore by *Ferdinand* King of *Arragonia*, whither the King used to retreat, when he desired to repose himself, and to recreate his minde from the fortunes of the Sea, in a blith and secure port.   This Palace is contrived in this manner, four square Towers, upon four corners, are bound together by great Porticues, so that the Palace hath two bredths in a length, each Tower hath fair and pleasant Chambers aboue and below, and you passe from one to the other by the means of those open galleries; the Court in the midst is ascended by certain little steps, and therein a fountain and clear fishpond, and on all sides by the nod of the Master, from the pavements rise sprouts of water, by meanes of infinite subtile Chanels there placed with art, and in such plenty that they suddenly wet all the aspicients not thinking of it, in the summer a sufficient cooling: these Fields by the *vicinity* of the *Vesuvius* enjoy great plenty of sweet waters, the Fire within forcing out many fountains of sweet waters purged and pure: hence also the *Sebeto* acknowledgeth its being and the greatnesse of its Chanel being conveighed into all the streets of *Naples* by Pipes under ground, to all the publique and private palaces and habitations: so great comodity of all things brings to its inhabitants, the Paradise of *Italy* (*as Corona Pighio* frequently and not improperly calls her) that flourishing part of the *Neapolitan* territory, although many times afflicted with wars and earthquakes.

IL MONTE VESUVIO.

VEfevo, or *Vefuvio*, or *Vefuvius*, (fo called by the Antients from the fparkling)was a moft fair mountain; and formerly a goodly Countrey for about four miles compaffe lay at top, which then produced the excellent *Greco*, but tis now layed waft: Tis an imitator, and companion or rather the Brother of flaming *Ætna*,and is begotten by earthquakes and fire, the materials whereof it continually retains in the profoundeft part of it: which as if withbeld within it felf for fome yeers till come to maturity, and as if the fpirits were fummoned and fomented,with fury evaporates fire,breaks open the firm parts of the Mountain, and vomits forth its inward parts, as earth, ftones, flames, fmoke and afhes, throwing them up into rhe air with horrid noife, and with fuch force, that the *Vefuvio* feems to imitate the war of the Gyants, by fighting againft *Jupiter*, and the Gods with flames,arms, and huge ftones,(fome whereof four porters can fcarce move)and feeming to draw the Sun down to the earth, to change the day into night, and laftly to cover the very heavens. Experience and the teftimony of *Strabo*, *Vitruvius* and other antient Authors affures us, that under *Vefuvio*, aud the adjacent Maritimate Mountains,and of the neighbouring Iflands,are vaft burning fires, of fulphur, pitch,and allume: the hot bathes and *fulphureous* boyling fountains fufficiently prove it: and therefore the *Vefuvio*,when abounding with fire,fometimes afends & fometimes ufeth to move earthquakes and vaft ruins and deftructions. That *incendium* was the greateft and moft famous which happened under the Emperor *Titus Vefpafianus*: defcribed in a print by *Dion Caffius*, and other Authors, the afhes of which fire, were not only exported to *Rome* by the wind,but over the Seas into *Affrick* and into *Ægypt*; the Fifh in the boyling Sea were dreffed,the birds were fuffocated in the air, and the famous and moft antient adjacent Cities *Stabia,Herculeano*, and *Pompeo*, were heaped and covered over with afhes and ftones), while the people were fitting in the Theatre: and *C. Plinius* the famous Naturalift, who then governed and commanded the *Armada* of *Mifenus*, too inquifitive after the caufe of this inteftine fire,approached too near,and by the heat and favour received his end,by being fuffocated near the *Porto Herculiano*: *Francefco Petrarca* noting this acutely (in his triumph of Fame) faies he wrote much but dyed little difcreetly.

> *Mentr'io moriua, fubito hebbe fcorto*
> *Quel Plinio Veronefe fuo Vicino*
> *A fcriver molto, a morir poco accorto.*

Yet for all,that to *Pliny* fucceeded fo fearfull his dalliance, *Stephano Pighino*, himfelf not thereby fore warned,could not forbear, but took a voyage (of 30. yeers old) in order to his ftudies, into *Italy* through *Campania* and *Naples*,to the end he might fearch out,and behold the place of fuch wonders, although very high, and no leffe

difficult

difficult to afcend which coft him an entire dayes labour. and with his two companions, he marched round the mountain, reaching the very top: where he could fcarce fatiate his view, in looking on the bourg, the Countrey round about, the Iflands and the Sea: *Vefu-vio*, rifeth in the midft of a moft fertile Countrey; the afhes fcattered over it, the ftones and clods of earth burnt by the fire, and diffolved by the rain afterward, infinitely enrich and frudifie all the countrey; in fuch fort that the vulgar to purpofe enough, call *Cam-pagna*, the mountain and the Caftle built at the foot of the mountain, *Sommano* from *Somma*, the fum and wonderfull abundance of generous wines, and excellent fruit; the *Vefevo*, as well as the *Cam-pagna*, and neighbouring hills, being furrounded with fair vineyards.

So alfo *Martial* fung, that in his time it was green, with the fprouts of the vines, bewailing in his firft book with a fair epigram that fierce fire, happening in *Vefpafians* dayes: the top in all times and ages hath been ever held barren through the burned ftones, as if eaten up by flames. Tis hideous to behold the deep cracks in the earth through which the ftreams of fulphur pafs, but when arrived at top the *Vo-rago* reprefents hell, fo terrifying is the fpedacle; Tis a hole about three miles compafs and round, as if formed like the middle and lower part of an Amphitheatre, tis called *Lazza* from the form of the Rock Fifh, the bottom of it reaches to the bowels of the Earth, The place is cold now, nor feems it to emit the leaft heat or fmoak which the faid *Pighius* teftifies, who defcended as far into that profundity as the the precipices and obfcurity of the place would permit; the firft entrance of the *Vorago*, is fertile through the earth and afhes caft on it, and growes green through the firre and other great trees growing in it, as far as the Sun can refled into it, or the rains penetrate; but the parts under, reftrained to a narrow compafs are as twere ftopped by the great pieces of ftone and ro cks, and arms and bodies of trees fallen down: which obftrudions, when the inward Materials of fire abound, like little bundles of ftraw are eafily raifed and mounted to the skyes, by the invincible force of its fmoake or flames.

The fire alfo is known to open it felf a way, not only by the ordinary mouth, but on other fides alfo, as occafion offers; whereof we have a memorial in the *Italian* Annales: To wit that two hundred fixty and fix yeers fince, in the Pontificacy of *Benedid* the 9th. from one fide of the Mountain gufhed out a ftream or river of flames which ran into the Sea, in a liquid fire like water: the iffue and footfteps of which Cavern tis faid appear yet: The *Roman* Hiftory tells us that befides the mouth, it had other iffues and courfes for the flames of old: for inftance, it faies that *Spartacus* the fword-player having begun to raife the war of the *Fugitives* againft the Ro-mans in *Campania*, and having poffeffed the mountain *Vefuvius* with his army, as a ftroug fortrefs and fure retreat for war, and being there afterwards befieged, he efcaped from the *Roman* fiege by an admirable way: for that covertly faftning chains at the mouth of the Mountain, he with his companions let themfelves down to the bottom: (as *L. Florus* briefly relates in his third book of the *Ro-man* hiftory) whence iffuing forth by an obfcure breach, he at una-

Zzz

wares

wares put to fack the quarters of the Captain *Clodius*, and of the rest who were at the siege: who never conceived the least th ought of it.

Whither at this day any *subterranean* wayes or caverns, leading from the Vineyards to the mouth of the Mountain, are found out, I cannot tell. *Pighius* assuredly tells us, that he observed at the top of the mountain about the mouth, certain vents, whence procee-ded a continual heat: wherein putting his hand, he perceived clear-ly a heat although small and without smoke or vapour: but our Countryman *Raymond* observed in his view there, a certain hill ri-sing in the midst of the *Vorago*, that still vomits thick smoke, which he saies the fire within hath raised within few years, that it dayly encreaseth, and when grown to a fuller bulk, *Caveat Neapolis.* Thus much touching the *Vesuvius.*

Between the mountain *Vesuvius* and *Attella*, in the *Mediterrane*, are scituate, *Aferellano, Acerra,* and *Sessola,* at present ruinated, of old possessed by the *Camps* of the *Liborini,* where the *Romans* and the *Samnity* fought most fiercely: hither reach those mountains of *Capua,* called by the Antients *Tifata,* and those that extended to-wards the *Mole* Northwards; here is *Forche Caudino,* and other Ca-stles with many inhabited places, among which the chief is the Castle of *Aciola:* at the foot of these mountains lies *Caferta* the City and Country of the great Cardinal *Santorino,* called *Santa Severina:* near which lye *Maddalone, Orazano* and *Argentino*; Behind *Tifata* on the back of the Mountain is scituate *Sarno,* flowing with waters by means of the River *Sarno,* which there takes its rise: these are *mediterranean* places about *Naples* and *Campana,* whence you go to the *Marca.*

The Kingdom, whereof *Naples* is the Metropolis, cōmenceth from *Latium* that part where the River *Ufente* runs into the *Terreno*; Then towards the *Apenines* it passeth to *Terracina,* thence to *Frigella,* or *Ponte curvo, Ceperano, Kieti, Tagliacozze* a Ducal City, and *Matrice,* where *Trent* begins its source,

Then follow the way along the River for eighteen miles to *Co-lonia de gli Ascolani,* where the River dischargeth it self into the *A-driatick Sea*: that part of the Kingdome opposite to the Promontory called of old *Leucoperta,* now *Capo Dell'armi,* respecting *Sicilia,* is di-stant from *Poggio,* forty eight *stadii,* each of which contains 125 paces; whose head is called *Tarlo:* Tis 418 miles of way to go by *Terracina, Bossento,* and *Reggio* towards *Naples.* This Kingdom of *Naples* is one thousand four hundred and sixty eight mile in circuit: whereto some have assigned ten provinces, others nine, others seaven and we thirteen.

The *Terra di Lavoro,* taking in *Naples,* hath three Arch-Bishops, twenty five Bishopricks, one hundred sixty six Castles surrounded with walls, and one hundred and sixty Towns: the Principality named *Di quà* on this side hath twelve Cities, two hundred and eigh-teen Castles; the Principality *Di là* beyond, eleaven Cities, one hun-dred forty and one Castles, the fairest among which is *Confa. La Ba-silicata,* hath ten Cities, ninety three Castles, the fairest *Venefa. La Ca-labria di quà,* hath ten Cities, one hundred sixty two Towers and Villages. *La Calabria di là,* wherein is *Reggio,* hath sixteen Cities and

one

one hundrd and thirty Caſtles. The Province of *Otranto* hath beſides *Brindeſi*, thirteen other Cities, and one hundred fifty eight
Caſtles or Towns. The Province *de Bari* hath fourteen Cities and
fifty Caſtles. *La Capitaota*, thirteen Cities and fifty Towns, whereof
the moſt notable is *Manfredonia*: The Countrey of *Moliſeo*, four Cities, one hundred and four Caſtles, the faireſt *Trivento*. *L'abruzzo
di quà* hath five Cities, one hundred and fifty Caſtles, the cheif *Tea-
te*. *L'Abruzzo di là*, beſides *Aquila*, hath four other Cities and two
hundred eighty four Caſtles: but with more brevity to ſpeak of
them, this Kingdom, hath twenty Arch-Biſhopricks, one hundred
twenty & five Biſhopricks, ten Principalitys, twenty three Dutchies,
thirty Marquiſates, fifty four Earldomes with authority over their
ſubjects, fifteen Lords who have juriſdiction, four hundred forty
three petty Lords with title and authority: a thouſand Towns encloſed with walls, and villages in great number. The moſt famous
Iſlands of this Kingdom are *Enaria*, *Procida*, *Lipari*: and thirteen o-
thers of ſmall fame.

The Offices of this Kingdom are great Comeſtable, who is Viceroy. Grand Juſticiary, Grand Admiral, Grand Chamberlain, Grand
Prothonotariy, Grand Mareſchal, Grand Chancellor: as alſo the
Sindico or Judge, who publiquely performs his office, in attending
the buſineſs of the City *Naples*: which hath five kindes of aſſembly
of the Nobles: *di Nido, di Porta Nova, di Capuana, di Montagna, di
Porto*; which congregations or aſſemblies, although under other
denominations, the City *Capua* likewiſe enjoyes

Many Cities moſt antient and adorned with ſignal conditions have
been in this Kingdom, whoſe memory is yet in being, except
Oſea, Metaponto, Sibari, and others hereafter ſpoken of.

The Foſter Children of this Kingdome, truly famous in Letters,
were *Archita, Eurito, Alemeone, Zenone, Leucippus, Parmenides, Ti-
mæus, Ennius, Lucillus, Pacuvius, Horatius, Ovidius, Statius, Juvenal, Saluſtius, Cicero*, and *San Thomaſus*, beſides others more modern

I wil be ſilent of ſuch *ſommi Pontifici*, or Popes, the Emperors,
Kings, the valorous Captains of war, and the thouſands of Prelates, Princes and Heroes, as likewiſe of the male and female ſpirits,
(who perpetually contemplate the Countenance of God) as this
Kingdom hath happily given birth to.

Theſe following have been Lords of the Kingdom of *Naples*, to wit,
the *Greeks*, the *Goths*, the *Vandals*, the *Longobards*, *Sarazens*, the
Turks, the *Hormeni*, the *Suevi*, the *French*, the *Catalonians* the *Arragonians*, the *Flemmings* or *Spaniards*, and ſometime, the not to be for-
gotten *Romans*.

The Journey towards *POZZVOLO*.

THe Mountain *Paufilippus*, though very high is well manured with vineyards, and rich Townes alſo in old time as we col-lect from *Pliny* and others ; it extends into the Sea in form of a Pro-montory, and ſhuts up the way between *Naples* and *Pozzuolo*, and was an intollerable toyle to the Travellers to paſs over or go round it; before twas cut in two; tis now by the induſtry of the paſſengers, through their hollowing it for the head, and levelling it for the feet become the miſtreſs of waies, being ſtrait, plain and eaſy : there-fore the *Græcians* to the purpoſe by a word in their tongue called it *Paufilippo*, as if they would ſay a remover of troubles and labour : by which ſurname the *Græcians* of old called *Jupiter*, as we read in *Sophocles*. The mountain is hollowed within for one thouſand paces in length, twelve foot wide, and as much more in heighth, on which as *Strabo* writes two Carts may commodiouſly meet and paſs under earth: *Seneca* calls the cavern *Cripta Neapolitana:* though now the name is changed for *Grotta*, where he writes to *Lucullus* in the 58. epiſtle, to have run the whole fortune of the *Atleſi*, for that he found copiouſly in a part of the muddy way, i mplaiſtrings, and in the ſame cavern, abundance of the duſt of *Pozzuolo :* we alſo have proved and tryed that duſt, as others did . for we find that troops in the paſſage by foot or horſe raiſe the duſt, and that at our iſſuing out of that obſcurity we were all yellow, and looking and laughing at one a-nother we much wondered at it, finding a more then deſirable in-convenience, in cleanſing our ſelves of that filth. The cauſe of which duſt is eaſily, known to proceed from the excluſion of the wind and rain, ſo that the raiſed duſt (as *Seneca* ſaies) having no Vent falls down on it ſelf, or on thoſe that raiſe it : whence we collect that in the time of *Nero* this cavern had no Caſements or breathings whereby it might receive air or light, more then at the entrance and end, becauſe *Seneca* calls it a long and obſcure priſon, where nothing is to be ſeen but darkneſs. Yet *Cornelius Strabo* teſtifies, by the riving or chops of the Mountain in divers places, that many win-dows gave it light, which being cloſed or earthed up, either through the earthquakes or the careleſneſs of the times, we may rationally imagine, rendred this long cavern ſo darkſom. *Pietro Raſſano* a *Sici-lian* Biſhop of *Lucerie* writes, that in his time, which we may count to be above 250. yeers ſince, this cavern was found without any holes, and without light, and that the entrance and the out-paſſage were ſo filled up with ruines and buſhes, that twas terrible to enter without light : and that therefore the King of the *Arragoni-ans Alfonſus* the firſt, having reduced this Province, enlarged and levelled the way and the entrance of the Caverne, and cloſing the top of the Cavern opened two lights, which obliquely enlighten it, whoſe reflection at a diſtance ſeems to the aſpicients, ſnow ſcatte-red on the earth : in the midſt of this darkſome way is a little ſacred place cut in the walls of the mountain, where night and day a lamp perpetually burns, which puts the travellers in re-

mem-

membrance of the eternal light, and shews in a painted tablet our salvation, proceeding from the virgin Mother *Mary:* a Lampe perpetually burns there, and the words at the Incounter are *Alla Marina, Alla Montagne.*

In our times D: *Pietro di Toledo,* magnificently restored and aggrandized this work so worthy of eternity, being then governor of *Naples* Kingdom by the favour of the Emperor *Charls* the filth: the way is now become so strait, that it seems to such as enter the cavern, a Star, to which they ought to direct their course in the darknels, by means whereof, with what pleasure they behold all such as enter on foot or horsback at the other end, who seem like Pigmies at that distance, is scarce imaginable. Divers are the opinions of the learned touching the time and beginning of this great work worthy of the mind of *Serse:* omitting the idle prating of the vulgar who attribute it to the magick incantations of the Poet *Virgil,* whose ashes by the opinion of many ly at the mouth of theCavern: or of others who make one *Basso* the author, of whom there is no record among the antients: we beleive we may draw from *Strabo, Eforus, Homerus* and other greek writers, that the *Cimmerij* a most antient people dwelt in that *Canton* of *Campania,* between *Baio, Lucerno,* and *Averno,* and that they lay in denns and *subterranean* Caves, and that running the one to the o her they dug out metals, and hollowed mountains, and in profound Caverns exercised (by means of their Priests,) Negromancy and inchantments, conducting travellers, and pilgrims to the oracles of the infernal gods: which people being destroyed, the *Greeks,* who succeeded them and built *Cuma* and *Naples,* accommodated as most suppose those Caves of the *Cimmerii* into hot baths, and baths, ways and other conveniences for humane use. So likewise the *Romans,* after the example of the *Grecians,* being chiefly enclined to great and magnificent impreses encreased these laborious under-ground structures, and at the time when they became the Lords of the world, they there erected their Palaces of Recreation, and Mannor houses little interiour to Castles when the rare quality of the dust of *Pozzuolo* was discovered (extracted from those mountains) to be very efficacious for binding, building, and establishing foundations of Edifices in the waters. *Strabo* affirms that in his time *M. Agrippa* under *Augustus,* cutting up the wood on the mountain *Avernus,* which corrupted the air, among the other antique & magnificent things found out a *subterranean* cavern hollowed even to *Cuma,* the which as was conjectured, together with another between *Naples* and *Pozzuolo,* was made by one *Corceios,* and that in his time the custom of the Countrey was to make such underground waies and Caverns: from whose words we collect, that for a long time before *Strabo,* the *Cocceian* family were got together in *Campania,* and that the place was called *Spelonca* though for truth we cannot set down any thing of certain of him that first made it: nor is it probable to me, that *Strabo* could be ignorant of the deeds of *L. Lucullus,* the which in those places were very great and of excessive expence, from which he was called *Serse Togato,* by *Pompeius Magnus,* by *Tuberone,* by *Cicero,* and the other principal men of *Rome:* wherefore their sence pleaseth me, who impose on him the concavating the *Pausilipus* for the conveniency of his

Villa: becaufe tis written by *Marcus Varro, Pliny*, and others, that *L. Lucullus* cut a mountain in the midft of *Naples*, with greater coft, then he expended in building his Manor houfe: for to what end fhould he? not to level and accomodate the way for paffengers: but rather to open a gulfe of the Sea whereby at his pleafure to admit and let in Sea water to his Fifhponds that fo the caves of the mountain might be a good receipt for his Fifh (which he kept alive) to lye in as well in Winter as Summer.

At the outgoing of this Cavern, you perceive by little & little the odour of brimftone in the air, which here and there proceeds out of divers vaults. By it lies the Lake *Aniano*, in fimilitude of an Amphitheatre furrounded and fhut in on all fides by the Mountains, and through a mouth of a hill cut with iron great plenty of Sea water, and great concaves, made ponds for Fifh, at prefent filled with mud, fand, and ruines of ftructures: *Leandro* and others write from the relation of the peafants there, that in the midft of the Lake there is no mud: and that in the fpring time, with great noyfe & fury fall down from the higheft præcipices of the rocks there round into thefe watersKnots of Serpents knit and bound together, which are never feen again to get out.

Near them are the fweatingRooms of *Germanus* vaulted: from under which, through the fuperficies rife vapours fo hot, that who enters though naked, fhall foon perceive a mighty fweat trickle down his body.

Wherefore thofe places are held of exceeding validity to fuch as fuffer under the gout by purging the bad and malevolent humours, they heal internal wounds, and are helpfull for many infirmities of the body: which if any defire ampler fatisfaction in, he may read the Tract of *Gio Francefco Lombardo*, who gives an account of all fuch as have writ in verfe or profe of the baths and wonders of *Pozzuolo* but we are obliged to too much haft, to relate with care and amplitude all particulars wee meet with.

In the *Campagnia* of *Pozzuolo*, *Baia*, *Cuma*, and the near Ifland *Enarie*, by the old *Greeks* called *Pythecus*, are found great quantity of the like Miracles, that it might be well beleived that there nature ferves *Apollo* perpetually, and *Æfculapius*, *Higia*, and the *Nymphs*: although the earthquakes, and the volleys of fire which frequently happen, demonftrate fufficiently that in divers places, that as well under the foundation of the Sea, as under the Mountains, and in the loweft parts of the Earth great fires are kindled, whofe boyling vapours and flames working their own way through the veins of Allum, fulphure, pitch and other materials, caufe to rife in divers places hot and boyling fountains, and create baths in the Caverns comodious for fweating. Yet the nature and faculty of thefe things are different, being conformed to the propriety of the materials and the earth whence the fource proceeds: fo that among the medicinal and healthfull faculty of thefe waters, we find fome waters and vapours mortal, which iffue out of fome muddy earth, evil in it felf. *Pliny* in the fecond of his natural Hiftories writes, that in *Italy*, and particularly in the *Campagna* of *Sinveffa*, and *Pozzuolo*, are vents or breathings, fo evil, that they evaporate a mortall air.

At

At the foot of the mountain which circles the Lak *Anianus*, not far from the said waters appears a Cave called *Grotta di Cane*, eight or nine paces in circuit, by which mouth two or more men may commodiously enter together: where from the inmost part of the stone, from its invisible pores proceed hot spirits, but so subtile and dry, that they carry not with them any similitude of smoke or vapour, although they condense the air, driven thither by the wind and the colds of the Cavern with great heat, and change them into water, as the drops demonstrate which hang at the entrance of the Cave, shining like little stairs, when they are beheld at the opening of the Cave, by those without in the light: they have been often taken for drops of quicksilver. All men generally believe this Grotta to have such an innate property that if any living thing should pass the prefixed term of a certain ditch in the entrance, it would without doubt suddenly fall upon the earth, and would be wholly deprived of life, if not immediately drawn out, and cast into the near standing waters or pool, called *Agnano*, by whose coldness only in a short time by little and little it recovers Life. Whereof Travellers dayly make experiments, if curious to know the wonders of nature, by casting in cocks or dogs or some other live creature to which they fasten a rope to draw them up by. *Leandro Alberto* writes that *Charls* the eighth King of *France*, when a hundred and 14. yeers since he drove out the Spanish and for some time Lorded over *Naples*, caused an Asse to be driven in, who suddenly whirled about and dyed.

Another who two hundred yeers since wrote of these baths, relates, that a foot hardy rash Souldier, run in armed and dyed miserably: *Corona Tighio* writes, that in the presence of *Charls* Prince of *Cleves*, the Spanish Captains cast two cheerfull dogs by force into the *Grotta*: who strove all possible to avoid it, as if they had formerly experimented the danger; the which being taken out dead, by means of the refreshing waters in the aforenamed Lake were restored to life: one of which being again cast into the cave, and being thence drawn & cast into the Lake, returning not thereby to Life, was left for dead on the bank, who not long after as waking from a profound sleep raising himself, and limping and staggering, so soon as possible ran away, every one that saw it smiled, and *Charls* praised the dog, that he would not for that time become a victime to the beares; after this tryal they cast a brands end lighted into the *Grotta*, beyond the prefixed sign, which come to the bottom seemed to extinguish, and raised up a little higher, to rekindle: which demonstrated that the spirits proceeding from the superficies, as more hot and dry in the bottom, consumed the more subtil nutriment of the flame, but having lesse vigour at more distance from the foundation, they rather rekindle the hot and grofs smoke and flames of the brands-end: as we see the flame of a lighted candle will pass to another newly put out, by means of the smoke; and the beams of the Sun when united by a burning glass, are very vigorous and will set tow or flax on fire if approached too near. *Fiebius* through his exceeding love to study, travialing over *Italy*, and having an extream desire to inquire into the nature of all things by which he might acquire knowledge, wondring at the reports of the miracles of *Pozzuolo*, reſolved to ſearch out the cauſe by a nearer ſcrutiny then had been made by others.

He could not beleive that thoſe drops that hung ſo reſplendent at the end of the Caverne, were quick-ſilver: wherefore being counſelled by a certain juvenile and youthfull audacity, he paſſed the propoſed meaſure in the Cavern; having enclined his body a little and getting ſomewhat nearer, he found they were drops of clear water, and taking them on his finger from the ſharp pendent of the rock, he demonſtrated the truth to his companions, requiring them either to beleive or enter and make proof.

Which alſo happened: for that _Antonio Aniſtelo_, and _Arnoldio Niveldio_, two _Holandeſi_, noble youths and companions in the journey with _Righius_, got near: who when he had for ſome time ſtood in the Cave, and perceived the heat, how it aſcended from his feet to his leggs and knees, yet underwent no other then a giddineſs and pain in his head; and ſweat only on the forehead and the temples through the heat of the place: he learnt by experience that that heat, and thoſe nocive vapours are not luſty and violent, but when near their riſe; and there they kill ſmall animals or great, but chiefly the four footed, becauſe they alwayes go with their head downwards, whereby being neceſſitated to draw in with their breath thoſe hot and boyling vapours, their vital ſpirits become ſuddenly ſuffocated with too much heat: the which alſo are as ſuddenly releived by the imediate refreſhment of the waters in the Lake, if the animal be forthwith caſt therein when drawn out of the Cavern. Whilſt _Righius_ was performing this, an _Italian_ who guarded ſome herds wondred ſtrangely at his temerity, and remained aſtoniſht at the ſucceſs, many times demanding if he did it not by the magick art, nor would he be perſwaded that _Righius_ could avoyd the nociveneſſe of that _Grotta_, otherwiſe then by enchantment or witch craft: which made him mock at the _plebeian_ ſimplicity, laughing at the vulgar, who for the moſt part attribute that to the Magick art, which appears wonderfull, and produceth ſtupendious effects, from their incapacity to comprehend the cauſe: but to return to our voyage.

From the _Bucca Coronea_, we are brought to _Zolfettara_, as at preſent they call thoſe places which were of old celebrated with the invention of various fables of old Poets for theſe wonders of nature: who ſing that the Gyants buryed under this mountain, even from hell caſt forth of their throats, Flames at that time when earthquakes happen.

Et montes, ſcopulos, terraſque invertere dorſo,

Theſe Mountains are full of Sulphure, Allum, and Vitriol, the chief whereof as _Strabo_ writes, ſtood pendent at a few paces diſtance from the _Colonna_ of _Pozzuolo_ now diſtant from the caſtle _Novo_, about a mile: from the form of which place, tis gueſſed, that the top of this Mountain was at laſt conſumed and emitted into the profundity of the near valley by the continual fires, whence that which of old was a high and eminent top or head, is now a great ditch in the plain of a valley and that which was of old the ribs and

flanks

flanks of a mountain, are now the upper part of (helfs and rocks, which surround the plain, with a certain fence in length about a thousand and fifty foot, in bredth about a thousand foot: *Pliny* writes that they were nominated from their whitenefs *Leucogei*, and the plain or Level, *Campagna Phlegerea*, from the flame and fire there ever extant: which *Silius* the Italian confirms.

Cornelius Strabo calls this place the *Piazza* and (hop of *Vulcan*, where likewife fome fable, the Gyants to be overcome by *Hercules*: here the Mountains feem continually to burn at their roots: for that on all fides they emit fmokes by many mouths which fmell of fulphure which fmokes are blowen by the wind all over the neighbouring Countrey, and fometimes to *Naples*. Antiently thefe Hills, as we draw from *Dion Caffius* and *Strabo* emitted greater fires, as alfo thofe about the *Lucrino*, and *Averno*, which are not a few, burnt and e-mitted like furnaces grofs fmokes and flames. Now the plain as alfo the hill *Phlegrei* are deprived of their perpetual flames and are caver-nous in many places and become yellowifh, as from the materiall and colour of fulphure: the earth when fpurned by the foot, re-founds like a drum, through its concavity underneath, where you may hear (with wonder) under your feet boyling waters, grofle and inflamed fmokes to make a horrid noife, and run too and fro through the fubterranean Caverns, which the force of the exhala-tion hath made, which how great you may thence gueffe; ftop any of thofe mouths or holes, with a good great ftone, and you fhall fuddenly and with violence fee it amoved by the ftrength of the fmoke. Here they compofe medicinable pots of brim-ftone.

In the fame plain or level lies alfo a great marifh filled alwaies with a black fcalding hot water: which fometimes ufeth to change place, and the waters making themfelves hard (as tryed fewit ufeth being cold to bind it felf to the fides of the Veffel tis melted in) do thereby and with the force of the exhalation increafe or diminifh. When I was there it boyled with great noife and fmoke, as if it had been a huge chauldron filled with blackifh mud, and therefore ex-ceeded not then its bounds and limits: but I remember, that at my view thereof, this *Vorago* mounted and caft up of afudden like a *Pyramides*, eight or nine foot high, (beyond the common ftature of man,) that thick water yellow and of the colour of fulphure: which alfo the people of *Pozzuolo* affirm, adding that fometimes twill rife from fixteen to twenty four feet.

When the Sea is in a ftorm, this water is of various colours; though for the moft part like fulphure, and fometimes other, accor-ding as the fubterranean winds are difturbed by the fea blafts, and being invigoured among the flames, with all poffible force expels fome of the earth mixed with divers colours from the deepeft veins. Thefe very winds, when moft quiet under ground, the top of the Fens or moors being only difturbed, caufe a grofs thick water, co-loured with black to be caft out. Thefe things of fuch occult na-ture, do certainly afford ufefull and welcome matter for confidera-tion and ftudy to fuch as love to fearch thereinto; which *Cicero* ve-ry pertinently terms, the natural food of the mind. And hence we certainly know, that the globe of the earth is not in every part fo-lid,

lid, and maſſy, but in ſome places hollow, cavernous, and full of vains and pores, like as is the living body of any animal: and that with the continual motion of the imbodied elements, water and air, it becomes penetrated, and is by the ſame nouriſhed, increaſed or diminiſhed together with its ſeveral kinds and changes of plants, and that the earth ſoops up vaſt quantities of the Sea waters, diſperſt on it by means of thoſe pores, the which being encountred by ſome fierce winds, occaſion a motion of thoſe waters in its inmoſt part, and in the ſtraiteſt paſſages; and the ſame winds there ſplit in ſunder among the rocks and ſtones, grow violently hot, and kindle vaſt fires, the which conſuming whatever they meet, empty the internal parts of the earth, and drawing to themſelves thorough thoſe pores the neighbouring winds, together with great ſmokes; they there augment beyond meaſure, ſearching out an egreſſe, with horrible noiſe and ſhakings of the earth and mountains.

Pellunt oppoſitas moles, ac vincula rumpunt.

As more at large *Cornelius Severus* a moſt learned Poet hath declared in his *Ænea*, and hence proceed the earthquakes, whirlpooles, and openings of the earth, the forcing out of flames, the rivolets of fire, boyling fountains, and hot vapours. *Dion Caſſius* writes that in his time, the ſaid Mountains of *Pozznolo*, had more fountains of running fire in the likeneſs of water, that through the exceſſive heat the water took fire and burnt, and the fires with the mixture of the waters acquired a fluxible corpulency; in ſuch ſort that theſe contrary elements, did not ſeparate: and we find even in our time that the flames and ſulphure, conſerve and nouriſh themſelves in theſe waters, and that they endure for ſo many ages and never conſume, but alwayes continue and guſh out in the ſame conduits, the which *Severus* the Poet graciouſly ſets down in theſe verſes.

Atque hæc ipſa tamen jam quondam extincta fuiſſent,
Ni furtim aggeneret ſecretis callibus humor
Materiam ſilvamque ſuam, preſſoque canali
Huc illuc ageret ventos, & paſceret ignes.

So alſo he writes of the *Phlegrean* Fields and of the ſame place between *Naples* and *Cuma*, whereof we now diſcourſe, *viz.*

Ejus ab æterno pingueſcens ubere ſulfur
In merces legitur.

As at preſent the King exhauſts a great toll from that brimſtone, and merchandize of allum. Wee obſerve furthermore, that theſe ſulphurious or brimſtone waters commixt with the ſaltneſs of the Sea, and with the aſhes of burnings, turn into ſtone after they have cooled themſelves by running a ſhort courſe: and that they communicate the ſame faculty to thoſe rivers and brooks with which they commix, whereof though a clear experiment cannot be had, yet that innate quality in all the rivers of *Italy*, as the *Tyber*, the

the *Teverone*, the Lake of *Luca*, in the *Nera* and others of veiling the sides or brims of the banks and the Conduits whereby they pass as also the conserves and receptions of their standing pools, give sufficient proof. Besides tis as clear as the Sun, and dayly observed that their continued washing of wood, plants, arms, bodies and roots of trees, the stubble of herbs, and the leaves by little & little are covered with a kind of scurf of stone, and by revolving become by chance formed like comfits of aniseeds, fennel, cinamon and almonds, and so much resembling such, that with no great difficulty some more greedy then wary have been coufened with them: and in truth what *Vitruvius*, *Seneca*, *Dione*, *Pliny*, and others have writ of the wonders of *Vesuvius* and *Pozzuolo*, seems beyond reason; to wit that the waters receive that nature and particularity from the tenuity of the ashes of the burned sulphure; which ashes the fire having in part reduced as small as atomes, in part dissolved into liquid moisture, and in part expelled by the vapours of the subterranean fires through the veins of the earth and by springs, we observe to be converted into that dust which the antients called *Pozzuolo* from the place; and that they unite so soon as they attain the waters, and cooling with them, attain the just substance of stone, and that the waters which run by those places mutually receive a certain nature of connexing to any thing, so that they easily cleave to the body they touch, and make it become stone,

And for wonders of this kind, scarce can any be found like those in the caves of the *Apenines* near the old chanel of the *Anione* by *Vico Varo*, where the waters distilling through the clefts and chinks in the Rocks, in their fall by little and little form it self like stone, in the likeness of high Collumns in divers forms, branchy bodies of trees, and monstrous bodies of *Centaures* and Gyants; in which Caverns or labyrinths of pure darkness, with candles may be found out objects which in one word, may worthily be said to feed and satiate the mind of the curious searcher into the secrets of nature: but beware that the light be not extinguished by the frequent flappings of the night bats, who thither retire as to a secure retreat by millions to avoid the light of the day.

Thus beholding the hills *Leucogei*, and the various surges of medicinal fountains, of baths, hot baths, and the Cavernes, you go to *Pozzuolo*, amids the great and spatious ruines of the antient *Colony*.

POZZVOLO.

THe *Roman* Empire flourishing, that maritime tract of *Campania*, about *Cumà*, *Misena*, and *Pozzuolo*, was in great reputation for the temperature of the air, the pleasantness of the scite, the quantity of good waters, and the extream fertility of the fields, and therefore replenished with great possessions of the Gentry, and proud Palaces, of the principal men: And to speak truth, no other part of *Italy* nor of the Provinces, or the world, appears more proper for the confumption of the *Romans* riches then that peice of *Campania* lying between *Capua* and *Naples*, and extending to *Cuma*, where with good reafon the common faying was that *Bacchus* and *Ceres* contended, for fuperiority. the luxury and fenfuality of which maritime places and Iflands, made the old Poets in their antient fables of delights call thefe the houfe and habitation of the *Syrenes* : And this caufed fome old Poets and them of no fmall efteem to aver thofe things which happened between *Ulijfes* and the Nymph *Calipfo*, to have been acted in the Ifland of *Pozzuolo* and not in *Ogygia* a place of the *Thebans*, or in the Ifland of the Promontory of *Lacinio*; which Goddefs by fome called the daughter of *Atlas*, by others of *Oceanus* and *Tethys*, was held a Nymph of the Sea, and reigned in the Ifle *Ogygia*, , receiving *Ulyffes* when he efcaped drowning ; and took this name from her adornments of body, and delights fhe liued in : *Homer* calls her a Nymph very well adorned with fair riches : And in truth who confiders the fhores of *Pozzuolo*, muft in truth conclude that to his imagination, a more pleafant delightfull and glorious place cannot be found out than it, nor a Seat more inclined by nature to receive and carrefs Travellers; thence tis that the Poets of old feign that *Ulyffes* there fixing and dwelling, recollected his many paft peregrinations and perils, and alfo in the Ifle *Ithaca*, whereof *Dion Caffius* and *Philoftratus Lemnius*, in the Life of *Apollonius* make mention. And although at prefent the whole is filled with ruines, and every thing lies even with the earth, through too intollerable fufferings by war and time, yet are the re objects enow, which fuch as will reape any profit from the curiofity of the antient arts and hiftories, ought maturely and with great induftry to confider. But to begin, *Pozzuolo* is a City fcituate on a hill in the midft of a fhore of the Sea, which though very fair and large, cannot yet be at all compared in any part with the riches and grandezza of the antient *Colony*, as may be clearly extracted from the wayes pitched with flint, and the foundations of publique edifices: whereof the Sea hath fwallowed up one part, & earthquakes and wars the other. It was a moft antient Colony of the *Grœcians* wch. the *Samii* conducted hither in the time of *Tarquinius Superbus*, in the fixty fecond *Olimpiad*, as the Chronologer *Fufebius* writes and *Stephanus Eyfantius* confirms: which happened about the time that the republique of the *Samii* was tyranized by the three Brothers, *Policrates*, *Silus*, and *Pantagnoftus*. At that time alfo *Pythagoras Samius*, flying from his own Countrey in *Morava*, attained the potent City of *Italy Crotone*; where he layed down a new Philofophy then called *Italian*, and by it acquired a high efteem: with whofe Laws the *Italian* Cities (being reformed from the *Grœcian*, by the indeavours of three hundred of his Scholars, as *Diogenes Laertius* writes) received the government of *Ariftocracy*, under which they lived happily for many Ages. Others will likewife that the *Colony* of the *Samii* from the obfervance of the Juftice of the moft holy Empire, wherewith it was governed was called *Dicearchia*, by which name all the *Greek* writers ftiled, it and many times after their example, the *Latin*. *Strabo* writes, *Dicearchia* was once the Piazza of the *Cumani*, and that afterwards the *Romans* called it *Pozzuolo*, either as fome will from the many deep pits, or as others from the fulphurious ftenches of the waters there arifing; It became

under

under the power of *Romans* in the warr with *Hannibal,* when *Capua* was taken by a feige, and feverely chaftifed for the perfidie and ingratitude it exercifed: from which was then taken its government and liberty, and annually fent thither from the *Roman* people a prefect to govern them, which happened the five hundred forty fecond yeer after *Romes* building: when many Caftles and Cities ran the like fortune with it, for that they had with arms defended *Hannibal* as *Titus Livius* fets down, wherefore *Sextus Pompeius* fets *Pozzuolo* among the ten Prætectures of *Campania,* on which the *Roman* People every yeer impofed Governors: for all which fome yeers after, they pulled farther by difpofition of the *Acilian* Law, to wit that they fent thither a Colony of *Roman* Citizens, and made it one of the five maritimate Colonies, which were drawn from *Rome* in the five hundred and fifty ninth yeer by force of the Laws of the faid *Acilius* the Tribune, as is clear in *Titus Livius:* being then Confuls *Publius Scipio Africanus* writes the fecond time, and *Titus Sempronius. Vellejus Paterculus* from the opinion of fome, that the Colony was later fent thither, to wit 3 luftres or 15 yeers after the above written time, and addes that in fum the verity is not punctually known.

Yet verily the old memorials of *Pozzuolo,* copious enough in the houfe of *Hadrianus Guilernus* the moft courteous, learned, and curious beyond meafure in antient hiftories, wholly agree with *Titus Livius:* where is extant one of thofe ftone Tablets, containing the fecond Law, the Regulation of publick edifices and expences there to be had: which was made in the *Confulacy* of *P. Rutilius* and *Cn. Mallius Maximus,* the fix hundred forty and eight yeear as the *Fafti Capitolini* demonftrate, which happened in the ninth yeer after the conduct of that Colony to *Pozzuolo,* as thefe words fet down on the beginning of the faid Law clearly prove.

Ab Colonia deducta anno X C.
N. *Eufidio N. F. M. Tullio Duum vir*
R. *Rutilio. Cn. Mallio Cos.*
Operum. Lex. II.

From which words we clearly comprehend, that the comencement of this Colony was under the Confulacy of *Martius Portius Cato* and *L. Flaccus,* in the five hundred forty eighth yeer, although *Livius* fets it down to have been the following yeer. *Auguftus* being at laft become Conqueror in the Civil wars, having reftored peace, and fhut up the Temple of *Janus*; for reward of the veteran Souldiers, difpofed them into the 28 Colonies of *Italy,* among which *Pozzuolo* was one, then made a military Colony, as *Suetonius* writes and as may be drawn from the fragment of the Military Colonies.

From the above written obfervations is certainly known, how antient the Colony of *Pozzuolo* is, and that many times Inhabitants were thither fent and inrolled. And therefore this Author holds for very imperfect, and ill treated from the infufficiency or inobfervancy of the remembrancer, what *Tacitus* fets down in the fourteenth book of his Annals: and fo *Juftus Lipfius* thinks alfo, for in the acts of *Rome* in the eighth hundred and twelfth yeer, the Emperor *Nero* and *Coſſus Lentulus* being Conſuls, we find theſe words of *Tacitus*. *At in Italia vetus oppidum Puteoli jus Coloniæ, & cognomentum a Nerone adipiſcuntur*, adding no more as if *Pozzuolo* for no preceding time had the quality of a Colony, whereas *Titus Livius* clearly proves it to have been in that condition two hundred and forty yeers before: but theſe two may be eaſily reconciled, by the adjuſting of one ſingle word, to wit the writing it *verus* inſtead of *vetus*: in theſe words. *At in Italia verus Oppidum Puteoli novum jus Coloniæ, & cognomentum a Nerone adipiſcuntur:* for that being at firſt called *Colonia Auguſta*, with *Nero* it was called *Auguſta Neroniana*, and thence tis that *Tacitus* ſaies that *Pozzuolo* obtained a new condition with a new name: but *Tacitus* not explaining the occaſion why then a Colony was ſent thither, or who gave it new condition, and what that condition was, the place ſeems to want more then one word: and becauſe the particle *At* ſeparates the word afore ſpecified and the difference of things and the particle *non tamen* is placed in the midſt of the period which followes, this place is therefore believed defective and that therefore theſe words ſet a cloud before the eyes, and ſcruples in the ſtudies of the curious, which this Author hath thought not eaſily removable without ſome ſupplement to that place of *Tacitus* to the effect following, viz. *At in Italia verus Oppidam Puteoli novum ius Coloniæ, & cognomentum adipiſcuntur æquè cladem paſſi: Queis arritum Principis beneficium facere Coloni ex diverſis legionibus undecunque coarti, numero licet frequentes, ut veterem Tarentium, & Antium adſcripti, non tamen infrequentiæ locorum ſubvenere, dilapſis pluribus in Provinciis, in quibus ſtipendia expleverant:* And thus will the difference be known between what fell out to *Pozzuolo,* and what to *Laodicea,* by the copulation *At:* of which Cities this returned to its proper ſtate by its own power, the other not, although it aſſiſted the Prince, as did happen to *Tarento,* and *Antio,* the occaſion of which misfortune *Tacitus* gratiouſly declares.

The learned are intreated to have due conſideration of this place, and to note the defects with a *ſtelletta.* To return then to our firſt purpoſe: the Author when he copied out thoſe inſcriptions, whileſt there permanent, it occurred to him, that a Colony was of new conducted to *Pozzuolo* under the Empire of the *Veſpaſiani,* and was called *Flavia,* for that he eſpied among thoſe old ſtones, a great ſquare marble one engraven with letters of a foot long a piece, the which by being continually expoſed to the ſurges of the Sea, hath its characters almoſt eaten out, yet not ſo wholly but that one may read the third part of the elogy inſcribed in the old Marble Arch, the which the *Flavian* Colony erected to expreſs a gratefull ſence to *Antonius Pius Cæſar* for his liberality in reſtoring the ports: which part of the Elogy will hereafter be repeated. In the mean time behold in *Pozzuolo* and its neighbourhood, the meritorious objects: Among others a vaſt Church now entitled *S. Proculo Martire,* the which of old *Calphurnius* had dedicated to *Auguſtus Cæſar:* tis built in a Corinthian order, as may be underſtood by the Porticue, containing one peice of the old title in the frontiſpeice in theſe words.

L. Cal.

All Authors question who this *Calphurnius* the Son of *Lucius* was, chiefly for that there were so many *Calphurnij*, and they famous in the time of *Augustus*: and if it be lawfull to make use of conjecture none comes nearer then mine, that *L. Calphurnius* Son of *Lucius* called *Pisone Frugi*, after he had been *Conjul* and Prefect of Provinces, was also Prefect of *Rome*, after *T. Statilius Taurus*, who was twice Consul and triumphed: he exercised this very charge in the time of *Augustus* and *Tiberius* for twenty yeers, as *Tacitus* in the fifth Book of his Annals sets forth; who writes that his father was a man appertaining to the Censor: whence tis impssioble but *L. Pisone* must have been his Father, of whom the eloquent tongue of *Cicero* speaks so much ill, as that he was banished whilst he was Consul. He was then Censor in the seuen hundred fifty and third yeer, whilst *Cæsar* Dictator warred against the confederates of *Pompey*. Among all the greatest charges and employments which the *Calphurnian* family participated, they only twice administred the Censorship. The first time *L. Pisone Frugi* was Censor after the Consulacy, in the 695 yeer of *Rome* who being Tribune of the People, prevailed for that Law against the rapine of the Provincial Magistrates: and the second time fifty eight yeers after,

This Temple is so well built, that in the space of so many ages neither Time the consumer of all things, nor the insolencies of enemies, who have many times destroyed the rest of the City, have been able to ruinate, which could not come otherwise to passe then from the beams being composed of marble, in which scarce a fastning appears: yet the impetuous force of the earthquakes have in part moved it out of order, in such sort that the right angle of the Frontispiece is faln with a part of the Title, where certain ruptures appear.

Of such esteem was this Fabrick, that the architectors were not ashamed the work being finished to place their name there: being *Luccio Cocino Liberta of Luca*, and *Caio Postumi*, as we read in the left wall of the Church in these words.

> *L. Cocceius*
> *C. Postumi L.*
> *Anctus Architect.*

Many other holy sacred places that were therein are either faln to nothing, or at leastwise very badly handled. The Temple of *Neptune* as *Cicero* affirms was the most famous, of which some great Fragments to this day remain near *San Francesco*, as vaults, arches, huge wals & other places with their nooks for the statues: but its columns and high ornaments of marble are taken away. Also nearthe Amphitheatre, are the footsteps & ruines of a Temple, which *Antonius Pius Augustus* had erected to *Adrian* the Emperor his Father who dy-

ed at *Baiæ* in the Mannor houſe of *Cicero* as *Spartianus* relates. Some
yeers laſt paſt many fair ſtatues and vaſt peices of Columnes and
Marbles were amoved, together with the Elogies of *Nerva, Trajan*
and *Adrian* the Emperors, that is to ſay of the Father, Grandfather
and great Grand-Father: to whom *Antonius* (having created them
Gods) had adorned ſacerdotal ſacrifices, of the *Flamins* and their
companions: and hence ſome believe he obtained the ſurname of
Pius the Pious, as we are inſtructed from the aforeſaid *Spartianus*,
and by *Julius Capitolinus*.

The Temple of the *NYMPHES*
extant on the Sea Shore without
POZZVOLO.

IT ſeems very likely that either the Sea or Earthquakes have ſwal-
lowed up the temple of the *Nymphs*, the which, we read in the
8th, Book of *Philoſtratus Cennius* in the life of *Apollonius Tiancus, Domitianus* the Emperour built on the ſea ſhore without *Pozzuolo:* he
writes that twas built with white ſtone, and that of old twas famous for divination, and that in it was found a fountain of running
ſpring water, from the which though any quantity were taken a-
way, twas never perceived to diminiſh; but this with infinite other
antiquities is now gone to nothing; yet now is evident at a little
diſtance from the Land near the *Via Campana* in the Sea a fountain
of ſweet water, which gurgles to this day with great force; whoſe
ſource may be alwaies perceived almoſt to admiration, if the Sea be
quiet and calm: let the ſtudious of antiquity conſider if in this
place the Temple of the *Nymphes* may have been, which conjecture
will not ſeem far from truth upon weighing the words of *Philoſtratus*, who relates, that *Apolloneus Trineus* appeared to his two Diſciples
Damicles and *Demetrius* was in the Temple of the *Nymphes* on the Sea
ſhore without *Pozzuolo*, who were diſputing the nature of the a-
bovenamed fountain, where alſo is the Iſland of *Caliſſus* to whom
the ſucceſſes of what happened with *Uliſſes* they relate in the fables.

 Furthermore, as twere in the midſt of the *Colony*, remains yet a
moſt huge Amphitheatre little leſſe then entire, compoſed of ſquared
ſtones, the which notwithſtanding its ill treatment by earthquakes
the taking away many of its ſtones, and the plowing of its ſoyl, yet
appears in its firſt form, enlarged into a more large circuit, then was
uſual for the Emperors, & *Leandro Alberto* ſaies that by meaſuring he
found it tobe in length in the plain within, 172 foot, in bredth only
92. foot.

 Ferrante Loffredo Marques of *Trevico* affirms, this the moſt antient
Amphitheatre, ſuppoſing it to be built before *Rome*, loſt its liberty

ty under the Emperours, from an old infcription in marble there found, demonftrating under what Confuls this Fabrick was repaired at the publick expence of the Citizens of *Pozzuolo*: which infcription although much fought for by me, I had not the good hap to fee.

Many fragments of Acqueducts are yet to be feen, which either paffed through or furounded the Mountains: nor is it an eafy matter to number the conferves for the waters made in divers formes, fome entire, and fome ruinated by earthquakes, many of which are under ground and very large, which who enters, without a clue of thread, a light, or a well practifed guide, may dwell there for ever, fo intricate are the labyrinths, built without gates, heads or turning ftreets: from which we may affuredly know, that the *Romans* with vaft expence thither drew, and therein preferved great plenty of thofe fweet waters, abounding on that Maritimate coaft. The vulgar unfkilled in old hiftory, as in all things very ignorant, have moft injurioufly expreffed themfelves, in giving ridiculous names to thefe edifices, calling them, *Pifcine mirabili*, wonderfull fifh pools, *Cento Celle*, the hundred Cells, and *Grotte Draconarie*, Dragons Caves. Soe alfo have they handled the fountains and baths in number forty or more between *Pozzuolo, Miffeno* and *Cuma*, of divers forts, and efficacious for fundry difeafes. But tis not our purpofe to look back and take notice by one and one of thefe things, having already fet forth whatever is there rare and worthy view; we fhall therefore referre fuch as defire more ample and compleat fatisfaction in the like objects to *Leandro Alberto*, and the other writers herein before mentioned.

The defcription of the Antient Port of
POZZUOLO.

SUch and fo great wonders, as here by degrees prefent themfelves to the view of the Traveller as he approaches the Sea fide, may well entertain him; for like mountains in the waters rife the immenfe moles of the old Port, that is, thirteen immenfe Piles, which fpring out of the water like fquare Towers, which in old time were conjoyned in manner of a bridge by frequent arches, but now by fortune and antiquity thofe grofs engines are feparated, and the falling down of fome of the Arches renders it unpaffable from one to the other: which muft have been caufed either from earthquakes or the furious Sea, the whole fabrick being compofed of burned earth like bricks of two foot fquare, not eafily to be divided and broke down by any other accident.

Tis certainly known, that when this Port was in being, it extended it felf into the Sea, in form of a large bridge, and bending it felf in the fashion of a bow, reached the fhore and the *Avernus*, and fo defended the place from the raging force and ftorms of the Sea, whofe haughtineffe was comodioufly bridled by means of thofe Moles.

And tis believed that the Antients there made thofe Arches, to the end that through them the fea waters might enter into the Port, and by its continual flowing and ebbing keep it cleanfed of the mud, which the rivers and rain waters brought down in to it from the *Terra firma* and the neighbouring hills, through which in their courfe to the Sea thofe waters muft firft paffe; and it had not been poffible to avoid the filling up of that port in few yeers, by that perpetual inroad of durt, had not the Sea waters through thofe Arches continually purged it of that mud and filthineffe fo drove into it : and this the inconvenience in the port of *Naples* and divers others, who are only furrounded with a bank without arches, fufficiently proves.

Suetonius in the life of *Caligula* from its vaftneffe calls it the Mole of *pozzuolo*, from whence thorough the midft of the Gulf of the Sea, *Caligula*, as he writes, to fhew his greatnefs and vanity, and to be able to tread and walk on the Sea as well as upon the Land; or as *Dion* faies becaufe he would imitate King *Xerxes*, who paffed his Army out of *Afia* into *Europe* over the ftreight of *Hellefpont* upon a wooden Bridge: commanded to be brought together and new built all the fhips he could get, which were infinite, and therewith caufed a Bridge to be made with the faid Ships fet in two Banks faftened and moored together with anchors chains and cables, which made them ftand fixt and firm, and extended even to *Baias* through the gulf of the Sea : he commanded this bridge to be made of boords fo ftrong and even and to lay fo much earth upon the fame, as it feemed to be firm ground and one of the ftreets of *Rome* like the *Strada Appia*. This being finifhed, he proudly attired in Robes of Gold and pearl, and a crown of Oaken boughes on his head (called *Civica*,) on horfeback entred at one end of the bridge and road to the other, accompanyed with the Band of the *Pretorian* Souldiers, and all the Nobles and Gentlemen of *Rome* : and the next day returned habited like a *Campanian*, in a Chariot, with a great multitude of his Friends. *Dion* writes that the night he lay on this bridge, he caufed fuch an infinite number of Torches, lanthorns and other Lights, to be lighted and fet up, that the clearneffe thereof did exceed the darkneffe of the night : *Caligula* boafting, that he had made of the night day, and of the Sea Land; & becaufe it happened that thefe two days the Sea was calm, he faid that *Neptune* did it for feare & to do him Reverence; *Suetonius* adds, that *Caligula* having invited many, who being on the fhore ready to goe on the Bridg where himfelf was, he turned them all over, breaking the bridg, and commanded fome that endeavoured to catch hold of the ropes of the Veffels, to be forced into the water with oars and other ftaves, which ferved for a jeft and pleafant fpectacle to this Monfter : *Seneca* in his 78th. Epiftle calls this *Machine* by the name of *Pila*, faying *Omnis in Pilis Puteolanorum turba confiftit, cum Alexandrinarum navium confpicitur adventus*. And therefore this *Machine*, in a ferene sky ferved to thofe of *Pozzuolo* to paffe and walk on, as if they had been in a

Piazza

Piazza, At the entrance on this Mole as aforesaid was a large Arch built of Marble, dedicated to the Emperor *Antonius Pius* by those of *Pozzuolo*, by way of gratitude for his remembrance of their Republique with liberality in moneys for repairing the Port, as we find from that piece of an Elogy aforementioned, here set down, for the benefit of such as delight in these particulars,

Æsari, Divi
hici, Nepoti Divi
onino Aug, Pio
olonia Flavia;
uper Cærera Ben-
us Pilarum vigin
quo, et Munition.

The entire contents whereof cannot easily be comprehended from these few remaining characters, but may in some sort be supplied from the said words, and the marks of the Lines wherewith those characters appeare, which being formed to our thoughts, seem after manner.

Imp. Cæsari Divi Hadriani filio Divi Trajani.
Parthici Nepoti Divi Nervi Pron. T. Ael. Hadriano.
Antonino August. Pio. Pont. Max. trib. pot. coss. pp.
Colonia Flavia, Aug. Puteo lanorum.
Quod super cætera beneficia, ad hujus etiam tutelam,
Portus Pilarum viginti molem cum sumptu fornicum,
Reliquo, et munition ex ærario suo largitus sit.

Julius Capitolinus much favors the subject of this elogy, by what he writes in the life of *Antoninus Pius*, to wit that he gave moneys to many Cities, to the intent they should either erect new publick structures, or restore the old.

The Promontory of *MISENO,*

THus having viewed the old and great foundations of the *Piazzza* and the Port, passe by bark directly from the Mole to the Promontory of *Miseno*, famous and immortal by the verses of *Virgil*, and the writings of other good Authors. This mountain lies in the Sea, and is boared and hollow, full of grotts and caverns, which made the Poet much to the purpose and with no lesse ingenuity to stile it *Aerio* or ayry, as if he would denote it windy, by reason of the waies and concavities in it self, saying further, that under it, *Æneas* gave sepulture to *Misenus* his dead Trumpeter & man of oars, or as *Servius* writes afterwards sacrificed to the *Avernus* as in his sixt he saies.

Imponit suaque arma viro, remumque tubamque
Monte sub Aerio, qui nunc Misenus ab illo
Dicitur, æternumque tenet per sæcula nomen.

Seeming by the Oare and the Trumpet, to glance at the future famousnesse of that Port, and of the *Armada* or Fleet, which *Augustus* had then placed there for defence of the *Mediterranean Sea*, under E. M. *Agrippa*, And *Dion* commemorates, that *Augustus* being made Captain, made use of it for the harbour of the Fleet in the *Sicilian* warr, against *Sextus Pompeius*, where they then lay in the sea between *Miseno* and *Cuma*, environed with hills, in form of a crescent, a place very capacious and more then opportune for the Navy at Sea, by reason of those three gulfes of the Sea, scituate between *Baia* and *Pozzuolo*, that is the Lake of *Baia*, the *Lucrino*, and the *Averno*, the which *Lucius Florius* calls by a most gratious Metaphor, the Ease of the Sea : of which the *Averno* now called *Mare Mortuum*, being included, where it issueth out with sand, seems a stagne or Moore about a thousand paces distant from the allodgment of the *Armada*. And therefore the neighbouring precincts, as also the *Miseno*, began to be accommodated for the Souldiers stations, for that the Fleet there was wont to winter, and both *Strabo*, and *Servius*: the Commentators upon *Virgil*, report, that the wood and Trees on *Averno* were cut down, because they through their thicknesse rendred the air offensive , and prejudicial to the health of the Inhabitants : furthermore hills were boared thorough , and leuel waies layed , to the end there might be a short and facile accesse to the shores of *Baia* and *Lucrino*. And that fresh water might never be defective, with infinite expence and no lesse labour, Rivolets from Rivers and fountains from springs were conveyed thither from a far off : cisterns and conservatories were built, (vast enough) in divers figures as the conveniency of the place afforded, both in the plain and under the ground, and in the very bowels of the hil, that so cold water might be at all times ready for refreshing the bodies in the excessive heat of the Summer: tis for these reasons that we find the *Miseno* in great part, hollow and concave within, and exposed to the air to the very top. In which we see sitting places for washing, baths, lakes, and tables for eating : being within full of grotts, waies and edifices arched, here and there sustained by frequent pillars, part built with brick, part cut out of the same rock; among which edifices the biggest conservatory of the waters called vulgarly *Grotta Dragonacia* is admirable, as are the conveyances into it: for the rain waters descending from the Promontory; the which *Grotta* is capable of many thousand butts, being large beyond measure, and twenty five foot deep : the largnesse not being to be measured, for that the vaults and ruines fallen into it have filled many parts of it : all these conservatories are incrusted or plaistered with a certain hard composition used by the antients for rendring them tenable of the waters, so that none could pass nor soak thorough : the inward space between the walls, is two hundred foot long, and eighteen broad : having four doors through which is entrance into four great chambers: near these are other conserves different in artifice and grandeur.

That which vulgarly they call *Cento Camere*, from the multitude

of abodes (by some thought to be *Nerva's* prison, where among the
other Fabricks they preserved their waters, is wonderful for the
vastnesse and art wherewith tis built: its walls within are conjoined within in squares, and support the vaults, forming every where
square chambers, which on all sides have small doors by which may
go from one to the other the servants, whose office twas when the
waters were spent to cleanse them of the dirt and soyle: the vaults
of these chambers have certain open holes, whereby the waters
might be drawn up as occasion required. The *Piscina Mirabili* or
Pool for water was admirable and famous, and known by this name,
the which is yet almost entire on the back of the Promontory of
Miseno, toward the Port for the Navy, and *Cuma*. This Fabrick *Leandrus Albertus* affirms, is inclosed by four walls, is five hundred foot
long, and two hundred and twenty broad: and the Vault somewhat higher: raising a little archwise from the walls, it riseth higher towards the middle, being supported upon forty eight columns,
each of which is three foot square, which being disposed into four
ranks represent a beautifull and proportionable object for the
whole length. The whole Fabrick is composed of brick, and the
walls being of a great thicknesse, render it of an extreamfirmnesse;
both the Walls and Pillars within are exactly incrusted as useful to
keep them from leaking: and in the arch are many open ovals for
drawing up the waters: at each end were forty steps for descent
to the very bottome. The Pavement on the sides is higher even to
the midst of the Porticue: whence was a descent by fiue steps into
a lesser chamber on each side, and thence was a descent into another very narrow inclosed place, into which tis supposed the waters
purged their filth and uncleannesse, the which was afterwards ex-
haled by the publique officers for this purpose called *Castellarij*,
from these conservatories of waters being denominated *Castella* in
Latine.

All the Pavement is *Terras* beaten, with all art and diligence,
so that to this day it holds the rain water like a dish in the lowest
part of it.

Many variously conjecture who should be the first builders of so
vast Fabricks: some whereof suppose, *L. Licinius Lucullus* to have
been the first Author, and that this was built out of the ruines of the
said *Lucullus* his *Villa*, which *Plutarch* and *Varro* write he built most
proud in the Tract of *Baia* neare the Promontory of *Misenus*: with
whom agree *Suetonius* and *Cornelius Tacitus*, who write that *Tiberius*
the Emperor dyed in the same *Villa*, whence (hindred by the storms
at Sea being sick) he could not sayle over to the Island *Caprea*. Others
think this was the Fabrick of *Nero*, and thence tis to this day called
Peschiera di Nerone, and *Suetonius* writes that he began a *Peschery* extending from *Baia* to *Avernus*, covered and shut in by porticues.

But this conjecture pleaseth not me much, nor any other who hath
diligently seen those places, who know the use of the like Fabricks
to have been meerly for conserving of waters: and for that these
three Fabricks afore described, lye so contiguous one to the other, it
may not be far from the purpose to imagine that *Augustus* and the
Princes his successors, built them for the use of the Fleet, since it is
assuredly known, the Souldiers thereof there continually lodged

E e e e

and

and wintred, ſome vaſt fragments of their military lodges yet being
extant: and I remember that I copied out ſome Epitaphs of the Souldiers of the *Armada*, from the near ſepulchres, wherein are placed the
names of the *Pretorian* ſhips, as *Fede, Iſede, Gallo*, wherein they had ſerved, whereof ſome brief ones for delight of the ſtudious of antiquity hereunder follow.

> D. M.
> *Ti Porroni celetis.*
> *Nat. Alex. Ex. III. Iſidevix.*
> *Ann. XL. Mil. am. XIIII. Titi.*
> *Us. Aquilibus Epidius Pariſi III. Iſid.*
> *H. A. M. fecerunt.*
> D. M.
> *G. Senio Severo.*
> *Manipulato ex III. Fi-*
> *de Natione Beſſus.*
> *Vixit annos XLVI.*
> *Emilius dolens Erei*
> *E. M. Fecit.*
> D. M.
> *C. Julio Quarto.*
> *Ver. Ex. Pr. N. Gallo.*
> *M. Cecilius Felix. S.*
> *Inonia. Heraclia*
> *S. & S.*

Theſe had the captainſhip of the Fleet, who conſtantly reſided
there: as was *Anicetus* the libertine of *Nero*, who was firſt his Maſter, by means of whoſe frauds, theſe there ſlew near the *Bauli, Agrippina* his Mother. In ſuch a command (though different from this)
was *Pliny* the writer of the natural hiſtory, in the time of *Veſpaſian*
at *Miſenus*, and there governed the *Armada* and *Navy*, at the eruption and burning of the *Veſuvius*, being with it ſhaken by the earthquake: but approaching too near with his ſhips, to aſſiſt the op-
preſſed Souldiers, and to ſatisfie his curioſity in the occaſion of thoſe
fires, he was ſtifled by the aſhes and vapours of this burning mountain as aforeſaid: where with his uncle *Pliny* was alſo *G. Celius* the
ſon of his ſiſter, who related this ſtory more at large to *Tacitus* the
Hiſtorian. And certainly waters were preſerved in theſe Fabricks
for uſe and delight, both in *Lucullus* his *Villa*, and many other places very numerous in that piece of a fair country, all over which
run pipes, ſhores, and chanels. All the Sea ſhore and ſtrond is deformed by the ruines of Towns and Villages, of old full of houſes
and inhabitants, in particular that part between *Formia* and *Suren-
tum* moves compaſſion in the paſſers by at Sea: which in the flouriſhing time of the *Roman* Empire, preſented to their view at a diſtance the effigies of a continued City, by the quantity of ſtructures,
and proud Palaces, beautifyed with all ſplendour, pompous and
vaſtly expenſive: and would any take that pains now as by a ſtrict
ſcrutiny to take a particular account, or to draw draughts, and
exquiſite deſcriptions; enough of importance might be found to
ſatiſ-

ſatisfie his own Curioſity, and to fill up a new commentary, nay a juſt volume.

. The Palaces were wont to be very pompous in thoſe parts on the *Maritime* coaſts, being 150 miles in length: Which was ſo filled with Palaces, Cities, Towns, Burghs, Baths, Theatres, and ſuch other proud and magnificent Fabricks, beginning at *Baia*, and ſo continuing to *F. Herculanus* and *Volturnus*, that they ſeemed not ſeparate, but one great and fair City, to which no proſpect could be comparable: But in this our time all things there are ruinated except *Naples* the head of the Kingdome, and reſidence of the Viceroy and ſome other great Princes.

The *Villæ* or Palaces of pleaſure of the ROMANS.

THat we may gratefully pleaſe the ſtudious in theſe things, we thought it not from the purpoſe to run over ſome of the more noble *Villæs*, which the *Romans* had built in theſe parts. That famous Palace then of *Lucullus* ſtood in the *Terra Forma*, near the Promontorie of *Miſenus*, diſcovering the top of the near high hill and the other leſſer between the port & gulf of *Baia*, where he firſt bought of *Cornelia* the *Villa* of *Sc. Marius*, baniſhed by *L. Sylla*, which he amplified with Fabricks, Gardens, and ſumptuous Fiſhpools; the ſpaces of which Gardens appear to this day, towards *Cuma* not far from the *Centa Cumæræ*, and footſteps of the Peſcheries at the ſhore of *Baiæ*, with grots, and ſtanding pools cut into the foot of the Rock by art, that they might be a refuge and defence to the Fiſh from the ſcorching Sun in hot weather: as *M. Varro* ſets forth, ſaying that *D. Lucullus* had given order to his architectors to conſume as much money as they pleaſed; ſo they made a ſufficient defence for the Fiſh againſt the heat of the Sun, and provided them ſecure retreats under the mountains, ſo that when this work was compleated he might ſay, he needed not envy *Neptune* himſelf for goodneſſe of fiſh: which ſhews that he had fiſhpools in many places. And in the ſaid *Marcus Varro*, ℒ *Hortenſius* the Orator reprehends *M. Lucullus* for that he had not after the example of *L. Lucullus* his Brother, provided for the conveniency of his fiſh, a retreat into the *Freſco*, from the ſcorching beams of the Sun. Tis thought the *Villa* of *M. Lucullus* ſtood at the foot of the mountain *Miſenus* towards the Iſle *Procyda*, antiently called *Prockyte*, where under the waters may yet be perceived great ruines of Peſcharies.

Villa Di Q. HORTEENSIO.

QVintus *Hortenſius* had his Mannor houſe in the breaſt of *Baiano* near *Bauli*, whereof ſome reliques yet appear on the ſhores, and ſome are covered by the waters: tis moſt certain and famous that he had then moſt fair fiſhpools, with ſome grots cut into the mountain for the refuge of his fiſh from the Suns ardour: ſo much were they then given to the like pleaſures: for which C. *Cicero* (taunting him) calls him God of the Sea, and the moſt happy in his peſcheries, in that he had ſo domeſticated the fiſh, that they came at his call when they heard his voice; and much condoles the death of his *Muræna*, the *Bennet* fiſh, which tis thought by ſome will ſtay a ſhip if it ſtick to it: of whom a friend of his requeſting a pair of his *Athliets*, he anſwered he woud rather give him two mules out of his litter. *Pliny* writes that after *Q. Horterſius*, *Antonia* the mother of *Claudius* the Emperor poſſeſſed theſe very Fiſhpools with the ſame humour, and that ſhe ſo much loved a *Muræna*, that ſhe cauſed earrings of gold to be put on him in the waters: and that thoſe places were ſo famous for this fact, that many reſorted to *Bauli* purpoſely to behold it. Tis not certain whether *Nero* the Emperor cauſed *Agrippina* his mother to be ſlain in this very *Villa*, but if not there, twas not farr from it, as may be collected from *Cornelius Tacitus* in the 14th book of his Annals.

Domitia the Aunt of *Nero* had a *Villa* in that neighbourhood: whereof in the 13 book of *Tacitus* is ſome memorial, and *Dion Coſſius* ſaies that *Nero* having poiſoned *Domitia* his Aunt, poſſeſſed himſelf of her Livings near *Bauli*, and *Ravenna*: the contrary whereof *Ælius Lampridius* reports of the Emperor *Alexander Severus*, to wit that beſides many Palaces he built in *Rome*, in honour of *Julia Mamea*, his mother, he built one moſt ſumptuous with its Peſcheries calling the place *Mamea*, which *Ferrante Loffredo*, Marques of *Trevico* ſuppoſeth to ſtand in the midſt of *Baia*, where he likewiſe erected many other in honour of his Parents.

The *Villa* Of *C. PISO.*

THis ſtood under the mountain near the hot fountains : hither *Nero,* (leaving the other charges of importance) often retired for his ſolace, as *Tacitus* declares in the 15th. book of his Annals. Tis ſuppoſed that in this *Villa, Nero* entertained his mother *Agrippina* at table many hours under pretence of the feſtival *Quinquatrus* : a feaſt celebrated to *Pallas* five daies, but with intention to make her return by night to her *Villa* at *Bauli,* having before hand given order that in the return, the Bark (wherein ſhe was) ſhould be ſunk, and ſhe thereby be drowned, as *Suetonius* and *Tacitus* relate.

The *Villa of* C. MARIVS, *of* CÆSAR. and of *POMPEY.*

IN theſe confines likewiſe *C. Marius, Cæſar,* and *Pompey,* had their houſes of pleaſure, as *Seneca* tells us in the ſecond Epiſtle, but they ſtood on the very tops of hills, ſo that they had more the faces of Caſtles and Forts and places made purpoſely to protect the Countrey below, then of Pallaces for ſolace. *Pliny* ſpeaks of that of *Marius* in the 6th chapter of the 13 book, which was afterwards poſſeſſed and amplifyed by *Lucullus,* near the *Promontory* of *Miſenus,* towards the Port. But the *Villa* of *Cæſar* ſtood above *Baia* and on the top of the Mountain, as *Tacitus* teſtifies in the 15th book of his Annals, whoſe vaſt foundations remain to this day under their old name, neare the Temple of *Venus.* That of *Pompey,* they ſay, was on the third Mountain, between the *Avernus* and the contiguous *Tritullian* hot baths, whence the ſurname they yet retain: and there ſome yeers ſince was found a ſtatue of *Pompey.*

The *Villa Academica of* Marcus Tullius CICERO.

Pliny in the ſecond Chapter of his thirty firſt book declares, that the *Villa* of *Cicero* (made ſo famous by his writings) was in theſe quarters between the *Avernus* and *Pozzuolo,* upon the Sea ſhore with a

F f f f

moſt

moſt delicious grove and a ſpacious hall to walk in, wherefore *Cicero* called it an Academy in imitation of that at *Athens*, wherein they ordinarily diſputed walking. Here *Cicero* made his ſepulchres: and ſo much was he pleaſed with it, that he often ſpoke of it, and entitled ſome of his books from it, *Queſtiones Academicæ*: Academick queſtions. *Atticus* being in *Athens*, *Cicero* in almoſt every letter recommended his Academy, that he might ſend to him from *Greece*, whatever could be had for ennobling it with fair ornaments, wherein *Atticus* failed not, according to the occaſions, in ſtatues, pictures and other the like ornaments. Whence *Cicero* in his Epiſtle *ad Atticum*, praiſeth his diligence and the things ſent him.

Cicero being retired hither in the calamitous times of the Republique to ſpend away the time, toyl, and troubles with Books, many of the Principal Romans repaired thither to viſit him, and take ſome counſel. Of them was *C. Cæſar* after the victory he obtained in the civil warr, *C. Octavius* the Succeſſour of *Julius*, yet before he made himſelf Emperour, with infinite others: but after that *Cicero* was baniſhed, the *Villa Academica* was poſſeſſed by *C. Antiſtius*, who was the Legat of *Cæſar*, and followed his faction in the civil wars. A little after *Ciceroes* death, in his *Villa*, ſprung up fountains of hot water, good among other things for the eyes and ſight, celebrated by *Tullius Taureus* the freeman of *Cicero*, with an Epigram ſet down among the works of *Pliny*, who wrote this ſucceſſe, and judged that Epigram worthy of memory. We muſt believe that this *Villa* ſtood where now the *Stadio* is, taking that name from the length of *Ciceroes* hall, whoſe ruines yet remain ſo diſtinctly, as that it may be meaſured how long twas: and although this *Stadio*, ſeem to ſtand too far from the Sea, in reſpect of that we read touching *Ciceroes* Academy, yet this will not create any difficulty: ſince the Sea may be in ſo long a ſpace of time through divers cauſes retired; becauſe truely this *Villa* in *Ciceroes* time ſtood over water, at leaſtwiſe conducted from the Sea, by certain channels, ſo that he eating at table, might caſt into the waters for the fiſh to eat, & angle and fiſh at his pleaſure. The hot fountains are extant in a neere field, in a cavern under ground at the root of the hill, which are alſo of wonderfull nature, becauſe they increaſe and decreaſe according to the flowing and ebbing of the ſea, by day and by night: in their increaſe they caſt abundance of water into the bath, and when full, part of the water returns to the fountain, and part runs into the Sea by a certain ſmall chanel or gutter made to that purpoſe.

This Bath vulgarly called *Bagno Ciceroniano*, the *Ciceronian* bath, and by phiſicians, *Prætenſe* or *Tritulliano* is as gallant and entire an antiquity as any in the Tract of *Pozzuolo*: Theſe waters were ſo ſoveraign not many years ſince over moſt diſeaſes, that over every bath was written for what cures twas good, of which inſcription ſome letters yet ſtand: but the phiſicians of *Palermo* (as they tell the ſtory) finding thoſe waters prejudicial to their cuſtom, went with inſtruments expreſly & demoliſh't thoſe writings (ſo that for the preſent they are unuſefull) the ſaid phiſicians being all caſt away in their return. Thus much ſhall ſuffice touching *Ciceroes* famous *Villa*, for that *Leander* and other writers treat ſufficiently of its nature and others thereabouts. From the commencement of *Ciceroes* Acade-

demical queftions is comprehended, that the *Villa* of *Ter.Varro* a
moft learned *Roman* was not far diftant, but the determinate place
is unknown.

The *Villa* of SERVILIVS VATIA.

SEneca demonftrates in his fifty fecond Epiftle to *Lucullus*, that on
the fhore between *Cuma* and the Lake *Avernus* ftood the *Villa* of
Servilius Vatia, the magnificence and vaftnefs of which Fabrick may
be comprehended from the fragments yet extant. He faies twoCaves
were here built with great expence, into the one whereof the Sun
never entred, and on the other it fhone from morning to night, into
weh ran a delicious water through as pleafant aMeadow with many
Fifh.   Hither *Servilius* a noble and rich Man retired himfelf at fuch
time as *Tiberius Cæfar* afflicted many noble *Romans*, and applyed
himfelf to honeft Labour far from *Rome* in peace, for which he
was ftyled happy, and obtained the fame of knowledge in his
affaires above others; by that meanes avoyding dangers. Touching
the dead and other notable things others have abundantly writ,
let this therefore fuffice, for the purpofe of the *Baianiæ* celebrious
Villa's, fince of the other particulars in the times of thofe old
Roman Princes, tis impoffible to treat exactly, all things being
fo wholly ruinated and deftroyed that fcarce any footfteps remain.

The old City of BAIA.

THe moft fair foundations and pitched *Piazzaes* of the old City
Baia, lye underneath the waters, fcarce any fragments remaining on the Land : but in the neighbouring Mountains in every
corner lye baths, hot baths, and ftructures of Admirable Architecture, notwithftanding that many great Fabricks were burnt, many thrown down by earthquakes and many fwallowed up by the
Earth. In the Sea may be clearly feen the great old Piles of the
Port of *Baia*, like thofe of *Pozzuolo*, built of Brick with intollerable expence, which now feem like Rocks, as do the the enclofures
and foundations, which of old ftood for defence of the Lakes *Lucrinus and Avernus*, againft the ftorms of the Sea : which was gene-
nerally believed to be made in this manner, to wit, that *Hercules* by
his ftrength, upon two carts abreft, drew as large a peice of Earth as

was requifite, and that a mile in length to the place, and there fixed it : and therefore Pofterity for a perpetual remembrance and acknowledgement of fo great a benefit, erected to him a Round Temple near *Bauli*, whereof fome fragments yet are extant.   But afterwards, that repair being wafted by the Sea, *C. Cæfar* again reftored and bettered it, as may be collected from *Virgils Georgicks* and from *Servius* his Commentator; with whofe opinion *Suetonius* feems to accord, faying that *Auguftus* perfected the *Julian* Port near *Baia*, whence tis fuppofed that *Julius Cæfar* had firft fetled it: which muft have been in his firft Confulfhip by Commiffion of the Senate, who gave him that charge at the inftance of the Receivers of the Cuftoms and Tolls, upon their allegation, that the cuftcmes and Tolls much decayed in value through the ruine of that Port: which was afterwards called *Julia*, from the Reaccomodators name *Julius Cæfar*. So faies *Servius* upon thefe verfes in the fecend of the *Georgicks*.

An memorem potius ? Lucrinoque addita clauftra,
Atque indignatum magnis ftridoribus æquor?
Julia qua Ponto longe fonat unda refufo,
Tyrrhenufque immittitur æftus Avernis;

A wonderfull Adventure.

In our times, that is in the yeer 1538 (thofe adjacent Fields and places being for two whole yeers before fhaken moved and difturbed) in the end, the night of the twenty ninth day of *September*, between the foot of the mountain *Gaurus* and the Sea near the aforefaid Lakes, there arofe a new mountain called *Monte Novo* a mile high in the upright, which now is in circuit at the bottome fcur mile. A miraculous thing to fall out in one night. At the birth of this mountain the fhore and the waters of the Sea retired the fpace of two hundred fpaces, one great and entire town called *Tripergolano*, was entirely fwallowed up by the *Vorago* and gulf of the earth, with fome of its baths which were very celebrious: and the near Lakes *Avernus* and *Lucrinus* were almoft filled up with ftones earth and afhes. This was thought to have proceeded from the afhes which came out of *Sulfatara*: how many other old memorials this new mountain hath covered cannot be known. On the top of it is a large mouth about 50. paces in circuit, which at the beginning vomited out fire, at the bottome whereof are now found warm waters.

The Lake *AVERNVS*.

THe Lake *Avernus* hath been illuftrated by the moft efteemed Poets, and diligently defcribed by *Strabo* and other Hiftorians, for the Fables fake (which the Antients gave credit to) appropriated to it. For this was confecrated to *Pluto* the God of hell. Hereabouts as Fame went was the Poets *Acheron* or defcent into hell, and here was the gate of hell thorough which they caufed to rife the infernal Spirits, when any hamane creature was facrificed unto them. And hence the *Cimerian* Priefts (the antient Inhabitants of this place fent down (by certain Caverns) into hell to find *Pluto,* fuch Travellers and ftrangers as came to be refolved in any queftions, or to receive counfel or anfwer from *Pluto.* To this day the vulgar believe, that through the Caverns in the neighbouring hill, (hence denominated *Monte della Sibylla*) one may defcend to the fubterranean refidence of the *Sibylla Cumana,* and that there fhe is feen and confulted by many, which things *Leandrus Albertus* in his *Italia* diligently adver ifeth. *Lactantius* faieth that fhe among the other Sybils prophefyed of Chrift. The Inhabitants further hold for certain, that Ghrift returning from *Limbus* with the fouls of the holy Fathers, arofe out of the earth through a certain mountain near the Lake *Avernus* and the *Monte Novo,* and therefore they call that Mountain by the name of *Monte di Chrifto :* which opinion fome old Poets confirm, writing of the Baths of *Pozzuolo.*

> *Eft locus, effregit quo portas Chriftus Averno*
> *Et fanctos traxit lucidus inde Patres.*

And another.

> *Eft locus Auftralis, quà Portam Chriftus Averni.*
> *Fregit, et eduxit mortuos inde fuos.*

Twas alfo believed by the multitude of hot waters fpringing out all over thofe quarters, that this Lake reached to a vein of the infernal waters, and therefore called *Palude Acherofia,* the *Acherontick* Fenns, from which *Ataro* difagrees not, when he faies.

> *Quando hic inferni janua regis.*
> *Dicitur, et tenebrofa Palus, Acheronte refufo.*

Though in truth this falfe opinion was augmented by the natural quality of the places, and other circumftances: to wit fome rare and ftupendious miracles which have there come to paffe. Then as to the *Avernus,* know it lies in a low Valley, almoft furrounded by high hills, clothed of old with thick and heavy Trees capable to keep out the wind.

Whence the Lake was not frequented by any, but emitting an unwholſome ſulphurous ſtink, it ſo infected the air above it (by being ſo cloſely beſieged by mountains and woods) that Birds flying over it fell down dead: and thence twas named by the Latins _Avernus_, that is to ſay, without Birds. So alſo may we collect from _Livy_, that in old time this Vale was a horrid place and eſteemed altogether inacceſſable: for ſaith he, the _Romans_ waging war againſt the _Samniti_, the enemies (when the _Romans_ put them to flight) by whole Armies retreated into the Woods in the ſaid Vale, as to ſecure places.

But _Strabo_ writes not ſo of it in his time, but ſaies, that then this vale and nearer hills were delitious places, in reſpect _Auguſtus_ had cauſed the woods to be felled, and a free paſſage opened to the air. At preſent the Lake is full of fiſh and water-foul, nor hath it any of thoſe incommodities attributed to it by the antients. Yet tis true that not many ages ſince, a vein of ſulphurous peſtilential water guſhed out of the bottome of the Lake, which ſuddenly killed a world of fiſh, their colour and ſmell (being caſt on the earth) confirming that to be the cauſe of their death. _Joannes Boccaccius_ in his little tract of Lakes, ſaies he ſaw it with his own eyes in the time of King _Robert_, about the yeeer 1380.

The Sybil _Cumana_ was ſhe which gave _Æneas_ free paſſage into hell, as _Virgil_ ſaith; ſhe was called _Cumana_ of the City of _Cuma_, (here under treated of) and was one of the twelve Sybils, all which prophesyed of Chriſt though ſome more obſcurely, yet two ſo fully that with ſubmiſſion I ſhall here inſert ſomewhat of their prophecies touching the Saviour of Mankind.

SIBILLA CUMANA.

G̲Reat _Rome_ ſhall then look high.
Whoſe proud Towers from ſeaven hills ſhall brave the sky,
And overlook the world.   In thoſe bleſt daies,
Shall come a King of Kings, and he ſhall raiſe
A new Plantation: and though greater far
Then all the Monarchs that before him are
In Majeſty and power; yet in that day
So meek and humble he ſhall daign to pay
Tribute to _Cæſar_: yet thrice happy he,
That ſhall his ſubject or his ſervant be.

And the SIBILLA ERITHRÆA,
to this effect.

THe times by the great Oracle affigned
When God himfelf in pity of mankind,
Shall from the heaven defcend and be incarnate,
Entring the world a Lamb immaculate;
And as himfelf, in wild m thinks it meet,
Walk on the Earth on three and thirty feet.
And with fix fingers all his fubjects then
Though a King mighty, fhall be Fifhermen,
In number twelve; with thefe war fhall be tride
Againft the Devil, world, and flefh; their Pride,
Humility fhall quell, and the fharp fword
With which they fight, fhall be the facred word,
Eftablifh't upon *Peter*, which foundation
Once laied, fhall be divulg'd to every Nation:

At one fide of the Lake *Avernus* is the Temple of *Apollo*, at the o-
ther this *Sibilla Cumana* her Grott, which is very fpatious, having
at the end a magnificent afcent where the oracle ftood, with the way
that led to *Cuma:* Her bath yet ftands, and her Chambers painted
in Mofaick woik; yet all under ground as moft of the aforefaid
Antiquities (except the Temples) are.

CUMA,

Leaving the Lake *Avernus*, you find on the way among the ruines
of the City *Cuma*, now altogether undone & defert) great foundations and ruines of Towers, Temples and Edifices of importance.
On the top of the mountain are yet the footfteps of a Temple of
Apollo, which in its time was infinitely celebrated, and is taken notice of by *Virgil* and *Servius* his Commentator. There is alfo an Arch
built with brick, now called *Arco Felice*, the happy Arch, of a ftupendious igh Vault, through which the antients wrought an even
way between two heads of Mountains: *Cuma* was built by the *Chal-
cidenfi* a *Græcian* people of *Negroponte*, who being arived in thofe Seas
with their fhips, to feek out a Country for their habitation, firft landed in thofe near Iflands, called *Pitherufa*, which lye over againft
Campania, and were fo denominated from the multitude of Apes
thereon found: and afterwards taking courage they paffed over into
the *Terra Firma*, where they built this City *Cuma*, calling her by this

name, either from one of their Captains so called, or from the Procurator in those maritimate Coasts, or from its good augury they there met with, to wit a woman great with child the which confirmed them in their determination to dwell there, as *Strabo Dionysius* and *Livy* relate: for to all these sences *Cuma* in Greek, (considering its significations) may be well applyed.

These people lived a long time governing their Republique with prudence, and increased so much, that *Pozzuolo, Paleopoli*, and *Naples* became part of their Colony: we read that the *Cumani* were under Tyrants, before the Romans expelled their Kings, but this happened not through their being subjugated by any, but because they chose to themselves a head and chief to obey, who after the Greek manner, was called *Tyranno*, that is, Lord, one of which was *Aristodemo Malaco*, elected for his meer valour, as *Livy* and *Dionysius Halicarnasseus* write: for that with a small party, he overcame a great nnmber of *Tuscans, Ombrians* and *Ansonians*, enemies of the *Cumani*, and slew with his own hand *Arunte*, the Son of *Porsenna*, their Captain. To which *Aristodemus* say the same Authors, *Tarquinius Superbus* (expelled *Rome*) fled for safety, and by him being well accepted, he ended his daies in *Cuma*. Afterwards the *Cumani* were overcome and for some time evilly intreated by the *Campani*, saies *Strabo*; but in subsequent times there being no Forts strong enough to resist the *Romans*, all those people were at one instant of time reduced under the said *Romans*, who set a *Præfect* over the City *Cuma*, for that that people would too obstinately have fought for defence of their Liberty. Afterwards that City run retrograde, loosing its splendour and inhabitants: for that the *Romans* by their greatnesse measuring their pride, possessed themselves of all that *Campania* or Country, erecting therein their luxurious and most sumptuous Palaces, which not only obscured *Cuma* but all the adjacent Cities: who being bereaved of their Land, first fayled of Inhabitants, and at last became desolate, yet *Cuma* was the last of those Cities that underwent this desolation; by reason that being built upon a mountain, when the *Roman* Empire began to feel its tottering condition, by the frequent inroads of the barbarous Nations into *Italy*, *Cuma* for the commodity of its site, was reduced into a Fortresse: which caused *Agathia Mireneus* in his first book of the *Gothick* warr, to say, that *Cuma* in his time was very strong, almost impregnable through its many grosse Towers, walls and other fortifications; and that for this reason *Totila* and *Teja* Kings of the *Goths*, thither conveighed their Treasure, as to a safe and secure place, together with their most estimable and dearest things: however *Narsetes* the Legate of *Justinian* the Emperor, after a long siedge made himself Lord of it.

But at present nought hereof remains, save only immense ruines, foundations and profound Ditches cut into the hard stony rock with Chisels. In the departure from *Cuma*, you often fall upon parcels of the *Via Domitiana*, (now interrupted in many places) and great Ruines of a stone Bridge, raised over the *Volturnus*. *Domitian* caused this way to be made, beginning from the *Via Appia*, between *Minturnæ* and *Sinvessa*, and so leading to *Cuma*: *Statius Papinius* in his *Hendecasillabi*, or verses of eleven sillables, makes mention of

Cuma

Cuma, the above named bridge, and a triumphal Arch of Marble placed on the same way: whereof no fragments are now to be found.

⁂⁂⁂⁂⁂⁂⁂⁂⁂⁂⁂⁂⁂⁂⁂⁂⁂⁂

LINTERNO.
And why now called the Tower of the Countrey.

ON the left hand of the *Via Domitiana* lye vaſt ruines of the old City *Linternum,* of old a Colony of the *Romans,* ſo in the midſt of that twas called the Tower of the Ccuntrey *Campania,* which name it ſeems to have acquired from the places old ſucceſſe, and was ennobled by the remainder of dayes which *Scipio Affricanus* the Greater ſpent there, after his voluntary baniſhment from hisCountrey *Rome*: Who being ill treated by his Citizens, whom with their goods and eſtates he had defended from their Enemies, and made them Lords of *Spain* and *Affrick,* in diſdain of ſo great ingratitude, retired himſelf to his own Palace in this place, that he might deprive his Countrey of himſelf living, & of his aſſiſtance, by this means dealing with her as moſt ingratefull: after his death commanding his body to be there entered, expreſly forbidding his bones to be tranſported to *Rome,* as *Livy, Strabo, Valerius Maximus, Seneca* and many others relate. *Pliny* ſaith further in the laſt Chapter of the ſixteenth book of his natural Hiſtory, that even to his tme they found in *Linternum* of the Olive trees planted by *Scipio Affricanus,* and a mirtle of a notable largeneſſe under which was a Cave inhabited by a Dragon the guardian of *Scipioes* Scul; from which fable aroſe this other, which theInhabitants tell of the *Monte Maſſico,* ſo renowned for the wines it produced, to wit that in a certain Cave on the ſaid mountain lay a Dragon, who ſlew and devoured all ſuch as approached to him, and that twas therefore called *Monte Dragone* and the Caſtle ſtanding thereon is called *La Rocca di Monte Dragone.* Iu theſe quarters is a ſpring or fountain of which was wont to be ſharp or ſower water and as twas ſaid would intoxicate: but now it hath the taſt of ſweet and pure water, and hath not the ſaid effect of inebriating, but when drunk cures the head-ache.

⁂⁂⁂⁂⁂⁂⁂⁂⁂⁂⁂⁂⁂⁂⁂⁂⁂⁂

SINOPE or *SINVESSA.*

UNder the Caſtle *Dragone* ſtood the antient City *Sinope,* firſt a Colony of the Greeks, and afterwards made a Colony by the Romans, calling it *Sinueſſa,* when they alſo made *Minturnum*

Hhhh

num a near City another Colony, by occasion of the warr they had
against the *Samniti*, in the four hundred fifty seventh yeer after *Romes*
foundation, *Appius Claudius*, and **L.** *Volturnius* being Consuls, the
latter the second time, as *Livius* relates, or the following yeer when
Pirrhus began to reign as *Velleius Paterculus* will have it.

Vast ruines of this City lye disperst on every side there, but chiefly towards the Sea, where the footsteps of a large port also appear.
'Twas a renowned City, having a healthfull air, and some salutiferous
hot fountains, for which the Poet *Silius* stiles *Sinvessa* lukewarme;
these fountains are now denominated *Bagni Gauani*, but *Tacitus*
calls them *Sinvessan* waters , saying in the 12th book of his Annals,
that *Claudius* the Emperor being restored to his senses, caused himself to be conveighed to *Sinvessa* for recovering his health , hoping
and depending much on the goodnesse of the aire and the benefit
of the *Sinvessian* waters , when his wife *Agrippina* had prepared for
him those poisoned mushrooms which himself and his Son *Brit-
tanicus* eat. This *Agrippina* was Daughter of the noble *Germanicus*,
Sister to *Caligula*, and by him abused, she was first married to *Domitius* by whom she had *Nero*, afterwards to *Claudius* whom with his
Son as aforesaid she poisoned , that her Son *Nero* might be Emperor,
But her falshood, abomination & cruelty was not unpunisht by that
Son, who though he had joined her in equal authority with himself,
and carnally known her as some suppose, yet caused her to be most
cruelly slain, after sundry attempts to do it privately and with least
trouble and pain to her. *Tacitus* saies further in the first book (speaking of the histories of his time) That *Onofrius Tigillinus* one of the
principal actors of *Nero* the Emperours misdeeds, had the wezel
pipe of his throat cut near the waters of *Sinvessa*, whilst disporting
himself among his Concubines he least thought of any such
thing.

♣ ♣♣♣♣♣♣♣♣♣♣♣♣♣♣♣♣♣♣♣♣♣♣♣♣♣ ♣♣♣♣♣

MINT*URNE*

The River *Garigliano* being passed, wherein the *Scille* or Seashrimp
or prauns are taken, a sweet little fish held very delitious by
the *Romans* , you may see the reliques of *Minturnæ*, of old a most
flourishing Colony of the *Romans*: and among them the footsteps of
vast publique and Private Fabricks, some despoiled of the marble
which embellished them , and some entire. As a very sumptuous
Aqueduct, a Theatre with its *Scenes* and all other necessary parts,
a work after the antient way of building but solid ; An Amphitheatre with its accomodation for sitting, one seat above another, but despoiled of its marble, wherwith for ought appears, the Castle *Trajetto*
standing on the neighbouring hill hath been adorned and fortified,
which Amphitheater is now used as an inclosed pasturage for goats
and sheep. Therein lye great footsteps of Walls and Towers, great
arches over gates, and vast foundations of edifices, from whence we
easily

eaſily collect, ſhe hath a been potent and noble City.

This place hath acquired an illuſtrious fame alſo from that great victory, which the Chriſtians there obtained againſt the *Saracens* and Infidels, under the Captains of the Chriſtian Army, Pope *John* the 10 and *Albericus* Marqueſs of *Tuſcany*, when all *Italy* was delivered from that curſed people, except *Monte Gargano*, whither ſuch as could eſcape, fled and poſſeſſed it a long time after, robbing both by ſea and land.

At the mouth of the river *Garigliano*, was the ſacred wood, where the *Minturneſi*, honoured the Nymph or Goddeſſe *Marica* the wife of *Faunus*, to whom on the banks they built a proud Temple, whereof nought now remains, no more then of the honourable City *Veniſta*, or of *Anſonia* a moſt noble City, which was ſo named of *Anſon* the Son of *Vliſſes* and *Calypſo*, which City afterwards gave name to all Italy, over all which it alſo Lorded: which Cities ſtood in thoſe parts along the aforeſaid river.

LE PALVDI MINTVRNESI.

THe adjacent Fenns now Medows called *Minturneſi*, are famous for that they reduce to memory a notable example of the various changes of Fortune: which was that *C. Marius* who had been ſeaven times Conful, and had ſeaven times triumphed, had the good hap to abſcond himſelf therein for ſaving his life; where not witbſtanding he was found by a *Frenchman* an Enemy, but one that had not the boldneſſe to offend him, being terrified and put to fear by the Majeſtick aſpect, and noble preſence of that great man. Whence *Marius* (having reached a ſhip) paſſed into *Affrick*, whereof *Juvenal* ſpeaks conciſely in theſe words.

Exilium, & carcer, Minturnarumque palludes,
Et mendicatus victa Carthagine panis.

FORMIA.

Thence the *Via Appia* leads by *Hercoleana* to *Formia*, which way is very pleaſant, but the Caſtle *Mola* now ſtands near if not in the place where *Formia* of old ſtood; *Mola* takes its name from the many Mills grinding in that quarter, by reaſon of the quantity of water. The Countrey is ſuch, that a more delicious cannot be fancied, wherfore *Martial* ſaies.   H h h h 2   O

O temperatæ dulce Formiæ littus!

And a little after follows.

Hic summa legi stringitur Thesis vento.
Nec languet æquor, viva sed quies Ponti.

Volaterrannus and others well skilled believe, that here was the *Villa Formiana*, appertaining to *Cicero*, famous for his slaughter there, which opinion cannot well be contradicted, becaufe the Epitaphs, infcriptions, & reliques of antiquity, on the *Appia* and near Towns, demonftrate that the City *Formia* was there, but chiefly thefe words to be read on the bafis of a Statue (in that place) following.

> *Imp. Cæfari Divi*
> *Hadriani Filio Divi*
> *Trajani. Parthici. Nep.*
> *Divi. Nervæ. Pronepoti.*
> *Tito Ælio. Hadriano*
> *Antonino. Aug. Pio. Pont.*
> *Max. Tr. Pont. XI. Cos. III. II. P. P.*
> *Formiani. Publicè.*

Strabo, Pliny, Solinus and other hiftorians concurring fay, that the *Lacedæmonians* built *Formia* in the antient Territories of the *Leftrigoni*, and therefore *Silius Italicus* calls it the houfe of *Antifata*, becaufe there *Antifata* the Son of *Janus* and Nephew of *Neptune* ruled over the *Leftrigoni*, and firft called it *Hormia* which in their Language fignified a comodious port, which that was. The *Lacedæmonians* were afterwards fubjugated by the *Campani*, and they by the *Romans*, who reduced that with *Capua* into the form of a Prefecture, yet leaving *Formia* in Liberty, or free, and making her participate of the *Roman* honours for fome time as *Livius* in his 33 book : at laft in the civil warrs, *Formia* was made a *Roman* Colony, and reduced with many others in *Italy*, into Caftles and Forts as *Frontinus* faies, by the *Triumvirate*, *Cæfar, Antonius*, and *Lepidus*. Twas moft flourifhing in the time of the Emperors through the goodneffe of the air it injoyed , as *Horace, Martial* and other authors worthy credit relate, which may alfo be conjectured from the more noble ftructures now extant. In the end the *Saracens* deftroyed it, with many other Cities in *Campania* or the *Terra di Lavoro*, when Pope *Gregory* the 4th. tranflated the Fpifcopacy to *Gaieta*. And thus then purfueth the *Via Appia* leading to *Fondi*.

VELLETRI.

VElletri was an antient and potent Caſtle of the *Volſci*, whereof the *Roman* hiſtories frequently ſpeak: *Livius* and *Dionyſius Hal-licarnaſſeus* ſay, that *Velletri* was beſieged and enforced to yeild to *Ancus Martius* King of the *Romans*: and *Livy* adds further, that twas ſeverely chaſtiſed by the *Romans* for its frequent rebellions, wherefore the walls were levelled, and the richer ſort of *Velletri* ſent to dwell beyond the *Tyber*, with penalty of impriſonement to whoſoever ſhould ſet foot on this ſide *Tiber* within a mile of *Velletri*. This Caſtle was alſo made a Colony of the *Romans*, and many times repleniſht with new Inhabitants ſent thither from *Rome*, becauſe the old (in the many warrs made on thoſe confines) became impotent and much decreaſed as *Livy* affirms. *Frontinus* in his *Fragments* ſaies, that he finds many people by precept of the *Sempronian* Law, to have been at ſundry times ſent from *Rome* to *Velletri*, and that afterwards *Claudius Cæſar*, made it a Military *Colony*, dividing his own Territory among the Souldiers. Twas renowned, becauſe the Anceſtors of *Cæſar Auguſtus* were of old Inhabitants in it, that is the *Octavian* Family, and the ſame *Auguſtus* had a certain noble Seat of his own there, from whence ſaies *Suetonius*, he cauſed many things neceſſary for ſuſtenance and livelyhood to be conveighed.

Yet now remain very few marks of the old Fabricks, notwithſtanding that tis yet a great and well inhabited Caſtle. It hath a lovely Territory repleniſht with gardens and Palaces through its vicinity with *Rome*, *Pliny* in his 14th. book reckons the wine of *Velletri*, among the moſt generous, but it is not now in that credit, being ſo crude at preſent, that they are fain to boyle it in a caldron, to make it drinkable: wherefore *Pliny* well obſerves, that even the Earth hath its age and decays as have all other things.

In the voyage preſent themſelves to view, *Lanuvium* or *Lanuvio*, a place famous for the Temple there dedicated to *Juno Sofpita*. The *Riccia* or *Agritia* built by the *Sicilians*, afterwards made the Seate of *Alba Longa*. The mountain ſo much ſpoken of for the Temple conſecrated to *Jupiter*, and the Latines Feaſt daies there celebrated. Some Lakes which lye under it. The Hill *Albano* ſo fatal to the *Vejenti*. The *Nemoreſe* famous for the barbarous ſacrifices there performed to *Diana Taurica*, and *Hippolitus Urbius*. In ſum all that tract of Land is worthy contemplation for the many records taken of it among writers. The frequent ruines of great Fabricks lying up and down the Countrey *Tuſcularum*, where *Cicero*, *Varro*, and divers other noble *Romans* had their Palaces, deſerve due conſideration: as do the Countrey ſeats of the renn Cardinals, and above all the fair *Villa* of *Freſcati*, a place deputed to the Popes recreation: The Territory of *Freſcati*, was the antient delight of the *Romans*, and conti-

Iiii

nues

nues now of such ravishing delights, as tis fitter for the Gods to inhabit then men. such is the quantity of trees the quality of verts alwaies flourishing, the murmuring of Fountains and the like.

PELESTINA.

VPon a mountain on the right hand stands *Pelestrina* the Antient Seat of the *Aborigini*, a people who first possessed the Country about *Rome*, living abroad without houses: of the original of this City is no certain knowledge to be had, being lost through its antiquity, but thereof divers are the opinions. *Virgil* in his seaventh (by authority of the Chronicles of the *Preneftini*) saies, that *Cæculus* the Son of *Vulcan* founded it: whose mother fitting by the fire fide a spark happened to light into her lap, by which she said she was conceived with Childe: when her full time was come she was delivered of a Son, whom because he had very small eyes, she called *Cæculus*. Of him the noble Family of *Cecilians* in *Rome* would need have their beginning deriving, their Original from him as their first stock.

Solinus by authority of *Zenodotus* faies that twas built by *Prænestus* the Son of *Latinus* and Nephew of *Vlisses*: *Plutark* in his parallels by authority of *Ariftotle* in the third of *Italian* things faies, that *Telogonus* the Son of *Vlisses* by *Circe* the witch, after he had built *Tufulum*, by advisement of the Oracle called it *Prenefte* from the name of the Crowns wherewith he first faw the Inhabitants of the Country to daunce: but be it as some say from the said *Prænestus* or as others will from the feituation of the place, a little pendent, or as others from the feites being so high, tis indifferent, fince the name *Prenefte* will eafily accommodate it felf to all or either of these respects.

Yet the more rational opinion for the name, feems to be derived from the Crowns aforementioned, not only for the aforesaid cause but also for that in that City there stood a most noble Temple of *Fortune*, famous for those diviners by Lots, who exercifed themselves in that fuperstition: and was therefore visited with many Crowns offered to the said Goddesse by vow: of which Temple some fragments yet remain, and a few years since, were there found divers figures of Fortune, in brasse, brick, marble and other materials, as also feveral Crowns, and divers medals, upon which were figured the various lots, fortunes, and chances, with their marks, fignes, and letters.

In it also hung divers Tablets and other things offered by vow to *Fortune*, *Jove*, *Hope*, and to the *Capudini*, which things would take up too much room to recite, yet one Epigram will not be too impertinent, fince so eminently inferibed on a marble bafis, dedicate in that Temple by *T. Cæfius Taurinus*, with the figure of *T. Cefius* the

first

firſt his Father, the moſt famous Merchant of Corn, who uſed every
yeer to preſent a hundred Crowns by vow. On the ſaid Baſis are carved two meaſures, called *Modii*, half buſhels filled with ears of corn,
on the ſides are ſome little pillers crowned with ears of corn, and in
the middle is the enſuing Epigram.

> *Tu, quæ Tarpeio coleris vicina Tonanti,*
> *Votorum vindex ſemper Fortuna meorum*
> *Accipe, quæ pietas ponit tibi dona merenti,*
> *Effigiem noſtri conſervatura Parentis.*
> *Cujus ne taceat memorandum littera nomen*
> *Ceſius hic idemque ritus Primuſque vocatur*
> *Qui largæ Cereris meſſes, fructuſque renatos*
> *Digerit in pretium cui conſtat fama fideſque,*
> *Et qui divitias vincit, Pudor ille perillos.*
> *Conſuetus portus cura ſtudioque laboris*
> *Littora qui præſtant feſſis tutiſſima nautis.*
> *Notus in urbe ſacra, notus quoque ſinibus illis*
> *Quos Vmber ſulcare ſolet, quas Tuſcus arator*
> *Omnibus his annis votorum more ſuorum*
> *Centenas addit numero creſcente coronas*
> *Fortunæ ſimulacra coleris, & Apollinis aras*
> *Ægeriumque Jovem, quoruum conſentit in illo*
> *Majeſtas longæ promit.ens tempora vitæ*
> *Accipe poſteritas quod poſt tua ſæcula narres.*
> *Taurinus cari juſſus pietate parentis*
> *Hoc poſuit donum, quod nec ſententia mortis*
> *Vincere, nec poterit fatorum ſumma Poteſtas,*
> *Sed Populi ſalvo ſemper rumore manebit.*

Cicero declares in his ſecond Book *de Divinatione*, by extraction
out of the Books of the ſaid people *Preneſtini*, how the obſervation of Chances Lots or Fortunes came to have its beginning in that
City : ſaying, that a certain nobleman of *Peleſtrina* named *Suffucius*
by frequent advices and menaces which he had in his dreams, was
commanded to break out of a certain place a great flint ſtone, wher-
at all the other Citizens his Compatriots fell a laughing, but when
the ſtone was broke, the Lots or Chaunces ſuddenly leaped forth
engraven in antient Letters, which occaſioned their honouring of
Fortune in that place: and thence became the place by little and little encloſed and ſhut up through reſpect of the Image of *Jupiter*
there devoutly adored by the Matrons, in form of a boy childe ſit-
ting with *Juno* in the lap of *Fortune*, in a poſture as ſeeking out the
breaſt and teat : and that at the ſame time, after the Temple of Fortune was built, there dropped honey from an olive tree, wherewith
by commandement of the Southſayers was made a cheſt, and therein
thoſe Lotts were repoſed, the which were mingled and drawn
out by a litle boyes hand when ever they would ſee the iſſue of any
thing : as *Fortune* had at large directed her intention to be, that after
this manner they ſhould draw out the Lots.

This obſervation was moſt antient, and ſuch as affirm *L. Sylla* to
be the builder of this Temple deceive themſelves. Which errour

they took up from their reading the thirty sixth book of *Pliny*, who doth not say *L. Sylla* built that Temple but that he began to make its pavement with small stones of various colours in small figures, of wch. pavement thus wrought, some yeers since certain parts were found under ground, and therein figured many forrein creatures with their names in greek.

It may then be rationally believed that *L. Sylla* being victorious in the civil warrs, after he had enforced *C. Marius* the younger to dye, and his other enemies who had saved themselves in *Preneste*, after a long siege took the City, killing some part and selling others of the Citizens: but repenting afterwards his impietie expressed against the sacred places, for expiation of that crime, he resolved to restore and embellish anew the Temple profaned and a'most wholly destroyed by him. It seems a notable advise and observation to me, that the strength of the scite of this City hath occasioned its own destruction, which hath had a much contrary event in all other strong holds. The cause whereof is attributed to the assured confidence of the strength of the place, for which cause in the civil warrs the weaker part ordinarily fled thither for safety: but their enemies being stronger and more potent immediately layed siege to it, so that at the end if they surrendred not themselves the besiegers ruined the poor City: whence we read that in the following times of civil discord the *Pelestrini* that they might not undergoe so great misery as formerly they had done, abandoned their City and retired to their dwellings.

To this day appear there many subterranean waies from the Castle to the foot of the adjacent mountains, (besides the Caves used as conservatories for water) which were made for introducing of assistance, or to fly the City occultly: into one of which *C. Marius* the younger having withdrawn himself, and perceiving himself to be beseiged on all sides, so that he could not fly, that he might not living fall into the hands of his enemies, agreed with *Telesinus* to run one against the other with their naked swords so to kill themselves: by which means *Telesinus* was slain, but *Marius* remained alive thorugh desperatly wounded, and soon after caused one of his Servants to make an end of his then begun death, by killing him. From which successes, the Inhabitants of the place believe the stones of those subterranean waies to be still reddish with the bloud spilt there: which yet is not so, for ever all those hills are stones red by nature, and not through any accident of bloud spilt thereon.

Preneste was first a free City and confederate with the Romans, having its own *Prætor* as *Livy* and *Festus* declare calling her *Municipal*. *Appianus* saies that the *Prenestini* at the time of the Italian war were made Citizens of *Rome* with the *Tiburtini*; but some time after *L. Sylla*, victorious (as *Cicero*, speaks, in *Catalines* conspiracy) having emptied this City by slaughters and banishments, and deprived her of inhabitants by the many expulsions, slaughters and banishments he made of them, there remained so few inhabitants that he sent of the *Romans* to dwell there, dividing its Territory among the new comers, and thus made it a *Roman* Colony. *Aulus Gellius* saies in the third Chapter of his 16. book that afterwards the *Prenestini* obtain-tained of *Tiberius Augustus* a reſtoration to their firſt ſtate, that is into the condition of free Citizens, having the form of a Colony wholly amoved from their City.

TIVOLI.

WHen arrived at *Tivoli*, firſt go ſee thoſe gardens which *Hippolitus Eſtenſe* Cardinal of *Ferrara*, planted with ſo much coſt many yeers ſince upon the back of the mountain, together with a proud Pallace, which alſo is beautifyed with old ſtatues, Pictures and royal houſholdſt uſſe, even to the emulation of the greatneſs and magnificence of the Antients.

But who is able with ſufficiency ever to diſplay in words the exquiſite delights, coſts & pleaſure, wherewith this place and palace is plentifully furniſhed? and who ſhall relate the Labyrinths, the Groves, the half circles, the triumphant Arches, the Arches laden with old ſtatues, the Caverns of the Nymphs, and the innumerable fountains which every where ſprout forth waters, the cloſe walkes, and beautifull arbours covered with trees, herbs, and tender branches and other like verts.

Ubertus Folieta of *Genous* heretofore deſcribed it moſt gratiouſly, But *Corona Pighio* cannnot ſatiate himſelf with praiſing of it, who publiſhed deſcriptions of that Palace and the gardens in *Rome* ſtamped from braſſe cuts, the view whereof in my opinion may draw as many perſons to behold it, as *Rome* doth with all its wonders. Although we have ſcarce courage enough, y● conformable to that publiſhed Table will we curſorily deſcribe it, for ſatisfaction of ſuch as have not had the good fortune to ſee them, or at leaſt their draught in picture. Firſt then the Hill is levelled at top, and upon the plain thereon is erected the Palace, built of ſquare ſtones with the grandure and magnificence of a Royal palace, and with exquiſite art and proportion.

On the right hand whereof lie encloſed gardens, called *Secreti*, and therein ſixteen great marble Goblets emit clear waters, in the midſt whereof ſits a *Janus Quadrifrons*, with four faces, higher raiſed then thoſe goblets, which makes four other fountains adorned like looking glaſſes: and on the right hand a Tennis Court, and other ſumptuous places for exerciſe. The forefront hath between the windows many old ſtatues of Marble, as hath the firſt Porticue, from which lead two fair ſtone ſtaire-caſes up into the palaces.

Before this Porticue in the midſt of a Piazza ſtands a *Leda*, which *Leda* was wife of *Tyndarus* King of *Laconia* with whom as Poets feign *Jupiter* accompanying, ſhe brought forth two eggs, of the one whereof came *Pollux* and *Helena*, (raviſhed by *Paris*) of the other *Caſtor* and *Clytemneſtra*. Thence the hill (a pleaſant deſcent) is reduced into four long Piazzaes, and ſo levelled contains before the front of the palace four great and spatious gardens, into each of which at each end and in the middle, three pair of stone stairs (artificially compofed) conduct by a facile defcent, whofe fides are bathed by divers purling ftreams, running towards their Lakes. Every garden is divided in its orders, hath places to fit in, and fair collumnes erected in divers parts, fo that fuch as go walking from one part to another, through places and paffages covered over with leaves and vines, and other verts alwaies flourifhing, enjoy a moft beautifull profpect and no lefs fweet odours from the circumjacent flowers which make a pompous fhew. In the appartments growes trefh graffe, which with the flowers by their variety wonderfully entertain the eye and fancy of whoever regard them, nor can any fatiate himfelf in the view of thofe infinite and wonderfull ftatues, pillars, Fountains and other objects there prefenting themfelves.

The paffage from the Piazza before the Palace on the right hand leads through divers walks, trees and fmall groves, wherein are placed feveral Fountains, as that of *Tothyde*, that of *Æfculapius*, that of *Nigga*, that of *Aretufa*, and *Pandora*, and that of *Pomona* and *Flora*. In the defcent into the firft garden, fhews it felf the Coloffus of *Pegafus* in *Pamoffo*, a horfe feigned to have wings, under whofe fhadow a fair Fountain cafteth up her waters very high; and in the wood & rocks is a Cavern, and near them a ftatue of *Venus* & *Bacchus*: near wch. is a Lake, into which fome rivolets run among rocks with a murmuring noife between two *Coloffus*, one of the *Sibilla Tiburtina*, the other of *Melicerta* the fon of *Athamas* and *Ino*, whom the Gentiles did honour for one of the Gods of the Sea. Below which lye the ftatues of the Rivers *Anicne*, and *Herculano*, conjoined to certain veffels out of which fome waters run into the Lake, as alfo out of the Urns, round which ftand ten Nymphs. In the midft are two Grotts, the one of the *Sibilla Tiburtina*, the other of *Diana* the Goddeffe of the woods, both which are adorned with fountains, ftatues, Curral, mother of Pearl, and a pavement exactly wrought with mofaick work. On the other fide of the garden you have a fair profpect of *Rome* in a femicircle, round which appear her moft memorable Fabricks; and in the midft fits *Rome* in the habit of a warlike Goddeffe, between her feaven hills: this ftatue is of marble, bigger then a man, in fhape of a Virgin in a fhort girt coat, with naked hands, military buskins, and a fword hanging in a belt from the right fhoulder. Her head is covered with a murrion, in her right hand fhe holds a fpear, in the left a fhield: fhe fits as aforefaid in the midft of her wonders in the City and on every fide appear her facred Fabricks, as the *Pantheon*, the *Capitolian* Temples, the Circs, the Theatres, the Amphitheatres, the Collumnes, the Obelisks, the *Maufeoli*, the Arches Triumphant, the Pyramides, the Acqueducts, the Baths, the River *Tyber*, with the wolf and Twin Brothers pouring water into the City out of an urn; in the midft of which running waters, rifeth an Ifland cut in the fhape of a fhip which bears on the main yard an Obelisk, and the fhip feems to be laden with thefe four Temples, the Temple of *Æfculapius* in the poope, and thofe of *Jupiter*, *Berecinta* and *Fauftus*, it beares in the prow.

Thence

Thence descending to the lower garden, you find on the left hand in a femy circle called the great, a green grove, placed between certain Rocks amid which run fountains this may be called the refidence for birds: for on the arms of the trees you fee many images of little birds finging more fweetly then the natural, who clap their wings as if alive, receiving their motion from the aire and the waters with miraculous artifice, by means of certain little reeds hid in the armes of the trees: fometimes to pleafe the fpectators, they will make a fcreech owle to appear, and then on a fuddain as if the birds were fenfible of fear, they are all filent, but that again withdrawn, in an inftant they all begin their notes and fing moft melodioufly.

In the middle of this garden is a round ftanding water Lake, and in it a capacious veffel and a fountain named from the Dragons, which vomit out of their throats great ftore of waters, having trumpets in their hands which alfo emit plentifull waters, with a horrid noife imitating the found of the trumpet. On the right hand lies the Grotto of Nature adorned with many ftatues, and in it an Organ with fair pipes, the which perform an harmonious confort of various and artificial mufick, by the motion of the waters.

The next garden is not only beautifyed by the fair fountains, but by the quantity of Swans, and fifh preferved in their feveral ftations feparated with rare artifice. In the three greater fountains are certain Beacons, called *Sudanti*, and other boundaries round them, which caft water very high in fuch quantities, that in their fall they feem natural fhowers, refrefhing the air, and cooling the earth making noife of waters in their fall, as if the winds were high, fprinkling and wafhing at a good diftance. In the midft of thefe conferves you fee the effigies of the great Father *Oceanus* placed in a femicircle like a Theatre, and in the middle thereof a marble chariot like that of the *Venus Marina*, drawn by foure Sea horfes, on which fits a great *Neptune* feeming to threaten with his Trident.

Laftly defcending into the laft garden near the rock, you find in one part a Fountain of *Triton*, and on the other a Fountain of *Venus Clonina*, and in the reft of the level befides the Pefcheries, four Labyrinths difficult enough for any one to get out of thats once in, placed one by another in foure compartments amidft forreign plants. The entrance and outlet of thefe gardens, are embellifht with great Fabricks built of *Tiburtine* ftone, with great expence. Thus much concerning the *Villa* of *Tivoli*, of Cardinal *Hippolito E ftenfe.*

The noble fepulchre of Cardinal *Hippolito da Fſte* in the Church will recompence your pains in the fight of it, being compofed with marble of various colours, on it ftands a great white marble ftatue of the faid Cardinal of great coft and fair appearance. The Caftle alfo affords many worthy objects, but what is more confiderable, is the precipitous defcent of the River, which falls with fuch noife and fury from high cliffs of mountains, that for the moft part its vapours render the air foggie, and many times at a diftance there feem to hang celeftial rainbowes, cloudes being at moft times over it. This River infamed by the writings of the antient, takes its rife at the mountain of the *Trebani*, and runs into three noble Lakes, which give name to the adjacent caftle, called *Sublaco:* which Lakes *Tacitus* feems to call *Simbrivini*, faying in the 14th. Book of his Annals, that near them ftood the *Villa Sublacenfe* of *Nerò* in the confines of *Tivoli*, from which Lakes the *Aniene* running afterward through woods and mountains, falls at laft in the plain near *Tivoli*, from high ftones, with fury and noife, then it goes fome fpace under ground, and at the foot of the mountain returns all again above ground, it runs through the three fulphurious veins, called *Albule*, from their white colour. Tis faid, and *Strabo* confirms the water there to be medicinal in drinking or Bathing, and *Pliny* writes that they heal the wounded. Nor does the *Albule* only but alfo the *Albunea* above *Tivoli* confolidate wounds. Regarding the *Campania* of *Tivoli*, about the *Aniene* you will find huge ftones encreafed by little and little in long time by vertueof the waters running by, and in the bottome of Lakes there you'l find of hard ftones generated by the fame means.

In this confine are many footfteps of old edifices worthy contemplation : *Tivoli* having been a moft noble City, and well Inhabited through the beauty of its fcite, the goodneffe of its foyle, and the falubrity of the aire : which made it be furrounded with the fair Villa's, and Lordly houfes of the rich perfons of that Country, although now like *Rome*, and all *Italy* alfo it lies wafte and ruinated by the various warrs and fucceffes which have deftroyed it. Tis certain that Greeks were the builders of this City, but who they were is not certain, the writers of the *Italian* antiquities not agreeing herein : yet the greater part fay that *Catillo* was its founder, who fome fay was of *Arcadia*, and Captain of *Evanders* Navy. Others affirm *Argivus* the fon of *Amfiardo* the Sooth-fayer, after the prodigious death of his Father near *Thebes*, came by command of the oracle with his family and Gods (long before the *Trojane* warr) into *Italy:* and by the affiftance of the *Enotri*, *Aborigeni*, drove the *Siculi* out of that place, naming the Caftle taken from them *Tibure*, from his eldeft fons name. Nor does *Pliny* much difagree from this, though he does not wholly agree with it : for in the 16th of his natural Hiftory writing of the ages of Trees he faies, that in his time there ftood 3 Holme Trees by *Tivoli*, near to which *Tiburtio* the builder of that Caftle, had received augure to build it. But faies he was the Nephew not the Son of *Amfiardo* and that he came with his two Brothers *Lora* and *Catillo* one age before the *Trojane* warr, and that he there caufed the Caftle to be built, calling it after his own name becaufe he was the elder, in which opinion *Virgil*, in his *Æneides* feems to concur: but *Horatius* on the other part calls *Tivoli* the walls of *Catillus* purfuing the others opinion : from which expreffions we conjecture that the City *Tivoli*, was before *Rome*. Thofe of *Tivoli* held *Hercules* in reverence above the other idols, as Protector of the *Grædian* people, at whofe feftivity infinite people reforted thither.

In it was alfo a Temple for the *Sorti*, lotts or chances no leffe famous for their oracles then that in *Bura*, or in *Achaia* a countrey of *Morea* mentioned by *Paufanias* : whence the Poet *Statius* faies, that fuch was the beauty of the place that even the *Sorti Preneftini* would have chofen it for giving their anfwers, had not *Hercules* firft poffeffed the place.   Thefe

Thefe are his words.

Quod que in templa darent alias Tyrinthia fortes,
Et Prcneftinæ poterant migrare forores.

He calls the *Sorti* Sifters; for that good and bad Fortune were reverenced as two Sifters. Tis thought that Temple under the mountain in the way of *Tivoli*, was that famous Temple of *Hercules*: but
this people had another Temple dedicate to the fame God, yet called
Hercules Saxanus, as appears by the fubfequent infcription found in
a Piazza attaqued to a particular houfe.

Herculi Saxano facrum
Ser. Sulpicius. Trophimus
Ædem. Zothecam. Culinam
Pecunia fua a Solo Reftituit
Fidem. Dicavit. K. Decemb.
L. Tupilio Dextro. M. Maccio Rufo. Cof.
Euthycus. Ser. Peragendum Curavit

But we cannot conclude with certainty where this other Temple ftood: yet many agree that twas called *Hercules Saxanus*, in refpect twas built with ftone differing from the other greater Temple:
juft as the *Milanefi*, called one *Hercules in Pietra*, from the fcituation
of that Church in a ftony place near them. Upon the ftone arifeth a
certain antient round Fabrick without covering, built with marble
in rare architecture of much efteem, which poffibly might be the
Temple of *Hercules Saxanus*: tis near the *Cataracts* which augments
this fufpicion; for that the Antients ufually placed their Temples
confecrate to *Hercules* near waters, long ports, and violent falls of
waters, to the end that *Hercules* by them efteemed the Protector of
the firm Land, might caufe the water to continue in its limits, and
not infeft the country with inundations: the which *Statius* clearly
fhews in the 11th. Book of woods, fpeaking of the *Villa Surrentina* of his
Pollius, which ftood on the fea fhore near a port with a Temple of
Hercules, and another of *Neptune* neare it: whofe verfes now
take.

Ante domum tumidæ moderator cærulus undæ
Excubat innocui cuftos laris, Hujus amico
Spumant Templa falo, fælicia jura tuetur
Alcides, gaudet gemino fub nomine portus,
Hic fervat terras, hic fævis fluctibus obftat.

He feigns alfo in his third book, that *Hercules*, having layed afide
his arms, laboured much in preparing the foundations of his Temple in that place, and with great ftrength prepared the inftruments
for digging the earth; for thus the *Pagans* or Gentiles beleived, *viz,*
that *Hercules*, during his life went through the world, operating for
the publick good of Mankind, what ever was difficult or laborious
to be effected; as not only in the taming and killing of Monfters, re-

L l l l
moving

removing Tyrants, reducing unjuſt Lords to the terms and conditions of Juſtice, and chaſtiſing the bad and evil ones: But alſo in building of Caſtles and Cities in deſert-places, ports and ſecurities for
ſhipping on dangerous ſhores, reducing bad and irkſome waies into
good, changing the chanels of damnifying Rivers, breaking the
courſe of the waters where requiſite, for preſervatiõ ofthe firmLand:
ſetling peace between diſagreeing nations with juſt Laws, opening
the method & way of dealing and negotiating between people far
eloigned from one another: and inſum reducing into a ſtate of civility
ſuch as were wilde and fierce: wherefore they built him Temples,
created him a God, and devoutly honoured him, giving him ſeveral
ſurnames according to the diverſity of the places where they ado-·
red him, or the quality of the benefits which the people held they
received from him, or according to ſome great work which they
ſuppoſed he had done.   Whence the weſtern parts of the world
had *Hercules Gaditani,* when on the north ſide of the ſtraight called of
old *Fretum Herculeum,* was Mount *Calpe,* on the South Mount *Abila,*
on which *Hercules* placed his ſo memorable pillars, with the inſcription *Nil ultra:* becauſe that   was then conceived to be the moſt weſtern
bound of the world. But *Charles* the 5th: after the diſcovery of *America*
coming that way, cauſed *Plus ultra* to be engraven either on the ſame
Pillars or on new, erected in their places.   The *Batani,* called him
Monaco. The *Genoveſi, Baulio.* Thoſe of the *Terra di Lavoro, Sur-*
rentino. and they of *Tivoli,* called him *Tivoleſſe* and *Saxanus.* The *Ti-*
voleſi, were ſuch Friends to *Hercules,* that they called their City
Herculea, as if the whole were eſpecially conſecrated to him, and in
the palace of *Tivoli* they honored *Hercules* juſt as *Jupiter* was honored
in the *Campi doglio* at *Rome,* and the heads or chief of the publick
Council and of the Prieſts, were called in *Tivoli, Hercoleani,* being of
great dignity : a thing clearly demonſtrable by certain inſcrip
tions and Epitaphs extant in antient marbles,   whereof enſue
ſome for the ſervice and advantage of the ſtudious in antiquity.

In the Church of *S. VICENZO* in *TIVOLI.*

Herculi
Tiburt. Vict.
Et. Cereris. diſ.
Præt. Tiburt.
L. Minicius
Natalis
Cos Augur.
Leg. aug. Pr. Pr.
Provinciæ.
Moeſiæ Infer.
Votis Suſc.

In the ascent of the mountain in a Fragment
on the way.

C. Sestilius
V. V: Tiburtium
Lib. Ephebus
Herculanius
Augustalis

In the great Church.

C. Albius. Livillæ. L.
Thymelus, Herc.
Augustalis.

The tenth Sybil named by the Latines *Tibuclina* and *Albunea* by
the Græcians *Leucothea*, was held in great honour in *Tivoli* in old
time : for they adored her as a Goddess consecrating to her a wood
a Temple and a Fountain called after her own name *Albunea*, from
the whitenesse of its waters, above *Tivoli*, in that mountain where
Fame saies she was born and gave answers to demandants: of whom
Virgil speaks and *Servius* his Commentator, as also *Horace*, with his Interpreters. Tis reported that the Romans going about to deifie *Augustus Cæsar*, demanded advise of this *Sybil*, who after three daies
fast, standing before the Altar, where the Emperor himself was then
present, after many hidden words miraculonsly spoken concerning
Christ, upon the suddain Heaven opened, and *Cæsar* saw a beautifull Virgin standing before the Altar, who held as lovely an infant
in her arms, at which apparition *Cæsar* affrighted fell on his face:
and a voice as from Heaven was heard saying this is the Altar of
the Son of God. In which place was after built a Temple dedicated
to the Virgin *Mary* called *Ara Cæli* the Altar of heaven. This *Policro-
nion* affirms, and for the truth thereof cites *S. Augustine. lib* 18. *cap.* 24.
She Prophesied of the coming of Christ, after the recital of the sea.
ven wonders of the world to this purpose.

> What at these trifles stands the world amazed?
> And hath on them with admiration gazed ?
> Then wonder ! When the troubled world t'appaise
> He shall descend, who made them that made these.

These things being seen, march towards *Rome*, and leaving the
Road a little on the left hand, bestow a view on the *Elia Tiburtina*,

which was the *Villa* of *Hadrianus* the Emperor, feated on a little hill, which now at prefent fhews the countenance of a great ruinated City: the footfteps of fo vaft edifices ftupifie the beholders, hardly difpenfing with any beliefe that it could ever have been but one fingle *Villa* or princely feat. There may yet be found the ruines of many Palaces, Houfes, Temples, Porticues, Acqueducts, Bathing houfes, hot baths, Theaters, Amphitheaters, and in fum, of all other kind of Fabricks whatfoever imaginable for fupream delights and pleafures. Among the reft you'l finde a very high wall drawn long-waies againft the South two ftades in length, which Wall hath alwaies on the one fide the fhade, and on the other the Sun; fo that tis moft comodious for walking by, or for any other exercife either in the fhade or in the Sun, according to the neceffity or humour of the perfon at all times. The vaft ruines of this *Villa*, fpeak not alone the immenfe charge *Hadrianus* was at in building the fame, but *Spartianus* alfo declares it in the life of *Adrian*, faying, that he in that his *Villa* caufed draughts or as we may better fay the fimilitudes of the moft celebrious places of the world to be made, caufing them afterwards to be called after the proper names of the imitated places: as among others, the *Liceum*, *Ariftotles* School in *Athens*, the *Academy of Cicero*, the *Prytaneum* or counfel houfe of *Athens*, the Temple of *Theffalia*, a place wonderfully pleafant having trees and meadowes marvelloufly delectable, wherein birds of divers kinds fing continually with excellent melody: the *Canopus* of *Egypt*, a place wherein the God of that name was worfhipped; and the like Fabricks made and nominated in imitation of the true. He further faies, that he there caufed to be erected the place or reprefentation of hell: all which things were undoubtedly accomodated and adorned with all conveniences and endowments, fo that one might well comprehend at the firft view, that, which in it felf comprehended every one, that is Pictures, Statues, Figures, Infcriptions, pourtrayes of men, wherewith every of thofe places were illuftrated, either with fome notable writing, or heroick action. Which ornaments are all ruinated and difperfed, part by the rage of warr, and part by the incivility of the barbarous people, invading Italy, who there fhewed not the leaft refpect. Not long fince in the fields of *Tivoli*, were found many figures, and ftatues, taken without doubt from this *Villa*, and applied to divers fabricks in the adjacent Countrey: many alfo have been found among the ruines of the faid *Villa* under ground, and among others fome carcafes of men with their names in greek letters, as of *Themiftocles*, *Miltiades*, *Ifocrates*, *Heraclitus*, *Carneades*, *Ariftogiton*, an orator of *Athens*, who for his lewd behaviour was called Dog, with others, whofe tronks or bodies poffibly and credibly *Pope Julius* the third caufed to be got together and conveighed to *Rome*, for beautifying his gardens: being advifed of this their accidental coming to hand by *Marcellus Cervinus*, Cardinal of *Santa Croce*, a Lover of the ftudious: the which his *Sainctety* afterwards put in good order with great expence in the *Via Flaminia*, on the this fide the *Ponte Milvio*.

Being freed from the ruines of the *Villa Elia*, you travel to *Rome* by the *Via Tiburtina*, along which appear fome antiquities worthy obfervation

fervation ; and among others on the Banks of the River *Aniene*, is a
great *Mauſeolus*, a grand Fabrick erected for the Sepulchre of theFa-
mily of the *Plauſi Silvani* both noble and antient, and framed of large
ſquare marble ſtones, near the bridge which conjoines on the one
and other ſide of the River the antient Road; and is vulgarly called
the *Ponte Lucano*, the reaſon of which name is not facilly known,
bnt in ſome ſpeeches tis called *Ponte Plauto*, and ſome ſuppoſe that
way was ſet out and the Bridge likewiſe built by thoſe noble and
triumphant *Plautii*, whoſe names we find engraven on the ſaid Tomb:
chiefly for that *Suetonius* teſtifies it was the cuſtom by order of *Auguſtus* for the victorious Captains, to accomodate the Roads with the
ſpoiles taken from the enemies, to wch. he connexeth this other conjecture, that is, that in the third elogie of *P. Plinius* (of whoſe memorial
or Epitaph, though a part be fallen in his *Mauſeolus* or Tomb, yet e-
nough remains to ſatisfie the ſtudious in antiquity) we read among
other Titles of honour, that this was not omitted, viz.   That by the
comand of *T. Claudius Cæſar*, he was elected by the neighbourhood
Procurator for accomodating the Road, or high waies.

Mmm   A

A DESCRIPTION
OF THE
ISLAND
OF
SICILIA
OR
SICILY.

Sicilia is an Island of the *Mediterranean* Sea, seated betwixt *Italy* and *Affrick*, but between the South and West tis separated from *Italy* by a neck of the sea. Its form resembles a △ in greek, for that it hath three corners, every one whereof makes a Promontory, which are *Peloro, Pachino, Lilibeo*, now called *Capo del Faro, Capo Paffero, Capo Boco. Peloro* looks towards *Italy, Pachino* towards *Morea*, and *Li-libeo* toward the Promontory *Mercurio f Africk*, and to speak according to the aspect of the climes, *Peloro* lies Eastward, *Pachino* between South and East, *Lilibeo* between South and West. On the North this Island is washed by the *Tirrhene* Sea, on the East by the *Adriatique* and *Jonian* Sea, on the South by the *African* Sea, and on the West by that of *Sardigna*. It was called *Trinacria*, either from its three Promontories or from the King *Trinaco*, son of *Neptune*, and *Triquetra*, or from the three points of the Triangle; and *Sirania* from the *Sirani*, and after that *Sicilia* from the *Siculi*, (descended from the *Liguri*) who beat out the *Sicani*. It is in circuit, as by the moderns is judged (setting aside the diversities of the antients) six hundred twenty three miles: from *Peloro* to *Pachino* one hundred and sixty miles, from thence to *Lilibeo* 183 miles, from *Lilibeo* to *Peloro* 211. Its length from East to west is 150 miles, but its bredth is not equal, though on the Eastern part tis 160 miles broad, diminishing afterwards in bredth by degrees, being most straite at *Lilibeo*. The head of all the Island is the Territory *Ennefc*. It hath on the north side ten Islands which lie round it (the Antients numbred but 7) whose names are *Liparee, Vulcania*, or *Giera, Vulcanello, Lisca-bianca, Basiluzo, Thermisia, Trongile, Didima, Fenicusa*, and *Ericusa*. *Sicilia* is divided into three provinces, which they call *Valli* or *Vales*, that is into the *Val di De-*

mino

mino or *Demona*, the *Val de Noto*, and the *Val di Mazara*, the *Val di Demino* commenceth from the Promontory *Peloro*, and is the shore on one side to the River *Terria*, and on the other to the River *Himera* which dischargeth it self into the *Tirrhene* Sea. The *Val di Noto*, begins at the River *Teria*, and with it extending it self inwards, and traversing *Enna*, it descends with the river *Gela*, and ends at the City of *Alicata*. But the *Val di Mazara*, comprehends all the remaining part of *Sicily* to *Lilibeo*. This Island was some time conjoined to *Italy*, whereof the modern authors as well as antient render a large testimony, though there are some who take it for a ridiculous opinion. It is esteemed for the salubrity of the Ayre, the abundance of terrene sustenance and plenty of all things necessarie for mans use very excellent, as placed under the fourth Climate much more benigne then all the others, whence tis that what ever this soyle of *Sicily* affords, either by its own nature or the Ingenuity of man is accounted next to those which are cryed up for the best. It produceth corn in such abundance, that in many places it yields 100 for one.   Wilde Oats grow there of themselves, as also the Vines, which gave occasion for the Fable of *Ceres* & *Proserpina*. Their wines are most delicate, as is the oyle of Olives whereof they make great quantities. Their Canes too are admirable, called *Ebosia* heretofore, now *Cannamele*, whereof they make Sugars. Their Bee hony is there so good that by the antients as a proverb twas used the *Hyblean* hony of *Sicily*, which affords great store of wax: the Bees using the very tronks of trees for their hives, there gathering excellent honey. Their fruits of all sorts, grow with much plenty and goodnesse; they gather all sorts of Plants and medicinal herbs, and their saffron is better then that of *Italy*, as are their roots of wilde palm trees, which are gustfull to eat. The mountains *Aeri* are so plentifully furnished with sweet waters, fountains, fruitfull and pleasant trees, that they have many times preserved a great Army of the *Carthaginians*, when near famishing. Other mountains produce salt, as *Enna*, *Nicosia*, *Camerata* and *Platanim*, where they take out salt stones. There also are the Caves or Pits for salt made of the Foam of the Sea resting upon the coasts, but neare *Lilibeo*, *Drepano*, *Camarino*, *Macanio*, and other places, they take up the sea water, put it into pits, and thereof make salt. They also draw salt out of other parts of *Sicily* from the Lakes, as near *Pochino*, (a wonderfull thing) what by the rain, and fresh waters falling from other fountains, the Lake maybe increased, in a little time, is dryed away by the Sun. They also make here great plenty of that silk which they draw from their silk worms. Nor is *Sicilia* lesse enriched by her Metals and Mines, having Minerals of Gold, Silver, Iron, Allum: and on the banks of the River *Acate* grow pretious stones, as the Emerald and Agat stone, and the clear Bartina, which is white in circuit, and black spots in the midst, and in forms of severall Creatures, as birds, beasts, men or any other, which they say is an Antidote against the biting of the spider or Scorpion. *Solinus* saies too, that twill make the Rivers stop, and that *Pirrhus* had one stone of this sort in a ring, wherein was engraven *Apollo* with his Scepter, and the Chorus of the nine Muses with their Ensigae, at *Graterio*, they dig the *Beril* or Sea water stone in great plenty, and Porphiry ſtone, red and traverſed with white and green ſtroaks. Here alſo they take up the jaſper ſtone being red, and varied with ſeveral clear green and white ſpots, which ennobles the ſtone. And in the ſea of *Meſſina*, and of *Drepano*, there growes Corrals a ſort of ſea Plant much commended and ſought after. *Sicilia* is likewiſeFamed for the Chaſe of the Goat and wilde Bore: for the fowling at Partridge and Godwit. And all other ſorts of Birds, and four-footed beaſts both for delight and profit are there in great plenty, beſide the Falcon and other Hawks, which there are taken. The Fiſhing alſo is greatly abounding, particularly for the Fiſh called Tunny Fiſh, whereof they take not only at *Pachino* (as the Antients wrote) but alſo at *Palermo and Drepano*, and in all the River which is waſhed with the *Tyrrhene*Sea,(this fiſh bears a great price in *MayorJune*)as alſo of the ſword fiſh particularly at *Meſſina*, which('tis written) they cannot take unleſſe they ſpeak Greek, and to ſay no more both the Seas and the Rivers abound with all ſorts of excellent fiſh. They have alſo in divers places many baths of hot, cool, ſulphurous and other ſorts of water, uſefull and advantagious in ſeveral Infirmities, but thoſe that are in the River *Scnuntina*, near the Cities *Sacra* and *Himera*, are ſalt and unwholſome to drink. We will not ſpeak of the Fountains of ſweet water that are found over all *Sicilia*, and many Rivolets accommodated as well for the life of Man, as the enriching their Lands by the overflowing. And to ſpeak in brief, this Iſland is not at all inferiour to any other Province, either for its fatneſſe or abundance; but ſomewhat exceeds *Italy* in the excellency of their grain, ſaffron, honey, Beaſts skins, and other ſuſtenance for the life of Man; in ſo much that *Cicero* not improperly called it the Granary of the *Romans*,and *Homer* ſaid that all things grew there of their own accord, and therefore calls it the Iſle of the Sun. *Sicilia* is likewiſe admirable for the fame of thoſe things which told, exceed our beleef as the Mount*Etna*,&*Mongibello*,who ſending forthcontinual firesfrom its bowels hath not witſtanding its head(on that part where the fire iſſues)deeply covered in ſnow to the midſt of Summer.Not far from *Agrigento*,or *Gergento* is the Territory *Matharuca*., which with aſſidual vomiting of divers veins of waters, ſends forth a certain Aſh-coloured Earth, and at certain times caſting out an incredible Maſs of that Earth, the one and the other fields may be heard,to roar.

In *Menenino* is the Lake *Naſtia* (called by *Pliny Ffintia*) where in three eddies you behold boyling water, which alwaies gurgles with an egregious ſtink, and ſomtimes ſpues up flames of fire: hither antiently reſorted all ſuch, as through their ſuperſtition were to be ſworn to any thing. It bath likewiſe in ſundry other places divers other Fountains of admirable Qualities and nature, for an ample account whereof the reader is referred to *Thomaſo Fazellio*, to the end we may abridge our relation here. *Sicily* was inhabited by the *Cyclopes*, which is verified (beſides what Authors affirm) by the bodies of immenſe bigneſſe and heigth,which in our daies are ſeen in the Grots, or Caves. Thoſe *Cyclopes*, being monſters of Men or Gyants, whom the *Sicani* ſucceeded, and them the *Siculi* or *Sicilians*. Then the *Trojans*, the *Candiots*, the *Phenici*, the *Galcidonians*,

the

the *Corinthians* and other Greeks, the *Zanclei*, the *Guidii*, the *Sara-sini*, the *Normans*, the *Lombards*, the *Swedes*, the *Germans*, the *French* the *Arragonians*, the *Spaniards*, the *Catalonians*, the *Genouans*, and at length many *Pisans*, *Lucchesians*, *Bolognians*, and *Florentines*: all which people at several times inhabited divers parts of this Island : untill *Charls* the fifth Emperor took *Corona*, and after a little time leaving it to the Turks, all those Greeks that dwelt there transported themselves into *Sicilia*. The People are of an acute and quick wit, noble in their inventions, and industrious by nature, and said to be of three tongues for their velocity in speech, wherein their expressions proceed with much grace to facetiousnesse and quicknesse: they are held loquacious beyond measure: whence the Antients borrow ed the proverb *Gerræ Siculæ*, the *Sicilian* bablings. Antient writers attribute the following things to the invention of the *Sicilians*, the art of Oratory, the Bucolick or pastoral verse, dyall making, the *Catapulte* a warlike engine, the illustrating of Pictures, the Art of Barbing, the use of skins of wilde beasts and Ryme. They are by nature suspectfull, envious, evil spoken, facil to speak Villany, and prone to revenge, but industrious subtle flatterers of Princes, and studious of Tyranny (as saies *Orosie*,) which at this day does not so generally appear.

They are more covetous of their own commodities or conveniences then of the publiques, and reflecting on the abundancy of the Countrey, sloathfull and without industry. Antiently their tables were so splendidly furnished, that it became a Proverb among the Greeks, but now they follow the frugality of *Italy*. They are valiant in warrs, and of uncorruptible faith to their King ; beyond the custome of the Greeks, they are patient ; but provoked they leap into extream fury. They speak the Italian Language, but roughly, and without the least sweetnesse, and in their habits and other customes live after the manner of the *Italians*.

MESSINA.

THat City of *Sicilia* that is most illustrious, is *Messina*, built with the ruines and reliques of the City *Zancla*: at a thousand paces distance from hence came *Diccarchus* the hearer of *Aristotle*, the most celebriou*s Peripatetick*, Geometritian, and eloquent Oratour, who wrote many books, whereof *Fazellius* makes mention, and *Ibicus* the Historian and the *Lyrick* Poet, and in the memory of our Fathers times lived there *Cola* the Fish, born at *Catana*, who leaving human society, consumed the best part of his life among the fish in the sea of *Messina*, whence he acquired the nick name of fish. Hence came also *Giovanni Gatto*, of the preaching order, a Philosopher, Divine, and famous Mathematician, who read in *Florence*, *Bologna*, and *Ferrara*, and was afterwards elected Bi-

Nnnn

fhop of *Catano*; and laftly hence came *Gio Andrea Mercurio*, a moft
worthy Cardinal of the holy Church.

Here ftood the City *Taurominio*, which gave birth (according to
Paufanias) to *Tifandro* Son of *Cleocrito*, who four times overcame
in the *Olympick* Games and as many times in the *Pythick*, and *Time-*
us the hiftorian fon of *Andromacus*, who wrote of the tranfaĉti-
ons in *Sicilia* and *Italy* and of the *Theban* warrs.

CATANA.

IT hath alfo the City *Catana*, one part whereof is wafhed by the
Sea and the other extends it felf to the foot of the Mountains
where antiently was the Sepulture or burying place for famous
and illuftrious perfons, as of *Steficorus* the Poet, *Himerefe, Xenofane*
the Philofopher, and of two young Brothers *Anapia* and *Anfinomo:*
who (the fire of *Ætna* raging and burning all the Countrey round)
took up upon their fhoulders the one his Father the other his Mother
but being difabled by the weight to proceed with fpeed, and the
fire overtaking them and at their very feet, yet loft not their mag-
nanimity and courage, but when almoft in defpair, the fire on a
fuddain divided it felf before them, and fo they miraculoufly efcaped fafe. In this City is a Colledge for all the fciences, but moft
particularly they here ftudy the Civil and Canon Laws, and from
her have iffued many illuftrious perfous, as *Santa Agatha*, (which
the *Palermitans* will call of their City) a Virgin Martyr, who under
Quintiano in the yeer of our falvation 152 fuffered Martyrdome for
Chrift; and *Carondo* the Philofopher and Legiflator, and he that was
reputed the great *Afagus, Diodorus* or *Liodorus:* Hence came alfo
Nicolo Todifco, called the Abbot, or *Panormitano* the great Cononift,
and Cardinal, who wrote fo many books of the Canon Laws, and
was prefent fo much to his glory at the Councel of *Bafilea* in the yeer
1440. It gave birth likewife to *Galeozzo,* or *Galeotto Bardafino,* whofe
vaft body and ftrength acquired him the title of a Gyant, of whofe
proweffe and noble Aĉts of Chevalry we have as large relations, as
any our Romances attribute to their *Heroes.* The City *Leontina* or
Leontio (antiently inhabited by the *Leftrigones*) was the birth place
of *Georgia* the Philofopher and Orator, and *Agathone* the *Tragick*
Poet: and fince the faith of Chrift planted there, *Alfio, Filadolfio,*
Cirino, became Martyrs for it. From the City *Megara,* came *Theo*
genes the Poet, and *Epicarmo* the *Comick* Poet, and Inventor of Comedies.

SYRACVSA.

Syracusa, (antiently the *Metropolis* of *Sicilia*, and enobled by ma ny titles) gave birth to many eminent men in all the sciences; as to *Theocrito the Bucolick* Poet, *Filalao* the *Pythagorean*, *Filomone* the *Comick* Poet in the daies of *Alexander* the Great, another *Philomene* a *Comick*, who also had a Son of the same name and profession, *Sofrone a Comick* in the daies of *Euripides*, *Corace* one of the prime Inventors of the Art of Oratory and his Disciple *Cesia* no lesse eminent in Oratory; *Dione Siracusano* who wrote of the Art of Rhetorick, *Sosane the Tragick Poet*, *Epicarmo* the most learned continued alwaies in *Syracusa*, and at his death had a statue erected in honour of him; *Fotino* the *Comick* Poe t *Carmo* the Poet; *Menecrates* the Physician and Philosopher, *Filosseno the Lyrick*, *Callimaco* who wrote in verse concerning this Island, *Mosco* the Grammarian, *Jaceta* the Pihlosopher, *Antioco* the Historian, *Filisto* an Historian and Father of *Dionygio* the Tyrant; *Callius* the Historian, *Theodore* the Philosopher who wrote of the Art of Warr, *Archetimus* a Philosopher and Histo rian, *Archimede* a Philosopher and excelling Mathematician, with many others: Amongst the holy Martyrs it afforded *Lucia* the Virgin, and *Stefano* the third Pope.

From the County of *Nea* came *Ducetio* King of *Sicilia*, *Giovanni Aurispa* a famous writer, *Antonio Cassarino* a surpassing Orator, *Giovanni Martasio* a most celebrated Poet, and here also is the sepulchre of *San Corrado* the *Placentian* to whose merits they Fa le many miracles. From *Agrigento* a famous City issued the Conquerour in the Olympick games before *Diodorus*, and *Phalaris* here exercised his cruel Tyranny which begot him the surname of Tyrant; hence also proceeded *Creone and Acrone*, both Philosophers and Physicians; *Polo* the Orator, *Dinoloco* a *Comick*, *Archino* a *Tragick* Poet, *Sofocle* and *Xenocorate* to whom *Pindarus* entituled two of his Odes.

In the City *Therme* now called *Sacra*, were born *Agathocles* King of *Syracusa*, and *Thomaso Fazellio*, of the order of *San Domenico*, who wrote the affairs of *Sicilia* in a large volume.

PALERMO.

THe City of *Palermo*, is the fairest of all the others of this Island, and at present the Metropolis and Regal Seat: of which much will here be spoken: she gave birth to *Andrea* the most antient and noble Philosopher, who wrote the Civil history of the *Sicilians*;

  but

but it was muchmore illuftrated for the firft breath it afforded to the Saints *Oliua* & *Nimfa* both Martyred for the Faith of Chrift: & *Antonio* called the *Palermitan*, of the KnightlyFamily of *Beccatelli* of *Bologna*, an Orator& a noblePoet, & much edeared to all the Princes of his time. When alfo flourifhed *Pietro Ranzano* of the Preaching order, a Divine, an Oratour, and a famous Poet, and at laft Bifhop of *Lucera*. It bred alfo *Monfignior Jacomo Lomellini* its ArchBifhop, a learned Prelate, and of great integrity of Life. *Sicily* nourifhed alfo many other famous perfons as well antient as modern, as *Sthenio, Thermitano*, the defender of the Cities of *Sicilia*, *Stefcoro* one of the new Lyricks of *Greece, Diodoro* furnamed *Siculo* a famous and renownedHiftorian, whofe life the Author hereof hath wrote at large in another Treatife; *Thomafo Caula* a Laureat Poet, and many others. Sharp and long wars were waged for the poffeffion of this Ifland, between the *Romans* and *Carthaginians*, but the *Romans* at length remained Conquerours, and reduced her into a province at the overthrow of *Hie ronie* (by *Claudius Marcellus* the Conful) who was the laft of thofe Tyrants under whom fhe had thentofore been fubjected. Then twas governed by Prætors till it fell into the power of the Emperors, and *Charles* the great; in which time the Empire and world being divided, *Sicilia, Calabria* and *Puglia* remained in obedience to the Emperors of *Conftantinople*, under whom it continued till *Niceforus* beame Emperor, in whofe Reign the *Saracens* poffeffed it and *Puglia*, the Mount Saint *Angelo, Nocero* with other places in the yeer D C C C G X I I I I. hence they made frequent incurfions into *Calabria*, and to the very walls of *Naples* and *Gavigliano:* againft whom Pope *John* the tenth with *Alberico Mafalpina* his Kinfman great Duke of *Tufcany* armed themfelves, and with much difficulty and great flaughter drove them into the *Monte Santo Angelo.* Which *Alberico* was Son of *Alberto,* brother of *Guido,* grand Marqueffe of *Tufcany,* fome of whofe medals I have feen with their *Tefte* or Motto, and on the reverfe the fleurifhing Thorn tree(the Arms of that Family) in the hands of the Marqueffe *Lodovico Mafalpina* a Gentleman no leffe facetious then curious in collections. The *Saracini* one hundred yeers after their inroad into *Italy* were drove out by the *Normandi,* who were Counts of *Sicilia,* who for forty three yeers increafed their Empire with much felicity, till *Ruberto Guifcardo* feized *Puglia* in his own name, and *Sicilia* in right of his Brother *Ruggieri,* ; whereupon Pope *Nicholas* the fecond conceded to him the Title of Duke, and created him *Feudatory* of the Church: which was afterwards confirmed by *Gregory* the feventh, who by him was freed from the injuries of *Harry* the third. After whom, *Guglielmo* the fecond was by *Innocent* the 4th. created the firft King, to whom fucceeded *Gulielmo* the third who deceafing without iffue, the Kingdome was ufurped by one *Tancredi* a baftard of the Family of *Guifcardi:* againft whom Pope *Clement* and *Celeftine* the third oppofed themfelves; & in the end *Celeftine* gave *Coftanza* the daughter of *Ruggier* the fecond (a Nun in *Palermo*) for wife to *Henry* the Son of *Frederick* the Emperor with the Title and right claim of the Kingdome: whereupon *Henry* made war againft *Tancredi,* befieged and flew him in *Naples,* and fo fucceeded in this Kingdome and Empire of his Father. After whom followed *Frederick* the fecond, his

Son,

Son, then *Manfredo* the baftard Son of *Frederick* got the Kingdom, but was thence drove out by *Charls* of *Anjou* Brother of Saint *Lewis* King of *France*, being called in and invefted therein by the Pope; under which *Charls* the *Sicilians* (being complotted with by *Pietro d' Arragona*, who married *Coftanza* daughter of *Manfredo*) at the found of the Vefpers Bell, cut in peices all the French which were in *Sicilia*, by which means *Pietro* became Lord of the Ifland, which happened in the yeer 1283. By which occafion arofe many contefts and wars betwixt the *Arragonians* and the *Anjouans* for the poffeffion of that Kingdom, with divers fortunes, till at length the *Arragonians* were wholly driven out of the Kingdome of *Naples* by *Charls* the VIII. But the *Arragonians* at laft regained the poffeffion by the proweffe of *Confalvo Ferrando* the great Captain, who drove out the French for *Ferrando* the Catholick King of *Spain*; from whom the Kingdomes of *Sicilia* and *Naples* paffed by an hereditary fucceffion to *Charles* the 5th. Emperor, and from him it defcended to *Philip* the fecond, who left it to his Son *Philip* the third Catholick King, who now injoyes them in quiet poffeffion.

A Defcription of the Ifland of *MALTA*

BEtween *Sicilia*, and the River of the one and t'other fhore of *Barbary*, are fixed the two Iflands *Melita* or *Malta*, and *Gaulo* or *Gozo*, the one diftant from the other five miles, but eloigned from *Pachino* or *Capo Paffero* a Promontory of *Sicilia*, (which they look towards) one hundred miles, and from *Africa* one hundred and ninety miles. *Malta* is 60. miles in circumference, being all as it were a plain, though fomewhat Rocky, and expofed to the windes, it hath many and fecure Ports, but towards the North tis wholly deprived of frefh waters, but on the weftern parts are excellent Currance, and it produceth moft fruitfull trees. Where tis broadeft tis 12 miles over, and in the longeft part 20 miles, and in all thofe feas is there not one Ifland fo great diftance from the firm Land as this is. In more then fix places towards *Sicilia*, tis hollowed, and hath Ports as it were formed by the Sea of *Sicilia* for receipt of its Pyrates or Rovers on the Sea, but towards *Tripolis* tis all full of Cliffes and Rocks affording no mannor of Harbour. Tis called *Melita* in Latine from the Bees which in Greek are called *Melitte* for that the abundance and goodneffe of Flowers caufeth in this Ifle the production of the moft excellent hony, but of late by corruption of the word we call it *Malta*. At its firft habituation it yielded obedience to King *Battus* famous for his riches, and for the friendfhip and hofpitality of *Dido*, whence afterwards it obeyed the *Carthaginians*. Whereof the many Collumnes placed up and down the Countrey, engraven with antient *Carthaginian* Characters (farr different from the *Hebrean*) give fufficient teftimony. But at the fame time when *Sicilia* was reduced to the *Romans*, it alfo rendered it felf and was therefore governed by the fame Laws, and the fame Prætor as *Sicilia* was. Wherewith alfo

                                          coming

coming afterwards into the power of the *Saracens*, it finally with *Gozo* in the yeer 1090. was poffeffed by *Ruggieri Normanno*, Count of *Sicilia*, till at length it obeyed the Chriftian Princes. The Ayr over all the Ifland is moft healthfull, but chiefly to them that inure themfelves to it: It hath Fountains and Orchards copioufly replenifhed wtth Date Trees, and its foyle every where produceth plentifully all forts of Grain and Corn, Flax, Cotton, Wool, Cummin feeds, and abundance of Rofes eminently fweet favoured: here alfo they have a kind of little neat white Dogs, which from their long hair we call fhocks, of much delight to the people. The Earth is fowed all the year with little busbandry, and they reap two harvefts and the trees likewife bear fruit twice in the yeer. In the winter every thing is green and flourifheth, and in the fummer is burnt up with heat, howbeit a certain Dew falls which exceedingly nourifheth the Corn. At the head of a long and ftrait point almoft oppofite to the *Capo Paffero* or *Pachino* in *Sicilia* is erected the *Fortezza* of *Sant Ermo*, but on the right hand towards *Sicilia* are fome other points, and between them and *Sant Ermo* is a Chanel of water upon one of which points is the Caftle *Sant Angelo*, and the other the *Fortezza* of *San Michael* with their Bourges: between the one and the other of which lie the fhips & Galleys in a Channel which is locked at the utmoft points with a vaft Iron Chain. Eight miles off which place up the Land ftands the City called *Malta* famoufed by the Reliques of very noble Edifices, and by the antient dignity of a Bifhoprick. This Ifle hath a Promontory whereon was built a moft antient and noble Temple dedicated to *Juno*, and held in great reverence, and another on the South to *Hercules*, whereof at this day huge ruines appear at the Port *Euro*. The men of this Ifland are brown complexioned, and their genius more approaches that of the *Sicilians* then any other. The women are beautifull enough but fly company, goe obfcured abroad, are kept clofe at home, yet following the fame manner of life as the *Sicilians*, and fpeaking a language more like and near the *Carthaginian* then any other language. The people are generally religious and particularly pay a great devotion to Saint *Paul*, to whom this Ifland is dedicated, for that here he by chance fell into the Sea, and was here entertained with great humanity: and on that fhore where he fell in, is built a venerable Chapel; for their refpect to whom they believe no noyfome nor venemous Creature can grow or live on this Ifland. And from the *Grotto* where that Saint ftood are ftones by many plucked away, and carryed through *Italy*, (called the *Gratia* of Saint *Paul*,) to heal the bitings of Scorpions and Serpents. In our Age this Ifland had and hath great fplendour for its Devotion, and the religious order of the Knights of *Sant Giovanni* or *John* of *Jerufalem*, the which having loft *Rhodes* (taken from them in the yeer 1522. by *Soliman* the magnificent the great *Turk*) had this Ifland given them by *Charles the* 5th. Emperour, where they have built the aforenamed Caftles and Forts, that they may there refide with perpetual fecurity. In the yeer 1565. they valiantly defended the fame againft a moft potent *Armada*, which the fame *Soliman* fent thither to conquer the Ifland and to drive out thofe Knights: which in time to come will not contribute leffe glory to *Malta*, then that which they reaped in times paft from the general

council

Council which under Pope Innocent the first was there celebrated by 214. Bishops against *Pelagius* the *Heretike*; among others there met Saint *Austine* and *Sylvano* Bishop of *Malta*. *Soliman* sent to this Attempt an *Armada*, a Fleet of 200 sayls, under the command of *Piali Bassa* General of the Sea, a man both valiant and judicious, and of *Mustapha*, the *Bassa* General of the Land, a man very crafty, and much experienc't in warlike affairs: who having disembarked and landed their Army on the 18. of *May*, besieged and battered the Castle *Sant Irmo*, and after many contests and attempts, having beat down that wall flat to the Earth, on the 23d. of *June* became Masters of the Fort, and put all the defendors to the Sword and cut them to pieces. There dyed then on the Turks part *Dragut Rais* the famous Pyrat, being wounded under the ear by the blow of a stone. Then they turned their force upon the two other *Fortezza's* of *Sant Michael*, and *Saint Angelo*. They planted a fierce battery against *San Michael*, which levelled the walls with the bank of the Fosse or Ditch by their falling therein, but in many and many assaults which they gave to the Castle, they were alwaies valiantly repelled by the Horse: *Giovanni Valetta* a French man the then greatMaster, a man of singular valour and prudence, not failing in any thing of conduct or necessary provision, that might merit the esteem of an excellent Commander. At last *Don Garcia de Toledo*, having selected sixty of the most nimble and polite galleys out of those of the *King* of *Spain*, and furnished them with nine thousand six hundred Souldiers between *Spaniards*, and *Italians*, advanced to land them securely on the Island. Which the *Turks* understanding forthwith imbarqued their Artillery, and advanced with 8000 Souldiers to view the Christian Army, who fell upon them with such ardour and fury, that they immediately most basely run away, and got into their Galleys, leaving 1800 dead, having killed but only four on the Christians side: And in this manner were the *Turks* *constrained* to abandon the Island to their foul shame and confusion, and the great honour of Almighty God, whose hand strengthning this small number, clearly demonstrated, that by his favour, the valour of a few can oppose the violence of many.

Verses

FOR *Pompe, and Pietie, old* Rome *is fam'd,*
Venice *is rich, the Sage, and Lordly nam'd,*
Naples *is noble, and of pleasant air,*
Florence *through all the world reputed fair:*
Milan *doth of her Grandeur justly boast.*
Bologna's *fatt :* Ferrara *civil most.*
Padoua *Learned ; subtile* Bergamo.
And Genoua's *Pride , her stately buildings show.*
Worthy Verona, *bloudy* Perugia,
Brescia *well-armed ; and glorious* Mantoua.
Rimini *good.* Pistoia *barbarous.*
Babling Siena. Lucca *industrious.*
Forli *phantastick. kind,* Ravenna's *styld.*
Singalia *with nauseous air is fill'd*
Pisa *is pendent : amorous,* Capua.
Pesaro *flowry ; and (as all men say)*
Ancona *far from a good Port doth stray.*
Urbin *in her fidelity is strong.*
Ascoli *round, and* Recanate *long.*
Foligno's *candied streets most pleasant are.*
The Ladies of Fano, *so smooth and fair,*
That said they are from Heaven sent to be
But Modena *more happy is then shee.*

FINIS.

www.ingramcontent.com/pod-product-compliance
Lightning Source LLC
Chambersburg PA
CBHW031129120726
47905CB00006B/1614